MER

Parts 1 & 2

Vol. V

of

THE STEWARD

M.D. IRONZ

Published in the United States of America

Professorial Holdings

professorialholdings@gmail.com

Also by M.D. Ironz

The Steward
The Steward, The Box Set, Vols. 1, 2, 3

THE STEWARD
Domaine Delafaire
Realms Of Possibility
Alas, The Best Laid Plans
Storm Haven
MER
The Expanded Box Set, Vol. 1, 2, 3, 4

Standalone
Dire Covenants

CH 1

THE *Doom Wind's* slender bowsprit rose through the crashing swell to jab at the ominous cloud bank, only to plunge down the following trough and rise once more into the face of the looming storm.

Her sails reefed and hatches battened, the sleek ship kept her bow into the wind, riding the turbulent waves with a confident grace, as if eager for the adventure, somehow knowing this petulant squall would be violent but brief.

Fearful yet thrilled, Salidar paused in his descent from the reefed topsail and gripped the mainmast rigging more tightly as the vessel crested yet another huge wave and dropped like a stone into its trough. His jaw thrust forward in defiance, he sneered and squinted into the salt spray.

As the ship rose with the swell, Salidar spied the first mate below gamely approaching the helmsman, despite the rolling and pitching of the slick teak deck.

Ah, no doubt a course correction to get us through this squall more safely. Even I can sense this storm will be furious but quickly spent—nothing the Doom Wind cannot handle.

In his reluctant tenure as an impressed crewman aboard the three-masted clipper, Salidar had developed a number of nautical skills, and estimating the impact of imminent weather was among them. He had also come to appreciate the resilient seaworthiness of the narrow-beamed and surprisingly swift ship. Few vessels would dare to sail the treacherous Southern Ocean of the water realm, Mer—especially during storm season—but the *Doom Wind* seemed indomitable.

"Ready the sea anchor and stand by!" boomed the ship's bosun.

Climbing down the last few feet of wet ratlines, Salidar dropped to the deck and scrambled aft to assist with the sea anchor, should it be deployed.

Twice before it had been needed when storms of significant strength had sprung up unexpectedly and pushed the *Doom Wind* days off course. Casting a weather eye about, Salidar had a strong hunch the *Doom Wind* would not need the sea anchor for this squall. This minor tempest would only be a temporary inconvenience, not a true impediment to their already delayed port-bound progress, but was nonetheless unlikely to improve the captain's current temperament.

Salidar shrugged off a chill and noted gratefully that the captain was either below-decks or in his cabin. The ship had been at sea for almost two months, and the pickings had been meager. Only two merchant vessels had been run down, and three raids made upon isolated island towns. Captain "Bloody" Bane was in a foul mood. Some crewmen were grumbling as well, not surprising considering the poor booty taken on this voyage.

Neither of the wallowing merchant galleys had been worth taking as prizes. Their cargoes had been equally unimpressive; perishable fruits and vegetables that would spoil, worthless long before the *Doom Wind* could make port. Besides, the *Doom Wind's* hold was comparatively small; even Salidar could see she'd been designed primarily for speed, not hauling copious cargo. So, the pirates simply restocked the *Doom Wind's* depleted larder, relieved the indignant merchant captains of their purses, and let the vessels go, much to the relief of their frightened crews.

Raids on the island towns had been somewhat more successful. Half a dozen women had been taken. They now languished below in irons, their fate as yet undecided.

The *Doom Wind* was only two days out from New Port Royal, an infamous pirate haven on a lonely island in the storm-cursed Southern

Ocean. However, Salidar sensed this angry wind-lashed squall would likely further delay her arrival by almost half a day.

In his heart, he was experiencing mixed feelings about making port.

On one hand, he was more than ready to stand upon solid earth, not that the constant pitch and roll of the ship bothered him. In fact, he had gotten his *sea legs* early on, and found that he actually enjoyed life at sea. Forced to serve as a crewman aboard the pirate ship while being held for a ransom, he proved to be a rather adept seaman, and earned begrudging respect from members of the motley crew.

On the other hand, however, his fate, like that of the women held below, was also undetermined.

Unfortunately, when Lady Diere finally received the ransom demand, she had pointedly refused. This rejection came as no surprise to Salidar; he'd secretly expected as much. He knew his only hope lay in becoming as indispensable a crewman as possible until he figured a way to escape this transit-warded ship.

The much bigger problem was to escape Diere's vengeful scrutiny as well. Her reach was considerable since she was now known as Mab LV, Queen of the Dark Elves, and Monarch of the Unseelie Court. He was no fool; he knew she'd consider him a loose end, one who knew far too much, and therefore a threat. He speculated that she had no doubt expected the pirates to slay him outright upon her refusal to pay the ransom; he prayed she believed that had been the case. Only his wits and consummate adaptability had thus far spared him from such a fate.

He was one of two dozen sailors, not all of whom were fully human, who presently comprised the ship's company, serving aboard a vessel intended to be crewed by thirty seamen. Although numerically understrength, the inherent genetic and cultural diversity of the crew was hardly a detriment. One simply did not ask about a fellow crewman's background; a dubious past and staunch belief in naval superstitions were common enough denominators. This compelled camaraderie, tempered with a well-deserved fear of their infamous captain's periodic rages, kept the shorthanded crew on their toes and functioning cohesively well.

Fortunately for Salidar, one's seamanship spoke volumes in the eyes of the other crew members. That and the willingness to stand by one's shipmates in the face of adversity were sufficient virtues to merit cautious tolerance, and eventually guarded acceptance.

Salidar had few options; his fate was truly in the hands of one of the most feared pirate captains upon the seas of Mer. He could only hope that he would be found useful, and thus continue to serve as a crewman, at least for now.

Early in his indentured servitude, he had been closely watched as he was set to various shipboard tasks, most of which were equally mundane and disgusting. Inspired by a strong sense of self-preservation, he had worked diligently and without complaint.

Eventually, he was included in a shore party sent to acquire replacement supplies and fresh water from a dubiously trusted source on a lightly inhabited island. Unnoticed by his less than attentive fellow crewmen, an island urchin slipped him a tiny rolled parchment, a coded communication from Gallenius, the senior mage of the realm of Storm Haven.

"Shelter in place. Far safer than otherwise. You will be contacted when appropriate."

No fool, Salidar would do as instructed, so long as he could stay out of harm's way, and Captain "Bloody" Bane's sights.

But now, his survival sense bordered upon anxiety. Making port in New Port Royal would herald a change in his circumstances; he could just feel it.

What he thought he felt, more than anything else, was an insidious tendril of *creeping dread.*

ELLEN HUNG UP THE RECEIVER and pouted at the wall-mounted phone.

Millie noticed her daughter's out-thrust lower lip. "So, is everything alright? Is Hawk coming for supper?"

"No, Mom, he can't. He's got to work late *again!*" She slumped into a kitchen chair.

"Yeah? What case?" Mark asked, wandering into the kitchen.

"The same one they've been working for the last week or so, missing cattle. He said they found something, a carcass. So, he and Trey are working late."

"Oooo, was it a mutilated carcass?" Mark leered theatrically as he perched on a stool.

"All right, that's enough." Millie snapped a dish towel in his direction. "That's not appropriate kitchen talk, young man."

"Sorry, Aunt Millie, I couldn't resist. But I am curious about the case." He turned to his cousin and lowered his voice. "So, Ellen, these aren't the only *remains* that have been found, are they?"

"No, this is the third instance, I think." She straightened up in the chair and shook her head. "But I don't have any details. You know Hawk can't discuss ongoing investigations."

"Yeah, but you guys talk. Did he mention any sort of location, by any chance?"

"No, Mark, he didn't say where it was found." Ellen glanced askance at him. "I know what you're really asking—if it had been found here on Delafaire Farm, or even nearby, he'd have told me."

"Where what was found?" asked Ellen's best friend, Stacy, sauntering into the kitchen.

"Trust me—you don't want to know," interjected Millie. "Now, supper will be on in ten minutes. So, y'all get ready. Mark, you go wash up. You've been in the garage all afternoon. I don't want you bringing any grease or oil to my supper table!"

"Yes, ma'am," Mark mumbled and winked at Stacy as he shuffled from the room.

Stacy smirked and commenced to help Ellen set the table. She noticed that Ellen didn't set the usual extra place for her boyfriend. "Hawk can't make it?"

"Nope, he's gotta work; you know, the cattle thing. That's what we were talking about before you came in. It was kinda grossing my mom out."

"Ha! You mean *Mark* was! I swear, sometimes he's such a kid!" Stacy looked to the ceiling and sighed.

"Yeah, but you don't seem to mind," Ellen teased as she placed extra napkins on the table.

Stacy grinned anew and changed the subject. "When is Miska due back? The dwarves at the still were asking this morning; but, I didn't know what to tell them."

"Midweek, I think. He was pretty vague when he left for Were. His visit with his clan was very important to him, so I wouldn't be surprised if he took a little longer than he initially anticipated."

"I understand, I guess. But do you think it was really *safe* for him? You know, with Diere, I mean Queen Mab, knowing about him being Boltar's, er, *Ivan's* brother?"

"Well, he seemed to think so. The way he explained it, he was honor-bound to share the truth with his entire clan about his brother's ensorcellment and death."

“Yeah, I get that.” Stacy nodded in approval, and handed Ellen containers of mustard, ketchup, and pickle relish. “He sure has a strong sense of honor. I like that about him.”

“Me, too,” Ellen agreed, carefully arranging the condiments next to the salt and pepper shakers. “Mark thought there might be an unintended but beneficial consequence to Miska spreading the word among his people. It could diminish the potential threat that Mab might represent to Miska personally. Basically, if more people knew the truth, he’d be that much less of a target, I guess.”

Stacy shrugged. “Well, maybe Mark’s right. But then everyone who knows the truth might become a target, wouldn’t they? I sure wouldn’t trust Mab as far as I could throw her!”

Ellen sighed, hands on her hips. “Yeah, as tempting as that sounds—the throwing part, I mean—I wouldn’t trust her *ever!*”

A FOUL STENCH, CLOYING and putrid, tainted the still air near the edge of the small clearing. The CSI techs who wore respirators seemed unaffected; but the two detectives and the Livestock Brand Commission investigator had to hold their breath while examining the carcass. Flies buzzed overhead and crooked lines of ants marched up to ragged rents in the torn flesh.

Trey stood up and motioned for Hawk and the LBC investigator to follow. At a comfortable distance, he took several deep breaths and posed a question.

“Well, Charley, what do you think?”

The LBC investigator nudged the brim of his Stetson up a bit on his forehead and spat a stream of tobacco juice in the dust behind him. “I’d like to hear what you boys think first, Trey, if’n that’s all right.”

Trey shrugged and turned to his partner.

"Okay, Detective, what do you notice about this scene?"

Hawk took a moment to survey the scene from this vantage point and pinched the bridge of his nose.

"Whew, aside from the smell, a number of things." He gestured toward the carcass. "First of all, there are no obvious bullet wounds or blade cuts, no attempt at butchering for meat." His hand swept the entire area. "I see no vehicle tracks, clear footprints, or any indication of human involvement."

"So, it's not your classic rustling case?" Trey probed.

Hawk shook his head. "No, I don't think so. This steer has no ear tag or brand, so it'll take some time to determine the owner. I know we've had half a dozen complaints from several cattle ranchers. Those are only about one or two missing head of stock each, not enough for a herd. We've found remains of three so far. I think something else is going on here."

"Meaning what, son?" Charley toed the dirt and smiled askance at Trey.

"See here? This carcass was covered with dirt, leaves, and small sticks; so, someone, or far more likely *something*, tried to hide it. Also, something's been feeding on it, but I can't really tell what."

"Okay." The LBC investigator nodded approvingly. "What else?"

"I don't think this steer was killed here; there's not enough blood." Hawk stepped closer to the animal and pointed. "Look here. Hardly any blood has soaked into the ground; and, there's none anywhere nearby, no spatter or drips. I think the blood we do see is just gravity leakage, or from the feeding. Overall, everything suggests to me that the kill happened elsewhere, and the carcass was brought here. However, I didn't see any drag marks."

"Well, the ground is pretty hard here, a lot of rocks and stuff." Trey swept his hands in an open arc.

"Yeah, but there still should be some sign, some significant disturbance of the terrain. But I can't seem to find anything other than some very indistinct tracks. I can't say for certain what made them. However, it wasn't a person; and, it was pretty big!"

Trey scratched his head and looked around at the small clearing. "Are you telling me that something carried this carcass here? Just what's left here must be over three hundred pounds!"

"Trey, I don't know what else to think. This is actually the third scene we've seen like this! We've never seen any bullet holes, blade or tool marks, no tire tracks or clear footprints, no evidence of any human activity at any of the scenes. So, I think cattle rustling is off the table. That just leaves me with one question; what the hell is making the kills and feeding on these carcasses?"

"So, you think it's an animal of some kind? Maybe the same one for all three kills?"

"I don't know about the *same one*; it's possible, I guess. But it's an animal of some kind, a predator for sure!"

Trey sighed. "I think I've gotta agree. After all, the game wardens from Wildlife and Fisheries thought so as well, but even they don't know for sure. So, unless LBC wants to take this case, we're the lead agency. How about it, Charley?"

"No, I'm happy to assist, but LBC resources are spread pretty thin right now. My current caseload is such that my boss would balk unless there's clear evidence of a rustling operation. We haven't seen any. All three of these incidents, the found carcasses, are within Chantilly Parish, clearly your jurisdiction. For what it's worth, I think I agree with your young partner; this looks more like predation to me. So, y'all can be lead, Trey, and LBC will be in a support role."

"Oh hell, Charley," Trey groaned. "Somehow I knew you were gonna say that. Well, tell us, is there anything like this going on anywhere else in Louisiana? LBC jurisdiction is statewide."

"Nope, sorry," the LBC investigator responded. "I'd have told you already. This situation is somewhat unique; I haven't seen or heard of anything quite like it."

"So, you agree," Hawk probed, "that it's most likely a predator of some sort?"

"Yep, think so." Charley spat another stream of tobacco juice.

Trey was not convinced. "Tell me this, how come the K-9 dogs haven't tracked a scent? They've been brought to all the sites, but each time they just seemed confused and wary. They didn't track anything. So, how is that possible?"

"You got me. That doesn't make much sense. I don't know what to tell you." Charley shrugged.

"Well, unless something *flew* this carcass here," Trey's open palms waved in the air, "there's gotta be a better explanation, right?"

Hawk shook his head. "*Flew?* Nah, no way! I think it was *carried* here, not flown. Can you imagine the size of a bird that could fly with three hundred pounds of dead weight? It was something else; something that I think used that path," he pointed, "the old fire road that winds through those trees."

"How about a cougar, a swamp panther?" Trey offered. "You know every so often one from the Atchafalaya Basin will follow the Red River all the way up to Shreveport, right?"

"Yeah, I know," Hawk acknowledged. "A cougar would certainly be strong enough to drag, and probably even lift that carcass. Sometimes they'll stash a smaller kill in a tree. But I'm not sure a swamp panther would carry this much weight for any real distance. Remember, there are no drag marks. I think it's gotta be something stronger."

"What, like a bear? Wouldn't a black bear be strong enough?"

Hawk shrugged. "I suppose it's possible, if it were a big one. But I still think I'd see some drag marks. I'd expect to see some other sort of recognizable signs; distinct tracks, scat, and so forth—but I haven't. That path is just an old fire road that's still maintained; it's rocky but wide. I couldn't find enough sign to track. Anyway, black bears generally don't go after cattle, unless it's carrion. I just don't think a black bear made these kills."

"Well, there are no grizzlies or brown bears around here." Trey stroked his chin. "There have been no reports of anything escaping from a zoo or circus."

"Yeah, I know," Hawk agreed, his eyes drifting to the carcass. "No exotic pets on the loose either. I don't know what to think, or even begin to speculate."

"Well, we've gotta come up with something to tell the bosses. Captain Miller told me this morning that the Ranchers' Association is really putting some pressure on the sheriff."

"I know. But, Trey, you know I can't just guess. I've got to have more to go on. So far, there really isn't enough for me. I'm in the dark here."

"Well, cheer up; maybe there'll be some trace evidence on this scene," Trey speculated. "Let's find Sgt. Melancon and see what his CSI techs can tell us. Maybe they'll get lucky here."

Seeing Hawk frown, Trey shrugged and admitted, "Yeah, I know they haven't gotten any lab results back yet from the samples taken at the other two sites. We gotta be patient; the lab stays swamped and this isn't exactly a priority case."

"Well, I wish you boys luck," Charley offered. "I gotta go—got a meeting in Baton Rouge. Give me a call if something develops, or you need anything from me."

"Will do, Charley," Trey assured him. "We're gonna have to get going shortly, too. Be safe out there." He waved to the departing LBC investigator and nudged Hawk. "Come on, let's find Mel."

"Yeah, okay, but first, I gotta tell you; there's something else that's bugging me, something that's different about this site."

Trey cocked his head in puzzlement. "Okay, what?"

"Bear with me, uh, no pun intended." Hawk smirked and lowered his voice. "This is a relatively fresh scene. Even the ants only recently found it, and you know they'd cover it in a couple of hours. So, we got here pretty quick, sooner than at the first two sites, right?"

"Yeah, so?"

"Well, at the other sites, there was ample evidence that scavengers, coyotes and vultures for the most part, had been at the carcass. I'm pretty sure something else made the kill, ate its fill, and then apparently abandoned those remains. Here, I see no indication of any scavenger activity other than flies and ants, at least not yet."

"So? The other scavengers haven't found it yet?" Trey frowned. "Where are you going with this?"

"Not sure, but I don't think that's it. Look, scavengers don't miss much, if anything. Remember, it was fairly clear that the other two scenes were the actual locations of the kills. I don't think the coyotes and vultures got involved until it was safe—*after* those sites were abandoned by the predator."

"What are you saying?" Trey breathed *sotto voce*, casting his eyes about.

Hawk leaned closer and whispered hoarsely, out of earshot of the busy CSI techs. "Think about it; this scene is different! The kill wasn't made here, but the carcass was brought here and hidden. Listen, predators are smart—they have to be! They learn that their kills draw competition, scavengers at a minimum; so, they move the carcass and make an effort to hide it."

"So, you think that's what's happening here? Whatever did this hid it, and the scavengers haven't found it yet?"

"Not exactly," Hawk cautioned. "Remember I said that scavengers don't miss anything. They know this is here, the *smell*, you know?"

"Then why haven't they . . . " Trey began, letting his voice dwindle into silence.

"Yeah." Hawk leaned toward his partner. "Trey, I don't think this site is abandoned. Predators will defend their kills."

"Oh, crap!" Trey scanned the thick underbrush and densely wooded tree line that bordered the small clearing in which they stood.

"Yeah, I know," Hawk acknowledged. "My gut has been uneasy since we got here. I can't shake the feeling that we're being watched."

PAPA GEORGE SIPPED from a silver goblet and grimaced. He found the wine, the sole variety known here in the realm of Olmus, disappointing—far too pale and bland for his taste.

There was a slight chill, a pervasive dampness, within the torch-lit scrying chamber beneath the old temple ruins that the tepid drink did little to ameliorate.

What I wouldn't give for some honest bourbon—even the cheap stuff would be a damned sight better than this!

"Daegon, I don't get it," he grumbled.

"What?" The alchemist tore his eyes from the scrying orb and held forth his own goblet for a goblin servant to replenish.

"This minion of *hers* the goblins caught, this so-called mage, Gaspar . . . I mean, look, you still keep Zerban around and he's damn near an empty shell of a wizard. So, why would you let Gaspar go? You know he knows more than he's telling us. If you let him go," the shade of fear tinted George's concern, "he's liable to go right back to Diere, Queen Mab, or whatever she's calling herself!"

"Patience, my apprentice. You see, I very much want him to go back to her." The alchemist allowed himself a smug smile and a solitary raised eyebrow. "He will be my eyes and ears, unwittingly, of course. If she accepts him upon his return to her, we will have penetrated and compromised her innermost circle."

"But he's seen us!" George cried in desperation. "Arrgh! He might not know exactly who we are; but if he describes me to her, she'll know! You know she wants my head on a stick!"

"Well, you have betrayed her and fled—or so she believes, heh-heh.

"As for Gaspar, he will remember only that he was taken and held by goblins. He will have no recollection of either of us! That obsidian collar around his neck does much more than render all of his sorcerous powers inert. His very memories have been completely open to me; and all the while he has been unaware. So, you see, he may not have *told* us everything—but he can hide nothing."

That impressed George, another trick of Daegon's that he'd like to learn. However, he kept his thoughts to himself as his mentor continued.

"When I have exhausted my examination of his most closely held secrets, I will wipe all memory of us from his mind. I will then give him to the Red Hat goblin tribe to hold as a slave for an entire moon cycle. That will seem an eternity, I assure you."

George shuddered. He knew the goblins did not treat their slaves well at all, or for very long, since few survived. "That's almost a month. Hell! They're liable to kill him."

Daegon raised a finger in caution. "Oh, they will be instructed to do no lasting harm, but it will be a most unpleasant experience, I am sure. At some point, I will arrange for this gem to come into his possession." A small diamond stud earring lay upon Daegon's open palm, and captured the flickering torchlight.

"A diamond?" George gawked. "Oh, a gem from a dragon's hoard, and a spell inside?"

"Very good! The spell will allow Gaspar to free himself from the collar. His powers will seem to return, but not his memories. He can then escape and even transit out of this realm of Olmus.

"I chose to fashion this gem as an earring because he wore a similar gold nugget upon his arrival. Of course, my servants relieved him of it."

"Wait a minute," warned George. "What's to stop him from taking revenge on the Red Hat goblins before he escapes? You know he's a vindictive bastard."

"Ah, that is true, but should not be a problem." Daegon savored a long draught of wine. "You see, he will have been warned that the duration of the primary enchantment held within the gem will be very brief, and that he must quickly distance himself from the collar lest the goblins use it to track him. Once he has reached sufficient distance, the secondary enchantment in the gem will obscure his presence from any attempts by his enslavers to find him, and allow token access to his restored powers."

"Oh, so Gaspar will think the collar is like a kind of GPS locator, and the diamond is a cloaking device, right?"

"*GP—what?*" Daegon's face pinched in puzzlement.

“Never mind. Trust me; I get it.” George leaned back and smiled. “Gaspar will want to keep that diamond with him for the rest of his life. Hell, he’ll probably wear it in his ear as a replacement for his lost nugget!”

“Let us hope so, since this gem is the means by which all that is said and done in its presence will be known to us through this scrying orb.”

“A *Gaspar-cam!* Oh, now that is slick,” George declared.

“What? I do not—” Daegon began.

“It’s nothing,” George interrupted with a dismissive wave. “How do we get the gem, and the warning, to Gaspar in the first place?”

Daegon smiled smugly and shrugged. “Through another slave, I should think, one who would seem to lack the drive and initiative to even try to escape.”

“Who?”

“I was thinking of *your* bespelled servant, Zerban’s former pupil, Stellara.”

CH 2

PADRAIC STROLLED DOWN the broad and opulent palace hall of the House of Hawthorne's Castle Diere, now the unchallenged seat of power within the Realm of Dark Elves. In smiling nonchalance, he nodded graciously to passing courtiers and bustling servants alike. Held in high esteem by all of Queen Mab's court, from the highborn Dark Elfin aristocracy to the harried servants, he had made a special point of being friendly with the royal household guards. Consequently, he was a favorite among them, frequently regaling the guardsmen with ribald tales of former libidinous conquests.

As he approached the queen's reception room, in answer to her recent summons, the two guards on duty immediately recognized and hailed him.

"Ah, Lord Padraic, tis good to see you, sir!"

"Aye," echoed the other guardsman, "and a fine day it is! Are you here for Her Majesty?"

"Aye, that I am, lads, in answer to her call. Alas, a consort's work is never done." He sighed theatrically, earning the expected chuckle from the guards. "She is within?"

"Quite so, m'lord. But begging your pardon, she is in conference with the Lady Malvana. So, if you do not mind waiting a bit?"

Padraic shrugged, raising an eyebrow. "Tis no problem at all, my friends. No doubt they confer about the next council meeting. That is in a fortnight hence, is it not?"

"True enough, m'lord." The guard leaned forward conspiratorially. "But *this* conference has to do with the ongoing negotiations of the Elfin Accords."

"Aye," agreed his partner. "Lady Malvana is today appointed to represent Her Majesty in further negotiations."

"Oh, I see. I should not be surprised, I suppose," Padraic acknowledged with a wry grimace. "I knew the queen found the first few meetings, uh, not to her taste—if not boring to the point of annoyance."

The amused guards suddenly snapped to attention as the doors to the reception room began to swing open, and the Lady Malvana came forth.

Padraic bowed slightly to the comely elfin maid, who curtsied in turn.

"Ah, Lord Padraic, you are to go right in. Her Majesty expects you."

"Of course, and a good day to you, m'lady."

AS THE DOORS CLOSED behind him, Padraic saw a hint of movement behind one of the elaborate tapestries hanging along the wall to his right. *So, this audience is to be observed. I must be careful.*

"Ah, Your Majesty, you sent for me?"

Across the room, Queen Mab, leaning over a table strewn with charts and maps, glanced up and favored him with a small smile. Her blue-green gown clung like a second skin; its plunging décolletage only served to emphasize the distracting effect her ethereal beauty had upon males of almost any species.

Padraic fed her ego by gaping for just a moment longer than deemed socially appropriate. As he expected, her smile widened.

Ye gods, she's predictable.

He saw that she savored the moment, allowing herself a small smirk and lone raised eyebrow.

"Yes, I did send for you. Come here, Padraic, and look at this map. Do you recognize anything?"

Standing before the table he leered at her cleavage as expected and forced his eyes downward to the map.

"If I am not mistaken, Majesty, this is a part of the Realm of Mer, a quadrant of the Southern Ocean, I think."

"Quite right, very good!" She sounded genuinely pleased. "I knew you had visited Mer often. So, I trust you can tell me about *these* islands?" Her elegantly long finger slid across the map, and tapped a manicured nail on a crescent string of isolated islands in the vast Southern Ocean.

Padraic leaned over the table and studied the indicated coordinates.

"As you know, Majesty, not a great deal is known about some regions in the Southern Ocean. This area is well off the usual trade routes. But as I recall, these islands do have a name, the *Keys of Osiris.* They lay too far from the equatorial region to be easily accessible. There are frequent storms, renowned for their violence, that make any such passage challenging, to say the least."

"What do you mean *Keys?"* she demanded.

"Oh, *key* is just another word for a small island, Majesty. It need not imply anything else."

"Perhaps," she mused aloud, pursing her lips.

His curiosity piqued, he dared to ask, "Why have these islands drawn your attention, Majesty? Are they somehow important?"

Mab stared at him in momentary silence, her lips drawn in a grim line.

His expression betrayed nothing, but his thoughts were otherwise. *Ah, what does this mean? She cannot know—could she?*

"Titania is interested in them. I suspect she is trying to acquire them!" she spat. "This fact is not well known; but I have my sources. She made inquiries, quietly, through intermediaries. I do not know why—not yet. *You* will find out for me!"

His mind reeled. *Titania? What does she know? I must not overreact! It may be nothing, or something simple. The Queen of Light Elves is interested in, or is trying to acquire a lonely string of islands in a forsaken corner of a storm-cursed ocean in Mer, and the Queen of Dark Elves is upset about it? What is truly going on here? Is some strategic plan underway? Or is it merely simple jealousy? What one queen might have, the other must also acquire for the sake of parity, and vanity?*

"Majesty, I am not sure I understand. Queen Titania would acquire these islands in their entirety, or some property thereon?"

"I do not know." She frowned and stared past him, into some private distance.

"Ah, I see. And what, Majesty, am I to do, exactly?"

Her eyes narrowed; a spark of jealous anger flared in their depths. "Heed my words, Padraic! I will know what scheme Titania has in mind, whatever it is! I do not trust her! Even if it is as simple as having an island retreat or holiday location, she will not have something that I do not! You, Padraic, will be my instrument to ferret out the truth of this matter."

He almost sighed and shook his head—*almost*. A stoic expression firmly fixed to his face, he responded evenly. "I understand, Majesty. Have you some strategy in mind?"

"Oh yes, I do indeed, just for you," she cooed, all trace of ire absent, her smile seductive yet demure.

Accustomed to her mercurial mood swings, he smiled blandly, tilted his head in apparent attentive subservience, and remained silent.

"The next session of negotiations over the remaining issues with the Elfin Accords is to be held next week in Mer, at the Merchants Hall in Derinseum. You will attend in my stead."

He balked, his eyes wide.

Mab scoffed. "Oh, do not concern yourself, I have appointed Lady Malvana to negotiate in my behalf. She has been suitably, um, *prepared*, and will follow my instructions."

She sighed and let her delicate shoulders slump. "I simply cannot stomach another tedious negotiation session; Malvana will so serve. You need only appear at the opening ceremonies, as my personal representative. Once the sessions are underway, you may go about making the appropriate inquiries into this *Keys of Osiris* matter."

Padraic nodded appreciatively. He would be free to do as he pleased once the initial formalities were observed. Of course, he would have his own agenda to attend to once he had learned anything relevant regarding Titania's interest in these islands. Mab would no doubt be most eager for any scrap of knowledge he might discover; so, he could keep her focused, and suitably distracted, by controlling that flow of information.

"Well planned, Majesty. Although, I fear it may take some time. How long are these negotiations expected to take? I need to know my window of opportunity, so to speak."

"The session is scheduled for a week. However, Malvana has been instructed to slow the process, if you find it necessary, for several more days. You may find that you have approximately ten days. Will that be sufficient?"

"I believe so, my dear queen, but it may be that I must travel off-realm in my quest. Will I have any other assets at my disposal?"

"Off-realm? No, you will not. And if you must be gone from Mer, make your absence brief and see that no one knows of it, save Malvana."

"I understand, Majesty."

"And Padraic?"

"Yes, Your Majesty?"

"I know you only too well. You are to leave Malvana alone! Do you understand?"

"Of course, Your Majesty." He grinned and winked. "And now, by your leave, I will go make my necessary preparations."

AS THE DOORS CLOSED, Mab paused a moment in thought, and then spoke to the empty room. "Come forth. We are alone."

A tapestry was brushed to one side as a short adult elf attired in the tasteful garb of a successful merchant stepped forth and bowed. "Your Majesty?"

"Lord Nightshade, you heard all? My instructions to Lady Malvana and Lord Padraic?"

"I did, indeed, Your Majesty."

"You will have two assignments; first, you will attend as the delegation's chief of staff. Have your agents embedded in the negotiation retinue. Their mission is twofold; to observe, and protect if necessary. Neither Malvana nor Padraic are to know they are being watched. Of course, neither should come to any harm; admittedly that is very unlikely in Mer. However, the Light Elves are not to be trusted. Nonetheless, I shall expect daily reports. Do you understand?"

"Yes, Your Majesty. But, um . . . " he hedged, tugging at the hem of his belted tunic.

"What? Out with it!"

"Your Majesty . . . Um, since the task you have given Lord Padraic may require him to transit off-realm, a situation that will surely preclude our continued surveillance of him, what would you have us do?"

She paused; she hadn't considered that possibility until Padraic had mentioned it only a few minutes ago. Lord Nightshade's operatives could not follow, unless they knew where he was going.

"If you cannot ascertain his destination, curtail his surveillance and notify me immediately. If I know of his intentions in that regard beforehand, you will be so informed."

"Of course, Your Majesty." The diminutive elfin lord fidgeted. "Um, Majesty, I believe you mentioned there was another assignment?"

"Yes, you are to commence a search for the mage, Gaspar. I want this done quickly and quietly. No one else is to know of this. You will oversee this matter personally!"

"At once, Your Majesty. Is there anything you can tell me? Um, the last place he was seen, perhaps?"

Her brows knit and her eyes pierced his with the cold light of barely restrained anger. "Understand this, Lord Nightshade; you shall hold the information I am about to convey as dearly as you would your very life! Fail me in this, and your appointment as the head of my Secret Police will be of the shortest tenure in memory!"

Lord Nightshade blanched at the vehemence in her voice, but remained silent.

"Gaspar was to return to me after our *visit* to Storm Haven; but he has not done so! It has been far too long. I know for a fact he is not there. I do not know where he might now be. He has something of mine and I want it back! I want him found! Am I clear?"

"Um, crystal clear, Your Majesty. You may rely upon me."

"Then go."

STRIDING PURPOSELY down the long hall away from the royal chambers, Lord Nightshade wondered just how big a mistake he had made in accepting the offered appointment as the head of this queen's Secret Police. He had been quite content running the network of informants in support of espionage operations at the direction of his friend, the late Earl of Tanist, who had always served as a buffer between the monarchy and the day-to-day operations of the Secret Police. But now, with this new queen, *he* would be the buffer, not an enviable position at all.

"Ah, Tanist, how I do miss you, my friend." His sincere whisper was lost in the echoes of his footsteps.

With these latest threat-laden assignments, his regrets were becoming ever more clear.

Worse yet, he was to put someone he liked and admired, Padraic the Rogue, the queen's own consort, under surveillance. It was no secret that Padraic was prone to engaging in the occasional dalliance, despite his elevated position at court. Was that really why the queen wanted him watched? What would she do if this surveillance yielded incontrovertible proof?

There was no way he could avoid complying with her orders.

Damn the gods! What have I gotten myself into?

CH 3

"LAND HO!"

Salidar shielded his eyes from the overhead sun and peered up at the crow's nest.

The lookout extended his arm toward the horizon and repeated his hail, "Land ho! Three points off the bow to starboard!"

"About bloody time," mumbled Crabs, the helmsman, a bit too loudly as he adjusted course with a slight turn of the ship's wheel. "More 'n two days lost to weather! Gods be damned! Cap'n's been in a foul temper this whole—"

"Belay that, Crabs!" bellowed the bosun. "Still your tongue, lest you lose it! Keep her on course and mind the shoals; we'll be on `em soon enough."

Crabs gave the bosun a sour look and shrugged.

When the bosun turned his back, Crabs winked at Salidar and mimed the bosun's harsh words. A natural mimic, Crabs' antics had Salidar snorting in amusement.

"Somethin' funny, Salidar?" The bosun spat as he glanced askance at the impressed seaman.

"Ah, nothin', bosun. Just clearin' m' throat, I be."

Crabs smirked unseen and rolled his eyes. Salidar almost laughed aloud, but managed to maintain a look of innocence by biting his lips.

"Throat all cleared now, is it?" the bosun probed ominously. "Or would I be needin' t' shove a belayin' pin down y' craw, just to be sure now, eh? No? Then shut y' face and attend me at the ship's bell!"

"Aye, aye, bosun."

Salidar joined him at the bell and kept his mouth shut. He'd come to learn that the bosun was an excellent sailor and ran a tight ship. However, the heavily tattooed senior seaman was neither fully human, a halfling of some sort, nor blessed with any sense of humor. So, naturally he was often the butt of subtle jokes among the crew; but woe unto the joker should the bosun perceive the jest. Salidar could only hope the big halfling had completely missed the incorrigible Crabs' mocking jibe.

The bosun's expression betrayed nothing. He just stared into the distance and let his hand come to rest on the brass bell.

Salidar could see something engraved along the rim of the bell. He tilted his head and made out the fanciful script, ARIEL 1865.

What's this? This vessel is the Doom Wind. Why would she have a bell bearing another ship's name? Or was she renamed? Or perhaps a better question, does it matter?

"Salidar, y've turned out to be a fair sailor. Cap'n says I can give ye more duties. So, when we make New Port Royal, ye'll pull the watch, one of four crewmen to remain aboard and man the watch, savvy?"

"Aye, bosun, the watch," Salidar acknowledged, his expression bland.

This wasn't bad news; but, it wasn't good either. Salidar had hoped to have the opportunity to go ashore. The varied amusements and distractions of New Port Royal were renown among all pirates. He, like the rest of the crew, had looked forward to a rollicking bacchanalia once in port. It wasn't like he had planned to escape; he had no where to go. After all, he was still in hiding, convinced Diere would arrange for his death the moment she learned he was alive.

"But first," the bosun cautioned, "satisfy me that y' can handle the ship's bell, as every man on the watch must, savvy?"

"Aye, bosun, I know, to mark the time, right?"

"Don't tell me y' know, y' slimy bilge-rat! Show me! Name me the watches. Then tap the bell with a fingertip—but don't let `er ring out! Savvy? Begin."

Salidar took a breath. He knew this—as would any competent sailor in this realm of Mer. Few crewmen had access to a timepiece; as a rule only the ship's officers could access the ship's chronometer. The periodic ringing of the ship's bell allowed the crew to track the time and perform duties as assigned. Once in port, with the captain and most of the crew ashore, the senior man on watch would be granted access to the ship's clock and would sound the bell accordingly.

"There are six watches of four hours each," Salidar recited. "First watch is from 8:00 p.m. to midnight. Middle watch is from midnight to 4:00 a.m. Morning watch is from 4:00 a.m. to 8:00 a.m. Forenoon watch is from 8:00 a.m. to noon. Afternoon watch is from noon to 4:00 p.m. Evening watch is from 4:00 p.m. to 8:00 p.m.; but the evening watch is split into two dogwatches. First dogwatch is from 4:00 p.m. to 6:00 p.m.; second dogwatch is from 6:00 p.m. to 8:00 p.m."

"Not bad, Salidar," the bosun acknowledged. "Y' be smarter than y' look. Now give me the bells. Let's say tis noon."

"Aye. There be eight bells at noon." He gently tapped the rim of the bell eight times, its muffled tone barely discernible. "At half past, there be one bell—*tap.* At one o'clock, two bells—*tap tap.* At one-thirty, three bells—*tap tap tap.* At two o'clock, four bells—*tap tap tap tap* . . ."

As he tapped out the final eight bells to indicate four o'clock and the conclusion of that watch, the bosun smiled, a grim proposition indeed. Salidar hoped his demonstration was sufficient, but was wise enough to remain silent.

The bosun nodded. "Tis good to remember an even number of bells sounds on the hour and odd at half past. Aye, I think you'll do. If we be in port more `n two days, I'll ask the cap'n about relief for you four, *if* you do a sound job. No reason you lot can't have a bit of fun in New Port Royal, eh?"

With a leering grin, Salidar bobbed his head. "Aye, aye, bosun, aye, aye! A *sound* job!"

"That's enough gum-flappin' now! Get below and check on the cargo. Get `em cleaned up. We're only a few hours out and the cap'n will want `em offloaded soonest. We've little enough to show for this voyage as tis. Go on now!"

As Salidar scrambled toward the hold, he caught a glimpse of Crabs, the helmsman, rolling his eyes and making an obscene gesture at the bosun's back. Descending the ladder, Salidar stifled his laughter and focused his mind.

For his own reasons, he'd wanted to talk to the captive women as soon as they'd been brought aboard, but he'd never gotten the chance. One of them had locked eyes with him and given him the ghost of a smile when they had been hustled below.

Did he know her? No, he was certain he did not. Even worse, did she know or recognize him? Was she one of Mab's minions? Whatever the case, this was an opportunity not to be missed.

FRESHLY REFILLED COFFEE mugs in hand, Hawk reached across his desk to hand his partner a steaming cup when Captain Miller stepped into the Chantilly Parish Sheriff's Office CID squad room.

"Bassett and Redhawk, my office!"

"What's up, Captain?" Trey asked as he and Hawk took seats at the captain's gesture.

"Y'all know where the old Johansen farm is?"

The detectives glanced at each other and nodded.

"Yes, sir, sure do," Trey acknowledged.

"Good. Y'all need to meet a patrol unit already on the scene. It seems we may have a crime scene."

"Okay, it'll take us about twenty minutes," Trey calculated. "What do we know?"

The captain leaned back in his chair and steepled his fingers.

"This came down from Sheriff Tatum, himself. He got a call from the lawyer, Claude Fornier, they're old friends, y' know, about old man Johansen. Seems he was having his will amended since his granddaughter had twins. He was supposed to meet with the lawyer this morning here in LaBorde; but, he never showed. The secretary, Miss Mavis, tried to call the farm and his cell phone with no luck. She's convinced that something's wrong; so, she had Claude call the sheriff. He had the patrol desk send a unit to check. They couldn't find Johansen; but, they did find what appears to be a crime scene. If it is, you two have a new case."

Trey nodded. "I see, sir. What makes patrol think it's a crime scene? What did they find?"

"I understand some blood; I don't know what else. I've notified the CSI unit; so, someone will meet y'all there. Any more questions?"

"Not a question, per se," Trey clarified. "You know we're getting nowhere on this cattle killing case; so, I assume we'll be putting that on a back burner if this Johansen matter is anything we can't wrap up right away. You know what I mean, Captain, old man Johansen is what, eighty or so? He might have forgotten about the appointment or maybe wandered off."

Hawk nodded in agreement, but he could see the captain shake his head.

"Not very likely, Trey. The old man is a tough old cuss and sharp as a tack." Captain Miller chuckled. "He still runs the farm pretty much on his own. Of course, it's a smaller operation these days, a good-sized garden and some livestock, mostly goats and some hogs. He leases the rest of his land to other farming operations. He also serves on the board of the Farmers Co-op; so, he's not slipping. Something is up. Y'all go find out what. As for the cattle case, back burner it is until we get a break. Okay? Get rolling!"

"On our way, sir!"

THE GUILDMASTER PLACED the lone candle on the rough-hewn table in the small anteroom off the Storm Haven portal room and eased into a chair. Sighing, he glanced up at his unexpected guest.

"Padraic, are you certain this visit is wise?"

The Rogue shrugged. "Perhaps not, but necessary, I assure you."

They were alone in the chamber.

The Guildmaster gestured to another chair. "Please, take a seat. I trust no one, other than the portal guards, saw you arrive?"

"No, no one else," the Rogue whispered and pulled the chair closer. The solitary flame flickered; the walls pulsed with shadows. "I apologize for the haste, but the need for discretion is great."

"So you indicated in your rather cryptic message. What is this all about?"

Padraic took a deep breath, and glanced around the room. "Ah, I may be completely misreading the situation, but I dare not take the chance."

"Go on, please."

"Mab is to send me to Derinseum in two days, ostensibly to represent her in talks regarding the Elfin Accords—"

"You?" The Guildmaster interrupted in surprise. "We were under the impression the Lady Malvana was the designated negotiator."

"She is. I see you are well informed as always. My presence is at best as *proxy* or *window dressing,* since Mab finds the negotiations boring and refuses to go. Her real reason for sending me is to ascertain Titania's interest in the Keys of Osiris."

The Guildmaster remained silent for a long moment.

Padraic studied his motionless friend. "You knew." It was not a question.

The Guildmaster leaned forward, the candlelight shimmering in the reflection of the masking spell that obscured his face within the hood.

"No, we only suspected. Several uncorroborated reports had come to our attention that the Light Elfin Queen had expressed an interest in the islands. However, now that Mab is so aware, there may be some truth to this after all."

"Does Titania know?" Padraic's breath stilled in his throat. He dared not say more.

The Guildmaster shrugged and shook his head. "Let us hope not. I should not have to remind you that some things are best not spoken of—*ever.* Other than you and me, only two others are aware of the truth. I have no reason to believe either of them have been compromised, but I will initiate appropriate inquiries. I am sure we will know soon enough. What will you do?"

Easing back in his chair, Padraic opened his palms. "I suppose that which is expected of me. I shall go to Mer, slip away from the negotiations, and find some sort of misdirected pretext to explain Titania's interest to Mab. But the real problem is that we do not really know why Titania is so interested. I assume you will also be looking into that?"

"Rest assured that we will. When must you return?"

"Now, actually." Padraic stood. "This visit to Storm Haven is a calculated risk. I must return before I am missed. But I do have one final question; Salidar, he is still aboard the *Doom Wind*?"

"He is. We believe him safe, at present."

"That may change now that Mab has focused her attention on Mer." Padraic leaned forward once more. "I still owe him."

"Perhaps, but it may be very unwise to make contact at this time. As it happens, we may have some need of his services in the near future. We must not act without ample forethought, especially in view of this *Keys of Osiris* development. As you know, Salidar is an asset worth keeping; provided, of course, he is used wisely, with much supervision."

"You will get no argument from me on that count," the Rogue admitted and grinned. "Now, I must go; the hour grows late."

The Guildmaster stood and extended his gloved hand. "I understand. Be careful."

"THIS IS NOT GOOD," Trey remarked, "not good at all."

"No," Hawk agreed and stepped to one side of the bloody ground as the CSI tech began taking digital photographs of the crusting pools on the dusty earth. "Oh, man, that is a lot of blood. All the livestock is accounted for; but, there's no sign of Johansen. Unless this . . ?"

"We don't know that," Trey cautioned. "This spot is what—about midway between the house and the barn? Blood could be from a critter of some sort; so, don't jump to conclusions. Just because the patrol units haven't found Johansen doesn't mean he's not around somewhere. Can you see any tracks that make sense?"

"No, not really. There are too many overlapping footprints, probably from our patrol guys. Unfortunately, whatever was there is now obscured. It's not their fault really; they didn't know it was a crime scene when they looked around for Johansen." Hawk sighed. "Maybe I can do a widening circle scan, once everyone else clears out."

"Okay, but that might be a while. In the meantime, let's check the house again; we can—"

"Hey! Detectives! Over here!" A patrolman waved from the area behind the barn. "I got something back here!"

A double-barreled shotgun lay in the weeds. It was in two pieces, the stock shattered at the wrist. CSI techs photographed it in place and prepared appropriate evidence tags and bags.

"Recently fired," announced a tech, "two spent twelve-gauge shells, one in each chamber—"

"Hey!" called out another patrolman. "I've got a cell phone in the grass over here!"

Once photographed in place, a CSI tech slipped the phone into a clear evidence bag and handed it to Trey.

"It's still on; battery must be good." He began to troll through the phone's menu. "Oh, man, no . . . "

"What?" Hawk asked stepping to his partner's side.

Trey tilted the bag so Hawk could see the phone's screen.

"No way . . . " Hawk whispered, his eyes widening.

"Not good," Trey breathed, "not good at all."

SEATED IN CAPTAIN MILLER'S office, Trey shrugged and opened his palms.

"It's not that big of a deal, Captain. An interview with *Teddy Pots* might not give us much, but I wouldn't want to overlook any potential lead. And right now, we don't have all that much."

Captain Miller grunted and leaned back in his chair. "Theodore Rasmussen is in federal custody on a parole violation. But if you think he might be helpful in the Johansen matter, I don't have a problem with you interviewing him. Why can't you just go out to Oakdale Federal Detention Center to do it?"

Trey exchanged a look with his partner before responding. "Well, the last time we saw him, he was pretty *hinky*—"

"More like scared out of his mind," Hawk interrupted, "but we know he saw something."

"True enough." Trey nodded. "And he knows that we know. He's not stupid. He'll probably talk to us; but, he also knows if he does while in the FDC the word will get around on the inmate grapevine, and he might be tagged as a *snitch*."

"He's in general population?" the captain asked.

"Yes sir," Trey acknowledged. "That's why we're asking you to talk to the D.A. and request that the U.S. Marshals arrange to have Teddy brought to their Alexandria office, ostensibly in regard to his pending state cases. There are state detainers on file at the Oakdale records office, so it shouldn't raise any eyebrows. In a worst-case scenario, we might need a writ of *habeas corpus*, but I don't think so."

Captain Miller sat up and raised his index finger. "You'd better hope not. There's no way we would want to assume custody until the D.A. has decided what he's gonna do with Teddy's pending local cases. All right, I'll call the D.A. How soon do you need Teddy transported?"

"The sooner, the better," Trey urged. "We'll only need an hour or so. We'll do the interview in the U.S. Marshals' office, or even their cellblock if there are no other prisoners."

"Okay, as soon as we're through here I'll make the call. Changing the subject, remember the limo driver who was injured in that chase, Vitorrio Smith?"

Trey nodded. "Oh yeah, Papa George's driver, hospitalized, like in a coma, right? What about him?"

"Well, he recovered sufficiently that the hospital released him yesterday. He claims to remember nothing about the accident or anything else relating to it. The doctors say that that sort of amnesia is possible—"

"Or convenient," Trey groused.

The captain scowled at the interruption. "Patrol took him into our custody on the traffic offenses. He went before the traffic court judge this morning and made bond."

"He's out?" Hawk blurted. "What about the federal firearms violations? Didn't they charge him with the constructive possession of the recovered machine guns?"

"No, not yet." Miller shook his head and shrugged. "Apparently the U.S. Attorney wants to sort out the details and take it to a grand jury."

"I get it," Trey offered and leaned toward his partner. "That way they can make it part of the overall RICO case against George Papadolis and his whole crew."

"That seems to be the case," the captain agreed. "Now, is there anything else?"

"No sir, that's it." Trey stood. "If you'll get the ball rolling with the D.A. on Teddy, we'll get going. Thank you, sir."

RETURNING TO THE SQUAD room, Trey asked Hawk, "Have you got those pictures? You know, the blowups from Johansen's cell phone?"

Hawk nodded. "Yeah, locked in my desk, why?"

"Get `em, and then call Ellen. See if we can pay her a visit."

"Sure, but a visit right now? Why?" Puzzlement clouded Hawk's face.

Trey lowered his voice. "Because, partner, I think we're gonna need a little specialized expert help with research and analysis. And Ellen's group of learned and discreet friends, the *Middle Earth Society*, comes to mind."

Hawk could only smile.

CH 4

IN THE REALM OF MER, the night held sway over the urban precincts of Derinseum.

Lord Nightshade, Chief of Her Royal Majesty's Secret Police, leaned across the trestle table in the dingy common room of a second-rate Derinseum inn and locked eyes with his two companions.

"Keep your voices down. Report."

"Here?" asked the Dark Elfin woman as she tried to keep her sheer sleeves from touching the begrimed tabletop. Her small mouth frowned in distaste.

"Of course, here—quietly," he cautioned, with a warning glance around the room.

The drably attired male elf seated beside her remained silent, but Nightshade easily noted the brief flash of amusement that betrayed the more seasoned operative's otherwise stoic facade.

Ah, he did not expect to be working in Mer with such a novice. Well, no matter.

Arranging the delicate skirts of her maid's attire off the filthy floor as best she could, she settled prim and erect, and began her report.

"The Lady Malvana has retired for the evening. The opening ceremonies of the formal negotiations went as expected, although a bit longer than anticipated. Lord Padraic excused himself midway through the afternoon session. I have not seen him since. Lady Malvana made it clear to the Light Elfin representatives that Lord Padraic need not be continuously present throughout the negotiations and that she was duly authorized to proceed on behalf of Queen Mab. There were a few raised eyebrows, but no objections."

"That reaction was predictable," offered the male operative at her side. "Lord Padraic's reputation precedes him. Everyone expects him to take advantage of the delights of Derinseum; and he does not disappoint."

"Indeed? How so?" Nightshade asked, a knot of unease growing in his gut.

"Upon leaving the afternoon session, he went to his guest quarters only to slip out within minutes, and make his way into the heart of the city. Our people followed, of course. In time he came to a well-known dwelling, an upscale brothel run by a woman known as Madam Iris. He was admitted, and is there still."

"Ah, I see." Nightshade sighed; this was as he feared, and, to be honest, expected. "I trust then that this *establishment* is being watched while he, uh, visits?"

"It is. When he leaves, our operatives will follow."

Lord Nightshade sat in silence for a long moment. "Very well. Have either of you learned anything about Gaspar?"

"No, m'lord, nothing," she answered.

Her companion merely shook his head.

"I see." Nightshade bobbed his head. "You may return to your tasks."

Alone once more the elfin lord wrung his hands in frustration.

The queen must have known Lord Padraic would pull a stunt like this. What did she expect? What does she expect me to do? Report this? How can I not? Ye gods, I am truly coming to hate this job!

SALIDAR IGNORED THE ripe smell of unwashed bodies wafting up from the *Doom Wind's* hold. Hefting the sloshing bucket of seawater, he made his way down the ladder. Holding his breath, he placed it within reach of the captive women. The large sliding rings along the length of chain bolted to the bulkheads allowed the prisoners considerable movement at the rear of the hold, but the cruel iron cuffs chafed their ankles mercilessly. Avoiding eye contact, they huddled together.

As he backed off, the prisoners crowded the water bucket, dipped pieces of rag within, and began to swipe at their grime-encrusted faces and arms. At first they watched him warily beneath sullen and guarded gazes, but soon lost interest since he seemed to ignore them.

Within a few moments the bucket was empty. A bolder wench kicked it toward him.

"A refill too much to ask, sailor?"

The other women froze in fear as Salidar snatched up the bucket and scowled at the speaker. It was *her,* she who had caught his eye when they had been brought aboard. The nearest women began to back away from her, as if to avoid any injury his retaliation would surely mete.

"Anything to improve the smell of you lot," he sneered. "Now, if m'ladies will excuse me." He made his way up the ladder, but not before he caught the bold woman's sly smile.

Upon his return, he found her alone at the near end of the chain. He thrust the full bucket at her and whispered, "Do I know you?"

Head bowed as she accepted the water, she hissed, "No, but I know of you, *Grimrald*. When you go ashore in New Port Royal, seek the *Fouled Anchor*, a brothel. Trust only the barkeep, Rumley, and the madam, Topsey."

Wide-eyed, he gasped, "You're of the guild! But how—"

"It matters not! Now I must slap you; you must strike me in return." With that, her hand lashed out at his surprised face with a resounding *smack!*

"I'm not your *whore!*" she screamed. "You filthy bastard!"

Smarting from the blow, he glared at her and swung a backhanded swipe at her head. He barely connected as she rolled away and pitched over backwards, appearing to trip over the chain. The overturned bucket rolled across the wet deck.

"Avast there!" boomed the bosun, clomping down the hold's ladder. "Stand to, Salidar! You were told to clean `em up! Not sample the wares!"

"Aye, bosun, b-but this one—got a m-mouth on her, she does," Salidar stammered, pointing.

The bosun squatted and grasped the felled woman by the chin. Turning her head to and fro, he studied either side of her face. Apparently satisfied, he mumbled, "Ah, you'll do."

Salidar felt the heated sting of his cheek. *Damn, she had not held back—that hurt! At least I pulled my blow, a little.*

The bosun grunted and stood. He leveled a finger at Salidar. "Be glad she is not marked! As for her mouth, heh-heh, she'll have ample use for it once she goes ashore. Now, get ye above decks and leave this cargo be!"

As Salidar preceded the bosun up the ladder, he glanced back to find the woman being helped to her feet by another captive. Catching her gaze, he nodded.

Her only response was a small wink.

DEEP BELOW THE OLD temple ruins on Olmus, Papa George heard something behind him. Tearing his gaze from the scrying orb, he glanced over his shoulder. He saw his mentor shuffling into the chamber; and clearly, something was amiss.

"Daegon?" George arose from the stool and faced him. "What is it? What's wrong?"

"Zerban is dead." The alchemist sighed and shrugged. "I suppose it is partially my fault. I was so preoccupied with delivering Gaspar to the Red Hat goblins, making certain they understood my demands, that I had neglected Zerban of late. My servants seem to have taken advantage of my oversight and absence, and tormented the weakened mage beyond his endurance."

George waved a hand dismissively. "You were pretty much through with him anyway, right?"

Daegon's lips drew into a thin line; he slowly shook his head. "No, I was not. This is a problem."

"What problem? You were gonna have to get rid of him eventually; so, now it's a done deal."

"You do not understand, my apprentice. The giant bats are the problem; I had not yet fully learned the secret to their control. I can barely keep them contained. My servants bumble about in abject fear of them and only do my bidding regarding the bats' upkeep because they fear me even more. Somehow, Zerban had some semblance of actual control of these bats, but just *how* has eluded me."

"Look here," George reasoned with open palms. "You got everything you could from him; don't worry about it. There may not have been much of anything worthwhile left. Could you have really gotten every last scrap of knowledge from him?"

"In time, my apprentice, in time, but alas . . ."

"Well, what's done is done," George declared with a brisk *slip-slap* of his hands. "And we have something else to discuss."

"Indeed? What might that be?"

"Remember how we agreed that you'd teach me sorcery, especially that transiting thing you can do with those black spheres? And that I'd work on getting us *organized* and getting some *earners,* you know, people to work for us?"

"Well, yes, but our servants—"

"No, I don't mean them," George interrupted. "I mean people who can do, uh, certain stuff for us in other realms; things that can show a profit, uh, control some turf, strengthen our position and standing, maybe even acquire more magic power or something."

"I am still not sure I understand all you are saying. I am confused."

"Look, it's gonna be easier for me to show you how it all works once I put the plan in motion; then you'll understand. But to get started, I'm gonna need your help."

"My help? I must admit, I am intrigued. Very well, how can I help?"

"First, I need to find some people in my home realm. I need your help to transit; I can't do what you can with those black transit globes. I think the scrying orb," he pumped his thumb over his shoulder, "can be of some help, to find people, I mean. But once I find them, well, that's where you come in. I need to go there and bring them back here."

"*Here? To Olmus?* This realm—this *place*—is our secret!" Daegon's voice rose in indignation. "Why would we compromise our very security?"

"We compromise nothing!" George insisted. "This place is perfect as a base of operations! I'm not talking about many people, just a few, some you already know, who can be trusted."

Puzzlement clouded the alchemist's face. "Just who are these people?"

George grinned. "We'll start with just one, Vito."

MADAM IRIS GAZED ACROSS her pillow, watching the steady rise and fall of Padraic's chest. It would be nice, she mused, to just lie here and let her cares drift away, but the sun had set and shadows had long faded into true dusk. Sighing, she realized the evening's customers would soon begin to arrive. There were preparations to make for this night's expected patrons—and more importantly, one would require particular precautions.

Her attention returned to Padraic, his eyes fluttering open.

"Ha! I knew you were not asleep," she teased.

"I am still asleep, and having the most pleasant dream. Come here." He leered and reached for her as she sat up.

"Again? Ye gods, you are ever the rascal!" She squealed, spinning away from him and reaching for her robe. "No, I have not the time! The night is nearly upon us, and I have much to do. Do you not have to return to the negotiations?"

"Soon enough, I suppose. I should—"

A knock on the chamber door interrupted him.

A servant poked his head in, his eyes downcast. "Forgive me, madam. The Captain of the Watch is downstairs to speak with you."

"About what?" She belted her robe.

"I know not, madam. He will only speak with you."

"Very well. I shall be down directly."

The servant bowed and took his leave.

"Problem, Iris?" Padraic asked.

"I do not think so." She gathered her clothes and began dressing. "I anticipate a rather unusual guest tonight, a sort of diplomat—a satyr. I was told there would be some security concerns. I suspect that is the reason for the captain's visit."

Padraic sat up, reached into the tousled bedclothes, and found his shirt.

"A satyr? And a diplomat no less? Whom does he represent?"

She shrugged. "I'm not certain, some group in the wild, I understand. They are certainly not of the Council Realms."

"Hmm, no doubt," he murmured, pulling his shirt over his head. "This is most interesting. You know, entertaining a satyr in your establishment could be *challenging*, if not dangerous."

"Oh, I am well aware. I understand he would require three of my ladies, and the utmost discretion."

He reached for her hand, his voice low. "It might be wiser still to so assign four of your most resilient doves, strength in numbers, and maintain discreet observation."

She squeezed his hand in assurance. "You need not worry. I will take appropriate precautions. Now, you must let me deal with the Derinseum Watch." She paused before releasing his hand. "Padraic, if possible, I would like to see you again before you leave Mer."

"I would like that as well." He grinned, spun her about, and gently smacked her butt. "Now, go act like the proprietress of this fine establishment."

She paused at the door, and glanced at him. A surge of endearment warmed her heart and almost prompted her to speak, but he was already preoccupied amidst the bedclothes.

"Now, where are my trousers?" he mumbled. "And where did my boots wind up?"

With a wistful grin and shake of her head, she slipped from the room.

MINUTES LATER, AS PADRAIC descended the stairs, he heard the rush of footsteps behind him. Turning his head he saw a small woman, her face hidden within a hooded robe, hurrying down the staircase. As he pressed to one side to allow her to pass, a small webbed hand shot forth from the folds of her robe and tugged at his sleeve.

"Follow!" she whispered.

Surprised yet curious, he hastened after her.

She led him through the kitchen and into an unoccupied pantry. Turning to face him, she dropped her hood.

"Selene!" he cried in delight. "What are you doing here? Not that I'm not happy to see you, of course; but here, now? Why?"

"Hush! Keep your voice down! Tis good to see you, too." The voluptuous undine regarded the Rogue with a twinkling gleam in her eye. "It came as no surprise that this brothel was your first stop once you slipped your leash. You do know you were followed, right?"

"Ah, I expected as much. A lone shadow?"

"Perhaps, but not likely. One lingers about across the street, and has been there since you arrived at this house. There was one other, a woman, who spoke briefly with him and slipped away several hours ago. She is probably still nearby, watching from another vantage point."

"I see, a team. It's gotten late; I suspect this afternoon's negotiation session has concluded. I suppose I should return; no doubt my shadows will follow. So, again, why are you here?"

She smiled as one might to a confused child. "To pass on information, silly. The Guildmaster sends his regards. Now, as to the Keys of Osiris, only two vessels are suspected of making periodic and, of course, clandestine visits; the *Doom Wind*, and the *Xanthippe.* Now the latter would be a junk with which I understand you are somewhat familiar, no?"

He grimaced. "All right, spare me your sarcasm, Selene. True, I was briefly an unwilling passenger; I can't recommend the accommodations. I assume that damned sea witch, Circe, is still her master?"

"Aye, she is. We can only speculate the reasons for her rare visits to those cursed waters. Smuggling is suspected, of course, but we have no proof."

He shrugged; this was not that helpful. "Anything about Titania's interest in these islands?"

"Other than it is confirmed that she has an interest, nothing of any real substance. However, there is a rumor."

"Go on."

She leaned closer. "Our sources indicate that the *Doom Wind* recently put in at New Port Royal and will stay to await the arrival of the *Xanthippe*—"

"Salidar is still aboard the *Doom Wind*?" he pressed.

"He is—do not interrupt. He is not your concern; he will have his own tasks soon enough. Pay attention! The *Xanthippe* is here, anchored in Essa Bay. We believe she is here to take on passengers and cargo bound for some undisclosed location. Who or where, we do not yet know for certain. However, since we do know the *Doom Wind* expects her at New Port Royal—"

"Ah, you suspect the final destination is the Keys of Osiris, do you not?" he deduced. "It makes sense. Tis storm season in the Southern Ocean, and the *Doom Wind* is far more seaworthy than the *Xanthippe*. The clipper cannot return to Derinseum since Bane and his crew of *sea dogs* have been declared pirates, and the junk cannot withstand the seasonal storms. So, a relay, the *Xanthippe* ferries the passengers and cargo to New

Port Royal, and once aboard the *Doom Wind* they make for the Keys. But who, the passengers, I mean, have we any idea who that might be?"

She cocked her head. "A relay is speculation, to be sure; but I think you have the right of it. As to the passengers, we do not know. However, whispers of a group in the *wild* have been circulating, someone supposedly interested in establishing a foothold within the Council Realms. Furthermore, they are said to have a powerful patron. The information is spotty at best."

"A foothold in the Council Realms? To what end? And why the Keys of Osiris?" His eyes pinched shut and his head dropped. He rubbed his temples, his utter confusion evident.

"I take it your questions are rhetorical," Selene observed dryly, "for I have no answers. In fact, I have conveyed all current information as instructed. Now, I must go. You should return as well."

"Indeed, be safe, Selene." He looked up.

The undine was gone.

CH 5

"MISS ELLEN, I'M SORRY for the short notice."

Trey stood in the foyer of Delafaire Farm's stately home as the Chow-Chows, Max and Sophie, sniffed at his shoes. The cat, Smokey, watched indifferently from the front parlor.

"Trey, we're friends, aren't we?" Ellen asked.

"Of course, we are. W-why wou—"

"Then please, stop calling me *Miss* Ellen. I'm not my mom's age. Just Ellen will do fine, okay?"

Chagrined, he mumbled, "Oh, of course. Sorry, uh, Ellen."

Hawk smiled. "Be patient with him. He's old school, you know."

Trey tried to scowl, but shook his head in smiling resignation. Turning back to her, he opened his hands and explained. "Ellen, I'm afraid we really need some help, some very discreet help. Your particular group of friends, who, um—"

"You know—the *think tank*—the Middle Earth Society," Hawk interjected. "Like I said when I called; that's who we need to consult now."

"It's not a problem." She grinned and tugged Hawk by the arm. "Come on, everyone's in the kitchen. My mom's got some snacks out."

"We saw Armand and Madeline's minivan parked out front. Who else is here?" Hawk asked as they passed into the dining room.

"Well, Mark and Stacy are upstairs; they'll be down in a minute. Zack and Marie came with Armand and Madeline."

"Miska's not back from the Realm of Were yet?"

"Nope. He might be gone a while; we really don't know. Do you think we're gonna need him?"

Hawk and Trey looked to one another and shrugged.

"To be honest," Trey offered, "we don't know. Let's meet with everyone and we'll explain."

TWENTY MINUTES LATER, silence descended upon the kitchen.

Comparing two of the enlarged photos, Armand broke the spell.

"Are you certain these images weren't captured from some other source, like the internet?"

Trey leaned forward and rested his elbows on the table. "Our CSI techs can't definitively rule it out, but the consensus is that these are first generation images that were taken with the cell phone recovered at the scene. They talked about stuff I didn't fully understand, like meta data and such."

"Let's assume, for the sake of argument," Hawk interjected, pointing to the two photos in the anthropologist's hands, "that these pictures are the real deal. What do you think we're dealing with here?"

Zack reached for the photos. "Armand, may I?"

Madeline stared at the other photos strewn across the table and pointed. "What is wrong with these other pictures? Something obscured or smudged the camera lens?"

"Yes," Trey answered, "blood, we believe."

"Blood?" Marie echoed. "But I thought you didn't find a victim, right?"

"We found no one," Hawk acknowledged, "at least not yet. We know the blood is human, but that's all so far."

Zack and Armand bent their heads together and murmured. Marie and Madeline exchanged worried glances and began rearranging the photographs displayed on the table.

Mark, who had been uncharacteristically silent, asked, "Do you think this has anything to do with that cattle mutila—uh, case you two have been working?"

"Oh, that would be too creepy," Stacy observed with a shudder.

"We don't know." Trey shrugged with open palms. "Anything is possible."

"I'm pleased to hear you have an open mind, Sergeant," Zack said with a nod to Armand, "because we have arrived at an opinion, if not a conclusion, that may be a little hard to swallow."

"Keep in mind," Armand cautioned, "that our analysis is based on these images; and, they're only partial images at best. Thus, we offer only an opinion. Absent conclusive proof, this is the best we can do. Do you understand?"

"Of course, I understand." Trey leaned back. "So?"

"We think," Zack breathed, "that this is *Smilodon*, or a facsimile thereof."

"What?" Hawk blurted.

Armand raised his hands. "It's a large cat, to be sure. These images look very much like Smilodon, a predator; more specifically, an extinct genus of *machairodont felid*. You probably know it better as the saber-toothed tiger, or more appropriately termed, the saber-toothed *cat*. It actually lived in North America during the Pleistocene Epoch."

"But it's extinct, right?" Hawk asked. "At least it's supposed to be, right?"

"That doesn't mean it's extinct *everywhere,*" Ellen softly remarked.

"Yeah? But then how . . ." Mark started to ask. "Oh, yeah—never mind."

"Okay, we get it. But from *where?*" Stacy probed. "I never saw a globe that held anything like that. Wouldn't some realm stuck in the Pleistocene be obvious?"

"Perhaps, perhaps not," Zack warned.

"It may be," Ellen mused aloud, "a naturally occurring phenomena, like a random portal. I know they do happen; that's a fact. But somehow, the more I think about it, the more I doubt it. It just doesn't feel random."

"Well, if it's not random," Stacy reasoned, "do you mean it's deliberate? Someone brought that cat here? Turned it loose?"

"I don't know," Ellen admitted, "but it just feels wrong in too many ways."

"Hmm, I don't disagree. However," Hawk proffered, "if that cat is from another realm, a parallel universe, or whatever, what do we do about it? I mean, if we can find it, what then? Catch it or kill it?"

"There's another question, maybe a bigger one," Trey warned with a wince. "Captured or killed *here*, in this realm, how do we explain it?"

VITO STIRRED THE BURBLING pot of marinara sauce with a practiced hand. The small kitchen in the third-floor New Orleans walk-up was overly warm, but rich with the savory aromas of freshly baked garlic bread, Italian sausage, tomato sauce, and a steaming bowl of whole wheat pasta. He sprinkled a generous pinch of oregano into the pot and gave the wooden spoon a deft flourish as he folded the fragrant herb into the red sauce. Closing his eyes, he leaned over the stove, waved a hand over the simmering pot and deeply inhaled; a smile creased his face.

He paused to sip from a rather delicate wineglass that seemed dwarfed in his large hand. The Chianti was almost past its prime; but he wasn't picky—it would do.

As he reached into the refrigerator for the plate of Parmesan cheese he'd grated earlier, his ears popped. The air pressure in the apartment had suddenly changed. Puzzled, he stepped into the small living room and gaped.

"What the hell?"

A black sphere, almost as tall as he, hovered in the center of the room. A figure stepped forth, George Papadolis, and then another, someone Vito didn't know, and yet seemed vaguely familiar.

"What? Uh, Boss? H-how—what?" Vito stammered.

"Yeah, good to see you, too, Vito. This is Daegon. Uh, Daegon, can we lose the globe?"

The black orb shrank and winked out of existence with a soft *pop*.

Vito narrowed his eyes at the stranger. "Uh, Boss? Isn't this the guy—"

"Yeah, yeah," George interrupted. "Long story, not the time. New place, huh? What smells so good? Are you cooking?"

"Yeah, a little pasta marinara, some nice Italian sausage, garlic bread, some wine. I got plenty; y'all wanna eat?" Vito asked with a trace of pride.

"You bet!" George exclaimed.

Disapproval etched upon his face, Daegon took a step forward. "We have not the time to—"

George raised a hand to forestall the alchemist's objection.

"Hold it, Daegon. When Vito cooks, you *make* the time. Besides, this is as good a place as any to talk without being overheard." He gestured to the small dining table. "Let's sit down, relax. Trust me, Daegon, you're gonna enjoy this. Vito, you can bring me up to speed while we eat."

As they savored the meal, Vito told his tale, occasionally casting wary glances at the newcomer.

"So, you said nothing, and you only got traffic charges?" George's surprise was evident.

"Yeah, once I woke up I kept telling them I didn't remember nothin'—you know, the old amnesia thing." Vito grinned. "I made bond; but I got a court date in about six weeks."

George pursed his lips and rubbed his chin. "That amnesia trick doesn't always work. You know, I bet something's up, maybe at the fed level. What about Ling and her muscle?"

Vito shrugged his massive shoulders. "I dunno about her—never saw her again. I heard her muscle, the two creepy bald guys, didn't make it. The limo got tore up pretty bad; the cops still have it."

George nodded. "You got a lawyer yet?"

"No, not yet," Vito admitted. "I was thinking I might just get scarce, you know?"

"No, bad idea," George cautioned. "I'm gonna need you to be clear of any legal crap, free to move around. I'll make some calls, get the right lawyer to deal with the traffic charges. If this is bigger than it looks, like *federal*, then we can think about having to get scarce. For now, let's not jump the gun. As you might guess, I have a plan."

Vito chuckled and leaned back in his chair. "Don't you always? What do you want me to do?"

"You'll be coming with us. But first, whatever happened to that meth cook, Teddy Pots?"

Vito scratched his head. "Last I heard, he was back inside on an old parole beef, the federal one he told us about. I think he's doing the better part of a nickel."

"A nickel?" Daegon echoed, clearly befuddled.

"A five-year sentence," George explained. "Vito, do you know where?"

"I'm not sure, but my guess would be Oakdale. Want me to ask around?"

George shook his head. "No, don't bother. I can *look into it.* Heh-heh, I found you, didn't I?"

SALIDAR FELT THE VAGUE world of his dream begin to sway and shake. He heard his name called from some distance, getting louder.

"Wake up, Salidar! Open yer eyes, matey!" Crabs bellowed as he shook his crewmate's hammock. "Time's a-wastin' an' we got shore leave!"

"Huh? What?" Salidar managed to mumble as he rubbed the sleep from his face and saw Crabs and the other two crewmen with whom he'd shared watch duty for the past few days. "Tis my watch?"

"Nay, y' bloody fool!" Crabs leaned into his face. "We be relieved! Granted two days shore leave! Now, up and at `em, me bucko!"

Shore leave? Ah, the bosun's promise! Oh, your bloody breath, Crabs! Ye gods! I'm damned well awake now!

Salidar pushed his shipmate back, rolled out of the hammock, and dropped unsteadily to the rough boards of the tween deck. He stretched and mirrored Crabs' wide smile.

"Two days shore leave? That's great! When can we go ashore?"

"Now, y' dunderhead! But gotta stay together; thems bosun's orders. Trust me, it be safer that way. Aye, New Port Royal be a wild `n' wicked place; she suffers no fools. Tis rife with thieves an' cutthroats—like us! Ha-ha! We watch each others' backs; we're crewmates, no? Remember, tis but two days we have. So, any notions? Know ye of a place we should put in?"

"Aye, mayhap there be a place," Salidar offered. "I once heard me a tale of this brothel with fair women and strong drink, the *Fouled Anchor.* Ever hear of it?"

"Aye, as much a gamblin' man's tavern as a brothel," agreed an older, peg-legged crewman, whose name no one could ever properly pronounce, so he was perpetually referred to as Gimp.

His companion, a pirate nearly as old and simply called Patch, no doubt a reference to the black eye-patch he sometimes wore over his empty left socket, leered and bobbed his head in agreement.

Crabs threw an arm around Patch's shoulder and declared, "Well then, tis settled! A-drinkin' an' a-whorin' we'll go! Let's begone afore th' cap'n changes his mind about stayin' in port; he's in the foulest of moods. I'd not tempt the fates, m'self."

"He's always in a foul mood," muttered Patch. "Now what's got `m all a-twist?"

"Lost some cargo, he did. Six women we took on this voyage, and six we offloaded," Crabs recounted. "When the lads marched `em to the slave mart, twas for only five they collected payment. The slavers argued that only five were brought over their threshold. Twas six, by the gods! Curse the buggers! There be no winnin' such an argument with the likes o' them slavers. Cap'n was furious when he heard! I don't ken this is over. So, tis best we steer clear of him, savvy?"

Three heads bobbed as one. They would definitely rather avoid Captain Bane.

Only the bosun was on the main deck to nod his begrudging approval as they quietly made for the gangplank and went ashore.

AS THE FOUR CREWMATES cleared the dock and entered into the boisterous streets of New Port Royal, their spirits rose. To be out of their foul-tempered captain's reach for two whole days was relief enough. Hopefully the missing cargo issue would be resolved or forgotten by the time they had to return.

Salidar suspected he knew exactly which one of the captive women had seemingly disappeared without a trace. His hand went to his cheek and a small smile creased the corners of his mouth.

"Ah, tis that a gleam in yer eye I see?" Crabs teased, slapping Salidar on the back. "Eager be ye, to find this Fouled Anchor, savor some fine rum and a willing wench, eh shipmate?"

"Aye, matey!" *You have no idea.*

CH 6

THEODORE RASMUSSEN awoke in a panic. A massive hand was clamped over his mouth and nose. Another gripped his wrists and pressed his chest down, crushing the thin mattress of the lower bunk. He tried to thrash about, but the vise-like grip tightened—his wrists flared in pain.

"Stop it, Teddy! Be quiet!" hissed a voice near his ear.

Teddy froze; he knew that voice. Vito! *Papa George's muscle! What's he doing here, in my cell?*

Another voice whispered, "Okay, get him up; we gotta go."

Teddy recognized that voice, too. Papa George! *What the—?*

He never finished that thought as he was jerked from the lower bunk to his feet in the dim cell. Vito's face was suddenly all he could see, mere inches from his own.

"Teddy, I'm gonna let you go; but you gotta stay quiet, *capisce?*"

Vito's big mitt still clamped to his face, Teddy tried to bob his head, moaning affirmatively.

As the hands released him, another face was now before him bearing a smug smile with more than a hint of superiority. Papa George! The boss' fist slowly rose; the blooded blade of a stiletto hovered in front of Teddy's nose.

"Not a peep now, Teddy," George warned as he wiped the tip of the blade on the upper bunk's mattress, mere inches from Teddy's cheek.

Teddy swallowed and took a quick personal inventory; no pain, no cuts or wounds. He was not injured. But the blood? He turned his head to peer at his sleeping cellmate.

Oh, shit!

"Yeah, sorry about that," George offered with a dismissive shrug. "He saw us arrive. We can't have that. Now listen, I'm gonna give you a choice. You can come with me now, get out of here, and work for me—you do remember that you owe me, right? Or you can stay here in the joint, do your nickel, and," he gestured with the point of his blade at the cooling body of the dead cellmate, "face the consequences when the bulls do the morning count."

Teddy felt his world collapse. He'd never admit it, but he was somewhat comfortable being institutionalized. He didn't exactly like being locked up, but he could deal with it. Truth be told, he felt safer inside. His nightmares of late had diminished in frequency and intensity. The horrors that haunted his sleep were out there, not in here.

But now, that would change. His dead cellmate was a member of a prison gang, a particularly well organized and vicious gang, infamous for excessive retaliation of any slight or disrespect. Any modicum of *street cred* and respect Teddy had enjoyed as a master meth cook would evaporate as soon as this body was found. No one would believe he hadn't done it. He was a dead man if he stayed.

But this is a federal joint! How did Vito and Papa George get in? How are they gonna get out?

"Daegon," George called softly, as he wiped his prints off the handle of the knife. "It's time to go. Bring the sphere back."

Teddy hadn't noticed the third man leaning against the wall at the rear of the cell, deep in the shadowed corner. He could barely see him in the dimness.

Slight of build and otherwise nondescript, the man straightened, made a series of small hand gestures and whispered, "Stand back."

Teddy gawked as a small black sphere appeared and grew to match the man's height. The mysterious man stepped into the black globe and disappeared.

Vito stepped to the globe, winked at Teddy, and disappeared within.

Alone with Papa George, Teddy was badly shaken and only managed to stammer, "Uh, w-what—"

"Shut up, Teddy. It's decision time—you can come with, or not."

George tossed the bloodstained knife onto Teddy's bunk, stepped into the globe and vanished.

Teddy looked over his shoulder at the still form of his cellmate on the upper bunk and shuddered. He turned and faced the ominous black orb; it was already starting to reduce in size. He was out of options. Closing his eyes and gritting his teeth, he plunged into the obsidian sphere.

A moment later, there was a soft *pop* as the shrinking globe winked out of existence. An ominous silence followed, softly punctuated by the steady *splink-splat* of dripping blood forming an ever-widening pool on the stark concrete floor.

SALIDAR NOTICED THE sour smell of the harbor dissipating as he and his crewmates made their way into the warren of streets rising up from the docks. Soon enough new odors assailed their senses; smoky cooking fires, the tang of unwashed bodies, and pungent pockets of sewage. His companions were wrinkling their noses as well. He hoped their destination was upwind of these poorer sections of this port town.

Salidar motioned to the peg-legged pirate and urged him to lead them. "Know where the Fouled Anchor lies, do ye, Gimp? Lead on, then."

"Aye," agreed Crabs, sniffing. "In your wake we'll be, the sooner the better. Mentioned gamblin', ye did! Have they dice games, then? Cards?"

"Aye, to be sure, but twas an age since I been there. I remembers the whores mostly, an' a tough old bird of a madam, Topsey. I had both legs back then, an' m' pick of the pretties! Har-har!"

Crabs made a face and groaned. "Oh, woe is us! Y've served aboard the *Doom Wind* longer 'n me, and I been aboard her for nigh on ten year. Y've had that oak stump since I knowed ya. Let's hope they got 'em a new crop o' pretties since then! Har-ha-ha!"

Gimp grinned, swatted at Crabs' head, and nearly lost his balance, but Patch caught him and guffawed. "Ha-ha! 'Ere now, Crabs! No respect f' yer elders, 'ave ye?"

Salidar snorted in laughter with his crewmates. He felt good, accepted, and comfortable with his companions as they walked through the streets of the raucous and randy port town; but he knew not to let his guard down. Aside from his personal circumstances, New Port Royal was an inherently dangerous place. No law held sway here, other than the general acceptance and adherence to a somewhat generic pirate code: might makes right, a man's word is his bond, and vengeance is a way of life. Life was cheap here; survival was assured to no one.

"Thar she be," announced Gimp, pointing to the largest stone and timber building along the cobblestone street. A weatherworn wooden sign, depicting a rusted anchor fouled by a length of loose line, hung out on a beam carved from an old yardarm that jutted forth above a set of open double doors. A cacophony of voices spiced with intermittent bursts of creative cursing and boisterous laughter echoed into the street.

Crabs smiled. "Methinks that likin' this fine establishment is to be our lot, lads."

As they walked toward the open doors, Salidar took the time to look around. The buildings to either side were of similar construction, but not as large. One held a carpenter's shop, the other an apothecary that had seen better days. Opposite the bar and brothel, a group of sullen young men, teens likely, sat under the leaning overhang of a decrepit facade that had been a storefront of some sort. An unreadable sign was faded and split, the window glass broken, and a shattered door hung off its hinges.

Salidar sensed these youngsters were watching his group carefully, and trying their best not to be obvious about it.

Ah, these boys are planning some trouble. I must keep them in mind.

As the crewmates crossed the *Fouled Anchor's* threshold, the din inside drained away and silence befell the common room. All eyes turned to the newcomers, who froze in cautious apprehension.

A short man with huge shoulders came out from behind the bar. A white apron was tied just below his barrel chest. His sleeves, rolled up to the elbow, strained against the bulges of his muscular arms. His hair was a scraggly nest of unkempt wire held back by a knurled silver circlet at the nape of his neck. Despite his welcoming, yet reserved, smile, his face was one of the ugliest Salidar had ever seen.

However, his voice was a surprise; deep, clear, and resonant.

"Welcome, sailors, surely ye be, to the *Fouled Anchor, if* ye can afford to partake of our hospitality. We offer no charity here. So, what's it to be? Be ye *guests* or no?"

Gimp nudged Crabs, who evidently got the hint and produced a small fat purse that clinked with the promise of coin.

"Aye, guests, to be sure, good sir." Patch added hastily.

The barman smiled broadly, an unsettling sight. "Well met and welcome! I be Rumley, the barkeep. We offer strong drink, games of chance," he leaned forward and winked, "rooms, and softer companionship, if y' take my meaning, upstairs." He nodded his head toward a flight of stairs along one wall.

At a landing about midway up, a lone woman attired in a bustier and slit skirt stood surveying the crowd in the common room. Salidar could see that beneath her elaborate hairdo festooned with colorful feathers she was very attractive, albeit middle-aged and running to plumpness. Her expression appeared to be that of mild boredom, but Salidar sensed that her gaze missed nothing.

Rumley noticed Salidar staring. "That be my partner, Topsey. If ye wish to spend time with her ladies, she be who t' see, savvy?"

The crewmates nodded as one.

Rumley grinned widely. "Well then, will y' be needin' rooms?"

"We can share a room," Crabs proffered as the rest shrugged and nodded.

"Fine, a shared room it is," Rumley agreed. "Eight coppers for the night, in advance, if y' please."

Crabs counted out the coins and dropped them into the barkeeper's large hand.

"Now, need ye a table, or will the bar suffice? The tables are for the games, y' see."

"The bar will do for now," Salidar decided. "If my crewmates would join a game underway, there be no problem?"

"None," Rumley assured them, "be there an open seat at the table, and no seated player objects."

"Fair enough," agreed Crabs, receiving nods from all.

"One moment," cautioned Rumley. "There be three house rules: no cheating, no credit, and no bloodletting. If y've a fallin'-out w' someone, take it outside."

They nodded once more and followed Rumley to the bar.

The murmur of low conversations began, and the interrupted games of chance resumed. Soon the common room returned to its state of rousing yet benign chaos. The crewmates began eagerly debating which of the offered distractions each man was inclined to sample first, and of course, how outrageously successful he would no doubt be.

Salidar took little part in that discussion, satisfied to sip his spiced rum grog and smile at the outlandish braggadocio his companions were so predisposed to spout. Smiling at another of Crabs' inveterate witticisms he happened to glance around and caught the woman on the landing, Topsey, staring directly at him.

A memory surged . . . *trust Rumley* . . . *trust Topsey* . . . He turned back to the bar and cradled his mug. When he dared to turn again, the landing was vacant.

THE PHONE TRILLED IN the CID office.

Hawk stretched across his desk and snatched it up.

"Squad room, Detective Redhawk, oh, hey Ellen . . . No, no problem . . . Yeah? He did? Okay, go on . . . I dunno . . . All right, maybe, we'll see. I gotta talk to Trey . . . No, I don't think so, not tonight . . . Yeah, I will . . . Okay, I'll call you . . . Me, too, bye."

Trey leaned back and propped his feet up on his desk. "Okay, you gotta talk to me about what? Is everything okay with Ellen?"

Hawk waved a hand to assure his partner. "Oh, she's fine. She just wanted to tell us that Miska is back."

"Uh-huh, and what else?"

Hawk leaned forward, glanced around the squad room, and motioned for Trey to draw near.

Trey sighed, dropped his feet to the floor, and scooted his chair closer. "Okay, what?"

"Bassett! Redhawk! My office!" boomed the captain from his doorway.

As they filed into Lou Miller's office, he pointed to two wooden chairs. "Shut the door and grab seats."

Trey settled in his chair and asked, "What's up, Captain?"

Hawk noted that Captain Miller remained standing. That was never a good sign.

"You're not gonna be able to interview that Oakdale inmate, Theodore Rasmussen, aka *Teddy Pots*. He's escaped, and—"

"What?" Hawk blurted in interruption, and immediately winced at the irritation that flashed across the captain's face.

"The U.S. Marshals' office called," the captain continued. "Oakdale can't find him; they have no idea how he got out. He was discovered missing at the morning count. His cellmate was found murdered, his throat cut. Needless to say, Teddy is their number one suspect."

"That doesn't sound like Teddy." Trey shook his head. "He's no killer; he's just a meth cook and user. He hasn't been a hard case for years. There was a time, when he was *young 'n' dumb,* that he'd fight the police; but he always lost, so he gave that up. I don't think he's ever really hurt anybody, much less killed someone. Are they sure about this?"

Miller shrugged. "You know what I know. Teddy's gone and all that was found was a knife and his dead cellmate. The U.S. Marshals and the FBI are meeting with the resident BOP/SIS officer to follow up on a gang-related lead; the dead man was a gang member."

Hawk nudged Trey. "SIS?"

"Oh, that's Bureau of Prisons intelligence; every BOP institution has someone assigned. They track illicit activity, gather and analyze intelligence, especially gang intel, and not always on the *inside.*"

"Oh yeah, I get it. Sorry to interrupt, Captain, but I gotta agree with Trey; this doesn't sound like Teddy at all."

"Be that as it may," the captain cautioned, "there will be a federal escape warrant issued and logged in NCIC today. That's enough to get him back in custody; they can charge him with the murder later."

"Yeah, I see the logic." Trey nodded. "They'll hunt him on the escape warrant. Then when he's caught, they'll take both cases to the grand jury and roll `em up into one indictment. Escape can only get him another five years, but murder can get him the death penalty. I dunno—my gut says something's not right here."

"Perhaps not. Nonetheless, Detectives, your interview will have to wait until he's captured."

"If other gang members on the *outside* don't get to him first," Trey muttered. "Is there anything else, Captain?"

"No, that's it. You're dismissed."

BACK AT THEIR DESKS, Trey leaned toward Hawk. "Well, talking to Teddy is gonna have to wait, if we get to do it at all. So, what were you going to tell me, before the captain called us into his office?"

"Oh, yeah." Hawk dropped his voice. "Ellen has an idea about the, uh, *cat problem,* and she thinks that Miska can help. She wanted to know if we could come by to talk about it. She offered supper, too."

Trey shook his head. "I gotta pass; the wife and I have dinner plans tonight. You go, see what Ellen has in mind. She's got a good head on her shoulders. Her theory about how it might have gotten here makes pretty good sense, knowing what we do, you know? And let's face it; the truth is that we can't afford to turn down any help at this point."

SITTING ON THE EDGE of the disheveled bed, Padraic poured the wine and smiled wistfully.

"I had hoped to spend even more time with you, Iris, but alas, I fear duty calls. If all goes well, I will make every effort to see you once more before I must depart Mer."

She accepted the goblet, careful not to spill a drop upon her tousled sheets. She sipped delicately and sighed. "Oh, I understand. We all have our responsibilities. How much longer do you expect these Elfin Accords negotiations to continue?"

The Rogue shrugged. "The rest of the week, I suspect. I have some other matters that require my attention, mere annoyances I can't ignore. Enough about me; how did it go with your special guest, the *diplomatic satyr?"*

She scowled. "About as well as could be expected, I suppose. It was wise to monitor the situation; it could have easily gotten out of hand. He had quite the appetite, and a strong sense of, ahem, *entitlement.* While I made no official complaint, no need to create a diplomatic issue for the Merchants Association, I would *not* welcome him back."

Padraic shook his head. "I am very sorry to hear that. What of your people? Was anyone harmed?"

"Not harmed, per se, perhaps ill-used. As you know, I generally do not allow any sort of sadism or the like; I had to interrupt his session more than once." Her lips drew into a grim line. "Had the Derinseum Watch not been nearby, ostensibly for his security, I'm not so sure he would have complied with my intervention. I'm certain I sensed his resentment. By the gods, I do not trust him."

"Iris, I have always known you to be a good judge of character." He lifted his glass in a gesture of toast. "If you wouldn't trust someone, then neither should I. By any chance did you learn his name, or whom he supposedly represents?"

She leaned back, pulling the sheet to her chin. "He is called *Silenos.* Be that *name* or *title*, I am uncertain; nor do I know whom he represents. He had two attendants, fauns, who stayed in the common room with the Watch. Some of my girls heard these attendants talking about shipping out aboard a vessel they seemed reluctant to name, as if to utter the very name was an ill omen of its own."

Padraic had his suspicions. "Indeed? Did they mention when?"

"Aye," she acknowledged, "on this morning's tide; and good riddance!"

CH 7

"IT'S SIMPLE, TEDDY." Papa George's smile and open hands did little to assure the nervous meth cook. The torch-lit cavern resounded with faint echoes of his voice. "You're gonna set up and cook right here, in this realm of Olmus. Think of this big cave as your new lab, okay? You'll be perfectly safe, no distractions, and these servants will be at your beck and call."

Looking askance at the pair of subservient goblins at whom Papa George tossed his thumb, Teddy suppressed an urge to cringe.

Jeez, pretty damn creepy for servants—or are they really jailers? Am I out of the frying pan and into the fire? Nah, I couldn't stay in the joint—I'd be a dead man. I just gotta make the best of this.

George leaned forward, dropped a hand on the frail man's shoulder and waved a finger under his frightened nose. "Look, everything's gonna be all right. Just tell Vito what you're gonna need to get set up. We'll take care of getting it. You just focus on production, *capisce?*"

Teddy bobbed his head, knowing he had little choice. Hearing a scrape upon the rock floor, he turned to see Vito enter from the mouth of a tunnel.

"You sent for me, Boss?" The big man towered over the goblin servants, who leaned away in a subtle display of deference, or perhaps fear.

"Yeah, I did." George took a step back from Teddy, unconsciously wiping his hands on a handkerchief. "Teddy here, is gonna give you a list, stuff he'll need to get cooking. Come see me when you're done."

"You got it, Boss."

"Good. Where is Daegon?"

Vito shrugged. "Dunno for sure. He was at the scrying orb when I last seen him."

GIMP LOOKED A BIT UNSTEADY to Salidar's eye as he made his way down the staircase and approached the bar. However, there was no mistaking the grin festooned upon the old pirate's face.

It had not escaped Patch's notice either. "Ah, Gimpy, me bucko! Did the pretties of the Fouled Anchor affix that smile t' yer ugly mug? Had yer pipes cleaned, did ye?"

"Aye, mates! Me pipes be clean!"

Patch and Salidar snorted in laughter, as Gimp waved to Rumley, the barkeep, signaling for another round of grog.

"Where be Crabs? I'll stand him another as well," Gimp offered genially.

Salidar shrugged and nodded to the other side of the barroom. "He's been at the dice games since right after you went up to see the madam."

"Pah! The fool! Got the luck of a scabby dog, he does—or be he winnin'?" Gimp scowled, and stole a glance at Rumley.

Salidar caught the inference immediately. "What? He'd not *cheat*—would he?"

His eyes wide, Gimp breathed, "He best not—twould not go well for us."

"*Us?* Why? What mean y' by that?" Patch pressed.

"Hush!" Gimp hissed as Rumley approached with three full mugs.

The three crewmen nodded to their host in thanks and drank deeply.

As Rumley left to wait upon another patron at the other end of the bar, Gimp leaned close. "Heed m' words, shipmates; ever seen a *Fenoderee* in full fury?"

His brow knit, Patch asked in *sotto voce*, "Y' can't mean of the *Ferrishyn,* or no?"

"Aye, that I do. Our host, the barman Rumley, a halfling he be. The blood of a Fenoderee runs in his veins, his father, or so the tale is told."

Patch blew a stream of air and reared back shaking his head. "Then, by thunder, tis not the man to trifle. Aye, seen the cut of his jib, 'ave ye? Twould be hell to pay."

Salidar had never dealt with any of the Ferrishyn before, but he was well aware of their reputation. Hardworking and industrious denizens of *Faerie*, they were renown for being true to their word and equally unforgiving toward those who broke their sworn trust. Among them, the Fenoderee, possessed of prodigious strength and stamina, were the most feared as they took the deepest umbrage to betrayal. They relished in retaliatory violence, and often tended to berserker rages that sometimes only abated upon complete exhaustion. To deliberately cross or mislead a Fenoderee was foolish in the extreme.

Yet it was Rumley and Topsey who Salidar had been told to trust. He certainly didn't need any more complications—like his shipmate Crabs cheating at dice, especially after they'd all been warned.

"Listen, lads," Salidar ventured. "We like this place, right? We can't have Crabs muck this up for us, can we now? Gotta make sure he's not cheating, don't we?"

"Aye," Gimp and Patch mumbled.

"So, you two go have a look, over his shoulder like, if need be. I'll keep the barman busy for a bit. If all be well with Crabs, just drift back here to the bar; if not, find some way to take him outside, savvy?"

"Aye, good plan, matey." Patch winked with his one good eye, and nudged Gimp. Their mugs in hand, they pushed off the bar and began to mosey through the gaming tables.

Salidar watched for a moment and then turned back to the bar. Hefting his nearly drained mug he caught the barman's attention.

"Another, good sir?" Rumley called out.

Salidar smiled, bobbed his head, and watched as the broad-shouldered barkeep approached with a freshly filled mug.

He is rather ugly; but, he does look powerful. Hmmph, no one to trifle with, indeed.

"Be ye in port long?" Rumley asked as he slid the grog before Salidar. "I ask `cause Topsey needs knowin' if ye `n' yer mates will want the room for more `n a night, y' see?"

Salidar shrugged. "Truly, I know not. Our captain hasn't consulted with the likes of us." *And I'm not of a mind to ask him.*

"Came in aboard the *Doom Wind*, did ye? Aye, Captain 'Bloody' Bane is not one to share his plans. Well, no matter—"

"Wait!" Salidar interrupted. "How did you know we crew aboard the *Doom Wind?*"

Rumley chuckled. "New Port Royal tis a small town, full of suspicious types. Word travels fast, especially when a ghost ship arrives."

"*Ghost ship?* What do you mean?"

The barman leaned back in surprise. "You crew aboard the *Doom Wind,* and you don't know?"

Salidar leaned forward, opened his palms, and lowered his voice. "I don't. Care to enlighten me, if you please?"

Rumley glanced around the common room, and leaned forward. "Never heard you of that vessel's origin? Know you nothing about her?"

Salidar shrugged. "I know she's a fast ship, stout of build and weather tight. But I've heard little of her history. Tis not something spoken of, above or below decks—passing strange, that."

"Well, truth be told, the tale be a bit muddled," Rumley admitted. "Seems she just appeared one night, well over a century ago, adrift in the Southern Ocean. The Mer found her, sails reefed and cargo hold empty. Twas no one aboard save a lone seaman whose mind was addled, his wits all askew. He made little sense to any who would listen, babbling on about an ax murderer on board who killed the captain and butchered the crew."

"An *ax murderer?*" Salidar gasped. "What happened?"

"No one knows for sure. As for the ship, the Mer towed her to Essa's port at Derinseum. Tis true that no trace of the captain or any other crew was ever found. Once ashore in Essa, the deranged man died within a fortnight. For months, no one came forth to claim the ship. Eventually she went to auction; sold cheap, she was. Y' see, many heard of the seaman's wild tale, the rumors runnin' rampant and all. Few honest men were willing to bid on so cursed a vessel, but sold she did. Even so, twas always a mystery who bought and renamed her."

"What? The ship was renamed? Why? What was she originally called?" A memory of the ship's bell surfaced in Salidar's mind. *Now, what was it? Ariel? 18-something? 1865?*

"Aye, renamed she was," Rumley nodded sagely. "Tis a bit of old sea lore to frustrate a vessel's curse; rename the ship to hide it from ill intent and confuse any vengeful spirit invoked. An old tale to be sure, but sailors be a superstitious lot, savvy?"

"Aye," Salidar agreed. "Know you then her original name?"

"Nay, not I." Rumley shook his head. "There may be some that do, but tis not likely they'd admit so, or give such to voice—bad luck, y' see?"

Salidar nodded, sighed, and sipped from his mug. This was interesting information, indeed, and he couldn't help but crave more. "If this was all of a century and more in the past, has this ship been in sea service all this time?"

The barman grinned. "To be sure. Oh, she's been refitted with fresh lumber and rigging as needed. She's been through a succession of owners. As you must know, since you crew aboard her, she's well maintained and as fit as the day she was launched."

Salidar leaned back and smiled. "Aye, that she is. Know a lot about the *Doom Wind,* do y' not? I find that interesting."

Rumley waved a hand in dismissal. "Ach, tis not so much. This be a port town, and we know our boats." He gestured with a finger over Salidar's shoulder. "Oh, it looks like y' crewmates are taking their friend outside—mayhap he be sick?"

Salidar blanched and twisted his head around. "Oh damn! Uh, I best check on them!"

"As y' will," Rumley responded and began wiping the bar with a small towel.

PAPA GEORGE FOUND DAEGON where Vito had last seen him, in the chamber of the scrying orb. However, the alchemist was not paying close attention to the crystal globe as was his habit; instead he sat cross-legged upon the stone floor, nose-deep in an ancient grimoire open upon his lap. A number of tilting stacks of dusty tomes lay haphazardly to his left, in contrast to a number of fragile scrolls carefully laid out to his right.

"Daegon, what are you doing? What's all this?" George swept his hands to encompass the apparent disarray. "Where did this stuff come from?"

"Oh, these are from the *late* Magus Atrellan's redoubt; he had quite the library. Now, it and all its sorcerous lore are mine." Daegon's smug smile and lone raised eyebrow spoke volumes.

"I get it," George assured him, "but why is it here, in this room? This is a cramped space as it is, so why spread it all out here? I mean you have your own chamber you use as a library, right?"

"Oh, I was there, researching bats and their control. Delving into some of Atrellan's more obscure volumes was enlightening, to say the least. I found something I did not anticipate, which led me to pursue an unrelated line of inquiry here, in this chamber. But leave that for the moment—how goes it with your *cooking endeavor*? Are the accommodations satisfactory?"

"We're good; that cavern will work just fine. Vito will get Teddy everything he needs. I'll help Vito with the transiting thing as much as I can, but I'm sure I'll need your help. I'm still not getting those black transit globes to work that well for me."

Daegon smiled and nodded. "Nonetheless, you have come a long way indeed, my apprentice. I am pleased with your progress."

George returned the smile. "Thanks. I think it'll be a coupla weeks before we'll have enough product for large scale distribution. Having the lab in this realm and my customers in another is gonna work out very well. I don't have to worry about cops raiding this place, and the distribution network in my home realm is already established. Hell, in time, I might even branch out to other realms—you never know. Once addiction takes hold, I can exert lots of control over people—and that's not magic."

Daegon raised a finger. "As we discussed before, it may not be wise to introduce this drug, *meth* you call it, to those who reside in realms other than that of Man. You know not what its effect may be, or on whom."

"Yeah, maybe. But believe this; to be addicted is to be controlled," George insisted in grim finality.

"To be *addicted* is to be *controlled*?" Daegon echoed, and began to grin. "I believe you may have given me the key to a most puzzling quandary."

"Huh? Well, whatever. You still haven't told me why you brought all these books and scrolls into this little chamber. So?"

"Ah, as to that," Daegon rose, stretched his back, and placed one hand upon the scrying orb. A minor flash, almost a spark of static electricity flared within and went quiescent. "My reading," he gestured to the books and scrolls strewn across the stone floor, "has been quite informative. Have you ever wondered about this orb, its abilities, or how it works?"

"Sure, I have; but it's magic right?"

"Indeed. Have you ever wondered if there might be more than this one?"

"I never gave it much thought. Are there more?"

"Perhaps, according to what I've read," he gestured to the books and scrolls. "It seems there were many once. They may have even been more versatile and powerful than we now know. This certainly merits more research."

George shrugged. "Research? Yeah, I guess that is your thing."

"Indeed." Daegon smirked. "Tell me, what do you know about the Keys of Osiris?"

"The *what?* Never heard of it."

"Ah, make yourself comfortable," Daegon said as he resumed sitting amidst his books and scrolls. "We have much to discuss."

George smiled. *So long as there's profit or power in it for me, I'm interested.*

STANDING OUTSIDE THE Fouled Anchor, Salidar winced in the sunlight. He squinted to his left and right; there was no sign of his crewmates. The street in front of the saloon was empty.

I can't be more than half a minute behind them. Where the hell are they?

In fact, there wasn't another soul in sight. Over his shoulder he could still hear the raucous din from within the bar, which was somewhat reassuring. He took a few steps to his right, in the direction of the old apothecary, and heard something.

Was that a groan? Where? Around the side of the building, I think.

He turned the corner and saw that deep shadow lay between the buildings. He could not see clearly into the gloom; his eyes had not yet adjusted from the bright sunlight. Two paces into the shadowed dimness and his vision began to improve.

Another groan caught his attention, and a shape, on the ground . . . *a body?*

Salidar tried to peer closer, however a scuffing sound to his rear distracted him. He began to turn his head, but a solid *thump* above his right ear stunned him.

Consciousness dwindled away.

CH 8

DEEP WITHIN THE FORGOTTEN and musty archives of the Council Realm, Elsbeth folded her tiny hands and leaned across her desk.

"I must say, Guildmaster, you rarely visit me these days. Am I to assume something has happened?"

"Yes, I suppose that assumption is warranted. I have heard from Padraic; this mysterious diplomatic envoy is a satyr called Silenos—"

"A satyr? Not the same, surely?" The aged brownie made no effort to mask her surprise, or her obvious concern.

"Unlikely, but in truth, I do not know." The Guildmaster shrugged and balled his gloved fists. "That name gave me pause as well. Padraic could offer little more, other than this Silenos is attended by fauns and is expected to journey to the Keys of Osiris. In fact, he may have already set sail aboard the *Xanthippe*, bound for New Port Royal."

"Ah! The *Doom Wind* is there—a relay, perhaps?"

"My thinking, as well. Of course, his name may be a mere coincidence, and he a legitimate diplomat representing some group in the wild. But what reason would he have to go to the Keys? They are of no importance to the Council, and of little to Mer itself."

Elsbeth sat back and raised a tiny finger. "Perhaps not, but the same cannot be said for Queen Titania. I do not believe in coincidence. We have heard rumors that she has developed a keen interest in these islands. If true, she would be wise to work through intermediaries. Could she be something of a silent patron to this presumed diplomat?"

The Guildmaster nodded. "A patron is rumored; so, that would make sense. But what does she have to gain? What could Silenos offer that would entice her support? We know she does nothing without sufficient benefit to herself, unless—"

"Unless it satisfies her thirst for vengeance. Bear in mind that Titania has a long memory—and nothing irks her more than her wandering husband's *not-so-secret* escapades." Elsbeth nodded sagely. "So, if this Silenos were to offer her the identity of her husband's current infatuation, or worse a location of Oberon's get—"

He slammed a gloved hand flat upon the desk! "She'd stop at nothing!"

"I agree. Worse, she could be easily manipulated with such bait. Of course, she would be most devious in her methods; but, she would be determined in her ruthlessness." The old archivist sighed and smoothed the pleats of her robe. "Even if our speculation is accurate, it does not explain Silenos' interest, does it?"

"No, it does not," he admitted. "Unless, as the use of that name might suggest, there is more to him than anyone presently knows, or—"

"Do not go there!" She waved her hands in interruption. "*That* Silenos is long dead, if the Dragon Lords are to be believed. It would be ominous indeed to begin to doubt them."

"I do not," he assured her. "But for the sake of argument, what if this Silenos does know *something*, and is, as we suspect, manipulating Titania for his own ends? What could we do?"

"An excellent question, Guildmaster. Silenos aside, assuming Titania knows no more than we suspect, then we have one other we must consult."

"Barnabas, you mean—do you not, Elsbeth?"

"I do. He must be warned, whether the threat be real or not. Beyond that, we can do little more than gather intelligence and prepare to muster our resources."

She leaned forward once more, dropping her voice to a mere whisper. "There may be another task before you that merits due consideration, and proper timing."

"Indeed?"

"In a worst-case scenario, we will need *all* our resources. And there is now but one Steward in all the known realms . . ." Elsbeth's words dwindled into a breathless silence.

The Guildmaster sighed heavily. "I know."

IN DELAFAIRE FARM'S kitchen, Hawk leaned back from the table and patted his stomach. "My compliments to the chef! I'm stuffed."

Millie rose from the table and smiled. "What? No room for some apple pie and a scoop of vanilla ice cream?"

"Oh, I think he could manage," teased Ellen. "How about you, Miska?"

"Yes, indeed," rumbled the big man, grinning. "I, too, can manage!"

"Okay, desserts all around," Ellen declared, and stood to help her mother. "Mom, don't we need to save some for Mark and Stacy? They're running late."

"Not to worry, dear. I baked two pies, and there's plenty of ice cream. Mark called to say they'd be tied up for at least another hour, so we shouldn't wait supper on them."

Miska muffled a belch, as Millie slid a plate bearing a huge slice of pie topped with a generous scoop of vanilla before him. "Oh, `scuze me.

Thank you, Miss Millie! Now, Mark and Stacy—I am confused. Who are they meeting, some *spider-person?*"

Ellen snorted in laughter. "Ha-ha! No, a *website designer*, someone who will create an internet web page for our farm business." She put Hawk's dessert before him. "It's basically advertising and a means to make sales, but it has to look good and professional. It's just the way one does business these days."

"Oh, I see I have still much to learn."

"Perhaps," Ellen conceded, "but we still can learn much from you, as well. Remember what we discussed, how you might be of help to Hawk and Trey?"

"Oh, yes!" Miska wolfed down another bite of pie. "Hawk, if you would allow, I believe I can be of help in tracking your *cat problem*."

"Okay, I'm listening. But I gotta tell you, we haven't had much luck, even with dogs. I took a risk and brought my grandfather out to the last site we found. He's the best tracker I've ever known, but he couldn't do any better." Hawk spooned up a puddle of melted ice cream and smiled as he savored its taste.

"I may surprise you." Miska leaned forward. "I can track anything, when I am in my bear form. I would gladly do this for you and Trey; but, it must be, how do you say *in secret . . . discreet?*"

"Discreet? Yes, very good, Miska!" Ellen beamed. "Your vocabulary continues to impress me. You are becoming much more articulate."

Miska smiled in return. "No doubt tis the company I keep."

Hawk finished mopping up the last of his dessert before replying. "Oh, that's some good pie, Millie! Thank you so much!"

Turning to the big man, Hawk shrugged. "Miska, I'll have to run this by Trey, but I don't think he'll turn down your offer. To be honest, we're kinda stuck, and can use all the help we can get."

"There is one thing, friend Hawk. I will need access to a fresh site, and no one but yourselves can be there."

Hawk paused. "We could probably arrange something. But there is a problem; the freshest site we know of may be weeks old—"

"No," Miska interrupted, "I mean a *fresh* site, a new kill, without any additional overlaid scents. Do you understand?"

"Yes, but we don't have any fresh kills, at least not that we know of."

Miska's voice grew somber as he looked up from his plate.

"If what our friends in the Middle Earth Society suspect is true, you will."

PAPA GEORGE WINCED as the light entered his sleeping chamber. His servant, Clement, was accompanied by a goblin servant who thrust the lantern too near George's face.

"Back off! Get that thing outta my face! All right, what is it?"

Clement's voice was a monotone drone. "Master, Vito returned. You said to tell you."

"Yeah, okay . . . I'm coming."

GEORGE FOUND VITO IN the lab cavern, in conversation with Teddy. Daegon stood to one side of a huge pile of crates and cardboard boxes.

"Hey, Boss!" Vito hailed. "Teddy tells me he's got everything he needs to get started. Daegon here was a big help transiting all this stuff; having him do that made it a piece of cake."

"Good. What about the generator, wiring and lights?"

"Got all that. It'll take me about a day to get it all set up. The generator will have to go in an upper chamber that vents to the outside—fumes, you know? We got enough lights for the lab and our spaces; all the rest will still need lanterns, torches, or candles. That's what you had in mind, right?"

George nodded. "Yeah, If we're gonna be spending time here, we're gonna have to have some basic creature comforts; power and lighting are priorities for us. The goblins can get by with their torches and stuff, so don't worry about their areas. That's okay, right, Daegon?"

"That should not be a problem," Daegon agreed.

"Okay, good. Teddy, get set up and let Vito know if there's anything you forgot. I wanna see some product sooner rather than later, *capisce?*"

Teddy bobbed his head and started unpacking boxes.

George motioned for Daegon and Vito to follow him from the cavern. He led them to the room of the scrying orb.

"What's up, Boss?" Vito wrinkled his nose in distaste as two goblin servants hastily departed the chamber. For some reason the goblins avoided the big driver.

"Did anyone see you or Daegon?"

"No, not that I know of. We were careful, Boss."

"Rest assured, my apprentice, we were not seen." Daegon smirked smugly.

"Okay. Daegon, we gotta talk about this trip you want us to make, you know, to those islands—"

"The Keys of Osiris," the alchemist offered.

"Yeah, them. Okay, I get why you want to go, because you think there's some elements of power to be gained. You think that's the source of this orb—"

"I am certain it is; and, this may not be the only one. As I have told you before, my research has given me a somewhat clearer picture of such things. There is a great deal to be learned, an opportunity not to be missed."

"Okay, I get all that." George opened his palms. "But I don't see why *I* have to go. This isn't a good time. It's not wise to leave Teddy alone here—uh, no offense, Vito. I need to personally monitor Teddy until this lab is up and running smoothly. You don't even know how long we're gonna be gone. That's just not gonna work with this lab just getting going."

The alchemist pursed his lips and tilted his head. "Did you not tell me that this *product* would appeal to many in the realms? *New customers* you called them. Are you not aware of the role the realm of Mer has come to play among the council realms? Its beaches, islands, and festivals are renown. It has become a holiday playground of sorts, and entertains visitors from all realms. Does this not pique your interest?"

"Oh yeah, I get it, new customers and all. It sounds almost too good to be true, a permanent Mardi Gras or Vegas! But, damn it, Teddy's gotta be watched, at least for a while."

"Uh, Boss, I could go," Vito offered. "I could check it out, you know. I know what to look for, as a potential market. Then you could keep an eye on Teddy."

"That might work," George acknowledged, "pretty well actually; but I'd need you back here within a week. Daegon, what do you think?"

"I will most certainly need more than a week. There is too much I must look into, and—"

"You're forgetting something," George interjected.

"What?"

"Gaspar! Your plan, remember? He's still a slave of the Red Hat Goblin tribe. You need to send Stellara on her mission, soon."

"Oh, yes." The alchemist sighed. "Very well, we will return in time."

George paused in thought, then smacked a fist into an open palm. "All right. When do you plan to leave?"

Daegon laid a finger aside his nose and pursed his lips once more. "I must consult my notes and make appropriate preparations. We could transit at any time to Mer with no problem; but, getting to the actual islands, since I have never been there before, will present a minor challenge. I must do some more detailed research, but I suspect a day with my books will be sufficient."

"So, you'd leave the day after tomorrow?"

"Yes, at sunrise," Daegon confirmed. "Now, if you will excuse me, I have much to do."

SALIDAR BECAME AWARE; he was flat on his back and his head throbbed with a vengeance.

What the hell? Where am I? A room? It's dark—no, just dim. This is a bed?

"He's waking up. Call the madam!"

A woman's voice . . . Where am I? How'd I get here? Where are my shipmates? What's going on?

"Easy there, sailor. No, don't try to get up; just stay still. The madam will be here in a minute. Would you take some water?"

He realized he was parched, and nodded emphatically.

The woman held a bowl of water to his lips; he drank greedily.

"Don't let him drink so fast, or he'll puke," warned another voice. "Stand aside."

"Yes, madam." She withdrew the bowl and stepped back.

Another figure loomed over him, and brought a candle to bear. In the light of the taper, he recognized the madam, Topsey.

"Tell Rumley I need him. See to it we are not disturbed."

"Yes, madam."

Alone with her, Salidar tried to speak, but his voice was a mere croak, his throat still too dry. He pointed to the water in a silent plea.

"If you can sit up, I'll hand it to you, understand?"

He nodded and struggled to sit up. His head pounded, but he managed.

As she passed him the bowl, the door opened and Rumley entered.

"Ah, he's awake I see." The barman closed the door. "Let's have another candle, shall we?"

Rumley touched the wick of a fresh taper to Topsey's lone flame, and faced the closed door. He made a series of small gestures and mumbled something under his breath. There was a subtle increase of pressure in the room, almost enough to make one's ears pop.

Salidar drained the bowl and found his voice. "What—"

Topsey moved faster than he could have imagined. Her hand clamped over his mouth, she hissed into his ear, "Silence, *Grimrald!*"

The empty bowl dropped from his fingers. His heart missed a beat and his eyes bulged—she'd *named* him!

Rumley turned from the door and nodded. "It is done. We may speak freely."

Topsey removed her hand and whispered, "Don't talk, Salidar, just listen. Yes, we know exactly who you are. We have instructions for you from Gallenius, understand?"

He could only nod.

Rumley sat on the bed, retrieved the upturned bowl and handed it to Topsey. "Let's hold off on any more water for the moment."

Salidar squirmed under the barkeep's scrutiny but kept silent.

"Your instructions are simple," Rumley began. "You are to return to the *Doom Wind* and continue to serve as a crewman. You are to be observant. It is believed she awaits the arrival of the *Xanthippe* for a transfer of cargo and passengers. Tis the passengers who are of interest; observe them closely. The *Doom Wind's* next port of call is thought to be the Keys of Osiris, and the likely destination of the passengers. If that is the case, you will be contacted there for your report."

Topsey sat on the other side of the bed and demanded his attention. "Heed my words, Salidar. Should the *Doom Wind* make any other port at the passengers' urging or request, you must notify us."

She produced a small piece of parchment that held an inked drawing of an anchor fouled with a length of loose line. "And this, Salidar, is the means . . . Lift your shirt, higher, off your left shoulder. Now, hold still."

She pressed the parchment to his shoulder and mumbled an incantation under her breath. Salidar understood not a word, but felt a slight tingling on his skin beneath the wrinkled paper.

Topsey removed the parchment and displayed it now blank.

He turned his head and twisted his shoulder to see the mark of the fouled anchor embedded in his skin.

"Looks like a maritime tattoo, does it not?" Rumley grinned. "Got yourself some ink when you went ashore, didn't you, matey?"

Salidar was surprised, and confused; his face showed it.

Topsey pressed the blank parchment into his hands. "Hold this scrap dear; tis what's important. Drop it in fresh running water and we will know where you are, anywhere in Mer. You will be contacted soon after, when it is safe."

"But beware," Rumley cautioned, "your tattoo will disappear once the enchantment is triggered."

"And remember," Topsey added, "it must be *fresh* water—not salt. It will work but once, understand?"

Salidar nodded.

"Any questions?" Rumley asked.

"Aye, a few. What happened? How did I get here? Where are my mates?" Rumley and Topsey shared a look of worried concern and shrugged.

"Tell him," Topsey said as she rose. "I must break the seal to check on my girls. Keep your voices down." Standing before the closed door, she made a small gesture and whispered under her breath. The pressure in the room abruptly diminished. She left, closing the door behind her.

"Ah, Salidar," Rumley sighed, "the short answer is you were mugged, and your mates as well."

"What? I remember looking for them, and . . ." His hand to the side of his head, he found a lump the size of an egg. "Oh! That smarts! My crewmates! What of them?"

"For the most part, they're fine; they're downstairs in the bar. They were beaten and unconscious when I found them. They'll live to tell the tale, and thank you for their rescue." Rumley grinned and winked.

"Me? I didn't do anything! I got knocked out, didn't I?"

"Aye, but they've been told otherwise. Tis to your advantage to be given the credit and held in higher esteem amongst the crew aboard the *Doom Wind*."

Salidar considered the implications; the idea had merit. "I see. And just what am I supposed to have done?"

"Sounded the alarm and lit into the thieving blackguards who attacked your mates. I came in answer to your hue and cry, dispatched two of the miscreants and captured three—with your help, of course." There was definitely a twinkle in Rumley's eyes. "You're the hero of the moment; enjoy it!"

Salidar gave the barkeep a wry smirk. "Right. Now, what really happened? Who were they, and what's become of them?"

"A gang of young thugs have been hanging around of late, some humans and Were. I've warned one or two against bothering my customers, but the only response I ever got was sneers and eye rolls. Until yesterday, I hadn't caught them in the act—"

"Yesterday? What? How long was I unconscious? How much time has passed? We only have two days shore leave!"

Rumley laid a big hand on Salidar's shoulder. "Fret not, tis only been a day. Your mates tell me you are all due back aboard your ship by first dog-watch this evening. You have plenty of time."

"Ah. Well then, what of these thugs?"

Rumley stood, glanced at the closed door, and lowered his voice. "The two who attacked you, both Were, saw me; they're dead. The other three did not see me; so, they do not know for certain who, or how many, caught them divvying up their booty and knocked them senseless. I've told any who've asked that the two of us were responsible for their capture. You sustained your injury in the confusion of the melee, understand?"

Salidar's hand rose once more toward his throbbing head, but he caught himself and smiled. "Don't worry, I get it. So, what happened to those three?"

Rumley smiled broadly. "Ah, we share a profit in this." He produced a money pouch and plopped it upon the bed. "Perhaps you know, according to the pirates' code as enforced in New Port Royal, thieves caught in the act are damned as slaves, a bounty upon their heads. This morning your crewmates and I marched these three down to the slave mart and gave evidence to all assembled. The three could have denied it and demanded trial by individual combat—I was more than willing, to be sure. But they admitted their guilt; I sensed some disappointment amongst the crowd. I collected the bounty. Now, as you are given half the credit, you deserve half the bounty, no?"

Salidar hefted the pouch and peered within; here was a good sum. "How much?"

Rumley's smile vanished. "It matters not. Heed my words. You will present this pouch to your captain as *booty,* for such it is under the pirates' code, to be equally shared amongst the crew. Consider what this will do for your standing aboard the *Doom Wind*. Do you catch my drift, *Grimrald?"*

He did, indeed, and sighed in resignation.

CH 9

SEATED ALONE WITH THE Rogue, beneath the mullioned windows of her guest chambers near the Merchants Hall of Essa, Malvana nodded.

“I understand, m’lord. How long will you be gone?”

“Two days, at the most, I should think,” Padraic answered, glancing at the fading light of sunset. “I trust you can prolong these last few points of negotiation?”

“Ah, there are some sticking points, so I foresee no problem. However, any time needed beyond two days will exceed that of the published agenda. I would have to have the delegation’s chief of staff, Lord Nightshade, craft some logistical reason for any further extension of the time frame.”

“I doubt it will come to that; two days should suffice.” He smiled in reassurance, rose, and bowed. “Now, by your leave, m’lady, I’ll be off.”

“As you will, m’lord.”

She watched him leave the chamber though a side passage, avoiding the formal reception area. She knew no details of his mission, only that it was at Queen Mab’s direction. That was enough for her.

HIGH IN THE HILLS ABOVE Derinseum, a black sphere materialized; sparks of static briefly arced to the ground as it hovered mere inches over a weed-strewn knoll. Two figures in hooded cloaks stepped out of the dark globe and watched it shrink into a mote of shadow. With a soft *pop*, it vanished.

“What now?” Vito asked.

"This is Essa, one of the larger islands in Mer, and below lies Derinseum," Daegon explained with a sweep of his arm. "I hope answers are to be found there. I need to find someone who has been to the Keys of Osiris, or failing that, adequate transportation to those islands."

"Oh yeah, you can't transit there unless you've been there, right?"

"Yes, and I'd rather not have to make a sea voyage. Unfortunately, finding the right person may take some time. Now, what must you do, and how long will it take?"

Vito and the alchemist gazed below as dusk flowed into deepening shadows and night crept upon the city. Tiny lights winked on in the distance as darkness slowly claimed a succession of small buildings on the outskirts of Derinseum.

The big man sighed. "Oh, I just need to hit the streets for a while. Cities are pretty much alike, no matter where they are. I'll know everything I need to know in a coupla days."

Daegon stroked his chin and mused aloud. "That should work for me as well. So be it. Let us meet back here at sunset on the second day."

"The day after tomorrow, right? Okay, then what?"

"Then, we shall see." The alchemist's voice grew somber. "Be warned! You must be careful, stay hooded, and make no use of *technology* while you are here."

"Not to worry, I didn't bring any, not even my cell phone."

Of course, he failed to mention the 9mm pistol and suppressor concealed under his robe.

"YOU'RE LOOKING WELL, Ellen. It's good to see you."

"You, too, Padraic." She swung the screen door open. "Come on in. Is everything all right?"

"Everything is fine." He stepped into the front hall and nodded to the dogs who commenced sniffing the cuffs of his trousers.

She smiled. "Well, you're not dressed so, uh, *elaborately* this visit. So what's the occasion? You just don't drop in without a reason, especially unannounced, do you?"

"Too true," he admitted. "Where is everyone?"

"My mom and Stacy are in the gardens working with the grape vines. Mark and Miska rebuilt the part of the arbor that fell down; but, that was a coupla days ago. I think they're both in the garage now. What's going on?"

"Can you slip away for a few hours? There's someone you need to meet, discreetly; and you can't talk about it, to anyone."

"Now hold on—I can't just drop everything and disappear with you. You're gonna have to tell me more. And I'm gonna tell my mother where I'm going. I'm not gonna have her worry."

He sighed. "Can we at least talk over a cup of tea?"

She relented. "Sure, come to the kitchen. I'll put a pot on. Don't worry, we'll be alone."

"SALIDAR, Y' DUN US all proud-like!" boomed the bosun as he clapped the impressed sailor on his shoulder. "A fine crewman y' be!"

Captain "Bloody" Bane hefted the coin purse in his hand and begrudgingly agreed, "Aye, tis fair booty y' brung to the *Doom Wind* an' her crew. Well done."

The rest of the crew crowded around, elbowing one another and laughing. They knew that per the pirates' code all would share in this unexpected booty, the slave price derived from those who had dared to attack their fellow crew members. Sorely beaten, Gimp, Patch, and Crabs would recover, all thanks, it was believed, to Salidar's timely rescue.

His standing among this motley lot had improved considerably, just as Rumley had predicted. But he could not let his guard down; the thought of Mab learning that he still lived was more than sufficient for him to keep a low profile.

Besides, he had new instructions. The *Doom Wind* awaited the arrival of the *Xanthippe*. Cargo and passengers were to be transferred, and a new course set for the swift clipper. He was to observe and learn whatever he could—and stay alive.

The deck tilted as the ship gently rocked on the swell of a passing wake, and the bosun cast a weather eye beyond the harbor.

"Avast, y' louts! There be a spot o' weather on the horizon. Get aloft an' check the reefed sails! Batten them hatches! Let's have her weather tight by end o' watch! Hop to it me buckos!"

The captain nodded to the bosun and made his way to his cabin, the hefty purse tight in his hand.

It did not escape Salidar's notice that no mention was made about the dispute days ago with the same slavers over a missing slave woman.

Ah yes, her . . . a Guild operative, I have no doubt—thus the less said the better.

He shrugged and joined the crewmen scrambling up the ratlines to check the reefed mainsail. He had every intention of losing himself in the routine of shipboard tasks, all the while trying not to think about the *Mad Elf.*

ELLEN PUSHED BACK FROM the kitchen table and rose.

"I'm going to reheat the water. Would you like another cup of tea?"

"No, thank you. We really should get going," Padraic insisted.

"I already told you. I'm not going anywhere without telling my mother, especially to some string of godforsaken islands in Mer. I don't care if it has to do with *our secret* or not! I'm just not gonna do that to my mother. She's already been through too much—"

The back door burst open—Mark stumbled into the kitchen.

"Oh! You *are* here! Both of you, come outside! Gallenius is here; he's looking for you, Padraic!"

"What?" Ellen balked in surprise. "Gallenius is here, outside? Why didn't you bring him in?"

Mark splayed his hands in frustration. "I can't, El'! The wards, remember? Just come outside. He's in a hurry and has to leave."

"Yeah, okay, we're coming."

She and Padraic found Gallenius standing with Miska in the yard a few paces from the back door.

The mage immediately grasped Padraic's arm and tried to pull him to one side, but the Rogue stood his ground.

"Whatever it is, Gallenius, I'm sure you can speak freely here. We are among dear friends, are we not? So?"

"Very well, you must return to Derinseum, as soon as possible. Titania has learned that Mab is not there and you are acting as proxy. Titania is planning to appear at the negotiations. We don't know when, but it could be at any moment."

Padraic knit his brows. "What the hell? Why would she? Unless, some aspect of the Elfin Accords?"

"Perhaps, but we suspect otherwise," the mage admitted. "Tis a strong possibility she is more focused upon you—"

"*Me?* What makes you—"

"Those believed to be in her retinue include Duke Briar and a particular pair of her personal guards, both of whom we have long suspected of being among her secret assassins. We don't know if *she* intends you any harm—but Duke Briar, ah, now that is another matter entirely."

Padraic nodded. "Damn, I see. Does she know I'm not there now?"

Gallenius shrugged. "We don't know for certain, but she most likely does not. Does it really matter?"

"Hmm, it might. I will return, of course, but I think I should make another stop first."

The mage tilted his head. "I'd be quick about it. We've risked considerable resources to learn of this, so the sooner you are back, the better. Now, I must beg everyone's indulgence, as I have another timely task before me, so I must go."

With a slight bow to the assembled company, he turned, summoned a transit sphere and stepped within. The familiar soft *pop* was its only trace as it disappeared.

Padraic turned to Ellen and shook his head. "Forgive me; our trip will have to be postponed, but not indefinitely. It is one we *must* make, and soon."

"We'll see; remember what I said," Ellen cautioned. "What are you going to do now?"

The Rogue offered her a sly smile. "I think I'm going to do just what would be expected of me; and in the process, play two huge egos against one another."

Ellen smiled in return. "You're gonna tell the Queen of Dark Elves that the Queen of Light Elves is coming, unannounced, to Mer, and will likely appear at the negotiations to further some unknown agenda. That is rather devious of you."

Mark chuckled. "Nice, Padraic! You'd have made a pretty good lawyer."

CH 10

LORD NIGHTSHADE LOOKED up from the scroll as the male operative knocked and entered the chamber.

"Forgive the intrusion, m'lord, but Lord Padraic has returned. He went directly to Lady Malvana's chambers."

Nightshade rose from the chair and walked around the small desk.

"Back already? How long was he off-realm?"

"Just over an hour, m'lord."

Nightshade was actually more concerned that the Rogue was now alone with Malvana in her chambers. Or were they alone?

"Where is her maid, in Malvana's chambers as well?"

"She is, m'lord."

So, his other operative was there, but that didn't mean Padraic wouldn't attempt a seduction with either—or both!

Nightshade's imagination flared and his breath caught.

The elfin operative cocked his head and hissed, "M'lord, someone's coming!"

The brief knock upon the chamber door was followed by Malvana's muffled voice.

"Lord Nightshade, are you there?"

The elfin lord pointed to an unadorned door in the rear wall; the male operative nodded and slipped from the room, closing the door behind him.

Upon opening the door to his chambers, Nightshade found Malvana, with Padraic at her side. The elfin lord's slight shoulders slumped in relief as his concerns of a moment ago evaporated, at least for now.

"Ah, m'lady, m'lord, please come in. How may I be of service?"

Malvana addressed him formally. "Lord Nightshade, I have learned from Lord Padraic that Her Majesty, Queen Mab will be joining us, perhaps as soon as in the next few hours—"

"What?" Nightshade blurted, forgetting himself. "Oh, forgive me, m'lady, I was taken by surprise—my sincere and deepest apologies." He bowed and groveled.

She sniffed and looked down her nose at him. "Ahem, I think it best if Lord Padraic were to explain further." She turned her head haughtily and deigned to ignore the diminutive elfin lord.

Nightshade noticed the ghost of an amused smile slip across the Rogue's face at Malvana's somewhat predictable, and typically self-absorbed, behavior.

Padraic simply sighed and came to the point.

"I was performing a duty at the behest of our queen when I learned that Queen Titania is planning on appearing here during the negotiations. Of course, I immediately informed Queen Mab. She has decided to attend as well, and, as the Lady Malvana just indicated, will soon join us.

"Her arrival is not to be noted or announced; it is to be as if she has been here all along. Should anyone inquire, the official position is to be that she arrived with our delegation, absent any pomp or ceremony. She simply elected for Lady Malvana and myself to represent her during the negotiations. These are her orders. Are we clear?"

"Of course, m'lord. I will see to the necessary preparations immediately."

STACY POURED GLASSES of lemonade and placed them on the kitchen table before Millie and Ellen.

"So Padraic couldn't stay because Gallenius came to get him?" Stacy took a seat across from Ellen and reached for the plate of pecan chocolate-chip cookies.

"Uh-huh, he said Padraic had to get back to Mer," Ellen explained. "It had something to do with Titania showing up there."

Millie took a bite of cookie and nudged her daughter. "Mmm, these came out good. I thought Padraic invited you to visit Mer; don't you want to go?"

Ellen sipped her drink. "Oh, he has a couple of times. He was being kinda pushy today, maybe a little too insistent. But then Gallenius showed up; well, plans change."

"Well, I wouldn't mind visiting Mer," Stacy chimed in. "Come on, a water world with islands and beaches! Sand, sun, and surf—what's not to like?"

"Yeah, I know." Ellen chuckled. "It does sound good, doesn't it?"

Stacy drained her lemonade and smacked her lips. "Mmm, tasty! So, when are we going?"

Ellen smiled. "We, huh? Okay, I dunno, but *we* will go—that's for sure."

Millie reached for another cookie. "Maybe just one more, hmm? Well, I'd feel better if Mark and Hawk went with you two. They'd probably like the beach as well, don't you think?"

Stacy gave Ellen an impish smile. "Oh, I suppose if we really tried, we might be able to convince them. Omigawd! Ellen, we've got to go bikini shopping!"

Millie snorted in laughter.

Ellen smiled and shook her head.

Yeah, this could be fun . . .

THE SUN HAD SET IN Derinseum. A lone lamplighter began his rounds as dusk faded and stars slowly became visible. It would be a clear yet moonless night; the stars would hold dominion over all, at least until a distant weather front made its way eastward.

Padraic wasn't sure if he'd heard a gentle knock on the door of his guest chambers or not. Uncertain, he rose from the desk and approached the door. He paused, listening intently, but heard nothing more. There was no security peephole, no way to check if someone was in the outer hall without opening the door. He sighed, unlocked and opened the door.

A figure in a dark hooded robe stood before the entrance. A soft voice, almost a whisper with a slightly musical lilt came from within the shadowed hood.

"Ah, do ask me in, if you please, Padraic."

While he found it vaguely familiar, he did not immediately recognize the voice.

Hmm, deliberately altered or disguised?

Curious, but nonetheless wary, the Rogue stepped aside and swept an open hand in beckoning.

"Do come in."

As the figure stepped to the middle of the room, Padraic closed the door. He had seen no one else outside in the vicinity of the entrance; but, that did not mean he assumed this person was alone.

The figure turned to face him, reached up and dropped the dark robe's hood.

Titania!

Padraic bowed. "Ah, Your Majesty, to what do I owe the honor of this surprise?"

She smiled, dropped her chin to her robed shoulder and considered him with a half-lidded gaze.

"Cannot old friends simply drop in on one another? You were not always so suspicious; and, you liked to have a bit of fun, did you not?"

Pursed lips and a shake of his head constituted his sole response.

"Oh, be not like that!" She pouted and stepped up to him. "Is not one supposed to have fun in Mer? Here you are, all alone—what fun is that?"

He tore his gaze from her haunting green eyes, and deliberately turned away. He knew better than to let his focus become entrapped in their depths.

She scoffed as if amused at this minor rebuff and began to unlace her robe.

"What are you doing here, Titania?"

She let her robe slide off one bare shoulder. "Oh, just passing through. I thought I would look in on the negotiations while here. When I learned you were here on your own, it occurred to me that I might pay you a visit. After all, I have always wondered what it is about you that so many women find so compelling, so intriguing." Her robe slid off her other shoulder. "Should I not find out for myself?"

He faced her and folded his arms. "Just passing through, eh? You have someplace else to be? I confess I feel mildly insulted."

Gripping her elbows to emphasize her cleavage, she leaned forward and coyly scolded him. "Oh, do not be, Padraic dear. I am simply doing a diplomatic favor while dealing with some other business in this realm."

"Diplomatic favor? Some other business? You think of me as a mere distraction? I am not a priority? Titania, I am hurt."

She clapped her hands and laughed. "Ha-ha! Ah, Padraic, you are ever the Rogue! I will see to your hurts, and banish your loneliness; upon that you may rest assured."

With that she tugged at the robe's laces—it dropped to the floor. She wore nothing more than a seductive smile.

Padraic pursed his lips once more and locked eyes with her. "I do have one question, Titania. What makes you so certain I am alone?"

Her brows knit in momentary confusion. At the sudden sound of another voice, her eyes widened and her face paled.

"My word, *sister!* Is this some new Mer fashion? I should think you might catch cold, being so *underdressed.*"

Titania turned to find Queen Mab standing behind her.

"Mab? What—? I was informed you were not here!"

With a grace that belied her embarrassment, Titania dipped, retrieved, and donned her robe.

"Hmmph, no doubt. Alas, I suspect you were *misinformed*, dear sister, for as you can see, I *am* here."

Mab's predatory smile had Padraic thinking of a cat considering a disadvantaged canary. That was not good. He knew this could get very ugly, very quickly.

A side door swung open and Lord Nightshade entered the room. He nodded to Queen Mab, but kept silent.

"Ah, Lord Nightshade, good timing," Mab acknowledged. "I believe my sister monarch, Queen Titania, is just leaving; perhaps you could escort her? That is, dear sister, if you have no further business *with my consort?"*

Mustering what dignity she could, Titania straightened to her full height, looked down her nose at Padraic and seethed, "No, *sister,* I do not!"

Flipping her hood up, she strode for the door, with Lord Nightshade in her wake.

Alone with Mab, Padraic asked, "What now?"

"We shall see. She is definitely up to something, more than her clumsy attempt at seduction. *Diplomatic favors? Other business?* A reference to this Keys of Osiris business, I would wager."

Padraic nodded. "No doubt, but I have yet to learn anything of proven value. It was simply good fortune that in making my initial inquiries I discovered her plan to appear here, in your reported absence. Of course, I informed you immediately. I did not know what to expect of her."

"Hmmph, I did. I am well aware of her interest in you, so I expected something like this. Forewarned is forearmed; and indeed we were. That was well played, Padraic. I must admit I thoroughly enjoyed it. Of course, she will tell no one of this—but *I* might."

Padraic thought Mab to be overly smug in relishing this minor triumph, in truth no more than an embarrassing incident.

Indeed a petty victory, but at what future cost?

Lord Nightshade returned, bowed to his liege, and offered his report.

"Your Majesty, m'lord, I bid Queen Titania farewell at the outer door. I slipped into the shadows to observe. She was met by three retainers who were lingering beyond the guest chambers facility. She was furious; she spoke harshly to them. I could not make out her words, but her tone was unmistakable. She bears strong anger for you both. It may be wise to expect some sort of retaliation. I may be mistaken, but I think one of the retainers was Duke Briar—he appeared particularly incensed."

Her eyebrows raised, Mab glanced at her consort.

Padraic met her gaze, sighed, and dropped his head. "Of course he is, and now burdened with further tarnished elfin pride." *At what cost, indeed. And so it begins anew.*

"Pah! *She* will not return, of that I have no doubt," Mab declared. "So be it. I have other matters I must attend to, so I will leave you to it. Lord Nightshade, how much longer do we expect the negotiations to take?"

"The Lady Malvana advised me that two days should suffice; that comports with the published agenda."

Mab nodded. "Padraic?"

"That is a very tight schedule for my task. This situation with Queen Titania was an unanticipated complication, and has cost me time I did not have to spare. Nonetheless, I shall do my best."

Mab made a series of small gestures; a transit globe appeared and grew to match her height.

"See that you do."

She stepped into the globe. It shrank and winked out of existence.

SALIDAR WAS ASSIGNED the first dogwatch once again. In fact, he was about to relieve the crewman on topwatch in the crow's nest atop the mainmast. Before he could ascend the rigging, the lookout hailed a sighting.

"Sail ahoy! Off t' starboard at amidships!"

Salidar guessed it was the *Xanthippe*, the junk they'd been expecting for the past day while the *Doom Wind* rode at anchor just out of sight of New Port Royal. Midway up the mainmast ratlines, he paused to peer at the horizon. There was no mistaking the black sails of the *Xanthippe*.

She was making good time. The two ships would be near enough to have their boats transfer cargo and passengers within the hours of his watch; and he'd have an excellent observation post.

Captain "Bloody" Bane hadn't informed the crew of their mission when he'd ordered the *Doom Wind* put to sea and then anchored just over the horizon from New Port Royal. It hadn't taken long for the crew-fueled scuttlebutt to have the right of it, a rendezvous at sea to take on a cargo or passenger better not seen in the town. The *Doom Wind* had often met the *Xanthippe* like this, away from prying eyes, so the sight of her solitary approach came as no real surprise to the crew.

Salidar watched the transfer of cargo with bored disinterest; it was all pretty routine. Only the collection of boxes and trunks bearing unfamiliar rune symbols managed to pique his interest; no doubt, he surmised, the personal property of the unknown passengers.

The final boat from the *Xanthippe* brought her mistress, the sea witch Circe, and the passengers; a large satyr, and two fauns. Salidar strained to get a better look.

This is who I'm supposed to observe? Circe, the witch, I recognize; but who are these others? Why were they transferred at sea rather than come aboard at New Port Royal?

He could see Captain Bane welcome the sea witch and the passengers on the main deck, but he couldn't hear what was said. Bane motioned for them to follow and made for his cabin.

The last to proceed, the big satyr, paused and looked up. For just an instant, his eyes locked on Salidar's own.

Salidar's breath stalled. A chill racked his spine and he shuddered, seized with a strong spasm of vertigo. It passed in a moment, but he was thoroughly shaken. Had he not secured the lookout's safety line to the mast—one of the bosun's cardinal rules for the crewman on top-watch—he'd now be a bloody splotch on the deck below.

He took several deep breaths to calm his racing heart.

So, I now know who bears watching—and from a safe distance, I hope.

CH 11

VITO FOUND DAEGON AT the appointed spot in the hills above Derinseum at sunset on the second day as they had agreed.

"Yo, Daegon, how's it going? Are we out of here?"

The alchemist greeted the big man with a noncommittal shrug. "I suspect so; I was not as successful as I had hoped. I found no one who could help me. I did learn of someone who could, but I have missed her. However, I know where she is going, a place to which I can transport, provided we return to Olmus first."

"Why go back to Olmus first? Can't we get there from here? We've still got some time, don't we?"

Daegon shook his head. "You do not understand. One cannot use transit globes to travel from one location to another within the same realm; the globes only work between realms. Although, it is said there were once exceptions, but—"

"Exceptions? Like what?" Vito's curiosity was aroused.

"Ah, not *what,* but rather *who,"* Daegon explained. "In some of the early lore I have read, there was speculation that some *stewards*, keepers and guardians of grand portals, had mastered the ability to use some unexplained versions of transit globes to travel from point to point within a single realm. Fascinating, if true, but the technique, if it ever existed, is lost to time."

"Well, it's not that big a deal, right? It just adds an extra hop to our travel plans," Vito reasoned, "from here to Olmus to *wherever*, right?"

The alchemist smiled at the simple logic. "I suppose you are right. It is only a minor inconvenience; and you can report your findings to your boss that much sooner. How did you fare, by the way?"

Vito rocked back on his heels and grinned. "Oh, he's gonna like what I learned. This place is great, basically a wide-open market! Almost nothing is illegal here, provided you have the coin and you don't openly hurt anybody. He can introduce meth, or any other drug with no problem, not even any significant overhead. He won't even have to bribe anybody! In fact there's only one person he'll be worried about; but if we can avoid her—"

"Her?" Daegon interrupted. "Who are you talking about?"

"Uh, *Diere* or *Mab*, whatever she calls herself. He wants to stay away from her."

"What?!" Daegon blurted. "Diere, the usurper, is here?"

"Yeah, that's what my sources, you know, street people, tell me. She's supposed to be at some visitors' accommodations. Is she a problem for you, too?"

Daegon's visage took on as dark an aspect as Vito had ever seen. The alchemist spoke through clenched teeth, but Vito understood every word.

"Not a problem—an opportunity! Something I've been planning just for that treacherous elf! This is unanticipated fortune, a chance of fate that I shall not miss!"

Vito was alarmed at Daegon's vehemence; hatred rolled off the alchemist in waves.

"Easy now, Daegon. What are you talking about?"

"We must delay our departure. Vito, you must show me where she is."

"Look, Daegon, are you sure about this?"

"I am! Trust me—your boss would approve." He balled his fists in anticipation.

Vito relented. "All right, but look, I don't wanna burn my sources; I'll probably need them again. So, I'll show you where, but you gotta keep quiet about how you know, *capisce?*"

The alchemist scoffed. "Pah! That will not be a problem."

The big man nodded, but he was still unsettled about this.

"Okay. Are you gonna need me to go in there with you?"

"No, that won't be necessary. In fact, once you show me where she is, you should return here, and wait for me. I will not be long."

"Well, okay, I'll meet you here. You sure you won't need me, or anything else?"

"Trust me—you would not want to be there." Daegon's voice dropped to an ominous tone. "I will only need one other thing, something I am certain to find there."

"All right," Vito acquiesced, still uneasy and apprehensive, but nonetheless resolved. "Let's go."

A MOONLESS NIGHT REIGNED over Delafaire Farm. Wisps of cloud softened the twinkle of starlight to the east. In his haste, Padraic turned his face to the breeze and sniffed. The increase in humidity was subtle, but he knew it to be the harbinger of a moisture-laden storm front that would pass through within the next few hours. It would not matter; he was running out of time. He briskly rapped the iron ring knocker on the farmhouse door, hoping Ellen would answer.

She did.

"Padraic, back so soon? Please, come in."

She swung the screen door open, but he made no move to enter.

"Yes, I'm back, but I—*we* don't really have the time. Can you spare me an hour? I assure you it's vitally important. Tell your mother if you must, but please come with me. I'll have you back here straightaway, I assure you!"

The dogs at her side, Ellen cocked her head. "Is this that little trip to Mer you wanted me to take earlier?"

"It is. It's important; it won't take long. Please."

Smokey seemed to appear from nowhere, twined around Ellen's ankles, then Padraic's, and finally sat on the wide boards of the front porch. He stared up at Padraic, then at Ellen, and slowly nodded.

Ellen smiled. "It seems Smokey wants me to go, or maybe he wants to come, too?"

Padraic chuckled. "That would be fine with me. Smokey goes where he will anyway. He's always welcome."

"Okay, let me go tell my mom; she's in the kitchen. Do you want to say hello?"

He deferred. "I would, but there's very little time. I'll wait for you here on the porch, with Smokey."

Within a minute Ellen returned. "All right, let's try to keep it to an hour."

Padraic nodded, trooped down the steps and into the yard. A transit globe shimmered into existence on the front lawn. "We will do our best to be quick. Now, if you please?"

At his beckoning gesture Ellen scooped up Smokey and followed her father into the globe.

A moment after the soft *pop* of the globe's demise, the gentle chorus of crickets and tree frogs resumed in the night air.

LORD NIGHTSHADE WAS tired and ready to retire for the night. He'd done as asked and reported his observations to Queen Mab upon her arrival. There had been some tense moments then, but he had remained as stoic as possible. Curiously, his queen offered no reactions to his reported observations.

He now knew that she had been preoccupied with planning for Titania's unannounced yet anticipated visit. Mab had manipulated the subsequent confrontation with Queen Titania with such aplomb that he both appreciated and rightfully feared such deft skill. It appeared to have gone well in Mab's view; she was obviously pleased. She departed soon afterward.

Now he just wanted to relax and get some sleep. Malvana had already retired, and Padraic was off-world. The visitors' facility was closed for the night, and secured by the Derinseum Watch. Nightshade was almost finished for the day; he only needed to hear from his two operatives. For some reason, both elves were late in reporting.

He stood, stretched, and unsuccessfully tried to stifle a yawn.

The door to his chambers burst open!

The male operative gripped the door frame and gasped, "M'lord, forgive me—we are breached! An intruder in Lady Malvana's chambers!"

"What? Malvana is—?" Nightshade blanched, his face paled.

"Unharmed, m'lord, but her maid is injured! Two of the Watch are injured as well!"

"The intruder?"

"The Watch has him; he lives."

Nightshade's face grew grim. "Take me there, now."

THE CAPTAIN OF THE Watch was barely able to constrain his anger; but, the man was a professional. He stood with a group of tense watchmen before a closed door to a windowless room; their prisoner was restrained within.

The captain acknowledged the elfin lord upon his approach; the watchmen stood a little straighter.

"Lord Nightshade, it is over. We have him, here in this transit-warded room."

"Well done, Captain. A sorry business, this."

All things considered, Lord Nightshade could appreciate how difficult it was for the captain to keep his men from meting out some street justice.

"Aye, he lives, m'lord, for now. He'll face the Merchants Guild justice for the harm he's done."

"To be sure, Captain, to be sure," Nightshade commiserated. "Two of your men, and one of my people. My, uh, *aide* and I must question him; I must know who sent him."

"Think he was sent, do ya? Aye, I'd like to know as well. The lads knocked him about a bit when they swarmed him, but he should bear some questions, right enough."

Nightshade nodded. "Shall we?"

The captain gestured and the door was opened, "I'll join you in a moment; I have to check on my injured men."

Nightshade and his aide, the clandestine operative, entered a small room well lit with half a dozen candles. The lock clicked as the door closed behind them. A bruised and bloodied man was tied to a rough wooden chair. He lifted his head; his eyes were almost swollen shut, but it was clear that he could still see. He coughed and spat blood.

Nightshade brought a candle closer and examined the man's face.

Recognition dawned. "I know you, do I not?"

The battered face creased with a broken smile. "Ah, Tanist's friend, Nightshade, is it?"

"Aye, and you are Daegon, the alchemist. You were thought to be dead, along with Atrellan, Tanist, and the late queen. How is it you are not?"

"I was not present, *cough-cough*. Twas Atrellan's treachery, *hah*, spared me their fate, *cough*. All Diere—all Diere."

Nightshade winced at the name and leaned forward. "And tonight? Why? What has Malvana to do with this?"

"Malvana? Tanist's daughter?" Daegon was clearly puzzled. "I thought Diere was here, in that room."

"Diere, er, Her Majesty *Queen Mab* was here, but she left hours ago. So, are you saying that you broke into the Lady Malvana's chambers thinking Queen Mab was within?"

Daegon shrugged, at least to the extent his bonds allowed. "Aye, the mistake was mine. Know this, Nightshade, I would never harm the daughter of Tanist. I greatly admired the man for he treated me well and with courtesy, a circumstance I rarely found amongst courtiers."

The door opened; the captain had returned.

"Your men, Captain?" Nightshade asked.

"The same," growled the captain, "unconscious, and we suspect bespelled."

"As is the Lady Malvana's maid," added Nightshade's aide. "Why harm any of them?"

"Ah, neither harmed nor bespelled," the battered man insisted. "They only sleep, by virtue of a potion. The men on watch foolishly accepted a flagon of rather potent wine, as bored guards are often wont to do. As for the maid, she attacked me and raised the alarm when I entered the chambers. A sleeping powder blown in her face was sufficient to overcome her, but it was too late. A host of guards fell upon me—you know the rest."

"If they only sleep," the captain pressed, "when will they awaken?"

Daegon grunted and spat a bit of bloody phlegm. "Soon, I expect; but they may not remember much. Tis but a harmless side effect, I assure you."

"Am I to understand," Nightshade probed, "that no one sent you? You breached these walls of your own volition?"

Daegon sat up straighter. "Of course! I, and I alone, undertook this—"

"Captain!" Nightshade interrupted the alchemist. "As you no doubt know, some sleeping potions can be dangerous, especially when the victims suddenly awaken. You should be there with your men, to take control and see to it they understand what has happened. You must be certain they have recovered their wits. Do you take my meaning?"

The captain appeared momentarily puzzled, but clearly did not want to appear ignorant. "Uh, yes-yes, of course, m'lord. If you'll excuse me."

As the captain departed, Nightshade placed a finger to his lips to silence Daegon. Turning to his *aide*, Nightshade said, "Double the guards on Malvana. Check on the maid; she should awaken soon. Stay with her. She speaks to no one; she must make a full report to only me."

The operative departed, closing the door.

Squatting to the side of Daegon's chair, Nightshade dropped his voice to a mere whisper, and spread his open palms.

"Now, Daegon, we are alone, and can speak in close confidence. Know this, as we were both friends to the late Earl of Tanist, who did indeed speak well of you at court, I accept your assertion that you meant no harm to his daughter, Malvana; I believe you. Now tell me why you sought out *this* Queen Mab, the former *Lady Diere*—I must know. What you tell me need go no further, certainly not to the Watch, who will no doubt insist that you face the Merchants Guild justice, which as you may know can be quite harsh. Help me to understand your actions this night. Perhaps I can offer the Merchants Guild some rationalization, some persuasive mitigating circumstance?"

"Pah! A gaggle of puffed-up merchants are nothing to me!" Daegon scoffed. "But you and I will speak, out of respect for our friend, Tanist—and respect for the truth!"

Nightshade smiled. "Very well, I'm listening."

MINUTES LATER, LORD Nightshade appeared at the guarded door to Lady Malvana's chambers.

Her surprise at seeing him in a hooded robe was evident. "M'lord! What has happened? All this excitement! Are we in danger?"

"No longer, m'lady," he assured her. "There was an incident, but it is over. Out of an abundance of caution, these guards will continue to stand post here at your chambers."

"Thank you, m'lord."

He lowered his voice. "There is another matter that merits your attention."

"M'lord?"

"Now," he whispered, "I must ask you to accompany me. There is someone who has certain knowledge, information you must hear—for your ears only. You will need your hooded robe; tis better that we are not seen."

"M'lord? But I—"

“No questions now, if you please, m’lady. Come, come now.”

CH 12

ELLEN SHIVERED AND winced as the cold wind chilled her very bones. She cradled Smokey tightly against her chest, his warmth reassuring. Padraic stood by her side on the craggy mountain shelf overlooking the crashing surf a great distance below.

"This is Mer?" she shouted over the wind. "Not what I was expecting!"

He grimaced and nodded. "This way; watch your step!"

She followed him along a narrow track, around an outcropping, past a few stunted trees clinging to the leeward side of the escarpment, and into a sheltered cave-like alcove. She rubbed her upper arms. The chill had diminished but it was still cold, too cold for what she was wearing.

Grateful to be out of the howling wind, she let Smokey drop to the stony ground. The cat promptly began exploring the alcove.

"Really Padraic? Think you could've warned me to wear something more than jeans and a light shirt? I thought Mer was supposed to be some sort of tropical paradise! What's going on? Tell me—right now!"

"My apologies, Ellen. I wasn't thinking. Mer is, for the most part, a very pleasant place, in the equatorial regions. We are presently more to the south of the equator, uh, quite a bit more actually. This is one of the smaller islands among the Keys of Osiris. The weather here is much cooler, especially at these higher elevations, and often somewhat unpredictable. This is also the beginning of storm season. And much like the weather patterns of your home realm, the northern and southern hemispheres tend to have opposite seasons."

"Oh, so we're here on the cusp of late fall and early winter?" She wasn't shivering any more, but she wouldn't have said *no* to a sweater or jacket. "Seriously? We couldn't have visited a nice sunny beach instead?"

Chagrined, he shrugged. "Sorry, but no. This is where we need to be. You can always visit the more hospitable locations Mer has to offer at some other time. But being here, right now, is important."

"So you keep saying. Remember, I don't have a lot of time; I need to get back. So, why are we here?"

"I told you, Ellen; you need to meet with someone."

"Who, Padraic? I don't have the ti—"

"Me."

The interruption surprised her; the voice seemed to come from all around her.

A man bundled in an oilskin parka stood in the rear of the alcove, with Smokey twining around his booted ankles.

Padraic smirked and shook his head.

"Ellen, this is Barnabas, your uncle, of sorts, I suppose. We three have a lot to talk about."

THE KNOCK UPON HIS door broke Lord Nightshade's concentration. He put the scroll he'd been studying aside on the desk as the male operative entered.

"M'lord, the Watch coach has arrived to take the prisoner to the Merchants Guild Hall."

"A *transit-warded* coach, I presume?" Nightshade leaned back in his chair.

"Indeed, m'lord—or so they have said. Did you wish to speak further with the Watch Captain?"

The elfin lord cupped his chin in a moment of thought. "Hmm, I do, but not now. Perhaps once his men have fully recovered, he'll be more receptive to my advice. I think we can afford to be patient a bit longer. No, for now they may be about their business. Anything else?"

"Yes, m'lord. The maid has regained consciousness and is coherent. She is prepared to make her report."

Nightshade sat straighter in his chair. "Good! You have been at her side, yes? Will her report bear any new information, anything we do not already know?"

The operative shook his head. "No, m'lord. She can only attest to that which we learned firsthand from the prisoner; that she attacked him when he broke into the Lady Malvana's chambers."

"I see. Very well, send her to me. I may as well get this over with." He sighed, but then paused as the operative turned to go. "One moment! Padraic? Is he still off-realm, or has he returned?"

"No, m'lord, he has not yet returned."

Nightshade nodded and waved the operative off. As the door closed, he leaned back in his chair and stared at the ceiling. Not knowing where the queen's consort was might not be too great an issue for the moment, but then again . . . *Mab knows he's not here; he's supposedly doing something for her.*

Then why do I feel so unsettled, so apprehensive?

ELLEN WRAPPED HER HANDS around the warm mug of mulled wine. This chamber, one among many in a virtual warren hewn from the granite of the mountain, was spacious, well furnished, and comfortable. Ornate tapestries hung upon polished stone walls amid a succession of heavily laden bookcases. A modest yet smokeless fire blazed happily in an iron brazier in the center of the large room. An ambient light of no apparent source radiated from a high domed ceiling, easily illuminating the entire space.

Ellen shifted in the soft wool nap of the sheepskin-covered armchair, sipped her wine, and considered the two men seated across the fire from her.

"All right, let me see if I've got this straight," she began. "Padraic, you and Barnabas are, uh, *half brothers?* The same father, but different mothers, right?"

The two men glanced at one another and nodded to her.

She grinned. "Okay. So, Barnabas, you're older, right? By how much?"

Barnabas shrugged. "Oh, I think you would say by about a century, as you understand time."

"Oh my, Padraic!" Ellen smiled in delight. "That makes him your big brother! Ha-ha!"

Her father rolled his eyes. "Yes, I suppose it does. Now, can we stay on point? You need to know certain things for your own protection—that includes family ties, especially now that we know Titania has a confirmed interest in the Keys of Osiris. Haven't you been listening?"

"Relax, Padraic, I haven't missed a word either of you have said; I get it. Oberon fathered the both of you, with different women, about a century apart. You're worried that Titania may learn of this—or worse, she already knows it. She's made it her obsession to eliminate any of her wayward husband's paramours and any progeny. She may have agents coming here, for whatever reason. And now, Mab is interested as well."

"Yes," Padraic confirmed. "Bear in mind that Mab knows you are my daughter. However, as far as we know, she is not aware that Oberon is my father—your grandfather. We don't know what Titania may know, or suspect, but it'd be best if the two elfin queens did not compare notes, you see?"

"I do. I told you; I get it," Ellen repeated, her patience wearing a bit thin. "Now I have some questions. Does my mother know any of this?"

Padraic sighed. "No, she does not—and it would be best for her that she not learn of it, at least for now. It'll be my task to tell her, not yours, when the time is right."

Ellen turned to her new uncle. "What about your mother, Barnabas?"

A hint of sadness passed over the older man's face. "She passed on, many years ago."

"Oh, I am sorry, my condolences," Ellen effused. "Please forgive my rudeness."

"I took no offense, my dear. My mother was quite the woman; I'll always miss her. In fact you remind me a bit of her—she was a steward, too. She was one of a long line of stewards in my famil—"

"Barnabas!" interrupted Padraic.

Barnabas blanched. "Oh! Was I not supposed to—"

"Enough!" Padraic demanded.

"No! Not enough!" Ellen declared and stood. "I know there is another reason I am here! Family reunion aside, Padraic, you could've told me all this in my home. Your insistence that we transit here has another purpose. I will have the truth—all of it, right now! Otherwise I will commence a thorough investigation on my own. Trust me; I have more than adequate support to accomplish that task."

The two men stared at her in wide-eyed shock.

Padraic paled and shook his head.

Barnabas began to smile. "Oh my, very much like my mother. Could she really do that, Padraic? She clearly has the will, but has she the resources?"

Padraic sighed and let his shoulders slump. “Barnabas, you have no idea. Very well, Ellen. Please resume your seat. We have little time, and much to discuss.”

DAEGON LOOKED UP AS the door to the room in which he was held opened. Three men of the Derinseum Watch entered. Without a word, they gagged him and placed a hood over his head. One freed him from the chair and forced him to his feet. They left his hands tied behind his back.

Another shoved him forward. “Walk where you are led. Keep silent.”

Daegon stumbled, and was caught by two men who dragged him forward.

“Make him walk!” commanded the third. “Move! The coach awaits.”

Battered, bruised, and blind, Daegon haltingly stepped wherever he was pushed. He concentrated on keeping his balance, despite an overwhelming sense of disorientation, and the harsh tone of impatient commands from his captors.

He had seriously erred in his thirst for vengeance in the name of his late queen. *Dire the usurper* was no longer present; he had missed his opportunity. And worse, he had underestimated the response of the Watch; they had taken him far too easily.

Now a captive, destined to face Derinseum justice, he could do nothing—not with his hands tied and his voice denied him by a simple gag. He could call upon none of his sorcerous skills under such circumstances, frustrating irony, indeed.

Oh, but he would not always be so bound and gagged. He would teach these foolish watchmen how badly mistaken they’d been to treat him so shabbily.

Distracted in his thoughts, he was jerked to a halt. He sensed he was outside. There was the creak of a coach door, as strong hands gripped his upper arms.

"Get him aboard. You two, in with him. I'll ride with the driver."

Pffftt—pffft . . .

"What the—"

Pffft—pffft . . .

The hands gripping Daegon's arms fell away.

Daegon was suddenly pulled to one side, the hood jerked off his head.

Vito!

The big man spun Daegon around and cut the ropes binding his hands.

Daegon pulled the gag down and gasped, "Vito! What have you done?"

Four unmoving bodies lay about; each watchman had a bloody hole in his forehead, like a macabre third eye.

"Saved your ass," Vito intoned as he unscrewed the suppressor from the barrel of the 9mm pistol. "You could show a little gratitude, you know."

"B-but, I warned you," Daegon stammered, "not to use any technology!"

"What's done is done; I had no choice," Vito reasoned. "I had to rescue you—the boss wouldn't have it any other way." He slipped the pistol and suppressor beneath the folds of his robe and scanned the ground. "Gimme a minute; I gotta find my spent brass. Don't wanna leave any evidence, you know. Then we can get outta here."

Daegon's mind was awhirl. True, the use of man's technology here may present a problem, but then again that may not be until well into the future. On the other hand, it may not become a problem at all—*if* he were to act decisively here and now. Why not? He had already decided to teach the Watch a lesson. He smiled in grim satisfaction.

Vito returned. "Okay, I've got the brass; we can go. Do we need to go back to that hill, you know, where we first arrived?"

"We do not. We can transit from here." Daegon paused. "But first, I need to leave a calling card, a token of appreciation for the way I was treated."

"Huh?" Vito was clearly puzzled.

"Just stand back," warned the alchemist, "and give me a moment."

Vito's eyebrows rose, but he kept silent.

Daegon half-closed his eyes and began a soft chant. As his voice rose and fell he carefully walked among the dead watchmen. As he passed each one, he briefly placed a hand upon the crown of each man's head, careful to avoid staining his hand with blood. Upon completing the circuit he stood in the midst of the corpses, let his voice rise in a discordant crescendo, and smartly brought his outstretched hands together in a resounding *clap*.

All sounds of the night ceased.

Vito looked around apprehensively. "Is that it?"

Daegon approached and nodded. "Yes. It will take a few minutes. I do not know their true names, so the spell may prove erratic—but so be it."

"Cool! Can we go now?" Vito was growing visibly anxious.

Daegon smiled. "Yes, we can go. Follow me. I'll open a transit globe over there, away from this area. Trust me, to linger nearby would be a mistake."

Moments later, as the dark transit globe winked out of existence, the reanimated bodies of the dead watchmen began to stir.

"YOU ARE CORRECT, ELLEN, there was once much more to these islands than is evident today," Barnabas admitted. "Some believe it was once a fairly large landmass, still an island to be sure, but according to the oldest lore and legends, a much larger island with a massive, albeit extinct, volcano near its center. Speculation holds that the islands now known as the Keys of Osiris are but the tips of peaks that once comprised part of the rim of the caldera."

"Ah, I see," Ellen said. "That would explain the apparent crescent layout of the island string."

"Indeed," her uncle agreed. "Of course, some few consider the islands to simply be the remnants of a large atoll. Whatever the case, storms and rising sea levels have slowly claimed many lower isles. The tides can be quite high, especially during storm season."

"And the storms of the Southern Ocean are renown for their ferocity," Padraic added. "There are few permanent residents of the Keys; a handful of clans mostly, who are, without exception, hardy and self-reliant folk."

"Are all the islands of the Keys rocky and mountainous like this one?" she asked. "No sandy beaches?"

Barnabas shrugged. "Mountainous for the most part, but there are a few narrow yet fertile valleys that bear fair crop yields. Some of the leeward Keys have remnants of black sand beaches on their lagoon sides—what was once very likely the center of the caldera."

"Black sand? You mean like volcanic residue, ash and pumice?" she reasoned.

"Yes, very fine, it gets into everything. Most people here find it annoying and avoid those places."

Ellen was finding this all very interesting. "Under the circumstances, the volcano theory makes the most sense. So, was there some sort of catastrophic event that sank most of the landmass, or was it simply a slow rise in ocean levels?"

Barnabas and Padraic shared an uncomfortable glance.

"Well, that depends upon whom you might ask," Barnabas hedged.

Ellen gave him a humorless smile. "I'm asking you, *uncle.*"

Padraic shrugged and shook his head. "You may as well tell her, Barnabas. I fear no one else will. Indeed, who better has the right?"

Barnabas nodded solemnly. "So be it. Ellen, the earliest lore holds that it was a catastrophic event, millennia ago, and cost many lives. There was an ancient city in the heart of the long dormant volcano's caldera, and a Grand Portal; my ancestor was its steward. The cataclysm occurred in a single day, perhaps within a single hour. The land sank in shocking suddenness beneath the waves; the city, the Grand Portal, and my ancestor were all lost.

"Thereafter, the title of *Steward* has been traditionally handed down through the line of my mother's family for untold generations. However, tis only a word, a sad and empty shell of a title, for the Grand Portal no longer exists. My mother had no other children; she did not bestow the title upon me. So it, too, effectively no longer exists."

Ellen was speechless in empathy.

"I know this is a hard tale to hear, Ellen," Padraic offered in sympathy, "but there is more to know. Barnabas, please?"

"Ah, this is difficult for me," her uncle admitted, "knowing that this calamity was engineered and orchestrated! Warnings were withheld from those who might have been saved."

"What?" Ellen blurted. "What do you mean *engineered and orchestrated?* No one was warned?"

Padraic looked to his half brother. "Barnabas, it is for you to tell her."

Barnabas sat in silence for a moment. He glanced to Padraic, who offered a sad smile in reluctant encouragement.

"Yes, tell me, please," Ellen urged, as Smokey leapt into her lap and went very still.

Barnabas stared at his clasped hands, took a deep breath, and sighed in resignation.

Her impatience building, her mind was awhirl with unfounded speculation. But in the next instant, his response left her stunned.

"Ellen, many believe that this event was carefully crafted by the foremost users of magic of that age, in closest secrecy, to rid the known realms of the scourge of the *Old Ones*. I have no proof, of course; but, I suspect the Grand Portal and its steward, my ancestor, were offered as *sacrifice* in the performance of that rite."

"*What? Sacrifice?* The *Old Ones?* I've heard stories. So, this is where . . ." Her voice dwindled into a breathless silence, as Smokey stared unblinkingly up at her.

"Yes," Padraic confirmed. "As you might surmise, that this is the actual, or at least presumed, location is a closely held secret. As far as I know, only four people knew the truth—now five, three of whom are in this room."

Barnabas stared into the fire in resigned silence.

"So, why tell me?" She leaned forward and studied her father's face in the firelight.

"Because, you are now a steward," he answered simply. "And to be honest, I'm not certain that either of the other two people who know of this truth, for reasons of their own, would tell you."

"Who?" she demanded.

"You must trust us, Ellen," Barnabas insisted. "It will be to your advantage not to know who else knows—not yet."

"That's right," Padraic confirmed. "Knowing that now may influence how you relate to or act around these people, and that may not be to your benefit. If either, or both, elect to confide in you, you will know in whom you can place further trust."

"So," she reasoned, "you're talking about people I already know and probably trust! Why would you want to undermine that relationship? You know I can probably figure out—"

"Please don't!" her father interrupted. "If you start down that path, you'll only poison all your relationships. Such speculation won't serve you well at all. I knew that telling you only this much here and now would be awkward and unsatisfying, but it could be far more dangerous to leave you in ignorance, however innocent."

"To be candid," Barnabas began, "we fear an ominous portent may be just beyond the horizon. I do not mean the machinations of Titania or Mab in pursuit of their own agendas. Those we do not now name are no doubt equally aware and concerned. We suspect this unknown portent is something far darker, that may eventually involve or impact you as a steward. In fact, keep in mind that you are the *only* steward in all the known realms."

"So that's your justification for only telling me half the truth? Something may or may not be coming that may or may not involve me? Are you kidding me? Have you so little faith—"

"On the contrary," Padraic interjected, "I have the utmost faith and confidence in you. And Barnabas, I have convinced. He and I have wrestled with this strategy and considered all feasible contingencies. There are aspects to the tactics employed in furtherance of such a strategy that will not be evident to you, but will nonetheless be to your advantage."

Ellen sat back in silence, mulling the situation over. Padraic and Barnabas glanced at one another, sighed, and stared into the fire.

"I see now," Ellen said. "You are testing me; and, you are testing these unnamed others as well. You might even suspect these people may not be worthy of trust. So, I am to be a pawn in this strategy, am I? Let me ask, what makes you so sure you can trust *me?*"

"It is simple," replied her father. "Remember, we are of the blood—*the old blood.* This is family."

CH 13

CAPTAIN MILLER OPENED his office door and peered into the almost empty squad room; only two of his detectives were present. Fortunately, those were the very two he sought.

"Bassett! Redhawk! My office!"

The captain remained standing as the detectives shuffled in, obviously curious about the sudden summons.

"What's up, Captain?" Trey asked.

"Got a call from Charley, from the Livestock Brand Commission." He handed the sergeant a slip of paper. "These are GPS coordinates for the scene he's at. He wants y'all to meet him there. It's just inside the parish off the old road, FM-1611."

"He's there now?"

The captain nodded. "Yeah, he asked for you two specifically—said it had something to do with one of your cases."

"Okay, I think I know where this is, but I'll still check the coordinates on a map. Charley called it a *scene,* but didn't ask for a patrol unit?" Trey asked as he and Hawk shared a quizzical look.

"Nope, just you two. He said there's no rush, but he is waiting for you."

"Okay, Captain, we're on our way. Hawk, if you'll get the car, I'll check the map. I think that's a heavily wooded area right near the parish line."

HALF AN HOUR LATER, the detectives found Charley leaning against his truck on the side of the old farm to market road. He waved in acknowledgment and spit a stream of tobacco juice into the roadside ditch.

Hawk parked the unmarked cruiser behind the LBC investigator's truck, and looked around. He saw nothing that put him in mind of a crime scene.

Trey scanned the area as well. "I don't see anything unusual. Come on."

Charley stood straighter as they approached.

"Hey, Charley!" hailed Trey. "So, what have we got?"

"You boys up for a little walk? Gotta show you somethin' about a quarter mile into these woods." Charley opened the cab of his truck and retrieved a lever-action rifle.

"Whoa!" exclaimed Hawk. "Are we gonna need long guns?"

Charley shrugged. "My .30-30 is all I'm gonna need. If you boys got a shotgun, it might be good insurance."

Trey nodded to Hawk. "Get it. Okay, Charley, what's got you spooked?"

"Not spooked, Trey, just careful; you'll see. Y'all ready? Follow me."

THE SMELL WAS PARTICULARLY rank; ants and flies were present in abundance. The steer had been dead for days; almost half the carcass had been eaten. The remainder was partially covered with leaves, small broken branches and bracken. It was very much like the previous scenes; but then again, it wasn't.

"Looks a lot like our last scene, weeks ago; but this is different." Hawk commented as he looked around. "There's a lot of blood spatter. The ground and surrounding brush around here are all torn up. Fight, maybe? I dunno, maybe the kill was here?"

Charley nodded. "Good eye! Caught my attention, too. Keep looking."

"How did you find this, Charley?" Trey asked.

"I didn't; coupla kids trespassing on a four-wheeler ATV did. This used to be the old Palmer place. Family still owns it, far as I know; but the property has been leased for a long time to the paper company as a tree farm. It ain't all fenced so kids trespass all the time. There's a watchman who runs them off when he hears any dirt bikes or four-wheelers. He was runnin' these kids off when they kinda stumbled across this here.

"He recognized the carcass as cattle and called LBC. When I got here and saw this, I thought of your case. I sent the kids home with a warning. I told the watchman to go back to his post and sit tight. They give him a little shack, you know, to keep outta the weather. I didn't know if y'all would wanna talk to him or—"

"Over here!" Hawk called out.

Charley chuckled. "Your boy's good, Trey. He found it in half the time it took me."

Trey smiled and shrugged. "What?" he yelled, making his way to his partner.

Hawk pushed the thick brush aside with the barrel of his shotgun and pointed with the muzzle.

"Black bear, dead, good size one, too."

The dead bear, severely injured, almost mangled, had obviously died on this spot. Its hide was torn and shredded; broken bones protruded through long rents in its side. Its throat was ripped out.

"This happened here." Hawk swept his free hand in an arc to encompass the entire area around the steer carcass. "I don't think this bear killed that steer. Black bears generally don't prey on cattle; but carrion is another story. I think the bear found the carcass; the smell alone would draw it in. Whatever did make the kill had been feeding on it, and probably hadn't abandoned the site. I think that's what killed this bear."

Trey and Hawk exchanged an ominous look.

"That's my take, too," agreed Charley. "This isn't rustling by any stretch. This is predation; so, it's not a priority LBC matter. Black bears are on the endangered list, and protected, which means I gotta loop in Wildlife and Fisheries. So, before I make that call, you boys wanna tell me what can do that to a full-grown black bear sow? A bigger bear, maybe?"

Trey blew a stream of air through his lips. "Now I see why we brought a rifle and shotgun. To be honest, Charley, we don't know for sure, but since our last case we have a hunch. We're thinking maybe a big cat—"

"You mean like a cougar, swamp panther? They can get to good size, but I dunno. There's a lot of damage to this sow. She might run close to a bit over two hundred pounds or so. Y'all thinking just one cat could do this?"

"You know, you might be on to something there, Charley," Hawk pondered aloud. "If we're right about a big cat, we might well be dealing with more than one. How long do their offspring stay with the mother?"

The LBC investigator shrugged and shook his head. "Beats me . . . Trey?"

"I dunno, but that's definitely something we should check," Trey confirmed.

"Charley, let me ask you," Hawk broached, "does anyone else know about this bear?"

"No, just us. The kids and the watchman only saw the steer."

"Okay, good. Now, how long before you gotta call in the agents from Wildlife and Fisheries?"

"Soon, but no set time. These critters ain't goin' nowhere. Why?"

"Can you give us a day or so? We might be able to track what made this kill."

Charley grinned. "Y'all got some fancy new bloodhounds or somethin' y'all wanna try?"

It was Trey's turn to grin. "Yeah, something like that. So, a couple of days, okay?"

Charley put another plug of tobacco between his lip and gum and mumbled, "Sure, why not? So, y'all got this? Good, I've got somewhere to be shortly, so *adios, amigos!*"

Trey waved. "Thanks! See you, Charley!"

Hawk was already on his cell phone.

ABOUT AN HOUR LATER, the muted rumble of an approaching vehicle snagged the attention of the detectives as they waited in their parked cruiser. Trey twisted around in the front passenger seat and peered through the rear window.

"I hear it, but I don't see anything. Oh wait, something's coming."

Hawk stared into the rearview mirror as the image grew. "I see it. It's the Chevy—you know, the black one."

"Oh yeah," Trey chuckled, turning forward again, "the hot rod! Mark will find any excuse to drive it, won't he?"

"Can you blame him?" Hawk countered. "That thing is a blast! Now that it's tagged and legal, Ellen likes to drive it, too. I wasn't too surprised when Mark offered to bring Miska out here to meet us. Given the choice, I didn't think he'd take the truck."

They climbed out of the cruiser as the old Biscayne pulled in and the throaty rumble died.

"I think you're in for another surprise." Trey pointed.

Miska was behind the wheel, grinning from ear to ear.

Mark opened the passenger door and climbed out. "Hi guys! We made pretty good time, don't you think?"

Hawk could only chuckle and shake his head. "I should've known."

"You let Miska drive?" Trey asked with a sly nod for the big man, who now stood smiling beside the Chevy, his hand affectionately on the hood.

"Sure, why not? He's got his learner's permit," Mark assured, "and we've been teaching him. He's really pretty good."

Miska beamed and bobbed his head. "It is so much fun! I love this car!"

"I'll bet you do," Trey conceded and looked askance at his partner. "You knew about this, didn't you?"

Before Hawk could respond, Mark answered, "Course he did, Trey. Hawk's been helping teach, too."

"Only in my off time, Trey, and only on the farm property. We kinda wanted to surprise everyone."

"I get it. I'm just surprised that you didn't ask me to help. You know I used to teach advanced police driving tactics and high-speed pursuit at the academy."

"Yes! Please, teach me *police driving tactics and high-speed pursuit!*" Miska boomed.

Trey, Hawk, and Mark erupted in laughter. Miska's smile only got bigger.

"All right already!" cried Trey. "Pass the test, get your regular driver's license, and then we'll see about furthering your driving education, okay?"

"Yes! Yes! Okay!" Miska declared in delight.

"Okay, now down to business," Trey announced. "Hawk, please explain."

"Right. Miska, we need you to track, like you offered to do. We have a relatively fresh scene in these woods not far from here. Two carcasses; a steer and a black bear. We hope you can track whatever killed both of them."

Miska nodded. "No one else is around?"

"Not now. Two kids and a watchman found the steer, but didn't see the bear. They've since been sent away. A friend of ours, a state Livestock Brand Commission investigator, called us here, but he's now gone as well. Other than Trey and I, no one else has been on the scene. Will that work?"

The big man stroked his chin. "It should, but I must be in my bear form. Is time a problem?"

Trey shrugged. "We're not sure. We've probably got two days. Remember, we're not really sure what we're gonna find."

"And we don't really know what we're gonna do if we do find something," Hawk hastily added. "So, we don't want you to engage with whatever it might be. All we really want to do at this point is locate and identify it, understand?"

"I can do this. You should not wait for me. I will return to the cabin and contact you once I have done this thing. Be patient, and do not worry. I will be careful. Can you show me this scene, now?"

Mark raised a hand. "Hold up—I gotta tell y'all something. I've gotta get back to the house and prepare for a special meeting called by the Council for tonight. Something is going on in Mer that has the Council all worked up. Don't ask, I don't know any more, and won't until tonight."

"Wait," Hawk cautioned, "wasn't Ellen just there, like a week ago? Is she okay?"

"Yeah, she's fine," Mark assured him. "She was there with Padraic, but only for about an hour. I asked her if she knew anything; she didn't. She's as curious about all this as I am."

"She's not going to this meeting, is she?"

"No, relax, Hawk. It's just for Council members, like an executive session. They're being pretty tight-lipped about it. I'll know more tonight."

"All right then, if there's nothing else?" Trey probed. "Okay, Mark, we'll see you later. Miska, if you're ready?"

"I am. Show me this place. Then leave me and wait for my call."

PAPA GEORGE SMILED at the meth cook and clamped a hand on the slight man's shoulder. Teddy flinched, but kept silent, as George leaned into his face.

"I gotta admit, you've done good, Teddy. The quality is acceptable, but I thought you'd have more ready." George backed off and gestured to the white plastic bucket. "This is what, about three kilos?"

"Close, just under three, about two and three quarters." Teddy replaced the clear plastic film over the bucket of methamphetamine crystals. "It's hard to make a bigger batch without help. I gotta do everything myself, and well, you know . . ." He cast a wary eye toward a pair of goblins hunched over in a corner of the lab-cavern, gleefully tormenting a captured rat.

George sighed in resignation; he understood very well that using the goblin servants for anything but the simplest and most mundane tasks had proven to be ill-advised. Anything the least bit complicated or delicate that might be required during the drug production process was well beyond their apparent capabilities. There had been several botched tasks, simple as they were, that could have been far more serious. As it was, the broken glassware, damaged equipment, and contaminated chemicals could be replaced. Some of the goblins had sustained minor injuries, but two were suffering from severe chemical burns.

After that last incident, Teddy had made it clear that if the goblins weren't kept away from what he was trying to do in the meth-lab area, a disaster was inevitable.

George had to agree; when Teddy talked about cooking meth, one had better listen.

Consequently, the goblins were to keep their distance from Teddy's operation. That was not much of a problem; one stern look from Vito would send them scurrying out of sight. The downside was that Teddy had to do everything; that took time and limited actual production. The only good news was that the quality of the product did not suffer. Teddy had a touch of *obsessive-compulsive disorder* when it came to cooking meth, and he was very careful. George couldn't fault that.

"You know, Teddy, we may have to get you some real help."

"Boss?" The cook's eyes glanced toward the preoccupied pair of goblin servants now dismembering the hapless rat.

George scowled in distaste. "Don't worry, it won't be their like. Let me think on it, *capisce?*"

Teddy's head bobbed up and down, but he kept silent.

Vito strode into the chamber. The two goblins grabbed up remnants of the rat, scrambled into a narrow side tunnel, and disappeared from sight.

Vito scoffed in mild disgust, and turned to George. "Hey Boss, you said you wanted to know when Daegon got back. He's in the scrying chamber."

"Good. Give me a minute, then meet me there."

Vito nodded and left them alone.

Turning to Teddy, George said, "This isn't much product for the time it took. Now I know you had to get all set up and iron out the kinks, and the *help* wasn't what we'd expected, but I need you to stay focused. You shouldn't have any more distractions, right? So, I need you to make more, twice what we've got here, as soon as possible. I can get started with what you've produced so far, but I'll need more. Let me or Vito know if you need anything, okay?"

Teddy just bobbed his head as George turned on his heel and left.

GEORGE FOUND DAEGON entirely focused on the orb in the scrying chamber. As Vito followed his boss in, two goblin servants beat a hasty retreat.

"Damn, Vito," George remarked, "why are they so afraid of you? Did you hurt any of them?"

The big man shrugged. "Dunno, Boss, I never touched them—oh yeah, except for the one I caught going through my duffel bag. I slapped him upside his big ol' head and kicked him outta my room."

George chuckled. "Yeah? How come I didn't hear about that?"

"Wasn't worth mentioning, I guess. They all give me a wide berth; come to think of it, they have since I got here. Whatever, that's fine with me. I got no use for them."

George scoffed. "Don't sweat it; they'll stay outta your way. Anyway, Daegon says they have their uses, right Daegon?"

"Huh? Oh, sorry, what was that?" The alchemist finally looked up from the orb.

"Nothing," George answered and waved a hand in dismissal. "What took you so long with the Red Hats? Stellara came back hours ago. Didn't she do as instructed? Was there something wrong?"

"No, not exactly," Daegon began. "She passed the gem and simple instructions to Gaspar as we planned, but he seemed to struggle with implementing the instructions. I fear his treatment during this period of captivity with the goblin tribe may have been more harsh and taken a greater toll on his wits than I had anticipated. I sent your servant back as soon as she completed her task. I waited and secretly observed Gaspar until he finally complied with the instructions and made his escape."

"So it worked," George declared. "See, Vito, now we can monitor Gaspar through the diamond we gave him—"

"Uh, there is a problem," interrupted Daegon.

"What? I thought you said he escaped?" George demanded.

"He did, but he put the gem in a pocket," Daegon pointed to the orb, "and that's all I can see, the inside of his pocket. The sound is muffled, too."

"Uh, Boss," Vito said, "I don't get it; what's the problem?"

George sighed. "Murphy's Law. The diamond, it's a stud earring. He's gotta put it in his earlobe so we can see in the orb whatever he sees, get it? If he leaves it in his pocket, that's all we get to see."

"Oh, now I get it. It's no biggie. I don't think he'll leave it there. I know guys like that, street punks full of themselves and all. He's too vain not to wear a diamond; you'll see." Vito chuckled.

"You may be right; he was kinda pompous and arrogant," George recalled. "I guess we'll see. Now, moving on to my plan; it's time to start the first phase.

"Vito, I want you to take two keys of product from Teddy's first batch to New Orleans and put it in our distribution network. We gotta get rolling on that so I can recover some return on my investment. When you get back, we're gonna see about taking the rest of the product from this first batch, about three-quarters of a key, to that town you checked out in Mer. That was uh, Derinseum, right?"

"Yeah, Boss, it's a wide-open town. It'll be a piece of cake."

George smiled and rubbed his hands together. "Good, very good. You know what we gotta do there. I don't care if we have to give the whole stash away in free samples. We gotta whet their appetites, create a demand, *capisce?*"

"You got it, Boss!"

"Now, Daegon, tell me about this other place in Mer, the place you said you need to get to, what was it again?"

"New Port Royal, a pirate haven that I would rather avoid, were the person I must seek out to be found anywhere else. It is frustrating, but without her help I cannot get to the Keys of Osiris."

"So, who is she? Can you trust her?" George demanded. "We don't want our operation compromised in any way."

"She is called Circe, and is known as a sea witch. She commands her own vessel, and has been helpful in procuring certain *things* for me in the past, things that should not come to the attention of any authorities—"

"Ah, a smuggler!" interrupted George. "Or a pirate? Perhaps both?"

Daegon smiled. "Indeed, a bit of both no doubt, although I suspect she finds smuggling the more profitable pursuit."

"Makes sense," he agreed. "So, she can get you to where you wanna go. But look, you said you missed her when you were there, in Derinseum; she'd already left, right?"

"True," the alchemist admitted. "But what—"

"For one thing, you got jammed up on your last visit; and I'm sure you made quite the impression with your departure. The whole town is probably still riled up; and they know who you are. That is never good. You can't go back there. Vito and I will."

"Derinseum is not where I must go," Daegon insisted. "I—"

George held up his hands to forestall further argument. "Hold on—I know you mean New Port Royal, and I'm not saying don't go. Look, Vito and I have to go to Derinseum for a few days to get *our thing* going. While we're gone, you've gotta keep an eye on Teddy, and keep the goblins away from his lab, okay? Besides, you and Vito have been back from Mer for almost a week now, so any information you picked up there is almost a week old. How do you know this Circe is in New Port Royal right now?"

Daegon gently laid a hand on the surface of the orb; a small spark flared and faded.

"I have found her vessel, the *Xanthippe.* It is now berthed in the harbor at New Port Royal. If her ship is there, I have no doubt she is as well. She is known to frequent this den of iniquity."

George grinned. "Actually, that place sounds pretty good to me. When we get back from Derinseum, maybe Vito should go with you, and take a little product to pass around. What do you think, Vito?"

The big man smiled and slowly bobbed his head. "Sounds like another wide-open market to me. Yeah, it might be good if I have Daegon's back; we've got some history with that now. This New Port Royal sounds like a pretty lively place."

"Yeah, we can't have anything *else* happen to our friend, Daegon, now can we?" George clapped his hands. "Very well, that's our plan!"

CH 14

"LAND HO!" CRIED THE lookout in the crow's nest, pointing forward only a point or two off the bow.

Salidar paused in coiling line on the forecastle deck and squinted into the distance, but he could not yet see what the crewman high above could, the *Doom Wind's* destination, the Keys of Osiris.

Made good time, we did, from New Port Royal. I hope the crew will get to go ashore once these passengers disembark.

I've seen little enough of them as it is—kept to their cabin for most of this voyage, only to come on deck briefly at night, near midwatch. Passing strange, that. These passengers deal only with Captain "Bloody" Bane, and only in private, at that. I trust them not.

Strangely enough, the captain had been markedly subdued the entire trip. His frequent angry outbursts, those distinctive characteristics of his infamous temper, were conspicuously absent. The crew didn't mind this one bit, but were sufficiently superstitious to avoid any further comment. Tis never wise to tempt fate.

The crossing had been uneventful, a surprise to all considering it was the beginning of storm season. But truth be told, the crew would be glad to be rid of these passengers; there was something unsettling about them, despite their preference for isolation and minimal contact.

Salidar resumed coiling loose line. He'd been treated well by his crewmates since they'd departed New Port Royal, his status suitably improved since enriching the crew's common booty cache. The incident at the Fouled Anchor had produced results as Rumley had predicted, all to Salidar's benefit.

“Helmsman, five degrees to starboard!” boomed the bosun. “We’ll make for the largest island. We’re to be at anchor in her cove by sunset. Steady on your course, now.”

AS THE BOSUN HAD PREDICTED, the *Doom Wind* rode at anchor in the cove of the largest island by sunset. What little wind there was died and the surface of the cove grew becalmed. A bow-shot away gentle waves lapped a black sand beach festooned with sharp rocks. There was nothing inviting about it. A settlement lay above the beach, a series of low thatched-roof buildings staggered in an array amidst a huge rise of tumbled boulders beneath the broken peak of what once had been a jagged mountain.

A narrow dock reached out a stone’s throw beyond the beach. Two men approached, one bearing a lantern, the other a crossbow. They walked out upon the dock in silence.

Captain Bane nodded to the bosun. “We are expected. Lower a boat; have the passengers taken ashore.”

“Aye, Cap’n!”

As the crew bent to the task, the bosun lowered his voice.

“Beggin’ y’ pardon, Cap’n, but once we’ve offloaded, and the boat secured, will there be shore leave f’ the crew? I ken tis a mean an’ desolate place to be sure, but there be ale house or such, I wager.”

Bane stared at the bleak shoreline as the shadows of dusk rose like a tide from low places and claimed the dismal town by inches.

He scoffed. “Pah! There’ll be no shore leave this night. In fact, double the watch until sunrise.”

“Trouble, Cap’n?”

“Mayhap, but tis not our concern. See to m’ orders, Bosun.”

"Aye, Cap'n."

IN THE NORTHERN REACH of Chantilly Parish the lone watchman peered through the western window of his small guard shack. The sunset bloomed amidst the lingering clouds, a cottony chorus of reds and golds. The magnificence of the display could not overwrite the horrible scene he had found today when chasing those kids off the property. That awful image was burned into his memory. He shuddered, checked that the window was locked, and checked the door lock—*for what, the third time?*

His shift would end within the hour, none too soon for him. He could get out of here, go home, and lock himself in. He didn't have to wait for anyone; no one was coming to relieve him. The paper company had curtailed the night shift over a year ago, as an economy measure, since they believed no one in his right mind would try to fell trees and steal raw lumber in the dark.

His seniority served to keep him on as the solitary day-shift watchman. His responsibilities were reduced to dealing with occasional trespassers, usually hunters or kids up to some mischief. However, today had shaken him, and those kids, too. He was getting too old for this.

A glance through another window at his nearby truck birthed a heartfelt wish that he'd parked closer to the door of the guard shack. Oh well, he'd waste no time getting into his truck and vacating these premises—*no sirreebob, no time at all.*

Movement snagged his attention; something was out there, just beyond his truck.

What is that? A bear? Yes! And it's huge!

Staring, mouth agape, the watchman didn't breathe. His wits suddenly clicked into gear; he fumbled for his cell phone.

Gotta get a picture o' this!

And so he did, just before the big bruin melted into the dusky shadows and disappeared beyond the tree line.

THE SCENT OF THE RESPONSIBLE predator lingered strongly in the vicinity of the steer and black bear carcasses; the huge bear had no difficulty following the trail.

The scent meandered from the scene of carnage through the managed woodland until it pooled in a low spot in the trees near the watchman's shack. Here, just inside the tree line, something had watched the shack for some time before moving on. A short distance further into the denser woodland, there had been a moment of confusion when another, similar yet different, scent crossed and overlapped the original.

Another? Stalking? Following? No, together? Yes, there are two—together.

The bear huffed, rose up on its hind feet and tested the wind. Satisfied, he dropped to all fours and resumed following the now mingled scent trail.

Miska mused to himself . . . *Now this is getting interesting.*

"SO HOW LONG ARE YOU going to be gone, Mark?" Millie asked as she rinsed off the supper dishes and loaded the dishwasher.

"I'm not sure," he hedged. "I hope it won't be too long, but I really don't know. Regular meetings can drag out, but this one, an emergency meeting, wasn't scheduled. I'm not sure what to expect."

"How soon do you have to leave?" Stacy asked hefting the coffee carafe and gesturing to his cup.

"No thanks, I'm good. I should get ready; I've gotta be there in an hour."

Ellen pushed her cup forward. "I'll take a half cup, please. Thanks, Stacy. Mark, before you go, there's something I've been meaning to ask you."

"Yeah, what?"

"Remember what I told everyone here about my meeting with Lord Ignatius on Olmus, you know, about Olmus being avoided, and the possible return of the Dragon Lords?"

"Sure, I remember. What about it?"

"Well, has the Council, or any of its members said anything about that?"

Mark paused and scratched his chin. "Come to think about it, there was something mentioned during the Council meeting right after all that happened. As I recall, the Council Clerk, Madam Moya, read aloud an agenda item, basically a reminder that Olmus was off-limits and to be avoided. But I don't remember her saying anything about the Dragon Lords, or your meeting their avatar. Of course, I didn't say anything."

Ellen furrowed her brow. "I guess the Guildmaster went through his back channels to get Olmus on the Council's agenda. He indicated that he wanted to *manage* the information about the Dragon Lords; it appears he *still* hasn't told anyone."

"Maybe he has his reasons," Stacy offered. "He didn't want *you* to tell anyone, right?"

"True," Ellen admitted, "but I made it clear I was going to tell y'all, and that we'd keep it confidential. Somehow, this just doesn't sit right with me."

"I know what you mean, too many secrets," Mark declared. "Do you think I should ask around at this meeting?"

Ellen shook her head. "No, probably not. For the time being, I'm willing to give the Guildmaster the benefit of a doubt. Tonight, just concentrate on what's going on right now with the Council."

"Will do. I admit I'm plenty curious."

She raised her finger. "Remember, you gotta let us know what's going on as soon as you can. You know we hate being left in the dark."

He rose from the table. "Don't worry, I will as soon as I can. That was a great supper, Aunt Millie. Thank you. Now if y'all will excuse me, I gotta get rolling."

AFTER MARK'S DEPARTURE from the kitchen, Stacy sat next to Ellen and wistfully sighed.

Ellen considered her friend's unusual silence. "Stacy, is something wrong?"

"Huh? Nah, probably not. Whatever is going on with Mark and this meeting, I hope it doesn't interfere with our beach plans. Is next weekend still good?"

Ellen shrugged. "I guess so, but Hawk hasn't confirmed yet. He's scheduled to be off, but you know how that can be. He's supposed to call this evening when he can; maybe I'll know something tonight."

"Well, even if it's just a day rather than the whole weekend, it'll still be fun," Stacy reasoned. "It's not like it takes us any travel time, you know?"

Ellen's pursed lips and raised eyebrow had no effect; Stacy just grinned at her.

Millie joined them at the table. "Were you girls planning to stay overnight in Mer? What was the name of that town again?"

"Derinseum," Ellen answered. "Padraic recommended an inn near a popular beach, but we haven't made reservations. He said that really wasn't necessary; he'd spoken to the innkeeper and we'd be taken care of if we needed any accommodations."

"I hope we do get to stay overnight. The only thing better than a day at the beach is *two days* at the beach!" Stacy declared.

THE BEAR HAD SPENT a restless night in the shelter of scooped hollow beneath a crossed pair of fallen trees. There had been no point in following the mingled scents in the hours of moonless darkness, despite the bear's excellent night vision. Trying to track two probable predators in an unfamiliar area, in the dark, was instinctively foolish—and Miska was no fool.

With the greying mists of first light, the bruin roused from an uneasy sleep, sighed heavily, and shook himself. Peering out beyond the crossed trunks he neither saw nor sensed anything of concern. With a final grunt, he arose and trundled forth from the makeshift shelter. Standing erect on his hind legs, he lifted his muzzle and scented the slight morning breeze. The day would be warm and humid. Dropping to all fours, the bear walked in a slowly expanding circle; within moments he found the trail of mingled scents he sought.

With a *huff* he followed.

BY MIDMORNING, THE heat and humidity were on a steady rise. What little breeze there had been in the freshening morning had long since died.

The scent trail led him through a thickly forested valley and across a streambed that held little more than a flowing trickle. However, it was enough; the bear paused to drink. An unanticipated rumble from his stomach announced the onset of hunger. He would have to find something to eat; but, he would maintain his focus and continue tracking, too.

Within moments of crossing the streambed, the bear smelled something enticing, wild blackberries. Led by his nose, he found a thick blackberry bramble patch. He was content to stuff himself with every blackberry he could find. This took the edge off his hunger, but didn't eliminate it. Temporarily satisfied, he reacquired the scent trail and resumed tracking.

Hunger was again becoming a serious distraction by midafternoon, when a trace of scent snagged the bear's attention. *Old meat? Carrion?* The scent trail lay in the same direction. The bear followed.

It led to a small clearing below the face of an escarpment, an area studded with tumbled boulders of considerable size. Strewn about the clearing were the bones of creatures small and large—clearly the site of multiple feedings. No meat was left on any of the bones; many were broken, the marrow sucked dry.

The bear pawed through a haphazard skeletal pile near the base of the escarpment, and froze.

Beneath his claws lay a cracked open human skull; there was no jawbone. No trace of any tissue adhered to the skull; it was empty and licked clean.

The bear sensed that he was being watched.

Backing away slowly, the bear stopped near the center of the clearing. All sounds in the surrounding forest dwindled into silence. Rising to his full height on his hind legs, the bear swung his muzzle in a series of wide arcs, testing the scents in the air.

There, at the top of the escarpment, where the scent was most strong, a shape moved into view.

A big cat—with very long fangs!

The two apex predators considered one another in silence.

The bear may have been a third larger than the cat, but the cat had the advantage of high ground. That could matter significantly in an initial encounter. On even ground, the size and strength of the bear would be an advantage.

A wafting draft caught the bear's attention, the other predator's scent that had co-mingled with that of the first. Another shape came to stand with the first atop the escarpment.

Ah, another long-fanged cat, but smaller, a female?

The two saber-toothed cats and the bear continued to stare in silence. After a long moment, the bear dropped to all fours, turned and shambled off into the forest. Competing predators rarely fought one another, unless in defense of offspring or over food; the risk of serious injury was far too great.

I saw no cubs, nor any kill to defend; so, they will not fight or pursue. They seem comfortable here; I suspect a den nearby. Nonetheless, I must be sure I am not followed to Delafaire Farm.

CH 15

SEATED ON A PLUSH DIVAN in her private chambers, Queen Mab straightened and tugged at the hem of her bodice, below which the delicate lilac-hued fabric of her gossamer gown tended to bunch in an unsightly roll—completely unacceptable.

She considered the small stack of scrolls on the low table before her, a collection of the mundane and annoyingly routine responsibilities that required a monarch's oversight, and decided she had read enough for one day. She picked up the delicate teacup, reclined on the divan, and sipped her tea. Her lips pursed in distaste; the tea had grown cold.

At her impatient gesture, a servant hastened forward and removed the tea service. The maid kept her eyes downcast as she backed away and mumbled apologies.

"Your pardon, Majesty. Shall I have the tea—"

Mab was having none of it. "Enough! Take it away; it's tepid and bitter. Leave me!"

The maid scurried from the room, nearly bumping into a short middle-aged elf approaching the queen's chamber, Lord Nightshade. She deftly curtsied, stepped around him and disappeared down the corridor.

He caught the chamber door before it swung closed and politely knocked as he stood in the open doorway in full view of the queen.

"Ah, Nightshade, come in. You have news?"

He gently shut the door. A quick glance assured him that he was alone with the queen—except of course, for her ever-present bodyguard, the warrior-elf standing silent watch by the far wall.

Stepping before her, Nightshade executed a brief bow, and wasted no time.

"Gaspar! We have him, Majesty, here, in this realm!"

"What?" She shot to her feet. "Where is he now? This instant?"

He smiled. "In seclusion, under guard, at the outermost gate tower. He simply showed up at the outer gate minutes ago, asking for you. I ordered that he is to be kept secure, *as a guest,* and not to be spoken to until further notice. I immediately hastened to Your Majesty."

"Well done, Nightshade! Does he appear well, in full health?" Her drawn brows belied the solicitous tone of her inquiry.

"Ah, that may be in question, Majesty. He is whole, but filthy, and appears haggard. He indicated he was thirsty and hungry. It may be best for you to judge for yourself, Majesty. Your orders?"

She paced about in a small circle, deep in thought.

He was patient.

She faced him. "Get him cleaned up, see to his thirst and hunger, and keep him isolated. He is to be closely watched. Be certain he is treated as a *guest.* However, he is not to leave his accommodations until I deem otherwise. Understand?"

"Of course, Your Majesty. I shall see to it personally."

"Do so."

For the merest instant, the ghost of a smile slipped across her delicate features as the head of her Secret Police bowed, spun on his heel, and departed.

SALIDAR CAME ON WATCH at four in the morning. Still dark, it was colder than he expected. He was to relieve Gimp who had been posted on the forecastle deck during midwatch. He found his crewmate at the port rail, staring at the darkened island.

"Oy there, Gimp, I be y' relief. What's got y' attention so fast, mate? Y' be staring off t' port all intense like."

"Ach, tis naught now, but at four bells there was a commotion of sorts on yon island. Dunno what, bit of a ruckus and queer flashes o' light twas. Been quiet since."

Salidar joined his crewmate at the port rail and peered into the starlit darkness. He could just make out the shape of the big island.

"Tol' the bosun, did ye?"

"Aye," Gimp confirmed. "Watched with me for a while, he did; but nothin' else happened."

Salidar nodded. "Anyone else on watch see?"

"Aye, topwatch, he saw, too. Had a better view from the crow's nest, he did. Bosun knows we saw somethin', but no tellin' what. He went below, I `spect to tell the cap'n. He ain't been back."

"Quiet ever since?" Salidar squinted into the night, but saw little.

"Aye, quiet." Gimp stretched. "I'm for me hammock. The fo'c'sle deck be yours. Keep a weather eye out, matey."

"Aye, that I will, Gimp, that I will."

AN HOUR OR SO INTO his watch, the northeastern sky just beginning to lighten, Salidar heard the crewman on topwatch call out.

"Boat to port at amidships!"

Leaning past the port rail Salidar spied a longboat approaching, but it was several minutes before he could discern its five occupants. Two unfamiliar men rowed, islanders no doubt. The other three were familiar, the *Doom Wind's* former secretive passengers, the two fauns and the satyr. There was some cargo as well, a thick rolled rug or canvas tied with rope and a metal-strapped strongbox.

Within moments, the bosun was on deck giving orders.

"Deck watch, drop a cargo net off the port rail! Help 'em aboard!"

The cargo and passengers once aboard, the longboat turned back toward shore as the morning light strengthened.

The bosun pointed to Salidar and two other crewmen. "Stow this cargo below—"

"No!" the big satyr interrupted. "This chest stays with me! Have the carpenter prepare a box with a lock for this bundle." He kicked at the rolled and tied bundle. "It is not to be untied, nor the prepared box unlocked. Store that in the cargo hold."

Turning his head, the bosun's eyes narrowed at the satyr.

Salidar and his crewmates froze; passengers do not give orders aboard the *Doom Wind*.

His countenance darkening, the bosun straightened to his full height and faced the satyr. Before he could speak, another voice sounded from the poop deck.

"Bosun!" hailed Captain Bane. "See to it—now!"

The bosun scowled and called for the ship's carpenter.

None of the crewmen present missed the murderous look the bosun gave the satyr as the captain descended to the main deck and hustled the passengers back to their former cabin. The fauns carried the iron-strapped chest under the careful eye of the satyr.

Salidar got a good look at the bundle as the sun broke over the horizon. Almost as long as he was tall, it had an overall familiar shape . . . *a body? And what's in that chest? Treasure?*

He had little time to ponder further, as the ship's carpenter arrived and huddled with the bosun.

"Enough gawkin' y' bilge rats!" boomed the bosun at the idle crewmen. "Yer watch ain't over! Back to yer stations!"

Salidar hastened back to the forecastle deck, his mind awhirl.

Methinks this is an interesting development—interesting, indeed.

LATE IN THE AFTERNOON, Mark walked into the Delafaire Farm kitchen and found Ellen on her cell phone.

"Oh, hold on, Hawk. Mark just came in . . . Okay, I'll ask him."

Her cousin opened his hands. "Uh, what?"

"What did you learn at the Council meeting? Hawk wanted me to ask, too."

"Okay, why don't you put your phone on speaker so I can tell you both?"

She did so. "You're on speaker, Hawk. Can you hear okay?"

"Yeah, so what's up Mark?"

"Well, in a nutshell, the Council is concerned that there may have been another incident of necromancy, this time in Mer."

Ellen gasped. "In Mer? Are they sure?"

"No, not exactly. Apparently the reports are vague; nothing has been corroborated yet. The Mer administration is looking into it and will report back to the Council."

"When?" Hawk probed.

"I don't know, as soon as possible, I guess. The chairman said they'd call another meeting when they have the facts in hand. Anyway, it might be no more than rumor, but it sure has spun up representatives of the other realms. In the meantime, we were advised to keep this confidential and on a need-to-know basis. There's always the potential for panic, something everyone wants to avoid."

"So, I presume," Ellen offered with a smile, "that you have decided that *we* have a *need-to-know?*"

"Of course, and I know I can count on our collective discretion, right Hawk?"

The detective couldn't help but chuckle. "Ha, no kidding! So, you're back until there's another meeting?"

"Yeah, I'm probably gonna—"

"You're gonna do what you promised, Mark!" Ellen interrupted impishly. "You have to take Stacy shopping like you said; she's gonna hold you to it!"

Mark dropped his head in chagrin. "Oops, I forgot. Yeah, I'll be shopping, very likely *all* tomorrow morning with Stacy. Oh, before I forget, did you hear from Miska?"

"No, not yet," Hawk answered. "I expect him to call today; he knows we only had two days or so for this gambit. Don't worry, I'll let y'all know when we hear from him. If that's all, I've got court, so I've gotta go."

"Anything else, Mark? No?" Ellen asked. "Okay, that's it. Be careful, Hawk. Call me."

THE NEXT DAY, TREY leaned over the large map spread out on the kitchen table of Delafaire Farm and studied the location Miska indicated with a thick finger.

“Here is the place, I am sure,” the big man insisted with a satisfied smile.

Ellen and Hawk, coffee mugs in hand, joined them at the table. Millie followed with a tray of mugs for the rest of the company.

Trey accepted the fresh coffee and blew across the hot mug. “Thanks, Miss Millie. Uh, Miska, this location might be a problem.”

“Oh? How?” Miska asked, nodding to Millie as she handed him a mug.

Hawk leaned over the map. “Oh yeah, I see. It’s in the Kisatchie National Forest.”

“Yeah,” Trey agreed, “although it is still in the parish. We gotta think this through.”

“Well, I’m confused,” Ellen admitted. “What’s the problem?”

Trey sipped his coffee and pulled a chair closer. “Y’all may as well sit a spell; this will take some explaining.”

As they settled around the table, Stacy and Mark came in through the back door.

“Hey, look who’s here, Stacy.” Mark swept his hand in an arc. “Hi Miska, Hawk, Trey! What’s up with the map?”

“The coffee’s fresh and hot,” Millie declared. “Y’all get some and join us.”

Mark pulled two more chairs to the table and winked at Stacy. “Wanna sit by me?”

Stacy scoffed, pulled her chair next to Ellen, and asked, “Okay, what did we miss?”

“Miska found the cat, er, *cats*. There are two of them; he saw `em both.”

Stacy leaned across the table and grasped Miska's wrist. "You were in your bear form, right?"

Miska's head bobbed. "Yes, a good thing, I think. They saw me, too. We did not fight. I walked away, and was not followed. But Trey says the place is a problem."

"*Might be a problem,*" Trey corrected. "The location of your encounter is in part of the Kisatchie National Forest. That's administered by the National Park Service; so, the Park Rangers have jurisdiction—"

"But you said it's in the parish," Ellen interjected, "so don't you and Hawk have jurisdiction?"

"Well, yes, but," Trey hedged, "think of it as concurrent jurisdiction; both agencies have authority to investigate. Wildlife and Fisheries will probably get involved as well. More often than not, we just cooperate in a mutual *ad hoc* investigation. The fact that we now know there is a human skull there is going to complicate the issues; bodies always do in cooperative investigations. Furthermore, in this case, we have another twist to deal with. I'll let Hawk explain."

Hawk cupped his mug with both hands and scanned the faces around the table. "This stays here, okay?"

Everyone nodded their assurance.

"On our way here, we got a call from our captain. It seems that sometime after we cleared this latest scene, and Miska began tracking, the witness, the watchman who found the scene, was back at his assigned post, a little guard shack, when he caught sight of a bear nearby. He got a photo with his phone and called the Sheriff's Office. The captain forwarded the photo to us." Hawk paused to display his own phone for all to see.

The grainy photo was clearly of a bear. However, absent a distance measurement, or anything but out-of-focus trees in the field of view for reference, the actual size of the bruin was impossible to accurately determine.

"Miska," Hawk continued, "we think this is you."

Miska nodded. "I did go by a small shack. The scent trail led to a place where something lingered near there, probably watching the shack." He pointed to Hawk's phone. "That may well be me."

"Actually, this may work out to our advantage," Trey announced with a grin. "If you take our prior scenes of cattle predation into consideration, it's no great leap to suppose a large predator may be responsible, right? *We* know it's most likely the cats; but, no one else needs to know that, at least not at this point—and if we're lucky, maybe *never.*

"You see, if the other involved agencies are willing to accept," he pointed to the photo displayed on Hawk's phone, "a *bear explanation*—uh, no disrespect intended, Miska—then we can focus on dealing with the cats, without having to explain them."

"Although we haven't got a clue," Hawk bemoaned, "what we're gonna do about them."

"Yeah," admitted Trey with a heavy sigh.

"Actually," said Ellen, "I think returning them to their home realm might be ideal."

"Perhaps so, if we can find it," Trey conceded, "and work out the logistics—no small challenge!"

Ellen smiled. "Let me get back to you on that; I might have some ideas."

DUSK IN THE MER CITY was passing into full night as a large figure slipped with deliberate purpose through the deepening shadows.

Vito kept his hood up and his head down as he made his way through the warren of cobblestone streets of this poorer side of Derinseum. He had made numerous contacts throughout the city and distributed tiny samples of product wherever he thought it would likely generate interest and subsequent demand. He had nothing to really worry about since little was deemed illegal here, absent force or harm, *if* one had the coin. Nonetheless, out of habit he had been circumspect in whom he approached, and managed to avoid speaking to anyone who might be an authority figure, especially the Watch.

He scanned the street and nearby alleys as he approached the tavern he and Papa George had agreed upon as a safe place to meet. Few people were about, many sought the shelter of their homes, especially during the hours of darkness.

Vito found Papa George in a shadowed corner of the dingy tavern, seated at a small table, his back to the wall. Vito pulled a chair over and sat opposite his boss.

"You're late." George groused.

"Yeah, sorry. The watch patrols are thick. I was careful `cause I didn't feel like havin' to deal with `em."

"You're paranoid. Didn't you tell me nothing's really illegal? So what if you're holding? They wouldn't do anything, right?"

The big man shrugged. "Maybe not, but I've got my *nine* on me. Daegon warned me they're funny about tech here. I don't wanna cause a stir, you know?"

George nodded. "Oh, yeah, good thinking. We don't wanna attract attention; Daegon sure stirred the pot enough. Here I thought this was gonna be a pure party town, you know, like the *Big Easy*, but they're damn near rolling the sidewalks up at night, all thanks to Daegon's *departure gift*. Did you hear any more?"

Vito leaned forward and dropped his voice. "Just that everyone knows, but don't wanna admit it was necromancy. Nothing's been said officially, almost like they're trying to keep it quiet. Word is that none of the reanimated guards have been caught yet, so everybody's kinda freaked out. It's put a real damper on the whole city."

George leaned back and waved a hand dismissively. "It won't last; this is one of those self-correcting problems."

"Huh? Meaning what exactly?"

George leaned forward once more. "Daegon explained it to me like this; it's not general knowledge but as a rule a reanimated corpse will deteriorate without continued support from the necromancer, unless it learns to feed. So, more than likely if you can stay clear of it for a few weeks, it'll just collapse and rot away."

"A few weeks? That sounds easier said than done." Vito scoffed. "Even if the locals know that, things could still get dicey around here. What if somebody, you know, like the Watch, catches one of `em before it collapses? Can they find out who the necromancer is?"

"That's a good question," George agreed. "I asked Daegon pretty much the same thing; he kinda hedged a bit. He said he put a time-delayed self-destruction spell on them, so that wasn't a real concern. He hinted at ten days to two weeks or so, but didn't say any more. I think the question made him uncomfortable. I could read between the lines, so I didn't press him on it. So, I'm guessing yeah, it's possible someone could figure it out."

Vito glanced over his shoulder and scanned the room. No one was paying them any particular attention. "And if they learn to feed before then?"

George shook his head. "That'd be bad, worse than it is now, and draw far too much attention, something we certainly don't need. Why, have you heard anything?"

"No, not about that, not yet," the big man admitted. "How long are we thinking about staying here, in Derinseum?"

"How much product have you got left?"

"Some, but not that much, about two ounces, I think."

George stroked his chin. "Hold on to it; we're gonna need it."

"Oh, yeah, you mean for that other place, New Port Royal, that Daegon's so hot to get to?"

"Yeah, a pirate lair, right?"

"That's what he called it." Vito grunted. "Sounds like another good market to me."

"I've been thinking." George cocked his head, raising a sole eyebrow. "When things do go back to normal around here, it'd be nice to have a sort of base of operations in Mer, maybe here in Derinseum."

"Here, in this city, not that pirate place?" Vito scratched his chin. "Derinseum might be pretty open, but they still have cops, you know, the Watch. That means *intel.* And don't forget that *she* was here."

George shuddered. "Yeah, you don't have to remind me. I like this place, but I don't wanna have to be paranoid either. I suppose we should check New Port Royal out. You're gonna go with Daegon once we get back—I gotta check on Teddy anyway—so, let's have you take a look and see if it might work out."

"You mean as a market *and* a base?"

George's smile was smug. "Yeah, or a backup base—can't be too careful, you know. Come on, let's get outta here."

Neither man noticed the two hooded figures at a nearby table who watched them unobtrusively as they departed the tavern.

"WELL, SELENE, TWERE `im, aye? Tol' ya, dint I?" The diminutive spriggan wiped his runny pointed nose on the sleeve of his robe and leered at his comely companion.

"Aye, tis no doubt, Twit, tis he. But I know not the big man," she answered in a soft yet clear melodious tone. "Done well, y' have. Tullos will be pleased. They've taken no lodging?"

"Nay, none. The man you know, been around here since daybreak, kept to hisself, he did. The other, the big'un, wandered all over like, and talked to many." Slipping a small folded paper packet across the table, Twit continued. "The big'un, he gave away these, a white powder inside. Claimed it sharpened awareness, strength, and speed, he did."

Selene pocketed the packet beneath her robe. "He took no coin in exchange? Anything of value?"

Twit shook his head. "Nay, nothing, even when offered. Passing strange, that. What now? Will you report `em?" The spriggan leaned forward, his small mean eyes agleam. "Be der a reward?"

The undine chuckled and shook her head. "Nay, no reward. Be content that y've done a good service that neither Tullos nor I will soon forget. Tis to your advantage to get involved no further—trust me."

"Aye, that I do, Selene, that I do. Canst y' at least tell me who hunts `em? M' sources within the Watch know naught of `em. Y've hinted that the Council be involved, but—"

"Hush! Keep your voice down," she warned. "Only the one I recognized is sought. The Council has questions, true, but that one is hunted by the Realm of Man—"

He scoffed. "Ach, tis that all?"

"And Queen Mab."

His small eyes flaring wide, Twit shut up.

CH 16

THE *Doom Wind* rode at anchor in the small cove sheltered by the largest of the Keys of Osiris. There was little activity upon her decks since the captain had gone ashore a few hours ago. If the bosun wasn't standing over a work crew assigned to a task, the crewmen were prone to relax. And so it was that Salidar and Crabs were on the forecastle, sitting on coiled lines in the narrow shadow of the foremast.

"Got first dogwatch w' me, Salidar?" Crabs asked as he picked at a scab on his elbow.

Six bells rang out from the poop deck.

"Aye, in about an hour. I've got topwatch; mayhap there'll be a breeze aloft." Salidar lifted his eyes to the crow's nest atop the mainmast.

"Ha, as like! I be standby for the helm, as usual." Crabs flicked the scab over the rail and studied the cloudless sky. "Tis strange how warm the days still be, considerin' how cold the nights be gettin'. There'll be no breeze on the deck for this watch. To be becalmed this long ain't natural, I'll wager, especially this well into storm season. Not that we have anywhere to go, I `spect. Y've not heard anything?"

"Nay, nary a whisper." Salidar shook his head. "Even the bosun, he's been too quiet, what with the cap'n all distracted an' all."

"Aye, passing strange, that." Crabs leaned toward Salidar and dropped his voice. "Ever since our passengers come back aboard w' whatever be that cargo they brought, me gut's been uneasy. Somethin' ain't right."

Casting his eyes about, Salidar probed, "What was that cargo, do y' suppose?"

"Dunno, but Patch says the carpenter thought the bundle be a body—without a head."

"W-what?" Salidar sputtered. "W-without a head?"

Crabs nodded and placed a finger to his lips. Both heard the creak of the ladder as someone ascended to the forecastle; but the staggered *clomp* announced the identity of the newcomer before his head cleared the edge of the forecastle deck.

"Ah, there y' be," declared Gimp, as he sat awkwardly upon another coiled line. "Listen here, I heard the passenger, the big 'un, tell the bosun to set sail with the tide. Wants to go to another of these islands, he does, a smaller one."

"A passenger givin' orders to our bosun?" Crabs chuckled. "Dint go well, did it?"

"Cap'n not even aboard either?" Salidar added. "So, what happened? Bosun light into 'im?"

"Nay, nothin' happened," Gimp responded, to their surprise. "Bosun, he just stood there, all silent like—but his eyes be smolderin'. He just nodded once an' walked away. Be no love lost there, I reckon."

"Won't matter," Crabs assured them. "The *Doom Wind* won't budge until the cap'n is aboard and gives the order. That be gospel true, lads, and y' knows it."

"Aye, you're in the right of it," Gimp agreed. "Dunno who this passenger thinks he be—some sea lord, he ain't!"

"Sure an' certain, he'll test our cap'n at his own peril!" Crabs cackled.

"A true word!" affirmed Gimp. "No treasure trumps our cap'n's command of the *Doom Wind*!"

"Treasure?" echoed Crabs and Salidar in unison.

Gimp's mouth slammed shut; his eyes darted side to side.

"Arrgh! Stand by to come about there, mate," Crabs intoned. "What be this treasure you speak of?"

"Has it to do with our passengers?" Salidar pressed. "Be it in that chest they brought aboard?"

Eyes wide, Gimp did not reply.

"Withhold such news from y' shipmates, would ye?" Crabs leaned into Gimp's face. "You know twould be yer fate accordin' to the articles, dun ye?"

Gimp sat back and waved his hands in denial. "Nay! Nay! Gots me all wrong, y' have, lads! I speak of treasure in the *general*—bein' that nothin' could tempt the cap'n to give up command of the *Doom Wind*, is all. Curse me for a lubber—twas all I be meanin'! Besides, there be no treasure in that cursed chest!"

"That be so? Know ye then wut in thar be?" Crabs' eyes bored into those of his frightened crewmate.

Salidar watched in silence. He knew withholding booty or information related to such spoils was a serious violation of a ship's articles, the agreement that specified the rules and principles of the pirate company and bound the crewmen thereto. Punishment could be severe. Whatever Gimp knew, he would have to share, or else.

"Listen close then, lads," Gimp sighed heavily in resignation. "I overheard the cap'n and the bosun talkin' real quiet like, after that *new cargo*, bundle and chest, come aboard."

"I remembers well enough," said Crabs. "The carpenter had to build a box for the bundle; tis now in the hold. But what of the chest?"

"Aye, that's the thing." Gimp bobbed his head. "The box be in the hold; but the chest be in the passengers' cabin. The two have to be kept apart—separate like."

Salidar hissed, his patience thinning. "Damn yer eyes, Gimp! What's in the chest?"

Gimp's eyes darted to either side and his voice dropped to a mere whisper. "I only heard, never saw f' meself—"

"God's blood! Gimp—what?" Crabs demanded.

"A head," breathed Gimp, his face going pale, "a human head."

"*A head?*" Crabs blurted, then mumbled, "Huh, Patch says a body be in the bundle, or so the carpenter thought. So, a head and a body to be kept apart? What in the wet world are we to make of that?"

"Dunno, lads," Gimp answered, giving a sailor's sign to ward off evil. "No clue—but given me druthers, I'll keep me distance."

Salidar tried to appear as bewildered as his crewmates, but his mind was awhirl.

A Dullahan? Could it be?

QUEEN MAB IGNORED THE two guards standing at silent attention as she paused at the door to the secured guest chambers and adjusted the long sleeves of her formfitting sheath; the iridescent greens and blues shimmered in the torchlight. Satisfied with her appearance she turned to her companion and nodded.

Lord Nightshade acknowledged her silent command and produced a brass key. The soft click of the lock was barely audible. He pushed the heavy door open, and with a flourish swept his arm in invitation.

"Your Majesty, your servant, Gaspar, awaits your pleasure within."

"Very good, Nightshade. See to it we are not disturbed. This will not take long."

He bowed and lowered his eyes. "As you command, Majesty. I shall wait without."

The door closed behind her, but the lock did not engage.

Before her, near the center of the large and comfortably furnished room, the prodigal mage knelt upon one knee, his head bent in obeisance. His hair long and unkempt, he appeared thinner than she remembered; perhaps the borrowed clothes were too big for him. However, he was clearly more haggard as well. She let the moment linger, savoring his discomfiture. He had displeased her—greatly. And yet, she had to keep her temper in check; she needed certain information from him.

Forcing herself to be patient, she acknowledged him. "So, Gaspar, you have returned. Rise. You are well?"

He scoffed. "As well as can be expected," he paused to dust off his knee, "Your Majesty."

Her eyes flared at his impertinence. She kept her ire constrained, her voice even and toneless. "Where have you been? Why did you not immediately return to me as instructed?"

The mage looked askance, as if reluctant to meet her eyes. "I was held—against my will—in a realm I later learned was Olmus."

"*Against your will?* A mage of *your* standing?" She made no effort to hide her surprise. "Indeed, by whom? I was under the impression that Olmus was uninhabited. In fact, I, uh, have reason to believe that even visiting that realm is proscribed."

His lips drawn into a grim line, he tossed a hand dismissively. "Hmmph, I know naught of any proscription; but, I assure you that place is inhabited—by tribes of foul goblins, who relish in the infliction of pain and harassment! Somehow they inhibited my powers."

She arched a lone eyebrow and observed dryly, "Goblins, eh? How interesting. Yet you managed to escape, yes?"

"Uh, yes, Majesty. It took, er, all my craft and guile to finally escape and return to you."

"So, goblins living in Olmus? Well, they are a secretive lot. I suppose they could have been there with no one the wiser for generations," she mused aloud. "So, how is it you came to be there? Were you not in Storm Haven, to do as I had instructed?"

"Aye, Majesty, I was, and I did. I had defeated their mage, Gallenius, when the Steward faced me—"

"The *Steward?*" Mab blurted, her fists instantly balled at her sides. "What was *she* doing there? What happened? Tell me!"

"She confronted me as I was about to deal the fallen Gallenius the final blow." He paused, staring into some private space, a befuddled expression upon his face.

"Go on!" she demanded.

"I-I do not fully remember—a spell, I think. Next I knew, I was in the cruel hands of the Red Hat goblin tribe." His hand drifted to his neck, but there was no obsidian collar to chafe and restrain him. Nonetheless, he shuddered.

"A spell? I doubt it," she spat. "The Steward is not a magic user. She may be responsible for your transit to Olmus; but, as for any spell, she had help, of that you can be certain!"

"I do not remember seeing anyone else, Majesty; but of course, I am sure you are right," he offered in placation.

"No doubt. I must ponder this development," she murmured as she began to pace back and forth.

He stared straight ahead in silence.

Stopping before him, she thrust out her open hand. "My ring, if you please."

He balked. "Uh, ring? Uh, Majesty?"

Her gaze burned into his soul; her voice chilled. "My topaz ring, Gaspar, the bespelled ring I entrusted to you to deal with those fools of Storm Haven, I will have it back—now."

He dropped to his knees, his face pale. "M-majesty, I-I now remember the ring, but I have it not. I have no memory of it beyond confronting the Steward—"

"The *Steward? Arrgh!"* she screamed in fury! "The Steward has *my* ring? How dare she! I'll-I'll—"

The door crashed open. Lord Nightshade and the two guards burst into the room.

"Majesty! Is all well?" Nightshade asked, not taking his eyes off Gaspar.

"Stand down, Lord Nightshade. I am in no danger," she assured him. "My outburst was merely a slip of anger, and not at my mage. You may withdraw."

"At once, Your Majesty." Nightshade and the guards returned to the hall and shut the door.

Silence hung heavy. Gaspar kept his eyes downcast and remained on his knees.

Mab began pacing once again. Her strides slowed and she stopped.

The mage looked up expectantly, his breath held.

"Gaspar, I am pleased you have returned to me. I am not pleased with the loss of my ring."

"I understand, Majesty. I will make every effort to recover your ring."

"Rise, return to your former chambers, and regain your strength. As for my ring, the Steward has it; so, I will deal with her." Her voice dropped to a whisper, "Oh yes, once and for all."

He rose and bowed deeply. "As you command, Majesty."

She nodded to the door, and he scrambled forward to open it for her. He inclined his head as she passed, and tucked his unkempt hair behind his ears. She did not miss the twinkle of a gemstone in his earlobe. A small smile creased her lips.

So, your vanity survives intact, Gaspar. Do you not know how malleable that renders you?

THEIR ARRIVAL UNOBSERVED, Vito and Daegon stood on a low hill overlooking New Port Royal's harbor. The morning sun was low in the eastern sky and the breeze was still blowing offshore.

"Feels like it's gonna be a cool morning at least," Vito observed, as he shrugged beneath his robe. "Can you see if her ship is there?"

"It is, the black junk," Daegon pointed, "there at that short pier. It has not moved for over a week. Nor have I seen it taking on any cargo."

"What? We just got here—oh, you mean in the scrying orb. Sorry."

Daegon smiled. "Yes, the orb. I have been watching closely, but I have not yet seen Circe."

"But you're sure she's here?"

"Indeed, if the *Xanthippe* is here, then she is not far. I will find her. What will you do?"

The big man sighed. "The same I did in Derinseum; hit the streets, check things out, maybe spread a little product around. Shouldn't take too long; this place ain't as big as Derinseum. We gonna set up a meet? Otherwise I won't know if you found her and what you're gonna do next."

The alchemist nodded. "You are right. Let us meet here, this day, at sunset. If I have found her, I will know my next move; if not, I will have found us accommodations for the night. We can continue tomorrow."

"Sounds like a plan," Vito agreed. "Be careful; this place isn't as safe as Derinseum."

"Oh, I am well aware; I have been here before. You should be cautious, too. Remember—"

"Yeah, I know," Vito interrupted, "don't use any tech, too much like magic."

"Yes, people remember, especially superstitious people."

AT SUNSET THAT EVENING Daegon had to admit he hadn't yet found Circe.

That didn't bother Vito one bit.

"Hey, no problem. We can spare another day here. In fact, that'll work out just fine for me. I've distributed almost all the product; I've only got a trace left, *two dimes* worth. I like this place, maybe even better than Derinseum. Now, didn't you say you'd arrange some overnight accommodations for us if you didn't find her?"

"I did," Daegon acknowledged. "As it happens, I did find the *Xanthippe's* bosun, with whom I have dealt on prior occasions. He would not disclose his mistress' current location, but agreed to send word that I sought her. He said to take lodging at the Fouled Anchor; if she is willing to meet, she will find me there."

Vito scratched his stubble beard. "Fouled Anchor? What is that? Like an inn?"

"Of sorts," Daegon lowered his voice, "more like a gambling saloon and brothel, but one can get a room overnight."

"And some willing company, I'd bet!" Vito smiled. "I'm in! Is it close?"

"It is not far; and to be candid, it is probably a smart move."

The big man's smile vanished. "How so?"

"Tis one of the few places in New Port Royal where you need not run the risk of having your throat slit in your sleep. The proprietor can be fearsome, and he runs a tight ship."

"Do you know him?" Vito asked.

"I know *of* him," Daegon explained. "He is called Rumley, and is not to be crossed."

"I get it. So, we stay low profile, right?"

"Indeed, let us go."

THE LATE MORNING WAS still relatively cool in the shade of the Kisatchie National Forest.

Miska led the way down a surprisingly straight and flat path that was nonetheless overgrown by thick brush from both sides. Towering pines and random hardwoods interlocked limbs overhead in a dense canopy. Only sporadic bursts of errant sunlight slipped through whenever a capricious breeze cavorted aloft.

Hawk, trailing behind Miska, adjusted the strap on his shoulder-slung shotgun and studied the screen of his phone. "According to my GPS, we're now within the national forest boundaries."

"But still in the parish?" Ellen asked, just behind him.

"Yeah, but this path—I think it's an old fire road—isn't on this GPS map."

"Actually, it's an old rail bed," Trey corrected, as he stepped up to Ellen and displayed his much-folded paper map. "See this light dotted line? That's what it means."

Hawk chuckled. "Heh-heh, I should've known you'd bring that old-school paper map. You see, Ellen, he doesn't trust these *newfangled* conveniences." He waggled his phone and snickered.

"Allow me to correct you once more, my young friend." Trey unfolded the map. "This is an old-school *topographic* map; the concentric lines are indicative of elevation. See the notations in meters and feet? I thought this may prove useful in our search for geographic anomalies, you know, like caves. Besides, I don't have to rely upon a battery, now do I?"

Ellen laughed. "Ah, the good sergeant has a point, wouldn't you say, Detective?"

"Arrgh! They're ganging up on me!" Hawk moaned in mock despair. "Miska, help me out here!"

"Ha!" Miska scoffed. "I need neither GPS nor maps; I have my nose. And more importantly, I know the way, having already been there." He winked at her. "Miss Ellen, you need only rely upon me."

"Oh, such chivalry, I might swoon," she teased. "Our adventure calls! Pray, lead on, Sir Knight!"

Miska grinned and bowed. "At once, m'lady."

HALF AN HOUR LATER the forest terrain changed to more severe hills and rocky outcrops. The old rail-bed path came to an abrupt halt at a massive pile of tumbled granite. Some of the boulders were as tall as Miska.

Trey scanned the area and stood silent as the others looked for any continuing sign of the old path.

"There's a very narrow path beyond these rocks," Hawk offered from one side of the obstruction. "Probably an old game trail, it winds around more big rocks, but it's passable."

"It is not the same path I used, but it will serve," Miska said. "In bear form I went through much thicker brush. However, this trail will take us in the right direction."

"Hey, Trey," Hawk called, "aren't we getting into Murrell territory?"

"Huh? John Murrell, the outlaw?" Trey asked. "That Murrell?"

"Wow!" Ellen exclaimed. "I haven't heard that name since I was a kid. Is this really the right area?"

Trey chuckled. "Yeah, I guess it is. You might wanna keep an eye out for his treasure."

Miska held up his hands. "Please, who is this person? What treasure?"

"It's a local legend," Hawk explained. "Although I guess it's not really a legend because most of it is true. I think every kid who grew up in East Texas or Louisiana back in the day heard the tale at one time or another."

"Yeah," agreed Ellen. "I know I did."

"Well, I have not," Miska pointed out. "So?"

"Go ahead and tell him, Hawk," Trey suggested. "But we gotta keep moving, okay, Miska?"

"Fine, stay close and speak softly. I must still be able to hear the sounds of the forest."

Hawk had a fine voice for storytelling.

"This goes back to a time after the turn of the nineteenth century, after the Louisiana Purchase but before Texas was a republic or a state. Spain still controlled Mexico, and that included what is now Texas. However, the borderline between the Louisiana territory of the United States and Spanish Texas was in dispute. So, until the two governments could work it out, they decided on a temporary compromise and declared the area along the Sabine River *Neutral Ground.* It was effectively *no-man's-land,* no law enforcement or courts. Needless to say, it became a haven for outlaws, and was known as the *Neutral Strip.*

"About 1825, a traveling preacher showed up in the Strip; this was John Murrell. But he wasn't about just spreading the gospel; he was a thief and a gang leader. He'd travel to different settlements and settlers' farms in the Strip ostensibly to preach, but he was also picking victims to later rob. While he was holding Sunday services, his gang would be stealing whatever they could from the homes of the unaware victims while they were sitting in church or a revival setting listening to Murrell's sermons."

"That's right," Ellen offered. "I remember he was called 'The Reverend Devil' after his victims caught on."

"Yeah, he was a nasty piece of work," Trey added.

"True dat," Hawk confirmed. "Now keep in mind that this was before there was any kind of acceptable currency as we know it, only silver and gold, most often as coins. This was what Murrell and his gang were primarily after. The more successful they were, the more other outlaws were drawn to him. Consequently, his gang grew; there were rumored to be seven or so clans within his outlaw band. They were well organized, used secret symbols and codes, and even had their own secret banks to hold their stolen wealth."

"Banks?" Miska echoed. "I do not understand."

"Not banks in the sense that we mean today, more like specific hideouts where the gang could stash their ill-gotten goods. Remember, they'd steal anything they thought was of value and resell it, most often on the western side of the Sabine River where people didn't ask too many questions. Murrell had lots of hideouts throughout the Strip, but the most important was his headquarters—probably more than one—believed to be somewhere near here, in the caves of the Kisatchie Forest. These caves were also the locations of his most important banks, the caches of stolen gold and silver."

"Supposedly there was quite a bit of gold and silver amassed over the years," Trey said. "The outlaw and his band had a pretty good run up until the late 1830s; then things changed."

"Right," Hawk confirmed. "You see, after Mexico won its independence from Spain, Texas successfully fought for independence from Mexico and declared itself a republic. Then law and order came to the Strip. Local sheriffs on both sides of the Sabine River, the Louisiana-Texas border, cracked down on the outlaws; even the Texas Rangers got involved. The Strip was still a wild `n' woolly place for years to come, but the days of the big and well-organized outlaw bands were on the wane."

"I see," Miska said. "So, what ever happened to this Murrell person?"

"No one really knows," answered Trey. "He just disappeared, and was never heard from again. Some think he was killed by his own gang; others think he fled fearing capture."

"And his treasure? The gold and silver?" Miska pressed.

"Ah, his treasure was never found," Hawk answered with an amused wink. "Lots of folks have looked for it over the years, but no one has found it."

Trey chuckled. "Well, I recollect there was something found by some railroad workers back in the nineteen-twenties, a silver bar, I think. I remember hearing about an old report about how it got turned in to the authorities. I don't know what happened after that; although, it did stir up *gold fever* among another generation of treasure hunters, and a lot of folks came to search. As far as I know, nothing else was ever found."

"Nothing at all?" Miska asked.

"Nope, nary a trace," Trey assured the big man. "Of course, that didn't stop people from looking. Unfortunately, many of those treasure hunters did a lot of property damage over the years, and a number of them got hurt. It got to be such a problem that the National Park Service had the known caves deliberately dynamited closed in the early nineteen-forties. However that still didn't stop some folks from nosing around. In fact, to this day some still do."

"All because this treasure was never found?" Miska concluded.

"Right," Hawk confirmed. "Not all the caves were closed because not all were discovered. As time goes on, the terrain slowly changes with erosion and such. Every now and then another cave is revealed; and that stirs up speculation that it might be one of Murrell's secret caches."

"So we know there are caves around here, right?" Ellen asked.

"Yes, there are," Trey answered, "and that's why we think the big cats will use one for a den. If Miska's hunch is right, it won't be too far from where he saw them both."

"Which is why we've got to find that spot, record the GPS coordinates, and see if that skull he saw is there." Hawk explained. "And at some point, we'll have to loop in the other interested agencies."

"Remember," Trey cautioned, pointing to Ellen and Miska, "you two aren't really here; officially it's just Hawk and I following up on the security guard's statement about his bear sighting."

"Oh, don't worry, I know," Ellen assured him. "I'm just here to see if I can sense any sort of active random portal. So far, I haven't."

"Keep in mind that we're not certain that a portal is how these cats got here," Hawk offered. "So it's important to keep an open mind, okay?"

"Oh, I'm open to whatever. It's just that I can't think of any other way to explain how they're here; and it suggests that we may have a means at our disposal to deal with them, maybe even return them to where they belong." She grinned hopefully. "Doesn't that make sense to you?"

"Maybe," Hawk allowed, "if we can figure out where they belong, and we can find them here, in this realm."

"Yeah, first things first. All we have to do today is find the clearing Miska described," Trey said.

"We will not search for a cave den?" Miska asked, a hint of disappointment in his voice.

Trey shook his head. "No, not now. We've got some tech that'll help us with that. It'll be quicker and a lot safer, trust me. Besides, we'd rather accomplish that before any other agencies get involved."

"Tech?" Ellen echoed. "What tech?"

"A new toy," Hawk answered with a smile, "a remote surveillance drone with infrared capability. We'll be able to identify all the warm-blooded wildlife in the vicinity—"

"That my *old-school topo map* indicates is prime real estate for caves," Trey finished smugly.

"But what if our quarry is *in* the cave," Ellen posed. "The drone can't register a heat source then, can it? It can't go *into* a cave, can it?"

Hawk shrugged. "Possibly, depending on the size of the cave, but it's probably not a good idea."

"It will not matter," Miska observed. "The cats must leave their den to hunt. They must find water, and they must feed. They will not likely return to that steer kill; we have been there and left too many overlaying scents they will not trust. No, they will need to make a fresh kill, and soon."

"All the more reason for us to finish this *recon mission* and get out of here," Trey cautioned.

"Yes," agreed Miska. "We are close. Now we must be quiet."

WITHIN TWENTY MINUTES they found the clearing at the base of the bluff. The surrounding forest was dead still and quiet. The merest hint of a breeze was at their backs. The companions beheld the disarray of scattered sun-bleached bones in a solemn silence.

Trey whispered to Miska, "Is this how you remember it?"

"Yes." He lifted his head and sniffed the air. "I can not sense any other creature nearby."

"Okay, I've got the GPS coordinates. Where was the skull?"

"This way. Follow me."

As Miska and Trey carefully stepped across the bone-littered clearing, Hawk nudged Ellen and asked, "So, no portal, huh?"

She shook her head. "No, nothing, I'm afraid."

He sighed. "Look, I don't object to your idea of sending the cats back where they belong, protecting that respective ecology and all, assuming we can figure out where that is, but I still have a concern. If we find them before we know where their home is, what do we do with them in the meantime? It's not like we can cage them up somewhere."

"Don't think that hasn't occurred to me," she assured him. "Trust me, I'm working on it."

He scanned the tree line at the edge of the clearing, and snapped his fingers.

"Oh man! I can't believe I only just now thought of it; but could you, you know, do *your thing*, see if we're really alone here?"

Ellen glanced across the clearing and shook her head. "Actually, I've been trying, but it doesn't seem to work here like it does in other realms. I mean it works a bit, but it's very faint. It seems like it works better right after I get back from another realm, but it kind of diminishes within a few days. I can sense portals with no problem, but that seems to be it. I'm not picking up much of anything right now."

Hawk kept his eyes moving along the tree line. "Hmm, I wonder if that's got anything to do with the laws of physics being a little different in each of the respective realms. Do you think?"

"Maybe," she slowly nodded. "We can run it by Zack the next time we see him."

"Oh great," he groaned, "another theoretical physics lecture, just what I need."

Ellen rolled her eyes and quipped, "Oh, you'll live."

Hawk pointed to her necklace. "Hey, your crystal is giving off a bit of light, kinda like soft yellow. Normally that's clear. So, does that mean anything?"

She lifted the crystal and gazed into its depths. "Not really, it does this when Miska is around. Padraic said it would; it's okay."

"Maybe, but it looks to me like it's getting a bit of orange tint, see?"

"Hmm, it's faint, but you're right. That's strange. I still don't sense anything."

"Hawk!" Trey waved and whispered hoarsely, "Over here—we'll need an evidence bag."

They'd found the skull.

Trey was on his phone as Ellen and Hawk joined him and Miska.

"Okay, thanks, Mel . . . Yeah, geo-tagged for now. You can log it as recovered. See you later."

"CSI?" Hawk asked.

Trey nodded. "Yeah, Mel green-lighted us recovering the skull, since this is only partial remains, and a John Doe for now. Even if we get a confirmed ID, we know it's unlikely this is our original scene. Besides, we don't want any other agencies coming out here until we've dealt with the cats."

"True dat!" Hawk agreed. "So, just a routine recovery makes sense, and maintains chain-of-custody. Although, to be candid, I don't see this ever going to court."

"Probably not," Trey conceded, "but we still have a job to do."

Within minutes the skull had been photographed *in situ*, tagged, and bagged. It now resided in Trey's backpack.

Miska scented the air once more, and shrugged uneasily.

Trey stood bedside him and scanned the perimeter of the clearing.

"Okay, mission accomplished. I'm getting a creepy feeling, like an itch I can't scratch. Let's get out of here. Miska, you're on point. Hawk, cover our six. Let's move out."

UPWIND, NEAR THE CREST of the bluff, a pair of tawny yellow eyes watched the four companions depart, slipping single-file through the underbrush and into the forest beyond the clearing.

Three of the four scents were new, strange and unsettling; the fourth was vaguely familiar, harboring an ominous taint of predator.

The saber-toothed cat had not moved a muscle during the encounter. He rose from his crouched position and stretched. He scented the air; the breeze had changed. With a short *huff,* he turned and padded silently into the rocks beyond the crest.

CH 17

MARK ENTERED THE KITCHEN to find Millie, Ellen, and Stacy enjoying their afternoon tea.

"Tea, Mark?" offered Millie.

"No thanks. Did Trey and Hawk leave?"

"Yes," Ellen answered. "They had to take the skull we found directly to their lab, you know, chain of custody and all."

"And Miska went to the cabin," Stacy added with a wink. "You were gonna ask, weren't you?"

Mark smiled and winked back at her.

"So, what's up, Mark?" Ellen probed. "What's going on?"

He opened his hands. "I just got a Council summons, another emergency meeting, tonight."

"Do you know why?" Stacy asked.

"Yeah, two issues. First, the necromancy in Mer has been confirmed; two of `em have been caught, uh, corpses, that is."

Stacy winced. "Eww, gross!"

"And what else?" Ellen pressed.

"Papa George has been seen in Mer, actually in Derinseum."

"Seriously?" Stacy exclaimed. "He's in Mer, and so is necromancy? Does the Council think there's a link?"

"It wouldn't surprise me. They suspected he was linked to the necromancy that occurred in the Council Realm; so, I'd expect the Council to assume a link with Mer, too. They're pretty paranoid about this whole necromancy thing. I expect they'll launch a full-scale investigation in Mer. I gotta tell Trey and Hawk; I know they're still holding outstanding warrants for Papa George."

"Hold on," Ellen cautioned. "What about extradition protocols? Nothing has really been established, has it?"

Mark shrugged. "No, not officially. But remember that the Council was willing to honor those warrants and turn him over at that initial meeting—"

"But he escaped," Ellen interrupted, "and from Queen Mab as well; which means she'll be looking for him, too."

Mark nodded. "No doubt. Sorry, but for now, I don't know any more, and won't until tonight."

Ellen stood. "I'll reach out to Hawk. Keep your phone with you, Mark; I'm sure he'll want to talk to you."

"I will, don't worry." He spun around, pushed into the dining room, and called over his shoulder. "I'll be in my room. I gotta research some stuff."

As the kitchen doors swung shut, Millie rose. "Hold everything, girls. Weren't y'all planning a beach trip to Mer this weekend? Aren't you going to have to postpone it now?"

Ellen and Stacy exchanged looks of pure mischief, smiled, and answered in unison, "We'll see."

CRABS' ASSURANCE THAT the *Doom Wind* would not hoist anchor until the captain's return proved true, notwithstanding the passenger's insistent demands. Captain Bane came back aboard just before high tide and gave the order to sail. Their destination was to be one of the smaller, yet more inaccessible, of the Keys of Osiris, a tall inhospitable rocky crag whose snow-covered peak was perpetually shrouded in swirling clouds.

Salidar was aloft, helping to reef the mainsail, when the big satyr came on deck and had words with the captain.

Although he could not hear the conversation, Salidar could read body language and gestures easily enough. The passenger wanted the ship to make haste, something the captain would not allow with these tides and such treacherous shoals. The *Doom Wind* would pick her way carefully on her approach to the island, and only then during the high tides. She'd be safely anchored in the deeper water between the shoals before the tide turned, and remain so until the next high tide would allow further progress.

Clearly the captain was not happy about having to rely upon such a tenuous anchorage in storm season; but thus far, the weather had held. Salidar knew that if the satyr could conduct his business on the island swiftly, the *Doom Wind* could soon be back upon the safety of the open sea, and the entire crew would breathe easier. There was something ominous about this lonely string of storm-cursed islands, something that no crewman dared speak of; yet every sailor, including Salidar, sensed it.

Sailors can be a superstitious lot, indeed—and me among them.

The frustrated passenger stormed off, his demands having fallen upon deaf ears. Salidar wondered just how much of this sort of disrespect Captain "Bloody" Bane would tolerate—he was not known for his patience or even disposition.

What is really going on here?

AT THE PEAK OF HIGH tide the following day, the *Doom Wind* arrived at the island and dropped anchor at her chosen spot. A boat was lowered, and the passengers taken ashore.

A second boat was lowered. The bosun sent Crabs, Patch, and Salidar ashore to refill three barrel casks with fresh water. The problem was that none of them knew anything about this strange island, much less where fresh water was to be found.

"Tis usually simple, lads," the bosun had instructed. "Find some fresh water runoff comin' across the beach, or a dry bed to the shoreline. Follow it back to the source, be it spring or rainwater, as long as it be fresh—not salt."

Crabs had his wits about him and suggested they stay in the boat and row parallel to the shore until they found something that looked promising. But all they found was a dry streambed strewn with small rocks and shards of shattered granite.

"Aye, tis better `n naught," Patch groused. "Best we beach `er here, `n' look inland."

They did so, among much grumbling.

Salidar stood among the rocks and coarse black sand, and stretched his back muscles; rowing was not among his favorite activities. He stared ruefully at the three hefty water barrels. "What say ye, me buckos, that we explore for water first?"

"An' heave them casks only after we find fresh water?" Crabs finished, getting the gist immediately.

"Aye, `at's a smart lad!" chimed Patch.

And so they set out, picking their way up the dry rocky streambed, into the dense foliage.

AMIDST THE USUAL DIN of the Fouled Anchor, Daegon did his best to appear inconspicuous. Alone at one end of the bar, he cupped his hands around the mug of spiced rum and kept one eye on the staircase.

An hour ago Vito had opted to take advantage of certain available distractions and engaged the madam, Topsey, in conversation. With a broad smile, she led him upstairs, only to return within moments and resume her post upon the landing.

Daegon didn't care what Vito did, so long as they were considered customers within the Fouled Anchor. As such, they were effectively under the protection of its proprietor, Rumley. Renowned for his propensity for retaliatory violence, it was well known that Rumley would permit no harm to befall any of his patrons on these premises, a rare thing indeed in this raw and raucous town of New Port Royal.

As if summoned by the very thought, Rumley appeared before Daegon and casually gestured to the mug. "Another, good sir?"

"Oh, aye, may as well." Daegon hefted and drained his mug.

"And one for your friend?" Rumley nodded over Daegon's shoulder, toward the staircase.

Daegon twisted to see Vito, smiling, troop down the stairs and pause at the landing to have a congenial word with the madam.

Daegon chuckled and winked at the barkeep. "Aye, and one for my friend as well. I suspect he's worked up a thirst."

Rumley chortled. "Mayhap, my friend, mayhap indeed." He turned to the task with a knowing smile.

Vito nodded to Daegon at the bar and joined him.

Rumley slid two full mugs before them. "Enjoy, gentlemen."

"Aye," Daegon acknowledged and raised his mug in toast. "To your health, good sir."

Vito mimicked the gesture.

"I thankee," murmured Rumley, who turned his attention to other customers and stepped away.

"Have you gotten us a room for the night?" Vito asked.

"I have," Daegon confirmed.

"So, now we wait?" Vito took a long draught, nearly emptying his mug.

"We do." Daegon turned to face the room, his elbows upon the bar. "Let us not get too much into our cups; we will need our wits about us."

"Perhaps, *if* she shows." Vito signaled for another round, earning a nod from the barkeep.

"Trust me, Vito. I know her; she will come."

A LITTLE LATER, RUMLEY retrieved their empty mugs and gestured toward the establishment's front doors. "I see who you asked after has arrived. Be wantin' a booth now, aye? For privacy, like?"

"Aye, we will," Daegon answered as he waved to attract Circe's attention.

Dressed as a simple sailor in men's attire, a faded blue-green bandanna wrapped tightly about her skull, Circe probably could have passed for a slight man with severe features. However, the twisted staff encrusted with dark gems and topped by a small amethyst octopus, and the amphibious lizard leering over her thin shoulder were well known. None within the bar failed to recognize the sea witch.

The din had diminished at her entrance, but resumed once she proceeded to the bar.

"Welcome, Circe," Rumley intoned. "These men have asked after you."

"So I have been told. Now, Daegon, I know." She pointed a bony finger at Vito, "You, I do not. So, I'll not—"

Daegon interrupted. "He is Vito." The alchemist quickly made a small sign with his left hand and whispered, "I vouch for him, by my oath."

Her eyebrows rose but she remained silent.

"I have a booth for you," Rumley announced. "Follow me."

The booth was almost hidden to one side of the staircase and shrouded in thick curtains. Once his guests were seated within, Rumley provided freshly filled mugs and addressed the group. "Once I drop this curtain, you will not be overheard. Do not lift the curtain until you have concluded your business, or care to order another round, aye?"

At their nods, the curtain dropped.

Circe lifted her lizard from her shoulder and put it next to her on the wooden bench. "Stay," she commanded, as one might a trained dog. She grasped her staff with both hands and murmured something unintelligible under her breath. Their ears popped as the air pressure seemed to modestly increase.

Setting the staff aside, she leaned forward. "We can speak plainly. What do you want, Daegon? Have you some new need that I am not aware of? You have not sought my services for some time."

Daegon kept his voice low. "I need to get to the Keys of Osiris."

She pulled her head back in surprise. "Ha! Now? In storm season? You should have booked passage aboard the *Doom Wind;* she is there as we speak. You know there are few who would even attempt such a passage in good weather. So, why there? Why now?"

The alchemist pouted. "I have my reasons. I just need to go. I did not really want to make a sea voyage. So, I would— "

"What?" she blurted. "You would *transit* there? Are you daft? You've never been there, have you?"

"No, but you have." His smile did not allay the hint of accusation in his tone.

"What? Me? Yes, of course I've been there. It's a dangerous gods-forsaken place, storm-cursed, and for the most part barren. Absent good, er, *business* reasons, no one in their right mind—"

Daegon interrupted and pointed at her. "Since you have been there, we could transit there, together."

"No! You do not understand. I have only been there by ship, aboard my own *Xanthippe* or the *Doom Wind.* I have never transited there."

"Why would that matter?" Daegon asked. "You only need to have been to a place to be able to transit there, so—"

"Hold on," interjected Vito, "I think I get it."

Circe and Daegon looked at him in puzzlement.

Vito smiled, obviously pleased with himself. "If I understand this right, Circe can't transit there because it's in the same realm, Mer. You can only transit between realms, right?"

Daegon drew the only logical conclusion. "Of course, she cannot—or rather *will* not—because that means she would have to go to another realm first and then transit to the Keys of Osiris." He leaned forward and locked eyes with her. "And Circe won't leave Mer. Now, why is that?"

Breaking eye contact, she stared at the tabletop and murmured. "I have my reasons."

Daegon stared at her. Now she seemed somehow diminished in his eyes, a fearsome sea witch afraid to even leave the realm? Or was it that some other realm held a genuine threat for her? Or did she merely think so?

"Circe, you know I have the highest regard and respect for you," he soothed, "and I want to understand. So, can you at least tell me if it is a particular realm that, uh, renders you so cautious? A Council realm, for instance?"

Her lips drawn in a grim line, she glared at him. "I will not go to any known realm—for any reason! That is the end of it!"

The alchemist leaned back and grinned. "Fine, we can respect that. However, we can offer you an alternative, outside the scope of known realms—a secret realm, known only to us, a very select few who have a vested interest in keeping it secret."

She locked eyes with him once more, but remained silent.

Daegon spread his open palms. "All but uninhabited, where one can conduct one's studies, or business, undetected, outside of Council reach or influence. Surely such is at least worthy of consideration, is it not?"

A long moment of silence ensued before she responded.

"I admit, I am intrigued. No Council interference or influence?"

Daegon smiled. "None whatsoever, I assure you."

Circe stared at him, a scowl still fixed to her gaunt visage.

"Would you not at least consider it?" The alchemist proposed as reasonably as possible. "It would seem you have nothing to lose, other than your self-imposed exile or imprisonment, or whatever you would care to call this stifling limitation to only one realm. And, it could very well be to our mutual benefit."

"Really? What's in it for me?" she probed cautiously.

"Possibly, many things," Daegon answered affably, and nodded to Vito. "Let us start with a gesture of goodwill."

The big man produced a small folded paper packet and pushed it across the tabletop.

"What's this?" She picked it up and held it between black lacquered nails.

Daegon smiled. "Speed, strength, and endurance—in powdered form."

"Indeed?" She returned his smile, although hers was far more predatory. "Let us talk."

THE DRY STREAMBED NARROWED as the three sailors picked their way uphill through the dense foliage. Patch stumbled over a tree root and floundered face-first into the streambed. As Salidar helped him regain his feet, Crabs broke out in a laugh and pointed to his awkward crewmate's face.

"Ha-har! There's mud in yer eye, f' certain!"

"Huh?" Patch wiped at his face; his hand came away damp and gritty.

"It is mud!" Salidar declared. "If it's wet, we're getting close! Come on!"

Within a few minutes, they clambered over a fallen tree to find a shallow pool fed by a trickle flowing down the old streambed.

Crabs dipped a finger and tasted the water. "Tis fresh, me buckos!"

"Won't be easy to fill the casks from this pool," Salidar observed. "Let's see what's upstream a bit. We might find a place with better flow."

"Aye, tis worth a look," agreed Patch.

Salidar raised his head and tried to peer past the thickening underbrush in the direction of the trickle, but to no avail. They'd have to trudge upward, paralleling the streambed, to see more. If only there was a path or a game trail, he thought, that would make it easier.

"Hold on, mates," Crabs hissed in alarm, "the water, changin' colors it be, reddish like."

The trickle was most definitely growing redder by the moment.

Crabs did a finger test once more; he grimaced and spat.

"Tis blood!"

The three gawked at one another in silence.

Patch broke the spell. "Let's away from here!"

"Aye," agreed Crabs in a breathless voice, "this water be tainted `n' befouled. Whatever this portends, tis not for the likes of us."

Salidar was torn, his curiosity raging; he *had* to know. He pulled his shipmates in close. "Right y' be, but we canna go back to the ship without water, or not tell the cap'n `bout this here, can we now?"

Crabs and Patch looked to each other, swallowed, and with raised eyebrows bobbed their heads.

"So, here's a plan," Salidar whispered and pulled them in closer. "This water be of no use to us. You two go back to the boat, row along the shore like we done before, and look for another water source. There must be more than one on this island. I'll follow this trickle upstream an' see what's what."

"But—" Crabs interrupted.

"No buts! Something be wrong here. The cap'n will want to know, right?" Salidar insisted.

"Aye, there be truth to that," Patch conceded, "but oughtn't we stay together? We be mates, no?"

"Mates, we be, to be sure," Salidar agreed, "but two missions have we now. The water be too important to us all, as y' well know. The fate of the crew lies with the two of you." He pointed to the blood-fouled trickle. "This needs knowin', too, mayhap for the crew's safety as well." He cast his eyes upward but the thick canopy hid the midday sky. "And time may not be with us."

Patch didn't appear convinced, but Crabs saw the logic. "Them be fair points, I reckon. And one can make way through this gods-forsaken brush a mite more quiet than three."

"True dat, an' there be no knowin' what's to find if'n one of us dun' go `n' look," Patch admitted.

"Fine, then," Salidar breathed easier. "On yer way back, look for me near where the boat lies now beached. If'n I've learned what we need, I'll be there; if not, take the casks back to the ship. The water be too important. Come for me with the tide; I'll stay hidden until I see yer ugly mugs, aye?"

Crabs snorted and slapped Salidar on the back. "Aye, that be a plan. We be off! Come on, Patch." He pointed a dirty finger at Salidar. "An' careful be ye."

Salidar nodded, turned, and slipped into the underbrush without a sound.

TWENTY YARDS FURTHER up the incline Salidar found the source of the water contamination. The body of an old man, clothed in coarse homespun, lay sprawled near the stream bank. A runnel of blood slowly drained from a deep slice across his throat and succumbed to gravity, thus tainting the water flow. The wound was recent, the body still warm.

There was not a sound of life in the vicinity, no birdsong, no insects scurrying, nothing.

Looking around carefully, Salidar spied a faint path that wound upward through the foliage. Making his way up the brush-encroached mountainside trail as quietly as possible, he soon came upon a rustic village perched precariously upon a wide ledge. Stacked stone walls and thatched roofs marked half a dozen dwellings, whose rear walls appeared hewn from the very mountainside.

He saw no one, but could hear voices coming from the largest of the stone-walled buildings. Stealing from shadow to shadow he crept closer. Finding a narrow defile between a stacked stone wall and the coarse rock of the mountainside, he clambered up to a smoke hole and wedged himself at its edge. There was no fire within the dwelling, so no smoke obscured his view as he peered stealthily down into the interior.

He'd found the voices. The satyr and his fauns were roughly questioning someone, a woman in homespun, on her knees, her hands tied behind her back. She was moaning and shaking her head. Salidar could not tell if she was trying to speak for her sobbing.

The satyr shook his head in disgust. "So, you do not know, or you refuse to tell me. Very well, it will not matter. I have no further need of you, or anyone else on this island—as you are now." He flipped a hand in dismissal.

One of the fauns grabbed her hair, pulling her head back. The other faun whipped his arm forward; a crimson arc of arterial spray followed. The woman's eyes widened in shock; her mouth gaped in a silent scream as her throat splayed open and her life's blood spurted forth in diminishing pulses. The faun holding her hair released her. She slumped forward in a growing puddle of her own blood.

The satyr glanced at the open doorway. "Is that all of them?"

"Yes, Master," a faun answered, wiping a viciously curved obsidian blade on the coarse clothing of the dead woman.

"He is not among them—gods be damned!" The satyr slammed a fist into his open palm. "We have much of what we came for, but we have not met her stipulation. We are running out of time! Did you plant the cursed scrolls where I told you?"

"Yes, Master, at each of the island's cardinal compass points, as you instructed."

"Master!" hissed the other faun from the doorway. "Someone comes! Ah, tis the merman; he is alone."

"Ah, about time. Bring him to me."

Salidar was growing stiff in his cramped hiding place. He suspected he now knew who was responsible for the body by the streambed. The poor man was most likely another villager who had tried to flee.

Daring to stretch his luck he squirmed forward a bit and tried to see more of the room.

He blanched. There were more bodies, at least five more that he could now see. *What the—?*

"You are late," the satyr declared. "Do you have it?"

The lanky merman stared at the satyr for a long moment. "I do." He produced a good-sized pouch of woven seaweed from beneath a worn robe of blue and green patches, a garment that had clearly seen better days.

The satyr reached for the pouch; but to his surprise, the merman pulled it back.

"Not so fast! First, the gold you promised. Twas not easy—there were, uh, complications."

The satyr's eyes narrowed. "You assured me you could do this." A money pouch appeared in his hand. "This is the agreed-upon fee. Why would you balk now? Are you overly superstitious about some ancient tribal taboo? Tis a bit late for that, is it not?"

"Taboo? Bah!" The merman scoffed. "I pay no heed; tis only the gold that interests me. This task was dangerous—life-threatening, savvy? Forbidden waters and lurking predators concerned me more than any superstition. Aye, twas a near thing."

"Then let us conclude our business; or, have you lost interest in the fee?"

The merman scoffed once more, and handed the seaweed pouch over. "I accept the fee, although methinks a bonus I deserve. Keep that in mind the next time business we do, aye?"

The gold changed hands.

The merman hefted the money pouch, and then seemed to notice the bodies in the dim room. "What happened here?"

The satyr tore his gaze from the contents of the seaweed pouch and glanced around. "I am searching for someone; I needed information. These were not cooperative."

The merman nodded. "Hmmph, this looks like the whole village. Too bad."

The satyr paused and considered the merman. "Oh, you knew these people? Of course, I should have realized that. So, perhaps you can help me. Do you know how to find a man called Barnabas? I know he lives on this island."

The merman's expression betrayed nothing. "I cannot help you."

The satyr's voice grew cold. "Cannot? Or will not?"

The stoic merman shrugged. "Does it matter?"

"No, in the end, it does not." The satyr flipped his hand in a gesture of dismissal.

The two fauns leapt at the merman.

In an instant it was over, his throat cut so deeply that he was nearly decapitated.

"Enough! Leave him his head—he'll need it." The satyr pointed to the money pouch. "I'll have the gold back."

The fauns backed off. One retrieved the money pouch. "Is our business complete, Master?"

The satyr sighed. "With him it is. Sadly, we did not find and slay this Barnabas as she demanded. But we are out of time and must return. However, we shall see to it that nothing on this island survives. If Barnabas is here, he shall be prey. Tis time to cast the spell and depart."

Salidar gaped as he witnessed, for the second time in his life, someone cast a spell of necromancy.

His shock passed; he realized he had to flee—before the corpses stirred.

He shimmied down from his cramped perch and stole away from the village. He found the path with no difficulty. A quick glance behind him showed no pursuit. He wasted no time and hastened down the faint track.

Soon he was running pell-mell down the mountainside, his imagination at full tilt. Surely he'd be chased—he'd seen too much. As he came past the body he'd found earlier, he couldn't help but stare.

He promptly missed his footing and sprawled on his face.

Before he could rise, something thumped him on the back of his head—everything dwindled into darkness.

CH 18

TEDDY POTS LOOKED UP from his beakers when he heard the goblins on the far side of the chamber suddenly scramble about and disappear into several tunnel openings. He then heard voices, growing louder. In the next moment, he knew why the goblins had fled; Vito entered the chamber, followed by Papa George, Daegon, and a gaunt woman in strange clothing, a blue bandanna tight around her head.

Teddy saw that she used a staff as she walked, but didn't lean on it. Something on her shoulder moved, flicking its tongue. *What the—a lizard?*

"This is our lab." George swept his hand in an arc, stopping to point at Teddy. "And this is our cook, Teddy."

"An accomplished alchemist of sorts, in his own right," Daegon explained.

Teddy wasn't sure quite what to do. He didn't know who this woman was, but if Papa George was showing her around, he'd better be careful. Keeping silent he bobbed his head, executing a brief bow.

Papa George smiled. "Teddy, this is Circe, our new associate. She will be representing our interests in the realm of Mer. She already has a considerable, uh, distribution network in place that I know will be mutually beneficial to us all."

Circe tore her eyes from Teddy's convoluted arrangement of beakers, tubing, and stainless-steel pots, and stroked her sharp chin with a bony hand. "I admit, I am even more impressed. This *association* may work out well indeed. I can come and go here—this realm—as I please?"

"Absolutely," George confirmed. "As I understand it, this will solve your transit problem, since this realm is, uh, for the most part, a secret. And we can warehouse and facilitate the transfer of certain goods that you've explained would otherwise be subject to import/export taxes—"

"Hah!" she interrupted. "No need to avoid the term—I am a smuggler, and a good one! This will mean I do not have to rely upon my vessel, the *Xanthippe* as my only method; I can transit goods as I see fit. Now, what of this new product, this *meth?* How will that work?"

"It's already begun," George said. "We've laid the groundwork, to create the demand. You monitor that demand and we supply you with the drug. Distribute it where you will. In time, we will mutually decide upon price increases. Trust me; the market will grow, as will profits. It's only a matter of time."

"And best of all," added Daegon smoothly, "it violates no laws on Mer. You would simply be seen as the proprietor of just another legitimate business. As for your other activities—"

"Ah, what is done in the shadows," Circe quipped with an evil smile, "stays in the shadows."

"So, do we have an agreement, an accord?" George thrust out his hand.

She returned a firm handshake. "We do."

"Then there is only one other matter," Daegon reminded her.

"Of course, the Keys of Osiris," she answered. "Let us go now, for I am soon expected in New Port Royal."

"Vito," George insisted, "go with."

"BOAT TO STARBOARD, at amidships!" cried the *Doom Wind's* lookout, pointing from the crow's nest high aloft on the mainmast.

The bosun glanced up, crossed the poop deck, and peered over the rail. "Aye! Tis our lads with fresh water! Lower a cargo net starboard! Get `em aboard. Right smart now!"

In no time the casks of fresh water were safely stowed in the hold.

Crabs and Patch stood before the scowling bosun.

"So where be yer crewmate? Did I not set the three of ye t' task? Where be Salidar?"

"Still on the island," Crabs explained. "Y' see, the first water found, tainted foul, it was—"

"Aye," Patch interjected, "a bloody taint at that! Another source we had to find. Took time, it did."

"True enough!" bellowed the bosun. "Ye've been gone most the day—even the passengers have been back aboard for hours. Why tis it Salidar not be with ye?"

"He went to find the source of the blood, y' see?" Crabs opened his palms. "Thinkin' the cap'n would be needin' to know an' all. Me `n' Patch searched for better water. But Salidar twern't at the meetin' place when we come back w' water. He `spected that might happen, y' see? So, the plan was to bring the casks aboard the *Doom Wind*, an' go back w' the tide to pick `im up."

"There will be no returning to that island," declared a new voice. Captain "Bloody" Bane strode forth and stood with hands on hips. "We sail with the tide, bosun. Set course for New Port Royal."

"Aye, aye, Cap'n, but a crewman still be on the island. Should we not—"

"Then he is lost! That island is cursed!" The vehemence in the captain's voice was startling. He seemed to catch himself; a haunted look stole across his countenance. He turned away, gripped the rail, and took a moment to regain his composure. "That'll be all. See to m' orders, bosun."

The three sailors were stunned; they'd never seen the captain like this.

"Aye, aye, Cap'n. We set sail with the tide for New Port Royal," the bosun confirmed, and avoided looking at the other crewmen.

Crabs and Patch could only gawk at each other in silence. To maroon a crewmate without just cause was unthinkable. This did not bode well—not at all.

SHROUDED IN DARKNESS Salidar felt he was in a numbing fog. Sight denied him and sounds muffled, he could not move.

Am I restrained? I cannot tell for certain, but . . . no, try as I might, I cannot move. My head hurts—a blow? Yes, I think so. My left eye, I feel something crusted across the lids—blood? Perhaps tis best to appear unconscious still, that I might learn something of this predicament. I can hear something—voices? I must concentrate . . .

". . . DO NOT UNDERSTAND, Yoshi. This is certainly a surprise. Why bring him to me?"

"In the hope you can make sense of this, *Barnabas-san.* As I said, I came to tell you of Brona, that she has not been seen and we fear she is missing. I know not if this one is involved. However, as to the slaying of your fellow islanders, he was there when the curse was cast, although in hiding."

"Why is his face so bloody?"

"Only a scalp wound; it no longer bleeds. Some members of the local *Yokai* clan saw him, and took him when he fled."

"Ah, the *Yokai* miss nothing, and yet are rarely seen—unless they choose to be. Tell me, Yoshi, did *he* see?"

"No, I was assured he did not. I trust you will make certain that our secret is safe, *Barnabas-san?*"

"Of course, please reassure *Daitengu-sama* that I will see to it, and take every precaution."

"Domo arigato, Barnabas-san. Shall I remove the stasis spell that you may question this one?"

"Not yet. First, please tell me of Brona. How long has she been missing?"

"Three, maybe four days, we are uncertain; the *nukekubi* tends to be solitary, as you know. There was some sort of sorcerous disturbance on her island a few days ago. When *oni* from that clan went to investigate, they found her abode in disarray, but no trace of her. She does not leave without telling the *Yokai.* We fear something is wrong; we knew you would want to know."

"Yes, thank you. None of the other clans on the other islands know anything more?"

"No, only that the ship, the *Doom Wind,* has returned and has been here for the same four days. We know this one came from that vessel. Do you think this is all coincidence, *Barnabas-san?"*

"A sorcerous event on her island, and my, uh, friend, the Dullahan, goes missing? And now human residents on this island are slain, and a death curse cast—coincidence? Not bloody likely, Yoshi, not at all. If this one has any answers, I will have them—of that you can be sure."

"I doubt it not, *Barnabas-san.* Can we be of further service?"

"Yes, We will need to clean him up before I question him. Take him to the cave behind the waterfall and wait for me there."

"Soka."

Salidar felt at least three sets of strong hands grip, lift, and carry him with ease. In a matter of moments, he was put down on a smooth shelf of rock. He could hear the churning roar of falling water nearby; a cold mist chilled his face. There were subdued voices, but he could not understand the language he heard—it was certainly nothing with which he was familiar.

A damp cloth was repeatedly wiped across his face. He still could not open his eyes, or move at all.

"Barnabas-san, now shall I lift the stasis spell? I can allow its grip to ease slowly, so that we might depart and not be seen, as is our preference."

"Yes, that would work. Leave the transit binding intact, since I have no way of knowing this one's transit skill level. I would not have him going anywhere until I am satisfied with his answers."

"If he is not to depart at all, we *Yokai* are at your service."

"We will see, Yoshi, we will see."

A LARGE TRANSIT GLOBE appeared on the rocky black-sand beach of one of the largest of the Keys of Osiris. Circe, Daegon, and Vito stepped forth. The globe shrank and winked out of existence with a soft *pop.*

"This is unusual," Circe commented, looking around. Perched upon her shoulder, her lizard turned its head to and fro flicking its forked tongue in the offshore breeze.

"What is?" Vito asked, scanning the area as well.

"I do not see or hear anyone. At this time of day, that is unusual." She pointed to a handful of fishing boats beached nearby. "Those boats should not be here. Fishermen would normally now be in the lagoon or out to sea."

Vito pointed up the rocky hill. "Is that the town?"

"Yes, but smaller, more like a village," she explained. "Something is off; it is too quiet."

"Yeah? Maybe." Vito grunted. "I don't hear anything, either. So, we check out the village?"

Her brow furrowed, the sea witch agreed. "Yes, I have dealt with the headman here; let us find him."

Their search was futile, the village empty, not a soul to be seen. An ominous tension seemed to permeate the very air; all three sensed it. It was too quiet, too still.

At the edge of an open market area in the heart of the village, Circe frowned and swept a hand at the deserted stalls. "This isn't right—not at all. Stay here, by this building, and give me a minute."

She strode a few paces to the middle of the central square, stroked her lizard to calm it, and closed her eyes. She began to murmur a breathless chant, her voice too faint to be distinctly heard.

His curiosity getting the better of him, Vito started to call out and ask her something, but Daegon placed a hand upon his arm and shook his head.

"Say nothing; do not move," warned the alchemist. "She is conducting a summoning."

"Summoning *what*, exactly?" Vito whispered, his apprehension apparent.

"That." Daegon pointed to an unwholesome mist that grew more dense and began to swirl in an unruly knot before the sea witch. An amorphous shape, too vague to identify, formed within the mist and hovered at chest height.

Circe spoke to the shape, then seemed to listen to something no one else could hear. Finally she nodded and snapped her fingers. The shape lost cohesion; the mist dissipated and was gone.

Her lizard flicked its tongue in nervous agitation.

She returned to Daegon and Vito.

"We were right; something is wrong—very wrong. Now, we must wait a few minutes. The headman will be here shortly. Say nothing, unless I ask you to do so. Do you understand?"

Both men nodded affirmatively.

Within minutes, a short broad-shouldered man in rough homespun appeared between two buildings at the opposite end of the market square. He clearly saw them, but went instead to the door of the larger dwelling and quickly went inside. After a moment, he reappeared in the doorway, hastily scanned to the right and left of the square, and beckoned Circe and her companions to come inside.

He wasted no time in securing the door after them and confronting the visitors.

"Circe, this is not a good time. Who be they?" His manner was brusque—yet, to her, deferential.

"All you need know, Elias, is that they are with me. This is Daegon, uh, a scholar of sorts, and Vito, an associate. Now, tell me, where is everyone? What is afoot?"

"Dark doings, Circe, dark doings, indeed—people missing, others slain, and some resurrected."

"What?" She blanched. *"Necromancy?"*

Vito and Daegon exchanged looks of shocked surprise, but kept silent.

"Aye," Elias confirmed. "There can be little doubt. An entire clan on one of the smallest islands was so cursed; their corpses now roam the island freely. Anyone left alive there is doomed. My people have taken to the caves and will remain in hiding."

Her thin lips drawn into a grim line, Circe leaned into his face. "Elias, who is responsible?"

He shrugged. "We cannot know for certain, but we have our suspicions. Come, I would be a poor host were I not to lay a fire in this cold hearth. Let us be seated and have some wine. I know not why you have come now, in this dark time, but believe me that no one is safe here—not even you."

"I shall be the judge of that," Circe declared. "Will you confide in me, or no?"

Elias nodded in resignation. "I will share with you what I know."

THE SMALL FIRE WARMED the room; however, the tale told by the headman held a chill of its own.

When he had finished speaking, Circe asked few questions, but kept most of her thoughts to herself.

After a prolonged silence, Vito pushed his empty cup aside, and glanced at Daegon. The alchemist returned the glance, but remained mum, his brow deeply furrowed. In unspoken agreement, they knew they would need to talk. But first, they would need more information, a lot more.

Vito looked to the sea witch, and asked, "May I?"

She spared him a nod; he nodded in return.

"Elias, let me see if I understand," the big man began, "and please feel free to correct me if I get something wrong, okay? Good. So, this ship, the *Doom Wind,* that comes here occasionally, came and brought this so-called *diplomat,* a satyr and two fauns. They came ashore here, said they were looking for some people, and then went off into the mountains, right? Who were they looking for, exactly?"

Elias looked to Circe, who nodded that he should answer.

"A woman called Brona, a recluse who lives in the mountains. We see her in the village on occasion, a pleasant and harmless woman who keeps to herself."

"And who else?" Vito asked.

"One other, a hermit, a man called Barnabas, who lives on another island, the same island that is now cursed."

"I see. And you don't know if this satyr and fauns found either one of these people, right?"

Elias shook his head. "I do not."

"I understand. Can you tell us more about this unusual storm in the mountains that you mentioned?"

Elias was at a momentary loss for words.

"Storm? It was . . . *like* a storm, but *not* a storm. Twas deep in the night, no rain, but much thunder and lightning. Everyone in the village could hear the rumbling and see flashes of light. It did not have a natural feel to it; no one dared venture forth. We stayed in our homes, behind closed doors, until the following day. We did not see the satyr or fauns again."

Vito probed further. "And the woman, Brona?"

Elias sighed. "We only know that she has not been seen since."

"Hmmph," Vito scoffed. "Did you even go looking?"

"No, where she abides is not known to us in the village; she is a very private person. We would not know where to look, you see?" Elias held his open palms up in supplication.

Daegon glanced to Circe; she nodded once more.

"Elias," Daegon broke his silence. "All of this was four days ago?"

"Aye."

"The *Doom Wind* set sail the morning after that mysterious storm?"

"Aye, she did. We know not where she was bound."

"But you suspect," Daegon interjected, "another island—Barnabas' island, do you not?"

"Aye, we do." Elias stared at his folded hands.

"Elias," Daegon asked softly, "did you ever learn the name of this *diplomat*, this satyr?"

"No, there was no introduction. He just acted all *haughty and entitled,* like some sort of nobility. I admit we were leery of him. The crewmen from the *Doom Wind,* who rowed them ashore, warned us not to ask questions. I think they, too, were intimidated. We never heard the fauns address the satyr by anything other than '*master*'. We know not what he may be called, much less his *true name.*"

Circe caught Daegon's eye and slightly shook her head, forestalling any further questions.

"Elias, thank you for this information; I think it may prove helpful," she assured him, as she pushed her mug aside, and stood. "We must go. You should return to your people; do your best to keep them safe. We will look into these matters."

Elias banked the small fire. He unlocked the door, checked that the square was still empty, and stepped aside.

"Tis safe . . . Be careful, Circe."

Circe paused at the threshold. "Trust that I will, Elias . . . Oh, by the way, it may be that our scholar, Daegon, will return to further his studies in quiet contemplation and solitude such that the Keys of Osiris may offer. I trust you will make him welcome."

"As you wish, Circe. I can only hope these terrible circumstances pass quickly." He bowed briefly. "Safe journey."

As they crossed the square, Vito started to ask a question, but Circe stopped him.

"Not here—wait until we are on the beach."

THE THREE STOOD IN silence among the rocks on the black sand. The shifting onshore breeze grew cool, carrying a hint of salt spray and the lonely cries of gulls wheeling in lazy arcs over the lagoon.

Vito scanned the empty beach once more. "All right, we're alone. You both know something—something about this satyr. We are partners now, so give."

Daegon sighed. "I may know his name, and something of his skills."

Circe looked to both of them. "I have met him. He is called Silenos."

"Aye," Daegon confirmed, "a dangerous, highly skilled mage, a *necromancer* of the darkest order."

"So, do we have a problem?" Vito asked. "Does the boss need to know about this?"

Daegon and Circe exchanged haunted looks.

"Oh, yes," they answered in unison.

CH 19

TREY DID NOT LIKE WHAT he was hearing; yet, it couldn't be ignored.

"Now hold on, Mark. Is this intel corroborated? Are we sure about this?"

Mark glanced around the comfortable Delafaire Farm kitchen, leaned back in his chair, and sighed.

"I'm telling you, Trey, it's as solid as it gets. Papa George was seen and positively identified in Derinseum; and, he wasn't alone."

"Source?" Trey pressed.

"Selene is our source; she was there and made the ID."

Mark pushed a folded paper packet across the table. "She secured this from another asset. Whoever was with Papa George was passing these packets out all over Derinseum. She thought you would want to have it analyzed."

Trey unfolded the packet and peered inside. "Crystalline powder, kinda off-white, looks like meth to me—we'll have to have it analyzed.

"Okay, I'm sure Selene is solid on the ID, and a good source for intel; but, it'd help if we could further corroborate the ID. Did anybody else see Papa George?"

"Yeah, a number of people saw him. He was there for almost a full day. The Guildmaster has further corroboration from other sources; so, it's *golden.* Of course, we don't know if he's still there."

Hawk pushed back from the kitchen table. "And he was with someone? No ID?"

Mark shook his head. "No ID. Selene didn't recognize him; a 'big man' was all she could report. There was no chance for her to gather more intel; she couldn't follow them. The Watch is already on high alert with this *necromancy* situation."

"What's the status of that situation, Mark?" Ellen asked, taking a plate of warm oatmeal-raisin cookies from her mother and placing it on the table.

"As of yesterday, two of the four known corpses have been captured; they were in pretty bad shape, I understand." Mark couldn't quite suppress an involuntary shudder. "The Mer Administration has the Watch hunting for the last two. But, based on the state of deterioration of the others, the mages in charge think the final two may not even be mobile any longer. So, they're pretty confident they'll be found soon."

"These guys—the *zombies*—were all watchmen?" Hawk asked, reaching for a cookie.

"Yeah," Mark answered, "although, I've never heard anyone from the other realms use *that* word."

"Zombies?" Stacy asked, putting a fresh carafe of coffee on the table. "So, we're the only ones who use that term, you know, for *reanimated corpses?"*

"Yeah, come to think of it," Mark admitted, "most likely thanks to our own folklore, and Hollywood, of course."

"Well, the term certainly fits the circumstances," Ellen submitted with a lone elevated eyebrow, as she sat down at the table and sampled a cookie.

"Wait a sec." Hawk reached for the carafe. "Wasn't there some speculation after the *zombie* incident at the Council meeting—y'all remember the one I mean—about some alchemist?" He poured himself another cup of coffee.

"Good memory, Hawk," Mark responded. "That was from Elsbeth, the Council Archivist. His name was Daegon, an alchemist in service to the *former* Queen Mab LIV, who was assassinated. Originally thought by most to have perished with the late queen, this Daegon clearly survived. Some of our *well-informed friends* suspected him in the necromancy—excuse me, *zombie* incident, but there was never any proof. There was no solid evidence that he was there; no one actually saw him. No one had a line on him or even knew where he was.

"Now, as it happens, the Guildmaster advised that it's been confirmed this same Daegon was in Derinseum during this latest incident. This alchemist is no friend to the current Queen Mab LV. In fact, it's been reported that he admitted to being there to assassinate her. But he was too late; she had already left Mer. He was taken into custody, of course, but he escaped. The four watchmen who became zombies were his prisoner transport detail."

"What? Are you kidding?" Trey blurted. "That's pretty strong circumstantial evidence right there!"

"Maybe, but there's a twist," Mark cautioned, raising a finger.

"Okay, what? Tell us already!" Stacy insisted, taking a seat next to Ellen.

Mark dropped his elbows to the tabletop and leaned forward. "Okay, this goes no further. The Mer Administration isn't releasing details, so it's not public information."

"You got this from the Guildmaster, right?" surmised Trey.

"Right. Here's the thing; the recovered corpses have various wounds, as would be expected. However, each one has a very similar head wound, a penetrating hole that I suspect might look a lot like a bullet wound. I admit this is speculation on my part—but it makes sense, because the mages on Mer wouldn't likely recognize a bullet wound. There are no guns on Mer."

"Oh, really? None?" Trey asked.

"Yeah, let me explain," Mark offered. "There's an old Council rule that one realm cannot interfere with another's pace of technological development. From what I understand, it's based on a belief that the more advances technology or science make, the more diminished it leaves that realm's well of magic. Whereas others simply fear it would forever upset the balance of power among the realms."

"I get it—kinda like a *prime directive,* right?" Hawk proffered with a knowing smile.

"Yes, that's a pretty good analogy," agreed Mark. "If a realm develops a major technology on its own, in its own time, that's fine; but another realm can't influence or gift the tech—"

"Or arm one faction against another," Trey deduced. "Okay, I understand; and I get that it doesn't have to be only about weapons. For example, any sudden technological advance could trigger an economic paradigm shift that could drastically upset several realms, right?"

"Yes, that too. That's why none of the significant technological advances from our home realm are typically seen in any of the other Council realms. Well, there is the exception of Storm Haven, but that's not a Council realm. Anyway, that's why there are no guns in Mer."

"You mean there aren't supposed to be," Hawk countered. "However, there may be evidence to the contrary. And now we have confirmation that Papa George is, or has been there; and, he wasn't alone."

"This is all within the same time frame, right?" Trey asked, with a smiling nod to Millie as she poured fresh coffee into his cup.

Mark shrugged. "Yeah, close enough, or so it appears—some coincidence, huh?"

Trey spent a moment in quiet reflection, slouched in his chair, sipping slowly from his cup.

His eyes fell on his partner. "Hawk, what was the status with Papa George's driver, Vitorrio Smith?Isn't he out on bond?"

Hawk bobbed his head. "Yeah, pending a court appearance sometime in the next coupla weeks; but, I'm pretty sure that's been bumped. He's got some new lawyer, not a public defender, so the court granted a continuance. I don't know the exact date, but we can find out."

"Let's do that." Trey sat up straight. "Let's get some photos and get them in front of Selene. In fact, let's do a regulation photo spread, and see if we can ID this 'big man' who was with Papa George."

"The driver, eh? Yeah, that could be," Hawk speculated. "Hmm, I guess photos wouldn't be the kind of tech that would draw undue attention—oh, never mind, Selene is connected to Storm Haven."

"Selene's whereabouts might be the question," Trey mused aloud. "Is she still in Derinseum, Mark?"

"I don't know—"

"We can take care of that for you," Ellen interrupted, "since Stacy and I will be in Derinseum this weekend."

"Oh yeah!" Stacy exclaimed. "We're going to the beach!"

"Oh man!" Hawk winced. "I forgot. That's *this* weekend?"

Mark shook his head in sympathy. "I guess I forgot, too."

Trey opened his palms. "What are y'all talking about?"

"A beach trip we've had planned for some time, that's all," Ellen explained. "Mer has some great beaches, and Derinseum has one of the best. It'd be no trouble for us to get with Selene and have her look at some pictures."

Trey could only chuckle. "Thanks, Ellen, but it's not that simple. There's a specific procedure we have to follow to corroborate confirmation of a witness identification using a photo array—"

"Hold on, Trey," Hawk cautioned. "Think about it; do you really see this going to court?"

"Oh yeah, right . . . Well, there's still the bodies with possible bullet holes; we have to see that for ourselves to be sure. *We*—you and I—are gonna have to do that."

Ellen nudged Stacy and said, "It's okay, Trey, we were gonna invite you to go with us anyway. You like the beach, don't you?"

Trey shrugged and grinned. "Huh? The beach, is it? Why do I feel like I've been manipulated?"

"Why, perish the very thought, suh," Stacy slurred like an innocent débutante from the Deep South. "We'd mos' certainly be `onored to be accompanied by y'all, such stalwart southern gentlemen."

"So, we'd all go?" Trey asked.

"Oh, not me," said Millie. "I'm not one for the beach. Besides, somebody needs to be here to log in our online and telephone orders. Don't worry, Miska will keep me company."

"He's at the cabin?" Hawk asked.

"Yeah," Ellen confirmed. "He and I already discussed this. He'll stay and help my mom out."

Trey and Hawk exchanged a knowing look.

"Well then, we have a plan. Hawk and I will have to go and make some preparations. When do y'all plan on leaving?"

"How about after breakfast on Saturday morning?" Millie suggested. "I'll be serving at eight o'clock."

With smiles all around, everyone agreed.

AS HAWK DROVE THE CRUISER down the long Delafaire Farm driveway, Trey remarked, "You know, it's probably a pretty good idea for Miska to be around while we're gone, since we haven't resolved the *cat* issue yet."

Hawk blew a thin stream of air between his lips. "Yeah, that occurred to me as well. Let's hope nothing happens while we're gone."

"True dat! We don't need any more incidents on the home front."

"So, Trey, do you think we can get all this stuff we're planning in Mer done in one weekend?"

Trey shrugged and adjusted his seat belt. "We should, but the truth is we don't have a lot of choice. We've both got court on Monday."

"Oh yeah, right. By the way, did you hear anything back from the lab?"

"No, I called but they couldn't give me any real answers. They're backed up, so there's no telling how long the lab's gonna take with that skull. I put the request in for old man Johansen's dental records, just in case."

Hawk looked at his partner. "Do you think that skull—"

"Doesn't matter what I think. What matters is what we can prove. Without dental records or DNA for an ID comparison, all we've got is a John Doe."

"Yeah, I know." His eyes back on the road, Hawk asked, "So, the cats—what about the drone?"

"The captain said the surveillance drone we need won't be available for another week at least, so our aerial surveillance and any cave exploring are gonna have to wait—unless, Hawk, you want to go spelunking on your own?"

"Uh, no thanks, I'll pass." He eased the car to a stop at the parish road, empty of any traffic.

"Smart man," Trey acknowledged and scratched his chin.

"Changing the subject—Mer—there's something bugging me about these watchmen, the zombies."

"Yeah? What?" Hawk didn't take his eyes from the road as he drove south on the two-lane blacktop.

"Mark described what he thinks might be gunshot wounds, head shots, right?"

Hawk glanced at his partner, "He did. So?"

Trey winced and shrugged. "Well, maybe I'm not up on my *zombie lore—*"

Hawk snorted in laughter. "Huh?"

"Seriously," Trey insisted, "I thought head shots, you know, to the brain, were supposed to neutralize zombies. Or is that just Hollywood?"

"Oh yeah, I think you're right; that is the common folklore," Hawk agreed. "But now that I think about it, we don't know when they got shot, or even if those actually are gunshot wounds. I mean, assuming we are dealing with gunshots, what if the head shots are what killed them, and then afterward they were resurrected?"

Trey shrugged again. "I dunno; wouldn't logic dictate that damaged brain tissue would somehow compromise a zombie's overall ability to function? Doesn't that follow the folklore premise that damaging the brain stops the zombie?"

"Maybe in our reality," Hawk conceded, "but we don't really know what the rules are in another. There may be different laws of physics, like Zack suggested. You've gotta admit, we've seen some strange things lately."

Trey folded his arms. "Hmmph, no argument there. I'm still more comfortable dealing with hard evidence in any reality."

"Me, too, for the most part." Hawk chuckled. "All we can really do is keep open minds, right?"

"Yeah, I guess so." Trey mumbled, "Damn it."

IN OLMUS, PAPA GEORGE looked up from the scrying orb and made no effort to hide his surprise at the return of Vito, Daegon, and Circe.

"What are y'all doing back here so soon? Daegon, I thought you wanted to spend a few days at the Keys of Osiris. What's up?"

"I did," the alchemist responded, "but something came up—"

"He can now transit there as he pleases," Circe interrupted, "since I have taken him there and returned him here. Now I have to go; I have an obligation and am soon expected—"

"Not so fast!" Vito interjected. "You've got some explaining to do before you leave, Circe—you, too, Daegon."

George's eyebrows shot up. He knew Vito didn't interrupt or take charge unless it was important.

The alchemist and sea witch exchanged glances.

"Very well," conceded Circe, "but time truly is short. I—"

George stopped her with a raised hand. "Hold on. Let's go to another chamber." He tilted his head in the direction of a pair of goblin servants lingering in a nearby passage. "I think this might call for a bit more privacy. Shall we?"

The other chamber was considerably larger, but had only one entrance. Vito made sure no servants were anywhere near its entrance or in the sole passageway.

"All right, this is much better," George declared and pointed to both Circe and Daegon. "So explain—leave nothing out."

And so, they did.

MINUTES LATER, SILENCE hung heavily in the chamber.

George cupped his chin in his hand, tilted his head at Daegon, and asked, "So this Silenos is a necromancer? How powerful?"

Daegon's eyebrows rose. "He is not to be underestimated. He made his reputation in the *wild.* What he is doing in the Keys of Osiris is anyone's guess. We were told he was searching for two people; we do not know if he found them."

"Well, Circe, what more can you add?" George pressed.

Her lizard flicked its tongue in nervous agitation. She stroked its back, a calming gesture that had little effect. She sighed, her own anxiety obvious.

"I really have to go. Time is a problem; so, I'll be brief. As I said, he is supposedly some sort of *diplomat.* He and his aides, a pair of fauns, were briefly passengers aboard my vessel, the *Xanthippe,* and later transferred at sea to the *Doom Wind.* I surmised his destination was the Keys of Osiris, even though Captain 'Bloody' Bane refused to confirm it. I am to meet the *Doom Wind* off New Port Royal, take Silenos and his fauns back aboard the *Xanthippe,* and return them to Derinseum. That is why I must go. The rendezvous is soon; my ship awaits me at New Port Royal."

"A diplomat? For whom?" George opened his palms.

Circe shrugged. "I do not know; I was never told."

"You didn't ask?" George scoffed. "Well, who approached you to arrange his passage in the first place?"

"That was a bit strange," she admitted. "In Derinseum I was called to a meeting in a tavern, a prospective client, I presumed, for some of my other, more lucrative pursuits. There was an elf—"

"What—an *elf?"* George blurted, a flash of panic in his face. "Who? Was it a Dark Elf? Lady Diere? Uh, Mab? Answer me!"

Taken aback at his outburst, she balked. "What? Calm yourself! It was a male elf, a Light Elf."

"Are you sure?" The tension had not left his voice.

"Of course, I am certain! I was there! He was a Light Elf; there is no doubt. He gave me a false name, of course, but I had him followed when he left. I learned that he is a servant in the House of Briar. He arranged for the passage of this *diplomat* and his aides. He paid in gold, half up front, and half upon return delivery. Now you see why I must complete this task—there is gold at stake."

"I get it—trust me," George assured her. "Something is up with this Silenos. We gotta watch him. It'd be good for you to be the one keeping an eye on him while he's in Mer. He knows you—in fact he's expecting you to get him back to Derinseum. Is he also supposed to meet with this Light Elf?"

Circe shrugged once more. "I know not. However, I will certainly meet with this elf to get paid!"

"All right, you can go. Just keep an eye on this Silenos."

The sea witch bristled at the implied order; her lizard suddenly hissed at George.

Taken aback, George hastily added, "Uh—if you don't mind, of course?"

"Very well, but before I go," Circe pointed a finger at George, "tell me of this Lady Diere. You reacted quite strongly; and now that we are *business partners*, I would know more. After all, I once had to deal with her, albeit through intermediaries. We could not come to any agreement; I found her rather curt and unpleasant. I also know she took the throne of the Dark Elves; rumors of treachery abound. So, what is she to *you?* Or more pertinently, what is she now *to us?*"

"She is no friend," Daegon answered frostily, "and is not to be trusted. She betrays and manipulates without conscience."

"*That* is an understatement," George confirmed. "Think of her as an enemy—to all of us. She has her own agenda, and she's dangerous to anyone in her way. She *did* take the throne through treachery—that's a fact!"

Daegon's voice grew colder still. "There shall yet be a reckoning—I swear it."

Circe paused and slowly nodded. "I see; and I understand there is more to this. But, now I must go."

George nodded and watched her call forth a transit globe. In the next instant, she was gone. The globe shrank and winked out of existence with a soft *pop.*

George let a moment of silence pass before he spoke.

"I have other news," he announced, "that I thought might best be shared with us alone; so, I waited until our newest *associate* departed."

Daegon and Vito looked up expectantly, but remained silent.

"Our *Gaspar-cam* is working! He put the stud back in his earlobe—just like you said he would, Vito!"

"And Diere, the usurper?" Daegon spat, as if her very name tasted foul upon his tongue. "Has he returned to her? Has she taken him in?"

George smiled broadly. "He did; and she has! I saw and heard everything. It worked!"

Daegon smiled smugly and rubbed his palms together. "So, it begins."

"Let's not share this with Circe just yet," George cautioned. "Let's see how she deals with distribution and sales of our product. And then there's this Silenos matter. Hmm, I wonder . . ."

"What are you thinking, Boss?" Vito asked.

"I think we need to know a lot more about Silenos. Can we use him in any way?"

"That might not be wise," Daegon warned.

"Why? Is he a more powerful necromancer that you?" George turned fully to Daegon. "Is he more than you can handle?"

"I-I do not know," Daegon admitted. "But I suspect he is in league with the Light Elves in some fashion; that alone bespeaks caution."

"Oh, I see. If the Light Elves know he's a necromancer, they'd be violating the Council prohibition just like the former Dark Elfin queen did when she brought you on board, right?"

Daegon shook his head. "That may be rather crassly put. She brought me on, for all intents and purposes, as an *alchemist*—but I fear you are essentially right. If Silenos openly performs an act of necromancy while in the service or patronage of the Queen of Light Elves, Queen Titania will have a problem, a most serious problem in the eyes of the Council, and perhaps even among the noble houses of her own realm. Her hold on the throne of the Light Elves could very well be at risk."

"Yeah? But wait," Vito interjected, "what about what Silenos has done in the Keys of Osiris?"

"Ah, yes, that is precisely what I mean; however, someone would have to have seen it," Daegon countered, "and then live to tell of it."

SENSING HE WAS ALONE for the moment, Salidar opened his eyes. The cave was not as small as he had thought, but no larger than the small hold aboard the *Doom Wind.* He sat up; a wall of falling water faced him. Diffused light passing through the waterfall offered dim, yet adequate, illumination. Turning about, he found walls of damp rock on all other sides. His head throbbed; a hand to the back of his skull confirmed that he'd suffered a blow. At least he was no longer bleeding.

"Ah, I see you are awake," a voice echoed hollowly. "Now we can have a conversation, or not. If we are not to have a conversation, you will not like the remaining options. So, what's it to be, eh?"

Salidar didn't like the sound of that. He rubbed his hands over his face and peered into every corner of the cave. He saw no one. He had little choice.

"A con-conversation? Yes, let's talk. Where am I?"

"The Keys of Osiris—but, you knew that. Your name, how are you called? What are you doing here?"

"I am Salidar, a crewman aboard the clipper, *Doom Wind.* I came ashore in search of fresh water for our ship—"

"Alone?"

"No, with two others, shipmates. We got separated in our search . . . and I-I don't remember . . ."

Silence ensued, making Salidar most uncomfortable. He felt the need to say something—*anything.*

He pointed to the waterfall. "This water—I have a great thirst—is it safe to drink?"

"Aye, tis fresh and cold, melt from the snows that blanket the mountain above us. Drink your fill, if you will, but ask not for food. There is no food upon this mountain; one would have to go down to the village that lies well below us. And for now, that is a problem, one that I had hoped we might discuss. But alas, your memory has failed, so—"

"Um, my apologies, I am sorry I cannot be of help. I really must get back to my ship."

"Oh dear, that presents another problem. The ship you named *Doom Wind* set sail with the tide; she departed these islands several hours ago. You may think of yourself as marooned here."

Salidar's mouth gaped open, yet he was speechless.

"I can see how that might upset you; but, things could be worse. This cave has water; you won't die of thirst. Of course, food is another matter. You could try to make your way down to the village, but you will no doubt encounter that *problem* of which I spoke."

"Problem? I-I," Salidar stuttered, "don't understand."

"Well, you see, everyone in the village was killed—and resurrected. Their corpses now roam the island, driven by an unholy hunger to slay and consume any living thing. You are probably safe here, hiding in this cave—for now."

"Safe? Wha-what do you mean?"

"Oh, it may be several days, or even a week before the voracious appetites of those roaming dead compel them to ascend this mountainside in search of living flesh. I would urge you to stay hidden, try to stay safe."

"Bu-but . . . I-I . . ."

"It may be that you possess a smattering of talent, and think you might transit out of here. A pity, truly, but you will soon see that is impossible. Any such attempt will cost you dearly; but, feel free to try if you must."

Salidar was speechless. His mind raced and within seconds he sensed it was true—he was trapped!

"I'll leave you now. Perhaps I'll check on you in a few days? Maybe your memory will return."

The cave was silent but for the steady rush of falling water.

CH 20

LORD NIGHTSHADE HASTENED down the corridor in answer to Queen Mab's summons.

He and the Lady Malvana had been back in the Realm of Dark Elves for some time. Despite his expectations, he had yet to be granted a private meeting with his queen. He sensed that something else held her focus and attention.

Perhaps the incident with Queen Titania? Or something to do with the returned mage, Gaspar? Now there is someone not worthy of trust, by any measure. He would bear watching.

Nightshade had heard the whispers at court; no one trusted this dark mage.

There were also dubiously optimistic rumors that the results of the negotiation sessions conducted in Mer regarding the Elfin Accords had finally been deemed acceptable, if not entirely satisfactory, by the Dark Elfin Queen. Most courtiers, ever attuned to palace intrigue and gossip, had wisely given her a wide berth ever since her return from Mer. To say her mood had been mercurial was an understatement; she had fluctuated between silent brooding and chuckling to herself for no apparent reason.

Nightshade had been waiting to deliver his most recent comprehensive report. He had sent word that he had news, but could not, would not, approach her without her leave to do so.

The summons finally came. The two stoic guards at her door nodded to him, and bid him enter.

Ushered into the reception area of the queen's private chambers, Nightshade was surprised to find Lady Malvana already there, alone, seated on a divan. Nodding to one another, they kept silent.

The queen entered through another passageway, and brightened at seeing her guests.

"Ah, you are both here. Very good!"

Nightshade bowed as Malvana rose and curtsied.

"Sit, sit," Mab insisted, gesturing to the divan. "I wanted to thank you both for your service in Mer. I've been going over your reports regarding the negotiations. Despite some unforeseen complications, like that unfortunate *burglary attempt* that you so courageously foiled, my dear Malvana, I think our current position with the Accords is as good as can be expected, for now. Well done, both of you."

Nightshade's mind whirled. *A burglary attempt? So that's what she thinks of Daegon's intrusion? Or, is that what she has chosen to believe—or have others believe? Hmm, that is far more likely. What does she know, or suspect? Hmmph, no mention of Queen Titania's visit—no surprise there, I imagine.*

He and Malvana briefly shared a knowing glance, but resumed bland yet pleased expressions. Both knew that certain relevant details had been omitted from their written reports—deliberately.

However, further speculation was moot for the moment—the queen demanded their attention.

"Here now, Malvana, what has the Council to say about this horrid necromancy incident in Mer?"

Her eyes downcast, the elfin maid folded her hands in her lap, and primly composed herself.

"Your Majesty, the Council has not released any formal statement. However, Lady Orla has confided in me that all the reanimated corpses have now been accounted for. The investigation continues, and plans for rites of execution are under consideration."

From beneath drawn brows Mab scoffed. “Ha! No doubt! So, who is responsible? Have they any clue?”

Malvana daintily shook her head. “No, my queen, I suspect not. Lady Orla did not know; and she is fully privy to the investigation.”

“I see.” Mab pursed her lips and considered her avatar to the Council. “Very well. Please, keep me informed. You may go.”

Nightshade rose as Lady Malvana took her leave. As the door closed behind her, he turned to find Mab reading a small scroll. He waited.

She rewound the scroll, slipped it into a messenger’s tube, and sealed its cap.

“Nightshade, resume your seat.” Mab gestured with the messenger’s tube to the divan.

Settling in an elaborate armchair, the queen faced him. “Now, your report?”

“May it please Your Majesty,” he began, sitting once more. “Our sources have confirmed that Queen Titania left the Realm of Mer immediately after your, uh, encounter with her. She returned to the Realm of Light Elves and has remained there ever since. However, Duke Briar did not return with her; he is still in Derinseum. His presence there is not well known; it appears that he is rather deliberately keeping a low profile.”

She leaned forward and asked, “Is he alone, or has he staff?”

Nightshade nodded. “He has staff, two unidentified persons, a male and female, and his usual pair of personal guards. We do not know why Duke Briar has stayed in Mer.”

She sat back and waved the tube in a vague arc. “It could be anything, or it could be nothing. Derinseum is renown for its distractions; and, the duke is rumored to have certain appetites. Keep an eye on him.”

"Of course, Your Majesty." Nightshade executed a small bow, even while seated.

Mab pointed the tube at him. "There is another matter that will require your attention, and discretion."

"Yes, my queen?"

"The Steward—I have unfinished business with her. I want you to track her activities when she leaves her home realm. I want to know where she goes and with whom she visits."

Nightshade was agog. *Track a Steward? That was nigh on impossible—and the queen should know it! What in the name of all creation was really going on here?*

"The Steward, Majesty? That would be most difficult—if even possible. I-I do not know if—"

She smacked the tube into her open palm; her voice frosted with an ominous chill. "You will do so, Nightshade—find a way! Even if you learn where she has been and whom she has seen after the fact, that may have value in establishing a pattern in her behavior. And of course, you will be extremely discreet in this matter."

"Your Majesty? I don't under—"

She rose and leveled the tube at him. "That means, Nightshade, that other than the necessary minions, you will not inform anyone else, but most especially Lord Padraic, of this assignment. Is that clear?"

He came to his feet and bowed deeply. "Of course, Your Majesty. It shall be as you command."

JUST PAST SUNSET, PADRAIC appeared at the door to the queen's chambers and was immediately admitted. He found her lounging on a divan in her boudoir, attired in a diaphanous gown that left little to the imagination.

"Ah, you're finally back," she cooed. "I've missed you."

He grinned. "I'm sure. We have some time before we dine, how shall we spend it? Would you have my report, or . . ."

She spared him a wry smile beneath a lone arched eyebrow.

"Padraic, you do not listen very well, do you? Did I not just say I missed you?"

AN HOUR LATER, A SERVANT knocked gently upon the chamber door and announced the evening meal.

"Very well," acknowledged Mab, rising to her elbows.

Padraic rolled over and watched as she rose from the bed, draped a sheer robe around her shoulders, and stared into her open wardrobe. He sensed that she was distracted, but he did not know why. He'd learn nothing if he couldn't get her to talk. He sat up and swung his legs off the bed.

"Now do you want to hear what I've learned before we sup? It will not take long, and I think you will like it."

She paused in selecting a gown and glanced over her shoulder. "Indeed? Then tell me as I dress. You should get ready, too."

"Oh, very well." He rose and started gathering his clothes in silence.

"Well?" Mab demanded, hands on her hips. "I know you can do two things at once, so?"

He grinned. "You were right about Titania; she hasn't told a soul about her embarrassing incident in Mer—"

"*Incident?* Ha!" Mab scoffed. "You mean her pitiful attempt at your seduction—what *cheek!*"

"Er, yes, quite so," he murmured, trying not to smile. "Shall I continue?"

Rotating her wrist, she spat irritably, "Yes, yes, go on."

"As I was saying, Titania has even withdrawn from most social interaction with courtiers of her own inner circle. I suspect she fears that some whispers or rumors of your encounter with her might be circulating beneath the cordial surface of the Light Elfin Court—or worse, the Seelie Court itself."

Her interest piqued. "And do any such rumors or whispers exist?"

He shook his head. "I could learn nothing in that regard. So, no, I think not."

She grinned evilly. "Not yet."

"See? I knew you would like hearing this. There is more."

"Oh? Then do go on." She turned once more to her wardrobe and began riffling through the hanging gowns. "I am listening."

He pulled his pants on, sat on the bed and reached for his boots. "Titania seems to have lost interest in the Keys of Osiris after your encounter with her. Whatever further plans she had in Mer, she canceled. Word is that she may have withdrawn support for some diplomatic mission—some group in the *wild,* who were in Mer. Apparently they were interested in the Keys, and for some reason she was acting as a silent patron."

She turned to face him once more. "You do realize that the incident that followed *after* my encounter with her, that foul necromancy, may have had some impact on her waning interest, do you not?" Turning back to the wardrobe, she let her sheer robe slide off her shoulders and drop to the floor. "That will most certainly be viewed as a stain on the reputation of Mer as a holiday destination. I would certainly lose interest."

Buttoning his shirt, he agreed. "Oh, of that I have no doubt. The repercussions will be felt in Mer, especially in Derinseum, for some time. I am sure the merchants are beside themselves; this is very bad for business."

Mab paused, held an amethyst sheath to her chin, and peered into a full length mirror. "One thing bothers me; what of these *diplomats* who were supposedly benefiting from Titania's patronage? What do we know about them?" She stepped into the dress and pulled its straps up over her delicate shoulders. "Why were they interested in the Keys of Osiris in the first place?"

Padraic stood behind her and addressed her reflection. "I do not know; no one I spoke with did. They may still be there for all I know."

She smiled smugly and locked eyes with his reflection. "Then you must find out. Return to Mer on the morrow. Now, Padraic, button me up."

He did so. "Tomorrow? So soon?"

"Yes. I do not like not knowing. Find out what I need to know. Do you understand? Good. Oh, by the way, be careful in Derinseum; Duke Briar is still there. I would like to know why that is so, as well."

"Briar?" He sighed heavily. "Oh, great! Just what I need."

Mab playfully swatted his arm. "Enough—no whining! Come, our meal awaits."

With a resigned shake of his head, he followed her from the royal chambers.

THE SATURDAY MORNING breakfast at Delafaire Farm was as sumptuous as everyone had hoped. Millie had prepared eggs, bacon, sausage, pancakes, grits, biscuits, and fresh fruit. The rich aroma of coffee permeated the entire kitchen.

Hawk and Trey watched in obvious amusement as Miska delved into his third helping of everything.

Mark chuckled as he shoved another plate of biscuits closer to the big man, and winked at the smiling detectives. Stacy scoffed at Mark's none too subtle gesture and shook her head, clearly deigning to ignore his puerile behavior.

Ellen looked around the table and smiled to herself. The people most important to her were now all gathered in her kitchen, enjoying the moment and each other's company. *If only life could stay this simple, this comfortable, wouldn't that be nice?*

"More coffee, dear?" Millie asked, appearing with a steaming carafe at her daughter's shoulder.

"Oh, no thanks, Mom, I've had plenty. I really need to get ready to go."

Stacy perked up. "I'm all ready! Yeah, the beach! Just say the word!"

Mark chuckled. "Well, I could use a few minutes. Besides, I gotta wait for something."

"Whoa!" Ellen blurted. "A transit globe just appeared! In front of the house, I think!"

"Oh, yeah." Mark stood. "That's what I'm waiting for. I've got this. Y'all just sit tight."

"No way, lover," Stacy declared, and followed fast on his heels.

Miska, Hawk, and Trey rose as well; but, Ellen raised her hand. "Hold on! I can sense that it's okay. Let them go. Trust me; she can handle him. She'll keep him out of trouble."

"Yeah, unless she starts it," quipped Hawk.

Amidst the ensuing laughter, Millie shook her head and rolled her eyes.

Moments later, Stacy and Mark returned, both grinning.

“Well?” Ellen prompted.

“Two bogies! You know, Council messengers!” Stacy announced. “Oh yeah, don’t worry, Miska, they didn’t touch us. One of them gave Mark something.”

“Yes, this.” Mark held up a small pouch of soft tan leather and handed it to Ellen.

“And this is?” she asked as she opened the pouch and let a small sapphire tumble onto her palm.

“An invitation of sorts,” Mark explained. “I’ve been in touch with Lady Orla, the Council avatar for Mer. She sends her regards, by the way. We’ve all been invited to spend the weekend at her villa by the sea, on the outskirts of Derinseum. This gem, Ellen, is for your use to transit us there.”

“I see, from a dragon’s hoard, right? Holding a spell of coordinates, or the equivalent, right?”

“Exactly! In fact, she is most eager for our visit; especially since I explained that Trey and Hawk were interested in looking into, uh, certain recent events in Mer, and could possibly be of help.”

“The zombies? Er, the recovered bodies of the watchmen?” Hawk asked.

“Yeah, of course I assured her you would be discreet. They’re very concerned about bad publicity and the impact on commerce. But the truth is that they may be in well over their heads, and need all the help they can get. So, you’ll be given some level of access; but, I don’t know how much exactly.”

“We have to look for Papa George, too,” Trey reminded everyone. “I trust there won’t be any problems or interference with that?”

Mark folded his arms. "I should think that a thorough investigation would include exploring the possibility of a potential link between the two sets of circumstances, would it not?"

Hawk and Trey grinned and nodded to one another.

"Jeez, Mark, sometimes you really do sound like a lawyer," Stacy teased.

A smug smile upon his face, Mark countered, "Yeah, don't I though."

Ellen fought the urge to laugh aloud. O*h, what sort of weekend are we in for?*

THEIR ARRIVAL IN THE spacious courtyard of Lady Orla's villa was not quite what they had expected.

Lady Orla herself was there to meet them. She was not alone; Selene stood at her side.

"Ah, Lady Ellen, welcome to my home," Lady Orla effused. "Thank you so much for coming to our assistance."

Hawk nudged Mark and whispered, "Psst, *what* did you tell her?"

Displaying a broad smile, Mark responded under his breath, "Just go with it, okay?"

"Thank you for having us," Ellen responded. "I hope we're not imposing."

"No, not at all," Lady Orla demurred. "I am honored to be your host. You know Selene, of course?"

"Yes, indeed, she is a good friend." Nodding to the undine, Ellen added, "It's good to see you, Selene."

"You, too, Ellen." Selene winked.

Lady Orla raised a hand; a host of liveried servants, under the direction of her major domo, were instantly in attendance.

"I have arranged accommodations for you all in the guest wing. My staff will see to your needs. Anything you wish, that I can provide, will be made available to you."

Ellen executed a small bow. "That is most gracious of you, Lady Orla, thank you. May I return your sapphire?"

Lady Orla gently plucked the gem from Ellen's open hand. "Thank you, these are quite dear to us, as you know."

Ellen nodded. "Of course."

"Unfortunately, it is likely that I will not be here for the entirety of your visit," Lady Orla lamented. "I have other duties that require my attention. So, I have asked Selene to act in my behalf, and see to it that your escort, the detectives, have access as needed—or at least to the extent that I could persuade the administration to allow. Please bear in mind that discretion is critically essential in these matters."

"We understand," Ellen assured their hostess. "We seek only the truth; we will share with you everything we can. Correct, gentlemen?"

Hawk and Trey nodded and mumbled, "Yes, of course."

"Thank you." Lady Orla sighed and offered a small sad smile. "Forgive me, but I must go. The staff will show you to your accommodations. Feel free to enjoy the private beach and the other amenities of my home. Luncheon buffet will be served at the noon hour. If I am free, I shall join you."

"Thank you, Lady Orla," Ellen repeated.

Selene took Ellen's arm and addressed their hostess. "I'll see that they're properly settled, m'lady. You needn't worry about a thing!"

Lady Orla chuckled. "Where you are concerned, Selene, I never do." To her guests she added, "May you all enjoy your stay. Now you must forgive me, duty calls." She turned and strode through a doorway, her major domo in her wake.

Staff personnel began directing guests to their respective rooms.

Selene tugged Ellen to one side. "Can you spare me a moment? I'll show you to your room, and we can talk on the way, okay?"

"Sure, what's on your mind?"

Selene glanced at some servants still within earshot; Ellen got the message.

Ellen's arm in hers, Selene sauntered toward the guest wing and proclaimed for all who might hear, "Ellen, it's about time you finally had some fun. You really must try the beach; it's great!" She grinned mischievously and stage whispered, "Very private—swimsuit optional, you know."

"What?" Ellen balked. "Uh, no, I don't think so, thanks anyway. Oh, you're teasing aren't you?"

"Me? Teasing? Perish the thought!" Selene's impish smirk implied anything but.

Another glance around assured them both they were now in no danger of being overheard.

"Seriously, Selene, I know Trey and Hawk want to talk to you about Papa George, and the bodies of the watchmen—"

"I know," the undine interrupted. "Keep your voice down. That's all set up. I'll escort them, so don't worry. But in the meantime you, Stacy, and Mark are supposed to be here on a holiday. Trust me, this is important. Knowledge of your visit has been carefully leaked by the Mer Administration. So, many people know you are here, ostensibly for a *holiday visit.* Understand?"

Ellen dropped her arm and stopped. "I might, if you'd care to explain. What's going on?"

Selene sighed. "Please, Ellen, keep walking, and I'll explain the best I can. Look, this recent necromancy incident has shaken the very foundation of this realm's economy, that carefully maintained holiday ambiance, the vacation atmosphere. The fear of necromancy is very real among the realms; its merest suggestion can cripple a tourism-based economy. Your visit, especially now that the situation is essentially well in hand, can help to mitigate that fear and its potential economic impact."

Ellen considered this for a moment. "Wait, what do you mean 'well in hand'?"

Keeping up a leisurely pace Selene glanced around once more and kept her voice low. "All of the cursed reanimated corpses are now in the custody of the Watch, and will be dealt with shortly. There is no more danger, to the best of our knowledge. Nonetheless, everyone is vigilant."

Ellen's eyebrows rose. "So, now the economy is the big concern? What about your people? The apprehension of those cursed corpses, was anyone hurt?"

"No, fortunately not—and yes, the economy here is a big deal. It affects everyone, directly or indirectly. It is not a small matter, Ellen. Please try to understand."

"I do understand economics," Ellen insisted, "but how is my brief presence here going to matter?"

"Look, I know you are only here for the weekend, but think about it," Selene reasoned. "Your visit is no secret, nor was it intended to be; the administration took advantage of that. Of course, what Trey and Hawk will be up to will not be made public. So consider what additional good you could do simply by being here, and being seen enjoying what Mer has to offer."

Ellen scoffed. "Oh, like being seen on a nude beach? Is that what you meant?"

Selene snorted in laughter as they entered the guest wing. "Okay, you got me! Maybe I was teasing, a little bit. What I mean is just be seen doing what any tourist or vacationer would do; spend time on the beach; go shopping in Derinseum; take a boat ride in the harbor—you know, that sort of thing."

Ellen relented. "Actually, that doesn't sound too bad. I think Stacy and Mark might go for it as well. Has anyone talked to them about this yet?"

Selene shook her head. "No, not yet. I wanted to discuss this with you first. See, you're the key; people pay attention to what the Steward does. You're kind of a celebrity among the realms, whether you know it or not."

"No way! I'm no celebrity!" Ellen was decidedly uncomfortable with the very concept.

Selene steered her through an oversized doorway and into a huge, lavishly appointed suite.

Ellen's jaw dropped.

"Think not?" Selene teased.

Mouth agape, Ellen could only shake her head. "No-no-no."

"Oh yes, this *is* your suite," Selene insisted. "The other suites are very nice, but not quite this grand. Face it—you have a certain celebrity status, and will likely be treated accordingly. Whatever you do, and are seen doing, will matter. Now do you see why it will be important for you to be seen savoring the enjoyments of Mer?"

Ellen sighed. "Okay, you've made your point. But I'm still not comfortable with all of this, uh, *pomp* and attention."

"Oh, Ellen, you don't have to be comfortable with this; all you need do is appear so. It is only for a couple of days. That should not be too much of a burden, now, yes?"

Ellen scoffed. "Ah, you're teasing again."

Selene shrugged, but her tone was serious. "Perhaps a bit, but if you consider the practical impact of such positive public relations, it is also a tactically sound strategy."

"How so?"

"Simple," Selene insisted, her palms open. "If the focused attention of the populace is on you and your holiday activities, then I can see to it that Trey and Hawk can conduct their investigation with far less scrutiny, or as you might say, below the radar."

"That does make sense," Ellen conceded. "Very well, I'll play the happy and carefree tourist. I'm sure Stacy and Mark won't mind either. However, I won't keep them in the dark. I'll talk to them at lunch. I trust you won't mind if I share this with them?"

"Not at all." Selene shook her head. "In fact, that works well for me since I'll miss lunch. If they're willing, I intend to escort Trey and Hawk to the Watch as soon as possible. The disposition of those cursed corpses is at hand; so, time may be of the essence."

"I understand, Selene. Go, do as you must. We'll keep up our end. Trust me."

"Oh, I do, Ellen, I most certainly do." Selene's smile was genuine. In the next instant, she was gone.

"ARE THESE HOODED ROBES really necessary, Selene?" Trey groused as he and his partner followed the undine through the back streets and narrow ways of Derinseum.

"Yes, tis far better neither of you is noticed," she insisted from beneath her own hood. "There is always a chance you may be recognized. You were introduced at a formal Council meeting; many persons of some importance from Mer were in attendance. Your presence here, especially now, would raise questions the administration would rather avoid at the moment. Please, trust me and stay close."

"How much further?" Hawk asked, peering warily overhead at tilting balconies and crumbling masonry. "This part of the city looks abandoned."

"Parts of the old city are," she admitted, "but not here, despite appearances."

"Hold up a moment," Trey suggested. "Are we safe enough here to speak privately for a minute?"

Stopping, she glanced around and nodded. "Safe enough—what is it?"

Trey produced a small flashlight, focusing its beam on a photograph, a mug shot of Vitorrio Smith.

"Do you recognize this man? Have you seen him before?"

"Hmmph, I have," Selene announced. "That's the big man who was with Papa George in Derinseum. Who is he? He was passing out those paper packets. I sent you one; what was in it?"

"His name is Vitorrio Smith; a known criminal who works for George Papadolis."

Hawk added, "The packet held a drug, methamphetamine, sometimes called speed. It's medicinal, but often abused. Without the proper license, its manufacture is illegal. Without a doctor's prescription, possession and use are also illegal in our realm."

"But not here," Selene reminded them.

"It ought to be; it's addictive and dangerous," grumbled Trey.

"Perhaps, but here we are . . . We need to get going—time is short," she insisted.

A few minutes later, Selene pointed to a rusted gate, leaning on one hinge. "We have arrived."

Two hooded men stepped forth from the old gate and blocked their path.

Selene dropped her hood and whispered to Trey and Hawk, "Stay here; say nothing."

She approached the hooded men and spoke quietly with them. After a moment, they stepped back through the gate and disappeared from sight.

Selene motioned for Trey and Hawk to join her.

"Watchmen, right?" Trey posited.

"Yes, this is a hidden Watch facility, a former marine garrison abandoned ages ago. Come, the Captain of the Watch awaits us."

She led them through the gate and across the wide paving stones of a dusty courtyard—empty but for windblown debris and a lone weathered post of great age, a thick wooden column twice a man's height thrusting up from the center. There were char marks on the post and the surrounding paving stones. Something had burned here.

Selene passed through a low arch and paused before a stout oaken door. She knocked in a distinct pattern, and received another pattern of knocks in response. A moment later, the thick door swung open on silent hinges.

A tall man in a hooded robe stood before her. Torchlight behind him rendered him a dark silhouette, but motes of reflected light danced upon the weave of delicate chain mail visible at his wrists. He spoke with a firm and even tone.

"Selene, you are early; but as it happens, that is good. Come in."

The heavy door closed behind them; a lock *clicked* home.

Within the torch-lit room, Selene stood with hands on hips. "Captain, these are the men of whom I spoke, Lords Trey and Hawk. Why is it good that we are early?"

Dropping his hood, the Watch commander sighed heavily and wiped a callused hand down the length of his careworn face.

"The mages have decided upon rites of execution, to commence at high noon, on the morrow. It will not be public. Tis just as well; these men were our comrades, their families our friends. This is not easy for my people." He turned away for a moment.

"Captain, we offer our deepest condolences," Trey offered.

"We are very sorry for your loss," Hawk added. "If we can be of any help . . ."

"Thank you." The captain sighed and pointed to another door. "They are held in the cells below. I understand you would see them, and possibly help in determining what may have happened. Is that not so?"

"Yes, that is the case," Trey assured him. "However, we don't yet know what we'll find; so, we are uncertain how helpful we can be. We will do our best."

"I understand. I must admit we are at somewhat of a loss. I hope you can help us."

"Okay, then," Trey urged, "let's have a look at these corpses."

"Of course," acknowledged the captain. "If you'll follow me. I'm not sure how to prepare you. This will be difficult, for all of us. Uh, Selene? Perhaps you might care to wait—"

"Nonsense! I'm coming, too. Please lead on, Captain."

CH 21

BARNABAS AND YOSHI winced as their ears popped. A transit globe materialized before them, crowding the small chamber in Barnabas' mountain retreat among the Keys of Osiris.

Yoshi crouched in an alert martial-arts defensive stance.

A figure stepped out of the globe—Padraic. At his simple gesture, the sphere shrank and winked out of existence with the usual soft *pop.*

Barnabas laid a hand upon Yoshi's arm. "It is fine, Yoshi. There is no threat here. This is my brother, Padraic. This is my friend, Yoshi—"

"Of the *Yokai,*" Padraic finished and bowed from the waist. "This is an honor, and a bit of a surprise. My apologies for my unannounced arrival, but I thought Barnabas was alone. I do hope I am not interrupting."

"This may not be," Barnabas cautioned, "the best time for a visit, Padraic. So, why are you here?"

Casting a meaningful glance in the direction of Yoshi, Padraic responded to Barnabas' question in a low voice. "Guild business, actually."

Barnabas pursed his lips. "I see." Turning to Yoshi, he said, "Forgive me, my friend, But I must ask you to excuse my brother and me. If you do not mind, let us continue our discussion later. Your people will be safe?"

Yoshi nodded. "We are in no danger, *Barnabas-san*. I cannot say the same for you and your *guest.* We will speak later." To Padraic he added, "It is an honor to meet you as well, Lord Padraic." Yoshi bowed, smiled, and faded into invisibility.

Padraic noted, "Ah, so tis true; the *Yokai* are not seen, unless they wish to be. Are we now alone?"

Barnabas nodded. "We are. So?"

"First, what is this danger Yoshi spoke of, that may affect you and me?"

"Necromancy. However, you are not the *guest* to whom he referred."

"Ah, then you mean Salidar, of course?" Padraic grinned.

"Salidar?" Barnabas balked, clearly taken aback. "How did you—"

"I'll get to that. Tell me of this necromancy. What has happened?"

Barnabas gestured to a pair of armchairs. "This may take some telling, so let's be seated. I'll pour some wine.

Padraic settled into the rather comfortable armchair and listened to his brother's tale.

SALIDAR WAS TRYING to sleep, despite the chill of pervasive dampness, the roar of the waterfall, and the insistent hunger gnawing at his gut. He needed a way out of here, and soon. Thirst was not a problem, but starving to death held no appeal whatsoever. Of course, there was always the alternative; fall prey to the voracious appetites of those re-animated corpses now roaming the island below this small hidden cave shrouded only by the persistent veil of snowmelt water.

Some twinge in the depths of his hindbrain alerted him that he was no longer alone in this cleft of wet rock. He twisted his head and squinted into the perpetual mist. One—no, two figures were silhouetted by the diffused light beyond the wall of falling water.

"Are you awake, Salidar? You have a visitor."

There was a series of sparks and a small oil lamp flared to life. The two men approached.

Salidar sat up, eyes blinking as recognition dawned.

"Padraic? M'lord, is it really you?"

Strong hands gripped his shoulders, pulled him to his feet, and spun him about. His shirt was yanked up, exposing his back. A firm hand passed across the back of his shoulder.

"So, your tattoo *is* gone," Padraic confirmed. "I have come for you, as you once did for me."

Salidar did not know what to say. Relief and anxiety flooded his mind; confusion reigned.

"We cannot linger here," Barnabas insisted. "We have much to sort out, but the roaming dead have begun to ascend this mountain. Have you somewhere in mind, Padraic?"

"I do, but we must go together. Take my hands and do not let go."

The transit globe enveloped them in an instant; they were gone.

The oil lamp flickered in the roiling mist of the waterfall, and succumbed to an errant splash. The damp alcove plunged into empty darkness.

THE CAPTAIN OF THE Watch led the way by torchlight down a narrow set of worn stone stairs.

"Watch your step."

As they descended Selene caught a whiff of an unpleasant scent and wrinkled her nose. Trey and Hawk exchanged knowing glances but kept silent.

At the base of the stairwell, they found a broad flagstone landing bathed in the light of flickering torches held in begrimed bronze sconces. A pair of stoic watchmen stood guard before an iron-strapped door. Centered on the door was a large bronze casting of a bull's head with a huge pull-ring suspended from its nose.

The guards stepped away from the door at the captain's nod. His hand upon the pull-ring, the captain faced his visitors.

"Noticed the smell, have ye? Aye, prepare yourselves, for it gets no better. This was the brig for these old marine barracks. There are only two cells, but sufficient for our present needs."

The captain tugged on the ring, twisted it half a turn, and pulled the door open.

A wash of foul air flowed from within; everyone winced and held their breath for a moment.

At a gesture from his captain, one of the guards handed Trey and Hawk lit torches and cautioned, "Stay to the center, away from the bars."

"Right," Trey acknowledged with a grunt. Exchanging nods with his partner, he gestured for the captain and Selene to proceed.

She frowned and followed the captain through the doorway. Their combined torchlight began to bring the darkened space to life, but deep shadows still hovered about. Selene silently wished she'd been offered a torch as well.

Hewn from the bare rock, the brig was smaller than she had expected. Two modest-sized cells sat opposite one another, separated by an open hallway almost the same width as a cell. The two sets of stout iron bars held cross pieces inlaid with thin rods of silver; that appeared to be the only ornamentation. She knew well enough the silver was functional, not ornamental.

Hawk thrust his torch toward the bars and gasped. "What the—"

"No closer!" warned the captain. "They are restrained in cold iron and silver, but can reach the bars. Do not let them touch you!"

Trey added the light from his torch.

Two disheveled forms shambled forth across the straw-strewn cell floor, waving outstretched arms and grasping hands. Only the silver-inlaid iron collars about their necks, chained to the rear wall of the cell, abruptly halted their lurching progress. They had almost reached the barrier of the bars. Each bore a blood-crusted hole the size of a small fingertip in its forehead.

"Oh, man," Hawk whispered, "this is not good."

"Their eyes," Trey noted, "they're glazed over with a milky film. How can they see us?"

"They sense us," Selene answered, "as living things, therefore prey. They are dead, yet reanimated and still decomposing."

"Unless they feed, right?" Hawk speculated.

"Yes," the captain confirmed. "We think these two have fed; they are in better shape than these others." He thrust his torch at the opposite cell.

"But I don't see . . . Oh." Hawk pointed. "There, on the floor, in the straw."

Two rail-thin bodies lay barely moving amongst the matted straw; but, they *were* moving, slowly trying to crawl toward the living. Their chained collars flopped loosely around their scrawny necks.

Trey fished a small flashlight from his pocket and nudged his partner. "We need a good look at their head wounds. We'll start with these two. Hold your torch lower and a little closer."

"Okay, got it. Oh man, the stench is worse closer to the floor!"

Selene gasped in alarm. "That's not the same smell. Something is wrong! Something is happening! The eyes—the eyes!" She pointed at the crawling corpse nearest the bars.

The milky film covering the eyes began to glow with a sickly green light. The eyes of the other crawling corpse began to follow suit.

Hawk quickly stood and turned to face the other cell.

"It's happening to the others, too!"

"Stay to the center! Stay out of reach!" the captain shouted.

As they watched in grim fascination, the green light intensified, streaming forth from dead eyes, ears, nose, mouth, and wounds; every orifice blazed with this verdant radiance. The shambling forms moaned, convulsed in erratic spasms, and collapsed in shuddering heaps.

The sickly green light suddenly flared in blinding intensity.

Instinctively cringing, everyone crouched back, shielding their eyes.

In an instant it was over. Flickering torchlight and pulsing shadows reigned once more.

"Look, the bodies!" Hawk hissed. "They burned! They're nothing but ash!"

"Yeah," mused Trey aloud, "and we've seen this before, haven't we?"

Hawk was about to agree when Selene gripped his arm. "Speak no further. The captain and I will deal with this. I regret you were not able to determine what you needed to know—"

"Oh, we're not done here," Trey interrupted and pointed. "Look, those green flames didn't even set the straw on fire; whatever that was only affected the bodies, leaving piles of ash. We just need to look through those ashes; that'll tell us if what we suspect is true. This won't take long. Captain, can you open these cells?"

The captain looked to Selene, who merely shrugged and nodded. Resigned, he motioned for a guard to open the cells.

Trey and Hawk spent a few moments sifting through the piles of ash.

"What are you looking for?" the captain asked after a few moments, clearly curious.

"Evidence." Trey stood and displayed a clear plastic evidence bag; within were four similar yet smaller bags, each containing a small ash-covered lump. "We suspect these are projectiles, and not very likely of this realm. We will know more when we can more closely examine this evidence."

The captain balked. "But—"

"Rest assured, Captain, we will share everything we can when we've reached a conclusion. For now, it would be best not to divulge that we have recovered any evidence. Selene, you agree?"

"I do, but Lady Orla must be informed. That is required. I assure you, she will be discreet."

"Very well," Trey acquiesced. "In that case, we are done here. Captain, is there anything we can do to assist you?"

"Thank you, no. I need only inform the mages that now there will be no need for the scheduled rites of execution. To be candid, I know they were less than keen to perform the rites—such duty can be quite taxing—so, I anticipate no problems. I am sure they, too, will be discreet in regard to this matter."

Trey smiled. "Excellent! Time for us to go."

TOPSEY LEANED AGAINST the rail on the stairway landing and surveyed the benign chaos of the barroom below. The Fouled Anchor had a good crowd this evening. All her girls were currently occupied with their regular patrons; she anticipated no problems. She saw Rumley behind the bar listening intently to an old man in sailor's garb whose half-lidded eyes scanned the room in a constant sweep as he bent over a mug of rum and whispered to the barman.

Moments later, Rumley nodded and straightened. He looked up and locked eyes with her. His swipe of a forefinger past the bridge of his nose told her he had news to share.

She casually made her way down the stairs, nodding to a few of their regulars. She meandered between the gaming tables with a slightly exaggerated sway of her hips, speaking a few words of encouragement to the gamblers and squeezing a shoulder or two in passing.

Ever popular with the clientele, smiles and good-natured bawdy comments followed her progress.

By the time she reached the bar, the old sailor was nowhere to be seen.

Leaning with her back to the bar, she blew a few kisses at some of the more creative invitations and waved her fans off. Her elbows on the bar, she sensed Rumley behind her. To her pleasant surprise, he slid a small snifter of cognac, a favorite of hers, within her field of view.

"Ah, this is nice," she cooed. "What news merits this?"

He leaned forward, his lips mere inches from her ear. "Good news, I think. The *Doom Wind* has rendezvoused with the *Xanthippe* at sea. The passengers are now bound for Derinseum."

"Salidar?"

"Not aboard. The crew of the *Doom Wind* think him lost at the Keys of Osiris and likely dead."

She sipped her brandy and sighed. "But safe?"

"Aye, although thought dead may be the best turn of these events. We did what we could."

"That we did. Tis out of our hands now, to be sure. So, what happened at the Keys?"

Rumley shrugged. "Rumors of death and mayhem, the hint of necromancy fuels the whispers."

Topsey's eyebrows rose. "Indeed? That is most ominous. Any more news?"

"Some, but tis equally vague," he admitted. "A strange cargo was transferred to the *Xanthippe,* a coffin-like box and an iron-strapped chest. Our source knew not the contents."

She drained her glass. "Curiouser and curiouser, eh? Will the *Doom Wind* put in here, at New Port Royal?"

"I think it likely." He wiped a towel over a wet spot on the bar top. "Mayhap we will learn more, if she makes port here."

Topsey straightened and turned to face him. "If Captain 'Bloody' Bane has no other scheme afoot and his crew has coin to spend, we should plan on their arrival. Where else can they go?"

Rumley chuckled deeply. "A-ha, there is that! There is that indeed!"

DUST ASSAILED SALIDAR'S throat; he gasped and coughed. Blinking in the dimness, he realized he was standing on a carpet of crumbling paper amidst towering stacks of random files and disorganized piles of old documents. He sneezed.

"Easy there, Salidar," Padraic cautioned. "Take short breaths through your nose; let this paper dust settle. I should have warned you both that our arriving globe might cause a stir."

"Well, I for one would have appreciated the courtesy," Barnabas groused as he brushed flakes of disintegrating ephemera from his shoulder.

Salidar wiped a sleeve across his face and spat at specks of confetti lodged on his lower lip. "Where are we?"

"The Council Realm," announced a new voice. Gallenius stepped out from behind a tilting mass of ledgers haphazardly stacked against an overstuffed bookcase. "Actually, we are in the archives, below the Council Library. And no, you will not speak of this to anyone."

Padraic offered his open palm to Gallenius. "I return this bauble to you; it worked well."

Salidar immediately recognized the topaz ring—he should, for he had used it himself on prior occasions. *Yes indeed, and at Diere, er, Mab's direction. I know that is her ring. How is it that Gallenius now has it?*

The Storm Haven mage simply nodded in acceptance. "I knew it would. Follow me."

He led them through a confusing warren of disheveled records storage to a relatively clear area hosting a small desk and a number of simple chairs, each bearing an erratic stack of papers and files.

Gallenius gestured to the chairs. "Please be seated; just put those files on the floor behind the chairs. The Guildmaster and Elsbeth will be joining us in a moment."

They cleared off the chairs and sat.

Gallenius came to stand before Salidar and demanded his attention.

"Heed me, Salidar. You are about to meet Elsbeth, the Council Archivist, and a dear *friend of ours—do you understand?"*

"I do." He did indeed. *So, this is Guild business; secrecy will be paramount.*

The Guildmaster seemed to virtually materialize at one side of the desk. "Very good. In that case, gentlemen, may I present Elsbeth, Dowager of the Mayfield Brownie Clan, Librarian Emerita and Council Archivist."

They rose in courtesy.

A small wizened woman, bent with age—obviously a brownie—stepped forth and took the chair behind the desk. "Greetings to you all. Please, be seated. Barnabas, it has been a long time; it is good to see you."

Barnabas bowed. "And you as well, Elsbeth."

"Padraic, I see you've brought a guest."

"I have, Elsbeth. This is Salidar."

Hearing his name, he stood. Her small bright eyes seemed to penetrate Salidar to his very soul. He instinctively knew this was no one to take lightly.

"Indeed," she murmured. "Salidar, we have not met before now; but trust that I know all about you."

Unsure of the protocol, Salidar bowed from the waist, but kept silent.

"Be seated, Salidar. Let's get started, shall we?" intoned the Guildmaster. "Salidar, you were instructed to remain aboard the *Doom Wind* and observe the passengers. Now is the time to report all you have learned. Please do so in chronological order, and leave nothing out. Do you understand? Good, begin."

And so, for the next hour, Salidar told his tale to a rapt audience.

AT THE CONCLUSION OF Salidar's narrative, the Guildmaster opened his gloved hands. "Thank you for that report, Salidar. Now, as I am sure you expect, we have some questions. Gallenius, would you care to begin?"

"Of course, Guildmaster. Salidar, after you saw this satyr, Silenos, perform a rite of necromancy, you said you fled and may have been pursued. Did you see anyone?"

Salidar shook his head. "No, I did not—but somebody knocked me out!"

"Yes, we are aware. Back to Silenos, have you seen him or his fauns since?"

Salidar stared into his open hands upon his lap. "No, I have not."

"I have an important question," Barnabas insisted. "This cargo brought aboard the *Doom Wind* by this Silenos, the chest and the rolled *what—rug?*"

Salidar bobbed his head. "Aye, that's what I saw. The captain had the ship's carpenter build a box for the rolled rug. There was something in that rug, I'm sure. The box was stored in the hold, but the chest stayed with the satyr, in the passenger compartment."

Barnabas' impatience was evident. "Whatever! Did you, or any other member of the crew see what was in either the box or the chest?"

"No, I did not; nor am I aware of anyone who did. Of course, there was talk amongst the crew, as tends to happen aboard ship—"

"What talk? Tell me!" Barnabas demanded.

Salidar leaned away and looked askance at his interrogator. "Scuttlebutt was that the cargo might be a body, and a head. They had to be kept separate, apart-like. Of course, that put me in mind of a *dullahan.* That may have been a flight of fancy—who knows?"

Barnabas paled; his mouth gaped but no words issued forth.

Elsbeth rescued him with a question of her own.

"Salidar, this merman who had some business with the satyr, did you learn his name?"

"No, it was never spoken."

"I see." Elsbeth raised a tiny finger. "You said this merman gave something in a seaweed pouch to Silenos, correct?"

"Yes, he did, in exchange for a fat purse of coin. I know not the amount. It was clearly the result of a prior arrangement, a deal struck between the two."

Elsbeth nodded thoughtfully. "I surmise that was the case. But Silenos betrayed the merman, and had his fauns slay him, yes?"

"Yes, he did."

"And he likely resurrected the merman's corpse, as he did in the case of the slain villagers?"

Salidar shuddered. "I-I have no doubt."

Elsbeth folded her small hands on the desk and fixed Salidar with her penetrating stare.

"Salidar, did you see, or come to know, what was in that seaweed pouch?"

The way she worded her question gave him pause; perhaps this was of far more significance than he knew. He would keep this in mind, but nonetheless answered truthfully.

"No, I do not know what it was. I only know it, and the purse of coin, were both in the satyr's possession when I, er, made my escape."

A somber silence followed. Salidar wondered what that meant; had he said too much, or not enough? Were there to be more questions, or not?

The Guildmaster stood. "I think that is enough for now. Thank you, Salidar, you've done well. Your shipmates now believe you dead, so your tenure as an impressed seaman is effectively over. Your presumed death is actually to your advantage; no one should be looking for you. For now, it would be best for you to disappear and let the rumor of your demise circulate. Gallenius will accompany you to Storm Haven; abide there and keep a low profile, for now. Do you understand?"

His mind awhirl, Salidar could not deny the immediate benefits of being presumed dead—*especially if Dire, er, Mab were to come to believe it.* He hoped his slight smile did not betray him.

"Of course, Guildmaster."

Gallenius came to stand by Salidar's side, clapping him on the shoulder. "Ready, Salidar?"

"I am."

The transit globe enveloped them, went opaque, shrank and *popped* out of existence.

PADRAIC COULD SEE THAT Barnabas was still agitated. Placing a calming hand on his brother's shoulder he said, "Take it easy, we can—"

"Take it easy?" Barnabas blurted. "You all heard him! A body and a head kept separate? Even Salidar suspects a *dullahan!* That damned satyr has *Brona!* We have to rescue her! *I* have to rescue her!"

"Calm yourself, Barnabas," warned the Guildmaster. "This is not helpful. There is much we do not understand. We must make some sense of this, before anyone acts rashly."

"We are missing something—something obvious," Padraic pointed out. "Silenos was looking for you, Barnabas. Now why do you suppose that was? You don't know him, so why?"

That got the anxious man's attention. He stared into his palms. "I don't know."

The Guildmaster leaned toward Barnabas. "Well, we have a working theory. I'll admit it's quite a bit of speculation. It may be that your, uh, parentage is not as secret as it once was."

"What?" Barnabas erupted. "No one outside the four of us knows Brona is my daughter!"

"That is true," the Guildmaster conceded. "But I was not referring to *her* father; I was referring to *yours.*"

"*My* father?" Barnabas balked. "Oberon? How could anyone know? What's that got to do with it?"

"Possibly quite a bit," Padraic offered. "Consider this; we know Queen Titania was acting as silent patron to this supposed *diplomatic mission* led by Silenos as some sort of *ambassador*. We know Titania has recently had an interest in the Keys of Osiris, and we suspect this was at Silenos' urging. We all know she does nothing that does not further her agenda unless she has something to gain—often something personal, yes?"

Barnabas scoffed. "Ha! That is no secret. She has always been self-absorbed and prone to act on whim."

"True," Padraic admitted, "however, keep in mind that she takes certain things—certain things of a personal nature, very seriously."

"And that may be precisely the case in this instance," the Guildmaster explained. "If Silenos became aware, or even suspected, that Oberon was involved in your lineage, he could offer that information to Titania as an enticement to secure her support. You know how she deals with any of Oberon's get; her price would be your life."

"So, you're suggesting Titania might not know about Brona," Barnabas reasoned, "but just me?"

"That would be most likely," agreed the Guildmaster. "Brona's secret has never gone beyond us four; on that you may rely. I should also point out that no one knows you've escaped your doomed island. You, too, will be presumed dead in time. Could that not be to your advantage, as well?"

"It could; I see the wisdom in that," Barnabas admitted. "But your theory does not explain why Silenos took Brona, assuming no one knows she is my daughter and thus in Oberon's descended lineage, too."

Elsbeth spoke up. "I have some thoughts in that regard, but allow me to digress for a moment. Remember the seaweed pouch described by Salidar, that is now in the hands of Silenos?"

Heads nodded amidst mumbled assurances.

"I suspect we may now know what that pouch contained," Elsbeth explained, "an ouroboros in silver, one of a pair, the other cold iron. When the pair are combined, they fit together to form the infinity symbol. Some of the oldest and most obscure sources of arcane lore we know of hold that this iron and silver infinity symbol is either a lock or a key of sorts, perhaps a seal of some kind. Admittedly, the ancient lore is sparse and somewhat vague."

"Wait," Barnabas insisted. "An ouroboros is a symbolic snake eating its own tail, right? And two of them can make this infinity symbol? I get that. But, what's all this got to do with anything? What's it got to do with Brona?"

"Patience, Barnabas, I will get to that momentarily. As I said, the silver ouroboros is only half of the infinity *key,* if you will. The other half, the iron ouroboros, is required to complete the key. If the old lore is to be believed, the intact infinity key was an integral aspect of the great work of the ancients that sealed away the Old Ones. In fact, it may be more than a symbol; it may be an actual key that secures the Old Ones in their banishment. We really don't know or understand its significance.

"What we do know is that some time in the long-forgotten past, the infinity key was separated, and its two component parts, the two ouroboros, were hidden in different realms. They were never intended to again be combined into the infinity key, lest the binding that confined the Old Ones be compromised."

"I must ask," Barnabas interjected, "why not simply destroy the two parts?"

"We don't know, for certain," Elsbeth admitted. "However, we suspect someone would have no doubt tried, but for a number of cryptic passages in old grimoires that essentially warn against any such action. There is a common belief that destruction of an integral implement used in a rite might compromise the old magic. This may well be true, for all we know. Those who knew best at the time elected instead to separate and hide the parts of the infinity key. The two ouroboros have remained hidden and presumably safe, until now."

"If I may, Elsbeth?" The Guildmaster took up the narrative. "We learned earlier today that the silver ouroboros was missing. A closely held secret, it had long been hidden on Mer, in a deep ocean vault guarded by an Aquatic Were clan; they've had this hereditary duty for generations. They still have no idea how the theft was accomplished, nor have they told anyone else, yet. We now strongly suspect, based upon Salidar's account, that this unidentified merman is involved, if not to blame."

"I still do not see what bearing all this has to do with my daughter," Barnabas insisted.

"Ah, you will, Barnabas," Elsbeth assured him. "There is something you do not know about Brona, something I only recently discovered in the research I've—"

"What?" he demanded, his patience exhausted.

Elsbeth sighed. "As you know, your mother did not approve of your periodic dalliances—especially your *liaison* with the Celtic dullahan, *Boand*, Brona's mother. However, your mother doted on the child, Brona, her granddaughter."

"Aye, that was true," Barnabas conceded with the ghost of a smile.

"What neither you, nor any of us, knew was that before your mother died, she bestowed the title and office of Steward upon Brona. Her gesture was formally recognized when she presented the child before the Council during an executive session meeting. An appropriate footnote was duly recorded in the minutes of the meeting; so, there is an official record. Apparently, the Council members in attendance indulged a well respected, loving grandmother who thought to make her granddaughter feel extra special, like a princess in that moment. It was no doubt only intended as a symbolic token, a simple endearing gift of heritage, since the Grand Portal of Mer had not existed since the time of the cataclysm and the banishment of the Old Ones."

"Tis been an empty title as long as I can remember," Barnabas admitted. "But why was I never told of this?"

Padraic pointed at his brother. “Probably because you had not cut ties with Boand until later, after your mother had passed on.”

Barnabas shrugged, yet remained silent.

“Which brings us to the salient point,” said the Guildmaster. “Brona is a Steward, albeit a Steward without a Grand Portal.”

“So?” Barnabas asked.

“Bear with me, for this may be difficult to hear,” the Guildmaster cautioned. “There are many, yourself among them, who believe that your ancestral Steward, who perished with the Grand Portal of Mer, and the portal itself were deliberate sacrifices in the casting of the great work, the cataclysm that banished the Old Ones. As we all know, such is the folklore that many hold dear. Unfortunately, we do not know for certain that *sacrifice* was, in fact, the case; it may be true, or it may be speculation based on mere coincidence. We simply do not know.”

Barnabas bristled, and was about to speak, but Padraic laid a restraining hand upon his arm.

“Easy, brother. The Guildmaster is not finished.”

“The truth we must face is clear,” the Guildmaster declared. “It does not matter what really happened at the time of the cataclysm. It does not matter what any of us might believe. All that matters right now is what the satyr, Silenos, believes.”

“Huh? Why?” Barnabas asked, clearly confused.

“We now suspect,” Elsbeth explained, “that Silenos intends to use the infinity key to breach the containment that holds the Old Ones; and, most likely use the Steward, Brona, as a sacrifice in the rite. We cannot be certain this is his intention, but it would be foolhardy not to consider it.”

Barnabas was speechless.

"As yet, we know very little about Silenos," Elsbeth admitted. "We do know he commands some dark arts to a level commensurate with that of a seasoned adept or advanced mage. We do not know his source of knowledge or power; but the use of necromancy suggests a comprehensive study of the Old Ones. If that is, in fact, the case, this apparent obsession with lore of the Old Ones is ominous indeed. Suffice to say, he is not to be underestimated."

"Worse," commented Padraic, "we're not really sure of what he wants."

"It may be that his goal is simply the acquisition of power," the Guildmaster speculated, "as was the case with the self-appointed priests and priestesses of the Old Ones who periodically arose in the ensuing years after the cataclysm. Or he may intend to bring the Old Ones back in their entirety to lord over the realms once again. We just do not know."

"And my daughter is to be a mere pawn to be sacrificed at his whim? By the gods," Barnabas declared, "I will stop him! I will save Brona!"

Padraic gripped his brother's shoulder and said solemnly, "Upon my oath, you will not be alone."

"We are together in this, all of us," Elsbeth said in firm finality.

Barnabas paused. "Thank you, thank you all." He shook his head. "Wait! We know Silenos has my daughter; but, he only has half the infinity key, the silver ouroboros. Am I right to assume he can do nothing without the other half, the iron ouroboros?"

"Yes, we believe that to be true," Elsbeth confirmed.

"So, if we can prevent him from getting his hands on the iron ouroboros," Barnabas reasoned, "then we may have time to rescue Brona! Where is it? We have to protect it!"

"Ah, therein lies the problem," the Guildmaster admitted. "We do not know where the iron ouroboros is hidden."

"What?" Barnabas was incredulous. "Someone must know!"

"The only person who did is dead," Elsbeth responded.

"Who?"

"Maude Delafaire."

CH 22

IN THE REALM OF DARK Elves, Lord Nightshade waited patiently in the hall outside the royal reception chamber. He had been prompt in responding to Queen Mab's summons; but she'd nonetheless kept him waiting for over an hour. The two guards to either side of the ornate doors looked on in stoic sympathy.

Finally one of the great doors opened. A servant came forth and curtsied to the elfin lord.

"Good day to you, Lord Nightshade. Her Majesty expects you. Please enter."

"Thank you." He stepped inside as the servant withdrew into the hall, closing the door.

"Nightshade! Attend me!" Mab commanded in a whirl of blue satin and black lace, one hand beckoning as she strode through another doorway that led to her private chambers.

But for the ever-present elfin warrior-bodyguard, they were alone in her sitting room.

The queen gestured to a set of chairs. "Be seated. Your report?"

He managed a small bow from his seated position. "May it please Your Majesty, I can report that the Steward spent the weekend in Mer, as a guest of the Lady Orla, and has returned to her home realm. She remains at Delafaire Farm."

Mab tugged at a sleeve and smoothed a swath of black lace that had bunched at her wrist. "Mer? Was she accompanied? Who did she see?"

Nightshade opened his palms. "She saw many people throughout Derinseum, and was typically accompanied by Lord Mark, the Counselor,

Avatar of the Realm of Man, and of course assorted attendants. Aside from Lady Orla, she visited with no other officials of the Mer Administration. We learned her visit was expected and planned as a simple holiday excursion. She spent time at a beach and shopped in the finer markets of Derinseum. She was seen by many doing that which any tourist might do. Of course, this may have been encouraged by the Mer Administration in light of the recent, er, *unpleasantness—*"

"Ha!" Mab scoffed. "Necromancy, you mean! I have no doubt the administration invited her to visit and be seen frolicking about, a sad attempt to mitigate any lasting effects that foul incident may have engendered. Pah! Those blasted merchants care only about lining their pockets. What else?"

"Nothing more, Majesty, regarding the Steward. However, we did learn that Lord Padraic arrived in Derinseum shortly after the Steward left. We do not know—"

"You need not concern yourself with Lord Padraic! He is performing a task at my direction. Am I clear?"

"Perfectly, Your Majesty." Her intense interruption surprised him; he dared not raise his eyes.

"What of Duke Briar?" she demanded. "Is he still in Derinseum?"

"He is, my queen. Rumor suggests he waits for someone. We know not who. Would you have me—"

"No, you need do nothing. You are to concentrate on the Steward. Understand? Good. You are dismissed."

Nightshade rose, bowed, and took his leave. *Ye gods! Now what game is afoot?*

THE EVENING SUN SLIPPED behind a dark cloud bank. Offshore winds picked up, chilling the few stevedores still laboring with cargo on the Derinseum docks. Seagulls wheeled overhead, their raucous calls buffeted by errant gusts.

Seated upon a worn wooden bench outside a ramshackle harbor pub, a pair of hooded men hunched their shoulders and snugged their flapping cloaks tighter in defiance of the brisk cooling wind. Padraic and Barnabas cupped their hands around warm mugs of spiced rum and watched the many vessels bobbing at anchor.

One in particular held their interest, a black junk anchored out near the channel, almost a full bow-shot from the docks.

"You're sure that's her?" Barnabas asked, his voice low.

"Aye, trust me. I'm quite familiar with the *Xanthippe.* We must be patient; just keep watching."

"So you keep saying. I still don't see why we can't board her. If our information is right, Brona is being held aboard. We *have* to rescue her!"

Padraic sighed and tilted his head toward his brother. "We will! But as I've told you, that vessel is *warded!* We'd never get aboard undetected. And worse, once aboard, we can't easily leave; she's transit-warded as well. Be patient; she's only dropped anchor within the past hour."

Barnabas took a long drink and wiped his mouth with his sleeve. "Why do you suppose they anchored so far out? There be plenty of room at the docks."

"I don't know," Padraic admitted. "Perhaps there's no cargo to unload, or none to take aboard—who knows? They are here for a reason, of that you can be sure."

Barnabas nodded at the vessel. "Look! Something is happening."

"Aye, they're lowering a boat; someone is coming ashore."

"Who?"

"Patience, we'll see soon enough."

As the longboat drew near, they could discern two crewmen rowing and two passengers, a gaunt woman and someone large, bundled in a heavy coat.

"As I expected," Padraic confirmed, "tis the sea witch, Circe; she is never without that staff. She usually has a lizard, too, but I don't see it. She must've left it aboard the *Xanthippe*."

"Who's the big guy with her?"

Padraic scoffed. "Who else? Unless I miss my guess, that's the satyr, Silenos."

"What do we do?" Barnabas asked, trying not to look at the approaching longboat.

Padraic scratched his chin. "Nothing. Let's just observe, and follow if necessary, without being noticed, of course. I doubt either of us are known to the witch or satyr by sight."

"So, we only observe and follow? What about watching the ship? Brona is still aboard! What if the ship weighs anchor and sails? What then? We abandon her?" Impatience and frustration harshened Barnabas' tone.

Padraic gripped his brother's arm. "Keep your voice down! Think! The *Xanthippe* anchored away from the docks for a reason. She'll not budge unless her master, Circe, is aboard. If Brona *is* aboard, she's not going anywhere for the moment. That's to our advantage, and gives us time to come up with a plan. You know we will never abandon her."

Barnabas stared into his mug. "I know that. Forgive me."

Padraic let his eyes scan the breadth of the harbor; the approaching longboat was the only craft underway.

"Barnabas, we need more information, before we can act. And just as importantly, we may need to know what business Circe and Silenos have ashore, here in Derinseum; and whether or not it has to do with Brona. Understand?"

Barnabas sighed in resignation. "Aye, I do, but still—"

Padraic clapped his brother on the shoulder and smiled. "Good! Now then, hold your tongue and pay fast attention to your rum. They've reached the quay."

The crewmen steadied the longboat as their passengers disembarked. Circe, a black bandanna tight about her skull, attired in sailor's garb and a long seaweed-patterned vest, led Silenos up a slick set of stone steps to the surface of the dock. The satyr kept his head down and his hands stuffed in the deep pockets of an oversized peacoat.

At a gesture from Circe, the crewmen pushed off and began rowing back to the *Xanthippe.*

A mere stone's toss away, Padraic and Barnabas sat focused on their mugs, ignoring the newcomers.

Fortunately, they too were ignored. Circe and Silenos walked right past them without a second look.

Padraic watched from beneath his hood for several long moments. When Circe and Silenos entered the streets of the city, he nudged his brother.

"Now?" Barnabas asked.

"Aye, now, all casual-like, but not too close—just keep 'em in sight."

FOLLOWING CIRCE AND Silenos proved to be no great challenge. The stylized octopus affixed to the top of her staff gave off a dull purple light in the growing dusk.

The sea witch led the satyr through the twisting streets of the lower city to the door of a dingy tavern. Despite the grimy ambiance, the place was clearly popular; boisterous groups of patrons were constantly coming and going through a wide propped-open door. Circe and Silenos stood to one side, away from the foot traffic, had a few words, and slipped inside.

From the shadows, Barnabas asked, "Do we go in?"

"Aye, I see no other choice," Padraic answered. "Look! Here come a handful of rough sailors. We'll follow them in as if part of the group. Quick now!"

Once inside, they peeled off and sought the shadows. Dimly lit, the interior was crowded and loud. A smoky haze hovered above the heads of the milling patrons. Somewhere a drum and penny-whistle accompanied an enthusiastic fiddler in a rollicking sea shanty.

In the din and dimness they scanned the crowded room. The clientele was indeed eclectic; fewer than half were human—not even a satyr would stand out.

"There," hissed Padraic, nudging his brother, "in one of the large booths along the far wall, see?"

"Be they alone?" Barnabas stood on tiptoe trying to peer past the surging mass of patrons, many of whom were well into their cups. "No, someone else is seated there—an *elf?* I cannot be certain."

Padraic shook his head. "This is no good. We have to get closer, within earshot at least." He pointed. "Head for the bar; we'll need mugs to fit in. Then make our way near the booth."

Barnabas nodded and struck out for the bar, Padraic in his wake.

Moments later, mugs awash with foaming ale, they eased their way through the jostling crowd, many of whom shouted ribald toasts and encouragement to other participants in the festivities. Despite the benign chaos, it was not that difficult for Padraic and Barnabas to maneuver closer, and position themselves quite near the row of crowded booths.

Keeping their backs toward the booth as planned, they were now within earshot of their targets. However, it was still difficult to hear over the din of the carousing tavern patrons. Fortunately, that meant those in the booth would have to speak up as well, no doubt louder than they'd wish.

Looking askance at one another, Padraic and Barnabas shared sly grins as they heard an irritated woman's shrill voice—that *had* to be Circe.

"Gods be damned! This is not a negotiation! I have complied with the contract—pay me you must!"

"You will be paid, but not until tomorrow." This voice was male, softer in tone but pitched almost as high as hers. "You must be patient."

"My patience is limited. A contract is a contract. I have other business to conduct," she stated with finality. "I set sail with the morning tide. You will pay me in full by then, or else."

"Indeed? Or else what?" The voice was now tinged with amusement.

Circe slid out of the booth, nearly bumping into Padraic's back. She faced the booth and *thumped* her witch's staff firmly upon the floor. "Or else, my dear elf, I will depart taking your client's cargo with me—as payment due!"

A shroud of silence fell upon the booth, broken a moment later by a deeply rumbling voice.

"You would not dare. You have no idea who—"

She cut the speaker off. "Oh, I do know, Silenos, and I would indeed dare, for *I* am not the problem—*he is!* This pompous buffoon of a Light Elf would toy with forces he knows nothing of. Tis he, or perhaps his master, who would breach a contract—not I! Tis in your best interest to see to it his master complies with the contract. There is no more to be said. I shall return to my vessel."

"Circe, please—" the elf began.

"Tomorrow! With the morning tide!" she spat, turned and pushed through the crowd.

Barnabas and Padraic shared a glance. At a nod from Padraic, Barnabas began to worm his way through the press of the crowd, trying to keep Circe in sight.

Silenos' voice was heavy with threat. "Hear me. Your master—"

"Is right here," announced a new voice to Padraic's rear right, one that sent his eyes wide.

The young Light Elf scrambled to his feet. "My Lord Duke! I did not expect—"

"No matter. I am here now."

Padraic pulled his hood lower as several people brushed past his back.

"Well, greetings, Duke Briar," Silenos acknowledged. "Please, be seated. Would you and your guards care for refreshments?"

There was shuffling as the Duke and two guards arranged themselves in the booth.

"No, I will not be here long."

"As you will," Silenos answered. "You heard the sea witch?"

"I heard enough. She will be dealt with in a timely fashion, you may rest assured. Now, your message was a bit cryptic; was there something else you need to discuss?"

"There is," Silenos dropped his voice, "the whereabouts of the *iron ouroboros,* if you would."

Duke Briar was silent for a long moment. "I cannot help you."

"Cannot or *will not?*" The satyr's tone was ominous.

Duke Briar sighed. "*Cannot.* I do not have such information; no one does. Indeed, what you speak of may be only a myth."

"I know better; tis no myth. If you have no such knowledge, then I must ask your queen. She—"

"You will not." Briar's voice dropped. "I am instructed to inform you that she has withdrawn her patronage. She will not see you, nor will she acknowledge any former arrangement she had with you. She will disavow all knowledge of you."

"What?" Silenos blurted, pounding a fist on the tabletop. "We have a deal!"

His outburst apparently attracted no undue attention; the near crowd ignored him. He glanced about and forced a harsh whisper that was almost lost in the din of the boisterous tavern.

"I did as she asked—he is surely dead! No one on that island could have survived!"

"Indeed? Even as we speak, in some select circles, certain rumors seem to indicate otherwise; your name is even whispered as the author of that dark deed."

"What are you talking about? Speak plainly!" Silenos demanded.

"It is rumored that there may be survivors, who may know far too much. If there is the slightest chance that might be the case, you will attract the scrutiny of the Council. You are no doubt aware that of late they are very much concerned with matters such as these."

"Bah! I am a *diplomat!* I have *immunity!*"

"So you keep asserting. However, you have not presented yourself, as is customary, before the Council as such, nor presented any sort of credentials to that effect. So, this presumed protection of *diplomatic immunity* may be as mere smoke on the breeze, an airy façade that the Sentinels of the Council will categorically ignore.

"In fact, you should assume that these rumors of which I spoke will assuredly reach Council ears within a day. It may now be in your best interest to depart the Council Realms entirely. You may even find it safer in the *wild*."

"*Within a day?*" Silenos repeated, his tone growing darker.

"Quite so," the duke confirmed. "Now, our business is done. Oh, there is one more thing—you are not to speak of my queen to anyone, about anything. Do you understand?"

"Oh, I understand," Silenos seethed through clenched teeth, "more than you and your vaunted queen will ever know!"

With that, Silenos suddenly stood, jostling several people in the crowd, to include the hooded Padraic, who kept his balance, but spilled some ale.

The incensed satyr faced the seated elves. Grinding his teeth, he jabbed a finger at Duke Briar's face, too angry to speak.

The Light Elfin guards tensed and gripped sword hilts; but the duke stayed their hands and addressed the fuming satyr.

"You should go—while you still can."

Silenos balled his fists and narrowed his eyes, his temper barely in check.

"I will not be treated so! To break faith with me is to seal your doom—all of you!"

Spinning about, the angry satyr plowed into the crowd, knocking several people down, among them Padraic.

Righting himself upon his elbow, Padraic realized he'd spilled the last of his ale, and his hood had flopped askew, falling back upon his shoulders. Looking up, he found the wide eyes of Duke Briar staring into his own.

"Padraic!" hissed the duke. "Seize him—quietly!"

The guards shoved the other fallen patrons aside, snatched Padraic up, and pressed him to his knees before the seated duke.

Leaning forward, his face twisted in aberrant glee, Duke Briar whispered for Padraic's ears alone, "Oh, how I have longed for this day!"

The Rogue remained silent. Duke Briar's eyes had gone wild, his shoulders shaking in anticipation.

"Bind and gag him!" the duke hissed.

Duke Briar led the way to a back door, the guards shoving their bound prisoner before them.

HIGH IN THE SOOT-STAINED rafters of the tavern, well above the tumultuous bacchanalia below, a pair of spriggans took long draughts from their mugs.

"Saw all that, did we, Twit?" asked one.

"Aye, that we did, Scratch, that we did." He wiped his long pointed nose on his sleeve.

"Think worth sumthin' it be, aye?"

"Oh aye, of worth it be—to the right people." Twit winked at his companion. "An' knows I just the right someone! But first, we follows `em, all invisible-like in the dark."

A CHILL ONSHORE WIND blew across the nearly deserted waterfront. Barnabas tugged his cloak tighter about him and hunkered down unseen amidst stacked crates of cargo. He kept careful watch on the sea witch pacing to and fro beneath a line of flickering torch baskets along the dock.

Circe had come straight here from the tavern, striding so purposely that anyone she encountered in the streets surely sensed her wrath and gave her a wide berth. In the fullness of the night, Barnabas had no difficulty following her.

She had somehow signaled to her vessel, the *Xanthippe,* and now awaited the longboat that had just shoved off from the junk.

Carried on erratic gusts of wind, her ill-tempered mumbling, well spiced with vitriolic curses, clearly indicated her mood had not improved.

Barnabas was uncertain what he was supposed to do if she went back aboard her vessel. Keep watch? Return to Padraic?

His perplexed musing was interrupted by the arrival on the dock of someone else—*Silenos!*

Circe stopped pacing and glared at the satyr. "Silenos? Now what?"

He tossed his thumb over his shoulder, spat and grumbled. "Treachery! I think we are *both* double-crossed! I expect betrayal will follow!"

"Speak plainly!" she urged. "What do you mean?"

"These Light Elves have no intention of paying you what you are owed; I think you know that."

"Aye, I do," she conceded. "What else?"

Silenos stared at the worn paving stones at his feet. "This duke made a *not-so-thinly-veiled* threat to expose or confirm some, er, *indiscretions* of mine to certain authorities who I am not prepared to deal with—not yet. This could be a problem for me."

She scoffed. "The Council, you mean? Oh, don't act surprised; spare me any denial. I know of you and your *rumored* capabilities. Yes, you would be wise to avoid any Council attention—I certainly do."

He paused, as if taking her measure; and, she clearly sensed it.

"What?" she demanded. "Scowl not at me! I am not your problem; this duke is!"

"Perhaps, but you threatened my cargo were you not to be paid; and that is now the case."

"True, I did," she admitted, "but the situation has changed. The duke expressed no interest in your cargo; so, tis nothing to me, certainly not leverage. I can offload here and now and be done with it—"

"No! That will not do!" he interjected. "It should not come ashore here; better to transit from your ship—"

"Not possible," she declared. "The *Xanthippe* is heavily warded against any sort of transit spell. Trust me; you would not like the results."

"What then? It would not go well for you should my cargo be found aboard your ship."

"Ha!" she scoffed. "I am a smuggler! Do you think such a trifling matter should concern me? My vessel will not be boarded against my will!" She slammed her staff upon the dock; sickly purple sparks flared in small arcs from the impact. "Do not underestimate me!"

"I do not. Nonetheless, we need to be away from this place, before tomorrow. Can we sail now?"

She shook her head. "No, not at night, tis far too dangerous; these shoals are treacherous. Tis impossible now at low tide. The earliest we can depart will be after sunrise, with the morning's high tide. We could make for a safe harbor; New Port Royal, I think. Once ashore there you and your cargo could transit anywhere you'd like."

"That would be acceptable, but . . ." He stared off into the night.

"But what?"

Silenos scratched his cheek. "I trust not this duke. It is now clear to me that he has planned this treachery for some time. I suspect he will act on his threat sooner than tomorrow—if not already. Besides, he has insulted and angered me. I do not like to leave such things unanswered."

"So?"

Silenos pointed into the dark harbor. The lantern in the bow of the bobbing longboat was now clearly visible, and much closer.

"I see your longboat approaches. I think I'll stay ashore a bit longer. Please send my fauns to me. I trust my cargo will be safe in your care for the next hour or so?"

Circe raised a lone eyebrow and chuckled. "Oh, I see. It will be safe, rest assured. When the longboat returns with your fauns, shall I have the crewmen wait?"

The satyr smiled and rubbed his large hands together. "Oh yes, we won't be long."

The longboat bumped against the stone steps of the quay. Circe paused before descending to board.

"A word of caution, Silenos. Do what you will with the duke, but perform no *Dark Art*—do you take my meaning? A similar event happened here not too long ago; the repercussions were economically severe, and merited Council scrutiny. Things have only recently settled down. This is a fledgling market for a new enterprise I am involved in, that could become quite lucrative. I'd rather you did not muck this up. Savvy?"

"Indeed? A lucrative enterprise?" His eyebrows rose. "Perhaps, we should talk later?"

She offered a sly smile. "Perhaps we will."

As Circe departed in the longboat, leaving Silenos standing on the dock, Barnabas tugged his cloak tighter about him. He had heard much of their conversation, but not all.

What to do—what to do?

With a heavy sigh, he decided to sit tight and maintain his watch on the *Xanthippe.*

After all, Brona was still aboard, or so he hoped.

CH 23

STANDING AT THE OPEN back doors of the SUV, Hawk leaned in and pulled a large plastic case forward. With a small key he unlocked a series of clasps along the lid. At the touch of a sliding switch, the lid opened on thin pneumatic arms with a slight *hiss*.

"So, what am I looking at?" Ellen asked, as Smokey slipped from her arms, dropped to the carpeted rear of the SUV, and began sniffing at the case and its contents.

Trey rested a hand on the open lid. "The latest tech in surveillance drones—actually the only set our department currently has, which is why we had to wait for it to become available to us."

"Set?" Ellen echoed. "There's more than one in there?"

"Yeah," Hawk answered, and began removing various parts from their snug foam enclosures. "There's a large one with six arms and propellers that's actually bigger than the case when it's fully assembled."

He began to lay parts to one side and brought out another foam enclosure not much bigger than an old-style big-city telephone book.

Trey took the block of foam and pulled the top half off, exposing within a small, fully assembled, four-arm drone about the size of his splayed open hand. He picked it up, holding its central body between two fingers.

"This smaller one works just like the big one but can get into smaller places. Unfortunately, it can't do as much or remain airborne as long as its big brother; it's still a good tool."

"They both look pretty sophisticated," she observed. "Are they hard to operate?"

"Not really." Hawk shook his head and grinned. "Although the captain insisted we spend a whole afternoon with the guys from tech support to learn how to fly these things. I gotta admit, it was a whole lot of fun! These bad boys are so cool!"

Trey looked askance at his partner. "Some had more fun than others, as you might imagine."

Ellen chuckled. "I'll bet. So, what's the plan?"

"First, we'll assemble the big one and do some test flights here on your front lawn. Oh, that is if you don't mind, okay?"

"No problem, Trey. Don't be surprised if Stacy and Mark want to watch—me, too."

Trey put the small drone back in its foam nest. "They're not here?"

Smokey sniffed at the small drone; Ellen plucked him from the SUV and cradled him in her arms. "No, they went into town. They should be back any time. I'll bet Mark is gonna dig this!"

"No doubt," Trey agreed. "Anyway, once we get everything squared away, we'll fly the big one over the area Miska led us to and see if we can get a fix on our *uninvited guests.*"

"There's some thick forest around there," Ellen remarked. "How will you be able to see—"

"Because, we can!" Hawk interrupted with a big smile. "The camera on the big drone is very sophisticated; it can livestream, record, transmit coordinates, and more. It can work in color, black and white, infrared, thermal, you know—heat signatures, and motion sensing. There are two monitor screens; a small one on the control unit, and a separate larger one. The techs told us they could even pair the drones to work with laptops, tablets, or smartphones. If there's anything alive in the search area, bigger than insects that is, we should be able to see it."

Ellen returned his smile. "I think you like your new toys, don't you? So, what about the caves in that area? Is that what the small drone is for?"

"Well, maybe, we'll see. The techs weren't exactly thrilled when we brought that up." Hawk shrugged and pointed to the little drone. "This little guy's camera isn't nearly as sophisticated, and its flight time isn't as long. So, we'll have to see what develops."

"Oh, what about flight times? Both drones are powered by batteries, right?" she asked.

"Right, lithium-ion rechargeable batteries." He hefted a small battery out of the case. "The big drone takes eight of these, with a projected flight time of up to two hours—"

"Think a realistic ninety minutes," Trey interjected, "depending on some variables, like wind and weather conditions, and what mode the camera is using. When the onboard charge diminishes to a threshold level, the drone is preprogrammed to return to the operator's coordinates and land."

Ellen smiled as she scratched Smokey's tummy and earned a rumbling purr. "And the little one?"

Hawk held another small battery between thumb and index finger. "The little guy carries only one battery, good for about twenty minutes."

Trey grinned and waggled a finger. "Twenty minutes may be stretching it; think fifteen minutes realistically, and a software-limited range of about a hundred yards. The range of the big one is limited to about five hundred yards. We don't really know what the maximum range would be, I mean without the limiter. I asked, but was told that was classified."

Hawk nodded. "Yeah, which leads us to think that this is a stepped-down law enforcement or commercial version of a *mil-spec* model designed for military use. I admit that's speculation, but I think we're close to the truth—especially since nobody would give us a straight answer."

"Not to change the subject, but," Trey began, "Ellen, you said you might have some ideas about what to do if we *do* find these cats. So?"

She looked around; they were alone in front of her house. She shifted Smokey over to one hip and dropped her voice.

"What I've been thinking is that the best thing we can do is send them back to where they belong, right? But we don't know where that is, not yet. So, the next-best thing is to send them somewhere away from here, *temporarily,* until we can figure out where they really belong."

"I can see the logic, but *where?*" Trey opened his palms. "I mean for the *temporary* solution. You know no other realm we know of would want to play host to a pair of saber-toothed cats, no matter how brief a time."

"I think I know," Hawk mused aloud. "You're thinking of an unpopulated realm, right? Something in the *wild?*"

"Yes," she acknowledged, "in fact, an unpopulated and *proscribed* realm—Olmus."

SOUND CARRIES RATHER well in the caverns and passages below the temple ruins on Olmus.

Papa George heard approaching footsteps in the nearby passage and looked up from the scrying orb to see his driver enter the chamber carrying a gym bag and a large brown paper bag.

"Hey, Vito! Back already, huh? How was *The Big Easy?*"

"Hot and humid as usual, but no problems, Boss." The big man unzipped the gym bag and displayed thick bundles of currency. "Collected deposits from our distributors, about a hundred and twenty large. I warned 'em how to cut the product, like you said, and not to put too much out there too soon."

"Good! We gotta keep demand up, keep prices up." George smiled. "If Teddy keeps producing at his current rate, it won't be a problem to keep the supply scarce—"

"Unless we get some competition," Vito interrupted.

"Competition? As if! Come on, Vito, is there anything out there as good as this meth? This pure?"

Vito shook his head. "No, not of this quality. You were right; Teddy really knows his stuff. But Boss, you know there are other cooks out there; it's only a matter of time before someone tries to push their own stuff."

"I know," George conceded, "that's the nature of the drug game. When we learn of any competition, and I mean *real competition,* not the overly stepped-on, bad-cut garbage that's usually on the street, we'll deal with it, *capisce?*"

"Gotcha, Boss. Our stuff is gonna move pretty well. I figure I'm gonna have to make weekly collections. Don't worry, I'll be keeping an eye on our distributors and my ear to the ground."

"Good, we gotta stay on top of this," George insisted. "So, what's in the paper bag?"

Vito grinned and opened the bag; tantalizing aromas wafted out. "I brought back some po'boys and muffulettas from the Quarter; I got enough for the four of us. To tell the truth, I may love that we can get carryout from back home, but I'm getting kinda tired of it—of course I won't touch whatever the goblins provide for Daegon. So, I'm thinking I could set up a little kitchen somewhere here, you know? I miss cooking. What do you think?"

George smiled. "That's fine with me—go for it! I don't know how Daegon can stomach that slop."

"Great! I'll get what I need and stock up on my next trip, okay?"

"That'll work. Was there anything else?"

"Yeah, coupla things." Vito closed the paper bag. "Before I left, when I picked up the last batch from Teddy, he told me that it was a couple ounces light because Daegon took some off the top. Daegon told him that you said it was okay. I told Teddy I'd talk to you about it when I got back. So, what's the deal? Was Daegon right?"

George wiped a hand down his face. "Oh damn, I forgot to tell you. Yeah, Daegon's been trying to exert some control over those big bats. I may have mentioned in passing that *to be addicted is to be controlled,* and apparently that gave him some ideas. I'm pretty sure he's been experimenting with getting the bats addicted; but I don't know if he's had any success. He may have mentioned that he'd need to use a little product—but *damn, a couple ounces?* I didn't think he'd be using that much."

Vito scratched his head. "Yeah, a couple ounces can be a bite outta our profits, you know? Besides, I thought bats were nocturnal; wouldn't getting them hooked on meth—*speed*—be kinda a bad idea? I mean those damn bats are creepy enough; I won't go anywhere near 'em."

George's eyes narrowed and brow furrowed. "Hmm, I hadn't thought about that. You may have a point. I'll have to talk to Daegon. He's already complained that his goblin servants are scared and don't want anything to do with the bats as it is now. I can't imagine them all hopped up on speed."

Vito shuddered. "Aw, hell no! Boss, this might be something that needs to be nipped in the bud, know what I mean?"

"Yeah, I do. Okay, any other news?"

"Uh, yeah, a message for you. Frankie Fingers outta Detroit sent word that he wants a sit-down. He says he's got some hook to get our product into Canada and says he can handle distribution there, too."

"Yeah, I'll bet." George scoffed, paused, and stroked his chin. "Through Windsor?"

Vito shrugged. "Dunno, didn't say. But I think it's gotta be; he's been working the border up there forever. He even claims Windsor as part of his *turf* these days to anyone who'll listen. I got a phone number for him, probably a burner. What do you want to do?"

"Lemme think about it. I guess you gotta go back to use that number, don't you? How soon does he expect an answer?"

"Dunno, whenever, I guess. And yeah," Vito chuckled, "phones don't work here, so I gotta go back to make any calls."

"No biggie, right?" George smiled. "You've gotten pretty comfortable using that transit globe technique Daegon taught you, haven't you?"

Vito shrugged. "Yeah, but I can only go from here to that permanent portal in the cemetery in New Orleans."

"And back," George joked.

"Oh yeah, and back," Vito echoed. "That reminds me; if I'm gonna be making regular trips, I'm gonna need some wheels back there. The cops have still got the limo, so I'm gonna need something else. I can stash it in a rental garage near the cemetery."

"You're right. I should've thought of that." George pounded a fist into his palm. "The next time you go, take what you think you'll need from the deposits there," he pointed to the gym bag, "and get something that won't attract too much attention. Stash it nearby, like you said."

"Will do, Boss."

"Maybe you ought to lease something, legit like. You gotta be able to move around and function as my eyes and ears back there without the law on your back. I sure as hell can't go back there, not right now."

Vito nodded. "Not gonna be a problem. We've still got our connections, and everybody knows I speak for you when you're not around. I just gotta keep a low profile while I'm on bond."

"Yeah, that's right. So, what's the status with your court case? Is that new lawyer working out?"

The big man nodded. "Yeah, he's pretty sharp. I got a hearing date in a coupla weeks; he's gonna ask for another continuance. He says the more we can push it off, the more likely he can get the charges reduced, maybe even get some dismissed. I guess we'll see."

George scoffed. "Ha! He sure is costing me enough; but, I like the sound of *dismissed.*"

"Me, too," Vito agreed with a broad smile.

IN A DIMLY LIT DERINSEUM stable, Selene scowled at the pair of spriggans. Without taking her eyes from Twit and Scratch, she spoke over her shoulder.

"Tullos, I don't know whether to believe them or not."

The centaur leaned forward from his waist and studied the two mischievous rascals. His voice was deep and rich, but carried no further than amongst the four of them.

"Tis an interesting development, and if true—one we cannot overlook."

"Tis d' gods' own truth—we swear!" Twit insisted, with no small degree of indignation, and nudged his companion. "Tell `em, Scratch!"

"Aye, tis true," echoed the other spriggan. "An' no doubt worth a lil' sumthin', tis it not?"

"We'll see about that," cautioned Selene. "Did anyone else see it happen?"

"Oh, aye! The tavern, full it be." Twit bobbed his head. "As like many saw, but none dared interfere."

"Aye," agreed Scratch. "Tis only a fool would mess about in elves' business, aye?"

Selene and Tullos exchanged looks of concern.

"You are certain you recognized Duke Briar?" Tullos asked.

"Aye, tis no doubt!" Twit chuckled. "Hard to miss is that fop!"

"This is important," Selene declared. "Are you sure Padraic was taken against his will?"

Twit scoffed. "Be a pig pork? Bound `n' gagged, he was! Aye, Scratch?"

"Aye!" Scratch laughed and added, "All trussed up like a fat goose, he was!"

The undine leveled a finger at the spriggans. "You followed and know for certain where he was taken?"

"Aye, followed we did," asserted Scratch, "to the grand house the duke's been renting. Stayed in, they did."

"So," Twit finished, "in search of ye we come. Tis not this of worth to ye?"

"As I said," Selene repeated evenly, "we'll see."

Tullos pulled her to one side. "Selene, if this is true, there may be no time to waste—"

"I know! That's why we must—"

"Wait!" he forestalled her response. "Hear me out. Despite the possible urgency, this is a matter for the Watch.

"Tis no secret that Duke Briar has a personal grudge against Padraic. Think of what it might mean were he to take his vengeance here in Mer. The duke may be prone to rash and opportunistic behaviors, but he is not overly stupid. You already know of the tension between the the Light and Dark Elves.

"At some point even Duke Briar will come to realize that he now has a problem. This abduction happened in a crowded public place, and was no doubt observed by any number of people. This could potentially be an incident of far-reaching proportions—entire realms could become involved. Harming the consort of the Queen of Dark Elves would be a regrettable mistake. That fact is bound to occur to him, sooner rather than later, I should hope."

"Yes, but we—"

Tullos stopped her again. "We *nothing!* Think! You and I cannot be seen to be directly involved; you know well of what I speak. The wiser course is to contact the Watch; let them handle it."

Selene sighed heavily in frustration. "Very well, I know you are right. So be it; let's not waste time!"

LESS THAN HALF AN HOUR later, in an upscale neighborhood of Derinseum, Selene stood with the Captain of the Watch before a palatial yet darkened townhouse. No light shone forth from within, in stark contrast to similar homes on either side whose windows glowed with the warm light of residents going about their normal lives.

"Are you certain this is the place, Selene?" The captain gestured at the ominous façade with a gloved hand. "We have confirmed that this is Duke Briar's temporary residence."

"Aye, our sources are certain," she insisted. "They are nearby, if you'd like me to check again."

"No, that is not necessary—your assurance is sufficient. It is time to act."

He motioned with an upraised arm, and six more watchmen seemed to materialize from the dark ends of the street. At his silent command, two slipped between the houses and made their way to the rear of the building. The other four men took up positions at the front, two watching the windows, and two at the front door.

Satisfied, the captain nodded and turned to Selene.

"We must knock, announce our presence, and seek permission to enter; that is our law. You must wait here, understand?"

"I do. But Captain, if he refuses . . ."

She could barely see his grin in the dimness.

"Well then, we shall see, won't we?"

With that he turned, ascended the wide steps, and stood before the door.

His gloved fist knocked but once—the door swung easily open.

Darkness beckoned beyond.

At his silent signal, four watchmen slipped inside. The captain followed.

It seemed an eternity to Selene before the captain reappeared at the open doorway and motioned her forward. She walked briskly up the steps, only to be stopped by him at the threshold.

"I cannot admit you. I have to preserve the scene for the inquisitors."

"What? What about Lord Padraic?" she demanded.

The captain shook his head. "He is not here. You are certain your sources saw him come here?"

"Well, yes," she insisted. "They said he was *brought* here against his will!"

"Selene, he is not here now. We very much want to talk to him."

"Why? Who *is* here, anybody? And why did you call this a *scene?*"

The captain hesitated.

She became unaccountably apprehensive as he lowered his voice and leaned toward her ear.

"There are five dead elves here—Light Elves. Duke Briar is among them."

SEATED ON THE STEPS of her front porch Ellen drained the last of her tepid hot chocolate, and placed the empty mug to the side. She stretched, crossed her legs and leaned back letting her elbows rest on the top step.

Smokey took that as an invitation to crawl into her lap and beg for a tummy scratch.

She smiled and granted his wish. Gazing up at the star-laden moonless night, she took in a deep breath. There was a hint of chill in the air.

She heard the screen door open, and turned her head to see Miska's bulk blocking the light from the foyer.

"Oh, Miss Ellen, I did not mean to disturb you."

"You didn't, Miska. Come, join me." She patted the wide step upon which she sat. "Have a seat and check out the stars tonight. They're brilliant!"

He eased his frame onto the steps and gazed upward. "Ah, the new moon; the stars are easier to see on such a clear night. It is very beautiful."

"Yes, indeed," she agreed and sighed. "It's nice and quiet out here. Is Mark going to play another movie on the new DVD player?"

"He is, but it's getting late. To be honest, I did not understand the last one we watched, the one Miss Stacy urged us to see, a *rom-com?*"

"Ha-ha-ha!" Ellen could not contain her laughter. "Oh, Miska, sorry—a *romantic comedy!* Don't worry about it; not all men get it either. The jokes tend to be subtle and primarily for women to appreciate—at least that's my take on it."

"So, my confusion is not a problem?"

She chuckled. "Not at all, and completely normal. Trust me."

He nodded. "Thank you, I am relieved. I think I will head to the cabin, no more movies for me tonight. Besides, once your mother went to bed, and you left to sit out here on the porch, I began to feel, uh, what is that saying? *Like a third wheel?*"

Ellen snorted in laughter. "Oh, Miska, you are becoming quite the wit!"

Miska smiled and winked. "Oh, I do not miss much."

She chuckled again, but suddenly stopped. "Something's coming—a transit globe!"

Alarmed, he stood and peered into the darkness. "Where?"

Ellen stood, spilling Smokey from her lap, and pointed to the lawn. "There!"

The cat seemed unimpressed. Smokey simply walked down the steps and sat down, staring unconcernedly at the transit globe coalescing on the lawn.

A familiar form stepped forth—*Padraic!*

"Padraic? What are you doing here?" Ellen asked descending the last few steps. "Were we supposed to expect you?"

"Oh, hello Ellen, Miska," He waved, but surprise marred his smile. "I, uh, well, this was an unexpected trip." At his gesture, the globe shrank and winked out of existence.

"Is everything all right? Why visit now, at this hour?" she pressed.

Opening his palms, he groaned. “Ah, I don’t have time to explain. I really have to go. Suffice to say, I needed to depart a place rather quickly; and now, I must be somewhere else. I only intended to pop *in and out* without disturbing you or your mother.”

“So, from one realm to another,” Miska deduced, “and yet to another—or to another place within the first realm?”

Surprised, Padraic brightened. “Why, yes, Miska, something like that. Now—”

“Hold on,” Ellen demanded. “At least tell us the gist of what’s happening; and whether or not we can help.”

Padraic sighed. “Very well, I’m trying to help orchestrate a rescue of your cousin, and—”

“What?” she blurted. “Mark is in the house! He and Stacy are watching a movie!”

The Rogue winced and shook his head. “Uh, not that cousin. Look, we’ll talk later, I gotta—”

“What—another family surprise? Oh, this just keeps getting better and better,” she observed dryly. “Well, at least tell me if I can be of any help.”

Padraic paused in thought. “You know, that just may be the case. I’ll let you know.”

“I, too, will help,” announced Miska firmly.

A smile creased the face of the Rogue. “Indeed? Well then, I will let you both know. Now, you really must excuse me. I must go.”

With that, he summoned a transit globe. Once it stabilized, he waved and entered without another word. It shrank and winked out of existence with the usual *pop*.

Miska grinned and nudged Ellen with his elbow. "I think this life is very interesting with him around, don't you?"

Ellen sighed, bent over and scooped Smokey up in her arms. "Miska, I think you're developing a genuine talent for *understatement.*"

BARNABAS WAS RUDELY awakened by someone shaking his shoulder. Jerking upright, he banged his head on a cargo crate and groaned.

Above him a familiar voice apologized.

"Oh, sorry about that. Are you all right?"

Rubbing his head, Barnabas looked up but could only discern the dark silhouette of someone leaning over him in the midst of the stacked cargo crates.

"Padraic? Oh, I must have dozed off. Wait—where have you been? What took you so long?"

The Rogue squatted next to his brother and peered at the crown of his head.

"That's a nasty bump; is it bleeding?"

Taking his hands from his head, Barnabas stared at his fingers in the meager torchlight along the dock.

"No, no blood; it hurts though. So, what happened?"

"Not much. I, uh, got delayed. More importantly, what happened here?"

"Well, the sea witch went aboard her junk, but the satyr stayed on the dock. His fauns came ashore and the three of them went into town. They returned within the hour and now they're all back aboard the *Xanthippe.* The ship still rides at anchor out in the harbor."

Padraic grunted and stroked his chin. "So, everyone is now aboard. They could leave with the morning tide. I'm betting that's their plan. There appears to be no reason to stay, since they surely feel they've both been double-crossed. Did you overhear anything?"

"Some . . . You are right that they feel they've been double-crossed, and they do want to leave as soon as possible."

"Where to?" the Rogue interrupted.

"Circe mentioned New Port Royal; but they can't sail before the morning tide. Silenos was anxious to leave soonest."

"New Port Royal?" Padraic echoed. "Well, I doubt we can accomplish any more here, so that might work to our advantage. However, we may need some help—*special* help."

"What do you mean? What kind of help?"

"We are probably going to need a thief, an expert thief, and one or two—"

"What? A *thief?*" Barnabas shook his head in disbelief.

"And one or two others, I suspect." Padraic finished. "Look, I'll explain later. Let's get off this dock; it'd be best we're not seen here."

"Why should that matter? All those who concern us are out there, in the harbor." Barnabas pointed. "There's not another soul around."

"Trust me," Padraic insisted with a clear note of urgency in his voice as his eyes peered toward the dark streets of Derinseum. "It'd be a good idea to get off the streets for the rest of the night. We can check the harbor in the morning to see if the junk sails like we expect her to. Come on, let's go."

Barnabas rose and stretched his stiffening back. "Oof, I was in one position way too long; I'm getting too old for this. So, where are we going?"

"It's not that late; I can check in with an old friend. In fact, you should meet her. I'll introduce you to Madam Iris; she runs a *friendly* house. Trust me; you'll like her."

Barnabas grinned knowingly. "Well then, brother, lead on."

AS PADRAIC AND BARNABAS reached the street that led to Madam Iris' establishment, Padraic stopped and pulled his brother into a dark shadow.

"What is it?" Barnabas asked, peering down the empty street.

"Something doesn't feel right," Padraic hissed. "Be still."

There was no movement, no sound, not even a breath of breeze; the entire street appeared deserted.

Padraic pointed and whispered, "Her house is about mid-block, the one with the red lanterns by the door. You stay here; I'm going to check it out. It may be nothing; if so, I'll wave you on. For now, just sit tight."

"As you wish, but I don't see anything wrong." Barnabas responded.

"Yeah, I know, neither do I," Padraic answered, "but my *gut* disagrees."

With that, the Rogue stepped from the shadow and sauntered down the street.

PADRAIC'S CASUAL STRIDES had taken him almost to the front steps of Madam Iris' home when two unseen watchmen stepped from the shadows and blocked his path. Two more were suddenly at his back.

"Uh, good evening, gentlemen," Padraic offered in greeting. "Is there something I can help you with?"

Another man, bearing the insignia of a Captain of the Watch, stepped forth from a darkened doorway.

"As it happens, Lord Padraic, there is, indeed. You can come with us to answer for the murder of five Light Elves—Duke Briar and his aides. Please comply and come quietly."

STUNNED WITH MOUTH agape, Barnabas watched as Padraic, offering no resistance, was taken into custody by the Derinseum Watch.

CH 24

"THE INITIAL REPORTS were vague, since our assets did not have firsthand information," Lord Nightshade explained, standing nervously before his seated queen. "However, we have now received formal notification from Mer that Lord Padraic is in custody and under investigation. He is suspected of slaying five Light Elves, to include Duke Briar."

"Five? And the duke as well?" Mab pursed her lips. "I assume Titania has also been notified?"

"She has, Your Majesty. However, as of this morning, there has been no formal statement from the realm of Light Elves."

Mab gripped the arms of her elaborate chair and scoffed. "Hmmph, there will be, just as soon as Titania decides how to play this to her advantage. What more do we know?"

"Only that the allegation that Duke Briar forcibly seized Lord Padraic in a tavern and spirited him away appears to be true. It was, in fact, witnessed by many who were present; the tavern was quite crowded at the time."

"So," Mab reasoned, as she considered her elegantly manicured nails in a shaft of sunlight, "Padraic could claim self-defense, could he not? Does not that principle apply in Mer law?"

"It would, my queen, but . . ." Nightshade hedged.

"But *what?"* She balled her small fists and pounded the arms of her chair. "Answer me!"

"Ah, there were some *unusual* circumstances, Your Majesty, rumors of certain *mutilations*. We do not yet have the specifics. Suffice to say that we understand that the circumstances are such that a simple claim of self-defense may strain any modicum of credibility."

The queen sighed, shook her head, and mumbled, "Ye gods, what has the Rogue done now?"

Nightshade paused, thinking she might address him, but she stared off into some private distance, ignoring him for the moment. He knew better, and kept silent.

"Nightshade, does the Steward know? Has she been informed?"

That surprised him. "The Steward, Majesty?"

She glared at him. "Yes, the Steward! You are keeping an eye on her as I directed, are you not? Does she know?"

"Of course, Your Majesty. No, my queen, as far as we know, she has not been informed." His mind raced—*and why should this matter?*

"She will be soon enough, I'll wager," Mab mumbled, rubbing her open palms on the arms of the chair.

"If I may, Your Majesty," Nightshade ventured, "what would you have us do, regarding Lord Padraic?"

"Do? Why, nothing, Nightshade. Let us see how this plays out." She sat back in her chair and steepled her fingers.

"Nothing?" he echoed incredulously. "But, Your Majesty, your consort—"

"Enough!" she declared with a slash of her hand. "Leave me! Send Gaspar to me."

He bowed and withdrew. Just as he closed the door to her reception room, he unintentionally heard a snatch of her final comment.

"... can always get another consort..."

GASPAR DISPLAYED NO emotion or expression as he listened to Mab. In truth, he was grateful to be given something to do. He had become bored while "recovering" from his ordeal; after all, one could only reread one's small library of grimoires so many times. His knowledge of sorcery had not grown appreciably, but what he had reviewed was now more firmly entrenched in his memory.

He realized his mind was wandering. He snapped his attention back on the queen. It would not do for her to perceive any lack of focus on his part whenever she was speaking—no, that would not do at all.

"So, as discreetly as possible, go to Mer, find out what is happening, and report to me alone. No one is to know of your mission. Am I clear?"

"Yes, Your Majesty. Should an opportunity arise, am I to take any action on behalf of Lord Padraic?"

She eased back in her chair and tapped her fingertips on the arms in a moment of contemplation.

"No, do nothing without my permission. For now, your role is to learn things—not do things. This may change as I see fit. Do you understand?"

"I do, Your Majesty. When would you have me leave?"

"Before this day ends," she insisted. "I would have you in Mer soonest."

"By your leave, my queen." He bowed and withdrew, careful not to let her see the satisfied smile that stole across his face.

"MARK, YOU'VE *got* to be kidding me!" Ellen bolted to her feet, nearly knocking the kitchen chair over, and stared at her cousin in disbelief. "Padraic was just here, late last night! Miska and I both saw him. We *spoke* with him! He never said anything about any of this!"

"Ellen, this came to me through the Council channels; it's gotta be true!" he insisted, pushing his empty coffee mug away. "I don't know any more than what I just told you. I'm sorry."

"This just doesn't make any sense—none!" Stacy declared. "Mark, can't you find out more?"

He shrugged. "Of course, I've asked, but not even the Council knows any more at the moment. I even sent a message to Gallenius, but he hasn't gotten back to me yet. I'm sure the Guildmaster is looking into the whole thing. We've just gotta wait and be patient."

Stacy gripped Ellen's forearm. "Come on, sit down. Have you called Hawk yet?"

Ellen sat and held up her phone. "Yeah, it went to voice mail. I'm sure he'll call when he can."

Ellen noticed her mother quietly sitting at the table, a twisted dish-towel in her hands. Millie had not said a word since hearing the news. Ellen's heart lurched. She stood and hugged her mother's shoulders.

"Oh, Mom, I'm so sorry! Are you all right?"

Millie smiled up at her daughter. "I'm fine, believe me. This is certainly disturbing, but I'm okay. You know, you need to have a little more faith in your father. It's true that he's been known to get into lots of trouble, but it always seems to come out all right. Like Mark said, let's be patient. It'll work out, you'll see." She patted her daughter's clasped hands.

Ellen stared into her mother's eyes, smiled, and gave the hug an extra squeeze. "Mom, you are one strong woman."

Millie smiled. "And don't you forget it, young lady."

THE GUILDMASTER HEARD the knock on his door, looked up from his desk, and motioned for Gallenius to enter.

"Guildmaster, Selene and Barnabas have just arrived in Storm Haven."

"Good. Send Barnabas in first. Give me a few minutes, then bring Selene in."

"As you wish," Gallenius answered and withdrew.

A moment later, the mage returned with Barnabas, and left them alone.

"Ah, Guildmaster, I need—"

"One moment, Barnabas, I must remind you that there are things not to be spoken of. We will be joined shortly by Gallenius and Selene, neither of whom are aware that Brona is your daughter. If you choose to keep this secret contained as it now is, you must think before you speak. On the other hand, if you are prepared to share this information, that is another matter. In fact, it may become virtually impossible to keep this effectively hidden any longer, since we now know that certain official records exist within Council archives. Do you follow me?"

Barnabas sighed. "I do. I'd much rather keep the secret, but I suppose I always knew the truth would come out someday. I would not insist on secrecy if it were to hinder her rescue in any way. Her well-being has to be my priority."

The Guildmaster nodded. "I am glad to hear it. I strongly feel you will need to make peace with a few more people knowing your secret; her rescue may depend upon it."

"What about Padraic? He said he had a plan." Barnabas shrugged. "But now?"

"I am sure he did," agreed the Guildmaster, "and now we'll have to try and figure out what it is, or was. His arrest is certainly a complication."

A knock on the door announced Gallenius' return with Selene.

The Guildmaster waved them in. "Do come in, please. Come, let us sit at the conference table."

They sat and gave the Guildmaster their attention.

"All settled? Good. Selene, please give us your report."

"Of course, Guildmaster. We now have confirmation that Padraic was forcibly seized and carried away by Duke Briar and his elfin aides. The Derinseum Watch also has this information, to include many witness statements. Two of our assets also saw the abduction, followed, and saw the house to which he was taken; the Watch knows this as well.

"We alerted the Watch to the abduction and the destination. I was there when they entered the house. Padraic was not there. There were five bodies, all Light Elves; Duke Briar and his aides. There was some evidence of mutilation to the body of Duke Briar. Neither the Watch nor we know for certain what happened; to the best of our knowledge, there are no witnesses.

"Within hours, Padraic was found some distance away by the Watch and taken into custody; he did not resist. I was not present when he was questioned; however, a *friend of ours* who was present confided in me.

"Padraic was initially cooperative. He admitted being seized and brought to the house against his will. He said they kept him bound and put him in a second-floor room that was somehow warded, so he couldn't use a transit globe. An elf was posted in the same room to watch him while the duke and his aides were making some sort of preparations. Padraic said there was some sort of commotion on the first floor that drew the elf watching him away. In that elf's absence, Padraic claimed to have freed himself from his bonds and escaped through a window.

"The Watch went over his story repeatedly, but he changed nothing, insisting he had made a clean escape. When questioned about the deaths of the elves, Padraic claimed to know nothing. The Watch pressed, but Padraic was resolute. One of the inquisitors asked what he did with the ears—"

"Wait! What—*ears?*" the Guildmaster interrupted.

Selene balked. "Er, yes, ears. The body of Duke Briar was mutilated; his ears were taken."

"Taken?" Gallenius asked. "They were not found there?"

Selene shook her head. "No, they were not found. All the victims had their throats cut, one deep slice each; but only the duke lost his ears. When Padraic was asked about the ears, he stopped cooperating and refused to say another word. He is still in the custody of the Watch. We have no idea what they intend to do now."

"I doubt they know what to do at his point," the Guildmaster reasoned. "This could have serious political ramifications. Is it possible for you, or any of our people, to get in to see him?"

Selene shook her head. "No, not at this time. My sources tell me the Mer Administration is very anxious and security is very tight. The Watch is especially vigilant."

"Hmm, that's too bad," the Guildmaster mused aloud. "We need more information."

"What did you mean about *political ramifications?*" Barnabas asked.

"The situation is dire enough," the Guildmaster began, "but it could easily spiral into something much worse."

"Worse than this? Ye gods! W-we must act! We have t-to—" Barnabas sputtered.

"Easy, Barnabas," Gallenius cautioned. "Let the Guildmaster finish. There is more to understand and consider here."

"Indeed, think about who is involved," the Guildmaster urged. "The consort of Mab, Queen of Dark Elves, is thought to have murdered Light Elves in a Council realm that is also a member of the Seelie Court. Worse, a high-ranking noble has been mutilated, a member of a distinguished house within the hierarchy of the Light Elves. Titania, Queen of

Light Elves, will have no choice but to formally demand justice and recompense. In turn, Queen Mab will have to respond. Don't you see?"

"Not to interrupt, Guildmaster," Selene interjected, "but it is rumored that some recent incident involving the two queens, some sort of social gaffe, occurred on Mer as well. Sorry, but we have yet to learn the details. We do know that Queen Titania left in a huff."

"In a sad way, that further illustrates my point," the Guildmaster conceded. "We all know that the Light and Dark Elves are often at odds. We also know that increasing tensions, however subtle, between the Dark and Light Elves have impacted relations between the Seelie and Unseelie Courts. The Council, fully aware of these tensions, cannot ignore this latest situation. In fact, it will no doubt view this mass murder as a potential flash point, a diplomatic crisis."

"Titania could even call this an *assassination*," cautioned Gallenius, "an act of *war*."

"And this all happened on Mer," Barnabas noted, "a realm presumed safe, a holiday destination."

"Aye, one that has only recently recovered from another discrediting incident," Selene reminded everyone. "It is no wonder the Mer Administration is so worked up."

"This could go well beyond further disruption of a realm's economy," the Guildmaster warned. "Should the Council get involved, a strong likelihood, and subsequently fail to mitigate the situation, that could very well portend the eventual collapse of the Council. Absent some level of Council control and oversight, the inherent strife between the Seelie and Unseelie Courts could escalate to unbridled chaos, benefiting no one. We must not underestimate these matters."

An ominous shroud of silence fell upon them.

After a moment, Selene broke the spell.

"Guildmaster, forgive me, but I have to ask about your reaction to the mutilation of Duke Briar—the *ears.* Was that news significant in some way?"

The Guildmaster nodded. "Yes, and I think Padraic may think so as well. In fact, it appears certain disparate facts may be more closely related than we have heretofore thought. However, before we proceed any further," he turned to Barnabas, "one of us has a decision to make."

Barnabas sighed heavily. "Yes, I can see we are at that juncture. Very well, Gallenius, Selene, please bear with me. I know I have been, uh, somewhat overly anxious; but, I have reason to be."

The Guildmaster laid a comforting hand on Barnabas' arm and nodded. "They need to hear it all."

Looking to Gallenius and Selene, Barnabas simply said, "I have something to share with you both, in confidence, of course."

And so, he did.

A FEW MINUTES LATER, Selene asked, "Are you certain the *Xanthippe* made for New Port Royal?"

Barnabas shrugged. "That is what I heard the sea witch say. Padraic thought that made sense, too. I know the junk put to sea the following morning. It was definitely gone from the harbor. I know they were eager to leave, but had to wait for the morning tide. I do not know how long it would take her to make the journey; several days in good weather, I suspect."

"It will be no trouble to learn when she makes New Port Royal," the Guildmaster assured him. "You and Padraic were confident that your daughter was still aboard while in the Derinseum harbor?"

"Aye," Barnabas insisted. "The *Xanthippe* never offloaded any cargo, never docked. She sat at anchor out in the harbor while in port. Circe and Silenos came ashore and reboarded by longboat."

"So, Circe and Silenos are aboard, Brona is likely still aboard, and the junk is headed to New Port Royal," the Guildmaster reasoned. "Was their hasty departure solely because they felt betrayed, or was there another reason?"

"Hmm, I've been wondering the same thing," Gallenius offered. "The taking of ears gave me pause, but enough of that for the moment. Barnabas, you said Padraic told you he had a plan?"

"Yes, he did. He said New Port Royal would work to our advantage, and we would need a *thief*—"

"A *thief?*" Selene echoed.

"Yes, an expert thief, and one or two others; but, he didn't tell me who or why."

"Ah, Barnabas," Gallenius broached, "can I ask you more about Brona? It may help us devise our own rescue strategy. I must admit my knowledge of *dullahans* is not without substantial gaps."

Barnabas initially balked. "Sorry, please forgive my reticence. It is something that I've always thought was best kept secret—but now? Very well, I suppose I should begin with her mother, Boand, a dullahan from the *wild.* She was named after a Celtic river goddess. We met a long time ago, and stayed together for a good while, during which we had Brona.

"Boand wasn't exactly the mothering type, I suppose. So, my mother took over most of the raising of Brona; they were very close. Suffice to say that Boand and I grew apart; eventually we parted on good terms. She left Brona with me. For what it's worth, my mother never did approve of Boand; but, she doted on her granddaughter, Brona."

"So, whatever happened to Boand?" asked Selene.

Barnabas shrugged. "I do not know. We lost touch years ago."

"Does Brona remember her mother?" Selene pressed.

"Brona was very young when Boand left. So, I am not sure, but I suspect she does remember something of her mother. You must understand that Brona was far closer to her grandmother than her mother. Brona may be *half* dullahan, but she was raised as a human. She displays none of the uh, more assertive or belligerent proclivities to which her mother was so prone. In fact, Brona is rather shy and prefers to keep to herself. She even has a modest skill with minor magics, but never showed much interest in more esoteric sorcery."

"Forgive me, Barnabas, but I have to ask," probed a contrite Gallenius, "Brona, her head . . ?"

Barnabas squirmed a bit. "Well, yes, she can separate her head from her body. However, she rarely does so—and never in the presence of strangers. As I said, she is very shy."

"We do not mean to make you uncomfortable, my friend," the Guildmaster assured him, "but understanding this sort of information may be essential in crafting an effective rescue plan."

Barnabas' shoulders sagged. "I know; but this is so *personal.* Ah, never mind, I understand."

Gallenius glanced at the Guildmaster, who nodded for him to continue.

"Barnabas, can Brona function without her head, as full-blooded dullahans can? And if so, do you know if her head needs to be within a certain proximity?" Gallenius opened his hands in earnestness. "Forgive me, but can you see why we may need to know this?"

"I do. Yes, she can function without her head, but I don't know if there is any sort of proximity requirement. I have never seen her without her head, uh, close by."

"So, it might be possible," Gallenius reasoned, "to rescue one and then the other?"

Barnabas shrugged. "I don't know; I never thought of it like that. I suppose it might be possible."

"Hold on a moment. I'm still not clear on something," Selene admitted. "Are we sure that this Silenos wants Brona only because she is a Steward, albeit without a Grand Portal, and thus, as we suspect, a potential sacrifice in whatever rite he's planning to undo the binding of the Old Ones? Or is there any other possible reason?"

"We are not entirely certain; this is to some degree speculation, as you know," the Guildmaster reminded her. "Why do you ask?"

"Because it occurs to me that it is obvious that Silenos also knows that Brona is a dullahan. Why else would he keep her head and body separate? Could he not have another agenda, something related to her dullahan nature? What more do we know about dullahans?"

"Anything is possible," the Guildmaster conceded. "As for what we know of dullahans, that's rather obscure lore, more within Gallenius' fields of study. Is it not, Gallenius?"

"Yes, but to be candid, Guildmaster, I suspect much of the related lore is equivalent hearsay and speculation as well. I can tell you that there are striking similarities within the essential gist of most legends and folklore.

"It is believed that clans within the *Tuatha De Danann* and the *Daoine Sidhe* consistently resisted the Old Ones; in fact, many openly defied them.

"A few of the Old Ones took umbrage and retaliated, in some cases, quite severely. Some of the defiant clans were almost wiped out; a few survivors scattered, disappearing into the *wild*. However, other survivors of those decimated clans who could not escape were enslaved. The remnants of one such clan were doubly cursed as dullahans and slaves, and bound into the service of an Old One who styled himself as Crom, the Dark One.

"This Crom was a nasty piece of work, one who declared himself a god and demanded periodic living sacrifices. He was also rumored to be the original source of the dark sorcery of *necromancy*—something that I believe would be wise to keep in mind.

"Crom's cursed servants, the dullahans, were tasked with collecting the souls of the condemned, and dealing with anyone else who ran afoul of the Dark One and incurred his wrath. The dullahans came to be associated with death, most often a harrowing and violent death.

"It is believed that when the Old Ones were bound and banished, Crom's curse of slavery was broken and the dullahans were freed. However, they could not change their unique nature. Consequently, they drifted into the *wild* as solitary beings. Over time they survived, and occasionally intermingled with other races. Halflings, like Brona, are rare and tend to be secretive. Pure bloods, like her mother, Boand, are extremely rare. Very few have been encountered, but they are known to still exist."

Selene shook her head and smiled. "I have heard similar tales, but I have never met one. I hope my luck is about to change. Do not worry, Barnabas, we will do everything we can to rescue your daughter. I have to meet her!"

Barnabas gave her a sad smile in return. "I only hope we have time."

The Guildmaster raised a gloved hand to make a point. "Remember that Silenos seeks that which he does not yet have, but believes is essential to his plans, the *iron ouroboros.* That may give us the time we need."

"True," Gallenius observed, "but we do not know its location either. Commencing a search of our own may well be a waste of time; and time is a scarce enough resource under these circumstances. Our ignorance handicaps us; we cannot accurately gauge Silenos' progress in his search. However, careful surveillance may be our best viable option. Fortunately, we do know where he is going."

The Guildmaster nodded to the mage. "Indeed, that would be playing to our strengths. See to it."

"Immediately," said Gallenius, pushing away from the table.

"One moment, if you please," Selene interjected. "I'd like to get back to something we sort of passed over—the *ears*. Guildmaster, you said that may be *significant.* What is that all about?"

The Guildmaster gestured for Gallenius to keep his seat; the mage nodded and complied.

"Needless to say, this information must be kept on a *need-to-know* basis," the Guildmaster cautioned. "There may be some significance in the act of taking the duke's ears as *trophies.* There may also be significance in this satyr's use of the name, *Silenos.* Gallenius, could you explain?"

"Of course, Guildmaster. We are aware that a very long time ago, sometime around the formation of the Council, there was another plague of necromancy that infested almost all of the known realms."

"What?" Selene blurted. "I've never heard of this!"

"That is no surprise—very few have," the mage offered. "When it was ultimately dealt with, any related records were purged or sealed at the urging and insistence of the Dragon Lords. These days very few, even within the administrating houses of the member realms, are fully aware that this happened. However, it *did* happen. There are secret records that our guild has been aware of for some time."

Selene nodded in acceptance. "So, what happened?"

"A magic user, well versed in the dark arts, including *necromancy,* arose. He was said to be a satyr who used the name *Silenos.* He traveled from realm to realm practicing the dark arts, taking advantage of whatever and whomever he found. The few who tried to oppose him were slain, and stripped of their *true names.* If the victims were of noble blood, or mages of some standing, their ears were taken and dipped in molten gold to be preserved as trophies. Like all of this necromancer's victims, their soulless bodies were resurrected as the walking dead, slaves to this self-proclaimed *Lord of the Dead*.

"It appeared no one could stop this necromancer. His persistent horde of rampaging dead feasted upon any living flesh. Few escaped. Victims fell, only to be resurrected as shambling infantry in an inexorable tide of corrupted conquest. In time, no realm was spared the ubiquitous horror; all suffered to some degree.

"In fact, some scholars have speculated that this may have inspired, deep in the genetic memory of many of the affected races, the frightening concept of a *zombie apocalypse*. Ah, forgive me, I digress.

"Finally, the Dragon Lords interceded. We suspect they recognized the taint of necromancy as a ploy of the Old Ones, likely an attempt to engineer their return. We may never know for certain. The actual fate of this Silenos is unknown. Thanks to the Dragon Lords' intervention, the threat of the risen dead was soon over, and quite literally buried.

"This was the genesis of the specific prohibition against necromancy within all spheres of Council influence. The Dragon Lords were adamant; necromancy was not to be tolerated.

"And now another satyr, well versed in the same dark arts, and using the same name has surfaced. Another instance of the taking of ears as trophies has happened. Is this all mere coincidence? We simply do not know. However, it would not be wise to ignore the similarities."

"Indeed," intoned the Guildmaster. "Of course, it is highly unlikely, nigh on impossible, that this is the same *Silenos*. However, I seriously doubt the use of this name is coincidence. We have firsthand accounts of his use of spells of necromancy. We know he has an agenda, and has harmed others in its pursuit. We are not completely certain of his endgame; but, we have our suspicions.

"Be that as it may, we have one priority before us now, one that is absolute; we must rescue Brona from his grip, and soon."

"Aye, but we need a plan," Barnabas insisted. "I have no clue what Padraic had in mind."

"Actually, he gave you some very good hints," Gallenius countered, "a thief, and one or two others, yes?"

"Yes, that's what he said. So?"

Gallenius raised a finger. "We know where Silenos is going; and, we know he has a pressing need to search for that which he lacks. We know he must offload his cargo, Brona, from the *Xanthippe.* Circe will insist on that once they make port. I doubt Silenos would want to be encumbered with this *extra cargo* in his pending quest. So, he will likely need someplace to safely keep Brona, probably someplace in New Port Royal, while he searches for the iron ouroboros. Remember, New Port Royal is a lawless place. If we can learn where she is to be kept, then we will have need of the thief."

The Guildmaster chuckled. "Trust me, we already have an expert thief."

Barnabas nodded. "I get it, but then we need to get her out of New Port Royal. Won't we need a ship?"

"We were thinking it might be best," the Guildmaster explained, "to transit her out of Mer entirely."

"Transit?" Barnabas echoed. "Won't we need the Steward for that?"

"I'm sure she'd be willing to help," Gallenius sighed, "if she's willing to work with our thief."

"Your *thief?* Oh no—*him?"* Selene snorted and clapped her hands. "Oh, good luck with that!"

THE FOULED ANCHOR WAS filling up with the usual evening crowd. Perched on the staircase landing, Topsey, attired in a black bustier trimmed in scarlet feathers, smoothed the front of her multiple petticoats of red lace. She leaned on the railing and cast her eye approvingly over the gaming tables; there were few empty seats. She caught her partner's eye at the bar and motioned with a tilt of her head to a few of her ladies bunched near one end of the bar.

Rumley nodded and sauntered down there. At the clearing of his throat and a smiling wink, Topsey's *hostesses* knew to start circulating among the patrons.

Topsey was a practiced hand at predicting the behavior of eager sailors newly come ashore. She knew a number of vessels had docked with the incoming tide, and their freshly paid crews would soon be venturing into town. It was likely to be a good night.

That reminded her; she had a bit of related news to share with her partner, the barkeep. Yes, better to do so now, before the night got too lively.

She sighed, pasted a practiced smile upon her face, and descended the stairs to the floor of the saloon. With an exaggerated sway to her hips she strolled through the gaming tables, patting a familiar cheek here, touching a favored patron's shoulder there, generally flirting with the regulars on her way to the bar.

Rumley met her with a small glass of watered sherry. "Looks to be a good night, I think."

She sipped and nodded. "Aye, the more ships in port, the more coin in our pockets."

"So? I can tell you have news."

She smiled at him. "Can you now? Gettin' a bit familiar, are we?"

He grinned. "Ah, love it, you do. Now, what is it?"

She turned, faced the room, and leaned against the bar, her elbows on the bar top. She sensed Rumley leaning forward and watching the room; he would easily hear her every whispered word. She let her eyes roam over the patrons as she spoke softly over her shoulder.

"The *Xanthippe* docked in the last hour, but her crew's not come ashore yet. Her master, Circe, and 'Bloody' Bane met dockside."

"Hmm, the *Doom Wind* has been here for days. Her crew is running short of coin. Have the captains some business with each other?"

Topsey sipped a bit more sherry. "Apparently some, but it may not have gone well. The junk was not expected this soon. I understand Bane was surprised at her arrival, and no happier after he and the sea witch met. It seems some expected payment was not forthcoming."

"Ah, let me guess, for his part in the relay they ran?"

She sighed. "So it seems. There is more; the *incognito passenger*, who no one was supposed to know about, is still aboard the *Xanthippe* with some questionably strange cargo."

"Oh, Circe won't like that. She likes to keep her junk's hold empty and ready for business."

"Aye, she's made no bones about it. She wants that passenger and his cargo off her vessel soonest. It seems Bane wants nothing more to do with that passenger or his cargo either. He's angry and has announced that the *Doom Wind* will sail with the morning tide."

Rumley scratched his wiry hair at the back of his neck. "Then something else has happened. Tis not like Circe to short Bane whatever is due him. Mayhap she did not get paid either?"

Topsey sipped from her glass. "Methinks that's the right of it. Word is that this passenger seeks storage space for his cargo here, while he tends to something else."

"I see," Rumley nodded knowingly. "And do we know of this passenger?"

Topsey turned to face him, raising one eyebrow. "Aye, we do; he is called *Silenos.*"

"Indeed? So," Rumley reasoned, "the Guildmaster was right. I suppose we now have our work cut out for us?"

"Indeed, we do, my love, indeed we do."

Topsey drained her glass, plunked it down, and spun away from the bar in a swirl of red lace.

She looked over her shoulder, gave Rumley a tired smile, and blew him a kiss.

(The tale continues in MER, Part 2, Volume V, of THE STEWARD)

[PART 2]

CH 25

HAWK WAS AT A LOSS for words—almost. "You gotta be kidding me—Padraic? Mass murder? I don't buy it!"

Trey leaned back in the kitchen chair and shook his head. "Yeah, something is off here. So far, Mark, everything you've told us is circumstantial at best. It sounds like there's no direct evidence."

Mark just shrugged and shook his head. "I don't know any more than what I've told you."

"Okay . . . So, based on that, *Counselor*," Trey asked, "what's your *legal assessment* on all of this?"

Leaning forward, his elbows on the kitchen table, Mark sighed and opened his palms. "Look, I agree with you—it's circumstantial. But I'm not sure there's anything we can do about it. I don't know that much about Derinseum's system of justice; what I've heard so far is pretty vague, and pretty harsh."

"So, they're still holding him," Hawk probed, "on what—*suspicion?*"

"I think so—but I'm not sure that's all," Mark admitted and nudged his cooling coffee. "I suspect there may be some political considerations as well. The fact is we just don't have enough information."

"Not yet," Ellen interjected, "but that's gonna change. Gallenius sent word that the Guildmaster wants to see me, and that it has to do with Mer. That means they know something—more than we do at this point. So, as soon as my mother and Stacy get back, I'm off to Storm Haven."

"They just went to the post office?" Hawk asked.

Ellen sipped from her coffee mug. "Yeah, right after lunch, so they shouldn't be too long. My mom had to send in a tax form and she wanted to send it certified with a return receipt."

Trey nodded in approval. "Always a good idea."

"So, you're going to Storm Haven alone?" Hawk asked.

"Yeah, I have to. The message from Gallenius was specific; they need to see me alone."

"How long will you be gone, do you think?" Mark asked.

Ellen shrugged. "I dunno, but I'm gonna keep this visit to under an hour, if I can."

Hawk looked to his partner. "What do you think? Can we wait?"

"An hour or so?" Trey checked his watch. "Maybe, let me check in with the office; give me a minute." He pulled out his phone.

"Hey!" Ellen grabbed Hawk's wrist. "I forgot to ask; how did your drone search go? Any luck?"

Hawk grinned sheepishly. "Aw, we gotta try again. We went out to the area and got all set up; but, we didn't have a lot of time to work with the drones. My fault, I screwed up and didn't fully charge all the batteries before we left the office; so, we only got about twenty minutes of flight time with the big drone. It looked like some weather was coming in, so we called it a day. Next time, I'll make sure the batteries are fully charged."

"Oh well, at least you'll get to play with your new toys another day," she teased.

He grinned, bobbed his head, and silently mouthed, *I know!*

Trey ended his call. "Okay, we're good for the next hour or so, but we gotta get back before the evening-shift briefing."

"Great!" Hawk stood, reached for the coffee carafe, and sloshed its meager contents around. "Anybody want some more coffee? I can make another pot."

The dogs suddenly alerted, rose from their sleeping pads on either side of the old iron stove, and shook themselves. Of course, Smokey was nowhere to be seen. After stretching, the Chows went to the kitchen door leading to the backyard and stood there patiently, their attention focused on the door.

Ellen chuckled. "Well, I think my mom and Stacy are back."

A moment later, the door swung open. Millie and Stacy entered the kitchen, each bearing an armload of shopping bags.

"Oh hi, y'all!" Stacy exclaimed, setting her bags down on the table. "We stopped at a roadside vegetable stand on the way back. Sorry if we took too long." She dropped to one knee to pet the dogs.

"Here, let me help you put this stuff away, Mom," Ellen offered, taking Millie's bags from her. "And then I gotta make a quick trip to Storm Haven. I'll be back in about an hour."

"Storm Haven?" echoed Stacy, rising. "Is this about Padraic? Can I go with?"

"Padraic?" Ellen shrugged as she emptied the grocery bags. "Yeah, I think so; and no—I have to go alone. I got a message from Gallenius shortly after you two left, but before Hawk and Trey got here. I was just waiting for y'all to get back. The sooner I go, the sooner I'll be back. So, if y'all will just sit tight—"

Smokey suddenly leapt upon the table, sat before Ellen, and stared up into her eyes.

Stacy snorted in laughter. "Ha! I think Smokey is telling you that he's going with you—you're not going alone after all!"

Ellen stared at the cat and sighed. "Uh-huh, and where have *you* been? Okay, I get the message."

Turning to the others, she declared, "Very well, *we* will be back shortly."

With that she scooped Smokey up in her arms and started for the backyard to summon a transit globe.

Millie shook her head and chuckled. "Never a dull moment around here."

AS SHE HAD PREDICTED, Ellen returned to her kitchen, Smokey in her arms, in just under an hour.

"Oh, Ellen, you're back!" announced Millie. "Wait—what is it? What's wrong?"

Her lips pursed and brow furrowed, Ellen sat down and let the cat spill from her lap. She looked around her kitchen to see that Miska had joined those waiting for her. Their conversations had paused, all attention now on her. She sighed heavily.

"This trip was not what I expected. Bear with me. I have quite the tale to tell—two tales, I think, that are quite likely to be related. To begin with, it seems I have another cousin . . . "

For the next few minutes, her audience sat in rapt, open-mouthed silence, as Ellen spoke of Padraic, Barnabas, and her newly discovered cousin, Brona.

When she concluded, the silence persisted.

Miska broke the spell. "So, that is what Padraic meant when he said that he was *trying to rescue your cousin?*"

"Right. He did not mean Mark," Ellen confirmed.

"But Padraic got arrested before he could do this?" Miska asked.

"Yes, the Guildmaster suspects his arrest may be tied to the kidnapping of Brona, in the sense that the same person may be ultimately responsible."

"This person being *Silenos?"* Trey asked.

Ellen nodded. "Yes. As I said, he's a *satyr,* and it's pretty well confirmed, a *necromancer."*

Hawk raised a finger. "Hold on a minute. So the reasons the Guildmaster thinks this Silenos is framing Padraic for the murders is the *name* he's using, and the fact that one of the victim's ears were taken? And that's consistent with a pattern of behavior believed to have been displayed by the historic Silenos?"

Ellen shrugged. "I don't know if those are his *only* reasons. I don't think the Guildmaster knows whether *framing* Padraic is even deliberate. It's more like he's *comfortable* with the idea that Silenos did commit the murders. However, he's absolutely convinced Silenos kidnapped Brona."

Trey leaned toward Hawk and murmured, "Taking ears as trophies . . ."

"Yeah, I know," Hawk dropped his voice, "that's a serial-killer behavioral trait."

Everyone had heard; a moment of awkward silence ensued.

"Uh, El', you said the Guildmaster had a plan," Mark reminded her. "Care to share?"

"Oh, yeah, but first . . ." She paused, biting her lip, and turned to her mother. "Mom, I gotta ask, did Padraic ever mention, or tell you about his half brother, Barnabas? Or Barnabas' daughter, Brona?"

Millie shook her head. "No, he rarely talked about any of his family—but I knew there had to be some family somewhere. Whenever I'd ask, he'd change the subject. Over time, he'd let some things slip, so I kinda got a vague picture. I once heard him and Maude arguing in hushed tones about Oberon, so I always suspected Oberon was somehow involved. I don't know why he or Maude never told me the truth—probably some misguided sense of protecting me. I'm glad to know now; although it doesn't really change anything."

"Either of them should have told you, Mom."

"Perhaps, but what's done is done—and I'm comfortable with the truth, even if it was late in coming."

"I see. Okay, let's focus on the problem at hand."

Ellen leaned back in her chair. "To be honest, I'm still having a problem wrapping my head around all of this.

"Here's what's weirding me out; Brona's mother was Boand, a *dullahan,* who hasn't been around for years. So, Brona is *half dullahan.* Like the dullahans in Celtic folklore, she can separate her head from her body—but she's still *alive!* When she was kidnapped, her head and body were separated and are being kept separate; somehow that inhibits her abilities or something. Anyway, to rescue her, both her head and her body have to be rescued."

Trey and Hawk were speechless. Millie's eyes grew wide. Mark stared slack-jawed at his cousin.

Stacy simply murmured, "Whoa!"

Miska looked around the table at the stunned expressions of his friends and chuckled. "Despite all you have seen and experienced, is this so hard to accept? I have met a few dullahans in my time. True, they are very rare, and often solitary, but they are no different from any other being who prefers to be left alone. Does not Miss Ellen's cousin, Brona, merit our help?"

Eyes dropped and heads bobbed in chagrin.

"Oh, Miska," Stacy mockingly scolded, "you know we're going to help! We're just surprised is all! So, Ellen has a cousin who's a dullahan; how cool is that?"

Hawk chuckled. "Can you imagine how our friends in the *Middle Earth Society* will react to this sort of news? That'll be priceless! But seriously, you know we will do anything we can to help, all of us, right?"

"Yeah, we're in!" Mark declared. "So what's the plan?"

"Yeah, the plan . . . about that," Ellen winced.

"What?" Hawk asked, a hint of suspicion creeping into his voice. "Go on."

"The Guildmaster told me that they know Silenos and Brona are aboard the *Xanthippe,* a ship that's headed for New Port Royal, an island seaport that's more of a pirate lair. Anyway, when they get there, Silenos will want to offload his cargo, Brona, and try to find someplace to keep her while he goes in search of something he believes he needs, some sort of amulet. The plan is to find out where Brona is to be kept, using a thief at this point, and then have me transit her away."

"So, you're supposed to go to Mer, this pirate lair, and transit her away?" Trey asked. "That's it?"

Ellen nodded. "Yes, essentially."

Hawk shook his head. "Sounds too simple and way too dangerous. Do they expect you to do this alone? I don't think any of us are cool with you doing this alone."

"Yeah, that doesn't sound good at all," Stacy remarked. "Would you be expected to help find her as well—you know, work with this thief?"

"Well," she hedged. "I might have to, it'll depend on the situation. You can't always predict what's gonna happen, you know?"

"Ellen," Trey asked evenly, "what aren't you telling us? What's the catch?"

"Yeah, there's gotta be a catch," Mark agreed. "Didn't you say that Brona's head and body have been separated? Doesn't that mean you'll have to find and transit both? Or can Brona, uh, reassemble herself?"

Ellen sighed. "Find and transit both if they're separated? Yes, of course. But I don't know if she can get herself together or not. I don't have all the answers; no one does."

"Wait a minute," Hawk interjected. "Ellen, you haven't answered the question; what's the catch? I'm guessing it's the thief. That's it, isn't it? Just who is this thief?"

Ellen looked into his eyes and nodded. The room grew very quiet.

"The thief is Salidar."

"Salidar!" Hawk bolted to his feet. "That bastar—"

Trey grabbed his partner's arm and pulled him back into his seat. "Enough! Let her finish."

"No way you're doing this!" Hawk declared at Ellen. "He's wanted for questioning in—"

"Do you think I don't know that?" she spat. "Do you think I'm stupid? Where do you get off—"

Millie laid a calming hand on her daughter's arm. "Easy, honey—he's just worried about you."

Ellen stared into her lap. "I know! I know! Please, just give me some credit." She looked up and around the table. "What makes you think I've agreed to do this—without consulting y'all and forming our own strategy?"

Crestfallen, Hawk apologized. "Ellen, I'm sorry. I just—"

She held up her hands. "I know. Look, rescuing my cousin is the goal; so, I'm willing to do this—but on *my* terms. Under the circumstances, working with the Guildmaster and uh, *certain unsavory assets* may be in our best interest. So, let's begin brainstorming with that in mind. Oh, and don't forget that we have another goal of equal importance—to clear Padraic. Now, shall we put our heads together?"

The mood in the kitchen had changed; a focused intensity prevailed.

HOURS LATER, AFTER Trey and Hawk had returned to their office, Millie bustled about in the kitchen, preparing supper and paying half attention to the quiet discussion going on at the table.

Ellen leaned toward her cousin. "So, Mark, you're sure you can get Trey and Hawk involved in the Derinseum investigation of Padraic?"

"Relax, El', and have a little faith in my powers of persuasion." He winked at her. "Trey already promised to share with the Captain of the Watch what they learned from the forensic exam of the projectiles recovered from the burned corpses of the *zombied* watchmen. So, if that report is back from the lab and they show up in Derinseum with a copy of it, that'll be perfect because it's expected. After that gesture of goodwill and support, I'm sure I can get them involved, or at least consulting, in Padraic's case."

"My, aren't we confident," Stacy teased, but relented. "Actually, Ellen, I think he's right; I don't think the Watch will turn down the help. But even if they did, our guys could still stick around in Derinseum for a while. They'd still be your backup, but like on *standby*."

"See? It'll still work," Mark insisted. "Having backup is the only way Hawk is gonna let you do this without a fight."

"Stop already! He doesn't control me, so don't even go there! He knows he goes along with the plan or he's out! He can stay home if—"

Mark threw up his hands in surrender. "All right! All right! I didn't mean to stir that pot. I'm sorry."

"Really, Mark," Stacy scolded, "you know Hawk was more amenable once Ellen said she'd take Miska with her. So why don't you focus on your role. We all have our jobs to do, right?"

"Hey, yeah, I get it. Sorry!"

Turning to his cousin, he said, "Ellen, don't worry, we'll be fine in Derinseum if you need us. But I still don't know how we'd get to you in New Port Royal in a hurry."

"You let me worry about that, okay? I've got it covered. Sorry, I didn't mean to go off on you," Ellen offered, slightly mollified.

Hawk mumbled in acquiescence, "It's okay."

Changing the subject, Millie asked, "Ellen, dear, when are you going to go back to Storm Haven and let the Guildmaster know your decision?"

Ellen stroked her chin. "You know, I may as well do it now; it won't take but a few minutes. Are you up for a quick trip, Miska?"

Miska grunted as Smokey leapt into his lap. "Oof! Yes, I am ready. I think Smokey is, too."

Ellen chuckled. "Why am I not surprised?"

"Don't be long now," Millie warned. "Supper will be ready shortly."

"Do not worry, Miss Millie," Miska assured her, "I would never miss your suppers!"

"True dat!" Stacy cackled, as they headed out the back door.

STANDING IN THE BACKYARD, Ellen glanced at her watch, and looked up to Miska. "Before I summon a transit globe, I want you to know we are going to make a detour and meet someone before we go to Storm Haven. It won't take long. However, it is important, and you are not to speak of this to anyone; do you understand?"

He cradled Smokey in one arm as he scratched his temple with his free hand. "I understand, but is this not part of our plan, our overall strategy?"

"Not exactly, it's more like *insurance.* I guess that's the best way to describe it. However, it works best if we keep it a secret for now, okay?"

He shrugged his massive shoulders. "Okay, whatever you think is best."

She smiled and summoned the globe.

In the next moment, they were gone.

THE GUILDMASTER HEARD the soft knock upon his door and put the stack of scrolls to one side.

Gallenius poked his head in and announced, "Guildmaster, Lady Ellen and Smokey have returned; they are not alone. Miska of the Ursus clan accompanies them."

"I see. Well, show them in. Then find Barnabas and have him join us."

As soon as Ellen and Miska entered, Smokey leapt from the big man's arms onto the Guildmaster's desk and began to groom himself.

The Guildmaster came from behind his desk and opened his gloved hands. "I bid you welcome, m'lady, and you as well, Miska. Have you come to a decision?"

"I have," Ellen answered. "I will participate in this rescue; but, I have conditions."

"Please, go on."

"Miska will accompany me at all times. My cousin, Mark, and my friends, Hawk and Trey, will be in Derinseum to look into the matter of Padraic's current difficulty, and act as my backup if needed."

"I see no problem with that," the Guildmaster assured her. "In fact, I hope they can be of assistance in getting to the truth of that matter. I do not doubt Padraic's innocence."

"Nor do I, so—"

A knock on the door interrupted her. Gallenius had returned with Barnabas.

"Ah, Barnabas, please join us." The Guildmaster motioned him in with a sweep of his hand. "Our friend, Miska, will be assisting Lady Ellen in our plan."

Barnabas nodded to the big man, but kept silent.

The Guildmaster raised a gloved finger. "Gallenius, would you find Salidar and—"

"One moment, if you please," Ellen interjected. "Before your *thief* joins us, let us further discuss my conditions, shall we?"

The Guildmaster motioned for Gallenius to stay. "Of course, please continue."

Hands on her hips, she nodded to Barnabas, but directed her words to the Guildmaster.

"As you well know, I have no reason to trust Salidar, and more than sufficient reason to *distrust* him. I hold him responsible in part for the death of my aunt, Maude Delafaire, and for harm that affected me personally. He is a wanted man in my home realm. If he ever sets foot there, he will be brought to justice; his freedom may be forfeit.

"Now, that said, I am willing to work with him to rescue Brona—*if* I have your word that he will not betray *any* of us. This is not negotiable. Am I clear, Guildmaster?"

Silence hung in the room for a long moment.

The Guildmaster sighed. "You have my word. In truth, I think you may find him a changed man."

He nodded to Gallenius, who slipped from the room.

"Lady Ellen," said Barnabas, "thank you for doing this."

She nodded in response, but remained silent.

Gallenius returned with Salidar, who stood with his head down, making no eye contact.

For the next few minutes, the Guildmaster instructed Salidar in his role in the rescue mission.

Salidar appeared to listen intently and asked no questions.

When the Guildmaster finished, he turned to Ellen and asked, "M'lady, have we overlooked anything? Have you anything to add?"

"Just this," she said and faced the thief, "Know this, Salidar, I do not trust you. Fail any of us in this endeavor, and I promise you will rue the day."

The Guildmaster faced Salidar and placed both gloved hands upon the thief's shoulders. "Your guild oath binds you. Do your best."

Releasing him, the Guildmaster turned to the rest of those assembled. "I believe that concludes our business. You are all excused. Lady Ellen, please stay a moment; I believe Gallenius needs a word with you. Barnabas will you join me for a meal?"

Of course, Miska stayed by her side.

Gallenius nodded in acknowledgment to the big man, and extended his open palm to Ellen.

"Lady Ellen, this topaz ring you may recognize. As before, the stone has been infused with a powerful spell. However, this time it is a transit spell that anyone may use, one that will permit the user to take large objects with them. We cannot anticipate every possible contingency, of course, but should you see a need for such a spell—well, you know."

She took the ring; indeed, she did recognize it. "You realize, of course, that *I* won't likely need it—but then again, you never know. I presume its destination is Storm Haven, with a number of diversions possibly triggered?"

Gallenius smiled. "Yes, essentially so, although the diversions and seemingly endless loops are only intended to thoroughly obscure any destination and defeat any tracing spells. There are no *dire* diversionary destinations; after all, we would like the ring back."

She grinned and slipped the ring on her finger. "I get it. I assure you, Gallenius, you'll get your ring back." She held the splayed fingers of her hand out at arm's length and noted the vibrant reflections of the coffee-hued gem. "Hmm, it's a bit much for my taste; nonetheless, I'll take good care of it. Now don't let me keep you from your supper."

Miska nudged her and whispered, "Or us, too?"

She laughed. "Nor us. Get Smokey; we're going home."

MILLIE HAD THE TABLE set for supper when Ellen and Miska entered through the back door. The aroma of Millie's cooking was, as usual, simply wonderful.

Miska grinned, letting Smokey drop to the floor, and nudged Ellen.

"Good timing, eh?"

She bobbed her head. "Oh yeah, that smells good."

Stacy and Mark entered from the formal dining room, followed by Trey and Hawk, now off duty.

Hands on her hips, Millie smiled. "It looks like everyone's here. Ellen, Stacy, would you help me serve? The rest of you, please take seats. The entrées this evening include Creole seafood bisque, crawfish etouffee, warm baguettes, and spinach salad. For dessert, we have lemon tarts."

"Oh man, that sounds good," Mark declared, pulling out a chair.

"Oh, by the way, I heard from the Council; Queen Titania issued an official statement regarding the murder of Duke Briar. It's pretty much what we expected, an expression of shock and sorrow, and a call for swift justice. She didn't name Padraic at all. However, sources within her court have whispered that he hasn't been held in too high a regard in her eyes lately. I don't know why—if something happened, nobody is talking."

"Did she indicate if she would go to Mer?" Ellen asked.

Mark shook his head. "No, there was nothing like that in her formal statement."

"What about the Dark Elves, has Queen Mab said anything?" Stacy asked as she put a wide plate of warm loaves of bread on the table. "You'd think she'd say something, since Padraic is her consort, right?"

Mark scoffed. "You'd think, but nope, nothing but silence so far. Of course, that doesn't mean she won't have something to say. In fact, a number of people at the Council are very surprised that she has yet to issue a statement, formal or otherwise."

Ellen gnawed her lip. She knew this meant something; but, she didn't know what.

Millie handed her a tray of filled salad bowls and tilted her head at the table. Ellen took the hint and distributed the salads.

As she placed a bowl before Trey, she asked, "Are you guys good to go to Derinseum like we discussed?"

"We are, if the day after tomorrow works for you. We're supposed to get the forensic report that we'll need tomorrow. After that we both have two days off. Do you think that will be enough time?"

She thought a moment and said, "Actually, that timing is almost perfect. Salidar is supposed to be in New Port Royal tomorrow; so, that gives him a day to search for the storage location of Silenos' *cargo*. When he finds it, he's to notify Gallenius who will in turn notify me. I'll be in Derinseum with you all until then."

Hawk grumbled. "I'm still not comfortable having to wait in Derinseum while you work with Salidar in New Port Royal. How are we supposed to be your backup if we're that far away?"

She smiled sweetly at him. "I told you not to worry about it. I've got it covered. Besides, Miska will be with me. You're just gonna have to trust me on this."

"All right, people, that's enough shoptalk," Millie insisted. "Your supper is served. Enjoy."

NIGHT HAD FALLEN ON Olmus when Vito entered George's private chamber.

"Sorry to bug you, Boss, but Circe just showed up and she needs to talk to you about some product. She's in the lab cavern with Teddy."

"With Teddy? That's a surprise," George grumbled. "I thought she freaked him out—right?"

Vito chuckled. "Oh, she does, and I think she knows it. She makes a point of speaking to him. He'd like you to come down there and bail him out. You comin'?"

"Yeah, let's go. I wish she'd leave him be. Disrupting his concentration affects production."

They found Circe hovering around the nervous meth cook as he was pouring some liquid from one beaker into another. Her lizard, perched on her thin shoulder, flicked its tongue and leered at Teddy's fingers like they were a potential snack.

George noticed there were no goblin servants in the vicinity; it appeared they gave the sea witch as wide a berth as they did Vito. *Jeez, as creepy as she is, who can blame them?*

"Circe!" he hailed. "Good to see you! How can I help you? Come walk with me and let Teddy get back to work."

She smiled at Teddy and sucked air through her teeth before turning toward George and nodding in greeting.

Vito nudged his boss. "Should I go get Daegon?"

George smiled at the approaching sea witch and murmured, "Good idea. We'll be in the next chamber."

Vito slipped from the cavern as Circe stood before George.

"Well, Circe, we weren't expecting you. Is there a problem?"

"Not one I can't deal with. A deal fell through, a temporary setback only. I need to push my plans up sooner than I would have liked. Can we talk?"

"Sure, follow me." He led the way into the candlelit chamber; a rough table and a number of benches were within. "Have a seat."

She sat, but wasted no time. "I need as much meth as you can supply me. I must establish myself in Derinseum as soon as possible."

Daegon and Vito entered the chamber; George waved them to seats as well.

"What is going on, Circe?" George asked. "Not that we can't accommodate you, but why so soon? I thought you wanted more time to deal with some other stuff you had going?"

Circe leaned her staff against the table. Her lizard curled its tail around her neck and flicked its tongue in nervous arcs. She stroked her pet until it calmed.

"I did want more time," she admitted, "but as I said, a deal fell through. I need to refill my coffers and meet certain obligations. The samples of your product have had the intended effect; there is now considerable demand in Derinseum. The time is right to capitalize on it."

Daegon glanced at George and Vito and posed a question of his own.

"Circe, has something happened with the necromancer, Silenos? Were not you involved with him in this latest deal you mentioned?"

She looked away, meeting no one's eyes.

"Circe?" George prompted.

"Yes!" she spat. "We were betrayed by Light Elves! They did not pay me as promised, which puts me in debt to others! As for Silenos, the Light Elves dropped their support and threatened him—a serious mistake, I think. I suspect he has resorted to certain extreme measures of retribution. He previously expressed an interest in my anticipated enterprise related to *our* business relationship. However, in view of his unpredictability and what he may have already rashly done, I would distance myself from him. I would advise you to do so as well."

"What has he done?" Daegon asked.

She shook her head. "I know not for certain, but I suspect he *has* done something. I am sure no good will come of it. I must avoid his taint. That is why I must push my meth distribution plans forward soonest, and become established in Derinseum."

"Just what does he know," George pressed, "about *our business relationship?*"

She dropped her eyes. "Nothing specific. He only knows that I believe Derinseum to be a potentially lucrative market. I said as much and warned him not to muck it up for me when he started considering retribution. But as I said, I do not know what he may have done."

"Where is Silenos now?" Vito asked.

The sea witch shrugged. "I left him in New Port Royal. He was in search of storage space for his cargo. I had my crew offload his cargo soon after we docked. My vessel is still there."

"I gotta ask," George pressed. "You know you can get our product directly from here into Derinseum, so why do you want it now when your boat is in New Port Royal? Won't you have to sail with it into Derinseum?"

"Yes, that is my intention. It is necessary for appearances sake," she insisted. "Let me explain. No one needs to know where I get my product—certainly not that it comes from off-realm. I intend to set up shop, an actual legitimate shop in Derinseum. The product will come in as shipborne cargo, aboard the *Xanthippe.* Since my vessel is heavily transit-warded, I must take delivery onshore at New Port Royal. Do you see?"

George smiled. "Oh, I do indeed. It makes sense; and, I think that's pretty slick. So, you're not doing anything so out of the ordinary as to attract undue attention from the authorities, right?"

Circe bobbed her head. "Right! So long as the Merchants Guild gets their cut, as an established and sanctioned businesswoman, I'll enjoy their protection. I can effectively operate anywhere in Mer."

George bowed his head in respect. "You're a smart woman, Circe. I'm sure this will be a beneficial arrangement for both of us, especially if we keep our operations as hidden as possible."

Daegon raised a finger. "But, Silenos? What does he really know about us? I would be remiss were I not to speak of this. There is something very disturbing in the flavor of his particular necromancy, something darkly arcane that smacks of the Old Ones. I find that frightening at best. He could be a problem, I think."

Vito nodded. "He's got a point, Boss. What are we gonna do about Silenos?"

George stroked his chin. "Yeah, that guy is bad news. For now we're gonna avoid him like the plague, *capisce?*"

Everyone nodded in silent affirmation.

No one, except Circe's curious lizard, noticed the pair of eavesdropping goblins lingering within a deeply shadowed crevasse high above in the craggy ceiling, missing nary a word.

CH 26

RUMLEY PLACED THE MUG of grog on the bar before the hooded customer who kept his back to the rest of the patrons seated at the Fouled Anchor's gaming tables.

The barman leaned forward and kept his voice low.

"Most do not know ye. A few patrons might remember your last visit; so, tis wise to keep a low profile."

"The *Doom Wind?"* Salidar asked.

Rumley shook his head. "Set sail days ago with all hands, after the *Xanthippe* docked and the captains met."

"And the sea witch? Gone now, as well?"

Rumley wiped at the bar top with a small towel. "Aye, took her vessel out with the morning tide, she did. So, there should be none ashore who might know you well. Nonetheless, draw no undue attention."

"What was the captains' meeting about?" Salidar sipped his grog.

"We know not; only that neither was satisfied, nor got paid. Bane was angry, but not at Circe directly. He left in a huff, and sailed the next morning with the tide. Circe offloaded her passenger's cargo and left it on the dock under the watchful eyes of his fauns. Her passenger then went in search of secure storage space for his cargo."

Salidar wiped a bit of grog foam from his lip. "Did he find some?"

"We suspect so." Rumley slid a small piece of folded paper across the bar.

Salidar deftly palmed the scrap as Rumley continued.

"He found a man called *Rathskellen,* a mercenary elfin halfling, who pursued a long career as a pirate, and now stores smuggled or stolen goods for a price. He maintains at least three warehouses in and around the town that we know of; there may be others. You should assume they will be guarded. We know not which one now holds the cargo in question. Determining *that* will be part of your task."

Salidar sipped deeply and whispered, "I understand. So, this passenger, *Silenos,* where is he now?"

Rumley shrugged. "We know not; only that he transited off realm once he secured storage space for his cargo. Our information is that he is now in search of some arcane amulet."

Salidar drained his mug and wiped his lips upon his sleeve. "And what of his fauns, did they go with him after his cargo was stored?"

Rumley nodded. "It would appear so; they have not been seen here since. What will you do?"

Salidar fingered the scrap of paper and grinned. "What is expected of me, of course. I will return to you, as planned, once I have the answers I seek. Is there anything else I need be aware of?"

"Perhaps there is," Rumley warned. "Circe transited off realm, after her crew offloaded the passenger's cargo and Silenos went looking for storage space. She was back within the hour. We do not know where she went."

"This is significant?" Salidar pressed, his curiosity piqued.

"It could be. For some unknown reason, she never travels off realm, or at least has not done so until recently. We think that such a change in her behavior may indeed be significant; but we know not why or how. Just keep it in mind, savvy?"

"I will." Salidar pushed his mug forward. "Another, well watered, if you please? I have some time to while away yet; I'll need my wits about me. Be assured I will be about my task after the full fall of night."

Rumley nodded in approval. "Good. As you were already told, 'do your best.'"

LORD NIGHTSHADE DID not expect to run into Queen Mab in the wide gallery hallway overlooking the grand ballroom of her castle. He had intended to seek an audience with her later in the day to offer his report. However, he realized now was as good a time as any, especially since it was unlikely he would hear again from his sources before tomorrow.

Her raised eyebrows were an involuntary reflex that betrayed her surprise. She looked down her nose at him in silence.

He held his low bow and waited patiently for his queen to acknowledge him. He knew not to read anything into her propensity to make her courtiers wait, frequently in less than comfortable circumstances, upon her whim.

She is either so self-absorbed that she is oblivious to the discomforts or concerns of others; or, she is indeed well aware, and takes perverse pleasure in savoring this minor token of petty sadism. Whichever the case, she always has been like this. So, despite the strain, I bide my time, as always.

She smoothed the front panel of black lace on her violet-hued gown. "Nightshade, you may rise."

He stood upright, a bland smile pasted upon his face. He glanced up and down the gallery. They appeared to be alone.

"May it please Your Majesty, I have a confirmed report that the Steward has traveled to Mer, and is there now."

"Indeed? Excellent! Do you know what she is doing there?"

"She has been seen shopping in the open markets, accompanied by female attendants, some of whom are from the household of the Lady Orla."

Mab pursed her lips and seemed to stare over his head. "She has not contacted the Derinseum Watch?"

"No, Your Majesty, she has not. Shall we continue our surveillance?"

Mab nodded. "Yes, but back off and give her some distance. She is not to know she is being watched. Inform me when she returns to her home realm."

"As you command, Your Majesty. By your leave, I shall return to my duties." He bowed once more.

She waved a hand in dismissal, effectively ignoring him, and turned toward the balustrade overlooking the ballroom below.

Nightshade held his tongue and walked away.

As he turned into a stairwell, he almost collided with Gaspar who was hurrying up the steps.

"Oh! I beg your pardon, Magus. I did not see you."

Gaspar scoffed and brushed Nightshade aside. "Out of my way! Where is the queen, in the gallery?"

Nightshade stepped back, his expression sour. He scowled with blatant distaste at the mage's atrocious manners. However, the unspoken rebuke was wasted upon the rude adept.

"Answer me! Is she there or not?" Gaspar demanded.

Nightshade squared his shoulders and faced the mage. "She was, as of a moment ago. Now, what is so—"

Ignoring him, Gaspar pushed past, and strode into the hallway without another word.

Stiffening his spine at the implied insult, Nightshade fumed for a moment, then silently followed, keeping to the shadows. His curiosity in full flare, he made his way unseen behind successive columns to an alcove, where he was within earshot of Gaspar and the queen.

"... BETTER BE DAMNED important!" Mab spat.

"The Steward is in Mer—" Gaspar began.

"Fool! I already know that! If that is all you have for me—"

"No, Your Majesty, there is more, if you please?" Gaspar groveled, physically hunching his slight shoulders and keeping his eyes downcast.

"Well? Go on!" she demanded, still in a huff.

"As we—er, *you* suspected, Your Majesty, the Steward has your *ring!* She wears it on her hand." He smiled smugly and crossed his arms.

She leaned into his face, her voice a blade of ice. "You are certain, Gaspar? There is no mistake?"

He scoffed, dropped his hands to his sides, and slowly nodded. He leaned forward as well, their faces now mere inches apart. He kept his voice low, yet heavy with earnest sincerity, and confidence.

"I saw it myself! I am quite familiar with that topaz, as you know, Your Majesty. There is no mistake; tis your ring. She *flaunts it!*"

Mab straightened. Her lips drew into a grim line; her eyes smoldered. The very air around her seemed to shimmer as pulses of anger rolled off her like the dissipating waves of a mirage.

Gaspar balked, took a step back, and smirked uneasily.

The queen, seeming once more to be in control of her ire, focused upon her mage and spoke evenly.

"I see. Is there more?"

"Yes, Your Majesty, considerably more," Gaspar assured her. "The Steward arrived in Mer with others from her realm, some of whom have been with the Derinseum Watch. Word is that they have provided assistance in the recent necromancy incident; however, I believe they are also now making inquiries regarding Padraic's current situation."

Mab laid an elegant finger along her delicate jawline. "That is interesting, indeed. I was told the Steward was shopping in the open markets? Is this true?"

"Aye, Your Majesty, she was. That is how I came to see the ring. I was in disguise, of course, lest she recognize me."

"So, she has not personally been to visit the Watch? Or check on Padraic?"

Gaspar shook his head. "No, my queen; there would be no need, not when others would do so on her behalf."

Mab scowled. "These others, do we know of them, their identities?"

Gaspar smiled once more. "We do, Your Majesty. Lord Mark, the Counselor, Lords Hawk and Trey from the Realm of Man, all three are with the Derinseum Watch. The Lady Stacy, also from the Realm of Man, has been with the Steward the entire time."

Mab nodded and tugged at the lace-trimmed sleeves at her wrists. "I see. Well done, Gaspar. It seems your information is far more complete, and perhaps even more reliable than his."

"Excuse me, Your Majesty?" The mage scratched his head.

She waved a hand in dismissal. "Oh, nothing for *you* to be worried about. Does this conclude your report?"

Gaspar executed a small bow. "It does, Your Majesty. Have you any questions?"

"Just one," she admitted. "Do you think these friends of the Steward will be of any real help to Padraic, in his current situation?"

The mage shrugged. "I would not be surprised, my queen. The Mer Administration is very unsettled, and the Merchants Guild is at a loss as to what to do with Padraic. A public trial is anticipated, but not desired by many who rightfully see this as a no-win situation for the realm. Their economy was already reeling from the recent necromancy incident. A public trial for a mass murder in a Council realm would only blight the realm further.

"The propensity for Council involvement has already escalated with Queen Titania's formal statement. And, forgive me, Your Majesty, but the fact that you, as yet, have said nothing, despite Padraic being your recognized consort, has encouraged untold speculation and rumor.

"The Mer Administration would very much like to find a way out of this quandary. So, if the Steward's friends were to offer some hope . . . well, you see?"

Mab studied Gaspar's face, and then smiled wryly. "I do see. You have a good grasp of the situation; and, I like your analysis. So much so in fact, that I have some thinking to do."

He maintained a bland expression, as she turned from him and mused under her breath.

"All things considered, I may have to make some changes around here, as well, perhaps sooner rather than later. I'd like more time, though . . . Hmm, we'll have to see. So be it."

She turned back to him and smiled. "All in all, you have done well, Gaspar."

"Thank you, Your Majesty. I am at your service, as always. Have you further instructions?"

"Yes, return to Mer and continue your clandestine observations. Do nothing overtly on behalf of Padraic. Let us see what the Steward's friends can do."

"At once, Your Majesty." He turned from her and hurried down the gallery hallway, passing Lord Nightshade, unseen in the shadowed alcove.

NIGHTSHADE HELD HIS breath, his mind awhirl.

Oh no! Gaspar's information is more 'complete' and 'reliable'? He has a 'good grasp of the situation'? She likes his 'analysis'? She may make some changes around here? Ye gods, what next?

ON THE OUTSKIRTS OF New Port Royal, a muddy track that served as a seldom-used road ran between staggered rows of dilapidated buildings.

In the pale light of the early crescent moon, Salidar could see that most structures in the vicinity were in some state of disrepair; many were clearly abandoned. The whole area held the air of desolation.

Salidar hunkered down among stacks of cracked barrels and broken crates to study the low stone building across the rutted road from his hidden position.

The information provided by Rumley had proven to be accurate, insofar as it went. The problem, as Salidar soon discovered, was that Rathskellen did in fact have another warehouse that was not among the three known to Rumley—this one.

Well, he did warn me that there might be others.

As Rumley had cautioned, the three known warehouses were guarded by hired thugs, who for the most part, were less than conscientious and easily bored. The buildings were secured with robust yet simple locks. Neither guards nor locks represented a significant challenge to one such as Salidar.

Undetected, he infiltrated each storage facility with little difficulty, and sadly little success. He found them well stocked, as expected, with goods most likely smuggled or stolen; however, none of the known warehouses held the specific cargo he sought.

That had sent him back to the streets for more information.

Salidar circulated easily among those *street people* who favored the hours of darkness. The bartering of information for coin or other consideration was a way of life for some; so, Salidar had no problem learning all he needed to know about Rathskellen's operations—or so he thought.

This took longer than he had anticipated, and considerably more coin; but, he did succeed in learning of Rathskellen's other secret warehouse, the one he now observed.

Curiously, he saw no guards. There had been no activity whatsoever in the area. This desolate end of town seemed completely deserted. He had a moment of doubt; had he paid for bad information? Had he been duped?

As that possibility gnawed at his gut, he focused on the stone building. Unlike its nearby neighbors, it did not seem in need of any repair, save the peeling paint on its sun-faded wooden trim. Dust and debris had accumulated in windswept corners, nooks, and crannies. However, its windows were tightly shuttered and the only visible door was securely padlocked. The gnawing in his gut began to subside.

Yes, this is very likely it; but. . ?

The lack of obvious guards gave him pause. What was he missing?

Of course!

He smiled at that flash of inspiration, and deliberately let his eyes go out of focus while he kept his gaze fixed on the building.

Ever so slowly, vaguely pulsating lines of dull crimson light grew in strength as they illuminated the perimeter of the building. Even the low line of the roof, the stones around the doorway and window frames were outlined in pulses of pale red—it was as if the very building had a visible heartbeat.

Salidar shuddered and blinked; the lights had vanished.

But, he knew better.

Oh man, this is going to be a problem.

"ELLEN, ARE YOU IN HERE?" Stacy asked, pushing into the lavish guest suite of Lady Orla's villa.

"Over here," Ellen called, waving from a windowed alcove. She closed the journal and left it on the cushioned window seat. "I needed to do some more reading. Is everything okay?"

"Yeah, as far as I know. The guys left shortly after breakfast; the Watch captain is supposed to let them see the crime scene today. Lady Orla asked if you were planning on doing any more shopping today, so I told her I'd check with you. So?"

Ellen rose and stretched. "To be honest, I'm kind of shopped out. But I guess we may have to, you know, for appearances sake."

Stacy flopped down on an overstuffed couch. "I never thought I'd say this, but I don't feel like shopping any more either." Her lower lip jutted out in a pout. "Do we have to? Can't we do something different, like go to the beach? Wouldn't that be *keeping up appearances,* too?"

"The beach, hmm?" Ellen brightened.

Miska was suddenly standing in the doorway. “Pardon the interruption, ladies, but Selene is here and needs to speak with you both.”

“Oh, okay.” Ellen shrugged, seeing Miska was alone. “Where is she?”

“Can’t she come in here?” Stacy uttered with a tired sigh. “Or do we have to go to her?”

“She is with Lady Orla, in her private office,” Miska explained, “so, yes, you will have to go to her. Please follow me.”

WHEN MISKA USHERED Ellen and Stacy into the office, Lady Orla was seated at her desk with Selene standing at her side, their heads bent in private conversation.

Their hostess rose and smiled. “Ellen, Stacy, I trust you are having a pleasant morning. Now, you must excuse me, I have a luncheon meeting at the administration building.” She gave Selene a knowing nod and slipped from the room.

Selene placed a finger to her lips and gestured for Miska to lock the door. When he had done so, she closed her eyes, folded her hands, entwining her webbed fingers in a particular way, and muttered a low incantation. The air pressure in the room seemed to increase incrementally. She gestured dropping her jaw and swallowing; everyone knew to follow suit lest their ears would pop.

Selene smiled. “Now we can speak freely.”

“What’s wrong? What’s happened?” Ellen demanded.

Selene held her open hands up. “Everyone is fine, as far as we know, and nothing is wrong. I’m here to tell you that Salidar thinks he’s found the location of Brona—”

“That’s great! Let’s go!” Ellen blurted.

"Hold on, there's more," Selene cautioned. "He *thinks* he's found her; that alone gives us pause. And there may be some complications."

"What do you mean?" Ellen pressed.

"Don't you trust him?" Stacy asked.

Selene sighed. "In this, we do trust him. However, he admits he has not gained entrance to the place he believes she is being held. It's a warehouse that is apparently heavily warded. He is willing to try to circumvent these wards; but, the Steward must be there. If successful, we gain access and find Brona; however, immediate transit from the realm will be necessary. Do you understand?"

"And if he's wrong? Brona is *not* there?" Miska asked.

"Our assets must depart without delay," Selene insisted. "There is no way of knowing what alarms might be triggered in attempting to breach any wards. Immediate transit is our only option, whether we are successful or not."

"I get it; I'm in." Ellen declared.

Miska smiled. "Me, too!"

"When do we leave?" Stacy asked.

Selene shook her head. "You don't, Stacy. We have another task for you."

"Huh? What?" Stacy's frown was growing darker. "What do you mean? I am too going!"

"Please, listen to me, all of you," Selene urged. "Haven't you realized you've been watched while you've been here?"

"I'm not surprised," Ellen admitted. "In fact, I sort of expected it. But wait, you don't mean by the local citizens of Mer, do you, Selene?"

"No, rather by agents of Queen Mab of the Dark Elves. We've known there are elements of other realms in Mer, and that some of them report back on what transpires here. For the most part we just keep an eye on them as well. Lord Nightshade oversees her *secret police,* in truth, her spy network."

"Is he here?" Miska asked.

"No, but his agents are; they have been observing you, Ellen, since shortly after your arrival."

"I never noticed; and, that kind of creeps me out. I guess I should be more aware."

Selene smiled, not unkindly. "They did not want to be noticed. Nightshade's people are very good; ours are better, trust me."

"You said they've been observing *me* since 'shortly after' our arrival, right?" Ellen asked. "So, they didn't actually *see* us arrive. Does that mean they don't know who came with me?"

"Well, yes and no," Selene hedged. "Since your transit globe appeared here, at Lady Orla's villa, your arrival was unobserved by Nightshade's people. However, you and Stacy have since been observed with some of your hostess' attendants on your shopping forays. We suspect that Mark, Trey, and Hawk may have been observed in their dealings with the Watch as well."

"I see," said Ellen. "So, they don't know about Miska, do they?"

Selene shrugged with open palms. "No, we think not, since he has not ventured outside the villa."

"A point to our advantage, I think," Ellen reasoned. "Let's keep it that way."

Still pouting, her lower lip thrust forward, Stacy asked, "So, what's this *task* you have for me?"

"Tonight, while Ellen and Miska slip away to New Port Royal, you are going to impersonate Ellen at a small dinner party, an *al fresco* affair on

Lady Orla's terrace, in full view of her gardens, where you are sure to be seen, from a distance. Of course, the guests will be our people, to help pull off the ruse."

"Wait! I get to impersonate Ellen?" Stacy beamed a mischievous smile. "Oh, this could be fun! I'll wear a wig!" She grabbed Ellen's arm. "Oh, can I borrow some frumpy clothes? You know I gotta look the part!"

Ellen arched a lone eyebrow. "I think maybe you're having a bit too much fun with this."

A splayed hand to her chest in feigned shock and dismay, Stacy cooed, "Oh, little ol' me? Perish the thought! Don't you worry about a thing, sweetie. I got this!"

CH 27

PAPA GEORGE WAS ON his way to the cavern that housed Teddy's meth lab when Daegon stepped into the passage and blocked his path.

"Daegon? What's up?"

"Come with me to the scrying orb; there is something I want you to see."

"Okay, lead on."

The chamber was well lit by several candles and a trio of torches, but George had always thought the resultant illumination was insufficient.

"You know, I can have Vito run some wiring in here," he offered. "A couple of light bulbs would make a big difference. We wouldn't have to rely on candles and torches all he time."

"Perhaps," Daegon admitted, "but as I have said before, the orb works best when the source of light in this chamber is natural flames. You really should trust me on this."

"Yeah, I get it. I just thought—oh, never mind. What did you want me to see?"

Daegon stepped to the orb and motioned for George to gaze within. "Remember Gaspar? Watch."

At the alchemist's gesture and murmured incantation, the orb went opaque. In a few moments what appeared to be a gray mist began to swirl within and eventually cleared to reveal a street scene.

"This is Derinseum in Mer; Gaspar is now there. Not long ago, he was in the Realm of Dark Elves with Diere, the *pretender*, or Mab as she is now known." Daegon's voice harshened at the very mention of the Dark Elfin queen. "He conveyed to her that the Steward and her friends are in Mer.

Some are shopping and some are consulting with the Watch. Mab wants them watched. It seems her consort, Padraic, is in some difficulty with the authorities. She wants to wait and see what the Steward's friends can do about it. So, I ask you, do we need to be concerned? Should Circe be made aware?"

George furrowed his brow. "There's no love lost between Mab and the Steward; so, as a rule there's no way they're gonna work together. Besides, I don't see a connection between the Steward's friends and Padraic. Do you know what this *difficulty with the authorities* is?"

Daegon shook his head. "No, not specifically; but rumors of violent deaths of Light Elves in Derinseum run rampant. Now, were we to speculate, in consideration of what Circe has told us . . ."

"Ah, you think maybe Silenos is responsible, and framed Padraic? That does make sense, but why—oh, wait!" George gasped in sudden epiphany. "I bet I know who these *friends* of the Steward are! They're the cops from my home realm, the same ones who were after me; they were at that Council meeting!"

Daegon shook his head. "I am not sure I follow you. What—"

"That's gotta be it!" George blurted in interruption. "If there's been deaths—*murders,* there's no way those cops aren't gonna stick their noses in it. If Silenos really did this, they will figure it out. I'll bet Mab knows it, too. She can just sit back and wait; she doesn't have to do a thing. She always manipulates or manages to get others to do her dirty work. Yeah, now it makes sense."

"I see. However, that does not answer my questions," Daegon pointed out. "Do we need to be concerned; and, should Circe be told?"

George held up a hand. "Nah, I don't think so. First of all, we don't have to be concerned now that we're aware of this development. However, we do need to give the Steward and her cop friends a wide berth; I'm still a wanted man back home. Given the chance, I don't doubt they'd try to grab me and take me back. So, we avoid them altogether.

"As for Circe, have you forgotten? She doesn't know about our *Gasparcam,* so we can't exactly explain how we know all this."

"Oh, yes." Daegon did remember. "That is true, but—"

"Keep in mind," George continued, "that she just took delivery of a sizable shipment of product; so, she's probably already sailing for Derinseum. She said her plans were to set up a legitimate shop under the Merchants Guild's sanction, right? So, if there are rumors running rampant around Derinseum, she's gonna hear them. You see, she's gonna find all this out on her own. I say, we let her."

Daegon nodded and tilted his head. "Tell me, do you ever intend to tell Circe about our monitoring of Gaspar?"

George pursed his lips and arched a lone eyebrow. "I don't know. Let's wait and see just how good her distribution ideas turn out; then we'll see if she needs to know." He gestured to the scrying orb. "In the meantime, you can continue to keep an eye on Gaspar."

Daegon shook his head. "Actually, I have other things I must do. If you like, you can monitor Gaspar to your heart's content."

George balked. "Huh? What are you talking about? What other things?"

Daegon sighed. "Sometimes I wonder if you ever pay attention. I have already told you that I planned to return to the Keys of Osiris to continue my research. Have *you* now forgotten?"

George scowled. "No, I remember. But you aren't talking about right now, are you? Remember what Circe said about the Keys? Right now may not be a good time to be there."

"I do not plan to go immediately. I have many preparations to make that will take some time and demand my full attention. I cannot waste time staring into the orb for days on end or—"

"Well, neither can I!" George groused. "Nor can I spare Vito; he's got too much to do and too many places to be as it is. Using Teddy is out of the question; he cooks—he *only* cooks."

The alchemist shrugged. "Then as I see it, we really have only one choice; we can periodically look in on Gaspar. It is not an ideal solution, but it may be the best we can do. Do you not agree?"

George fumed in silence. This was not a good solution at all; but, all things considered, it might well be their only option.

"Damn! Well, can we at least leave the orb focused on Gaspar? That way whenever either of us comes by here we can quickly look in on him and see what he sees without having to call up and cast the viewing spell. Do you follow me? Save some time, you know?"

"We could; it would save time. However," Daegon cautioned, "be aware that any other spells we have in place that require the orb would be suspended. For example, the perimeter triggers that would alert us to anyone arriving from off realm will be inert; the orb will neither alert nor show us who might arrive or where. Are you comfortable with that?"

George shrugged. "Look, we haven't had any visitors, except Circe, in a long time; so, I'm not that worried about it. What does worry me is those cops who are in Derinseum right now. And fortunately, our boy Gaspar is keeping an eye on them. So for now, we've got somebody else doing *our* dirty work; and, we get to watch. So, yeah, I'm comfortable with that."

"Very well," the alchemist conceded. "I will adjust the spell to keep this channel open."

"That's cool!" George chuckled. "It's like having one channel playing on a TV you leave on all the time. Heh-heh, you just can't use the remote to change channels! Ha-ha!"

"What? I do not—" Daegon began.

"Forget it! It's just a joke!" George smirked and shook his head. "Never mind; don't worry about it. Just do what you gotta do."

IN THE DARK ALLEY BETWEEN the old apothecary shop and the Fouled Anchor, a transit globe shimmered into existence. Two hooded figures stepped forth and paused in near complete darkness as the globe shrank and winked out with a muffled *pop.*

The larger of the hooded forms pointed to the cat cradled in the arms of the smaller form.

"Smokey?" whispered Miska. "How did he—"

"Hush!" Ellen hissed. "I'll tell you later. We're not alone; someone's coming!"

Several paces away, a side door on the building to their left swung open. Muted barroom clamor echoed from within as a slash of diffused light sliced across the alley. A stout figure stood exposed in the barely adequate illumination, took a step into the alley, and faced the darkness to the rear.

"Come forward; you are expected. I am Rumley."

Ellen stepped into the light and displayed her fist, the topaz ring flickering.

"I'm Ellen; this is Miska."

Rumley noted the ring and nodded. As his eyes found the cat in her arms, one corner of his wide mouth twitched in an involuntary smirk.

"Where is he?" Ellen pressed.

Rumley nodded toward the open doorway. "He waits within; we must go to a room on the second floor. Remain hooded and speak to no one, understand? Good. Follow me."

Rumley led them into the crowded saloon. He picked their way through the milling patrons to the staircase and ascended with Ellen and Miska on his heels.

A woman wearing heavy makeup and brandishing a large fan of ostrich feathers met them at the entrance to the second-floor hallway, effectively blocking any further progress. Rumley had a whispered word with her, and she stepped aside. Once they slipped past her, she resumed her post, thus restricting access to any who might have dared to follow.

Rumley stopped at the last door on the left, knocked in a distinct pattern, and waited.

The lock *clicked* and the door swung open.

Salidar stepped back, waved them into the dimly lit room, and closed the door.

Rumley gestured to Salidar and Ellen. "I understand you are acquainted?"

Ellen replied coolly, "We are. Salidar, you remember my friend, Miska?"

"I do," the thief replied, glancing at the big man. His stare dropped and lingered on the cat.

Ellen noticed. "My friend Stacy tells me you know Smokey as well. He will be joining us. I trust that will not be a problem?"

He tore his eyes off the cat. "Uh, no, m'lady."

"Good, then let's be about our business. Take us, unobserved, to the location; and, let's see what we are dealing with. Any questions?"

Salidar shook his head.

"It would be best," Rumley cautioned, "if your party was not seen leaving this establishment. There is another stairwell hidden within the rear wall. Tis narrow, I admit, but serviceable. Follow me."

Outside in the still night, Rumley offered some parting words of advice. "Of course, you will speak of that stairwell to no one. Now, I understand very few know of your mission. If anyone asks about any of you, I will only say that travelers unknown to me took rooms for the night, and left before daybreak. And as it happens, that is a carefully parsed truth. If questioned, your stories must match mine. Do we, by your oaths, have an understanding?"

"We do," answered Ellen.

Rumley looked to Miska.

"Aye," agreed the big man.

As Rumley's gaze found Salidar, the thief dropped his eyes. "Of course."

Rumley nodded and intoned solemnly. "You are all so bound. Best of luck!"

JUST UNDER AN HOUR later, in the rather shabby outskirts of New Port Royal, Salidar, Miska, and Ellen crouched hidden among stacks of empty crates directly across from the targeted warehouse. Despite the modest light of the crescent moon, they had easily avoided being seen on their way here. It appeared they were still alone. No one had passed by on the old rutted road; there were no guards to be seen.

"I found it thus last night," Salidar whispered, "no one in the vicinity and no guards. However, it *is* warded. There is an old trick to see—"

"I know the trick, Salidar," interjected Ellen. "Be still a moment."

She stared at the low building, letting her eyes go out of focus. She sensed Miska doing the same thing. Smokey dropped from her lap and disappeared into the nearby shadows.

Ellen held her breath as the lines of ruddy light became visible. There was no doubt the building was warded. She tried to assess details without changing her focus. That was hard; it took several attempts before she was satisfied.

She looked to Miska. "You saw?"

"Aye, tis warded as he says. No other building around here is so warded."

She turned to Salidar. "You said this Rathskellen is a halfling, part elf?"

"Aye, why, m'lady? Is that important?"

"Maybe. What color light do you see?" she asked.

"Red, m'lady, it fades off and on like a pulse; but tis red," Salidar insisted.

"Miska?" she asked.

"Aye, I saw red, too. What does this mean?"

Ellen peered into the dimness. "It means we are probably dealing with an old spell of elfin origin, that has been often modified, and very likely reapplied countless times under different circumstances and at other locations. If I understand correctly, that tends to weaken its effectiveness. I can sense its constrained energy is nowhere near what it once was. In fact, I think it now has only two aspects that still work to a degree that may concern us. One is to alert someone if it's triggered; the other, much stronger, is to prevent any transit spell from working."

Salidar stared at her in open-mouthed surprise.

Miska grinned. "You can *sense* that much? Ah, you've been reading again, haven't you?"

"Well, yes," Ellen admitted in chagrin, "and I'm very glad I did. If that counter-transit aspect is as powerful as I think it might be, we definitely do not want to trigger it."

"That would be most wise, m'lady," Salidar agreed, clearly impressed. "I have had the misfortune to have firsthand experience with such an elfin counter-transit spell. I cannot recommend it."

Ellen mused in thought for a few moments. Smokey reappeared, crawled back into her lap, and stared up into her eyes. She stroked his back and scratched beneath his chin. A smile slowly spread across her face; she winked at her cat.

"You know, there just may be a way. However, we must be certain there are no guards, or anyone else, nearby. Salidar, are there any other doors? What about the rear of the building?"

The thief shook his head. "No other doors that I saw, m'lady, and only shuttered windows at the rear. Why, what do you have in mind?"

"First, we need to be absolutely sure we are not observed. I need you to to check the perimeter of the building again; double-check for any signs of guards. Then I need you to check the nearby buildings for anyone who might see us. The state of disrepair doesn't matter; you must check each one. We will keep a watch on the road and the front of the building. Take your time; look everywhere. This is important. Do you understand?"

"I think so, m'lady. This may take some time; please, be patient."

With a respectful nod, Salidar slipped into the shadows and disappeared.

The thief out of earshot, Miska nudged her. "Miss Ellen, I know you could have done that *perception thing* you can do to see if we are alone; was it necessary to send Salidar off like that?"

She sighed. "Actually, it was. Sometimes, depending on where I am—you know, which realm I'm in—my *perception thing* doesn't always work so well, especially if someone is deliberately shielded from me. I was serious in that we really don't want to be seen here. So, why take the chance? Let's sit tight and keep our eyes open."

"Okay. I do have a question, if now would be a good time?"

"What?"

"How did Smokey get here? He wasn't with us in Derinseum; and I am certain that only you and I entered the transit globe you summoned. That brings up another question; how did we go from Derinseum to New Port Royal anyway? They're both in Mer. One can only transit from one realm to another, right?"

She smiled. "Yeah, I thought so, too. And that may still be true to a large degree, but right now may not be the best time to explain. Suffice to say my reading has been most enlightening. In short, the more I learn, the more I understand, and hopefully, the more I may be able to accomplish."

"And Smokey?" he pressed.

The cat crawled into Miska's lap and purred.

Ellen smiled. "Well, you know Smokey; he goes where he will."

SALIDAR RETURNED WITHIN half an hour. "I was thorough, m'lady. I am confident we are alone."

Ellen rose from her crouched position and stretched. "Well done, Salidar. Come on, let's have a closer look at this warehouse."

Miska rose, stretched and groaned. "Are you sure?"

"Yeah, let's not waste time," she urged. "This is either gonna work, or not."

She strode across the rutted track and stood three paces away from the front door. Hands on her hips, she said, "All right, visualize the wards again, and pay particular attention to the front door."

Salidar and Miska stood to either side of her and did as she asked.

As they stared in silence, she spoke in a soft tone so as not to disrupt their focus.

"You should easily see the pulses of red light. Now, notice that there is no such light at the door jambs, hinges, or the threshold. The padlock bears no light that I can see. Do you agree?"

"Yes, I do," Miska answered. "But what does that mean?"

"Oh, of course!" Salidar blurted in sudden realization. "Well done, m'lady!"

"Keep your voice down!" she hissed.

Miska winced, shook his head, and displayed his open palms; clearly, he still didn't get it.

Ellen laid a hand on the big man's arm and pointed. "I think to open this door, we may only need to defeat that padlock, which does not appear to be protected by any warding. Since we see no warding lines across the threshold, it may be that entering the building through that opened door will not trigger any spell either. Do you see any flaws in this logic?"

Miska shrugged. "No, I do not."

Salidar scratched at his narrow beard. "I think you are right, m'lady. I have seen many rely on magic as an acceptable deterrent and overlook the integrity of locks they may employ. In truth, I think some are simply lazy. I know that Rathskellen is one such; he hires common thugs as guards at his other warehouses." He scoffed. "I had no difficulty in breaching those walls, right under their easily distracted noses."

"So, you think he relies on this warding, instead of guards for this warehouse?" Miska asked.

Salidar shrugged. "Yes, very likely. This location is some distance from the docks, so it is probably used for long-term storage and would not be frequently visited. I doubt he would pay for guards. However, while I agree that we may be able to defeat the lock and enter, it would not be wise to assume that Rathskellen would not be alerted. I think he will respond in some fashion."

"Yeah, that would make sense," Ellen agreed. "Once inside I would not be able to transit us away without triggering the other aspect of the wards; that I most certainly do not want to do."

"Well, can't we just carry what we find out through the open door?" Miska asked. "Can't you then transit us and whatever we've found without worrying about these wards?"

"Of course!" Ellen chortled. "Why didn't I think of that? Thank you, Miska!"

"We must be very quick," Salidar warned. "I found no one in the vicinity, but it would not take long for Rathskellen's thugs to respond from the other warehouses."

"Indeed, speed will be paramount," Ellen conceded. "Salidar, can you deal with that padlock?"

"Yes, m'lady, I will need only a moment."

She looked to Miska, who shrugged, grinned, and nodded.

"Very well, Salidar," Ellen decided. "Do it."

AS EXPECTED, THE PADLOCK was hardly an impediment. The door swung open on well-oiled hinges in anticlimactic silence. The dark interior beckoned.

Ellen paused at the threshold; but Smokey didn't hesitate and promptly slipped into the building.

"I think our tactic has worked, so far," she muttered, and nodded to the entrance. "Shall we, gentlemen?"

Miska preceded her across the threshold, produced a flashlight, and sent a wash of light inside.

Stacked crates, barrels, and boxes were arranged in haphazard rows and piled in precarious mounds along all the walls. The air smelled old, stale and musty; dust was everywhere. However, in the rows between the stacks, the dust had been disturbed and bore evidence of many recent footprints.

Ellen stepped past Miska and activated her own flashlight. Smokey was nowhere to be seen.

"Okay, Salidar, what are we looking for?" she asked.

The thief came to stand beside her. He held his hands shoulder-width apart as he peered into the dim room. "An ironbound chest about this big, m'lady, and a long wooden box not quite the size of a coffin. They may be together; although, I doubt they are. Silenos was adamant about keeping them separate."

"Over here!" Miska called from one side of the packed room. "Is this the box? It is almost as big as a coffin. Looks like it's nailed shut. There's some sort of seal painted on its lid; the paint is sticky."

Ellen and Salidar bent over Miska's find. Her added light helped them make out the fresh marking.

"It's like heraldry, or some sort of symbolic seal," she remarked. "It looks like a griffin holding a large egg; there are distinct marks on the egg." She panned her light around and found similar depictions of the seal on every crate and box within view; only the marks on the egg were different. "This seal is on everything in here."

"So, this box," Miska prompted, "is this the one?"

Salidar leaned close. "Yes, I think this *is* the box from the *Doom Wind*. I can see where the lock hasp was affixed by the ship's carpenter, which would have been removed, once offloaded and nailed shut. As for this seal, I saw this on items in the other warehouses as well. I think the seal is Rathskellen's and the marks on the egg are how he keeps track of just who owns whatever he is storing."

"You're certain?" Miska pressed. "How do we know for sure this is the right box? Miss Ellen, do we open it?"

Ellen shook her head. "I don't know if we can take the time. Let's find the chest and see if the marks on the seal are the same; that might indicate it belongs to Silenos."

They immediately began searching. In less than five minutes, Ellen was successful.

"Hey! Found something—actually, Smokey did." She chuckled. "You gotta see this."

Atop a wide crate near the back of the room were *two* ironbound chests of approximately the same design and size; Smokey was sitting between them. Both bore griffin seals that matched that of the larger box.

Ellen pointed. "Look, these marks on the eggs are the same as the ones on the box. This paint is fairly fresh, too, still tacky. I think all three have been recently stenciled. If Salidar is right about Rathskellen's seal, this system makes sense as a kind of basic inventory control. Everything in here bears the seal; but, the marks on the eggs are all different. However, the box and these two chests all bear identical marks."

Miska stroked his chin. "So, all three belong to Silenos? What do we do now?"

"I only knew of *one* chest. But I think one of these is the one we seek," Salidar conceded. "They look too much alike; I cannot be sure which one."

"Fine, we'll take all three outside," Ellen decided, "and open them there."

Miska nodded. "Good! The sooner we're out of here, the better. I can manage the big box."

Ellen hefted each chest in succession. "These aren't too heavy. If you get the big one, Miska, we'll manage these two. Let's do it."

ON THE STONY GROUND outside in the pale moonlight, the chests and box appeared smaller, somehow diminished.

Ellen panned her flashlight across the front of the chests. Small brass plates bore keyholes.

"Salidar, there are locks." She pointed. "I assume you can deal with them and get these chests open?"

"No problem, m'lady." He bent to his task.

"Do you need more light?" she asked bringing her flashlight to bear.

"No, m'lady, tis done!" He grinned at her as he flipped the lid of a chest open.

Ellen shone her light within and gasped. "What the—?"

Miska stepped to her side as Salidar reached in and withdrew a thin golden chain; a dozen golden ears were attached.

"Ye gods," Miska murmured.

Salidar lifted the entire chain out and peered into the depths of the chest. He reached in with his free hand and lifted another such chain with its similarly macabre ornaments.

Ellen's shock and disgust were quickly displaced with focused anger and cool logic. Her lips drew into a thin line as she pointed to the chest.

"I've seen enough, Salidar. Put the chains back and close the lid." She shuddered and took a calming breath. "Please open the other chest."

"Yes, m'lady, at once."

Turning to Miska, Ellen pointed and asked, "What about that big box? Can you open it?"

"It is nailed shut. Without a stout tool to pry at the nails and the time to do it patiently, I would be forced to break it open. There could be too much damage, perhaps to the contents as well." He opened his hands in concern.

She understood, equally concerned that harm might come to Brona, if indeed she was inside.

Salidar cleared his throat. "Uh, m'lady?"

Ellen saw he had the other chest open. She stood over him and shone her light into the chest; a woman's head lay nestled in thick coils of auburn tresses. Eyes closed, her expression was composed, almost serene, the face of a sleeping woman in a pleasant dream.

Ellen remembered to breathe. "Wow . . . Brona, I presume?"

Of course, there was no answer.

Miska, at her side, peered over her shoulder. "I do not know if she can hear you, Miss Ellen. I think this is a stasis spell, like is sometimes used among the Were."

"Do you mean that someone did this to her? The spell, I mean?"

Miska nodded. "Yes, I think so. Dullahans have no need of stasis spells. Someone did this for reasons of their own."

"I think we know who," she seethed. "That bastard will—"

"Down!" Salidar screamed and tugged Ellen to the ground.

A furious rush of wind passed over her. She rolled away from Salidar and saw Miska grab his shoulder and tumble forward, striking the ground.

Salidar's face blanched in the pale moonlight; he jabbed a finger into the night sky.

"Griffin!"

Ellen saw Miska rise to his knees and wince. His hand came away from his shoulder; the blood looked black in the moonlight. He looked to where Salidar pointed and then to Ellen.

"Miss Ellen! Stay down! It's coming around for another pass!"

This time Ellen saw it. She dove to the side as the beast swooped past her and careened off into the night air.

"Miska!" she called, scrambling to her feet. "Are you all right?"

"I'm fine! And you?"

"I'm good! Salidar, are you okay?"

"Yes, m'lady! Where did it go?" He slammed the lid of the chest closed.

"I don't see it," she answered. "Is it gone?"

"No," Miska warned, "it will be back. Be alert!"

"There!" Salidar pointed up at a nearby building. "On the peak of the roof! It landed!"

Ellen strained to see, but then remembered her flashlight. She dialed the lens to a tight beam and spotlighted the creature. Miska followed her example.

The creature paused cocking its eagle-like head one way then another. It seemed curious about the two sources of light on the ground. It spread its wide wings and leapt into the air.

"It's airborne! I lost it!" Ellen cried. "Watch your backs!"

"M'lady! Behind you!" Salidar's shout was almost lost in the creature's deafening screech.

Ellen dove to the ground beside the long wooden box; the attacking griffin's wicked talons just missed her, slashing across the top of the box, gouging the wood.

A wing awkwardly hit the ground, and sent the griffin tumbling out of control, bouncing down the rutted road. Finally coming to a sliding stop, the creature righted itself, gave its disheveled wings a mighty shake, and paused as if taking stock of its surroundings.

Breath caught in Ellen's throat. Ten paces from the standing griffin, Smokey sat in the middle of the old road, his eyes fixed on the creature and his tail twitching languidly.

The creature could see Smokey, too. The griffin's neck stretched straight out, the eagle beak centered on the cat's position. It began to slowly stalk toward the seemingly unconcerned cat.

Ellen rose; she had seen enough.

"Oh no! Not my cat, you don't!"

Ellen sprinted to her cat.

The griffin balked, flared its wings, and hissed!

A silvery stream from Ellen's fist splashed across the huge beak, into its eyes, nasal pits, and down its open throat.

Ellen snatched up Smokey at a run and veered off to the side as the griffin collapsed, gagging and writhing in the dirt.

At ten paces distance, Ellen stopped and faced the suffering beast. The immediate danger apparently passed, she let Smokey slip to the ground.

Miska and Salidar joined her.

"M'lady," breathed Salidar clearly in awe, "what magic was this?"

"No magic, Salidar," she opened her fist to display a black aerosol canister, "just pepper spray. It does no lasting harm."

"Oh, well in that case . . ." Salidar produced a dagger and began to approach the hapless creature.

Smokey streaked forth placing himself between Salidar and the griffin. Staring into Salidar's eyes, he emitted a low, yet distinct warning *growl.*

Salidar froze.

Ellen stepped up and laid a hand on the thief's arm. "Sheath your blade, Salidar. If Smokey wants no harm to come to this beast, then none shall by our hands. Do you understand?"

In that moment Salidar could neither speak nor take his eyes off the cat. He nodded, sheathed his dagger, and stepped back.

Miska panned his flashlight on the prone griffin. "Look, it wears a metal collar with a short length of chain! Is this someone's pet?"

"More like someone's slave," Ellen reasoned. "What do we know about griffins?"

"Not much, I fear," Miska admitted. "Tis a good question to put to Gallenius, I'd wager."

The griffin was no longer in that much distress, but was still breathing somewhat erratically. It was clearly exhausted. Smokey walked up to the beast and gently batted its great beak to get its attention.

Ellen held her breath as the cat and the griffin stared for long moments into each other's eyes.

Finally Smokey turned away and approached Ellen. She scooped him up in relief and hugged him close. She sighed and scratched his stomach, earning a contented purr. Their eyes locked for a moment.

"Okay, it's time to go," she declared. "I think we're about to have more visitors, Rathskellen's thugs."

Miska nodded. "How soon?"

"Soon enough." She glanced at the box, and two chests. "Hmmph, nothing ever goes as planned, does it? Okay, we have a change in plans."

The men looked to one another and shrugged.

"Salidar, can you use the padlock to secure the warehouse door again?" she asked. "Make it look like no one has been here?"

"Yes, m'lady, no problem." He ran to the task, finished, and again stood before her. "It is done."

"Good." She opened her palm; the topaz ring lay there. "Salidar, take this."

"M'lady?" he asked as he took the ring.

Smokey still in her arms, she faced Salidar and Miska. "I was made aware that there might be tracing spells on the chest and the box. I had a plan to deal with them; but I did not know about the other chest, nor can we ignore it. Its importance, and what that might mean, changes things. Do you follow?"

Both men nodded; the significance of the contents of this chest was undeniable.

"We now have little choice. You, Salidar, must use this ring to get that chest and its contents to Gallenius at Storm Haven. The enchantment within the gem is designed to defeat any tracing spell. Do you understand?"

"Yes, m'lady, but—"

"No buts, Salidar! We don't have time. I will deal with the spells on the other chest and the box."

She pointed to the chest of ears. "That chest is of critical importance. I entrust it to you. Smokey will accompany you. Now go!"

The cat dropped to the ground, stood beside the chest and pawed it once.

Miska chuckled. "Smokey is telling you to do as she says, Salidar. You really don't want to keep Smokey waiting."

Salidar paled. He stood by the chest and activated the ring. A transit globe shimmered into existence. In an instant, it enveloped the thief, the chest, and the cat, shrank and winked out with the usual *pop.*

Miska leaned toward Ellen. "Do you think he'll do as he's told?"

Ellen smirked. "He'd better. Smokey is not to be underestimated."

"Are we ready to go?" He placed the other chest next to the box.

"One moment."

She stepped closer to the panting griffin. Miska started to object, but she forestalled him with a raised palm. She stopped within a pace of the exhausted creature.

"I don't know if you can understand me. We bear you no malice, and did you no permanent harm. We did defend ourselves; for that, I do not apologize. I suspect your circumstances are not of your choosing, as that chain and collar suggest; for that, I am sorry. We wish you no ill, and hope that you will find your happiness."

THE GRIFFIN WAS FAR more sentient than most would believe; she understood that she had been bested, but not truly harmed. This had been a most interesting and unexpected encounter for her.

She now had much to think about.

ELLEN RETURNED TO MISKA. "Okay, now we can go."

CH 28

ON THE WINDSWEPT PLAINS of Olmus, at the edge of a thick forest, a large transit globe appeared in the pale moonlight. A passing cloud darkened the scene for a mere moment, long enough for the globe to wink out of existence, leaving a man holding a large box and a woman holding a smaller chest.

Miska gently laid the long box on the ground. Ellen placed the chest next to it.

"No Salidar?" asked a voice from within the trees.

"Change in plans," Ellen answered.

"Ah, I see. Tis probably just as well; placing any trust in the likes of him is ill advised."

Lady Leanan of the Sidhe and her senior mage, Jalash-el, stepped forth from the dark forest.

The mage smiled and inclined his head. "Lady Ellen, Miska, tis good to see you both."

Ellen returned the smile. "And you, Magus."

"Is this she?" Leanan asked, gesturing to the two containers.

"Her head is here for certain." Ellen pointed to the chest. "However, we were not able to open the long box. It is nailed shut. We had neither the tools nor the time."

Leanan nodded to Jalash-el. "Would you?"

"Of course, m'lady." The mage stepped to the box, made a few hand gestures, and murmured an incomprehensible incantation.

As Ellen and Miska watched, one by one the nails in the lid began to rise amidst wrenching squeals, the wood creaking in complaint. The nails dropped away; the freed lid rose several inches, slipped to the side, and settled upon the ground.

Miska grinned. "Who needs tools?"

Ellen was impressed. "Nicely done, Magus. Thank you."

"What have we here?" Leanan asked, peering inside, "a rolled carpet?"

"Yes," Ellen answered, "and according to Salidar, a body within."

"Let us see, shall we?" Leanan gestured to Jalash-el, who nodded and raised his hands.

The rolled carpet rose from the confines of the box and began to unwind. A headless woman's body wearing homespun clothing was soon revealed. At a gesture from the mage, the floating body came to rest on the ground.

"There is some sort of stasis spell on this body," Jalash-el noted.

Ellen opened the lid on the chest. "We suspect the same spell may be on her head."

Jalash-el looked into the chest. "You are correct; it is two aspects of the same spell."

"Can you break this enchantment, Magus?" Leanan asked.

"I have no doubt, m'lady, but it may take some time to identify the exact spell." He looked to his mistress and then to Ellen. "Will that be a problem?"

Leanan shrugged and deferred to Ellen, who shook her head.

"I think not, Magus; take all the time you need. As Lady Leanan and I have discussed, it would be best to keep Brona safe and hidden while we further investigate this satyr, Silenos. Miska will stay with her. There will come a point when her father will be fully informed and they will be reunited."

Ellen turned to Leanan. "Until then, Lady Leanan, I will rely on your discretion. You have my deepest thanks."

Leanan smiled. "I am merely returning the favor. You extended your protection and hospitality when it was necessary to hide and shield Miska, for which I am grateful. How could I not come to your aid?"

"I, too, am grateful!" Miska added grinning.

Leanan and Ellen shared small smiles at the big man's sincerity.

"Uh, begging your pardon, m'ladies," Jalash-el interjected, "but I detect a set of tracing spells on the box and chest. Lady Ellen, you may be followed here."

"Hmm, I suspected as much, Magus. Can you tell if these spells are only on the box and chest? Are there any on Brona, or rather her two parts? Oh, and what about the carpet?"

"One moment, if you please." He closed his eyes, held either hand over the containers, then repeated his actions over the body and the head.

"May it please you, m'ladies, the tracing spells are only on the containers. The carpet is not bespelled. The only spell on *our guest* is the stasis enchantment, albeit in two aspects."

"What strategy do you have in mind, Ellen?" Leanan smiled. "I know you have something clever up your sleeve to deal with these tracing spells."

"Oh, I do indeed," Ellen countered. "We will leave the box, chest, and carpet here, on Olmus. I'll ask Miska to take each well inside the forest and hide them—but not too well. Let whoever follows the tracing spells find the empty containers and carpet. Hopefully, they will think Brona has broken the stasis spell on her own. I'd like them to think she is now in hiding somewhere in this realm—a realm in which *no one* is supposed to be."

"I see, leading to a prolonged search," Leanan deduced. "That would be a considerable distraction, giving all of us more time to focus our efforts in defeating this evil."

"A distraction for time, precisely," Ellen acknowledged.

"Time we will surely need," Leanan confirmed. "We must leave no trace of our presence. We will take Brona with us, and focus on restoring her, keeping her safe and hidden until you advise otherwise."

"Good. We should not linger here." Ellen cautioned. "I don't know how soon Brona will be missed, but someone will surely notice and raise an alarm. They will no doubt pursue the tracing spells and find this place. In fact, I may even arrange a surprise or two for anyone who will come searching."

"Indeed?" Leanan's eyebrows rose. "I know not what you may have in mind, but I must warn you; you are effectively *baiting* a suspected *necromancer.* This could not be more dangerous. You do understand that much, do you not?"

Ellen sighed. "I do, trust me. I know this is a dangerous game; and, I loathe putting anyone else in jeopardy. Aside from the four of us, no one else knows of this plan. I intend to keep it that way for as long as necessary."

"That is wise," Leanan conceded. "Is there anything more we can do?"

"No, I think not. Miska, you'll take care of hiding the box, chest, and carpet? Good. Now, I must go—I'm late for my own dinner party."

ELLEN WAS CAREFUL TO arrive within her assigned guest quarters at Lady Orla's villa. The hour was later than she had planned; she was certain the dinner party was over. She made her way to Stacy's guest room and fortunately found her alone.

"Ellen! You're back; but, later than you said," Stacy whispered. "How did it go?"

"Mission accomplished; we found Brona. She's safe and I think she's gonna be okay. Miska will stay with her. For the time being, I think it's best to keep her hidden. I'm not gonna get into details right now, okay?"

Stacy shrugged. "Uh, okay. Is something wrong?"

"Not exactly," Ellen hedged. "I need you to do me a favor. I've got to make a quick visit to Storm Haven; I'll be back in less than an hour. Please tell Lady Orla I'll need to speak with her when I get back; I'll need Selene here, too."

"No problem." Stacy waved a hand in assurance. "Does this have to do with Padraic?"

Ellen smiled; Stacy was sharp as ever. "Yeah, I think it does. What about our guys? Are they here, too? They're not still with the Watch, are they?"

"No, they're back. They were here for the dinner party; which went off without a hitch, I might add." Stacy smiled smugly. "Impersonating you was kind of fun; you even got a little drunk."

"What?" Ellen's jaw dropped.

Stacy threw up her hands. "It was only *playacting*, remember?" She grinned mischievously. "Trust me; I sold it!"

Ellen rolled her eyes and groaned. "I'm sure. So, do you know if you were observed by Nightshade's agents?"

"Well, I certainly hope so! My performance was *Oscar-worthy!*" Stacy snorted in laughter. "Seriously, we don't know; but, we think it likely."

"Okay, it's just as well," Ellen surmised, "having a bit of *plausible deniability* may come in handy."

"So, anything else you want me to do?" Stacy asked.

Ellen sighed and paused in thought. "Yeah, there is; can you get the captain of the Watch here, too? But we'll need to be discreet about that, okay?"

Stacy nodded. "I think so. I'll ask Selene to handle that."

"Good idea . . . I can't think of anything else at the moment. All right, I gotta go; I'll be back as soon as I can. I'll depart from my quarters and return there. That's where we should meet."

"Don't worry, I'll have everybody there," Stacy assured her.

THE MOOD AT STORM HAVEN was grim. Everyone seated at the conference table found it difficult not to stare at the ironbound chest placed in the center. The lid was now closed. Those in attendance had already examined the grisly contents.

"As I am sure you now understand, that the finding of this chest, unexpected as it was, changes things, potentially many things," Ellen proffered.

"I fear you are correct," the Guildmaster reluctantly agreed. "I had hoped to distance Storm Haven from this as much as possible. I have reservations about possible Council involvement. I would not care for such scrutiny."

"You saw the contents," Ellen countered. "Involvement of other realms will be inevitable, and most likely through the Council. The potential threat is too great; too many lives are already affected."

"She is right about that, Guildmaster," Gallenius remarked, and gestured to the chest. "Our examination of the ears suggests at least twenty victims of various races are represented. Identification of individuals, like Duke Briar, will be possible in some cases. It would be wrong to withhold such information from the surviving families."

"I still do not see what this has to do with Brona. Explain," Barnabas insisted, "why I cannot go to her. Why must she be kept hidden, even from me?"

"There are three very important reasons," Ellen answered. "Firstly, since we rescued her from someone acting on behalf of Silenos, the satyr will soon learn of this—assuming he does not already know. We have ample reason to suspect that he believes she is essential to his plans; so, he will no doubt search for her.

"Secondly, keep in mind, Barnabas, that Silenos was also searching for you. Now, we do not know for certain that he is aware of your paternal relationship to Brona, but we strongly suspect he was sent to find you by Titania.

"Consider this . . . If by some means Silenos was aware of your father's identity—even if it were no more than wild speculation or unsubstantiated rumor—he may have used that information, vague as it may have been, as leverage to entice support from Titania. Many are aware, of course, of Titania's inherent paranoia and subsequent predilection for the elimination of any of Oberon's offspring. That being the case, Silenos most likely intended to kill you, at her insistence.

"However, since Silenos did not find you, he resorted to an alternative plan in the hope you would succumb. He killed all the inhabitants of your island that he could find and cursed them with necromancy. We know this because we have a witness; do we not, Salidar?"

"Aye, Silenos did as the Steward said." The thief kept his eyes downcast.

"A witness we would rather not have come to light," intoned the Guildmaster. "Everyone believes Salidar is dead. And as such, he is a far more valuable asset. Were he to come forward, that would seal his doom; Queen Mab would seek his head."

"Precisely, which brings me to the third and most important reason," Ellen emphasized. "Murder was committed; necromancy was performed *again* in Mer, this time at the Keys of Osiris. Someone, a rumored survivor of this horror, must tell the tale, even if it is to spawn and circulate more rumors—and this must happen in Derinseum. Suspicion must be heaped upon Silenos; public opinion must be damning in the extreme.

"This chest and its contents will soon be in the hands of the Derinseum Watch. Bolstered by rampant rumors of carnage and necromancy, public outrage will be considerable. A demand for justice will reach the Mer Administration and the Council, whose member realms will be equally shocked and moved to act. Silenos will become *persona non grata* in all Council realms. He will have no choice but to seek refuge in the *wild*."

"So, I am supposed to be this *someone,* this *survivor?*" Barnabas asked.

"Yes, because it is essentially the truth," Ellen admitted. "Somehow, a similar rumor—possibly mere fanciful speculation—has already begun to circulate in Derinseum; you need only to add fuel to the flame. Simply retell Salidar's account, but be vague as to whether it is firsthand knowledge—hint that there may be multiple survivors. Of course, you will not mention Brona or her kidnapping; focus only on murder and necromancy. Those are the important issues that will motivate the Council realms."

Barnabas did not appear convinced.

"Consider how this could potentially solve a number of problems," Ellen urged.

"How?"

Ellen nodded to the Guildmaster. "Storm Haven could remain in the shadows; and, Salidar remains presumed *dead*."

Leveling a finger at her uncle, she added, "And just as important, the few who actually know of Oberon's role in your parentage can continue to keep that knowledge confidential."

Barnabas shrugged. "I see . . . And?"

"Think it through," she urged. "Once the Council becomes aware, Titania will have to distance herself from Silenos and his necromantic taint. Even if she does not believe you dead at present, Barnabas, she will be effectively constrained from pursuing any vengeance upon you. As her realm's queen, and monarch of the Seelie Court, she will be expected to openly condemn any and all acts of necromancy, known or suspected, and fully support any subsequent Council action."

"She must leave me be?"

"Oh, yes! She would not dare harm any possible *surviving witness,* lest suspicion fall upon the nature and scope of her involvement," Ellen confirmed. "In fact, her full attention will be required by the Council. It would not be surprising if the Council were to order the Sentinels to hunt down Silenos and any co-conspirators. And with Silenos on the run, he would have little time to devote to seeking Brona."

Barnabas scratched his chin. "That does make sense."

"And lastly," Ellen gestured to what lay upon the conference table, "this chest, its contents, and growing public outrage will clear Padraic of any suspicion in the deaths of Duke Briar and his aides. You see, Barnabas, you are the key to all of this."

"And Brona?" Barnabas asked.

"Safe and protected, I assure you. In fact, she is safest if no one knows where she is, to include you."

"But—" he began.

"Hold that thought," Ellen interrupted. "Consider this; if you do not know, not even a truth spell of the strongest magnitude could wrench such information from you. If, by chance, anyone else is aware that she is your daughter, you would be targeted for information as to her whereabouts. Even under maximum compulsion or duress, you cannot divulge what you do not know. I am sorry to be so blunt; but these are the facts."

Barnabas sighed. "I do understand. I do not fault your logic. In truth, I feel better having something I can do. I just want this to be over."

"As do we all," confirmed the Guildmaster.

"Are there any questions?" Ellen asked.

There were none.

Ellen rose. "Very well. I must go; I will take the chest with me. Barnabas, can you be in Derinseum by tomorrow?"

"Yes, I will be there. Trust me, I understand my role."

"Good. Now, where is Smokey?" Ellen looked around the room. "I planned on taking him with me."

Gallenius stood. "Oh, he left hours ago."

Ellen shrugged. "Oh well, you know Smokey; he goes where he will."

ELLEN FOUND HER GUEST chambers in Lady Orla's villa a bit crowded upon her return. Stacy had managed to get everyone Ellen had requested assembled.

Lowering the chest to the floor, Ellen addressed her guests.

"Thank you all for coming. Please make yourselves comfortable. I'll explain, but it may take a little time. Whatever we discuss in this room must, for now, stay in this room. Does everyone understand? Any questions before we begin?"

There were none; so she began with the good news.

"First of all, we have successfully rescued Brona . . ."

AS THE ENTIRETY OF her report wound down, the captain of the Watch pointed to the chest which now lay open, its contents in plain view.

"M'lady, am I to understand that I am to take custody of this chest and its contents as evidence of Lord Padraic's innocence?"

"That is correct, Captain," Ellen answered, "and more to the point, it is evidence of Silenos' guilt in the deaths of Duke Briar and his aides. And to be even more accurate, it is further evidence of Silenos' past crimes, many of which may have been perpetrated in other Council realms."

"This must be shared with the other Council realms," Lady Orla insisted. "They have a right to know. However, there will be questions—like how we acquired this, you see?"

Ellen smiled. "That's to be expected. May I suggest that the Watch receive the credit for acquiring the chest and the damning evidence within? It was, in fact, found on Mer, through confidential means available to the Watch. It was found in the constructive possession of a criminal, a pirate and documented minion of Silenos, known as Rathskellen."

She pointed to the stenciled seal. "That is Rathskellen's seal and the identification mark that establishes Silenos as the owner of the chest and its contents."

"Hence the documentation?" Mark asked with a smirk. "Captain, if I may ask; would you need further corroboration for any local court proceeding? Like producing this Rathskellen to give testimony?"

The captain shook his head. "I do not think so; but, I am not entirely certain. Rathskellen is known to us, of course; at one time he was quite the scoundrel. We know him to be in New Port Royal, which is generally presumed to be out of our reach. Of course, that assumption may change with the Steward's suggested strategy—not a bad thing, I think. Nonetheless, actually producing him before a legal proceeding could be a problem."

"Uh, Captain, if necessary," Trey offered, winking at Hawk, "I'm sure that my partner and I, in a cooperative consulting role, could handle that for you—with the Steward's help of course."

The captain smiled. "Why, thank you. I will let you know."

"Let me remind you all," Ellen gestured to the contents of the chest, "that this evidence is of much wider concern and scope than might impact only one realm. No one knows how many are already aware of Silenos and his dark deeds. Speculative rumors of an atrocity and walking dead on the Keys of Osiris circulate as we speak."

The captain and Selene shared a glance and nodded affirmatively.

"That is true," the undine confirmed, "and the name of Silenos is so whispered in Derinseum."

"Time may become an issue, as well," Ellen warned. "As Lady Orla so wisely pointed out, this must be brought to the Council's attention soon. The scourge of necromancy is anathema to the Council. It would not do at all for such rumors to reach the Council before an official notification from a member realm is lodged. We all know that these rumors are inevitable, and will likely grow to frightening proportions."

"Quite so," agreed Lady Orla. "I will make a request to call an immediate executive session. Lord Mark, I would appreciate your support in this."

"You have it, Lady Orla. I am at your disposal."

"Captain, send for your men," Lady Orla commanded. "Keep this chest safe until we can bring it before the Council."

“Yes, m’lady.” He opened the door, stepped into the hall, and spoke in a low voice to an aide.

Before Lady Orla could stand to take her leave, Selene laid a gentle hand upon her host’s arm.

“M’lady, before you make that request, would you indulge me?”

“Of course, Selene, what is it?”

“Something Lady Ellen said . . . This may well be evidence of a possible conspiracy of necromancy that may threaten the integrity of other realms, perhaps even the Council itself. If the Watch receives credit for discovering this evidence, Mer will be regarded by all in a most favorable light. Not only will the recent unpleasantness that so compromised our economy be relegated to dim memory, but our Watch, who serve and protect all who reside *and visit*, will be deemed most efficient and professional. I suspect the Administration and the Merchants Guild will see this as a most beneficial development. Do you not agree?”

Lady Orla chuckled. “Do not worry, Selene. I fully understand the implications. Rest assured the Watch will receive the credit, as Lady Ellen suggested. Now, if you will excuse me? Lord Mark, join me, please; we have a formal request to make.”

As the door closed behind Lady Orla and Mark, Selene smiled and nodded gratefully to Ellen.

The captain closed the lid on the chest, and turned to the undine.

“Well, Selene, you did say this would be an interesting meeting.”

She batted her eyelashes coyly. “Do I ever disappoint, Captain?”

Laughter ensued, the mood lightening.

Stacy nudged Ellen. “So, what now?”

Ellen thought a moment. "I suspect Mark will stay, depending on how soon the Council will call their meeting. We should probably go home."

"We should stay with the captain," Trey offered, "until his men get here."

The captain nodded in appreciation. "Thank you. They will arrive shortly."

"Okay, then we can go home," Ellen agreed. "I kinda lost track of Smokey; maybe he's at home."

BROW FURROWED AND LIPS drawn in a thin line, Malvana hurried down the corridor of Castle Diere and nearly collided with Lord Nightshade emerging from a side passage.

"Oh! Forgive me, m'lord!" Her hands fluttered in agitation. "I did not see you!"

"Nonsense, dear lady, tis no one's fault. What has you in such a hurry? Tis all well?"

Somewhat calmed, she took a breath. "I was in search of Her Majesty. The Council has called for an emergency executive session meeting. I must inform our queen."

"Yes, you certainly must. When is this meeting?"

"Tonight at moonrise."

"Oh, I see," Nightshade acknowledged, glancing up and down the corridor. "Spare me a moment, m'lady?" He guided her into the side passage.

"Of course, m'lord. Forgive me, but I thought you were in Mer. When did you get back?" she asked.

"Only a few moments ago," he admitted. "I learned that Gaspar was in Mer as well. Did you know about that?"

"No, I did not. But then he only does as the queen directs. She does not share her plans with me, as you know." There was a hint of distrust in her voice.

"Careful," cautioned Nightshade, with raised eyebrows. "This Council meeting, has it to do with certain situations in Mer? Like suspected incidents of necromancy, or perhaps Padraic's current difficulty?"

"Both, I think. The wording of the proposed agenda was sparse and rather vague—deliberately, I suspect. Of course, I will know more after the meeting—"

He pulled her into a shadowed alcove, finger to his lips for silence. They could hear footsteps hurrying down the corridor, growing louder in their approach. He held up two fingers and silently mouthed *two people.*

She nodded, edged deeper into the shadowed alcove, and pressed her back against the smooth stone of the wall. She could still see a slice of the corridor.

Queen Mab and Gaspar strode past.

Malvana started to follow, after all, she had been looking for the queen; but Nightshade gripped her wrist and pulled her back.

"Wait," he hissed in her ear, "and watch!"

Peering from the shadows, they saw Queen Mab come to a stop before a blank wall and look around. Mab whispered something to Gaspar, stepped up to the wall, and murmured some sort of incantation. In the next moment, she stepped *through* the apparently solid wall; Gaspar followed.

Malvana's jaw dropped, but she kept silent.

"Come." Nightshade pulled her into the corridor and strode away from the mysterious wall. When they entered the great hall, Nightshade paused to be certain they were alone.

"What just happened?" Malvana asked breathlessly.

His voice low, he simply said, "I have seen her do that before—something she does *not* know. I even know the incantation she uses. That wall—tell me truthfully; did *you* know? Has she ever taken you into her confidence and shown you?" He watched her reaction carefully.

She shook her head. "No, never."

He sighed. "Me neither."

"But, Gaspar, he—" she balked when he gripped her upper arms.

"He is completely her creature! Do not trust him! Do you understand?"

"Yes, of course. So, tell me; what lies behind that wall? You know, do you not?"

He released her and glanced around the great hall; they were still alone. "I do; a small room, a crystal orb this big," he held his hands slightly less than shoulder width apart, "held in the fingers of a large golden hand."

"You have been in there." It was not a question.

He smiled. "I told you I knew her incantation. Patient observation is a worthwhile skill."

Her eyes wide she asked, "The orb, what is it? What is it for?"

Nightshade shrugged. "I am uncertain; but, I suspect it is some sort of scrying device. I have tried to do some research, but the resources here are limited. I have learned that there are some in other realms who probably know a great deal more. Someday, I may seek them out, given the right circumstances, of course."

"What about Gaspar? He knows something," Malvana reasoned, and frowned. "But I realize asking him is out of the question. He is such a snake! I never liked him, never trusted him."

"You are a wise woman. He cannot know that we know anything," Nightshade warned. "You must never share a confidence with him; he will tell the queen everything."

Malvana nodded, her lips drawn in a grim line. "I understand. I do not make a habit of speaking to him beyond common courtesy; nor will I in the future."

"A *most* wise woman," Nightshade repeated smiling.

The ghost of a smile floated across her delicate features as she nodded in acceptance of the compliment.

"Now, you should go to Her Majesty's reception room," Nightshade suggested. "That is where you would be expected to await her pleasure. You have news for her, the hurried notice of the Council's executive meeting, remember?"

"Ha! As if I would forget!" She scoffed. "Be careful, m'lord. You are the only person here I know I can trust."

"Likewise, m'lady," he whispered as he bowed, "likewise, indeed."

CH 29

THE BREAKFAST DISHES done, Ellen and Stacy were lounging at the kitchen table with cups of hot coffee when the phone on the wall rang.

Millie answered. "Hello? Oh, hi Hawk. Yes, she's right here—hold on."

Ellen rose as her mother held the handset out to her. "Thanks, Mom."

Millie tossed a dish towel over one shoulder and sat down at the table. She pointed to Stacy's cup and asked, "Need a warm-up?"

Stacy sipped and shook her head. "No, thanks, it's still hot enough. Just sit for a while and relax; you've been on your feet all morning."

"I'm fine; don't worry about me. Have you heard from Mark yet?"

"No, not yet. He said the meeting was supposed to start at moonrise last night. It probably dragged on; he thought it might. What do you have planned for today?"

Millie leaned forward resting her elbows on the table. "I'm almost caught up on the outgoing orders; but our website is getting a lot of traffic. I'll just need to see what orders come in online today. It's getting so that we're seeing more online orders than we expected."

"But that's good, right? We're in the black, aren't we?" Stacy reasoned.

"Oh yes, we are doing very well, better than expected. In fact, we'll need to order more of the smaller shipping boxes sooner than I thought."

Stacy cocked her head. "You mean for the jams, jellies, and the potpourri sachets? Are our small item sales getting that good?"

Millie smiled. "I'll say! I've been thinking; you know how we've been using two sizes of small shipping boxes? Maybe we should use the same size box for all the small orders. We'd only need to change the amount of packing materials. Besides, if we were to use just one size small box, we could order them in larger bulk amounts and get a better unit price from the distributor. From what I can tell, by eliminating the smallest size box the impact on our shipping costs by weight would be negligible. What do you think?"

"Makes sense," Stacy agreed. "Have you crunched any numbers?"

Millie chuckled. "Only on a paper napkin, but I think it's feasible. I was going to wait until Mark got back to talk to everybody about it. Maybe I'll put some hard numbers on paper today for our consideration."

"That'll work. I'm sure he'll be back by supper time; you know he won't miss a meal!"

Ellen resumed her seat. "Who are we talking about, Mark?"

"Yeah, he *loves* your mom's cooking, and so does *Hawk*, I might add. So, have you learned anything from her, yet?" Stacy nudged her friend and teased, "You gotta study up on becoming a good wife, you know."

Ellen snorted in laughter. "No, *you* gotta study up on being a good wife!"

"Is Hawk coming over for supper tonight?" Millie asked.

"I don't know; but I'll ask him. He and Trey are on their way to pick me up. We're going out to play with the drones and try to find where our *cats* are hiding."

"Speaking of cats," Stacy probed, "has Smokey come home yet? I still haven't seen him."

"Me neither," Millie added.

"No, but I'm not worried," Ellen assured them.

At least, not yet.

STANDING ON A HILLTOP under the overcast sky, Hawk kept his eyes on the small monitor screen attached to the drone controller in his hands.

Ten yards away, Ellen leaned against the fender of the SUV and tried to steady her grip as she peered through a set of binoculars. She found it increasingly difficult to keep the distant airborne drone within the optics' reduced field of view, an unavoidable result of the 10X magnification factor.

In the front passenger seat of the vehicle, Trey stared at the larger monitor screen and blinked; the faint thermal glow of the pale pattern held steady.

"Hawk," Trey called out, "bring the drone back over the grid coordinates you just passed to the south, and put it in a hover."

"Have we got something?" Hawk glanced up from the onboard camera's live feed displayed on the control monitor.

"Maybe," Trey said. "It looks like thermal traces of large animal tracks. Get in position and hover."

"Got it—gimme a sec . . . Okay, we're in a hover at those coordinates. Now what? Remember, on my screen I need the daylight mode to safely fly this thing; I can't see well enough if I have to switch to thermal mode."

"Just hold your position. I've got thermal covered," Trey assured his partner. "Ellen, come look at this screen. See the pattern? Good, now go look at Hawk's screen and tell me what you see."

Ellen went back and forth from one screen to the other. "Oh, I see what you mean! The pattern of prints on your screen matches a game trail on Hawk's screen. Does that mean those prints are recent?"

"Yeah, very recent—the glow will diminish and fade as the prints cool. So, whatever made them is still in the vicinity."

Ellen pointed to the screen. "Trey, there's more than one set of prints going to the same point; but, then they just abruptly stop. What does that mean?"

"Probably that we've found a cave," Trey offered. "Hawk?"

"Yeah, that's what I think, too," Hawk agreed. "If we're lucky, this is where our cats are denning."

"Well, it's not that far from the clearing where we found all those bones; and there's water nearby in the bayou to the west," Ellen reasoned. "It does make sense. What now? Do you use the smaller drone for a closer look?"

"We may as well, but we won't have as long a flight time," Trey warned.

"We won't need it," Hawk countered. "We know the precise coordinates. If we don't try to get into the cave, we won't need the infrared, so the battery will last longer. But we do need to take a closer look."

"Okay, bring the big drone back," Trey said. "We'll try its little brother."

Ellen pointed skyward. "We might want to hurry up. I think it's gonna rain."

Trey glanced out the window. "Yeah, although we should be grateful for the overcast. It kept things cooler and really helped with the thermal mode."

In less than fifteen minutes, they had the large drone back in the SUV, and the small drone airborne. Sitting in the SUV, Trey and Ellen watched the larger monitor screen as Hawk, standing near the front bumper, piloted the diminutive drone in a modified grid search from treetop level.

"The canopy is pretty thick through here," he groused. "I'm gonna have to try getting a little lower."

"Be careful," Trey warned. "Try to keep it at least ten feet or so from the ground."

His focus on the monitor, Hawk nodded. "I'm trying; this isn't easy."

"Look there!" Ellen pointed. "That patch of shadow—no, back up. You went past it!"

"Gimme a sec," Hawk retorted. "Like here?"

"Almost," she said. "Can you get any lower?"

"Not *too l*ow," warned Trey.

"Whoa! Stop—I mean *hover!"* Ellen blurted. "That shadow—*it moved!"*

"Altitude! Now!" Trey shouted.

The drone abruptly rose just as something flashed beneath it.

Hawk panned the camera straight down. The monitor screen filled with the image of a crouching saber-toothed cat suddenly leaping upward. The ascending drone was just out of the reach of the massive paws. The cat dropped to the ground, spun about, and disappeared into the foliage.

"Wow," murmured Trey. "I'd say we've found our cats. I think you'd better bring the drone home."

"I'm on it." Hawk answered. "Man, I'm glad it didn't get the drone; that would've been hard to explain."

"You weren't recording, were you?" Trey asked.

Hawk didn't look up as he responded. "No, that was a live feed. Did you want to record?"

"No, definitely not!"

Hawk chuckled. "Didn't think so."

Trey just shook his head. "Okay, Ellen, now what?"

She pursed her lips and sighed. "I'm gonna open a portal somewhere on that path and try to get these cats to go through it. If I can get them to

Olmus, then we'll have some breathing room. You know what I mean, time to figure out where they really belong, and hopefully get them there."

"Sounds to me like you're gonna need some bait," Hawk observed.

"Bait?" she echoed. "I gotta think about that."

"It's starting to rain." Trey observed. "Let's secure the drone and get out of here."

There were no arguments.

IN A SMALL CAVERN ON Olmus, George gaped at the scrying orb, hardly believing his eyes. He stepped into the passage and grabbed a passing servant.

"Fetch Daegon here, immediately!"

The startled goblin hastened away. It returned in moments, following Daegon.

George simply pointed into the orb. "Our *Gaspar-cam. S*ee for yourself."

Daegon looked into the crystal and gasped.

There, in the heart of the orb, stood Queen Mab, eyes closed and mumbling, her hands outstretched around another scrying orb in a small candlelit room draped in heavy dark curtains. She dropped her hands and leaned forward, peering into the crystal.

"This will bear watching," Daegon decreed.

Despite being in another realm, George and Daegon could hear her voice, somewhat faint, yet clear.

"SO, GASPAR, I SEE YOUR information is accurate; the Watch does not want to keep Padraic in custody any longer than they must. However, no one in authority will give the order to release him."

"Not yet, Your Majesty." Gaspar's voice sounded somehow hollow. "However, the rumor amongst the watchmen is that there is now strong evidence that he did not commit these murders. The order for his release could come at any time."

"Evidence, eh? Do you know what it is?"

"No, Your Majesty, I returned to you immediately when I learned this much."

"You did well, Gaspar. This evidence, I wonder . . ."

She murmured something unintelligible and waved her hands a hairsbreadth over the orb, never quite touching the surface of the crystal. A rolling grey mist gathered within and began to fold in upon itself. The roiling cloud accelerated as small green and purple sparks flared in its core.

There was a sudden flash of foul purple light streaked with black tendrils. Mab's orb filled with an ominous black cloud of malevolent sentience.

Gaspar gasped and stumbled back, accidentally knocking over one of the candlesticks; the flame flickered out.

Mab convulsed, ground her teeth, and dropped to her hands and knees. Grimacing in pain, she pointed a shaking finger at Gaspar.

"Right the candle!" she spat, fighting to speak through gritted teeth. "Relight it! Now!"

He scrambled to follow her instructions. His hands were shaking so badly, he could barely manage to get the slim taper lit. Once done, he stepped back and held his breath.

The dark entity contained in the befouled orb pulsed in seething frustration, once more constrained.

Mab forced her jaws to open and and her panting to slow. She slowly rose to one knee and beckoned for Gaspar to assist her. Once standing, she pushed his arm aside and folded her arms across her chest.

Gaspar found his voice, but could not take his eyes from the cursed crystal.

"Y-your Majesty, w-what is th—"

She cut her eyes at him. "The *soul-stealer.* It lies in wait in the *void,* and preys on the unwary who would make use of this orb. I have taken precautions, of course."

"Ah, um, the candles, Your Majesty?"

She brushed at the front of her gown and scoffed. "Of course! These candles carry spells of my own design. When arranged in a pentagram, they force containment on whatever might lurk nearby in the void when the orb is in use. The activation of the spell is, naturally, *my* secret."

"Of course, Your Majesty." Gaspar bowed. "You are a most adept user of magic."

She sniffed. "Indeed, I am."

He pointed to the quiescent orb, all trace of the malevolent sentience now gone. "You bested a most powerful entity, before my very eyes. I am in awe, my queen."

"Enough. I now know what I need to know. I have other matters that require my attention. Find Nightshade and send him to me in my reception chamber—but tell him nothing about any of this."

She waved a hand in dismissal, leading him beneath a heavy curtain and through what appeared to be a blank wall.

A REALM AWAY, IN OLMUS, George and Daegon stared at one another in a long moment of silence.

"Well, our *Gaspar-cam* has certainly answered one question for you," George remarked. "There is definitely more than one of these scrying orbs."

Daegon nodded, still obviously deep in thought.

"What the hell is a *soul-stealer?*" George asked. "Ever heard of such a thing?"

Daegon shrugged. "I do not think so. I'll have to check my sources. I must admit, this was most enlightening. We have learned something of value; and this gives me some ideas."

"Yeah? Like what?"

"Patience, my apprentice. Suffice to say, we may have found a way . . . Oh, enough, for now. As it happens, I know this Nightshade, of whom she spoke. He may be a potentially worthwhile ally. Time will tell."

RIDING BACK TO DELAFAIRE Farm in the rear seat of the SUV, Ellen voiced her concerns.

"Don't take this the wrong way, guys, but I'm not comfortable with using bait with these cats. They're predators, right? So, they would probably only be attracted to *live* bait; I just don't wanna go there! There has to be some other way."

Trey and Hawk exchanged glances.

"Come on," Ellen insisted, "let's put our minds to it."

"Well, if we're sure we've found their den," Hawk reasoned, keeping his eyes on the road, "there might be another way."

"Yeah? Like what?" Trey asked, fumbling with his seat belt.

Hawk looked into the rearview mirror and sought her eyes. "Ellen, you can place a transit globe anywhere you want it, right?"

She shrugged. "Within reason, if I know some details about the location, but yeah. Why?"

"We pretty much know the location of the den. We know the cats will have to come and go, you know, to get water and to hunt, right? So, Ellen, could you open a transit globe right at the entrance, or really close?"

Ellen gnawed at her lower lip. "Possibly, but I can't leave it open. I'd have to open it long enough for the cats to pass through and then close it right away."

"Yeah! I get that," Trey deduced. "You don't want them to turn around and come back. So, that means you'd have to see them go through in one direction, and then close it, right?"

"Assuming they went through together, right," she echoed. "Of course, I could open and close it twice if only one went through at a time. However, it means I'd have to be there, for both possibilities."

"Does it, really?" Hawk proffered. "What if you could see everything remotely? Wouldn't that work for you?"

"You mean like with the drones?" Trey asked. "You know our time is up. We have to return them to the tech unit; they've got another case pending."

"I know, I know," Hawk answered in a rush. "I didn't mean the drones; although, they did give me the idea. I'm thinking about digital CCTV cameras that can transmit real-time wireless signals. If we can get a set focused on the specific area, Ellen could open and close the transit globe from a distance—a *safe* distance. What do you think?"

Trey shrugged. "It sounds plausible. Ellen?"

She nodded. "Yeah, it is: I like it. You mean like those game cameras that hunters like to use, you know, small camouflaged cameras they can strap to trees along game trails?"

"Not exactly, but the same principle," Hawk explained. "I think we'll need something a bit more sophisticated. And we know just who to ask for advice and guidance, don't we, Trey?"

His partner grinned. "Yeah, I get it—your grandfather's casino security surveillance gurus."

"Exactly," Hawk confirmed. "They stay abreast of the latest in surveillance gear and are sure to have whatever is currently *state of the art*."

Trey twisted around in his seat and stage-whispered to Ellen. "Sometimes, it really matters who you know."

"And who is willing to trust us with some expensive equipment," Hawk added.

Ellen smiled. "Okay, I gotta admit I like this plan better. I really didn't want to go the *bait route*."

Hawk nodded in the mirror. "Okay, I'll talk to my grandfather tonight. If all goes well, I think we could get the gear and get set up in the next day or so. For now, let's get you home."

"Well now, you know you would be just in time for supper, if y'all were so inclined," Ellen teased.

Trey brightened. "Oh really? You don't think Miss Millie would mind?"

Ellen chuckled. "I don't think that's a problem." She pulled her phone out. "I'll call her to confirm, but I'm certain she'd be disappointed if you didn't come."

Trey looked askance to his partner. "See? Sometimes it really does matter who you know."

UPON ENTERING THE KITCHEN, they found Millie and Stacy setting the table.

Mark had returned in time for supper. He stood by a window and tried to stay out of the women's way. His expression was grim.

"What's wrong, Mark?" Ellen asked. "What happened at the meeting?"

He shook his head. "A lot of confusion, wild speculation, and a number of arguments. I'm not sure anything was actually accomplished. No one wanted to commit to any one plan of action without consulting the powers that be in their home realms. We're scheduled to meet again in two days."

"Two days? Jeez . . . What about Padraic?" she pressed.

"Oh, he's to be released tomorrow morning. Lady Orla made it clear that he is no longer suspected in the recent deaths of Duke Briar and his aides in Derinseum. In fact, thanks to the evidence *found by the Derinseum Watch*, which Lady Orla produced at the meeting, the satyr, Silenos, is now considered the prime suspect. However, to be honest, some sound like they aren't convinced."

"What do you mean, Mark?" Trey asked.

Mark sighed and scratched his head. "Remember, you've gotta understand that there are essentially two voting blocs within the Council, the Seelie and Unseelie Courts. They are usually in opposition to one another on almost any matter. To some degree, that's the case here. Everyone is alarmed and frightened at the evidence of necromancy; hell, they're freaked out, if not borderline paranoid. Of course, that means there's plenty of unfounded speculation and insecure finger-pointing going on, even more than normal. Let me explain.

"The Light Elves have been making backhanded accusations and innuendo that the Dark Elves were somehow responsible for the death of Duke Briar and his aides. Everyone knows that Padraic and the house of Briar have some history, even though, thanks to the evidence, the focus is now primarily on Silenos.

"I should mention that since the satyr is now under suspicion, any claim he and his fauns may have made of diplomatic status is considered blatantly bogus; they would now enjoy no such protection.

"The Dark Elves are suggesting that Queen Titania of the Light Elves was silent patron to Silenos, and therefore bears some responsibility for the death of her own courtier, Duke Briar. Clearly, there is some level of personal animosity between the two elfin queens. I think the representative avatars, Lady Rowan of the Light Elves and Lady Malvana of the Dark Elves, are essentially out of their depth in these present circumstances and are merely adhering to their respective *party lines.*

"The unfortunate result is that the other member realms are equally unsure and tend to share the perspective of the Faerie Court to which they belong. This effectively stalls any action on the part of the Council. The bottom line is that they haven't a clue what to do; they're just dithering about and endlessly arguing."

"Paralysis by paranoid analysis," Stacy observed and nudged Mark's arm. "So, what do *you* think they should do?"

Mark sighed. "They should all get a grip! Seriously, they should authorize and conduct a thorough investigation of these incidents of necromancy *and* Silenos, and let the chips fall where they may. However, neither court sufficiently trusts the other; so paralysis rules the day. Now, I *do* have an idea, but I need to run it by all of you first."

"I'm ready to serve supper," Millie announced. "Y'all take your seats, now. You can talk during the meal, you know?"

"Yes, ma'am," Ellen responded and gestured for her guests to sit. "Okay, Mark, what do you have in mind?"

He settled in his chair and smiled as Stacy placed a big bowl of crawfish etouffee before him.

"It's simple, really. I would suggest that the Council entrust the investigation to us, the Realm of Man. As a nonaligned realm, we have no Faerie Court-based agenda, no reason to slant the findings. And to be brutally honest, if perhaps a bit insensitive, the other realms really don't have the skills to mount an effective investigation."

"Whoa," Stacy warned, "that sounds a little harsh. You'd better explain."

Mark looked around the table sheepishly. "Yeah, I know. I could be wrong, but I gotta admit I've seen nothing in any of the other Council realms that suggests any depth of creativity or curiosity. In fact, those aspects are more often than not discouraged, if not actually suppressed. Think about it; their societies and social development are for the most part static. I'm no expert, but even I know that effective investigation requires intuition; curiosity and creativity are essential elements of intuition. Am I wrong? Trey, Hawk, what do you think?"

The detectives shared a glance and shrugged.

"Nope, you're right," Trey confirmed.

"And I bet you had us in mind when you cooked up this idea, right?" Hawk smirked.

Mark grinned. "Maybe a little, but I think we'll all be involved in some way. Look, if I brought this up before the Council as a proposal in the spirit of compromise, they would debate it for a while; but, eventually they'd go for it. At least then they'd feel like they're doing something rather than arguing in circles. Of course, I'd expect the Council to be pressured to have someone from each court assigned to actively observe the investigation, if you know what I mean."

"Hmmph, we're used to that," Hawk countered.

"Yeah, so long as they don't interfere," Trey added in a solemn tone.

"All right everyone. Your etouffee is getting cold—eat!" Millie insisted.

CH 30

AT THE KNOCK UPON HIS office door within Castle Diere, Lord Nightshade looked up from his desk as the servant entered and executed a brief bow.

"Forgive the disturbance, m'lord; a messenger delivered this scroll for you." A small sealed scroll tube lay in the servant's outstretched hand.

"A messenger, hmm? Do we know him?" Nightshade pointed to his desktop; the servant laid the tube down where indicated.

"Aye, m'lord, a lad from a local village. He claimed a hooded man paid him some coppers to deliver this scroll to you. The boy was stopped by the guards at the front gate."

Nightshade scoffed. "Hmmph, of course he was. Is there anything else?"

"No, m'lord." The servant withdrew, gently closing the door behind him.

Nightshade leaned back in his chair, steepled his fingers, and stared at the curious scroll tube. He slowed his breathing and let his eyes slip out of focus.

Ah! As I suspected, a privacy spell, a rather strong one, protects this scroll. Hmm, there seems to be a trace of something else, but it does not appear harmful. I was not expecting any missives; so, who sent this? I may as well find out.

He picked up the scroll tube and broke the seal. He felt a barely perceptible tingling in his hands as the privacy spell dissipated; clearly, he was the intended recipient. He removed the scroll and unrolled the parchment.

Wary, yet curious, he studied the simple message.

Midnight – south tower observation deck – alone ~ D.

His brow furrowed, Nightshade peered closely at the entirety of the parchment. There was nothing else to be seen; that brief instruction constituted the whole message. He laid the open scroll on the desktop.

"Curious, indeed," he mumbled. "Very well, we shall see what we shall see."

After a moment, a vague mist arose from the parchment and quickly evaporated.

The unrolled scroll was now blank.

AT THE APPOINTED HOUR, Nightshade stepped from a stairwell doorway onto the flagstone walk that led to the wide observation deck of the south tower. To his right the tower continued to rise above him, girdled by an outer staircase. A mere sliver of a crescent moon offered the barest of light; nonetheless, he could see he was alone. He walked to the far side of the observation deck, gripped the balustrade, and looked down into the empty stable yard; nothing stirred that he could see.

His ears felt a slight increase in pressure. He turned to see a black transit globe appear near the center of the wide deck. A familiar form stepped forth.

"Daegon!" Nightshade gasped. "So, the scroll *was* from you; I suspected as much. Why are you here?"

"Greetings, friend Nightshade. We have to talk, in private."

"Here? You *do* know where you are, do you not?"

Daegon chuckled and opened his hands. "Absolutely. In fact, I am very familiar with this very spot. I am certain we can speak candidly here."

Nightshade glanced around; they were alone. "So be it. You know, some think you are dead, after that *incident* in Derinseum; others seek you for questioning in that same matter. Your name has been whispered about, even as the possible author of that suspected necromancy. You do know you are, in effect, a wanted man?"

Daegon shrugged. "Yes, well about that . . . I have a favor to ask of you; in return for which, I am in a position to share some very interesting information, with you alone."

"You have my attention. What sort of information?"

Daegon dropped his voice. "The sort of information that has essentially confirmed our suspicions regarding the deaths of our late queen, her *magus primus*, and our mutual friend, Tanist."

"Confirmation?" Nightshade echoed. "And Tanist as well? Is this not something that his daughter, Malvana, should hear?"

"Hmm, possibly," Daegon hedged. "However, I think this would not be easy for her. You know I would wish her no ill or discomfort."

Nightshade offered a knowing smile. "Trust me, Daegon. There is a spine of steel in that young woman. Do not underestimate her. If this concerns her father, she will want to know; she would insist."

"Very well, but first—"

"Ah! The favor?" Nightshade guessed.

"Yes, the favor . . . We both know you have a long reach and considerable, ah, *influence.* I ask that you have your resources in Mer, especially those in Derinseum, circulate rumors to the effect that *Silenos* is responsible for *all* acts of necromancy in that realm. Any mention of my name should be disregarded—quashed, if possible. I know you can do this."

"Perhaps . . . Why would you ask this of me?"

Daegon smiled. "Simply because I have further business in Mer, research essentially. If I am no longer under any suspicion, I can continue my research without any unwelcome scrutiny."

"I see. So, Silenos, eh?" Nightshade stroked his chin. "Tis true that he is presently the topic upon many tongues. Indeed the rumors are most ominous and likely inflated; credibility is in question. I have my own suspicions regarding the incident in Derinseum.

"Do not take me for a fool, Daegon; I would not be surprised if you were somehow involved. But be that as it may, we do find ourselves living in interesting times. So, aside from your vaunted *information,* why should I help you?"

Daegon stepped closer, their faces inches apart. "Because sooner or later, you will come to realize you cannot trust your current queen. She has a hidden agenda; and, she is willing to sacrifice anyone and everyone in that pursuit. You are within her inner circle; surely, you have seen enough to have your own suspicions. Mark my words; the time will come when you will need a strong ally outside her reach and influence—especially if you want to protect yourself and anyone you hold dear."

There was the weight of truth in Daegon's words; and Nightshade knew it.

"So, Silenos?" the elfin lord repeated.

"Indeed," Daegon confirmed. "It has already become common knowledge that he is responsible for what happened in the Keys of Osiris. It should be no great leap for him to be assessed the responsibility for the incident in Derinseum as well."

"Derinseum? Ah, you refer to that incident in which members of the Watch were attacked, and you were somehow spared and made your escape?" Nightshade's eyebrows rose at the blatant irony.

"The very same, in truth!" Daegon placed a splayed hand upon his chest and smiled.

"And I suppose the attacking satyr cast some spell that narrowly missed you as you fled the scene, but compromised and jumbled your memory of the event? Surely that is why you did not report it?"

“Oh, that is good!” Daegon grinned. “Yes, that is exactly what happened.”

“This rumor will be no problem to spread; it will develop a life of its own within a day.” Nightshade waved a hand dismissively. “Manipulating public sentiment is easy when you have such a ready and deserving scapegoat available.”

“So, do we have an agreement?” Daegon asked and extended his hand.

“We do.” Nightshade shook the offered hand. “Now, your information?”

“Ah yes . . . Tell me, Lord Nightshade, how well did you know the late mage, Atrellan?”

“Not well. He was an aloof sort, and truth be told, a bit insufferable. He had little regard for anyone of a lesser station. Even Tanist, who got along with everyone, did not care for him. Why do you ask?”

“Because I have learned that Atrellan had many secrets,” Daegon confided, “some of which led to the deaths of those we cared about, and ironically, his own.”

“Indeed? How so?”

Daegon sighed. “Bear with me; I will share all I know. Then we must decide what to do about it.”

“Very well,” agreed Nightshade, “but remember, the Lady Malvana must be fully informed as well.”

Daegon nodded. “So be it.”

SEATED IN THE SUV, parked once more in the vicinity of the suspected cat den, Ellen peered at the laptop screen. Two views of the spot were depicted on a split screen. She knew the portal was there, very near the entrance to the cave, but it was not visible. Of course, it wouldn’t be.

Hawk leaned over the back of her seat and spoke softly over her shoulder. "So, it's in place? We're good to go? I don't see anything."

She chuckled. "We're good. It's there, but I haven't opened it yet. You won't see it on this screen. If I crafted it right, Trey won't see it with the binoculars either."

Hawk leaned out of the vehicle. "Hey Trey! See anything?"

Ten yards away, Trey lowered the binoculars and scowled at his partner. "Don't shout!"

Hawk smiled as Trey shook his head and started walking toward the SUV.

About halfway there, Trey's phone rang; he stopped to take the call.

Hawk leaned back in his seat and smiled. "I don't think Trey saw anything. Now what?"

"I'm not sure," she admitted. "I can open the portal any time. In a best-case scenario, I'd really like to view everything, you know, see the cats first; but it may not work out that way. It'll be dusk soon. I'm not sure how well the cameras will work in low light. We don't even know if the cats are nocturnal or what. There are just too many variables."

"Ah, whatever—don't sweat it. We'll just roll with it." He scoffed and waved a hand. "The techs said the cameras will work pretty well in low light, automatic aperture settings and such. In full dark we'd probably need the infrared mode; but that'll drain the batteries quicker. They told me to only expect a couple of hours if we use the infrared."

Ellen nodded. "What about the laptop? How long will that battery last?"

"Oh, don't worry about that," Hawk assured her. "That's my new laptop; I've only had it about a week. I understand the battery's good for six to seven hours."

"This is *your* laptop?" she asked in surprise. "This is a nice computer! And here I thought you borrowed everything from the casino's tech crew."

"No, not everything, just the two CCTV cameras. They offered one of their laptops, but I passed when I found out mine would work. I just had to let them temporarily install a proprietary software program to receive and record the encrypted wireless signal. To be honest, I didn't want to be responsible for any more equipment than necessary. Those cameras and lenses are expensive enough."

"Trust me; I get it." She smiled and coyly stroked the edge of the monitor screen. "And I really do like your sexy new computer."

He returned her smile. "Me, too."

Trey climbed into the backseat, sat next to Hawk, and groaned. "Oh man, I'm tired of standing; I'm gonna sit for a bit. Oh, am I interrupting?"

Ellen grinned at Hawk.

"Would it matter?" Hawk asked. "So, who was on the phone?"

"Sgt. Melancon from the CSI unit. We've got some lab tests back; he's gonna leave the reports on my desk. The DNA tests on the skull we found confirmed the victim's identity as our missing person, the farmer, Johansen."

"Damn, I was afraid that was the case," Hawk uttered. "What else?"

"Remember the packet of suspected meth Selene got in Derinseum? We knew it field-tested positive for meth, but now we know it's of very high quality. In fact, it bears remarkable similarities to the high-grade stuff Teddy Pots was known to cook. The lab doesn't think it's from an old batch of his; it's too fresh. *Somebody* cooked it up recently."

"What? Teddy Pots in Derinseum?" Hawk shook his head. "That doesn't make any sense."

Trey shrugged. "I know. However, nobody has gotten a line on him since he disappeared from Oakdale. I only told the lab we got the packet from a CI, so they don't have any details. It'd be nice if we could find Teddy before anyone else does."

"Yeah," Hawk agreed. "We still need to talk to him about what he saw that night at Tippet's store—or more likely confirm what we already suspect. Anyway, was there anything else from Mel?"

Trey nodded. "Yeah, they ran ballistics tests on the 9mm slugs we recovered in Derinseum. All rounds were fired from the same gun; but, there's no match in our database. I'll work up redacted copies of that report for both our friend, the captain of the Derinseum Watch, and Lady Orla."

"Wait, how did we get CSI to process those slugs?" Hawk asked. "We didn't have a case reference number, did we?"

"No, I told Mel it was from something that turned out to be out of our jurisdiction, not linked to an ongoing investigation, and may not even be related to a crime. So, I suggested he use them as training aids for his rookie techs. You know he's always on the watch for stuff like that he can use for in-service training. Besides, if we were to need them for some reason, we know where they are, and the chain of custody is intact."

"Oh yeah, that was pretty slick," Hawk reasoned.

"On the other hand, the Johansen matter is gonna be a problem," Trey cautioned. "Animal attack is likely gonna be the official COD; so, the other concerned agencies will be getting more involved. Of course, the cell-phone photo of a bear in the vicinity is being viewed as pretty conclusive. Wildlife and Fisheries agents will definitely be looking to track in the area. Which reminds me, is Miska still off-world?"

"Yes, he is," Ellen confirmed.

"Good." Trey nodded. "It would be wise for him to stay there for a while."

Ellen shrugged. "That won't be a problem for now. At some point though, he'll have to come home. Just let me know when you think it's safe."

"I will," Trey assured her. "I don't think it will take too long."

"Well, that means we'd better deal with these cats before the guys from Wildlife and Fisheries get started with their own search protocols," Hawk warned.

"True dat!" Trey chuckled. "They don't miss a trick; if those cats are still here, they'll find `em for sure."

"Well, then," Ellen declared, "let's get started. I'm ready to open the portal, but I'll wait until you're back in position, Trey. Don't worry too much about having a clear view; I crafted the portal so you wouldn't notice it until you're right at the event horizon. You'd almost be in it before you'd see it."

"Okay, that's good. To be honest, I can't see that much even with the binoculars. The shadows are getting long and the light's gonna fade soon enough. I'll try for a little while more, but I'll probably join you two in pretty short order."

He slipped from the vehicle and went back to his former position. When ready, he waved.

"Okay," Hawk acknowledged. "Do it, Ellen."

"It's open. Now, I guess we wait."

IN LESS THAN TWENTY minutes, Trey gave up and returned to the SUV.

"No joy?" Hawk asked.

"Nope, too dim now that dusk has set." Trey returned the binoculars to their case. "How are y'all doing?"

"We've got good resolution, even in low light," Ellen answered, never taking her eyes from the screen. "These are really good cameras. Hawk, make sure you thank your grandfather; this is a really big help."

"I will," Hawk assured her. "Say, isn't it about time you got to know him? He's family, you know."

"Huh? What—meet your family?" Her eyes locked on his in surprise. "Well, I-I guess we could—"

"Look!" demanded Trey, jabbing a finger at the laptop screen. "Who, or *what,* the hell is that?"

A short, rotund figure stumbled forth, seemingly from thin air, and fell forward onto splayed oversized hands and thin bony knees. Righting itself quickly on the game trail, it spun about, grasped a shapeless red cap off its misshapen head, and balked in surprise and confusion. Its arms and legs were rail-thin, its feet large and long. Wide eyes darted to and fro; pointed ears twitched in agitation.

Two more figures, fauns, carrying wicked black-bladed knives, stepped from the portal and confronted the gangly, quaking figure.

"Have we got sound?" whispered Trey.

"No, just video," Hawk breathed. "They can't hear us, either."

"Damn! Fauns!" muttered Ellen. "I didn't expect them in Olmus this soon."

"Silenos' fauns?" Trey probed.

"Yeah, probably," she groaned. "I've no clue who, or what, the other one is; but I think he's afraid of them."

"No doubt," Hawk confirmed. "Look at those blades."

One of the fauns gripped the frightened creature by the shoulder, spun him about, and shoved him in the direction of the cave. With a worried glance over his thin shoulder, he pulled the red cap down on his head, and hesitantly disappeared into the cave mouth. The two fauns followed.

"So, you were expecting Silenos and his fauns?" Trey asked.

"Yeah, in Olmus." Ellen scoffed, and shook her head. "But not this soon, and certainly not here! I kind of *baited* them to go to Olmus, but I wanted to have the cats already there."

"Oh, a little welcoming surprise?" Hawk reasoned. "You can be quite devious, can't you?"

Smiling impishly she said, "Nobody should mess with my family—not ever."

"No sign of Silenos himself, just the fauns so far," Trey observed. "How did they find the portal, I mean the other end on Olmus? They obviously used it to get here, right?"

Ellen sighed. "That's probably my fault. I didn't think to craft the other end so it wouldn't be easily seen, like I did this end. It would look like a normal transit globe, once I opened it."

"But wait," Hawk interjected, "isn't Olmus supposed to be uninhabited?"

"Supposed to be, yeah," she echoed. "In rescuing Brona, I knew Silenos would try to follow; so, I thought to lead him to Olmus—"

"And have a surprise waiting for him—the cats, right?" Trey concluded.

"Basically, yeah," she admitted with a shrug.

"But Murphy's Law, right?" Hawk grinned.

She cut her eyes at him and pursed her lips.

"Uh-oh, look!" Trey pointed at the screen once again.

The two fauns ran pell-mell down the path from the cave; upon reaching the portal, they appeared to vanish into thin air. An instant later, the red-capped creature, fleeing in full panic, scrambled after them and disappeared as well.

"What the—?" Hawk never finished the thought.

The saber-toothed cats bounded from the cave mouth, paused to sniff the air, and stared down the game trail. In the next instant, the larger of the cats leapt forward—and disappeared! The second cat sniffed the air, looked to either side, and with a mighty leap followed.

The game trail lay empty.

"Ellen, close the portal!" Trey urged. "Do it now!"

She did. "They both went through, didn't they?"

Hawk nodded slowly. "They *all* did. God help `em."

"I think we're done here," Trey said. "Let's retrieve the cameras and get out of here."

Hawk looked to Ellen. "Are you okay?"

"Uh, yeah, but—"

He took her hand. "Look, there's nothing we can do. There's no way of knowing anyone would find the other end of the portal. No one was even supposed to be there! This isn't your fault!"

She shook her head. "No, you misunderstand. I'm not having second thoughts, nor do I really care about the fauns. I'm pissed because I've inadvertently led them here, to our home realm! I didn't want to do that!"

Her phone vibrated.

"It's a text from my mom; Mark is back and needs to see us."

THEY FOUND MILLIE IN the kitchen, preparing supper.

Stacy paused in setting the table. “Hey! You’re back! You’ve got good timing. Supper will be ready in about ten minutes.”

Seated at the kitchen table, Mark grimaced, clutched his iced tea, and offered an apology.

“Man, I’m sorry. I tried, guys—I really did. But I couldn’t get the Council to make a final decision. The political posturing and petty nit-picking is beyond annoying.”

Ellen accepted an iced tea from her mother and sat opposite her cousin. Hawk sat next to her.

“So, what happened?” she asked.

Mark nodded to Trey and Hawk. “I may have written a check you guys are gonna have to cash.”

“How so?” Trey asked, taking a seat to Hawk’s right.

Stacy topped off Mark’s tea.

“Thanks.” he mumbled. “Remember, y’all said something to the Watch captain about helping to produce Rathskellen if he was needed? Well, the Light Elves have taken the position that the ‘evidence’ needs corroboration; specifically, that it is, in fact, the property of Silenos. So, Rathskellen must appear and attest to that fact. So now, the Watch needs your help.”

“That’s all?” Ellen asked looking to Trey and Hawk. “This is no big thing, right?”

“Shouldn’t be,” Trey assured her. “He’s supposed to be operating in New Port Royal. If you can get us there, he shouldn’t be too hard to find. Where would we have to produce him?”

"The Council Realm," Mark answered, "before an executive session, with only the representatives of the member realms present, and as soon as possible."

Ellen leaned forward and propped her elbows on the table. "So Mark, what do you think is really going on?"

"Truthfully? I don't know for sure; but it's clear the two elfin queens are at odds with one another. Padraic's release somehow has Titania miffed. She still insists the Dark Elves bear some responsibility, but offers no proof. Mab is apparently ignoring her, which is just adding fuel to the fire. Remember that neither queen is present, just their avatars; so, the bickering is secondhand, filtered through at least two degrees of separation, and cloaked in pithy court-speak. Make no mistake, the animosity, however subtle, is real and escalating.

"If the two queens would just back off and take a breath, the rest of the members would go for my suggestion of letting us, the Realm of Man, conduct the investigation. I'm hoping that producing Rathskellen will negate Titania's objection."

"Maybe," Stacy offered, "but how do you know she won't just raise another?"

Mark shrugged. "That's true; she might. But I think the Council will have had enough of this squabbling, and will vote to proceed."

"So, we have to produce Rathskellen in the Council Realm," Ellen reasoned, "and then we can commence a sanctioned investigation, have I got that right?"

"Essentially, yes." Mark leaned back in his chair. "I'm sorry I couldn't do any better."

"I don't think it'll be a problem," Trey proffered and glanced at his partner.

Hawk grinned and shook his head. "Not at all. How soon?"

Mark winced. "As soon as possible?"

"Tomorrow?" Ellen suggested. "Hawk, you've still got to return the cameras, right?"

"I'll do that tonight."

"Oh, that reminds me," exclaimed Stacy, "how did your *cat project* turn out?"

Trey caught Ellen's eye before she answered. She understood.

"Oh, uh, it worked," she said simply. "The cats are gone, off to a realm in the *wild* for now."

MAB ROSE FROM HER THRONE, looked down her nose at her consort and sniffed. "Well, you do not look any worse for wear; but you do need to bathe."

Padraic scowled, but remained silent.

Mab gestured to her servants. "Leave us; see that we are not disturbed."

As the last departing servant closed the door to the throne room, Padraic put a finger to his lips and pointed to a small seating alcove beneath a tall diamond-mullioned window.

The queen's eyebrows rose, but she nodded and followed him into the alcove. She carefully arranged her skirt and sat, her curiosity obvious.

"What now? Secrets?"

He sat and leaned close. "Tis best we are not overheard."

"Go on," she insisted, her impatience growing.

He kept his voice low, barely above a whisper. "I have learned that this Silenos is very likely a real threat, not to be underestimated."

"Ha!" She scoffed. "That is common enough talk among Council members. Malvana keeps me well informed. What has this to do with me?"

He sighed. "You know he slew Duke Briar and his aides, a crime for which I was suspected. He has slain many, and wields the power of necromancy to some unknown degree. The Council has proof of this, yet they still bicker among themselves, and accomplish nothing."

She waved a hand in blasé dismissal. "So? I should care because. . ?"

His gaze hardened; his eyes locked on hers. "You must stop this petty feud with Titania. Set aside your differences, at least for now, so the Council can work cohesively to deal with this pressing issue."

Her ire smoldered. "What? You dare to speak to me like this! I—"

He grabbed her wrist, crushing the delicate lace of her sleeve.

"Yes! I dare! Because no one else would! You are greatly feared; you know that! None would tell you the truth, lest they incur your wrath. But the fact remains; this animosity between you and Titania, stoked by the acrimonious public sniping you are both so fond of, is at the core of the Council's present ineffectiveness. The members of the Seelie and Unseelie Courts are reluctant to act or speak, lest they run the risk of offending their respective monarch. Thus, the Council cannot act. Silenos will be free to pursue his own agenda, whatever it may be. Rest assured, that will no doubt be to the detriment of some, if not all."

He released her wrist, balled his fists, and sighed heavily.

For a long moment she stared at him in silence, her bloodless lips drawn in a grim line.

"Padraic, you have overstepped."

He shrugged. "Perhaps, someone had to . . . before it's too late."

Her eyes narrowed. "So, Silenos? What would you advise?"

"Send an emissary, perhaps your Council avatar, to Titania with an offer to work together to get the Council moving. Surely she will realize it would be to your mutual advantage to have the Council take point and deal with Silenos. The alternative is that each realm must face him in turn—on their own."

"Let the Council take the responsibility, strength in numbers and all that, hmm?" Her lower lip in a pout, she straightened out the crushed lace of her sleeve.

He nodded in agreement. "Indeed, all things considered, tis the wisest course."

"So, an emissary?" She cut her eyes at him and asked, "You would not go?"

"Ah, no. I understand Titania is not happy with me, not since her unannounced visit to my rooms in Derinseum not so long ago."

"Ah-ha-ha!" Mab cackled and clapped her hands in delight. "Oh, I have not forgotten, not in the least! Very well, I will send Malvana. Now, go clean yourself up—bathe—you are long overdue."

CH 31

BENEATH AN OVERCAST sky, a light rain fell on the begrimed town of New Port Royal. It had been raining most of the day; the evening was slipping away into what promised to be a very wet night.

Three robed and hooded figures stood under the dubious shelter of a leaning porch roof that was somehow still attached to a dilapidated vacant storefront.

"That's the place?" Trey asked, peering through the drizzle, at the faded sign hanging above the door of the Fouled Anchor, across the street.

"Looks like a worn-out saloon from an old Western," Hawk observed with a grimace.

Ellen chuckled. "You're not far off the mark; but the clientèle will be mostly nautical types; sailors, smugglers, and probably a few pirates. We should watch our backs."

"Duly noted," Trey intoned.

"I hope it's at least dry inside. Our contact is the barman?" Hawk asked.

"Right, Rumley is his name," Ellen confirmed pulling her hood down to obscure her face in shadow. "I can vouch for him; I've dealt with him before. Ready?"

Trey and Hawk tugged their hoods down a bit, hunched their shoulders, and followed her across the street, avoiding what ruts and puddles they could, and into the Fouled Anchor.

The din in the crowded barroom diminished at their entrance, but soon resumed as they were generally assessed and subsequently ignored. Ellen led the way to one end of the bar, and signaled for the barkeep's attention.

Rumley tossed a bar towel over one wide shoulder and sauntered to that end of the bar.

“Welcome to the Fouled Anchor, mates. What’ll it be?”

Ellen looked up from under her hood, smiled and winked. “Three grogs will do us.”

Rumley smiled, a twinkle in his eye, and nodded. “Comin’ up.” Under his breath, he added, “Been expectin’ ye.”

Surprised, Ellen asked, “How?”

Rumley shook his head. “Not here. Finish yer grogs `n’ ask for a room.”

She nodded once. “Got it.”

TWENTY MINUTES LATER, in the confines of a fair-sized second-floor room, lit by half a dozen candles, Ellen introduced Trey and Hawk to Rumley.

“I am pleased to know you both.” Rumley gestured to the two beds in the room. “Please, let us be seated. We can speak freely in here.”

“Good. This won’t take long,” Ellen began. “We are on a tight timeline.”

In a low voice she explained their need to locate Rathskellen, to do it quietly and as soon as possible.

Rumley’s brow shot up in surprise. “Rathskellen, is it? Ach, you don’t know, do ye?”

“Know what?” she asked.

“He’s dead—dismembered and shredded. Most of his body was found two days ago. What was left has already been consigned to the pyre. Tis naught but ashes now.”

Surprise washed over Ellen; her mind raced—*Silenos?*

"What happened?" Trey asked, ignoring the creaking bed as he leaned forward.

Rumley shrugged his huge shoulders. "No one knows for sure. Most suspect that a griffin he kept turned on him 'n' killed him."

"Griffin?" echoed Hawk.

"Aye, tis a beast—"

"Oh, I know what it is," Hawk assured him, "I'm surprised anyone would keep one as a pet."

"Truth be told," Rumley sighed heavily, "I suspect twas more slave than pet. Word is that some time ago he found the griffin's eggs and hid them from her. The threat to do harm to her eggs was sufficient to ensure her subservient compliance. You see, they are more intelligent than most beasts, and are possessed of a strong maternal instinct. Rathskellen took advantage. She was sometimes used as a threat in his business dealings, and as we now know, served to guard certain of his warehouses."

Rumley looked to Ellen, but said nothing.

"So, why would the griffin turn on him? Did she find her eggs?" Trey probed.

"It would appear so," Rumley bobbed his head, "and she took her revenge. At least, that is what most believe."

"Where is the griffin now? What happened to her?" Hawk asked.

Rumley offered his open palms. "No one knows; nor is anyone eager to go in search of her."

"I'll bet," murmured Trey.

"More power to her," Ellen mumbled *sotto voce*, then looked up. "So, this mission is a failure before we've even begun?"

Trey shrugged. "Hey, it happens."

"So, what now?" Hawk asked. "We go home?"

"We may as well," Ellen agreed. "But first, I have some questions, Rumley."

"Yes?"

"You said you were expecting us," Ellen reminded him. "How did you know, and when?"

The bed creaked under him as Rumley leaned back. "Ah, I received a communication from Gallenius this morning, so I knew to expect the three of you. He asked that I assist you in any way possible; but he did not advise me of your specific mission."

"Gallenius?" Ellen smiled and shook her head. "I should have guessed."

Rumley smiled and leveled a finger at her. "However, I have thought that you, Lady Ellen, would visit since early yesterday."

"Early yesterday?" she balked. "How? We hadn't even firmed up our travel plans until late yesterday evening. How is it you expected me?"

"Oh, because your cat is here. He's been here since yesterday morning."

"What?" Ellen jumped up and blurted, "Smokey is here? Where?"

Rumley grinned and pointed to the floor near the foot of the bed upon which she'd been sitting. "Oh, he's right there; he's been here since we sat down. I think he's been listening to us."

Smokey looked up from under the bed and blinked languidly.

Ellen scooped him up in her arms and hugged him, earning a strongly vibrating purr. She scratched vigorously behind his ears as he leaned into her nails, purring in pleasure.

"Where have you been, you rascal? What have you been up to?" *Never mind; I think I can guess.*

Noticing that the men were now smiling indulgently at her, she paused to take stock of the situation. The trip wasn't a complete failure; she had her cat back.

"Well, I guess we're done here," she announced.

"Yeah, for now," Hawk agreed, rising to his feet.

Trey rose as well. "Right, we need to go."

Standing once more, the barkeep was about to speak, but Ellen cut him off.

"Rumley, I assume it'd be best if we weren't seen departing?" she proffered.

"Aye, that would be best," he agreed. "We'll use the hidden staircase. If you are ready, follow me."

"We are ready," she assured him. "Let's go home; you too, Smokey."

ON OLMUS, IN A SMALL candlelit chamber off a passage near Teddy's lab cavern, George leaned against a rocky wall and considered what Daegon had just shared with him. To say that it piqued his interest was a gross understatement.

"Now hold on, Daegon. Let me see if I've got this right. You believe we now have an ally within Diere's, er, Mab's inner circle, someone willing to betray her?"

The alchemist nodded. "Yes, two people actually; Nightshade, of whom we have previously spoken, and Malvana, the *usurper's* avatar to the Council. She is the daughter of the Earl of Tanist, who was slain along with my queen and Atrellan."

"Slain by Diere, correct?" George confirmed.

"Yes, all three, and a host of others, in one fell swoop of foul sorcery, a deliberate act of treachery that presaged her ascension to the throne of the Dark Elves. Nightshade and Malvana are aware, and thus so motivated."

George stroked his chin. "Vengeance—I get it. This is essentially a vendetta. So, what do they want to do? Have they got a plan?"

Daegon dropped his eyes and shrugged. "That is a problem; they have no idea what to do. I fear that I do not know how to help. Planning such as this calls for a level of guile and creativity that I must admit I lack—but that you, my apprentice, do not."

George grinned. "So, you need me to craft a strategy, something that yields the vengeance the three of you seek, and removes Diere from the board, with luck, *permanently*. Yeah, that would work out just fine for me."

"Board?" Daegon asked, clearly puzzled.

"It's a chess reference—never mind." George waved a hand dismissively. "Tell me; what happens with the throne if Diere is gone? Who takes over the Dark Elves?"

Daegon hesitated. "I-I do not know. I had not given that any thought."

George shook his head and explained. "See? That's the problem with vengeance and vendettas; there's a tendency to act on emotion—that's shortsighted. Revenge is sweet, but that moment passes. Then what? You gotta think several moves ahead. Do you follow me?"

His brow creased, the alchemist nodded. "What then should we do?"

George waved his hands. "First things first. Let's focus on Diere, er, Mab. What assets does she have that she can rely upon? Who would help her? Who do we have to worry about?"

Daegon gnawed at his lower lip. "Her mage, Gaspar, I suspect. According to Nightshade, he is totally her creature, blindly dedicated to her. And then, there is also her consort, Padraic, but . . ."

"But what?"

Daegon shrugged once more. "Nightshade is uncertain, as am I, as to Padraic's loyalty to her. Court rumors paint him as a lusty Epicurean who has dalliances under her very nose. If she is aware, she ignores it. He may simply be a bawdy opportunist who finds there are certain benefits to his position at court. I do not know that he would actually support her in a crisis. Nonetheless, I would think he bears consideration."

"Hmm, I'll have to think about that," George mused aloud. "One thing for sure, whatever plan we come up with and execute, it will have to address Gaspar at the same time. We can't take her out, and leave her mage to retaliate. It's gotta be both; and it'll have to be simultaneous."

Daegon nodded in agreement. "That would be wise. Gaspar is not to be underestimated."

"We won't. The good news is that the scrying orb is still fixed on him, and has been for a while. There's not a lot about him we don't already know. Don't worry; I'll come up with a solid strategy and a simple plan." George smiled smugly. "It'll be something *elegant*."

Daegon folded his arms in confidence and returned the smile. "I knew you were the right person for this task; your creative planning is unrivaled."

George smiled and basked in the compliment.

Vito entered the chamber from the passage. "Oh, here you guys are! Sorry to interrupt, but I need to talk to both of you."

"What's up?" George asked.

“Teddy’s complained again,” Vito turned to Daegon, “about the goblin servants *you* assigned to feed the bats. It seems that every day they’re still taking a couple ounces of product—”

“What the hell?” George blurted. “The goblins are doing meth?”

“No-no! Lemme finish!” Vito held up both hands. “They’re still giving it to the bats, lacing their food and such.”

“You gotta be kidding me!” erupted George. “Daegon, we talked about this! You can’t keep giving meth to the bats. They get addicted, you’re gonna create a bigger problem than the one you’re trying to solve.”

Clearly surprised at the outburst, Daegon took a step back. “But *you* told me *to be addicted is to be controlled.* I have had a measure of success; I can exert considerably more control over the bats. They have even stopped harassing those servants who are responsible for their feeding.”

“Yeah,” Vito scoffed, “probably because the bats associate the appearance of those servants with the delivery of the drug! Come on, this ain’t brain surgery, you know.”

George shook his head. “Daegon, you’ve gotta rethink this *control* plan; meth is not the answer. Find some other way. Jeez! Giant *meth-fueled* carnivore bats are a ticking time bomb. We can’t have that here. You gotta get them off that shit.”

“Yeah,” Vito agreed, “and you can’t go *cold-turkey* either. You gotta wean ‘em off it.”

“Cold turkey?” Daegon whined, clearly befuddled.

“Aw, jeez!” George moaned and wiped a hand down his face. “Vito, take him aside and explain. I got something I gotta see to, and then check on something.”

“You got it, Boss. Anything else?”

George paused. "Yeah. Let's meet back here in an hour; we've got some plans to make."

TAILS WAGGING, THE Chows met Ellen at the front door upon her return home.

Mark and Stacy were in the front parlor watching television.

"Ellen!" Stacy cried, jumping up from the couch. "You're back early! And you've got Smokey! What happened? Where was he?"

Mark stood and turned the TV off. "What's wrong? Where are Hawk and Trey?"

"Here you go." Ellen let Stacy take Smokey and hug him. "I know you missed him."

Mark pointed to the couch. "Sit. Explain, please."

Ellen sat. "Hawk and Trey already said goodbye. They left once I got inside the house. They're all right; they've just got an early morning, court and stuff."

"Okay, so?" Mark pressed.

She held her palms open and shrugged. "Mission failure; Rathskellen is dead."

"Silenos?" interrupted Stacy, sitting next to her and letting Smokey spill from her lap.

"Don't think so. It looks more like Rathskellen was killed a couple days ago by a griffin he supposedly controlled. I understand there wasn't much left; and that's been cremated. So, we can't produce a dead man for the Council."

Mark scratched his head. "Man, that's gonna be a problem. I gotta send the Council the news, and soon. I have no idea how this will be received."

Ellen sighed. “You may as well do it now. I’m too tired to worry about how they’re gonna react.”

“Yeah, I’ll do it now.” He turned and left the room.

Stacy gripped Ellen’s arm. “I know you’re tired, but before you go to bed, please tell me about Smokey. Where did you find him?”

Ellen smiled. “In Mer, he was in New Port Royal at the Fouled Anchor. I almost think he was waiting for me there.”

Stacy’s eyes widened. “That pirate town? Oh, isn’t he a rascal! Wait a minute—do you suppose he had anything to do with this Rathskellen situation? Wasn’t he with you when you and Miska encountered a griffin?”

A lone eyebrow raised, Ellen sighed. “I admit I’ve had a sneaking suspicion about that—but there’s no way to know for sure.”

Stacy folded her arms, smiled smugly, and leaned back. “Well, it wouldn’t surprise me one bit.”

“To be honest,” Ellen chuckled, “me neither.”

They both looked up expectantly as Mark returned, his face a mask of confusion.

“I don’t get it. There was hardly any reaction to the news.”

“What do you mean?” Ellen asked.

“It was like Rathskellen was no longer a big deal. The news that he’s dead just didn’t seem to faze them. All I was told is that there is to be another executive session meeting in two days. Something is up.”

“Maybe,” Stacy offered, “they’ve worked out their differences, and are ready to act cohesively?”

Mark scoffed. “I’ll believe that when I see it.”

"Well, you'll know in two days, right?" Ellen concluded. "I'm going to bed. Goodnight, you two."

THE DOGS FOLLOWED ELLEN to her bedroom and promptly found comfortable places to sprawl. Within minutes they were asleep. Smokey had yet to find his way upstairs; so, she left the door open a few inches knowing he would soon join them.

In fact, she *was* tired. She changed, got into bed, and turned the light on her nightstand off. She would welcome sleep, but her mind would not slow. She sighed heavily and tried to let herself drift.

Did Stacy have the right of it? Did Smokey have something to do with the death of Rathskellen? Was that really too far-fetched? Smokey had definitely confronted the griffin; and, he stopped Salidar from harming the defeated beast. Had he developed a rapport with her? Perhaps I shouldn't be so surprised—I know there's more to him than meets the eye . . .

. . . Indeed, you do know this to be true.

. . . What? Maude, that's you, isn't it?

. . . Who else?

. . . Oh, I get it. I've slipped into sleep and I'm dreaming—that's how we can communicate.

. . . Of course, although, it has been a while.

. . . Yes, it has—my bad. A lot has been happening.

. . . So, I see. Now what's on your mind that your subconscious would seek me out?

. . . Wow, maybe too much—I'm not sure where to begin. Mer? Silenos? Brona? I just don't know.

. . . Well then, how about we just talk—we'll see if that can't ease your mind.

. . . I think I'd like that. I know I need to think more clearly. This might be a long night.

. . . So be it. Have faith in yourself, child—others certainly do.

OUTSIDE THE DOUBLE doors to the Royal Reception Chamber, Lord Nightshade straightened his tunic with a brisk tug and nodded to the guards. The guard to his right nodded in return, rapped three times upon the right door, and pushed it open.

A servant stationed just inside announced the elfin lord's entrance.

"Your Majesty . . . Lord Nightshade."

Nightshade saw that the queen was not alone; Gaspar sat at a small table to one side, studying a set of old scrolls.

Seated upon her throne, Mab smoothed the skirts of her pale green gown trimmed in scarlet lace, and motioned him forward. "Come, Nightshade. You may report."

As Nightshade approached the queen, he noticed Gaspar glance up from the desk, dismiss him as unimportant, and resume his close attention to the scrolls.

"Your Majesty." He held his bow until she acknowledged him.

"Yes, yes." She dismissively waved an exquisitely manicured hand. "Rise and report. What of *my* ring?"

He stood erect and nodded. "Majesty, your information was correct; the Steward did in fact have the ring. She was seen to wear it in Derinseum some days ago. However, she has since been seen in Mer and in her home realm, but without the ring. We are unable to determine what she did with it, or its current location."

Lips drawn into a thin grim line, Mab asked, "Where is she now?"

“In her home realm, at Delafaire Farm, my queen.”

Mab stood, glowering.

Before she could speak, three sharp raps sounded upon the chamber doors.

The door swung open and the servant announced, “Your Majesty . . . the Lady Malvana.”

Malvana stepped into the room and curtsied, her grey skirts and black lace petticoats flaring gracefully.

Her expression now impassive, Mab waved her forward.

“Ah, Malvana, come, come. Did we have an appointment?”

Dropping her eyes, Malvana curtsied again before the queen. “We did not, Your Majesty. Please forgive this interruption; I have important news.”

Mab extended a hand and gestured Malvana to rise. “I see. Tell me.”

“Yes, Your Majesty. I have just received word that the Council has called for an executive session meeting the day after tomorrow.”

“Indeed?” Mab stroked her delicate chin. “May we assume this is in regard to the Silenos matter?”

“I believe so, my queen. It appears that your strategy to send me to Queen Titania with the tentative proposal of *quid-pro-quo* cooperation has borne fruit.”

Mab scoffed. “That, or the Council has grown tired of her petty petulance and would now come to a decision with or without her.” She raised a finger. “However, we also know that the witness she demanded be produced cannot be. Is that not so, Nightshade?”

"Quite so, Your Majesty. Rathskellen is dead. It appears Queen Titania is out of options; she can stall no longer, nor prevent the Council from authorizing a full investigation into all these matters."

"Excellent!" Mab declared. "Her hidden support of this Silenos, this vile necromancer, will be exposed! I am going to enjoy this." She leveled her finger at her avatar. "Malvana, you will, of course, vote for a full investigation, and urge that it commence immediately. Is that clear?"

"Absolutely clear, my queen." Malvana curtsied deeply. "If that is all, Your Majesty, may I be excused to prepare?"

"As you will," Mab uttered with a flick of her wrist.

When the doors closed once more, Nightshade spoke up.

"Your Majesty, there is another small matter that has come to my attention, of which you should be aware."

She tugged at the hem of her chartreuse bodice and sat more erect.

"Go on."

"As you may recall, while in service to our late queen, her late *Magus Primus,* Atrellan, was in possession of certain holdings, the disposition of which has not yet been addressed."

"Holdings? What holdings?" she demanded.

"A small castle, a mountain redoubt actually, and the lands in its immediate vicinity. He used it, with the queen's blessing, of course, for certain research in arcane sorcery and spell crafting. It holds a library, a workshop laboratory, stables, and rather extensive dungeons. I understand there are no servants; it has been abandoned.

"It seems that several prominent noble Houses are aware of these holdings and are crafting plans to assume possession. As you know, such holdings are at the discretion of the Crown, it would be up to Your Majesty as to who would take and maintain possession."

Mab sat back and steepled her fingers. "I see."

Gaspar was suddenly at Nightshade's side. "My queen, may I be heard?"

A knowing smile crept across her face. "Of course, Gaspar."

"I would beg Your Majesty's indulgence, and ask that you would consider me, as *your* Magus Primus, the appropriate, and *most loyal* retainer to assume possession of such a holding. I am well aware of Atrellan's modest efforts in sorcerous research and spell crafting; and while my own skills far surpass his, I admit this holding would serve my—*our* interests very well. It would be the perfect place to conduct certain, ah, *experiments* as we so recently discussed. I might—"

"Say no more," she interrupted with a raised hand.

Gaspar immediately stopped and bowed his head in silence.

Mab turned to the head of her Secret Police and paused. He returned her gaze guilelessly and waited.

"Tell me, Nightshade, is this holding, this castle and its lands, of any strategic value? Would it serve me in any tactical way, from a military perspective? Or would its best use be in Gaspar's capable hands?"

"My queen, I know not; this is not my area of expertise," he admitted. "Perhaps you should judge for yourself?"

"Yes, I think I shall." She smiled smugly. "Tomorrow—and Gaspar, you will accompany me."

CH 32

THE MORNING DAWNED clear, but damp from the previous day's rain. Mab knew that traveling by coach with only a small escort of mounted warrior-elves to inspect the late Atrellan's holdings would take something over two hours.

Unfortunately, the going would be slowed by muddy water pooling in low places, and slick patches of wet clay. Once out of the lowlands, loose shale and rocks in the mountain ascent would offer further unsure footing for the horses.

Sighing in the rocking coach, she was starting to doubt the wisdom of personally inspecting this mountain redoubt. However, one look at Gaspar's eager face, sitting across from her, reminded her of her long-term strategy and banished any second thoughts. She had every intention of bestowing this small castle and its lands upon him, thereby further cementing his loyalty.

She anticipated molding him into a sorcerous weapon of her own design. Making long-term use of him as a most dangerous and dedicated minion greatly appealed to her.

In fact, this *inspection* was pure theater, intended to impress and ingratiate her mage. Truth be told, Mab hoped to also intimidate certain noble Houses among the elite of the Dark Elves, something she liked rather immensely.

Settling back in her seat, she allowed herself a small, satisfied smile.

UPON THEIR ARRIVAL at the deep ravine yawning before the castle gatehouse, they found the drawbridge down and the portcullis up.

Mab instructed her escort of four warrior-elves to enter the small castle first to be certain it was safe. She, Gaspar, and her ever-present warrior-bodyguard would wait at the coach for the return of the escort.

Gaspar was overly excited, and fidgeted constantly. He seemed oblivious to her warning glance.

That was beginning to annoy Mab.

"Gaspar, settle down! Look, they return even now."

The senior elfin warrior bowed before her. "Your Majesty, it is as described, vacant and abandoned. Nothing is locked. It appears safe."

"Very well," she acknowledged. "We shall inspect for ourselves. Please see that we are not unnecessarily disturbed."

"As you command, Your Majesty."

Mab, Gaspar, and the ever-present bodyguard strode across the drawbridge, past the raised portcullis, and into the shadowed interior courtyard.

Left at the coach, the elves of the escort sighed in collective relief. They picketed their horses and sought out dry patches of earth to sit, rest, and wait.

GASPAR WAS NEARLY BESIDE himself with excitement; but, he forced himself to appear outwardly calm.

They took their time, exploring by torchlight the keep and most of the outbuildings. In general, the place was dusty and disheveled; furniture overturned, the library ransacked, and the kitchen stripped of utensils, pots, and pans. If the servants had helped themselves, as it so appeared, they had certainly left in a hurry.

None of this seemed to dampen Gaspar's enthusiasm, despite Mab's cautionary comments.

"This will take some work to put right," she warned, looking about. "You will need a full staff of servants."

"Only a small staff, I think, Your Majesty. I will not need much. I must find Atrellan's workroom, the laboratory. I know it to be below this level. Shall we?"

"Lead on," she commanded with a wave of her hand.

Torches held high, they descended a flight of stone stairs and found what they sought at a lower landing.

Gaspar paused and held his torch near the dark doorway. "I believe the dungeons are located below this level, my queen. But what I seek, Atrellan's workroom, his laboratory, is here."

He stepped through the doorway, his torch dimly illuminating a large chamber hewn from the very rock of the mountain.

Mab and her bodyguard, his torch held high, followed.

The additional torchlight further revealed the chamber's secrets.

Smooth rock walls, laced with veins of metallic ores flickering with reflections of torchlight, rose in graceful arcs only to be lost high above in pulsing shadows. The floor was a dust-covered mosaic of dull colored stones, its pattern inscrutable. A large rectangular slab of stained stone was centered in the space, much like an altar. Near the foot of this slab stood a short stone shaft, a waist-high pedestal, its top concave.

Mab went to the pedestal and studied the depression. She nodded to her bodyguard who brought his torch closer. Ancient runes were visible on the shaft of the pedestal. She pointed to the top of the stone.

"A scrying orb once sat here," she murmured, "a long time ago."

She motioned for the bodyguard to bring his torch to the large altar-like slab. More runes became evident, completely surrounding the great stone in an unbroken chain.

"That is very old; these runes are ancient," she said, and paused to look around. "Some of this work is old Dwarven, I think; and some is yet older. This was a place of some power."

Gaspar nodded in silent agreement . . . *and would that it were mine!*

Mab pointed. "What lies beyond?"

Two more doorways led from the chamber. One led to another descending stone staircase cut from the rock of the mountain.

Standing on the landing, Gaspar held his torch out over the abyss. "I assume this leads below, to the dungeons."

"I see," she acknowledged. "I will forgo any further exploration below for now. What of this other passage?"

His torch before him, Gaspar led them into a large anteroom. Tables and broken wooden chart frames were shoved to one side. Hollow bookcases lined the walls. Some shelves held a few sparse books and scrolls. Broken shards of clay pots and cluttered debris lay about; dust was everywhere.

Gaspar walked slowly around the perimeter of the room, examining everything he could by torchlight. He felt his previous enthusiasm diminishing, his disappointment incrementally rising.

"My queen, I am certain," he sighed, "this, at one time, was actually Atrellan's workroom."

Leaving her bodyguard standing near the door with his torch held high, Mab strode to the center of the room and turned about with open palms. "Seriously, this pig sty?"

Gaspar flinched, but held his ground.

"I believe so, my queen; although, I am dismayed at the lack of research materials. There should be many more books, charts, and scrolls here, in this very room. Someone has been here before us."

Hand on one hip, she waved the other dismissively.

"Well, it *was* abandoned. The servants likely stole what they could and fled. What did you expect?"

Gaspar dropped his gaze in silent recognition of that truth, his resolve nonetheless undimmed.

It matters not—I still want it!

Looking up, he found her gazing at him, impatience in her expression.

Pffft—pffft!

The bodyguard toppled forward, his torch smashing to the floor, sending up a shower of hot sparks!

Gaspar froze as three men burst into the room.

One man thrust his hands at the queen, who was instantly encased in a bright column of sparkling green light.

Another man was suddenly at Gaspar's side, snatching his torch away! "I'll take that! Nighty-night!"

A blow to the back of his head sent Gaspar spiraling into unconsciousness.

All was darkness.

AT THE REALIZATION she'd been attacked, an unstoppable flood of red rage rose in Mab—but she could not move! She was trapped in what she intuitively knew was an overpowering stasis field. Only her eyes responded to her commands; and yet everything she could see was tinged with a horrible green tint.

A full pace away, a smug face appeared before her; recognition was slow in coming.

Who? Daegon? My late cousin's pet alchemist? I thought him dead.

Another face was now there—one she immediately recognized.

George! You spineless offal! What is the meanin—

George smiled. "Right about now I'd bet you're asking yourself what's the meaning of this, right?"

Daegon placed a hand on George's arm. "Not too close. Do not speak to her; she is still dangerous. We must be about our business. Do not worry, you will have your moment to gloat. Now, help me clear off the brass ring; then we can proceed."

Mab fumed, but she was still trapped like a fly in amber, unable to even speak, much less move. Her mind raced; but denied movement and voice, there was nothing she could do, except to let her gaze drop and watch as Daegon and George bent to some task.

As they brushed accumulations of dust and debris from the floor, she saw that she was standing in the midst of a large brass ring inlaid with runes of tarnished silver.

A master sorcerer's ring? How did I miss this? This is not good. Think! What sorcery uses such a focal aid? Ye gods, far too much, I fear.

Apparently satisfied with his preparations, Daegon stepped back. "All right, we're ready. No one crosses the ring; stay at least a pace away."

"Got it," George acknowledged.

Daegon nodded to someone Mab couldn't see, behind her.

"Vito, prepare him, a candle in each hand; then stand by."

"Duct tape okay?" asked a deep voice.

Daegon shrugged and nodded.

George stepped out of her field of view. "He's still out? I'll give you a hand, Vito."

Daegon was before her once more. "Look to me, *usurper!* I have waited long for this moment. Now you shall atone for the crime of *regicide—killing my queen!*"

Mab was surprised. *What? Ye gods! That's what this is about?*

Daegon opened his arms wide and began an incantation in an ancient elfin dialect. Tilting his head back, his voice changed, grew deeper and more guttural. His eyes rolled up in their sockets, only the whites showing.

Mab blanched. The ancient dialect was not completely incomprehensible to her. She sensed that part of this casting was an obscure yet very powerful form of arcane transit spell.

As Daegon droned on, a sheaf of purple light sprang up from the brass ring. The inlaid silver runes began to pulse with a dull inner light. Inky black tendrils slowly arose from each symbol and probed the foul purple encasement like pulsing sinewy veins.

Long moments later, Daegon stopped chanting and motioned with one hand. "Bring him."

A disheveled man bound in lengths of silvery tape was shoved forward—Gaspar!

The silvery tape was wrapped many times around his head. His nostrils were spared, but his mouth was taped shut. Only his wild eyes were visible. His upper arms were taped to his torso and elbows bent; a lit black candle was taped into each hand.

Turned by rough hands to face her, just beyond the brass circle, the paltry candle flames flickered as he shook in abject fear.

George and Daegon took positions behind Gaspar. Daegon began a new, barely audible chant.

Mab heard the unmistakable *snick* of a switchblade; Gaspar had heard it, too—and froze.

Their eyes found each other; the fear was palpable.

“Stop!” echoed throughout the chamber.

Hope flooded Mab’s heart.

Who? A woman’s voice! Malvana? Yes! Thank the gods!

Malvana was suddenly in the room.

“I’ll take that!” She snatched the stiletto away from George.

Eyes closed, Daegon continued his chant, seemingly oblivious to Malvana’s interruption.

George simply smiled.

Her young face devoid of expression, Malvana looked directly at her queen, helpless in a sorcerous cocoon of foul lights.

Mab’s hope faltered. *Something is very wrong here . . .*

Daegon completed his chant and was silent.

Malvana stood behind Gaspar, looked past his shoulder, and locked eyes with Mab.

“I am Malvana of the noble House of Tanist. Know this, Lady Diere of the House of Hawthorne; I know it is true that you killed Queen Mab LIV so you could seize the throne of Dark Elves, regicide most foul. But worse, beyond your treason, you killed my father, the Earl of Tanist!”

George whispered, "Now, just like I showed you."

With a single thrust, Malvana shoved the blade up to its hilt into the base of Gaspar's skull.

Gaspar's eyes bulged and he sagged, but George and Daegon held him upright. They snuffed out the candles and ripped them from the dying man's hands.

George nodded to Malvana, who pulled the knife free and shoved Gaspar past the brass ring into the ominous purple light.

In a brilliant multicolored flash, Mab gasped and succumbed to a numbing unconsciousness.

FOLLOWING THE BRIGHT flash, it took a moment for their eyes to adjust once more to mere torchlight.

All trace of sorcerous light was gone; no hint of purple or green remained.

The brass ring now stood empty and quiescent, absent any trace of Mab or Gaspar.

Her eyes wide, Malvana whispered, "Ye gods! Wha-what have I done? Am *I* now guilty of regicide? Have I killed her?"

George gently took the bloody stiletto from her hand and murmured, "No, you have not killed her—don't go there. Think of it like this; she has been banished for her crimes."

"Quite so," Daegon agreed, "to a realm from which she cannot return."

George looked sharply at Daegon, but remained silent as the alchemist continued.

"She lives and is unharmed, I promise you." Daegon patted Malvana's arm in assurance. "She is now in a harsh and dangerous place; so, her survival will depend entirely upon her. You have done no more than simply administer some long-overdue justice. Let your mind rest easy."

Neither George nor Daegon mentioned Gaspar.

Vito spoke up. "Uh, Boss, we gotta stick to the schedule."

"Right," George agreed, and took both of Malvana's hands in his own.

"Malvana, now it is time for you to return to your chambers, where Lord Nightshade awaits you. Daegon will take you there. It's very important that you be seen by many there now, at this time. Besides, don't you have to get ready for an upcoming Council meeting?"

Malvana hesitated. "Y-yes, that is true. I must."

George gently squeezed and released her hands. "Don't worry about a thing, doll. We'll finish up here."

Daegon stepped up. "Yes, let us go now."

Vito tugged at the alchemist's sleeve. "On your way back, bring all of those barrels I prepared in the chamber next to Teddy's lab."

"All of them?"

Vito nodded. "Yeah, if we want to thoroughly collapse this place I'm gonna need all the fertilizer and fuel oil mix I whipped up." He hefted a black gym bag. "I've got enough plastic to initiate, but I need the low explosive to complete the entire collapse."

Seeing the confusion on Daegon's face, George clapped a hand on his shoulder and said, "Don't worry about it; just bring what Vito says he needs when you come back for us. Okay? Now, go on, take Malvana home."

Daegon nodded and summoned a dark transit sphere. In the next moment, he and Malvana were gone.

Vito looked askance at his boss. "You were really pretty good with her, the kid-glove treatment, eh? I gotta admit she surprised me; I thought she'd hesitate."

George shook his head. "No, I knew better. Nightshade insisted she was a lot tougher than she looks. Still, I was impressed. In fact, I've something more in mind for her."

Vito nodded. "I'll bet you do, Boss."

George stepped over the body of the dead bodyguard and toed the black gym bag. "You sure this is enough plastic?"

"This? Oh, yeah, with the *ANFO* I prepped, this high-yield plastic is more than enough. The blast will be mostly contained in the lower levels, but everything above it will collapse pretty much straight down. Gravity will do most of the rest. This whole side of the mountain will be just a huge pile of rubble. To most people it'll look like a natural rockfall."

George nodded. "That'll bury this brass ring forever. She'll never be able to use it to come back."

Vito chuckled. "True dat!"

THE ELVES OF THE ESCORT were getting bored and kept glancing back at the castle. The queen and her mage were taking too long.

One voiced what all were thinking.

"Should not one of us check on them, Sergeant?"

The senior elf looked askance at the young soldier. "Have you a death wish, fool? The queen does not suffer interruptions gladly. She will return when she is ready, and not before."

Another elf mumbled something that set the others to chuckling.

"What was that, Corporal?" the sergeant demanded.

"Nothing, Sergeant, nothin' at all."

The sergeant stood and loomed over his subordinate. "Not be havin' that for an answer, now will I?"

The corporal raised his palms in mock surrender. "Easy, Sarge. I only said that her pet mage might be tryin' to, uh, impress her. You know he's such a suck-up, always underfoot an' the like."

"Aye, that be truth!" another agreed. "He thinks he'll be the new lord of this gods-forsaken place. Me, I trust him not."

"None of us do," the corporal confirmed. "The queen would be better served were he well away from her court."

"Best watch your tongues," the sergeant warned, "lest you lose `em. He has *her* trust; so, keep talk like that to yourselves."

"Aye, I'll admit that be sage advice," the corporal conceded, "for well we know, no warrior ever trusts a mage."

Elfin heads bobbed in silent unison.

The sergeant turned and looked at the castle once more; they *were* taking too long.

He turned back to his detail personnel, and suddenly stumbled, nearly losing his balance.

The very earth shook! The sergeant dropped to his hands and knees and looked wildly about.

A deep keening rumble built in volume and seemed to vibrate in the elves' very bones.

Sprawled outstretched on the ground, the elves grimaced wide-eyed as the shaking intensified.

Screaming in panic, the horses tugged loose from the picket line, fleeing pell-mell down the mountain road. The coach team followed, pitching the frightened driver from his high seat at the first turn.

The rumbling and shaking grew to a crescendo.

The castle seemed to vibrate in the dusty air, and then slowly collapse in upon itself.

The elves scrambled to their feet and ran, few daring to look back. Those that did saw the mountainside above the castle shudder and begin to slide. It built speed horrifyingly fast and crushed the castle like the fist of an angry mountain god.

A choking cloud of dust arose and obscured the sight. Chunks of debris, rocks and stones rained down and tumbled about.

The rumble faded to a strained lingering moan and quieted; the shaking abated.

Heart pounding, the sergeant stood unsteadily, coughed and spat. He could see only a few yards through the choking dust. Smaller and smaller stones pattered down like diminishing rain, finally stopping. The silence was too eerie.

Half expecting some sort of aftershock, the sergeant crouched tensely; but nothing more happened.

The air was still thick with dust, but somewhat less than moments ago. He could see a little better; clods of earth and loose rocks were everywhere.

He straightened and took a few tentative steps. Knowing he had a duty, he set out in search of his people.

Within a few minutes he found and gathered most of the scattered escort team. Scared and filthy, none were seriously hurt, but for a host of bumps and bruises. Unfortunately, the coach driver was dead, killed in his fall. The panicked horses were long gone.

"S-sarge, w-what happened?" managed the disheveled corporal.

The sergeant wiped grime from his face. "I-I do not know; an earthquake, a rock slide? Who knows?"

"But that sound, that shaking!" The corporal spat dirty phlegm and coughed. "That was no natural earthquake; that was sorcery!"

The sergeant had no answer for that. He started walking through the dust, in the direction of the castle. His dispirited troops paused in disbelief; then, one by one, followed in a shambling line.

It was soon evident that the castle was no more.

As the dust settled, the elves could not even find the ravine; rubble from the rock slide had completely filled and obscured it. There was no trace of the castle. It was as if the mountain itself had extended a mighty crushing arm to smash down and claim everything within its reach. All that remained was boulders, rubble, and dust.

The elves stood in uneasy silence. They all knew there was no saving anyone; no rescue to be had here.

"By the gods," mumbled the corporal, "what has that damned fool mage done now?"

None had any words; nor had they any doubt who was responsible.

ON A LONELY OUTCROPPING of rock, at the edge of a dark conifer forest and a rolling plain of tall grasses, a lone elfin woman lay curled in a fetal position. She shuddered, chilled in the brisk wind, and squinted one eye open.

What happened? I am not injured; but, where am I? I am alone? Do I know this place?

She opened her other eye and forced herself up to a sitting position. The cool wind was constant; she pulled her clothing tighter around her shoulders.

Is this the wild? It must be . . . So, I have been betrayed . . . This merits special vengeance.

Lips pursed and jaw clenched, she forced herself to calm down; unbridled anger and rage would do her no good at the moment. She sought her calm center. Moments later she stood and studied her surroundings.

A realm I am unfamiliar with . . . So, I have much to learn.

She paused and held one hand out at arm's length. Holding her thumb and forefinger about three inches apart, she furrowed her brow in concentration.

A bright blue spark arced between her fingers with a mighty *snap-crackle!*

She smiled.

Oh yes . . . much to learn . . . and much to do.

CH 33

ELLEN POCKETED HER phone and nudged her mother. "Hawk and Trey are on their way. You don't mind that I invited them to supper?"

Millie smiled and paused in stirring the contents of the huge pot bubbling on the stove. "Not at all. I made this big pot of gumbo and cooked plenty of rice; but, we might need some more cornbread. Could you help me with that?"

"No problem. One egg and a third of a cup of milk for one eight-ounce box mix, right?"

Millie balked. "A box mix? For goodness sake—you kids these days! What's wrong with making it from scratch and using cornmeal from the pantry? A store-bought box mix is like cheating. I don't like to take such shortcuts."

Ellen shook her head and chuckled. *Oh boy, here we go.*

This wasn't the first time her mother had teased or critiqued anyone of the younger generation for their *easy cooking solutions;* and, no doubt it wouldn't be the last.

"Oh, come on, Mom. It's faster, and after all, even I can't screw it up."

Millie glanced at the wall clock and waved her stirring ladle in surrender. "Oh, all right. At least use the small cast-iron skillet. Use plenty of shortening and preheat it to—"

"Four hundred degrees," Ellen interrupted, pulling the refrigerator door open. "I *know,* Mom. Then in the oven for twenty minutes. I *have* done this before, you know."

Millie shook her head. "Ha! A box mix! Someday, young lady, you're gonna need to know how to prepare meals from scratch. Trust me; a husband will always appreciate a wife who can cook."

"What? A husband? Trying to marry me off?" Ellen exclaimed in mock shock, but couldn't keep a straight face. "Besides, a worthwhile husband should know how to cook, too. I have standards, you know."

"Oh, are we interrupting?" Stacy teased, as she and Mark entered the kitchen.

"Whoa, we can come back later," he offered backing up with a grin, winking at Stacy.

"What? And get out of setting the table? Not a chance!" Millie decreed. "You know where everything is. We'll be serving in about thirty minutes."

Ellen placed the box mix, an egg, and a milk jug next to a mixing bowl on the counter. "Oh, set extra places for Hawk and Trey; they're on their way."

"You got it," Mark acknowledged. "Is something up, besides supper, I mean?"

Ellen shrugged. "Yeah, I got that impression; but, I don't know what. I tried to ask, but Hawk wouldn't get into it over the phone. I think he was driving; you know he tries not to use his phone too much when he's behind the wheel."

"That's smart of him," Mark remarked, "considering the stats on distracted driving these days."

Stacy began placing fresh napkins around the table. "Speaking of distractions, when do you have to leave for your meeting, Mark?"

His fist full of silverware, he glanced up at the kitchen's big wall clock. "Oh, I'd say about seven."

"Will you be back tonight?" Ellen asked as she cracked the egg open and let it plop into the bowl holding the coarse yellow cornbread mix.

He shrugged, placing the appropriate eating utensils at each place setting. "I have no idea. I'm hoping there will be minimal discussion or debate before they can put the issue of authorizing an investigation to a vote; but I really don't know."

"If it looks like you might be gone overnight," Stacy asked, "could you at least let us know? Send a message with a bogie or something?"

Mark nodded. "Yeah, I should be able to. I really don't think it'll be that long, late maybe, but not overnight."

"You never know," Ellen warned, stirring the milk into the mix. "Getting the Council to agree on anything never seems to happen as quickly as anyone hopes."

"Who wants wine?" Stacy asked. "I'm pouring. Oh, Millie, should I open white or red?"

"The entrée is seafood gumbo, so open the white, please."

"I'll get the glasses," Mark offered.

"Oh, I almost forgot," Millie looked to Mark. "There's a plate of chilled oysters on the half shell in the fridge. Can you get that out? We'll have that for an appetizer."

Mark smiled. "Oh good! Any hot sauce?"

"There's some homemade hot sauce on the same shelf. Be careful; it's in a crystal serving-dish."

"Okay, cornbread is in the oven," Ellen announced. "Twenty minutes until supper. Let's enjoy our wine."

"Hear, hear, it's happy hour!" Stacy declared.

HAWK AND TREY ARRIVED just in time for supper. The aromas wafting throughout the kitchen left no doubt that any serious conversation would simply have to wait until the meal was finished.

In time, the satiated diners placed spent napkins next to now-empty bowls, leaned back sighing in satisfaction, and offered rousing compliments to the chef.

Millie smiled self-consciously. "Enough already! I hope you've saved room for a little dessert. I've done something a little different—a little something I'd like y'all to try. Would y'all be my *beta-tasters?*"

Everyone enthusiastically agreed.

"Okay, give me a few minutes. I'll be right back." Millie left the table and busied herself on the other side of the kitchen.

Ellen nudged Hawk. "So, what did you want to tell me, that you didn't want to talk about while you were driving?"

He looked at her in surprise. "How'd you know I was driving?"

She scoffed and playfully punched his arm. "I can tell. Fair warning—you have no secrets from me."

He rolled his eyes. "I'm doomed!"

"Believe it! Now, tell me; what was it?"

"Oh, we think it's safe for Miska to return. The game wardens in Texas trapped a black bear, a very big male, that had gotten into some livestock. A farmer got hurt when he heard a ruckus at night and went to check on his animals. It's okay; he's gonna be all right."

Trey leaned forward. "That's on the Texas side of Toledo Bend, near the Sabine National Forest area. Everyone involved is ready to accept that this bear is probably the same one that was causing all the problems on our side of the Sabine."

"What will happen to this bear?" Stacy asked.

Trey shrugged. "That'll be up to Texas. Black bears are rare and protected. Since he attacked a human, there's a rabies concern. If he checks out okay, he'll probably be fitted with a radio collar and relocated in a remote wilderness area. If he's got rabies, it's a pretty good chance he'll be put down."

Everyone went quiet for a moment.

Mark broke the spell. "So Miska can come home?"

Trey and Hawk bobbed their heads in unison.

"Good," Ellen declared, "I'll send that news this evening."

"What about Brona?" Stacy asked. "Isn't she with him?"

Ellen nodded. "She is. I'm thinking about bringing her here, too. I've got to reunite her with her father, but I can't really do that in Mer, since we don't actually know what's going on there or what Silenos is up to."

"We might," Mark offered, "after tonight, *if* the Council will act on my proposal."

"Yeah," agreed Hawk as he and Trey exchanged knowing nods.

Millie returned to the table with two big serving plates. Each held about a dozen warm crescent rolls. There was something enticing about the aroma.

"Mom, what is this?" Ellen asked, reaching for a roll.

"No, not yet," her mother warned, touching her daughter's arm. "I have something else to put out. Just be patient."

Her hand suspended in midair, Ellen balked. "Huh? Uh, okay. Don't be too long; they smell wonderful!"

Millie returned with a tray holding half a dozen smaller bowls of whipped cream and placed them within reach of each diner. Hands on her hips, she gestured to the two serving plates.

"Okay, these are crescent rolls with semisweet chocolate chips baked in. The whipped cream is for dipping. Let me know what y'all think. Feedback is important to a cook, you know."

They needed no more encouragement to dig in. The next few minutes went by in wordless bliss, punctuated with broad smiles, dramatic eye rolls, and small moans of pleasure.

"O-M-G!" Stacy finally exclaimed. "Millie, how did you make these? They're really good!"

Millie beamed. "They're really simple. I just put a series of lines of chocolate chips in the little triangles of dough as I rolled them up, you know like you normally would with crescent rolls. Then put them in the oven at three hundred-seventy-five degrees for about fourteen minutes. That gave me plenty of time to prepare the whipped cream. That's it."

"That's really simple, Mom. Wait a minute! The crescent rolls—didn't I see a ready-made tube of dough in the refrigerator? A pre-mix *from the grocery store? A shortcut?"* Ellen fought to keep a straight face.

Millie grimaced. "All right, already, guilty as charged. The crescent roll dough was store-bought."

"What's going on?" Mark murmured.

Stacy snorted in laughter and waved her hand. "Nothing to worry about! It's an old tease they do with each other about cooking stuff from scratch. Personally, I'm delighted these rolls are so easy to make. Even I could do it!"

"Hmmph, me, too," Hawk managed with his mouth almost full.

Trey just grinned and popped another roll smothered in whipped cream into his mouth.

Ellen smiled at her mother. "Well played, Mom; but, I still gotcha!"

Millie shrugged and thumbed her chest. "Maybe, but *I* know how to cook. *You* still need to learn, sweetie."

THE FOLLOWING MORNING Ellen came down to the kitchen to find Millie and Stacy huddled over mugs of coffee. A large platter of pancakes and sausages lay untouched in the center of the table. The Chows, Max and Sophie, were sitting together by the cast-iron stove, ignoring the meat and pancakes in their food bowls, their attention focused on Stacy.

Ellen immediately sensed that something was amiss.

"Good morning . . . What? Is something wrong?"

There were circles under Stacy's reddened eyes. Millie grasped Stacy's hand and looked to Ellen.

"Mark didn't come home last night—"

"He didn't even send a bogie with a message!" Stacy blurted in interruption.

Millie patted Stacy's arm, and addressed Ellen. "Have you heard from him?"

Shaking her head, Ellen sat next to Stacy. "No, not since he left after supper last evening."

Gripping her crystal necklace, Stacy asked, "Could you check, you know, send a message to the Council, to see if everything is all right?"

"You can do that, can't you, Ellen?" Millie urged.

“Of course, I . . .” her voice dwindled as the crystal in Stacy’s grasp began to glow with a dull blue light. Glancing down, she saw that her own crystal dangling at the end of its fine gold chain had begun to glow as well.

Millie noticed, too, and tugged at her own necklace, pulling it up from deep in her blouse. It too glowed blue.

“What does this mean? All our crystals are glowing! What—”

“Easy, Mom. It means we have a visitor. I just sensed a transit orb, on the front lawn, I think.”

“Mark?” Stacy asked hopefully.

Ellen rose. “I don’t think so; his presence wouldn’t make these glow.”

Stacy was still hopeful. “Maybe he’s not alone? I’m coming with you!”

Ellen knew there would be no stopping her. “Okay, let’s see who’s here.”

The dogs in the lead, the three women went to the front door.

Before Ellen opened it, she paused and faced her mother and Stacy. All their crystals were glowing a bright blue. She took a deep breath.

“Remember, the house is warded. Whatever happens, don’t leave the porch, okay?”

Stacy and Millie nodded in assurance.

Ellen pulled the door open.

Two bogies, Council messengers, stood at the base of the steps. An almost transparent transit orb floated mere inches above the grass on the nearby lawn.

As the women stepped out onto the porch, both bogies bowed.

One spoke. “We come from the Council. We seek the Lady Ellen Doyle, Steward of the Grand Portal of the Realm of Man.”

Ellen nodded. "I am she. How may I help you?"

The other bogie produced a scroll tube from his robe and held it out on the palms of his gloved hands, as his colleague explained.

"M'lady, Madam Moya, Chief Clerk of the Council, sends this message, and begs that you give it your immediate attention."

Ellen descended the steps and accepted the scroll tube.

"Thank you. You may assure Madam Moya that I shall do as she asks."

The bogies bowed once more. "Thank you, m'lady."

Turning on their heels they entered the transit globe. In the next instant it was gone with the usual *pop*.

Ellen returned to the porch and noted that the crystal necklaces were no longer glowing.

"Ellen!" Stacy whined. "You didn't ask—"

Ellen held up a hand to forestall whatever Stacy was about to say.

"Inside, quickly."

Standing in the foyer, Ellen broke the seal, opened the tube, and removed the scroll.

"This isn't from Madam Moya . . ."

"What? Who is it from?" Stacy pressed, her anxiety unabated.

"Moya may have sent it, but it's from Elsbeth—and it's not good. I need to go the Council realm, right away."

"Why dear?" Millie asked. "What's wrong?"

Ellen rolled the scroll back up, slipped it back into the tube, and reactivated the seal. She handed the tube to her mother.

"Hide this somewhere. Neither of you can say anything about this, not right now, understand?"

"But what—" Millie began.

"The Council is missing."

"W-what?" Stacy blurted.

Ellen sighed. "The Council—the members, the avatars, are missing. Late last night, they were in their meeting, and then they were just *gone.* That's all I know. That's all that was in the message; and that Elsbeth needs to see me as soon as possible."

"So, Mark is missing, too?" There was a slight quaver in Stacy's voice.

"Yes, but you know he can take care of himself," Ellen assured her friend.

"Well I'm going, too!" Stacy declared.

"No, I have to go alone. Elsbeth was clear about that. This all has to be kept secret for now."

Millie asked, "Would that include not telling Hawk and Trey? I don't think keeping this from them would be very smart. Do you?"

Ellen frowned. "That's a good point. No, we're gonna tell them—but no one else, okay?"

Millie bobbed her head. Stacy pouted but reluctantly nodded.

"All right," Ellen declared, "I'll call Hawk. He'll want to argue, but I'm gonna go before he can get here."

Smokey was suddenly at their feet, looking up at Ellen.

Stacy pointed to him. "Well, at least take Smokey with you."

Ellen smiled. "Oh, I was planning on it."

IN THE CAVERNS OF OLMUS, Vito entered George's chamber and found him seated at a small desk illuminated by a pair of pharmacy lamps, another benefit of the generator running in an upper chamber.

"Uh, sorry to bug you, Boss, but—"

"Vito? What are you still doing here? I thought you were supposed to make a delivery in New Orleans—ten keys, right?"

The big man shrugged. "Right. I got the product from Teddy and was all set to go, but Daegon grabbed me and told me to get you to meet him at the scrying orb. He didn't say why."

George stood. "Wait a sec. Why did he send you? Why not a goblin servant?"

"I dunno. Come to think of it, I didn't see any around. But you know they tend to give me a wide berth; they pretty much stay away from me."

George pursed his lips. "Yeah, but not Daegon. Now that you mention it, since we got back from the Realm of Dark Elves, I haven't seen that many either."

"Yeah, even Teddy said they haven't been a problem around the lab. He was able to focus on cooking this last batch without any interruptions." Vito scratched his chin. "Do you think it means anything?"

"Got no idea. I may as well go see what Daegon wants. You're good to go now, right?"

Vito nodded. "Yeah, I'm heading out. I've got some collections to make, so I might be gone overnight. We'll see."

George waved him off with a knowing grin. "Cash and carry."

"Always," Vito grunted, and departed the chamber.

GEORGE FOUND DAEGON staring into the scrying orb.

"I'm here, Daegon, what's up?"

Daegon gestured to the orb. George leaned forward and peered at the scene depicted within; a low hill, little more than a stark jumble of rocks, boulders, broken plinths and shattered columns. It appeared vaguely familiar.

George furrowed his brow. "Isn't that the, uh . . ."

"Yes, this is the outer entrance to the Red Cap tribe's warren of caves," Daegon assured him. "Tell me; who or what do you see?"

George squinted and tilted his head from side to side. "All I see are rocks and broken stuff. Am I missing something?"

"No, but something *is* missing, the outer sentries. The Red Caps always post sentries deep in the shadows at this entrance. The other goblin tribes do the same at their home caves. I have looked at several other known tribal cave entrances; all are unguarded."

Hands on his hips, George asked, "So, something is wrong with the local goblin tribes?"

"Not just them," Daegon cautioned. "Haven't you noticed that our own goblin servants have become scarce since we returned? I've had to assign our human servants, Clement and Stellara, to tend to the bats."

George scoffed. "So, *that's* where she is. So, what's going on? Where are all the goblins?"

Daegon opened his palms. "I can only surmise they have gone into their deepest caverns for some reason, completely abandoning the surface and their upper-level caves. I do not know why."

"What happened? Did we miss something?" George mused aloud. "We weren't gone that long."

"No, we weren't," Daegon agreed, but then frowned. "However, at *your* insistence, we have had the scrying orb totally focused upon Gaspar for some time. We did not change that until our return from the Realm of Dark Elves. I warned you that we would be blind to all else. *Anything* may have happened during the time the orb was so narrowly focused. Thus, we would be—no, we *are* none the wiser!"

George scowled. "We're not having this argument again! We had good reason to stay focused on Gaspar! Thanks to that we were able to solve multiple problems, including your revenge on Diere, in one fell swoop!"

Daegon had nothing to say to that.

George relented and spread his open hands.

"Look, whatever is going on with the goblins might be nothing much at all, some cultural thing or other—we just don't know. It's inconvenient, sure, but it's not having that big an effect on our operation. So, there's no sense in worrying about it."

"Perhaps, perhaps not," Daegon countered. "I fully intend to look into it further."

George waved his hands. "Hey, whatever. Do what you gotta do."

Daegon sniffed, clearly still piqued. "I will."

George turned to leave, but paused.

"Daegon, uh, listen, about the bats . . . Did you tell Clement and Stellara about weaning the bats off the meth? You know, seeing that they got less and less in successive doses?"

Daegon's expression went blank. "Oh, I should probably speak to them again."

George ground his teeth, and tamped his flaring temper down.

"Yeah, you should probably do that."

CONSIDERING THE URGENCY of the message, Ellen decided to waste no time and crafted a transit globe that would take her directly to Elsbeth's warren of files and documents in the archives of the Council Realm.

To her surprise, Elsbeth was not alone.

"Ellen?" exclaimed Padraic. "What are you doing here?"

"I asked her to come," the wizened brownie answered, "before you *unexpectedly* arrived."

"Well, hello to you both. Now, tell me what's going on?" Ellen insisted, stooping to set Smokey down. The cat immediately sniffed at the papers strewn about the floor and began to explore these new surroundings.

"I shall explain," Elsbeth began, and looked to Padraic. "If you don't mind?"

"Of course not, please go ahead," he insisted.

"Ellen, I fear my message, while terse, was rather complete; the Council members are missing. We know very little about the actual circumstances. They were in a protracted, and as I understand it, a rather loud and heated executive session when the meeting room grew very quiet. Sentinels posted outside the chamber thought that strange and opened the doors to check; they found the room empty of avatars. Everything else, papers and documents, was in order; however, the chairs were vacant. There is but one way in and out of that room; no one passed by the Sentinels."

Ellen pursed her lips and frowned. "No signs of any struggles? Was anything displaced?"

Elsbeth shook her head. "No signs of struggles, nor was anything out of place."

"Could they have transited out? Aren't there wards?" Ellen probed.

"There are wards, although it appears they were insufficient—"

"Or compromised," interrupted Padraic. "Sorry, please go on."

"So, yes," Elsbeth concluded, "transiting out is likely. We did not know how or why, or if it had been of their own volition or not—not until several minutes ago."

"Of their own volition or not?" Ellen echoed. "You mean someone *took them?"*

"It appears so." Elsbeth placed a scroll on her desk. "Sentinels carefully searched the room and found this on the floor beneath the conference table. No one could read it; so, it was brought to me."

Smokey leapt upon the desk, sat, and watched intently as Elsbeth unrolled the scroll.

Ellen locked eyes with the aged brownie. "You can read it, can't you." It was not a question.

Elsbeth nodded. "Yes, it is written in an ancient pictograph sort of text, much like old runes."

"And?" Ellen prompted.

"It is addressed to the Steward of the Grand Portal—"

"What?" Ellen blurted! "To me?"

Elsbeth threw up her tiny hands. "Not you by name, just to the *Steward.* I doubt its author knows your given name."

"The author, who is it?" Ellen demanded.

"Silenos."

"I see." Ellen scowled. "And what does it say?"

Elsbeth cut her eyes to Padraic, who gave the briefest of nods.

"Essentially it says that to secure the release of the Council *unharmed*, the Steward is to bring the iron ouroboros—"

"The *what?*" Ellen interrupted.

Padraic put a hand upon her arm. "It's a sort of uh, talisman. I'll explain later. Elsbeth, please continue."

"Yes, of course." She glanced at the scroll. "Ah, bring it to a particular temple ruin on Olmus no later than sunset three days hence."

"Really? Or else what?" Ellen pressed, her mood darkening.

Elsbeth stared at her hands. "Otherwise, each member of the Council will be slain, resurrected as the mindless walking dead, bereft of true name and soul, and loosed upon their respective home realms."

Ellen pointed to the scroll. "Anything else?"

"No, not on this scroll," the brownie said. "However, you should know that before their disappearance the Council did vote to authorize the Realm of Man to conduct an investigation into the incidents of necromancy, to include Silenos and his activities; that much is in the official record."

"Really?" Ellen scoffed. "Under the circumstances, you know we'd have done so anyway."

"Perhaps, but now such actions will have Council sanction," Elsbeth pointed out. "There may come a time when that will matter."

Ellen shrugged, and turned to Padraic. "Now, what's the deal with this iron *ouro-whatever?* Is that why you're here?"

Her father shook his head. "No, I knew nothing about any of this. I came, at the request of Lord Nightshade, to notify Malvana, the avatar for the Dark Elves, that she is needed in her home realm and must return immediately to—"

"Wait!" Ellen interjected. "Who? Lord Nightshade? Mab didn't send you?"

"No, that's the problem—Mab is missing, and so is her mage, Gaspar."

"Gaspar?" Ellen scowled. "Oh, I remember him, what a piece of, uh, never mind. So, Mab is missing, too? Is this connected with the Council's disappearance, or should I say *abduction?*"

Padraic shrugged. "Possible, I guess, but I think it's unlikely. Mab and Gaspar went to inspect a holding in the realm of Dark Elves, a small castle on a mountainside and its surrounding lands. While there, something like an earthquake happened; the castle was destroyed in a massive rock slide. Mab, her elfin bodyguard, and Gaspar were inside, alone. She had an escort, of course, who were outside when it happened; most of them survived."

Ellen tilted her head. "You do realize that either Mab, Gaspar, or both could have transited away unharmed, right?"

"True, I suppose," he admitted, "but that would have been to another realm. Surely they would have come back by now, unless . . ."

"Unless *what?*"

Padraic dropped his voice. "Unless, as the surviving elves of her escort believe, her mage did something foolish that may have *caused* the disaster, something sudden that happened before either could escape."

A lone eyebrow arched, Ellen offered, "You mean like Gaspar showing off, trying a spell that backfired? That certainly does sound like him."

"These surviving elves," Elsbeth asked, "they are convinced this mage is complicit?"

"Quite so; they insist it was sorcery, not a natural occurrence," Padraic confirmed. "It may be wise to take their story with a grain of salt. As we all know, little love is lost between warriors and mages."

"Nonetheless, they may be right about Gaspar," Elsbeth concluded. "Occam's razor, you know."

"Well, whatever may have happened, Mab is at least missing. Some already whisper that she is dead; which I think is unlikely. Thus, Nightshade asked me to come get Malvana, since she has been named temporary *regent* in Mab's absence. And now, I find out that Malvana is missing as well. This is not good."

"Not at all," echoed Elsbeth. "The throne may be truly vacant. Elements within the noble Houses of the Dark Elves will surely seek to gain advantage. This will be very disruptive at a minimum."

"Disruptive may be an understatement," Padraic observed.

"You think?" Ellen scoffed. "Come on, focus! We've got more immediate things to worry about. So, back to the Council's abduction, what about this iron thing, the ouro-whatever?"

Elsbeth held up her hands. "Not here! We now know our wards have been compromised. That conversation is best held elsewhere, somewhere secure. You should go."

Ellen and Padraic exchanged a knowing glance. They knew precisely where to go.

Ellen scooped up Smokey and crafted a large transit globe.

In the next instant—*pop*—she and her father were gone.

IN HIS STORM HAVEN conference room, the Guildmaster patiently listened to Padraic's synopsis of recent events, glancing occasionally toward Gallenius, whose expression betrayed nothing.

Padraic concluded and asked,"Why do I get the impression you already knew most of this?"

The Guildmaster leaned forward and splayed his gloved hand on the table. "We've only heard snatches of speculation and rumor. Some of what you have shared has filled in some gaps. Gallenius?"

"Of course, Guildmaster. We also suspect Silenos to be the architect of the Council members' abduction. We had heard of Mab and Gaspar's misfortune as well, but we have not yet found a link between the two events. At this point, we suspect they are likely unrelated, and possibly coincidental."

Ellen's impatience was getting the better of her. "Can we get back to the Council problem, please? My cousin, Mark, is among the missing. Padraic needs to find Malvana, who is also missing. They are very likely together! Can we focus on that?"

"Of course, we haven't forgotten," soothed the Guildmaster. "We understand that Silenos had made a demand that you produce the iron ouroboros on Olmus within three days. That he has chosen Olmus has given us pause for concern. We do not—"

"Pause for concern?" Ellen echoed. "Hold it right there. I have a concern as well; and now is a good time to address it."

"I beg your pardon?" the Guildmaster balked in surprise.

"Some time ago, when I was in Olmus dealing with Mab, I had occasion to meet Ignatius, the avatar of the Dragon Lords. Do you remember me telling you about that upon my return to Storm Haven, Guildmaster?"

"I do."

"I conveyed a message from him to you, one that was meant to be circulated far and wide, heard by everyone. Do you remember that, as well?"

"Yes, I do."

"Can you tell me why that message went no further than a select few? I know I told my friends and family. I remember you telling me that this sort of information was better off *managed*. We both know that information was a warning, a serious warning. So, why was that information not shared?"

Smokey chose that moment to leap from Ellen's lap to the tabletop, sit before the Guildmaster, and stare up into the masking spell within the hood.

The room was dead quiet.

Gallenius broke the spell. "Lady Ellen, I can—"

"No." The Guildmaster raised a gloved hand. "I will answer."

"But—" Gallenius began.

"Enough! I will answer."

Ellen sat back in her chair. "I'm listening."

"There is a prophecy, a rather old one likely forgotten by most, that holds that the Dragon Lords will only return when chaos reigns and entropy has ensued. They will return to purge the realms of all living things and allow the cycle of life to begin anew. A collateral aspect of the prophecy tells of an avatar of the Dragon Lords who will periodically assess the realms as needs may be and render a judgment, or perhaps a recommendation in support of such a judgment. To be honest, the old sources almost never agree on the wording; interpretations tend to be vague and overly dramatic.

"Admittedly, many in the realms do not remember or were even aware of the prophecy; but some do, more than enough to warrant concern. Perhaps you can understand why any report of a return of the Dragon Lords, or even a visit from their avatar, might spark wild rumors or even wholesale panic. That is why such information must be *managed*."

"Perhaps," Ellen leaned forward. "However, that does not address the *warning,* that the realm of Olmus was off-limits, proscribed—*verboten!* Why wouldn't that information be circulated?"

"Primarily because that is, or at least was, considered to be common knowledge, and *has been* since the banishment of the *Old Ones.* We did see to it that the old prohibition was mentioned—a *reminder,* if you will, in the course of a Council meeting. However, we were reluctant to push the issue further for fear it might arouse undue curiosity."

Ellen pursed her lips. "So, why is Silenos demanding I go to Olmus, and bring the *ouro-thingy?* And just what is it anyway?"

Gallenius raised a finger. "Guildmaster, if I may?"

The Guildmaster nodded.

"As you may know," Gallenius began, "the realm of Olmus was once a place of power, a stronghold of the Old Ones. We have some very old maps that depict a series of ley lines, old paths of power. We are certain some of that power lingers, and Silenos probably plans to make use of it. What he intends to accomplish is open to speculation, but we have a theory, based on what little we do know about him.

"Before I get into that, I must explain about the ouroboros. This may take a little time, so please bear with me."

Ellen leaned back in her chair and folded her arms. "Very well, I'm good at listening."

ELLEN WAS IMPRESSED, but not convinced. "That was quite a bit of information. How much do you know to be factual, and how much is speculation?"

"Half and half," Gallenius admitted. "We believe the historical data on the Old Ones is reliable. We are equally certain that Silenos has found some access to a cache of forbidden sorcerous lore from the time of the Old Ones. That would explain his necromancy and his suspected fascination with the Dark One, Crom. His pursuit of a dullahan in preparation for a rite of unbinding further suggests a strong link to Crom. We know dullahans were compelled to serve Crom. We do not know if Silenos was aware of Brona's status as a Steward; which may, or may not, possibly be a sacrificial aspect he believes necessary to his plans."

"But you suspect so," Ellen concluded, "since he has demanded a Steward produce this iron thing on Olmus. So, he'd settle for *me* instead of Brona. What a piece of work . . . Do we have anything more on Silenos? Is this the extent of available intelligence?"

"Well, yes and no," Gallenius hedged.

Ellen folded her arms. "Meaning?"

"An asset of ours observed Silenos for some time, and was present when the silver ouroboros came into his possession."

Ellen raised a lone eyebrow. "Of course, Salidar. Well, get him in here. Let's see if he can contribute anything worthwhile. And I want to hear all about these *ouroboros* things, in detail this time."

SALIDAR'S OBSERVATIONS were only of moderate help. He hadn't actually seen the silver ouroboros, just the seaweed pouch that contained the suspected amulet. He sat quietly, eyes downcast, as the conversation moved on to related subjects and speculations.

"So, no one knows," Ellen groused in frustration, "the whereabouts of the iron ouroboros? Only Maude Delafaire knew?"

"Unfortunately, that is the simple truth," the Guildmaster said with finality. "However, you must understand that even if we did have the iron ouroboros, letting Silenos get his hands on it is out of the question."

"Quite so!" Gallenius added emphatically. "If what we suspect is true, that Silenos intends to conduct a rite of unbinding and loose the Old Ones—"

"Crom in particular," interrupted the Guildmaster.

"Indeed," Gallenius bobbed his head. "Life as we know it, in all the realms, would never be the same, if any were to survive at all."

Ellen grimaced. "That would be bad news—I get it. So, what can we do about the Council? Those are innocent people, kidnapped and threatened with a horrible fate. We can't abandon them; there's gotta be a way to save them. We've got a little time; there's gotta be something we can do. I'm supposed to show up on Olmus in a couple of days with the iron ouroboros—which, of course we don't have. But a couple of days is better than nothing."

"Believe me, Ellen," Gallenius urged, "we have all our resources searching everywhere for the missing avatars. By now most of the member realms are aware of the situation and have commenced their own searches. Everyone is looking."

Ellen shook her head. "They probably won't be looking in the right places. The member realms will likely only look among themselves; and that will lead to further distrust and accusations. Only Storm Haven would consider searching in the *wild,* a task too vast for even your resources."

The room grew quiet.

"Well, I know one thing," Ellen declared. "If we don't find them in time, I'm going to Olmus—even if I have to go empty-handed!"

That stunned everyone in the room; an awkward silence descended.

"It would be a mistake to go empty-handed," Salidar murmured, shaking his head.

Ellen stared at him, her eyes narrowed. "What? What do you mean?"

All attention on him, Salidar stood, faced Ellen, and splayed his open hands. "Silenos expects you to show up with an iron ouroboros. So, do so. It need not—"

"Weren't you listening?" interrupted Padraic. "We don't have the iron ouroboros."

Salidar waved his hands. "M'lord, I know that. It need not be *the* iron ouroboros Silenos seeks, but he will not know that, at least not right away. This may allow Lady Ellen to buy more time."

Padraic bolted to his feet. "It may also get her killed!"

Ellen held up her hands. "Wait-wait! Let's think this through. Do we even have another iron ouroboros?"

"Of course not!" Padraic spat. "This is idiocy!"

"Enough!" Ellen leveled a finger at her father; he resumed his seat and scowled in silence.

She looked at those seated around the table. "Now, can anyone answer my question—is there another ouroboros that we could use?"

Gallenius shook his head. "I don't think so. I—"

"You don't even know what it looks like!" Padraic grumbled through gritted teeth.

"Actually, we do," corrected the Guildmaster. "The old records are rather specific; and we know the size of the seaweed pouch that Salidar saw."

Padraic scoffed. "But you don't have another ouroboros, do you?"

The Guildmaster shrugged. "No, I'm afraid we—"

"We make one," Salidar interjected.

A cacophony of voices erupted.

Ellen shushed the room with a wave of her hand. "Explain, Salidar."

"Uh, m'lady, this ouroboros is just an amulet made of iron. Iron can be cast or wrought; any blacksmith has the skill. A collection of confusing spells can be attached, something obvious yet indeterminate. I, uh, have had some experience in crafting such implements—"

"*Fake* amulets! *Hustling,* Salidar?" Padraic huffed in disgust.

"Yes, fake amulets, false icons, worthless spells—I have had experience with all such," Salidar admitted.

"And it may now be just what we need," Ellen mused aloud. "How long to make one?"

"A day."

"Do it."

CH 34

PADRAIC ACCOMPANIED Ellen back to Delafaire Farm. However, he declined her invitation to come into the house.

Standing by the back porch, she tilted her head toward the kitchen door. "Are you sure?" She let Smokey slip from her arms to the ground. "Mom will be serving supper in a bit."

"I can't stay. I have to let Nightshade know what's going on. He was expecting me to return with Malvana."

"I understand; but, he probably already knows she's among the missing," Ellen pointed out.

"Nonetheless, I should go."

As he turned, she reached out and tugged his sleeve. "Look, I know you're not happy with me right now—"

He pulled his arm free. "You'll be walking into a trap!"

"Hmmph! You think I don't know that?"

"Then why would you do something so foolish?" He balled his fists. "You know we suspect Silenos wants a Steward to sacrifice—you'll be delivering yourself to him! You're going to get yourself killed!"

She shook her head and sighed. "Oh Padraic, you're just gonna have to learn to trust me."

"Oh, ye gods!" He moaned, his shoulders slumping. "Ellen, you know I do; but, I just can't help worrying. It's a parent's prerogative." He sighed in resignation. "So, all right, what are you planning?"

She grinned. "Oh, I've got a few things up my sleeve, and some details to iron out. Let me worry about that. Meanwhile, I have something else to ask of you, if you don't mind?"

Rolling his eyes, he clucked his tongue and asked, "*Tch!* What?"

"Barnabas is still in Mer, right?"

He nodded. "Yes, as far as I know. Why?"

"I think it's time to reunite him with Brona. I'm going to have her brought here tomorrow after sunset. Could you bring him here?"

"Really? Yes, absolutely! He'll be delighted! Oh, I know he'll ask—will they be able to go home?"

Ellen frowned. "No, I don't think so, not for a while yet. Everything is too unsettled right now—and not just with this Council mess. There's too much going on in regard to Mer; I don't think it's safe for either of them. So, I'm going to make arrangements to put them up here, at least for now."

"That's probably wise," he agreed. "Look, about earlier, I'm trying not to worry so much. So, at least tell me this; you're not planning on confronting Silenos alone, are you?"

"Alone?" Tilting her head, she frowned. "Of course not. You should know by now that I am not without exceptional friends and access to some very creative resources. Just trust me, okay?"

"Ha!" He scoffed, and chuckled. "Like I've got a choice?"

She grinned. "That's the spirit!"

TREY AND HAWK WERE seated in the kitchen talking with Millie, nursing mugs of cooling coffee. The men were clearly uncomfortable with the situation. Their eyes kept going to Stacy seated at the other end of the table, head down on her folded arms, a small pile of wadded damp tissues at her elbow.

Millie glanced up as Ellen entered. Trey and Hawk stood.

"Ellen! Any news?" her mother asked.

Stacy's head came up. Hope flared in her reddened eyes, but died when she read Ellen's face.

"Some," Ellen answered, pulling up a chair. "Everyone's still missing; but I know a lot more now." She waved the men back down to their seats. "Sit. I'll tell you everything I know."

And so she did.

GEORGE LOOKED UP FROM the scrying orb in surprise. "Vito? Back so soon? What's going on?"

The big man dropped an empty gym bag to the floor of the chamber.

"We got a problem, Boss. Before I could get started on my collections around New Orleans, I got word that Detroit and Toledo are in town lookin' for a *sit-down*. They gotta talk to you. So, I figured I'd better come right back to Olmus to tell you."

"Damn!" George smacked a fist into his palm. "I forgot about Frankie Fingers and his Windsor proposal. I was supposed to get back to him, wasn't I? So he came?"

"Yeah," Vito confirmed. "You never told me what to tell him. So, I didn't reach out."

"I guess he got impatient. He's got no other reason to come to New Orleans that I can see," George mused aloud. "Who came from Ohio?"

The big man shrugged. "Dunno, no other names were mentioned, just *Toledo.*"

George furrowed his brow. "Probably somebody from Don Giovanni's crew; Frankie's been on pretty good terms with them."

"Wait, a sit-down is a big deal. So, what do you mean *somebody?* The Don wouldn't come?"

"Nah, he's getting too old. He'd send one of his trusted higher-ups, probably a *capo.* I just hope it's not his nephew, Paulie—"

"Paulie the Torch? Are you kiddin' me—he 's a *psycho!* He's not a capo, is he?"

George shrugged. "Paulie Scapulante may not be a capo, but he is Don Giovanni's blood, his sister's son—that matters. Besides, Don Giovanni is old school; he doesn't really approve of the way Frankie likes to conduct business, too flamboyant, too much flash—you know, lotsa bling and all that. He wouldn't deal face-to-face with Frankie; he'd send somebody."

"But we know they do business," Vito began.

"Yeah, I know," George conceded. "They may have a profitable arrangement, but Frankie is too much of a showboat—that always rubs the old families the wrong way. See, he wants to be the Don of his own family, and pretty much acts like he already is—which is way stupid in my book.

"The Dons of the established families think he's an upstart who doesn't know his place. He's been pushing hard for a seat at the Dons' table. However, he's been told, more than once, that he doesn't deserve the title or the respect. He wants that power and prestige more than anything."

Vito scratched his chin. "You think that's why he's so hot to push our product into Windsor?"

"Yeah, it makes sense," George agreed. "If he can control the flow of product into Canada, that's the leverage he needs to raise his status. However, he needs the blessing of an established family, so he'd take the proposal to Don Giovanni, the only family who will still work with him. The old Don would need to know if the concept is feasible, and of course, profitable for him and his family."

"So, you think that's what this sit-down is all about?"

"More than likely, although . . ."

"What?" Vito prompted.

"Don Giovanni has friends in Canada, too, especially in Windsor. He already has an established, but small scale, import/export/distribution network for other stuff, like cigarettes and booze. If Frankie doesn't play nice, he may find himself squeezed out of the whole deal. Or, he could wind up being played for a patsy. Yeah, this could get interesting."

"So, are you gonna go for this sit-down, Boss?"

"Oh yeah, I can see a good angle for us in opening up the Canadian market, no matter who does the importing. Go see Teddy, get two ounces from his latest batch, and deliver one to each group, Detroit and Toledo. Tell them the sit-down is on. However, we'll set it up on *our turf, our terms*. Follow me?"

"Oh, yeah, you mean the room over the old club near the French Quarter, right? When?"

"Yeah, have it swept for bugs, and secure it for tomorrow night, say ten o'clock. No women or entertainment, this is strictly a business meeting."

Vito chuckled. "No broads? Frankie won't like that."

"Yeah, I know—in fact, I'm kinda counting on it."

"I get it—he'll probably complain and make an ass outta himself," Vito concluded.

George smiled. "Yeah, he won't be doing himself any favors. Remember, this is business; Toledo is who we must impress, not Detroit."

"But you're still gonna play `em against each other, aren't you?" Vito smiled in admiration.

George shrugged. "Be a shame not to, right? Besides, I never trusted Frankie Fingers. With that ego, he'd make a terrible Don."

Vito laughed and threw up his hands. "Ha-ha! Got it, Boss. Leave it to me."

Daegon burst into the chamber, nearly out of breath.

"The Red Hat tribe . . . I went to their cave . . ." Daegon gasped and held up a finger as he tried to catch his breath.

"This is about the goblins?" George asked.

The alchemist bobbed his head and gulped air.

"Okay, gimme a sec." George turned to the big driver. "Vito, you should go on and take care of that *thing*. I'll stay here and see how I can help our friend, Daegon, with whatever this goblin problem is."

Vito nodded and left the chamber.

George placed a hand on Daegon's shoulder. "All right now, catch your breath. You good? Okay, start at the beginning. What's up with the goblins?"

More composed, the alchemist explained. "Remember I told you that I suspected they had gone, most likely retreated to their deepest caverns, yes?"

"Yeah, so?"

"I went to the primary cave of the Red Hat tribe. There were no sentries and no one in the upper chambers."

George nodded. "Yeah, you said you could pretty much see that using the scrying orb. So?"

"Correct, but I had to see for myself; so I went. It is true; the goblins are all in hiding, deep in the bowels of this realm. Even our servants are gone!"

"Yeah, we kinda noticed. So, why?"

Daegon opened his palms. "I know not for certain, but I suspect it may have to do with what I *did* find in a lower-level chamber—bodies!"

"Bodies?" George echoed. "Dead goblins?"

"No! Not dead, and not goblins!"

"Huh? Explain."

Daegon took a deep breath. "There are seven bodies—not dead, but in heavy stasis fields. They're *not* goblins. We *know* one of them—Malvana, the Dark Elf who helped in taking vengeance on Diere the *usurper!"*

"Malvana? You're sure? Damn, we had plans for her," George muttered. His eyes widened and jaw dropped. "Wait—she was named to the Council as the Dark Elves avatar! Who else did you see?"

"I didn't recognize any of the others. I can only tell you there was a dwarf, another elf, a female, perhaps a Light Elf? All the rest, three men and a woman, appeared to be human. Do you have any idea what this means?"

George shook his head. "No, not sure—not yet. Did you touch any of them?"

"No, I tried to touch Malvana, to be sure it was her, but my hand got no closer than a few inches before she started to float away—"

"Float?" George blurted. "They're not on the ground?"

"No, I told you this was a heavy stasis field. Each one floats a few inches above the floor of the cavern. I have seen strong fields like this before; these are very old, very powerful spells. Whatever is in the stasis field can be moved with ease. It is akin to spells used by the dwarves of old in moving and placing large boulders once crafted into building blocks."

George stroked the back of his neck. "Now that is very interesting. So, they can be moved? This may be an opportunity for us; but first, we need to find out what's going on."

"How?" Daegon asked. "Do you want to go and see for yourself?"

George paused, pursing his lips. "No, not just yet. First, we need to do our due diligence."

He let his hand glide over the surface of the scrying orb, activating a number of small sparks within. "Let's see what's happening in the other realms; then, we'll make our plan."

MOMENTS LATER, DAEGON stepped back from the scrying orb and mumbled, "This cannot be—the Council? How? Why?"

George stepped back, as well. "Hmmph, better questions might be *who* has done this? And why bring them here?"

"Are we certain these are the Council members, the avatars of their realms?" Daegon asked, wringing his hands.

"Based on your description, I think there's little doubt." George gestured to the orb, its surface gone opaque and quiescent. "Every realm we looked in on had a frantic search going on. Everybody's looking for these people."

"But why here?" Daegon whined. "This was supposed to be our safe, secure, and *secret place!*"

"Calm down, and let me think," George muttered, and began pacing in the small chamber.

"Let's assume these are the Council avatars. Someone snatched, bespelled, and stashed them here, on a realm that's supposed to be off-limits to everybody. Somebody doesn't want them found, or . . . Daegon, are they hurt or harmed in any way being in these stasis fields?"

Daegon shook his head. "I do not think so. The Were make use of stasis spells on occasion without harming the subject."

George nodded. "I see, kinda like *suspended animation.*"

"Like *what?*"

"Oh, never mind," George waved off the alchemist's concern. "The point is that someone has further plans for these people, because they haven't been harmed. We need to find out who did this, and what their agenda is. Once we know that, we can see if there's any advantage for us."

Daegon scoffed. "Ha! I can think of a big *disadvantage* for us; someone may think to search here! This realm may officially be off-limits, but that does not preclude someone from thinking to search here, does it?"

"You have a point," George conceded. "It may even be inevitable. But don't forget, those stasis fields, and whatever is in them, can be moved, right?"

"Well, yes, but where—"

"Don't worry about it. I have an idea." George plucked at Daegon's sleeve. "Come on; follow me. I gotta ask Teddy something."

THEY FOUND TEDDY, A respirator masking his lower face, in his lab carefully pouring a cloudy liquid from a small beaker into a larger flask. The chemical odor was very strong and cloying.

George paused at the entrance and stopped Daegon from entering the cavern.

"Wait! We shouldn't go in there when the smell is this strong. I'll get his attention and we'll talk in the passageway."

Daegon crinkled his nose and squinted his eyes. "Whew! Fine by me!"

George waved until he caught Teddy's attention and beckoned him.

Teddy nodded and raised a finger. It took him a moment to secure the chemicals. He followed George and Daegon into the passageway and removed his respirator.

"Yeah, Boss, uh, what can I do for you?"

"Is everything coming along all right with this batch?" George asked.

"Uh, yeah, everything is fine. These last three batches are definitely the strongest I've ever cooked. When you get it to street level, you'll really have to step on it—a lot."

"Really? It's that strong?"

Teddy bobbed his head. "For sure! It's a killer at this strength and purity. You gotta step on it more than usual or a lot of users will OD the first time around. I could do it here—"

"No, not here and not you," George insisted. "It's easier to get smaller amounts to distribution points and cut it there. That way the blend is always a little different, the labeling, too. Users think there are different products out there, like competition in the marketplace. But in reality, we'll control it all."

"Oh, I get it. No problem, Boss," Teddy acknowledged. "Was there anything else?"

"Yeah," George said, a grim scowl settling upon his face, "there is."

Teddy blanched. "Oh no! Is something wrong? Are the goblins back? I'm really doing just fine without 'em. I don't—"

George shook his head. "No, that's not it. Listen, remember the place I found you, that house on Toledo Bend?"

"Oh, yeah-yeah!" Teddy nodded and scratched at his stubble. "You mean Brewster's fish camp, right?"

"Right! Now think, did he tell anybody else about that place, bedsides you, I mean?"

"No, Boss, I thought I told you this before. Brewster said that he only told me about it. Now, I don't know if he was lyin' or not; but he did give me the code to get in past the alarms an' all. If anybody else knew about it, wouldn't do `em no good without the security code."

George folded his arms. "And you never told anyone about the house, or the security code?"

"No way, Boss," Teddy insisted, "never told a soul!"

"Good!" George clapped the meth cook on the shoulder. "All right! We'll let you get back to work. Oh, one other thing; you know Vito had to go make a delivery and do collections, right? Well, Daegon and I have to go take care of something, too. So, when Vito gets back, tell him I need him to wait for me here. We won't be long, okay?"

Teddy bobbed his head. "Got it, Boss."

TEDDY WAS ALWAYS APPREHENSIVE when the boss sought him out. Fortunately, this encounter hadn't been that big a deal, so he relaxed a bit. But he still felt the need for a cigarette. Smoking in the lab was out of the question; but no matter, he'd recently found a better spot.

Since the goblin servants had seemingly disappeared, Teddy had been nosing around some of the lesser-used passages looking for a well-vented chamber where he could indulge his smoking habit. He'd found one, a small chamber whose walls were honeycombed with vent tubes; it was a perfect candlelit smoking lounge. He had even decided to keep a pack of cigarettes and matches here.

The funny thing was that sounds from other parts of the cavern complex could be heard here, thanks, no doubt, to the host of vent tubes.

GEORGE LED THE WAY back to the scrying room. He let Daegon enter first, and paused to scan the passage to be certain they were still alone.

"What?" Daegon asked, clearly confused.

"I don't want to be overheard," George admitted. "I know the goblins are gone, but I don't know where Clement and Stellara are."

Daegon furrowed his brow and brightened. "Right about now, they should be tending to the bats. Why?"

George rolled his eyes. "I just said *I don't want to be overheard!* Look, we gotta move those bodies in the stasis fields to a secure place; and, no one else needs to know it!"

"Move them? Where? Why?"

"Yeah! Because we can work this to our advantage. We gotta get them to a place I have in mind in my home realm."

Daegon was aghast. "What? How? Oh wait, you mean to use a *transit globe* to take them there, to the place you and Teddy were talking about? A *transit globe, really?"*

"Sure, why not? But not me—*you!* Don't you see? You could do this easily. It'd be no different than all that stuff you moved for Vito when he was setting up electric power for us, or the stuff Teddy needed to set up the lab. You said these stasis fields were easy to move; you've even done it yourself with one hand. This will work!"

"But—"

"But nothing! And best of all, by moving those bodies to another realm, we run less risk of our operations being discovered here. Not to mention that we'll have seven bargaining chips of very high value. And maybe best of all, we'll have screwed over whoever tried to pull this off in the first place. Daegon, this is a golden opportunity!"

"All right, I can see the logic," Daegon admitted. "However, I have never been to this specific place in your home realm; so, transiting there, with seven bodies no less, could be a problem."

"I've been there, so I can help you focus," George countered. "And here's one more thing; that's the place your servant, the crow, found me and conveyed your message that allowed me to later rescue you from that, uh, other realm."

"The crow—really? You actually used the ensorcelled gem I sent, at that place, that location?"

George leaned back against the wall and folded his arms. "I did. Does that help?"

"Indeed, it should; that was a very strong spell. A lingering trace of such energy can be a rather precise focal point. Yes, this could work."

"Yeah, like GPS waypoint!" George ignored Daegon's look of sudden befuddlement and pushed off the wall. "Whatever, don't ask. Come on, let's do it—the sooner, the better!"

QUIET SETTLED OVER the kitchen at Delafaire Farm.

Ellen splayed her open hands atop the table and leaned back in her chair. "Well, that's it. Now you know everything."

Hawk shook his head. "Seriously? That's it? And that's your plan, as well?"

"Well, the gist of it." Ellen winced. "There are still some details to iron out; but I'm open to suggestions."

"Here's one," Trey offered. "This meet is supposed to take place on Olmus, right? If you know the location of a planned meet, you always do prior reconnaissance; know everything you can about it. Plan for contingencies, because nothing ever goes exactly as you expect—ever. And most importantly, don't try to do this alone, always have backup."

"He's right," Hawk insisted. "I know you think this will buy time, but it also puts you in danger. We have no idea what Silenos really wants. How do you know it isn't you?"

Ellen shrugged. "I don't; none of us do. What I do know is that Mark, and six others, are missing. Silenos claims to have them, and will harm them if he doesn't get what he wants."

"This iron ouroboros?" Trey asked.

"And her!" Hawk spat, scowling.

"Yeah, maybe," Trey conceded. "But this ouroboros will be a fake; and there's no way to know how soon he'll realize that fact, is there?"

"No," she admitted. "We hope to find the missing people before the meet, or at least before Silenos discovers we've tricked him. And of course, everybody's looking." Ellen opened her palms. "Look, I know this is a huge gamble, but I don't see any other options here—does anybody?"

The kitchen grew quiet once more.

Her eyes reddened, Stacy looked up. "Excuse me." She sniffled into a tissue. "Ellen, you said everybody's looking. Yeah well, we all know the Council realms will only search in their own realms; they won't venture into the *wild.* But, Olmus, that's in the *wild,* right? Shouldn't that be searched, too? You said that even Storm Haven doesn't have the resources to do much searching in the *wild.* So, Olmus, who's gonna look there?"

"We are," Trey answered. "First thing tomorrow, Hawk and I will do the recon for the meet and conduct a search, uh, if Ellen can get us there."

Ellen balked. "That's not—"

"I'm going, too!" interrupted Stacy, who leveled a finger at Ellen. "And don't you *dare* say I'm not! There's no way you're keeping me from looking for Mark!"

Hawk stood. "We are going to do the recon, conduct the search—and we will cover the meet as your backup. Don't think for an instant that this is negotiable. Do you understand?"

Ellen locked eyes with Hawk, his expression stern and determined. Gratitude swelled in her heart.

"Actually, all I can say is *thank you*. I'd be grateful for your help."

CH 35

TEDDY DIDN'T MIND BEING alone in his lab; in fact, as a rule, he preferred it.

What he *really* liked was that the goblin servants were nowhere around. They made him nervous. He felt like they were always *watching* him, hovering nearby, peering with those strangely luminescent eyes from the shadows.

Of course, Papa George had made it clear the goblins were to leave Teddy alone; and for the most part, they did. Nonetheless, the goblins still gave Teddy the *creeps.*

Now, for some unknown reason, they were gone—all of them. In fact, they'd been gone for a while; that suited Teddy just fine. If they came back, he might lose his new smoking lounge. That would be a problem, especially since he'd developed an interest in eavesdropping. He wondered just how much eavesdropping the goblin servants may have done.

Footsteps coming down the passageway drew his attention.

"Hey, Teddy," hailed Vito, as he entered the lab chamber and dropped a heavy gym bag to the stony floor. "Where's the boss man?"

The meth cook shrugged. "Dunno for sure. Him an' Daegon had to go take care of something. He didn't say what. He did say when you got back to wait for him."

"Okay, I'm gonna be in my room." Vito picked up the gym bag and suddenly froze, cocking his ear toward the passageway.

"What? Are they back?" Teddy asked.

Vito dropped the gym bag and waved him into silence. Crouching, he hissed, "It ain't them."

Teddy's eyes widened at the sudden sight of a pistol in the big man's hand. Teddy ducked behind his lab bench and kept quiet.

"Hello? Is anybody here?" echoed down the passageway.

A woman's voice? Teddy strained to hear more. Peeking around his lab bench, he saw Vito straighten and relax.

"Circe? Are you alone?" Vito demanded, slipping his pistol beneath his jacket. "What are you doing here?"

Teddy saw the sea witch step into the lab chamber. He relaxed and stood.

She was dressed in an upscale female merchant's garb, a simple dun-colored dress fringed in black lace, rolled-up sleeves, and an orange bandanna wrapped snugly around the dome of her head. She gripped her ever-present staff as her pet lizard balanced upon her thin shoulders.

"Yes, Vito, I am alone." She nodded to Teddy, who dipped his head in response.

"So, what are you doing here?" Vito repeated.

"Where is your boss, George?" she asked.

"Not here, but could be back any time. So, why?" Vito folded his arms.

"I have been in Derinseum, setting up my shop. I am ready to open for business, so I need some product." She gestured toward Teddy. "That is, if our talented alchemist can so provide?"

"No problem. So, your shop is ready? That's good." Vito bobbed his head. "I know the boss has been waiting to hear from you. He'll be pleased. You don't mind waiting for him, do you?"

"Not at all. As it happens, we need to talk. Strange things are afoot in Mer."

Before Vito could inquire further, a familiar voice echoed down the passageway.

"Oh yeah? Like what?"

"Hey, Boss! You're back!" Vito cried. "Look who's here, Circe. She's ready to open for business."

George and Daegon filed into the chamber.

"Well now, that's certainly good news." George noticed the hefty gym bag at Vito's feet and let his eyebrows ascend in an unspoken question.

Vito smiled. "Yeah, it was a good day. We're all set up for tomorrow." He picked up the gym bag. "I'm gonna put this away."

George nodded. "Do that. Then join us. Meanwhile, I want to hear what Circe meant by *strange things*. Circe?"

The sea witch tilted her head and gently scratched beneath her lizard's chin. "Two things, actually."

George shrugged. "Go on."

"The Derinseum Watch has been searching throughout the city. Rumors abound that members of the Council are missing—hard to believe, I know. However, my sources tell me this is true, and that searches are underway in other realms as well. There are even whispers that Silenos is responsible."

"The Council is missing?" George repeated. "Wow, imagine that. Silenos is supposed to be responsible?"

George ignored Daegon's sudden glance of concern, and maintained an expression of mild surprise tempered with bland innocence.

However, Teddy had seen it all; George playing it too innocent, and the alchemist stifling his momentary lapse of composure.

Uh-oh, something's goin' on here. That was definitely a reaction from Daegon. What's this mean?

Teddy glanced away, but listened more carefully as Daegon questioned the sea witch more closely.

"Circe, I must ask; do you think this is all true? Do your sources know any more?"

She shrugged. "That members of the Council are missing, is likely true. That Silenos is responsible? I know not what to think. As I said, my sources have heard only whispers."

Daegon nodded. "Do you think Silenos is capable of such a thing?"

"I do not know," she admitted, as genuine concern slipped across her angular face. "But in truth, I would not be surprised. That he is powerful is not in doubt. What he ultimately seeks is anyone's guess. I do not trust Silenos—no one should. He is not to be underestimated."

"You said there were *two* things, Circe," George reminded. "What else?"

"A cursed fog! Sailors throughout Mer are baffled. I know not what to make of this development," the sea witch confided.

"What, just fog? Explain," George insisted.

Circe waved a bony finger in warning. "Seasoned sailors do not take fog lightly. This is a strange thick fog spreading out in the Southern Ocean, a clinging miasma said to have a foul stench, much like that of rot and corruption. It emanates from the region of the Keys of Osiris."

"You mean something like an algae die-off, a red tide?" George suggested.

Circe shook her head. "No, tis no red tide. It imparts no color to the sea—unless it be black! Tis far larger than any known tide or current, and spreading quickly. It leaves the darkened sea stagnant; ships not moored in socked-in harbors drift blind and becalmed in fouled waters. Already spread past New Port Royal, this choking fog will reach beyond Essa within days. Many whisper tis not a natural fog, but a sorcerous curse."

George scoffed. "Well, sailors are a superstitious lot."

"Aye," she conceded, "but that does not make them wrong."

"And your vessel?" Daegon asked.

"The *Xanthippe* is anchored in Derinseum's harbor, safe for now. No sane ship's master would venture forth." She made a small sign with index and little finger, a warding against the *evil eye.* "No amount of coin would tempt me to sail in these conditions. A fool's errand, twould be."

"If it's only weather," George reasoned, "it will pass. Be patient. Now, let's talk business; how much product do you need?"

"As much as you can spare at the moment. Normally, I would take delivery in New Port Royal, but that is impossible now. I must make it appear as recently offloaded cargo. I must return to Derinseum soon."

"We'll take care of you." He turned to the meth cook. "Teddy, see what we have left from last week's batch—*not* the stuff you've been working on this week, *capisce?*"

"Sure thing, Boss. We've got plenty left from that batch. I just need to know how much to package."

George smiled. "Give me a minute; we're gonna work that out right now."

As George and Circe discussed business, Teddy noticed Daegon appeared distracted and worried.

Hmm, Daegon is no dummy; something's bothering him. My gut is uneasy, too; not a good sign—no, not at all.

THE MORNING WAS COOLER than expected, and overcast.

Trey and Hawk were running late. Hawk had called to explain the delay.

Ellen and Stacy were sitting on the front porch savoring mugs of coffee when Trey and Hawk pulled up in a borrowed departmental SUV.

"About time," mumbled Stacy into her mug.

Hawk, at the wheel, waved.

"Sorry for the delay," Trey called as he climbed from the vehicle. "We had to load this rig with our gear." He opened the right rear passenger door, and waved them forward. "Come on, hop in. We'll drive to the cabin."

Ellen and Stacy climbed into the backseat and buckled in.

"We're good. Let's go," urged Stacy.

Hawk steered the SUV around the outbuildings and started down the fire road. He looked over his shoulder and asked, "What, no Smokey? I thought for sure he'd go with us."

"Yeah, I thought so, too," Ellen responded, "but, I haven't seen him all morning."

"Me neither," Stacy murmured under her breath, "and wasted too much time looking for him."

Ellen nudged her friend. "Chill already. We couldn't have gotten started until the guys got here; we only spent a few minutes looking. And now we're saving time because we don't have to walk. Lighten up."

Stacy pursed her lips. "Yeah, okay. I'm just anxious to start searching for Mark. I'll be all right."

Ellen nodded. "I know."

"What are y'all talking about back there?" Hawk asked looking in the rearview mirror.

"Coffee," Ellen answered. "Do y'all want some? We brought a full thermos and extra travel mugs."

"Yeah, I'll take some," Trey twisted around in his seat to accept a mug.

"No thanks, I'm good," Hawk said, his eyes on the worn path of the old fire road.

"If I might ask, Ellen," Trey began. "Is there a reason you wanted to use the Grand Portal to go to Olmus? I thought you didn't really need it."

"Actually, I don't, but there are certain protections, wards and such, that are integrated into the Grand Portal that I think would be wise to take advantage of, especially since I'm transiting all of us."

"Do you think," Stacy asked, "there's a globe in the Grand Portal that'll take us right to Olmus? Would that save time?"

Ellen shrugged. "An Olmus globe? I don't know; there might be. However, there are a lot of existing globes; we're not gonna waste time looking. I can get us there, no problem. It'd just be best if we were within the standing stones when I do it."

"That's where the protection, the wards and such, are in effect?" Trey concluded.

"Sorta," Ellen began. "The area of protection is bigger than that, but it's kind of *focused* there. Does that make sense?"

"Yeah, it does." Trey grinned. "I feel better about it already."

IT DIDN'T TAKE LONG to get to the cabin.

Trey and Hawk began unloading gear from the back of the SUV; utility vests, extra flashlights, and a pair of twelve-gauge shotguns.

"Shotguns?" Ellen pointed.

Trey nodded. "Definitely . . . Have you forgotten what you sent there?"

Ellen winced. "Oh, yeah."

Stacy gripped Ellen's arm. "*That's* where you sent those saber-toothed cats, to *Olmus?*"

"Uh-huh," Ellen admitted in her chagrin. "But it's supposed to be only temporary, until we can figure out where they really belong."

Stacy released Ellen's arm. "And we're gonna search in the same realm you sent these cats to?"

Offering a weak smile, Ellen slowly nodded.

Stacy pointed at the pump shotgun in Trey's hands. "I'd like one of those, too!"

"Sorry, Stacy, we've only got the two pumps. Hawk and I are trained and qualified in their use."

Hands on her hips, Stacy fumed, "Well, give me something!"

"Hold on." Trey rummaged around in the back of the SUV and produced a thick black aerosol canister with a pistol grip. "Here, this is heavy-duty OC pepper spray used for crowd control. Aim it like this at arm's length, push the safety off, and pull the trigger. It'll spray a straight stream out to about twelve feet, and then start to dissipate; so, it's actually effective to a bit over twenty feet, or just over a car length."

She hefted the canister and held it out at arm's length. "Hmm, not too heavy. How many shots does it hold?"

"Depends on how long you hold the trigger down," Trey explained. "If you can keep it to about a two-second burst, there are about a dozen shots in that canister. Of course, you'll know when you're running out, because it'll get lighter as you use up the contents."

"That makes sense," Stacy agreed. "It's kinda cumbersome to carry, though."

Trey reached back into the SUV. "Here, this is a tactical pouch with a shoulder strap. The canister will fit in the wide zippered compartment; try it."

She did. "Okay, cool! This'll work. What are these extra loops on the side for?"

"Those are usually for grenades; tear gas, colored smoke, or flash-bangs. I doubt we'll need any of those."

Hawk paused in loading shells in the magazine tube of his shotgun. "Trey, you might wanna rethink that; having a couple of flash-bangs might be a good idea. If we don't need them, then fine."

"I see; better to have and not need, than need and not have," Trey reasoned. "Okay, give me that tac-bag for a second, Stacy. Thanks."

When he returned it to her, two flash-bang grenades were secured in the bag's loops.

"Here you go. I hope you don't mind carrying these, too. Whatever you do, do *not* pull on these rings, understand?"

Stacy nodded. "Don't worry, I won't mess with `em. Hey, what about Ellen? Shouldn't she have something, too? Do you have another pepper-spray canister?"

Trey chuckled and pointed to a large tank on a backpack frame strapped into a recess in the SUV.

"Just that one; it's the big brother to the one you've got."

She gasped. "That looks like a flamethrower!"

Trey shrugged. "Almost the same size, and damn near as heavy. That's not coming with us."

"I don't really think I'm going to need anything," Ellen said. "I'll feel plenty safe just being with you guys. Can we get going now? I have to be home before sunset."

"Sunset?" Trey repeated.

"Miska is coming home!" Stacy exclaimed. "And he's bringing Brona. Her dad is supposed to come, too, right?"

"Right, Barnabas," Ellen confirmed. "Come on, let's go."

As they walked toward the stone-ringed clearing, Hawk spoke softly to Ellen.

"So, *before sunset,* eh? Some significance to that?"

"Some," she admitted. "I'll explain later."

"You know, this has got me thinking," Hawk mused aloud. "It's about time we got serious about teaching you some firearms skills."

"What do you mean? We've been out plinking at targets, cans and stuff. I've shot twenty-twos and your forty and a forty-five."

"I'm not talking about simple target practice; I mean some real handgun training, combat survival stuff. I know it's a skill set you might think you'll never need; but it's like Trey said, *better to have and not need, than need and not have.*"

She smiled. "I'm game. After all, I like learning new skills, especially if you're my teacher."

Once in the center of the clearing, Trey announced, "Last chance everyone—check your gear. Okay? Good. We're ready when you are, Ellen."

"Okay, stand together. Here we go."

The hemisphere of a large transit globe suddenly enveloped them, went opaque, and shrank out of existence with an audible *pop.*

An errant breeze off the lake teased the grass in the now empty clearing.

THE FOUR COMPANIONS stood near the edge of a thick forest. Hawk and Trey immediately scanned the area in all directions. With the tree line at their backs, they faced a wide grassy plain beyond which rose a succession of rolling hills covered in low scrub, intermittent copses of twisted trees, and erratic rocky escarpments.

"This feels a little familiar," Stacy said, looking around. "Ellen, is this where we were when we came here before?"

"Not exactly, but it's close. This is the edge of the same forest; but, we were a bit south of here. I've brought us here because it's supposed to be close to the ruins we need to scout."

"The meeting site?" Stacy asked.

"Yeah, about half a mile in that direction," she pointed across the plain, "in those hills. Gallenius told me that there are lots of old temple ruins in this area, mainly because of the ley lines."

"Ley lines? What's that?" asked Trey.

Ellen shrugged. "Some say they're ancient highways of power, but more likely old paths of energy. They run through the ground in different directions, close to the surface, and usually in straight lines. I guess the easiest way to explain is to visualize a lingering static electricity charge, or a faint line of dormant current that hasn't been discharged."

"You mean like in a battery?" Hawk asked.

"Kinda, but more volatile—you know, like it'd give you a shock if you mess with it the wrong way."

"Oh, yeah," Hawk reasoned, "that's more like a capacitor. I've used them on older motorcycle ignitions. They'll hold a charge and *zap* you if you're not careful."

"That sounds right; think of a ley line like a long capacitor and be careful it doesn't zap you," she teased. "The good news is that I can sense them, and they're really strong here."

"Is that how we're supposed to find the right ruins? Tracing the ley lines?" Trey deduced.

"Right!" Ellen confirmed. "It's the place where several ley lines converge, in that direction." She pointed once more. "If we start walking that way, we'll hit a ley line going in roughly the same direction; then we follow it. If Gallenius' old maps are right, we should find the right ruins in those hills."

"Hold on! We're also here to look for Mark and the others," reminded Stacy. "So, give me a minute to search this forest."

"Huh?" Trey balked. "We don't have the time to—"

"Sure, we do!" Ellen cut him off, and grinned at Stacy. "Do it."

Stacy smiled and walked past the tree line, into the forest. She went to the biggest oak she saw and gently laid her hands upon its rough bark.

"Oh man, of course." Trey toed the dirt and let his shoulders sag. "I forgot what she can do—my bad."

They watched Stacy's face take on a serene expression as she communicated with the great tree. It was several minutes before she broke contact, stepped back, and bowed in gratitude before the old oak.

"Well?" asked Ellen.

Stacy sighed. "Several things . . . These trees know nothing of Mark or any other Council members. However, their knowledge is limited to what the trees observe, and they're not everywhere in this realm. Also, despite what most believe, this realm is not uninhabited. There's a sentient native species here, but they haven't been seen of late. Something else is here, and has been hunting; that might be the reason."

Ellen bit her lower lip. She had a pretty good idea what might be hunting here.

"Any more info about this *sentient native species?*" Trey asked.

"Not really. Trees don't tend to differentiate species by details, other than the simplest of terms; whether or not they can move, you know, fly, walk, or swim, and the number of legs," Stacy explained. "These sentient natives are two-legged."

"What do they mean by *not been seen of late?* What's the time frame for *of late?*" Hawk asked.

Stacy shrugged. "I don't know. Trees tend to view things in the long term, so there's no telling. But my gut says it hasn't been that long."

"Whatever's the case," Trey intoned, "we need to be careful."

"I agree. Let's get going," Ellen urged. "We can search any ruins we encounter while we look for the meeting place."

AS ELLEN HAD ANTICIPATED, finding and following ley lines was no great challenge; she sensed them easily. The path took them through several sites of old ruins—weatherworn piles of tumbled blocks and shattered columns. Some had accessible subterranean chambers. However, all were devoid of any signs of life.

Nonetheless, they searched each site. Ellen tried her best to sense any life energy in the vicinity, but aside from insects and small creatures, she found nothing.

By late afternoon, they worked their way past another ring of blasted blocks and broken columns to find a large, debris-strewn stone circle. In its center sat a raised dais bearing an altar-like stained stone.

Ellen closed her eyes and let her awareness fully open. She shuddered and almost stumbled.

Hawk reached out and gripped her arm. "I've got you! Are you all right?"

"I'm okay," she insisted, pushing away. "Just give me a second."

"What is it? Is this the place? Are you sure you're all right?" Trey pressed.

Seeing three concerned faces staring at her intently, she smiled. "I'm good; and yes, this is the place. There are a number of ley lines converging here. Feeling them all at once was kind of overwhelming. I was just surprised, that's all."

Stacy pointed to the central stone. "Is that some sort of altar, do you think?"

"Yeah," Ellen agreed, "I think so. I want a closer look."

"Me, too," insisted Stacy. "We gotta look for clues. Think maybe Mark's been here?"

Ellen shrugged. "Dunno, but we should check it out."

"Okay, but be careful." Trey warned. "Hawk and I will check the perimeter. Stay alert."

As Hawk and Trey began a careful inspection of the area, Ellen and Stacy approached the altar stone.

Stacy pointed and whispered, "Are those old bloodstains? They're almost black."

"Hard to say; I think bloodstains do blacken with age. There's no way of knowing for sure without some sort of testing, I'd guess," Ellen cautioned. "Look, symbols kinda like runes are chiseled into the side of the stone."

Stacy stared and then walked completely around the altar. "Yeah, they go all the way around the whole thing. What do you suppose that means?"

Ellen chuckled. "If I could read ancient runes, I'd tell you."

Stacy rolled her eyes. "Well, duh! What now, *Miss Smartypants?*"

"I don't know. We should look around some more, I guess. What are you doing?"

Stacy was toeing through a small pile of stones at the base of the altar. She squatted down and picked through them. "Now this is a strange rock."

"What is?" Ellen leaned over her friend's shoulder.

"This is," Stacy answered holding up a rounded shape. "All the rest of these stones and rocks are irregular and jagged, but not this one. It's smooth and different. Here, see for yourself."

Ellen took the stone and brushed off as much dirt as possible. "You're right. It's not just smooth, it's carved into a shape, see?" She held it between thumb and forefinger. "It's a figure, I think."

Stacy squinted. "A fat woman with pendulous breasts? Oh-oh, I know! It's a fertility symbol!"

Ellen smiled. "I think you're right! There's no telling how old it is."

Stacy nodded. "As a symbol, it could go back to the neolithic. I think it's cool."

"Yeah? You ought to keep it as a souvenir; maybe show it to Armand when we get home?"

Stacy beamed. "You bet!"

"Find anything?" Trey asked as he and Hawk joined the women.

"Not much," Ellen admitted, and held up the small stone figure, "a little carved figure—"

"And some old carved runes on this altar stone," Stacy interjected, smirking and nodding toward Ellen, "that *no one here* can read."

Ignoring the teasing jibe, Ellen returned the figure to Stacy and asked, "How about you guys, find anything?"

"Maybe," Hawk offered, "but it might be nothing. I found some faint deer tracks, and maybe some goat tracks."

"What?" Stacy caught her breath. "You mean like faun and satyr tracks?"

"Don't jump to conclusions," Trey cautioned. "It might just be deer and goats. We've never seen the real thing, genuine faun and satyr tracks; so, we have no basis for comparison."

"Well, we don't know if deer and goats are even in this realm, do we?" Stacy reasoned hopefully.

"Nor do we know they're not," Ellen countered.

Stacy was unbowed. "But it makes sense that Silenos and his fauns would come here to check this place out, wouldn't it? They'd want to see this place before they'd pick it for a meeting site, wouldn't they?"

Hawk nudged his partner. "She makes a good point."

Trey nodded. "True, they would come here. There's got to be a reason why they picked this site."

"There's power here; the ley lines converge here. That's got to have something to do with it." Ellen concluded.

Stacy let her shoulders slump. "Unfortunately, there's no trace of Mark or the missing Council members here, or anyplace else we've searched today. So, what do we do now?"

"It's getting late," Ellen announced. "We now know more about this place. We need to get back; other things will be happening this evening that will demand attention."

"We also need to plan for tomorrow," Trey insisted, "when this meeting is supposed to take place here, sometime before sunset, as I recall."

"Right," Hawk agreed. "What now, Ellen, can we leave from here? Or do we have to retrace our route and leave from where we arrived?"

She paused in thought. "Retrace? No, but not from here, either. I don't think that would be a good idea. Let's get some distance from this place and depart from somewhere else. Just humor me on this, okay?"

No one disagreed; so, they set off, Hawk in the lead and Trey bringing up the rear.

AS THEY WENT FURTHER into the hills, scrub brush gave way to stands of twisted trees. The rocky ground offered difficult footing, slowing the companions' progress.

Passing a thick copse of gnarled live-oaks, Stacy paused, raised her head, and sniffed.

Ellen stopped beside her. "What is it?"

Stacy shook her head. "Dunno. For a second there, I thought I caught a whiff of something—it wasn't pleasant."

"Yeah?" Ellen wet a finger and stuck it up into the air. "There is a slight breeze. Wait, the wind's changing." She suddenly made a sour face. "Oh man! That stinks!"

"Yeah, that's it, whew!" Stacy grimaced and pointed. "It's coming from those trees."

"Wait! Don't—" Ellen began.

Ignoring her friend's warning, Stacy was already at the trees, pushing the underbrush aside.

Trey caught up to Ellen. "What's the holdup? What's Stacy doing?"

"Looking for something, I think. A moment ago we both smelled something kinda nasty, but the wind's changed again. I don't smell it now."

Stacy suddenly straightened and stumbled back from the trees. Her face was ashen, eyes wide, and mouth open in a soundless scream. All she could do was point, her finger trembling.

Trey was at her side in an instant, his shotgun leveled at the tree line.

Ellen hastened to Stacy and pulled her back a pace.

Hawk came running to join them. "What? What is it?"

Pulling away from Ellen, Stacy found her voice, jabbing her finger at the trees. "A b-body!"

A hand on her shoulder, Hawk turned Stacy to face him. "Stay with Ellen. We'll check it out."

Nodding to each other, the men spread out and approached the trees from different angles, their shotguns leveled. The capricious wind changed again; the scent of corruption fouled the air.

Ellen and Stacy held their breath. An uncomfortable silence reigned, until Trey and Hawk stepped out from the trees and motioned that it was safe.

Strengthening their resolve, the women went forward.

"Who is it?" Ellen asked. "Someone we know?"

"No," Hawk assured her. "In fact, we don't know that it's human."

"What?" Ellen blurted. "I have to see!"

"Yeah—me, too," Stacy insisted. "I'm fine now."

Trey shrugged. "Okay, but prepare yourselves. It's not pretty; the smell is worse when you get closer. Follow me, and don't touch anything. It'll help if you think about what you're about to see as evidence."

They spent a long moment staring at the mangled body.

"Bipedal, but definitely not human," Ellen observed. "The skull is large, but the eye sockets and the mouth are way too big. Those ears, are they *pointed?"*

"Looks like it," agreed Stacy. "This is too weird. Look, the hands are too long, the feet, too. The arms and legs are too skinny. The torso is very round, like a beach ball; but, *eeeww*, it's all torn open. Not human, for sure."

"Hmmph, not likely." Trey grunted. "You ladies would make pretty good detectives. What else do you notice?"

Ellen pointed to scraps of fabric clinging to the distended limbs. "Is that cloth, like for clothing?"

Trey nodded. "Probably. What does that suggest?"

"Innate intelligence—a culture," Stacy answered. "Would this be the sentient native race here?"

"Good supposition, and very likely true," Trey agreed.

"What's that?" Stacy pointed to something red on the ground in the nearby brush. "Something blood-soaked?"

Hawk used a stick to pick it up. "No, it's not bloody; it's fabric, just dark red in color. It looks woven, like a cap."

"Our victim's?" Trey asked.

"Yeah, more than likely." Hawk returned the cap to the precise place he found it.

"Ellen, have you got your phone?" Trey asked.

"Yes, why?"

"Why don't you take some pictures? Later you can ask Gallenius if he can identify this species."

She nodded. "That's a good idea. But, I gotta ask, don't you have your phone?"

Shaking his head, Trey explained. "No, Hawk and I have department-issued cell phones. We figured it would be best not to bring them along whenever we weren't in our home realm. I know we had done so before, but we came to realize it wasn't a good idea. We didn't want to take the chance on having text or photos stored in memory that would be awkward to explain. And I don't really know the extent of the phones' GPS tracking ability. So, we leave them at home when we're gonna be *elsewhere.*"

"I see. Have you given any thought to having some personally owned phones? Wouldn't that be something your department couldn't arbitrarily examine?" Ellen reasoned.

"Possibly," Trey admitted. "We have talked about it, but they still wouldn't work as communications devices. As far as we know, there's no established infrastructure, no cell towers or repeater systems, in any of the other realms. Whenever we've needed individual point-to-point communications, we've used handheld radios that neither record nor have memory."

"That makes sense. I'd forgotten about your radios," Ellen admitted.

"No problem. We'll get out of the way so you can take the pictures."

"Okay, give me a few minutes," she grinned, "while I play *crime scene technician.*"

As the three of them stood clear of the trees, Ellen bent to the task. She heard Hawk ask Stacy how she found the body.

"It was the smell," Stacy explained. "I tried to find its source. When I pulled a bunch of limbs and leaves away, I saw the body."

"Limbs and leaves? It was covered up?" Hawk pressed.

"Yeah, pretty much."

Trey and Hawk shared an ominous look.

"Ellen!" Hawk called. "Are you about through?"

"Yeah, I'm coming!" In a moment she stood with them. "What's wrong?"

"We need to go, now!" Hawk urged.

Trey gently pushed the women away from the copse of trees. "We think this body might be a predator's kill. Predators try to hide their kills; and, they'll protect them. Let's go."

They hastened away, following a faint trail.

Hawk hissed under his breath, "Ellen, how soon can we get out of this realm?"

"Anytime, but I've got to find a spot away from all these ley lines. I don't want to try crafting a transit globe too close because I don't know what effect that residual energy might have. We might wind up someplace we really don't want to go."

"Well, start looking," he insisted. "In the meantime, could you *do your thing?* You know, see if we're still alone?"

"Yes, but we've got to stop for me to do that, and it'll take a moment or two."

"Okay, I get it." Hawk *stage whispered* out to his partner. "Hey Trey, find a spot to stop for a minute, someplace defensible!"

Trey pointed. "How about that knoll? It's pretty clear of brush and trees, good sight lines."

"Yeah, that'll work!"

They made their way atop the small rocky knoll and stopped to catch their breath.

Ellen took a moment to calm herself and projected her awareness like subtle ripples on a pond. The further she probed, the less distinct were her perceptions—but something was there.

No, two somethings . . . stalking us . . . creeping closer . . .

"Oh no! We've got company!"

"Where?" Trey demanded.

Ellen pointed to one side, then pointed with the other hand in another direction. "There are two! There and there!"

They could see nothing beyond the thick scrub and stunted trees; but they all sensed that something was out there.

"They're trying to flank us," Trey reasoned. "Ellen, can you tell what they are?"

"Animal, I think, but cunning, and definitely working together."

A moment later Hawk hissed, "There! In that stand of trees, something moved—something big!"

Stacy whispered to Ellen, "This might be a good time to call up a transit globe, don't you think?"

Ellen balked. "We're right on top of a convergence of ley lines; that could be disastrous!"

Stacy frowned. "Worse than this? Come on, we both know what's probably stalking us."

Ellen knew Stacy was right. "I'll need a moment."

"Hawk!" Trey cried. "Can you still see it?"

"Yeah, but just a shape—still can't tell what it is!"

Trey kept swinging the muzzle of his shotgun in a broad arc in the other general direction that Ellen had indicated; but, there was no sign of a flanker.

At the top of the knoll, Ellen stood concentrating, totally focused—she never heard the faint snap of a twig a short distance behind her.

STACY HEARD IT AND spun in that direction. She could see little beyond the thick underbrush at the tree line. She took several steps down the knoll in that direction and peered more closely at the trees. A breezy gust fanned the leaves and set limbs to swaying, but for an upright sapling whose limbs seemed immune to the wind, even to the point of slightly bending the wrong way.

There, almost at ground level, Stacy saw a saffron glint of reflection, and realized a pair of tawny eyes were watching her closely. Her breath caught in her throat; a memory surged.

Another set of yellow eyes had once stared at her in much the same way, as prey—*Ling.*

Stacy shook the memory off, and slowly backed up.

"Uh, guys," she announced in a conversational tone, "I think I've found the other one."

Trey came to her side just as the male saber-toothed cat rose and stepped out from the trees.

"Walk slow and steady," he hissed. "Get to the top of the knoll with Ellen."

Trey kept his shotgun leveled at the big cat, who just stood there sniffing the air.

Hawk shouted, "This one broke cover! It is one of the cats, but it's just standing there. I think it's confused because we didn't run."

"Same with this one," Trey called. "Keep eye contact and don't show any fear. Make your way to the top of the knoll. We need to be together for Ellen to get us out of here."

Neither saber-toothed cat moved as Hawk and Trey began slowly backing up the knoll. The cats watched intently, sniffing at the air to catch the prey's scent.

It was going well; but halfway up the rise Trey caught his heel on an unseen protrusion of rock and stumbled back into a sitting position.

In an instant, the big male cat crouched and leapt, landing at the foot of the knoll. Another such leap would have him in Trey's face. Clearly focused on his prey, the saber-toothed cat raised his head, opened his massive jaws and rent the sky with a bloodcurdling screaming howl.

Shotgun to his shoulder, Trey scrambled to his feet, but not quite fast enough.

Stacy was suddenly at his side, arm extended, firing a silvery stream of liquid into the open maw of the great cat.

The saber-tooth's shrieking howl was abruptly cut short. Slamming its eyes closed, it grit its teeth and shook its head vigorously.

A shotgun's *boom* sounded from the other side of the knoll.

"To me—quickly!" screamed Ellen.

Everyone scrambled up the knoll. Once together, a transit sphere instantly enveloped them.

Pop!

The knoll was empty.

THE FEMALE SABER-TOOTHED cat cautiously approached her growling and whining mate.

He was frantically wiping at his eyes and muzzle with his paws and forelegs. His growling and whining diminished to whimpering.

She sat down with a *huff* and watched the male. Her mate was soon reduced to panting and wiping at his squinting eyes. She *huffed* again.

The prey was gone. This hunt was done.

She rose and started back to their cache, instinctively knowing *somebody* had to guard their recent kill.

CH 36

ELLEN BLINKED—THEY were still atop a knoll!

What happened? Didn't it work—or did it?

"Hey! This isn't home!" Hawk declared.

"Maybe," Trey agreed, looking around, "but no cats. Where are we?"

They were standing upon an earthen mound, in a clearing ringed by huge sets of standing stones, some of which supported lintel stones spanning the gaps. Several more large stone blocks, perhaps fallen lintels, lay haphazardly around the clearing amid tufts of wild grasses and bracken. A conifer forest thickened beyond the clearing. The air was cool, almost chilly, and crisp with the scent of pine.

Stacy peered at the encircling standing stones, glanced up at the overcast sky, and tugged at Ellen's sleeve. "So, Ellen, where are we? Some kind of *Stonehenge?*"

"I don't know. Not our home realm, that's for sure. Give me a second." She closed her eyes and opened her awareness. "I don't sense anything nearby—but I don't know where we are."

"Okay. Everyone, keep your voices down," Trey whispered. "Hawk, let's check the perimeter."

"Right," Hawk acknowledged. "Ladies, this is a good vantage point—please watch our backs from here."

"You got it," Ellen assured him, as Stacy simply nodded.

IT DIDN'T TAKE LONG for the men to determine that they were alone, at least within the stone-ringed clearing. However, they did find signs of life; in fact, the place was littered with splintered bones, large and small.

"Something has been feeding here," Hawk remarked, stepping cautiously and scanning the ground.

"Over here!" Trey hissed, standing over the upper portion of a large bleached skull. "What do you make of this, Hawk?"

"Wolf, a big one," he pointed, "and there's a jaw over there. Hold on." In the next moment he had put the skull and jawbone together. "Hmmph, they fit, like they belong together." He stood and pointed to the reassembled skeletal head. "That's it; this is the complete skull."

Trey looked on in amazement. "Are you kidding me? That thing is huge! Are you sure it's a wolf?"

"Oh yeah, although it's probably twice the size of the largest timber wolves in our home realm." Hawk tilted his head. "I'm thinking it's a *dire wolf.*"

"Dire wolf? They're extinct, right? In our realm, I mean." Trey quickly corrected himself. "Of course, I guess that may not mean anything here, wherever *here* is."

"Or *whenever,*" Hawk mused aloud. "If dire wolves are indigenous to this realm, what else from that era might be here?"

"Good question. Stay alert," Trey cautioned. "By the way, I heard you fire your shotgun before Ellen got us out of Olmus. Did you shoot the other cat?"

Hawk shook his head. "No, I fired over its head. The report surprised it; and it froze. In those few seconds I was able to get to you guys."

Trey pointed to Hawk's shotgun. "What about your spent casing? Did you leave it there?"

Hawk grinned and produced the fired shell from a pocket. "Nope, I knew better that that. I always police my brass."

Trey returned the grin. "Good man. Leave no clear evidence of our presence. Now that we've wound up here, it might be wise to conserve our ammunition."

"True dat!" Hawk nudged the massive wolf skull with the toe of his boot.

Trey turned back toward the knoll. "Come on, we gotta tell Ellen and Stacy."

"DIRE WOLVES?" STACY exclaimed. "Oh, that's just great! How did we wind up here anyway?"

Ellen opened her palms. "I'm not sure, but I think it had to do with the ley lines, specifically the residual energy they held. I tried to warn y'all that trying to use a transit globe too close to such an energy source could have unanticipated effects."

"At that moment, it wasn't like we had a lot of choice," Stacy rationalized. "We're here now. So, does anyone think there's any chance Mark or the other missing people are here?"

"I didn't sense anyone other than us in the vicinity," Ellen confirmed, and gestured to the scattered bones. "But we now know there are signs of life here, animals at least."

"There may be more than animals," Trey cautioned and pointed to the standing stones and lintels. "No animal did that."

Hawk nodded. "Yeah, but we have no way of knowing *when*. This doesn't look recent. We've seen no other evidence of humans or any sentient life. I don't think our missing people are here."

"I agree, but what does worry me is the other animal life," Trey admitted. "Dire wolves aren't extinct here; so, what else might be around as well?

What equivalent era would this be, the Pleistocene? What else should we expect?"

"Actually, the Pleistocene is an *epoch,* the first of the Quarternary Period in the Cenozoic Era," Stacy corrected, earning her three surprised looks. "What? I know things!"

Ellen raised her hands. "Wait a minute! Could that mean those saber-toothed cats might belong *here?*"

Hawk shrugged. "I guess it's possible. Of course, that would mean there might be more of them around here. Who knows what else?"

Trey scanned the tree line. "Jeez, that's a comforting thought. So, the real question now is can we get home from here?"

"Well, yes and no." Ellen opened her palms. "I think I can get us home, but not from here, this spot, I mean. It's the same problem; there are a bunch of ley lines converging here. We're gonna have to find some location where they won't be a factor—unless y'all want to take a chance on going realm-hopping again?"

"Sounds like fun, but I'll pass," Stacy said, hands on her hips. "Look, let me try my thing with the trees—gimme a minute."

Moments later she returned, frowning.

"Nothing worthwhile—I only got a glimmer of confusion from the tree. It's like it didn't recognize the contact or something."

"Hmm, different realm—different rules?" Ellen mused.

"Maybe," Stacy allowed. "I don't think there have been people here for a long, long time. I've got a strong gut sense that Mark and the others aren't here. If I felt there was a chance—any chance—I'd want to search, but something tells me it'd be a waste of time—and it's too dangerous to linger here. So, lets do what we gotta do to get home, the sooner the better."

"First, we have to move somewhere else, not so close to any ley lines," Ellen declared. "I'll let you know when I can't sense their energy nearby, then we'll try transiting, okay?"

"Right," announced Trey. "Hawk, you've got point. Let's move out."

BEYOND THE STANDING stones, where the conifer forest thickened, shadows seemed deeper and more ominous beneath the overcast sky.

Hawk led the way, following a thin winding trail between the trees. He couldn't shake the feeling that they were the aliens here; and somehow, this realm knew it. He knew that his friends, following in silence, must feel the same sense of other-worldliness. If their current speculation about this being the equivalent of the Pleistocene was even close to the truth, they were woefully unprepared. Who had erected those standing stones? Some humans, or others? And when? In his mind, that project alone was a sufficient hallmark of considerable sentience.

Clearly, we are the interlopers here.

Was he naïve to hope, or assume, their presence here was undetected? Or worse, were they even now the subject of some sentient native species' curious scrutiny? He shuddered at such disquieting thoughts. He had to stay focused.

No bird or insect sounds were audible, which only enhanced a pervasive sense of being watched.

The itch between his shoulder blades would not be ignored.

He turned and whispered, "Ellen, how about this area, any better?"

She paused. "Some, but if we could go a little further that way," she pointed just over his shoulder, "I think it'd be better."

He looked in that direction, but the trees were too thick to see beyond a few yards.

“Is something wrong?” she asked.

“I dunno; it’s too quiet. Can you check, you know, see if we’re alone?”

“Sure, gimme a second.” She closed her eyes.

His eyes kept moving, watching all around as Stacy and Trey caught up.

“Sit-rep?” Trey asked.

Hawk nodded. “Ellen’s checking now.”

“Hmmph,” Trey grunted, “too quiet.”

Ellen gasped. “Something *is* following us! Not like the cats, something else. I don’t know what; it’s too far away and it’s kinda vague, fluctuating. Hmm, it might be more than just one.”

“Can’t we—” Trey began.

“No! Not here!” Ellen warned, pointing. “We need to go that way, twenty-five yards or so.”

Trey nodded to Hawk. “Go!”

Wasting no time, Hawk pushed through the conifers, his companions close on his heels. In a few moments he found himself pushing through thick fronds of huge ferns. He could hear the burble of water running over rocks. He slowed, pushed through a wall of ferns, and stood on the bank of a shallow fast-running stream.

Ellen, at his shoulder, pointed upstream to a wet shelf of flat rock jutting out into the stream from the opposite bank. It appeared to be only a stone’s throw away, and barely above the flowing water.

“There, that flat rock, that’ll do!”

"Okay! Come on!" He splashed into the ankle-deep water and led the way to the flat rock shelf she'd indicated.

With all four finally standing uneasily on the slick rock, Ellen warned, "Stay together. This'll take about a minute. I gotta be sure we're clear of any errant energy." She closed her eyes.

Trey nudged Hawk and pointed downstream toward where they had just been.

Hawk raised his shotgun to his shoulder and peered in that direction. *What had Trey seen?*

There was slight movement on the right bank; he strained to see. Something stepped out of the thick ferns and into the water—man-sized bipedal reptiles.

Stacy pointed. "There! Two of 'em—no, three!"

To their right, there was the faint sound of movement just beyond the foliage.

Trey swung the muzzle of his shotgun toward the ferns on the opposite bank, much closer to their position, and whispered, "There are five, three downstream on our six at twenty-five yards—they're yours, Hawk. Two flanking us in the ferns at nine o'clock, fifteen yards—they're mine—some kind of big lizards."

"Velociraptors, a pack of 'em," Stacy offered, her head swiveling. "How about that—they *do* have feathers."

"Huh? What?" Hawk blurted.

"Don't you ever go to the movies, or watch science shows on TV?" Stacy asked incredulously. "They hunt in packs, and attack with a big claw on their feet—a toe, actually. They're fast; don't let 'em get any closer!"

"Ellen?" Hawk urged.

“A few more seconds!” she spat.

The three downstream charged in great springing leaps!

Shotguns roared—and roared again!

Startled, Stacy lost her footing on the slick wet surface and slammed to her butt, almost taking Hawk down with her. Trey grabbed her arm and pulled her to her feet.

A shimmering transit globe enveloped them.

Pop!

WATER SLUICED OVER the edges of the rock shelf, empty now but for a small rounded stone figurine and a spent shotgun shell rolling to a wet stop.

Three of the lizards lay unmoving, bleeding in the streambed as the flowing water flushed the blood away. Another thrashed about in the nearby ferns, biting at its own shattered leg. The last lizard, uninjured, leapt upon the rock shelf and sniffed the air in confusion. The scent of fresh blood and the thrashing in the nearby ferns drew its attention. With a mighty leap, it was amongst the ferns. The thrashing increased in a crescendo, and stopped.

The ferns swayed as something moved among them, dragging a fresh kill away from the area.

For long minutes there was no sound other than the burbling of the water over the rocks of the streambed.

A twig snapped; the surrounding forest seemed to hold its breath.

Grimy hands reached down and picked up the carved stone figurine and spent shotgun shell. Violet eyes studied the figurine and the fired shell held in dirt-stained fingers, fingers that had once been kept elegantly manicured. The staring eyes allowed their focus to relax.

An amused chuckle, softer than a breeze, broke the silence.

"Well-well-well, who would have guessed that you, of all people, would find your way here? And, then find your way out of here? Oh, I am delighted! True, I cannot follow, but I need only find your entry point. Yes, that will suffice, quite nicely in fact."

A chill wind blew down the streambed, but the flat shelf of wet rock was empty once more.

TEDDY WASN'T HAPPY. Circe had left Olmus and taken all of the older batch of meth, leaving nothing but the three containers of the most recent batch, by far the strongest and highest quality meth he had ever cooked. He wasn't keen on Papa George's idea of letting the distributors in their home realms do the cutting. He'd warned the boss that this batch had to be handled carefully and stepped on a lot more than usual just to make it safe, but he wasn't sure he was being heard—really heard.

"Don't worry about it," George had insisted, "we got it covered."

Teddy went back to his lab. There was no point in arguing or repeating himself; he'd only be ignored. The boss and Vito were way too preoccupied planning this sit-down meeting.

Teddy didn't feel like starting a new batch this soon. He wasn't really sure he wanted to cook up another super-strong batch anyway. He figured he'd be better off seeing how things went with what he had left. That prompted him to check on it; maybe he ought to weigh everything again, just to keep track.

One of the plastic buckets felt lighter than it should. He reweighed all three.

One was light, by just over six ounces—that couldn't be right! He was sure he'd weighed everything after Vito had packaged two ounces in preparation for the sit-down meeting tonight. He checked his notes and weighed all three buckets again. Damn! He was right; this bucket was six ounces short.

This was not good.

Had Circe taken it? No, he was right there when Vito weighed and packaged her order; and that was all from the earlier batch. In fact, as it turned out, she took it all; there was nothing left from the old batch to weigh. He had nothing left to do but clean up the used containers.

So, not Circe . . . who else could've taken it?

Daegon hadn't even been around much. When he was here, he hardly ever came into the meth lab.

The goblin servants hadn't been around either—not that Teddy missed them.

That just left Clement and Stellara.

Teddy knew he had to tell the boss. Should he do it now? But they're all focused on this sit-down meeting tonight, and they already weren't listening to him. No, he'd be better off waiting until after this big deal meeting. Yeah, that's what he'd do; just tell the boss tomorrow.

GEORGE FOUND DAEGON in the scrying chamber, staring into the orb and murmuring something under his breath. The scene depicted in the orb did not appear to change.

"Is something wrong, Daegon?"

The alchemist looked up, his concern obvious. "I am uncertain; but, I think something is amiss."

George gazed into the orb. “What are we looking at? All I see is a dark grey mass.”

“Derinseum, or rather the fog that Circe spoke of. Most of Mer is now so enshrouded.”

George shrugged. “Bad weather, right?”

Daegon shook his head. “I think not. There is something ominous about this. I do not think it natural.”

George scratched his head. “You can’t tell using this scrying orb?”

“No,” the alchemist admitted. “We have not made much use of this orb since monitoring Gaspar—”

“Yes, we did,” interrupted George, “when we looked into the Council going missing.”

“Ah yes, but that was the work of little more than an hour. My point is that we have not been using this orb as much as we had been previously. True, we have been otherwise occupied, but there may well be many things that we have missed. I do not know if we have missed something related to this unnatural fog in Mer.”

“I get it, but there’s nothing we can do about it now, so we just let it go for now, right?”

“No, wrong,” Daegon insisted. “It would be foolish to overlook this development. I would return to Mer to see for myself.”

“Are you sure?”

“I am. In fact, I would go tonight. You and Vito have your meeting to attend; I have nothing else planned. So, I may as well look into this now. I can also check on Circe.”

George shrugged. “Okay, suit yourself.”

THIS TIME, ELLEN'S transit globe deposited them in their home realm, in the stone-ringed clearing at the cabin.

"All right! This is more like it." Stacy sighed. "But we still haven't found our missing people."

Ellen also breathed a sigh of relief and remarked, "Not yet—we're not giving up."

She scanned the overcast sky, still daylight, but the sun would set within an hour. "We need to get back to the house."

"Right," Trey acknowledged, opening the rear of the SUV. "Let us stow our gear and we'll go."

As Hawk unloaded his shotgun, he cursed under his breath, "Oh, damn!"

"What?" asked Trey.

Hawk laid two live rounds to one side, and two spent shell-casings next to them. He spent a moment going through his pockets.

"I'm short one spent round."

"You sure?"

"Yeah, I know I fired three rounds; one over the cat, two at the lizards. One of the last two must've ejected into the stream. Man, I'm sorry."

"I fired two rounds, too; but I've got both of my spent shells. So, we might have left one back there." Trey shrugged. "Oh well, it's too late to worry about it now. Come on, let's roll."

Once in the SUV, Trey turned in the front passenger seat to check that the women had secured their seat belts.

Stacy hadn't. She was busily going through her own pockets.

"What's wrong, Stacy?" Ellen asked. "You gotta buckle up."

Lip in a pout, Stacy whined, "I can't find that little stone figurine. I know I had it."

"Maybe you dropped it back there?" Ellen suggested.

"I probably did, darn it," Stacy admitted, giving up and buckling her seat belt. "I must've lost it when I slipped and fell. Oh man, I liked that little thing."

Trey faced forward and nodded to Hawk. "Okay, we're good. Let's go."

HAWK PARKED IN THE front driveway. "Is it okay to leave the SUV here?"

Ellen nodded. "Sure. While I am expecting visitors, I don't think anyone else will be driving. How long will y'all be able to stay? You know my mom will have prepared a big supper."

"Oh, I think," Hawk grinned widely, "we can stay a coupla hours or so, right Trey?"

"Absolutely! Give me a minute." Trey fished out his phone. "I gotta make some calls."

Ellen and Stacy climbed out of the SUV and headed for the house.

Stacy asked, "Who all is coming?"

"Padraic will probably get here first. He's bringing Barnabas, who's been overly anxious about his daughter. They could arrive at almost anytime now."

"So, when will Miska bring Brona?"

"Not until after sunset."

"Oh, how dramatic! He wants to make an entrance, huh?" Stacy chuckled. "Maybe he has been watching too much TV!"

The men joined them on the porch where they could hear eager *yips* and *whines* from behind the door.

"I think somebody is glad Ellen is home," Stacy teased.

Upon entering the house, Ellen was enthusiastically met by her obviously very happy dogs.

She stooped and cuddled Max and Sophie. "Yes, I missed you guys, and I'm glad to be home!"

NO SOONER HAD THEY made their way to the kitchen and greeted Millie, than Ellen had to excuse herself.

"Oh, I think some of our guests have arrived. Y'all stay and get comfortable. I'll be right back."

Ellen returned with Padraic and Barnabas, the dogs sniffing at their heels.

"Everyone," she announced, "this is Barnabas, Brona's father; and since he's Padraic's half brother, that makes him my uncle."

Ellen introduced everyone, and added. "Now, Brona won't be here for a little while yet; so, please be patient. In the meantime, shall we talk, or eat?"

Millie insisted they all sit down to supper.

No one objected.

AFTER DESSERT WAS SERVED, Ellen noted the sun had set.

As Millie served Irish coffees, Ellen raised a hand, garnering everyone's attention.

"Barnabas, we expect Brona to arrive very soon. So, this would be a good time to explain things to everyone, all right?"

Barnabas hesitated.

Ellen locked eyes with him. "Trust me, *uncle,* you are among friends, whom I assure you are good listeners."

At Padraic's urging, Barnabas told his tale and patiently answered a host of questions.

Noting that full darkness reigned beyond the windows, Ellen nudged Stacy and whispered, "Come with me."

As they rose from the table, Ellen said, "Keep your seats gentlemen. Excuse us girls, we're just gonna freshen up." Max and Sophie trotted after them.

Following Ellen, Stacy whispered, "She's here?"

"Yeah, Miska, too. They're not alone; but, I think it's gonna be okay. I'll need you to stay on the porch with the dogs, okay?"

Stacy nodded firmly. "You got it."

THERE WERE FOUR PEOPLE standing together on the front lawn of Delafaire Farm. Ellen recognized only three; the fourth, a woman, had to be Brona.

"Good evening, Ellen," said Lady Leanan. "I trust we are not intruding?"

"Not at all, Leanan. Thank you for coming."

Leanan tilted her head to the person at her side. "I trust you remember Lord Addecus of the Were?"

"I do." Ellen nodded; however, she had no idea why he would be here.

The Were lord politely inclined his head, but kept silent.

Leanan gestured to the big man whose smile could not be any broader. "And of course, Miska?"

Ellen returned his infectious smile. "Of course! Welcome home, Miska!"

"Thank you, Miss Ellen, it is good to be back!"

Leanan smiled as well, and then gestured to the young woman. "Ellen, may I present Brona, late of the Keys of Osiris. Jalash-el was able to restore her fully."

The woman appeared to be in her late twenties or early thirties, an inch or so taller than Ellen and broader of shoulder and hip. Plaited coils of auburn hair rested upon her shoulders. Even in the dim light, her eyes were striking, the irises a pale brown ringed in black. She had prominent cheekbones and a dimpled chin. Ellen sensed she was nervous, as she kept glancing up to Miska, as if for reassurance.

Ellen tried to convey her warmest welcome, and gave her newly introduced guest her most earnest smile. "I am delighted to finally meet you, Brona. Thank you so much for coming."

"Miska tells me," her voice was far more delicate than her somewhat robust appearance may have suggested, "that I have you to thank for rescuing me. Thank you."

Ellen shook her head. "Many were involved, some of whom you know. Some of them are here now, to welcome you, as I now formally welcome and invite you into my home."

"Here? Now?" Again she glanced to Miska.

"Indeed." Ellen turned to the big man. "Miska, would you be kind enough to take Brona into the house? Stacy is on the porch at the door; you'll find everyone else in the kitchen. If y'all are hungry, my mother still has some supper on."

Miska beamed. "Yes, Miss Ellen, right away." Taking Brona's hand, he led her to the house.

Ellen turned back to Leanan and Addecus. "I gather we need to talk?"

"We do," Leanan confirmed and nodded in the direction of the parting couple. "Let's give them a moment."

Once Miska and his charge were behind the closed door, the night seemed to sink into a velvet silence; but there was something unnatural about it.

Ellen did not miss the subtle yet deliberate flourish of Leanan's left hand.

"A small spell of privacy," the Sidhe explained. "Best not to be overheard."

"I understand. So?"

"It has become common knowledge that the Realm of Man is to investigate recent incidents of necromancy, and by extension, the disappearance of the Council. We know that you will be involved in any such effort. All the realms have conducted exhaustive searches for the missing Council members within their realms with no results. If there is anything more we can do, please do not hesitate to ask. It is not an easy thing for any realm to admit to any weakness; but, the facts are what they are."

Ellen could sense the sincerity, and surprisingly a hint of fear, in her words.

"Leanan, I appreciate the offer, and I will not hesitate to ask for assistance should the need arise. You are correct, we are investigating, and have tentatively determined who may actually be responsible."

Leanan gasped. "Who?"

"The satyr, Silenos."

"The suspected *necromancer?*"

Ellen nodded. "The same. Unfortunately, we have not yet found him, or the missing people. I'm afraid we don't know about *Queen Mab* either."

"Mab? You mean Diere?" Leanan asked. "What about her?"

"It appears that she is missing, too." Ellen shrugged. "We don't know if the two circumstances are related."

The Sidhe and Were lord stared at one another in shock.

"Thisss isss newsss to usss," Addecus insisted. "I wonder, isss Sssalidar sssomehow involved?"

"Salidar?" Ellen echoed.

Leanan shrugged. "Diere would have his head, if she could. Many think him dead since she has been obsessed with killing him. Is it possible he survives and may have turned the tables on her?"

"Sssalidar annoysss me greatly." Addecus admitted. "I would have ssslain him myssself, had I the opportunity."

"Be grateful you haven't," Ellen cautioned. "There are things you may not know."

"So, he does live?" Leanan pressed. "Has he moved in some way against Diere?"

Ellen shrugged. "While I am no fan of his, he does survive. It may be unlikely that he has anything to do with Diere's disappearance; but we will, of course, look into that. I can tell you that we know he is not part of the problem of the missing Council members; but, he may contribute in part to a possible solution. I'm sorry, but I can't go into details at this time."

"And to think, I would have ssshredded hisss sssoul long ago." Addecus sighed and shrugged. "Fate isss indeed fickle."

"Just to be sure," Ellen probed, "neither of your realms have heard any rumors about Diere, er, Mab being missing? The timing seems conveniently coincidental with the disappearance of the Council members."

Leanan and Addecus looked to one another and shook their heads.

"Asss to Diere, we had no idea," Addecus assured her. "The timing isss curiousss, but may well be only coincidental. But, that assside for the moment, permit me to explain why I have accompanied Lady Leanan here tonight."

"It was, in part, at my suggestion, Ellen," Leanan interjected. "Lord Addecus has certain information that I thought might be of use to you. I thought it best you hear it from him directly."

"I see," Ellen acknowledged. "Very well, Lord Addecus, I'm listening."

"Lady Ellen, I know our interesssstsss in the passst may have been at oddsss, but I hope the weight of thisss presssent crissssisss, that clearly affectsss usss all, will allow you to put assside any ill feeling toward me or my realm. We sssincerely want to help. Our avatar, Lord Talbot, isss a lifelong dear friend to me; I am willing to do anything to sssecure hisss sssafe return. Pleassse believe me."

"I am willing to take you at your word," Ellen said. "Now, this information?"

Addecus dipped his head. "Thank you. It hasss to do with Mer. You may be aware of the aquatic Were who ressside there. There are clan tiesss to some Were who ressside in my home realm; vissitsss and regular communicationsss are quite common. Many of the aquatic Were on Mer are alarmed; sssome have even fled to other realmsss."

"Why?" Ellen spread her palms. "We've heard nothing of this."

"Sssomething foul is creeping acrosss the entire realm of Mer. On the sssurface, it appearsss like a thick fog, bessstirred by neither breeze nor wave. Below the becalmed ssseasss, it darkensss the very water asss if it were night. Thossse living on the sssurface and thossse living below have sssimilar complaintsss; a pervasssive lethargy asss if one'sss very life energy isss being ssslowly drained. Thisss isss no natural phenomenon; sssorcery isss sssussspected!"

"Indeed? Do you think there is any connection to the Council's disappearance? Or perhaps Mab's disappearance?"

The Were lord simply shrugged. "We know not, on either count. I only hope thisss information may be ussseful to you in your invessstigationsss."

"Any information may have value. Thank you for sharing it," Ellen said and added, "Is there anything else we need to discuss?"

Addecus nodded. "Pleassse accept my belated thanksss for protecting and sssheltering Missska when he wasss in sssuch need. I regret that I have not expresssed my gratitude sssooner."

"It was no problem," Ellen assured him.

"Speaking of Miska," Leanan remarked, "I think he has developed a rather fond attachment for our guest, Brona. They were quite inseparable during her recovery from her ordeal. As I said, Jalash-el was successful in restoring her; but, it was a challenge—the stasis spell was particularly pernicious. I think she found Miska to be a reliable rock in a very uneasy and emotional sea."

Ellen smiled at the image. "So, you think perhaps this *rather fond attachment* might be mutual?"

Leanan returned the smile. "Uh-huh, I wouldn't be the least bit surprised."

Ellen nodded. "Well, thank you again for sheltering Brona."

"Twas the least I could do," Leanan assured her. "Now we must away. We wish you luck! Call upon us—for anything!"

With a wave of her hand, night sounds resumed.

Addecus dipped his head in a modest bow.

A dark transit globe enveloped the Were lord and the Sidhe.

Pop!

Ellen was alone once more; she turned and walked to the house.

So, Miska and Brona, eh? This could get very interesting, indeed.

CH 37

DARKNESS REIGNED OVER New Orleans. The overcast sky had threatened rain throughout the afternoon and early evening, but none had fallen. The ensuing hours of darkness brought a modest token of relief. The cloying air, heavy with humidity, had cooled in low places, blanketing parts of the old cemetery in a thin wispy fog.

The effect within the Crescent City was even more eerie than usual. Something just felt *off*.

Even an opportunistic street hustler, who perpetually hovered around the cemetery entrance and occasionally acted as an impromptu tour guide, couldn't seem to spark any interest in a tour of the spooky cemetery from among the sparse groups of wandering tourists. In fact, as hours crept by, not even the hardiest of tourists lingered in the vicinity. The frustrated hustler finally gave up and headed into the *Vieux Carre,* the French Quarter, to try his luck drumming up some other quasi-tour business; after all, pub crawls were always popular.

Deep in the shadows among the old crypts, cracked statues, and graffiti-stained mausoleums, a pale oval of twisted fog began to waver and solidify.

George and Vito stepped forth from the portal.

"Jeez, it's still pretty warm," George complained.

"Yeah, muggy, too," Vito agreed. "It must've been sweltering when the sun was up."

"How much time we got? Where's the car?"

"We got, uh," Vito peered at his watch, "almost an hour. The car is close, stashed in the rented garage off Conti Street; but we really won't need it."

"Yeah, you're probably right; although, the air-conditioning would've been nice." George grumbled. "What the hell, it's only a coupla blocks."

"Yeah, besides, parking would've been a bitch. The city still hasn't allowed parking anywhere within those blocks even though most of the trash and debris from the storms has been cleaned up. The clubs and all the nearby businesses still can't get permits to open."

George scoffed. "Ha! You know why, don't you? Some of the owners are still hassling with the city over FEMA funds. Insurance claims are still pending, too; so, a lot of repairs have yet to be done. Then there's all the city inspections, and all the licenses that gotta be reviewed before they're renewed."

Vito chuckled as he led the way out of the cemetery. "I get it; certain palms gotta get greased, right?"

"As always," George groused. "But I'm not complaining—so long as we all get our cut."

THE SECOND FLOOR OF the defunct strip-club housed a large room, now almost empty. Its four walls, floor, and ceiling, bare of any ornamentation or fixtures, were painted flat black. All the windows were taped over with yellowing sheets of old newsprint.

Near the center of the room stood an old billiards table, its tired green felt stained and torn. Neither balls nor cue sticks were anywhere to be seen.

A rectangular light housing hung above the table at head height. Its stark fluorescence provided the sole illumination for the entire room, its opaque shade rendering a harsh shadow line halfway up the walls. Bits of trash, crumpled food wrappers, and dust collected in abandoned corners and littered the scuffed linoleum floor.

The room smelled stale, musty, and forgotten.

George nodded his approval. "This'll work. How much time?"

Vito checked his watch. "About fifteen minutes. I'll go downstairs and stay by the door. I'm gonna have to tell the drivers to park over in the next block."

"Tell `em to stay with their cars, too," George cautioned. "Cops cruise through here about once an hour; we don't need any hassles. Besides, I wanna keep the number of people in the room down to a minimum. Did Frankie Fingers say who was coming with him?"

"He only mentioned his driver." Vito shrugged. "But you never know with Frankie, right?"

George shook his head. "Yeah . . . I wish Don Giovanni hadn't sent his nephew, Paulie Scapulante; but, I guess I should've expected it. How many men did Paulie bring?"

"Dunno for sure," Vito admitted. "When I delivered our sample, I only saw two. I think one's a bodyguard and the other a driver."

"Okay . . . If the drivers stay with their cars, and you man the door downstairs," George reasoned, "that puts three in here with me. So, we got enough seats." He jerked his thumb at a row of old bar stools along one wall.

Vito's brow furrowed. "You gonna be all right with the three of them in here?"

George waved such concerns off. "I'll be fine. Just keep your phone handy; I got you on speed dial. This is a business sit-down; there are rules, you know?"

Vito nodded, but was obviously not convinced. "Yeah, I know. Look, Frankie doesn't bother me; I know you can handle him. But, *Paulie the Torch?* He can be a hothead, a real loose cannon."

"It'll be okay. You'd better get downstairs and man the door."

A FEW MINUTES LATER, Vito called up the staircase, "Boss, Frankie's here, alone. I'll send his driver down the block to stay with the car. Oh, I think I see Paulie's car coming, too."

"Okay! Send Frankie up!"

George backed away, as footsteps ascended the stairs.

Frankie "Fingers" Del Marco entered the room and sniffed disapprovingly. Attired in a white linen suit and a straw fedora, he carried a small briefcase in one hand. He whipped out a silk handkerchief and held it to his nose and mouth.

"Welcome, Frankie." George extended his hand.

Frankie ignored it, waving the handkerchief. "Is this it? *This* is our sit-down?"

George dropped his hand and his voice. "This is business, Frankie—just business."

"This is bullshit!" Frankie blurted. "Ain't this New Orleans? Where's the booze? Where's the broads? Ain't you got no class, *Papa George?*"

Before George could respond, another voice sounded from the doorway.

"Ah, now I understand why my uncle declined to come; and sent *me* instead."

Paulie Scapulante stood near the doorway, smirking at Frankie Fingers. Standing past his shoulder, a hulking man, no doubt Paulie's bodyguard, remained silent but never took his eyes off Frankie.

George stepped forward and offered his hand. "Welcome, Paulie. I'm sorry that Frankie doesn't seem to appreciate that this is a business meeting—strictly business."

Paulie took George's hand in both of his. "Papa George, my uncle, Don Giovanni, sends his respect and greetings. He also told me," glancing at Frankie, "what to expect. My uncle appreciates how you conduct business when it is time to do business. Any celebrating is for after business has concluded."

George was impressed. Paulie was making an effort to play the refined and respectful *capo*, a representative of his Don. Clearly, he'd been learning, modifying his behavior in anticipation of assuming more *family* responsibility. After all, he was Don Giovanni's heir apparent.

"My thoughts exactly." George gestured to the pool table. "Shall we begin?"

At a nod from Paulie, the bodyguard arranged stools around the table.

Clearly still miffed, Frankie wiped the seat of the stool with his handkerchief and sat.

"Fine, let's get this over with. George, you've got some good product. I think we're all in agreement, yeah?"

Paulie nodded. "Speaking for my *familia,* we agree. My uncle wishes to know more."

George smiled. "Thank you, both. Now, as I understand it, Frankie wanted this meeting. So, Frankie, the floor is yours."

Frankie preened a bit, then placed the briefcase on the felt.

"George, I have the means to open the Canadian market for your product. I am prepared to offer export/import and distribution north of the border for a reasonable division of profits." He nodded deferentially toward Paulie. "And of course, my patron's cut; I have Don Giovanni's blessing in this."

"Not exactly," Paulie corrected. "It is true that Don Giovanni is interested; however, he is not yet convinced it is in the best interest of *our family*. So, at Don Giovanni's direction, I am here to learn more details."

Frankie gave Paulie an insincere smile. "When he hears about the profits, he'll be convinced."

"Perhaps," Paulie shrugged, "but there is more to such an enterprise than just profits. There are logistics, and considerable risk as well. My family will need to understand all aspects of this proposal."

"Ah, there's always risk," Frankie waved a hand in dismissal. "We have to act now, while the market is wide open. I've already done some preliminary distribution sampling with some other products, so I know the time is ripe. We can—"

Paulie raised his hands. "Wait! You've done what? *Preliminary distribution?* What other products?"

Frankie grinned and opened his briefcase. "I was hoping you'd ask!" He plopped three sealed clear plastic bags on the green felt.

"This one," he pointed, "is George's meth, the sample his guy delivered earlier."

To George's eye that looked like about *half* of what Vito had delivered to Frankie.

Frankie pointed to the remaining bags. "These other two are samples of what I put into distribution."

George noted that one was a white crystalline powder, the other tan, almost light brown.

Frankie shoved the white bag forward. "This is cocaine, ninety-five percent pure, from a cartel south of the border."

George blinked in surprise. *Cartel? Oh-oh, Don Giovanni has rules about the cartels; all deals must be sanctioned by him. What have you done, Frankie?*

George wasn't the only one surprised. He noticed the brief flare of shock and indignation that slipped past Paulie's otherwise stoic facade.

Frankie either missed, or ignored, the implications. He shoved the brown bag forward. "This is some cheap-ass heroin—and I do mean low quality, inexpensive, street smack. However, it's got a higher profit margin than the coke, because it's laced with fentanyl, which is easy for me to come by, and comparatively cheap. I can even get *carfentanil*, but that'll be for later, when I—*we* expand."

Fentanyl? Carfentanil? George was stunned, at a loss for words.

Not so Paulie, whose stoic reserve evaporated as he stood and leaned into Frankie's face.

"Are you out of your mind? You've actually pushed *cartel* coke and fentanyl-laced heroin into Canada, using *our* established distribution networks—*without Don Giovanni's permission?*"

Frankie waved his hand again. "What? It was no big deal, just a preliminary, uh, marketing test. The profits are well above what any of us are used to. This could be astounding!"

George had heard enough, and slammed his palm on the felt. "*Astounding?* You fool! This could be *deadly*! Fentanyl can kill your customers—and carfentanil *will!* You won't even have a market!"

"Nah, you just gotta watch your cut ratio," Frankie insisted. "You can take trash heroin and get top dollar for it. It's good business."

"No, it's not, you idiot!" Paulie seethed, trying to maintain his composure. He resumed his seat, sighing heavily. "You may have ruined the family's distribution network—tainted it, at least. There is no way you're gonna get Don Giovanni's blessin—"

"I won't need it," Frankie interrupted and pulled out a cell phone. "Let me explain—see, this is a new day." He pressed a speed-dial key.

A pale wash of muted light flared beyond the newsprint-covered windows; a muffled rumble sounded, not too far away.

However, the sudden *pffft* sound was much closer.

The bodyguard stood and tried to pull Paulie to his feet—but Paulie had gone limp, blood beginning to ooze from a small round hole in his forehead.

George dove for the floor, and saw Frankie turn the suppressed semi-auto pistol on the bodyguard.

Pffft—pffft!

The bodyguard grabbed at his midsection and crumpled.

Frankie turned the muzzle of his gun on George, now prone on the floor, and smiled.

"Well now, change in fortunes, eh? It looks like only you and me are gonna be in business now—unless you have some objection, no? On the other hand, I'm not sure I even need you—I just need your cook. That's gotta be Teddy Pots—who else, right? Oh, you think I didn't know? I had your guy followed—yeah, that's right—when he delivered your sample. So, I know you've got Teddy cooking in a lab somewhere in that old cemetery, probably in one of those big mausoleums, right? Well, it don't matter 'cause you're gonna show m—"

Blam! Blam!

Two deafening gunshots echoed in the room.

The back of Frankie's head had exploded, staining the black wall with gore. In his death spasm, Frankie's fists clenched; his suppressed .380 pistol fired one last time before slipping from his grasp.

Something seared down the back of George's arm; the bullet had furrowed a thin crease in his flesh.

A heavy clatter drew his attention; a .45 semi-auto pistol lay on the floor, near the hand of the dying bodyguard. Somehow, he had managed to draw his own weapon and shoot Frankie in the face—twice.

George's phone rang; it was Vito.

"Boss, I think it's a hit! Frankie's driver went up to Paulie's car and tried to lob a grenade through a window at the driver, but the glass didn't break. It rolled under the car and blew! It got both of 'em!"

George grimaced; the pain was setting in.

"Vito, listen! Frankie's pulled some shit! He shot Paulie and his guy—but his guy shot Frankie. I think they're all dead. I got winged in the arm by Frankie, but I'm okay. Can we get outta here?"

"I don't think I can get to you. The cops and fire department are already here. The car's on fire and the streets are all blocked off. They're pushing people back and putting up that yellow tape. I'm outside the tape in the next block, standing with the crowd. How bad are you hit?"

"Not bad. Listen, you need to go back to Olmus and get Daegon. If you're with him, he can transit right into this room. I'm gonna need him here to deal with all this. There's more to it, but not on the phone, *capisce?*"

"Yeah, got it. Go back, get Daegon, and we come to you, right?"

"Yeah, go!"

VITO WASTED NO TIME in returning to Olmus; but he was not prepared for what he found—their headquarters was in shambles, and apparently deserted.

The generator was still running, so there was light in most sections, but not all. Some of the low-slung overhead wires he had run for lighting were pulled from their stanchions and now lay on tunnel floors, leaving some passageways in darkness.

Vito headed for Teddy's lab, but almost lost his footing on a section of flat slate-like rock that was slick with something wet. He recognized the coppery smell of blood.

He backed off, drew his semi-auto 9mm pistol, and made his way to his own chamber. He retrieved a flashlight, then retraced his steps to Teddy's lab.

Blood was in the passageway, a lot of it, but no body. Watching his step, he pushed into the lab.

His flashlight beam showed the lab was wrecked; glassware broken, and tables overturned. He wrinkled his nose at the astringent fumes wafting about.

Vito panned his flashlight around and marveled at the scope of the destruction. A battered steel cabinet lay on its side against one wall. There was no sign of Teddy; but there was no blood in the lab either.

"Damn!" He grumbled. "What the hell happened here?"

"*Pssst* . . . Vito, that you?"

The big man swung the flashlight about. He still appeared to be alone.

"Vito! It's me, Teddy! I'm stuck in the cabinet!" Small thumps came from within the overturned cabinet. "You gotta get me out!"

"Teddy?" Vito went to the cabinet and banged a fist down on the side. "You in there?"

"Not so loud—they hear good! Yeah, I'm in here; doors are stuck. Get me out!"

Vito tried the cabinet doors; they were indeed stuck, no doubt from the battering they'd taken. Vito set his pistol and flashlight down and gripped the door handles.

"Hold on, Teddy. I'm gonna get this open."

The handles yielded to Vito's grasp—but the doors were wedged tight against their bent frames. Vito put his back into it; one door bent, buckling near its center and allowing Vito to get both hands in the gap. With a mighty pull, the door sprang open, its metal squealing in complaint.

Teddy stared wide-eyed up at Vito. "Shit! They'll hear that for sure!"

Vito held the door open, as Teddy crawled out of the damaged cabinet, obviously frightened, but apparently uninjured.

Vito demanded, "Who's gonna hear? What the hell happened here? Why were you in that cabinet?"

"The bats! Those damned bats have gone berserk! Somebody's been giving them too much meth from the *wrong batch!* I heard `em coming and I hid. They trashed my lab! We gotta get outta here!"

"Wait! Where is Daegon? I didn't see him."

"Huh? Daegon? He's in Mer, and hasn't come back yet! Come on—we gotta go!"

"Damn!" Vito chewed his lower lip. "What about Clement and Stellara?"

Teddy spat. "Who do you think screwed up and gave the bats the wrong dose? I think they're both dead. I heard some screaming; then it went all quiet-like. That can't be good."

"Oh man," Vito wiped a hand down his face, "I really don't need this right now. I need Daegon—is there any way to get him back here? Can we contact him?"

Teddy opened his palms. “How the hell would I know? All I know is we gotta get outta here before the bats come back—they’re craving meth! Daegon can deal with this when he gets back. Let’s go!”

Vito sighed, seeing no other choice. “All right, come on. The boss needs help; it looks like you and me are it!”

THE CAR FIRE NEAR THE edge of the *Vieux Carre* had spread to a nearby vacant building. The gawking crowd had grown larger; tourists and locals from other parts of the French Quarter were drawn to the scene out of morbid curiosity. The police were pushing them back, and stringing more yellow tape.

Vito and Teddy, taking advantage of the chaos, made their way from the cemetery through the growing crowd to the line of police tape strung across an intersection. A pair of uniformed NOPD officers were stationed there for crowd control.

Vito spoke into Teddy’s ear and pointed to a recessed doorway in the middle of the block, twenty yards past the tape. “We need to get to that doorway; the boss is on the second floor.”

Teddy squinted down the dark street. “The smoke is starting to blow this way. Is that the only way in? No back door?”

Vito shook his head. “That’s it; the back door is chained shut. We gotta get in and get the boss out.”

Some of the crowd started to move away from the smoke.

Vito nudged Teddy. “Come on. Let’s move down by the edge of the corner building. When the smoke gets thick, we’ll run for it.”

“Are you nuts?” Teddy balked, but changed his tune when Vito snatched him up by the nape of the neck. “Hey-hey, whatever! I’m on board! Just say when—jeez.”

It didn't take long for the smoke to thicken. Holding their breath, Vito and Teddy made their move. They were at the doorway and inside in a matter of seconds.

"Don't let the door close all the way," Vito warned. "I'm not sure what we'll find upstairs, so, watch yourself. I know the boss is hurt, and we gotta get him outta here."

Teddy shrugged. "We made it in here and we weren't seen, right? We've been lucky so far, right?"

Vito shook his head. "I *hope* we weren't seen. I don't trust luck. Come on; stay quiet."

The hanging light over the pool table was still on. The smell of blood and gunpowder hung in the air. Three bags of dope lay on the stained green felt of the pool table. Four bodies lay on the floor.

"Oh, shit," murmured Teddy, eyes wide.

One of the bodies moved, waving an arm.

"Over here," George managed, wincing in pain.

Vito rushed to his side and quickly looked for injuries. "Just the arm?"

"Yeah, flesh wound I think. Where's Daegon? Gotta get this mess cleaned up. What's Teddy doing here?"

"Long story, not now. We gotta get you outta here!" Vito insisted, still smelling smoke.

"Wait!" George demanded. "Where's Daegon?"

"Mer, he hasn't come back. And worse, the shit hit the fan in Olmus." Vito rolled his eyes. "The damned bats have gone berserk on meth."

"What? Are you kidding me?" George asked incredulously. "This ain't good—I gotta think!"

"Look, Vito," George pointed, "there's Frankie Fingers and Paulie the Torch. There's dope on the pool table; our meth, some cartel coke, and Frankie's fentanyl-laced heroin. We can't leave all this like it is! Who do you think Don Giovanni is gonna hold responsible?"

Vito understood, all too well—then inspiration struck.

"Boss, listen, the grenade set Paulie's car on fire and it looks like it spread to the building at the end of the block. If it were to, you know, spread to this building, then all of this . . ."

George brightened. "Yeah, yeah, I get it. Maybe we could help it along? Help me up."

Vito helped George stand, and nodded to the meth cook. "Teddy, grab the dope; use the briefcase. You got any matches?"

Teddy shook his head. "No way—no source of flame in my lab, remember?"

"Oh yeah, never mind, I got a lighter." Vito leaned George against the wall. "Will you be okay for a minute? I gotta shove some of this trash in a pile; that ought to get things going."

George grimaced but nodded. "I'm fine. Do it."

Vito bent to collecting trash while Teddy put the bags of dope in the briefcase.

"What about the guns?" Teddy asked, pointing to the two pistols on the floor.

George shook his head. "Leave 'em, right next to the bodies."

"I'm ready," Vito announced, and flicked his lighter. "We'll let the fire take care of everything. It's amazing how fast this one spread, ain't it?"

"Freeze!" Two uniformed NOPD officers stood at the doorway, guns leveled. Four more officers, weapons drawn, rushed into the room. "Hands! Show me your hands! Now!"

One of the patrolmen approached Vito, took the lighter from his hand, and said, "Actually, the fire department has that fire under control; we can't have you starting another one." He glanced at the bodies. "By the way, you are all under arrest. You have the right to remain silent . . ."

Gripping his wounded arm, George sighed, rolled his eyes toward the black ceiling, and mumbled, "Aw, shit!"

THE RINGING PHONE WOKE Hawk. It was early, the sun had barely risen. Caller ID indicated Trey's number.

"Uh, yeah, Trey? What's up?"

"Get dressed. I'm on my way to pick you up. We gotta get to the the U.S. Marshals office in Alexandria. They've got Teddy Pots in custody."

Hawk was awake now. "Teddy Pots? Where did they find him?"

"They didn't; NOPD did. There's more to this, but not over the phone. Get a move on. I'll see you in twenty minutes. Gotta go, bye."

HALF AN HOUR LATER they were on the road to Alexandria, bolstered by go-cups of hot coffee.

Trey sipped carefully without taking his eyes off the road. "So, here's the sit-rep, per our captain. NOPD found George Papadolis, his driver, Vitorrio Smith, and Teddy Pots at what was clearly a crime scene, and took them into custody. They're tentatively charged with a laundry list of felonies; multiple counts of murder, possession of controlled substances with intent to distribute, possession of prohibited weapons, I could go on and on."

Hawk chuckled. "I bet the OCDETF investigators are happy."

"For the most part, yeah, but I get the sense that something else is going on, too."

Hawk shrugged. "Well, that's no surprise in any case with concurrent jurisdiction; there's clearly gonna be a lot of state and federal overlap. Think of the logistics involved, assuming nobody makes bond—court appearances and attendant custodial issues alone could necessitate habeas corpus writs back and forth. Of course, one jurisdiction may just wait until the other is finished; that's pretty typical."

"Yeah, you're right. Anyway, I get a heads-up call from Todd Simmons; he and his partner Willis had to make a quick run to the USMS New Orleans office to assume custody of Theodore Rasmussen, aka Teddy Pots, and ostensibly bring him back to be processed and ultimately returned to BOP custody."

"Oh, I get it, because he's an escapee. Once back in custody he can be indicted for the escape and the murder of his cellmate at any time. Smart move, but what did you mean by *ostensibly*?"

"Caught that, did you? Good!" Trey smiled. "I'll get to that. Keep in mind that Willis and Todd knew that we wanted to talk to Teddy, back before he escaped."

"Yeah, but, that was before, you know . . ."

Trey shot him a warning glance. "Yeah, I know. But here's the thing; they may have let slip that we wanted to talk to him—in Teddy's presence—sorta accidentally, I'm sure."

Hawk chuckled. "Yeah, right. Those guys are too slick."

Trey smiled. "Be that as it may, here's the crux of the matter; now Teddy is willing to talk. In fact, he very much wants to talk to us—you and me, specifically. He's not willing to talk to anyone else."

"Just us, huh?" Hawk pondered that for a moment. "Think maybe it's got something to do with what happened at Tippet's Store?"

Trey shrugged. "Probably. Now, here's the rest of the story; the details get interesting.

"The NOPD bagged Teddy, George Papadolis, and Vitorrio Smith with dope *and* three bodies of deceased gunshot victims on the second floor of an old club of Papa George's at the edge of the French Quarter. George has a minor gunshot wound on the back of one arm, so it's pretty clear he was present for at least some of the gunplay."

"Yeah," agreed Hawk, "a bullet wound would be hard to explain under the circumstances."

Trey scoffed. "Hmmph, no kidding. He was treated at a hospital, and remains in NOPD custody.

"Now here's the kicker. Around the same time as what happened in the club, there was some sort of confrontation on the street in the next block; an explosion, and car fire. Two more bodies were recovered from that scene."

"So, two scenes? Related?" Hawk asked.

Trey nodded. "Suspected, and very likely confirmed by now. The two bodies in the street and the three in the club are all out-of-town wiseguys. Todd didn't have positive IDs yet; but he said confidence was high that they were well-connected organized-crime figures out of Detroit and Toledo. He said things are still a bit confused; the U.S. Attorney and the District Attorney are trying to work it all out. No doubt it'll take some time."

"It always does," Hawk acknowledged. "I'd expect both prosecutors to take these cases to grand juries; they've got the time now with everybody locked up."

"Oh, I'm sure they will," Trey confirmed. "In the meantime, Papa George and Vitorrio Smith aren't talking. But the prosecutors thought Teddy might; so, they had the U.S. Marshals in New Orleans assume custody of Teddy as an escapee. Then Todd and Willis got the call to transport Teddy back to their Alexandria office, pending further removal to FCI Oakdale. That effectively gets him out of New Orleans, separated from the other two, and just maybe more willing to talk."

"Isolate the weak link, that's typical prosecutor's strategy," Hawk noted. "Wait! Let me guess. They're very happy that Teddy is apparently willing to talk, but not so happy that it's only to us, right?"

Trey nodded. "That's about the size of it."

Hawk sipped from his go-cup, and murmured, "I guess we do live in interesting times."

THE U.S. MARSHALS SERVICE office was on the second floor of the U.S. District Court/Post Office building in downtown Alexandria, a concrete and granite WPA *art deco* edifice from the 1930s that held an esteemed certification on the National Historic Register.

The USMS field office was compact, consisting of a reception area, office space, cellblock, and attorney interview room. The burnished oak trim, thick pebbled glass, heavy doors, and old brass fixtures contributed to that grounded ambiance of deliberate solidity and permanence that characterized a flurry of government-sponsored building programs decades ago when the country was trying to claw its way out of the devastating Great Depression.

Their footfalls echoing down the wide granite-floored hall, Trey nodded toward the marbled wainscoting and said, "I've always liked government buildings from this period. There's a lot of history here—if only these walls could talk."

"Yeah, I know what you mean," Hawk agreed, as they arrived at the door to the U.S. Marshals office. "I gotta remember to call Ellen to bring her up to speed. She expects us, but we might run late."

Upon entering the reception area, they ran into Willis who was on his way out, keys in hand.

"Oh, you guys made it! Come on in—now, I won't have to lock up. I gotta run to court for a bit. Todd is in the judge's office; he should be back shortly. Can you wait for one of us to get back?"

Trey pumped Willis' hand. "Sure, we'll wait for you. Good to see you, Willis. So, is Teddy here?"

"Yeah, he's in the cellblock, the only prisoner. You can go ahead with your interview, but you'll have to do it through the steel mesh of his cell. No firearms allowed in the block; check your weapons in one of the blue gun lockers. I'll be back as soon as I can."

Glancing up, Hawk noticed the camera monitors. "CCTV in the cellblock?"

"Yeah, but we're not recording. Do you want to record the interview?"

"Nah." Trey waved the suggestion off. "We'll listen to what he has to say, then we'll decide."

Willis nodded. "Okay. I gotta go."

They found Teddy sitting on the long steel bench affixed to the wall in the second cell. He stood when they entered, grasping at the thick wire mesh.

"Hello, Teddy," Trey said. "Do you remember us? You asked to talk to us, right?"

Teddy stared at them for a long moment. "I remember y'all, Sergeant Bassett and Detective Redhawk. You were there, both of you, at the store, that night."

Hawk nodded. "Yes, we were there, Teddy. How are you doing?"

Teddy shook his head. "Not good . . . I gotta tell somebody; but, no one will believe me! I know I'm in trouble; but, it's not my—well, most of it, is not my fault. Th-this is bad."

"Teddy, why did you want to talk to us?" Hawk asked. "I mean *us* in particular?"

Teddy's eyes grew wide. "Because you were there—you saw! You'll believe me—you gotta!"

Trey and Hawk exchanged a knowing glance and realized Teddy was probably right. They very well might believe him.

"You know, Teddy," Trey cautioned, "you don't have to talk to us. You have the right to remain silent. You can have an attorney—"

"No! I don't need no damn lawyer hearing this!" Teddy insisted. "I'll tell you `cause you'll believe. You were there—you know!"

"Okay, Teddy, chill." Trey sighed and gestured to the frightened man. "We're listening. Sit down, take it easy, and start at the beginning."

TWENTY MINUTES LATER, Hawk stopped Teddy. "Hold on, Teddy. This place on Toledo Bend, you're sure that's where George and Daegon meant? Do you know the actual address?"

"Of course I'm sure! The address? Hell yeah! I even know the security code to get past the alarms and stuff. Listen . . ."

A moment later, Hawk looked to Trey. "I gotta make a quick call, you know?"

Trey nodded emphatically. "Yeah, do it."

Turning back to Teddy, Trey encouraged him. "Okay, so tell me more about this Daegon guy."

"ELLEN, HI . . . NO, everything is fine—in fact it might be great! Listen, I'm gonna give you an address, a house on Toledo Bend. You need to go check it out; our missing people might be there! No-no, I don't have the time to explain. Just go check out this lead . . . Yes, if you find them, you gotta get them outta there right away . . . Whatever you think is best, okay? Call me back and let me know—no matter what you find. Now listen . . ."

HAWK RETURNED TO THE cellblock to hear Teddy's tale winding down.

". . . then Vito and me, we saw the bodies. We found the boss, er, Papa George on the floor, too. I thought he was dead at first, but he wasn't. I dunno what happened before we got there. Once Vito got the boss up on his feet, they talked about what to do. Vito was gonna start this fire; but, the cops busted in and stopped him. Then we all got locked up.

"But I swear that dope was already there! I just put it in the briefcase like the boss told me!"

"Okay, I get it," Trey soothed. "Now, back in your cell at Oakdale—"

"Damn it! I didn't kill my cellmate! I told you! Papa George did him, and made it look like I did so's I'd go with him! I ain't never killed nobody!"

Trey cocked his head. "And this is when Daegon made like a hole in the wall—"

"No-no," Teddy corrected. "It's like a big black ball, a *transit globe* he called it. We went into that, and we were . . ." he shook his head and shrugged his shoulders, "just someplace else."

"Okay. What about—" Hawk began, only to be interrupted by the ringing of his phone. "Oh, excuse me, I gotta take this."

STEPPING INTO THE VACANT office, he answered his phone.

"Ellen? Yeah, go ahead . . . What? All of them? That's great! No—say no more, not over the phone. I'll call when I can . . . Yeah, me too. I gotta go, bye."

HAWK WALKED BACK INTO the cellblock, caught Trey's eye, smiled and flashed him a thumbs-up sign.

Trey's eyes widened as the ghost of a smile flit across his face.

"Teddy, quick question," Hawk posited. "Let's go back to when you were talking about where Papa George found you, you know that house on Toledo Bend. You said that some guys from the cartel came sniffing around, and that woman bodyguard, uh, Ling, took care of them, right?"

Teddy bobbed his head. "Yeah, that's right." He shuddered. "That is one creepy woman."

"What," Hawk pressed, "did she do with the bodies?"

"I think she had her two bald-ass goons, her *muscle-heads,* bury them somewhere on the property. Why?"

Hawk smiled. "You see, Teddy, if we can find these bodies that'll help to corroborate what you're telling us; it supports your credibility."

"I get it; but y'all believe me, right? I mean, you were there—you saw!"

Trey sighed. "Teddy, it's not about what we believe; it's about what we can prove, see? All you need to do is keep telling the truth."

"I am telling the truth to you two!" Teddy scoffed, crossed his arms, and reclined against the back of the bench. "But if I tell the truth to anybody else, people will think I'm nuts!"

Trey leaned forward. "Think about that very thing for a minute, Teddy."

Hawk had a sudden flash of comprehension; he understood exactly what Trey was thinking. He smiled and lowered his voice.

"Come to think of it, Teddy, don't you have the better part of a nickel to do on your parole violation? You know there's no getting around that, no matter what happens with any new beefs involving Papa George, right?"

Teddy stared up from under a sullen brow. "Yeah, so?"

"Would you rather do that back at Oakdale in gen-pop, or," Hawk shrugged, "oh, I don't know, maybe in a monitored ward at some federally contracted mental-health facility?"

Teddy sat up straight. "But, I'm not . . . crazy . . . am I?"

"We don't think so," Trey responded opening his palms, "but it's not up to us. The best thing we can tell you to do is tell the truth, the absolute truth, to anybody who will listen."

"Yeah, that'd be best." Hawk nodded. "At some point you'll be offered an attorney again; it'd be smart to take that offer. Of course, you should tell your attorney the truth. If you get to talk to some doctors, you should tell them the truth, too."

"But, that'll get me . . ." Teddy's expression soured, but then cleared. "Oh-oh, yeah, I see. Gee, maybe I really do need the help, at someplace safe, you know?"

Trey nodded. "All you gotta do, Teddy, is just keep telling the truth. I think it'll all work out for the best. We can talk again if you like, especially if you remember anything else."

"Yeah," Teddy bobbed his head. "I'd like that. I'll try to remember everything."

Trey smiled. "Good man. We gotta go now; but we'll see you later."

WILLIS AND TODD WERE back in their USMS office.

"All done?" Willis asked.

"Yeah, for now." Trey shook his head. "We might get some bits of worthwhile intel from him, which we'll have to corroborate or refute. However, I have serious reservations about him ever being a credible witness."

"What do you mean?" asked Todd. "We got back in the office in time to hear y'all encouraging him to tell the truth. Wasn't he cooperative?"

"Cooperative? Oh yeah, definitely." Hawk bobbed his head. "He's probably being truthful as well, at least what he believes to be the truth. However, it's all just too . . . I don't know, bizarrely delusional."

"Huh? Delusional?" Willis echoed.

Shrugging, Trey offered a sad smile. "Oh yeah, most of what he says is like science fiction and fantasy stuff; other worlds, magic spells, goblins, teleportation, and the like. We humored him and listened. It's pretty clear that his reality is not necessarily the same as this one. He waved Miranda, but we're pretty sure his competency may be in question. He's gonna need a thorough psychiatric examination before anybody even thinks about using him in any kind of case, much less as a witness."

"Really?" Willis scrunched his face. "Is he high?"

"Nah, he's not high." Hawk chuckled. "But he's got one helluva imagination; and, he believes it's all real. But you don't have to take our word for it." Hawk jerked a thumb toward the cellblock. "Just let him know you're willing to listen. If he warms up to you, he'll tell you *all* about it, and then some."

"That's funny, like in *weird,*" Todd remarked. "You know he wouldn't talk to anybody else; he insisted it had to be y'all. Any idea why?"

"Dunno, for sure." Trey shrugged. "We arrested him once before, just a trespassing charge, refusing to leave a store. He was pretty well freaked out and seemed pretty delusional then, too. But we treated him well and got him calmed down. Maybe he remembered? Who knows? I think he'll talk to anybody now; but it'll probably help if you humor him a bit."

"When does he go back to Oakdale?" Hawk asked.

"We don't know," Willis admitted. "The U.S. Attorney wants us to put him in Rapides Parish Jail so he can be further interviewed in reference to this new case. He'll probably be appointed counsel from the public defenders office, too."

"Well, it'd be a good idea to mention his, uh, mental state, when you arrange a jail bed for him," Trey cautioned, "just to be on the safe side."

"Oh, don't worry." Todd waved that concern off. "All our contracted jails have to do medical workups as part of routine in-processing. We'll mention the mental-health concerns for sure when we drop him off. Any indication he's a potential danger to himself or others?"

Hawk and Trey looked at one another and shook their heads.

"Nope," Trey answered. "I think we're done here. Thanks, it was good to see you guys."

DRIVING BACK TO THEIR office, Trey mused aloud, "You know, I don't think Teddy has ever actually hurt anybody."

Hawk looked up from his notebook. "You mean aside from cooking meth?"

Trey scoffed. "Well, yeah, aside from that. The point is that we both know if he keeps telling the truth, he'll never be used as a witness, and probably won't face prosecution—"

"Because he most likely wouldn't be found mentally competent," Hawk finished. "I get it. However, you do realize that he could be remanded by a court as an involuntary commitment to a mental-health facility indefinitely, right? That could be a lot longer than what he's got left to do on his parole violation, or even what he might be facing if a prosecutor wanted to bring new charges."

"True, but I think Teddy knows that as well." Trey slowed the cruiser as he approached the I-49 on-ramp. "He's not stupid; he knows if he were to be convicted of killing his cellmate, he'd potentially face the death penalty. Trying to prove in court that Papa George did it and then compelled him to escape is a waste of time—and Teddy knows it."

"Hell, Trey, if he goes back into Oakdale, even if they put him in administrative segregation, he's a dead man; that inmate gang will find a way to get to him."

Trey accelerated onto the interstate. "Think Teddy doesn't know that? He'll opt for the mental-health facility, for the rest of his days if necessary. He's pretty close to having that *institutionalized mentality.* He'd be safe and cared for; and, he knows it. Not to mention that would also spare the federal and state courts the cost of trials and related proceedings—don't think that won't be a consideration."

Hawk shook his head. "Isn't it always?"

Trey simply grunted and stared straight ahead. "So, changing the subject—did Ellen say any more about the people she found at Toledo Bend?"

"No, just that they were all there, and in some sort of stasis. We didn't get into any details over the phone. We'll have to wait until we see her later."

Trey nodded. "Okay. As soon as we meet with the captain and file our report on Teddy, we'll head to the farm. We've still got tonight to plan for."

"Yeah," Hawk agreed, "but now the deck has been reshuffled, and the dealer's lost his leverage."

"And with any luck," Trey added, "he may not even know it yet."

CH 38

ELLEN MET HAWK AND Trey as they arrived at her home. She forestalled any questions until they were standing inside the foyer, the dogs sniffing at their shoes and trouser legs.

"Let me give you a quick synopsis. We found all the missing Council members, including Mark, at that house you told me about. All of them under some sort of stasis spell—and floating a few inches off the floor, like in zero gravity. Otherwise, they appear to be all right. Anyway, we moved them like you suggested. I thought—"

"Who is *we?*" Trey interrupted.

"Padraic, Stacy, and I, okay? Can I finish?"

Trey winced in chagrin and held up his hands. "Please."

"They've been moved to Were, under Lord Addecus' protection. He sent for Jalash-el, the Magus Primus of Shadow, to deal with the stasis spells. It appears the spells involved are somewhat similar to the one that held Brona in stasis, which Jalash-el managed to overcome. No one else knows we have recovered these missing people or where they currently are. Padraic and Stacy stayed with them."

Hawk smiled. "Stacy wouldn't leave Mark, would she?"

Ellen nodded. "You'd better believe it!"

Trey raised a point. "Forgive me, but why Addecus? Do you trust him?"

"Well, there wasn't a lot of time. I didn't have much choice; and, he had offered. He has his own reasons, which he shared with me, for wanting to help. So, yes, I do trust him.

"Just moving them from that house wasn't enough. I thought it important to move them to another realm for a couple of reasons; to keep them safe while Jalash-el deals with the stasis spells, and to keep their recovery a secret from Silenos and anyone who may be working with him."

"According to Teddy," Hawk interjected, "Silenos didn't put them there; Papa George and Daegon did after finding them on Olmus. Silenos probably hid them on Olmus. So, it doesn't look like Papa George and Daegon are working with Silenos. It's probably a good bet George and Daegon found them, figured out who these people are, and were trying to work their own angle. After all, it has become common knowledge that the Council is missing."

"So, if Teddy's right," Trey reasoned, "the only other players who we know for certain are working with Silenos are his fauns. However, we don't know the extent of their abilities, or those of Silenos either. The big concern of the moment is that we don't know whether or not Silenos knows he's lost his bargaining chips."

"Yeah, and if not yet," Hawk cautioned, "at some point, he will."

"Another good reason to hide his victims," Ellen rationalized. "I'm sure there's more to learn from these folks; but, they can't be interviewed until they're conscious. So, I think it best to keep their rescue a secret for now."

"That makes sense," Trey conceded, "but I'd have thought you'd call on Lady Leanan rather than Addecus."

"Uh, Trey," Ellen smiled and gestured toward the windows, "she's a vampire—it's daylight."

"Oh, yeah." Trey winced. "My bad—sorry."

"Now that I think about it," Hawk mused aloud, "you found them pretty quick. I thought it might take you like half an hour or more to drive out to Toledo Bend."

"We didn't drive." Ellen smiled impishly.

"Huh? Then how . . ." Hawk scratched at his stubble. "Ah, something new?"

"Yeah, something like that." She opened her palms. "You know how one can only transit between realms? Well, that may not always be the case."

"Uh-huh, so, I guess you've been reading in the journal again," he surmised, "haven't you? You've learned a new trick with the transit globes, right?"

"Yeah," she admitted. "Under the right circumstances, I can transit within the same realm. The procedure is a little different, but it's not too difficult."

"And you can take others with you, like you did with Stacy and Padraic?" Trey asked. "Wait, that's what you could have done in Mer, if you had needed our backup, right?"

"Yes, precisely—and I think it might be best to keep this new skill of mine on the *QT,* or at least among those with a need to know. So, for now, let's keep it in the *family*."

"No problem," Hawk assured her. "Speaking of Padraic, I gather Diere—er, Mab, is still missing?"

"Yes, that's another reason he is staying in Were. The missing avatar of the Dark Elves, Malvana, is among the recovered Council members. While she was in that Council meeting, her home realm named her as *regent* in Mab's absence."

"What? You mean," Hawk probed, "before anyone knew the Council went missing?"

"Right!" Ellen confirmed. "She doesn't even know about her appointment yet, since the Council was incommunicado in an emergency executive session. Padraic intends to inform her and bring her back to her home realm as soon as we determine it's time to let the rest of the realms know their people have been recovered and are safe."

"That won't be until after we deal with Silenos," Trey said firmly.

"Yeah, so what are we gonna do about Silenos?" Hawk asked. "Now that we've got the missing people relatively safe, there's really no need for you, Ellen, to meet with him, is there?"

"Of course there is!" Ellen insisted. "We don't know what he's really after; we aren't certain what his endgame is. We have to play this out."

"She's right," confirmed Trey. "What's to stop him from pulling another kidnapping stunt, or harming somebody else? We've got a Council sanction to investigate and deal with him; that's what we're gonna do."

"Absolutely! So, what's our plan?" Ellen pressed. "Y'all got something in mind, don't you?"

"Yeah, we do," Hawk reluctantly conceded. "We've thought it out. It's still dangerous, but I kinda knew you'd insist on doing this."

Trey started counting off with his fingers. "We've already scouted the meet; and, we know when it will go down. We'll get there early, secure the site and our positions. We'll have you wired and monitored. We've already got appropriate gear with us to back you up. The only thing we don't have is the prop you mentioned."

"The *iron ouroboros*," Ellen clarified. "Salidar is preparing it. Gallenius will bring him and it to Olmus just prior to sunset. I didn't want Salidar coming here."

"We'd lock his ass up," Trey grumbled, as Hawk scowled.

"Trust me; he knows that," Ellen assured them.

"Well, we've still got a couple of hours," Hawk offered glancing at his watch. "Our gear is ready; we can go at a moment's notice. So, what now?"

"An early supper," Ellen answered. "My mom's got everything laid out in the kitchen. That's where Barnabas, Brona, and Miska are. So, let's eat."

"Your wish is my command, m'lady," Hawk intoned, making a modest bow. "To the kitchen, once more into the breach!"

"Ah, you love it!" Ellen teased.

Tugging him by the sleeve, she headed for the kitchen, the dogs at their heels.

Trey just smiled, rolled his eyes, and followed.

DAEGON FOUND DERINSEUM mired in dense fog, all sense of normalcy suspended.

Few people were about in the normally crowded streets. Those who had to traverse the fog-choked thoroughfares kept their heads down and their pace as brisk as the limited visibility would allow.

Sounds were strangely muffled in the cloying greyness. Everything smelled *wet.* Shrouded in a pervasive and damp dusk, the usual colorful signs fronting the small shops seemed leached of all hue and vibrancy.

Late afternoon should have been bathed in daylight, but was not. The lamplighter had already made his rounds. Street lamps hosted pale encapsulated glows that offered little illumination beyond an arm's length in the woolen grey of the persistent fog.

It was pure chance, or perhaps fate, that led Daegon down a narrow way to a cobblestone street near the harbor. He spied a faint light of fuzzy amethyst, bobbing slightly as it seemed to be coming closer. The light stopped near a building. He was now close enough to discern that a person stood there.

He, too, was seen.

"Declare yourself!" a sharp voice commanded.

The voice seemed vaguely familiar, yet somehow distorted in the fog.

Daegon hesitated, but stepped forward.

"Daegon? Is that you?"

He breathed a sigh of relief. "Circe?"

"Aye, come closer. Alone be ye?"

"I am." Now, within a pace of her, he could see it was indeed the sea witch, her pet lizard perched as usual on her shoulders. The amethyst octopus still glowed atop her staff.

He began to explain, "I came to—"

"Not here!" she interrupted. "Inside—quickly now!"

A door was suddenly open before him; she shoved him unceremoniously through it.

She shut and bolted the door. Aiming her staff at the secured door she murmured an incantation under her breath. The air pressure in the room increased incrementally. She swept the staff in an arc, encompassing the rest of the room; a number of candles sparked to life. The glowing octopus atop Circe's staff dimmed; she set the staff aside. She extended her arm, allowing her lizard to creep down and drop to the the floor.

"It is wisest not to tarry, nor be overheard in this fog," she cautioned. "We can speak safely now. I must say, I did not expect a visit so soon. Nonetheless, Daegon," she opened her thin arms in a deliberate gesture to indicate the entire room, "welcome to my new shop."

To Daegon it appeared to be a typical apothecary shop, albeit very well stocked.

"This is impressive, Circe. You've done well, I see."

She smiled. "A façade, of course, but this is what the Merchants Guild expects. So long as I keep up appearances, and pay my guild tithes, I'll be left to my own devices. Sales of our new product have been encouraging, and the interest is growing. Our *arrangement* will very likely flourish. Now, why are you here?"

Daegon tilted his head toward the door. "Your report and concerns about this fog intrigued me. I have been scouring my research materials—"

"As have I," she interjected. "This is no natural weather phenomenon."

"I am convinced so, as well. To be honest, there are few with whom I can consult." He gestured to her in respect. "I think you and I need to talk."

She considered him for a moment. "Indeed, we do. This may take some time. Tea? Or perhaps something stronger?"

He sighed. "Tea will be fine. I suspect we will need our wits about us."

She chuckled. "Verily, Daegon, verily indeed."

OLMUS SEEMED DECEPTIVELY quiet under heavily overcast skies.

Ellen, Hawk, and Trey stood quietly just inside the tree line and kept careful watch on their surroundings. Close by, on the grassy plain just beyond the edge of the forest, a pocket of air began to shimmer.

"They're coming," Ellen whispered and pointed to the transit globe forming before them.

"Let's stay back in the trees until we know who it is," Trey cautioned.

Trey and Hawk took up covered positions to either side of Ellen, holding their shotguns waist-high, the muzzles leveled at the fully formed transit globe.

Gallenius and Salidar stepped forth. The globe shrank and winked out of existence.

Pop!

Ellen stepped out from the trees. "Welcome, gentlemen."

"Ah, Lady Ellen." Gallenius bowed.

Salidar bowed as well, but kept silent.

Trey and Hawk stepped from cover, lowered their weapons, and nodded to Gallenius. They simply glared at Salidar, but remained silent.

"You have it?" Ellen asked, slipping her backpack from her shoulders.

"We do," Gallenius confirmed, and gestured to Salidar, who held out a package wrapped in stiff parchment.

"I'll take that," Trey insisted, snatching it from Salidar.

Never taking his eyes off Salidar, he handed it to Hawk, who unwrapped the package and presented it to Ellen.

She picked up the iron ring. "It's heavy . . . Is there anything I need to know?"

Gallenius shrugged. "It is as close as we could conceive, based on our research, to the real iron ouroboros. Personally, I think Salidar did a fine job. It appears ancient, despite the fact it was crafted in a blacksmith's forge only days ago, thanks to an aging spell that may have left it a little brittle; but then, that is the nature of very old iron. Of course, there are a number of interlocking spells infused within, harmless but deliberately convoluted and quite confusing. Hopefully, it will appear to be genuine."

"I can sense the energy of the spells," Ellen remarked, hefting the ring, well cognizant of its weight. "Well, iron is heavy; it certainly does look old. Hmm, somehow this seems . . ."

"M'lady?" Gallenius asked.

She waved it off. "Oh, it's nothing . . . Well done, Salidar. Now, tell me, have *you* any advice?"

Hawk stiffened—but at a glance from Ellen, he held his place and his tongue.

Salidar bowed again. "M'lady, I can only repeat what you, no doubt, already know; do not trust Silenos. Remember, his fauns can be deadly; never let them out of your sight, or behind you."

She considered him a moment, and hefted the iron ring once more. "Thank you, Salidar, for your craftsmanship, and your words of wisdom." She wrapped the ring in the parchment and put it in her backpack.

Hawk ground his teeth—audibly.

Ellen turned to Gallenius. "What will you do now, return to Storm Haven?"

"No, m'lady, if you do not mind, at the Guildmaster's urging, we would stay to observe, and offer any assistance as needed—with your approval, of course."

She glanced to Trey and Hawk. She knew both would welcome Gallenius, but had reservations about Salidar. Nonetheless, it was her call.

"Stay if you like, but remain hidden. I'm supposed to be alone," she cautioned. "We have a plan in place; so please, do not interfere."

"Time to get into position," Trey announced and glanced upwards. "I think we're gonna get wet. Comm check?"

The air felt heavy and humid as Ellen touched the earwig in her left ear. "Loud and clear. Let's go."

"Good luck!" called Gallenius as Ellen and her two companions struck out across the grassy plain in the direction of the rolling hills.

THE SKY IN OLMUS WAS growing darker, more overcast.

The dank air in the outermost chamber of George and Daegon's cavern headquarters began to shimmer. A large transit globe appeared; Daegon and Circe stepped forth.

"What is that rumbling sound?" she asked, as the globe shrank and winked out of existence.

"Oh, that's Vito's generator running in the next chamber." Daegon paused, noting the look of confusion on Circe's face. "Oh, right, you have not been in this outermost chamber before. The generator is a device that provides simple power and light wherever Vito can string his wires. It is not magic, just technology."

"Power and light? It would seem magic to me," she countered, gently stroking her pet lizard perched across her shoulders.

He smiled indulgently. "It did to me, too, at first; but one gets accustomed to it."

She shrugged, "So be it. I would know more, when we have the time. So, your scrying chamber?"

"Of course," he swept a hand toward a wide passage. "This way."

As she followed, she said, "I must admit I was surprised that once we identified the nature of the problem we found nothing helpful within my reference resources."

"Nor mine, as well," he offered in consolation. "I had hoped there would be no need to turn to the scrying orb. There are unknown depths within that I have been reluctant to plumb. I know it to be dangerous; I can feel it in my very bones."

"That may be the case," she conceded, "but we may now have little choice, having exhausted all other resources. I confess, part of me looks forward to it. I have heard of scrying orbs, of course, but I have never seen one."

"It is quite an experience," he admitted. "I do not profess to fully understand its subtleties or nuances of its usage, but I get by."

"Oh my, how modest," she teased. "How much further? It is quiet; where is everyone?"

"Just through this passage and one more. Most of our servants, the goblins, that is, have left us for some reason. Hmm, that is strange."

"What is?"

"It *is* quiet, too quiet; and, some of the lights are out. But we heard the generator running." He pointed to a dark passage and a chamber beyond. "That goes to the lab—you have been there. The lab is never dark; Teddy is always working. One moment."

He turned down the passage, but soon came to a stop.

"What is it?" Circe asked, a degree of tension in her voice.

"The floor, sticky . . . blood, a great deal."

She came to him and thumped her staff upon the stone floor. Bright amethyst light flared from the top of the staff illuminating a huge black stain of coagulating blood. "Ye gods," she murmured.

He stepped around the blood and made his way to Teddy's lab, Circe right behind him.

The bright purple light washed over the chaos of the destroyed lab.

Shock momentarily robbed Daegon of his voice.

Circe hissed, "Whatever happened here, it was not that long ago. That puddle of blood is somewhat fresh, a few hours old. I see no bodies in here. Can your scrying orb show us what happened?"

That got his attention. "Yes, I think it can. This way."

Once in the chamber of the scrying orb, Daegon made sure all the candles were lit.

"How long will this take?" Circe asked, unable to take her eyes from the crystal orb. "I am getting an ominous feeling just being here." Her lizard was uneasy, frequently flicking its forked tongue.

"I'm not sure. I have not done this very often, looking into the recent past. It is exceptionally taxing. The procedure is difficult; it will require my full concentration. I shall try to see what has happened here since I left yesterday."

"Will I be able to see, as well?" She stroked her pet, calming it.

"Yes, now let me be about it." Daegon held his open hands near the surface of the globe and began his murmured incantation.

The clear orb gradually lost its transparency. Smoke-like clouds began to roil within, growing darker and more frantic. Small sparks flared in its depths, spinning about in a chaotic whirlwind until burning out one by one. The dark clouds slowed their mad dance, their energy dissipated. The scene within the orb cleared to display Teddy working in his lab.

"I see him!" Circe cried out in delight. "It works!"

Daegon scoffed irritably. "Yes—now let me concentrate!"

They turned back to the orb to see Teddy suddenly look up and drop a flask. His face a mask of panic, he scrambled under his worktable as something large and dark obscured the view. Light flared as something tore the wiring from the overhead stanchions and lightbulbs burst in rapid succession. The scene went dark, but not before Daegon and Circe saw the cause of the chaos—the bats on a rampage.

"This is not good," he mumbled.

"Ye gods! What are those things? They look like wolves with wings!" Circe exclaimed.

"An apt description, I suppose," Daegon conceded. "They are giant bats, and like wolves, they hunt in packs. I thought I had them under control, but—"

"What? They are yours?" she blurted. "They are not under any control! They are savage! Are they still here?"

"Probably, they are kept in a lower cavern and would likely return there. They seek darkness during the day; being nocturnal, they should now be asleep. It would be best not to wake them."

"Look!" Circe pointed to the orb. "Something is happening!"

The scene was quite dim, but they could make out someone coming into the lab, someone with a flashlight.

"That's Vito," Daegon whispered and pointed, "He's found Teddy in that overturned cabinet . . . then they leave. Well, at least neither one of them were hurt."

Circe scoffed, "Ha! That blood came from somewhere—or someone. We did not see George, did we?"

"No, we did not . . . Maybe I can expand the scope. Let me try something." Daegon hunched over the orb and began reciting another incantation.

The orb clouded for a long moment and then cleared, but the scene was outside, on a trail across a rocky knoll somewhere on the surface of Olmus.

"Where is that?" the sea witch asked.

"I-I am not sure . . . It could be anywhere," he admitted, turning to her with open palms. "At least we know it is in the very recent past, and probably close by. But I do not know why the orb would show us this."

Circe pointed at the orb. "Maybe because of that."

An oval of distortion began to waver and shimmer at the top of the knoll. A woman seemed to step from nothingness onto the trail and turn about, assessing her surroundings.

Circe squinted. "Is that a portal? Who is that? Do you know her?"

Daegon's jaw dropped. He gasped, balled his fists, and hissed, "No! Not possible—the *usurper!*"

ELLEN STOOD AT THE edge of the dais in the debris-strewn stone circle. Scanning the perimeter, she saw no one, but knew Hawk and Trey were watching from concealment.

"I'm in position. I don't see or sense anybody else. I'm gonna head for the altar stone."

"Copy that, be careful." Trey's voice sounded tiny in her left ear.

She approached the altar stone and paused; it appeared no different from when she had seen it last. She walked carefully around it; nothing had changed. She glanced up at the darkening overcast sky; not even a bird was to be seen. The unseen sun had set moments ago; dusk was slowly encroaching. The air was humid and dead-still without a hint of breeze. It was all too quiet.

She spoke softly, knowing the earwig would pick up and transmit the sound of her voice.

"No changes; everything looks like we left it."

"Copy. Now we wait . . . Hawk, comm check?"

"You're both ten-two. I've got good field of view; all clear."

Ellen gasped! "Wait! I sense something, a big energy spike! I—"

She never finished her warning.

CIRCE GRABBED DAEGON'S sleeve. "Who? What do you mean *the usurper?"*

"That is Mab—Diere! There is no way she should be here! She could not have . . ."

"Diere?" the sea witch echoed. "You mean Diere the Dark Elf—*that Diere?"*

"You know her?" Daegon made no effort to hide his shock. "How?"

"Not personally, but certainly by reputation," she quickly assured him. "I told you and George about this. Some time ago, I had some dealings with her, through an intermediary, a business matter, a ransom, as I recall. We did not come to an agreement, a pity. Anyway, we have had no contact since."

"So what is she doing here? *Here!"* He glowered at her, his suspicion evident, and growing stronger by the moment.

"You are asking *me?"* Circe opened her palms. "How in the seven hells would *I* know?"

His expression darkened, his hands flexed in anger.

She glanced over his shoulder and pointed.

"On the other hand, you could just ask her."

Daegon spun around to find Mab scowling at him from the chamber entrance.

In a voice of crystalline ice, she hissed, "Did you really think I would not return—*and find you?"*

Daegon blanched. "B-but h-how did you . . ."

"You underestimated me, you fool! I—"

"Uh, not to interrupt, but," Circe interjected, "Lady Diere, or Mab, or whatever you are called these days, you came here through a portal from someplace *unpleasant*, right?"

Mab turned on Circe. "How dare you interrupt me! I will—"

Circe thumped her staff, the amethyst light flashed, and her lizard hissed. "You will listen, if you are as smart and cunning as rumored! You came through a portal—but you did not close it, did you?"

"What?" Mab paused in confusion.

"Look!" Circe stepped aside and pointed to the orb. "You left the portal open. You are not the only thing to come through!"

"A scrying orb? You have a scrying orb?" Mab shrieked.

"Really? You think that is what is important here?" Circe rolled her eyes and murmured to her lizard, "Elves, ye gods—spare me." She jabbed a skeletal finger at the orb. "Here! Look within! These creatures have followed you! What are they?"

All eyes looked into the orb where half a dozen large bipedal lizards milled about, sniffing the air and scratching at the ground with vicious scimitar-like toe claws.

"Ye gods," Mab mumbled, "they tracked me . . . I—"

The air suddenly felt charged, surging with static electricity; a massive energy wave rocked the chamber with a deep *boom*. Circe, Mab, and Daegon were thrown to the floor. The scrying orb blackened, cracked and fell apart in rough chunks of shattered crystal.

Circe, shielding her pet, was the first to recover. "What in the seven hells . . ."

"No, not the orb!" Daegon cried, on hands and knees.

He suddenly paled. "Oh no! That will surely stir the bats up—it is past sunset! We must transit away from here now!"

"Wait!" demanded Mab, sitting up. "I am not through with you—*either* of you!"

"Fine!" Circe scoffed. "Then you can wait here and entertain a pack of giant bats the size of wolves who have probably already killed every living thing in these caves." She got to her feet, cradling her lizard, and leaned on her staff. "I am out of here!"

"Me, too." Daegon found his courage, stood, and leveled a finger at Mab. "Stay if you like; the bats aren't picky eaters. Or take your chances with those lizards who seem so intent on following you!"

Mab got to her feet, her confusion evident. "What are you—"

"Hush!" Daegon held up a hand. "Listen! I hear them; the bats have roused! We must—Circe, what's wrong?"

"I-I cannot summon a transit globe. I keep trying, but the energy will not coalesce!"

Daegon tried, and tried again. "Oh no . . ."

Mab looked on with disdain, and scoffed—but she could do no better.

"What does this mean?" the angry elf spat.

"It means we must flee these caves—now!" Circe tossed over her thin shoulder as she pushed Daegon before her into the passage. "Lead the way out, Daegon! Quickly, like your life depends upon it!"

Clearly frustrated and angry, Mab followed.

HIS EARS RINGING, SALIDAR struggled to rise and leaned against a tree. A freshening breeze had sprung up, punctuated by a few large raindrops plopping through the leaves of the canopy. Shaking his head, he mumbled, "What was *that?*"

Gallenius stood unsteadily and brushed at the dirt stains on the front of his robe. "An energy wave of some sort, I think. Are you all right?"

"Aye, just shaken," Salidar answered, looking around. "And you?"

"I am not injured. Where did it come from? Did you see anything?"

"No, I saw nothing; but I heard it and felt it." Salidar pointed into the gathering gloom, across the grassy plain at the rolling hills beyond. "I think it came from that direction."

More rain began to fall as Gallenius peered into the dusk. "That is where the Steward and her companions went."

"Aye. Do you suppose they are all right? It will be full dark soon. Should we not check on them?"

Gallenius shook his head. "Our instructions were to remain hidden, were they not?"

"Yes, but . . ." Salidar shrugged in exasperation. "Gallenius, something is wrong—very wrong. I feel it in my gut! We must check on them!"

His eyebrows rising in surprise, Gallenius paused. "I must say, Salidar, demonstrating such concern for others is not typical for you."

Salidar sighed in resigned confusion. "I know, sometimes this surprises me as well. I cannot explain it. However, I trust my gut. Right now, my gut is telling me that something bad has happened—and we will be needed."

"Very well, that is good enough for me," Gallenius conceded, and motioned into the rainy night. "Can you follow their trail, without exposing us to anyone else?"

Salidar scoffed. "Hmmph! Who do you think you are talking to? Just stay quiet; and keep up."

THE PASSING ENERGY wave startled, but didn't particularly frighten, the saber-toothed cats. More than anything, it rather annoyed them, disturbing their nap. The big male rose and stretched. He padded to the mouth of the cave, peered into the wet night, and growled irritably deep in his throat.

His mate watched, sighed heavily, and rose to join him.

The sudden disruption of moments ago, had rendered them alert, and piqued their interest.

Their muzzles in the air and jaws thrust forward, they sampled the scents wafting past the rocky outcrop. The growing darkness was no hindrance to their kind, whose night vision was as acute as any nocturnal predator; nonetheless, they relied most upon their sense of smell. Despite the rain, this night was already replete with unfamiliar scents of potential prey.

The female grunted softly in satisfaction—*prey*. This pleased her, triggering a primeval urge to hunt.

Truth be told, of the mated pair, the female was the more accomplished hunter, a most stealthy stalker. More often than not, the male was content to follow her lead and assist in the final kill. They were an effective team, and feared little.

And so, like cats of any variety, they succumbed to instinct and curiosity, slipping soundlessly into the moist velvet dark.

CH 39

THE PELTING RAIN HELPED Ellen regain consciousness. Lying facedown on the wet stones of the circle, she managed to lift her throbbing head and squint her eyes open. A string of burning torches ringed the dais a few paces away. Someone, or *something,* was moving among the deep shadows beyond the reach of the flickering flames. She rolled onto her side and forced herself to sit up. Hands to her damp temples, she squeezed her eyes shut and took several deep breaths; the throbbing abated.

What happened? Torches? Where'd they come from? I was standing on the dais, there, by the altar stone, wasn't I? Oh no—the energy surge! What was that? Hawk and Trey? Are they all right? Are our comms still working?

Before she could speak to test the comm link, she heard an unfamiliar voice.

"Ah, you are awake. You will answer my questions."

There, palms flat upon the altar, stood the satyr. Leaning slightly forward, he leered at her across the stained slab and motioned to someone behind her.

Suddenly seized by her arms, she was brought to her feet. She stumbled, but the fauns did not release her.

"Who sent you?" Silenos asked.

Ellen stood straighter. "What? You did! You are Silenos, right?"

"I am *the* Silenos! I left instructions for the *Steward* to bring me," he hefted the iron ring, "this iron ouroboros. You are not her! So, I ask again, who sent you?" He set the ring down on the altar.

Ellen had not realized she no longer had possession of the iron ring. She saw her backpack laying to one side, its flap open and contents dumped out upon the wet stones.

So, they searched me while I was unconscious. Hmmph, they missed a few things; the earwig is still in my ear. I hope it still works. I've gotta get him talking.

"You want to talk? Fine! Have these goons unhand me. I can stand on my own, thank you!"

Surprise and mild amusement flashed across the satyr's face. At the flick of his fingers, the fauns released her.

She rubbed her arms where she had been so cruelly gripped. Steeling her resolve she faced him, hands on her hips. *So, Silenos, let's see how much of a conversationalist you can be.*

"As much as I hate repeating myself, it seems I must. If you are in fact, Silenos, then *you* sent me, or sent for me. Whether you believe it or not, I *am* the Steward!"

Silenos slapped an open palm down upon the altar stone and jabbed a finger at her. "Do not lie to me, girl! I know the Steward is an aged woman, Maude Delafaire! You are not her!"

Ellen's surprise was genuine. "What? Maude Delafaire?" She crossed her arms and nodded. "Oh, now I see. You do not know, do you?"

He scowled and uttered menacingly, "I do not know *what?*"

As she pondered how to answer, a tiny *squelch* sounded in her ear, followed by Hawk's voice.

"We're okay. There's just the three of 'em. Keep him talking."

Relief flooded through her; but she maintained a poker face and kept her eyes on the satyr.

Okay, I can do this. Play to his ego; but mess with him just enough to keep him going.

"Silenos, it appears you really are out of touch. You do not know that Maude Delafaire died, or that I am her successor."

"You? A mere slip of a girl?" Palms flat on the altar stone he leaned forward, his disbelief blatant. "Do not make me laugh!"

"Oh, really?" she countered. "Shall I conjure a transit globe—right here, right now, as proof?"

He waved a hand dismissively. "Oh, you could try; but it will not happen. Even if you were the Steward, no transit globe to take you from this realm will even form within the boundaries of my stasis sphere."

"Stasis sphere?" Ellen echoed. *Seriously?*

"Yes, that is what I call it—a specialty of mine." Silenos smiled smugly. "But by all means, if you are the new Steward, do try to summon forth a globe."

"Very well." She did try—and failed.

The satyr chortled. "Ah, such a look of disappointment and defeat! Mayhap, you are indeed the Steward after all." His voice dropped to a low murmur—but not low enough. "If so, you will do."

Alarmed at his *sotto voce* comment, Ellen pressed on, careful to appear equally confused yet interested. She had to keep him talking. "A stasis sphere? But how? I have never seen such a power."

Silenos scoffed. "Ha! You mean until now! I am the most powerful mage—the ultimate! My command of stasis spells alone is unsurpassed! Tis but a taste of the breadth of my power!"

Ellen shrugged. "All right, I will admit I am impressed. But come on, *this* stasis sphere," she swept her hands about, "is fascinating on its own! So, no transit globe will form within it? That is a skill of staggering proportions. Is the scope, or the size, any sort of impediment? The energy drain must be significant, yes?"

"For me? Hardly worth noting." Silenos preened in his gloating. "I have cast this spell for some distance in all directions. No one, with the skill to do so, will be able to transit out of this realm; the energy to do so is held in stasis."

"I see. Wow, that is just," Ellen shook her head, "amazing, simply amazing. This is not—no, *you* are not as I expected." She dipped her head. "My compliments, Silenos. Now, if I might change the subject?"

Basking in the perceived admiration, Silenos blinked in surprise. "What?"

She pointed to the altar stone, upon which the iron ouroboros rested. "As you can see, I complied with your instructions; I brought the iron ouroboros. In return for that, you promised to release those persons you took from the Council Realm."

"Oh, did I?" Silenos smiled.

Ellen let her voice grow cold. "You did—you know you did. Would you break an oath?"

"I swore no oath." All manner of civility slipped from the satyr's countenance. "I have other plans for them—and you as well."

Folding her arms, Ellen raised a lone eyebrow in scorn and took a few steps forward. "Oh really, other plans, indeed?"

"Yes, observe!" Silenos commanded, picking up the iron ouroboros with dramatic flair.

She leaned back in caution.

"Oh, do try not to swoon, girl." Leering at her, he opened his tunic baring his hairy chest. The silver ouroboros hung suspended from his neck on a chain of oversized silver links.

Defiantly standing her ground, she confronted the smug satyr. “So, you have a penchant for jewelry?”

“Ha! I do like your wit, girl! This is no mere adornment.” He slipped the silver ouroboros from the chain.

Ellen did her best to appear unimpressed. “Indeed?”

“You see, my fledgling Steward, now I have both halves of a *key.* With both, I can now perform the rite I have been researching for a very long time.”

He held the two rings out at chest height over the altar, and mumbled an obscure incantation. In a flash of sickly green light, he twisted the two together forming a recumbent figure-eight.

“Behold, the *infinity key!* At long last, I can release my master—Crom!”

Ellen gasped. “One of the Old Ones?”

Silenos offered her a wicked smile. “Indeed, the darkest of the Old Ones, in whose service I have long been dedicated. In fact, I am the strongest among his followers. Only I had the wits and skill to arrange a suitable sacrifice—the entire realm of Mer!”

Her shock genuine, she blurted, “Mer, the water realm? Are you out of your mind?”

The satyr scoffed. “Hmmph! You know nothing! The so-called *great work,* the banishment of the Old Ones, took enormous collective energies from several realms to accomplish. To undo such a thing would take at least as much. But, to briefly open the door wide enough for Crom to return to this side, here in his favored realm of Olmus, I need the collective life energy of but one realm—Mer.”

Ellen was speechless. Sacrifice all life of an entire realm—the very idea was *monstrous!*

However, Silenos was not finished gloating.

"Of course, for any living mage short of my standing, this rite is not without potential peril, and cost. However, I now have the power and the skill to mitigate both."

He leaned over the altar and leered once more. "Unfortunately for those Council fools, the rite demands sacrifices of token beings of those assorted races who participated in the crafting of the first cursed *great work*—and a Steward."

CIRCE CALLED OUT TO Daegon, "By the gods—hold on a moment! Let us stop and catch our breath!"

She leaned heavily upon her staff, her thin chest heaving. Her lizard's eyes were wide with fear, its forked tongue flicked incessantly.

Daegon slowed and stopped running. Panting heavily, he wiped the rain from his eyes. He turned and sloshed back along the puddled forest path.

Next to Circe, Mab stood drenched, hands on hips, winded but scowling. "What are we running from? I saw nothing pursuing us in this damned rain."

Daegon pointed to the dripping canopy overhead. "The bats are no doubt on the wing. In the dark of night and with this overcast, you will not likely see them. Rain will not stop them. We are relatively safe beneath the trees of the forest. They tend to attack in more open areas, hunting as a pack."

"Why can we not summon transit globes?" Circe asked, sucking deep breaths. "Tell me that!"

"I have no idea," Daegon began, "but—"

"A spell," Mab interrupted, "of some kind; I can sense it. That means someone cast it. Think! If none of us is responsible, then someone else is—someone else is here."

"Yes, and that someone must be fairly close," Circe reasoned. "Spells have limits in range and duration. We must find this person—"

"And deal with them!" Mab spat.

A snapping twig to their rear caught their attention; they froze.

Mab locked eyes with Daegon and Circe. "What else," she hissed, "might hunt in this forest?"

Daegon shrugged. "Nothing that I know of, but I do not—"

Circe raised a hand to forestall Daegon, and tilted her staff in Mab's direction. "How about those creatures that followed *you* through that portal?"

Mab paled. "We need to get out of here!"

"At least out of these trees," Circe added, "so we can see what's coming."

"But the bats," Daegon whined with open hands, "they—"

"Enough!" Mab fumed. "Do you want to stay here and take your chances? We have no choice; we must find whoever is responsible for this cursed spell! Now we go!"

Daegon slogged after the two women, mumbling under his breath, "I have a bad feeling about this."

SALIDAR COULD MOVE as silently as a ghost in the wet night. Gallenius was hard pressed to match the thief's stealth. As they crested a scrub-covered hillock, Salidar stopped and dropped to a crouch; Gallenius followed suit.

"The wind has changed," Salidar whispered. "Good."

"Why? It's just raining harder."

Salidar pointed. "Because we need to go there. See that faint glow against the night sky? However, we need to approach from another angle, staying upwind. The rain will help."

"Upwind, why?"

Salidar shook his head. "Because I have taken great pains to lose whatever has been following us."

Gallenius was aghast. "Following us? By the gods—what?"

"I do not know—nor do I want it to find us again. So be silent, and follow my lead."

Gallenius could only nod and comply.

ELLEN FOUND HER VOICE. "What do you mean *sacrifices?*"

Silenos set the infinity key on the altar. "Just what I said. The lives of the Council members are to be offered during the rite, and yours as well." His expression betrayed no emotion.

The intensity of the rain increased incrementally as she stared into his eyes. She saw a hint of madness flickering within.

Not good—there may be no reasoning with him after all. Hmm, new tactic.

Hands on her hips, she asked, "What makes you think I would permit any of that to happen?"

"Ha-ha! Permit?" Silenos roared with laughter. "Oh, what wit! There is nothing you can do to stop me! It will happen this very night!"

She offered him a sad smile and shook her head. "Oh, I think not. These anticipated sacrifices, the kidnapped Council members, are no longer yours. Oh, you did not know? You did not think to check?"

The satyr's face darkened, but before he could speak a voice called out.

"Silenos! It *is* you! What have you done?"

The satyr squinted into the rain. "Circe? What are you doing here? Who is with you?"

The sea witch came forward, trying to avoid the growing puddles. "I know you have done something because I cannot transit out of this gods-forsaken realm!" She stopped, made a sign to ward off the evil eye, and spat at the ground.

"Answer me, Circe!" Silenos demanded. "Who is with you?"

Ellen stepped back, trying to keep one eye on Silenos while peering through the falling rain at the interlopers.

Her earwig *squelched;* Hawk's voice followed. "Ellen, two women, one man; one of the women is Diere—Mab! She looks worse for wear."

Circe, mere paces away from the dais, answered, "A mage called Daegon, and a Dark Elf, Diere—"

"That is *Queen Mab* to you—all of you!" The wet elf, beyond angry, stepped up to Circe's side. "What is going on here? Are you responsible for interfering with transit globes? Answer me this instant!"

Silenos chuckled. "Oh, is she not full of herself—a queen, no less."

He smiled at Ellen. "It seems I may have sufficient sacrifices after all."

Her earwig *squelched* again. "Ellen, there's something coming up behind them, five or six of 'em! Wait, they're staying within the trees. We can't get a good visual."

"Come forward and be welcome!" Silenos shouted, waving a beckoning hand to the three newcomers. "You are just in time for the ceremony!"

Ellen and Mab locked eyes. Recognition was immediate, despite both being soaked.

"What are *you* doing here?" Mab demanded. "Are you responsible for this transiting debacle?"

"Not me," Ellen replied, jerking a thumb at the satyr, "all him."

Mab focused on Silenos, her angry impatience evident. "Now see here! I demand—"

"Silence!" Silenos bellowed. "You demand nothing here!"

Shocked, Mab screamed in fury and thrust her hands out at him. A flare of bright crimson energy shot forth from her fingertips, only to splash against an unseen shield around the satyr, and dissipate as roiling steam in the rain.

Silenos scoffed. "Hmmph! You call that power? Ha! Pathetic!"

Mab was clearly beyond rage, and took a step forward. "You infuriating bastard! I will—"

He pointed a single finger at her; her voice went silent.

"Ah, that's much better," Silenos declared.

Hands to her throat, Mab sucked in great gobs of air. She could breathe; but, despite her best efforts, further speech was denied her. Murderous intent bloomed in her eyes. Her arms dropped and stiffened at her sides; ominous red sparks danced upon her balled fists.

Silenos noticed. "Oh no, we will have no more petty displays of temper." He waved his hands in an arcane gesture.

In the next instant, no one within the stone circle, save Silenos and his fauns, could move.

Ellen immediately recognized it as a stasis spell. She could move her eyes only. She was still standing, fully aware, yet held completely immobile. She was not alone; neither Circe nor Mab were moving. She could not see the man called Daegon.

"Ah yes, that will do." Silenos rubbed his hands together and turned to the fauns. "Bring them up to the altar."

Ellen could only watch. Her earwig *squelched*; it was Trey this time.

"We saw and heard. We're changing position. The things in the trees are still there; and now there are several things flying around overhead, big things."

Ellen watched as Circe, Mab, and Daegon were brought upon the dais and placed around the altar.

The fauns came for her as well and placed her next to Mab. Circe and Daegon were at the head and foot of the rectangular stone. The four sacrifices were now on three sides of the altar. Silenos stepped to the vacant fourth side.

The fauns stepped back as Silenos began a strange monotone chant. They took up positions at his elbows, like acolytes in dedicated service to a mage.

Silenos droned on in a cadence as steady as the rain. The temperature began to drop, the unnatural chill of ill-intended sorcery.

Ellen felt the fine hairs on the back of her neck stand on end.

LYING PRONE, GALLENIUS peered out from under the pile of wet leaves beneath the thick scrub at the tree line. The wind and rain were in his face. Squinting, he could make out Ellen and three others stationary around the central stone. He could see the satyr and his two fauns as well, but he couldn't hear them.

He nudged Salidar, hidden inches away. "I can see, but not hear—you?"

"Same. Quiet; don't breathe. Something is coming and will pass right in front of us."

Gallenius froze.

Moments later, something did pass in front of them—two *big* somethings, on four legs.

Gallenius held his breath for a long time.

TREY AND HAWK HUNKERED down in the dripping underbrush. They'd been careful to avoid the area where half a dozen big lizards lay in wait watching the stone circle. A good look at a couple of them confirmed the men's suspicions—velociraptors, those sparsely feathered monstrosities they'd dealt with before in another unnamed wild realm. However, the men had no clue why such creatures were in Olmus. Nonetheless, these reptiles merited a wide berth.

Trey and Hawk had a good view of the altar stone area. They could easily hear Silenos' monotone incantation, picked up by Ellen's earwig mike.

"What now?" whispered Hawk, wiping beading raindrops from the receiver of his shotgun.

"We watch. What's your magazine load?" Trey asked, nodding to his partner's shotgun.

"Alternating slugs and 00-buck, slug in the chamber. You?"

"Same. When it's time to act, we'll know."

"Right, but let's watch our six."

Trey softly chuckled. "True dat."

GALLENIUS WAS DOING his best to maintain his calm. He would have considered meditating had not the situation been so perilous. He was attuned to every sound no matter how subtle; the constant rain didn't help. He kept hearing what he thought were gusts of wind through the trees, a *whooshing* of sorts, but it made him uneasy and apprehensive.

He nudged Salidar once more. "Listen, above us, I hear—"

"Yes, I know. Bats, big ones, predators. They are native to the Realm of Were and very rare. I know not how or why they are drawn here. Stay quiet."

Gallenius needed no further urging.

SILENOS CONCLUDED HIS monotone chant and held the infinity key above his head. His lips moved in a silent invocation.

High above the altar stone, a pale sphere formed and began to pulse with an inner purple glow. With each slow pulse it grew until it was almost as large as the dais, easily ten feet in diameter. Black tendrils of crackling energy crept up its circumference. Raindrops striking the sphere sizzled to steam upon contact. A wind began to whirl around the the stones beyond the dais, picking up wet debris and leaves, sending them hurtling erratically about.

Within the sphere, the pulsing increased. Patches of throbbing shadow and profane light constantly churned, folding in upon themselves, until stabilizing to resemble a wavering demonic face, a bespoke horror of vicious cruelty and deliberate malice.

"My Lord Crom!" cried Silenos.

The hellish image smiled upon the satyr.

Silenos dropped his hands from the infinity key; it hung there, unsupported, in midair just below the pulsing sphere.

The satyr could not be more pleased with himself. "I am ready, my lord; the sacrifices are in place. I shall free you now!" A large obsidian-bladed athame appeared in his hand.

However, the infernal image now frowned upon the satyr.

Silenos balked. "My Lord Crom, what is it? Is something amiss?"

Receiving no answer, Silenos' mind raced through his preparations. "Ah, the order of the sacrifices—that must be it!"

Silenos motioned to his fauns and pointed to Ellen. "The Steward. Lay her on the altar. I must release her stasis spell and make her the *first* sacrifice."

THAT WAS ALL HAWK AND Trey needed to hear. They broke from cover and sprinted for the dais. Hawk went left; Trey went right.

The fauns had Ellen up and on the altar in a matter of seconds. They stepped back and turned to face the oncoming men. Brandishing their wicked obsidian-bladed knives, the fauns leapt toward their prey.

Boom-boom! Twin shotgun blasts echoed in the night.

For an instant, the fauns seemed to hang suspended in midair, then fell, crumpling on the wet stones before the dais. Both bore slug wounds in their chests and massive exit holes in their backs.

Trey and Hawk trained the muzzles of their shotguns on the satyr; but Silenos only smiled and repeated his earlier arcane gesture.

They were held motionless—another stasis spell!

Silenos walked over to one of the fallen fauns, and shook his head. "Now this is inconvenient."

Standing over the body, he made some gestures while mumbling an incantation, and placed his hand upon the faun's head. He then repeated the ritual with the other slain faun.

Within a few moments, both fauns stirred and rose to stand before their master, the bloody holes in their bodies slowly repairing.

Silenos sighed and gestured to the altar. "Now, let us be about our business."

GALLENIUS AND SALIDAR were aghast!

"We have to stop this ritual!" Gallenius hissed.

"I know," Salidar responded through gritted teeth. "I have an idea, but I have to get to the infinity key. I need a distraction!"

Gallenius scanned the area around them and then looked up. "I believe I can help you with that. Be ready."

Salidar considered the mage, and nodded.

Gallenius stood and closed his eyes in concentration. He could feel that this place was rampant with errant energy from the converging ley lines. He knew what he needed to do. It would be taxing; but, it just might work.

Collecting as much ambient energy as he dared, he thrust his arms out from his sides and let balls of energy-fused lightning coalesce in his open palms. With a flick of his wrists, he sent the lightning balls streaking at shoulder height in opposite arcs through the tree line just beyond the stone circle. When they met in the trees on the other side of the clearing, lightning flashed and a massive clap of thunder erupted.

He looked skyward, and repeated his actions; this time sending the two balls of lightning spiraling into the sky to clash in another great flash of lightning and clap of thunder within the cloud bank overhead, well above the swirling bats.

Gallenius dropped to his knees, nearly exhausted, and saw that Salidar was gone.

WITHIN THE STONE CIRCLE, a pack of tense velociraptors, having fled the unexpected lightning within the trees, skittishly sniffed the air, twisting their reptilian heads about. On the other side of the clearing, the pair of irritated saber-toothed cats growled ominously and sampled mingled scents of prey, fear, blood, and ozone.

Overhead *whooshing* heralded the arrival of the drug-fueled rampaging bats, sorely aggravated by the sudden discharge in the unpredictable cloud bank, and drawn by the scent of prey.

All the predators were now fully aware of each others' presence. Screeches, spitting hisses, and roaring howls of challenge shredded the rain-cursed night. Instinctively wired not to tolerate one another, and maddened by the scent of freshly spilled fauns' blood, the competing predators attacked!

Utter chaos ensued!

SILENOS IGNORED THEM all, mumbling another incantation as he raised the deadly athame above his head. "Observe, my Lord Crom! In your name, I sacrifice this Steward with one thrust to the heart!"

His eyes rolled up, only the whites showing; gritting his teeth, he plunged the athame down.

The obsidian blade shattered on the rough stone of the altar—she was gone!

Looking up, Silenos spotted her amongst the battling creatures, wrapping an arm around one of the men who had attacked his fauns. Then they were both gone!

Suddenly she was back, by the other man—then both were gone!

The hair on Silenos' arms stood on end. He looked up into the demonic face within the roiling purple orb—not smiling now—no, more a look of angered surprise and fury!

"My Lord Crom," he pleaded, "I can fix this!"

The black tendrils of crackling energy faltered; the orb began to diminish in size, its purple intensity fading.

Unsure of what to do, Silenos looked around frantically. Desperation and ratcheting panic birthed a solitary hope.

"The key—the key! Yes-yes, of course! I will renew the spell using the infinity key!"

He reached up for the key—it was gone!

"Looking for this?"

Silenos spun to find a small man at the edge of the altar, just out of reach, holding the infinity key.

Key in hand, the interloper scoffed and slowly shook his head. "Hmmph, too bad."

Silenos lunged!

The small man deftly stepped to one side, around an immobile and wide-eyed Daegon, effectively keeping the altar between Silenos and himself.

"Give me that! This instant!" the satyr demanded, his hand out.

"No, I think not," said the strange man, his tone taunting. "In fact, I think no one should have this."

Raising the infinity key above his head, the man smashed it down upon the altar stone. The iron ouroboros shattered, pieces skittering across the altar and spilling onto the dais.

Mouth agape, Silenos was too stunned to speak. He blinked in disbelief.

The strange man was gone; only shards of brittle iron remained, scattered in all directions.

High above the altar, only a trace of the pale purple glowing orb lingered.

Silenos climbed upon the altar and cried out, "My Lord Crom! I will—"

An angry beam of foul purple light shot out from the lingering glow, illuminating Silenos. Its intensity flared white-hot for an instant, then streaked back into the pale orb. The glow faded in the persistent rain and winked out.

Silenos was gone; there was no trace of him.

In the stone circle, the predatory bloodbath continued unabated.

WITHIN THE TREES BEYOND the clearing, Ellen shook off Hawk's embrace. "I'm fine, now let go! I've got to get the others out of there!"

Trey shook his head. "Are you sure? One of them is Mab. We don't even know the other two."

"Doesn't matter!" she insisted. "You two stay here and keep an eye on Gallenius. Salidar should be around somewhere, too."

"I am here," the thief announced, stepping through the dripping trees. He held up the silver ouroboros. "Mission accomplished. How is Gallenius?"

"I am fine, just tired," the mage replied. "Are you all right?"

Salidar nodded. "I am not injured."

"I gotta go," Ellen insisted. "Be right back."

"Uh, Ellen, before you go," Hawk cautioned and pointed. "Look!"

Peering past the trees, she could see that nothing was now moving within the stone circle. The battling predators were frozen in place, like a state of suspended animation.

"What the—?" she breathed. "Another stasis spell? Even the rain has stopped. Don't look at me; I can't explain it."

"Perhaps I can."

Turning to the new voice, they saw a short, broad-shouldered man step forth from the trees. Attired in a knee-length cloak, he was cradling a good-sized grey cat.

"Smokey!" Ellen exclaimed in joy, as he literally leapt into her arms.

Everyone smiled indulgently as she cradle-rocked her cat.

"Oh, forgive me," she begged, forgetting her manners. "This is Lord Ignatius, Avatar of the Dragon Lords. And I gather he has something to do with what has happened, correct, m'lord?"

"Quite so. We do need to talk, but I think you were about to recover some people who are still bespelled, yes?"

"Yes, I am," Ellen answered. "But how did you know to come here? Now? I mean—"

Ignatius simply nodded to her cat and smiled.

"Oh, yes, of course, I should have known." She smiled and scratched under Smokey's chin, earning a rumbling purr. "Wonderful cat! He does go where he will."

"Indeed, and thankfully so," Ignatius agreed. "Now, first things first. Salidar, is it? I shall take the silver ouroboros, if you do not mind."

Salidar looked to Ellen, who simply shrugged. "May as well, it wasn't that well hidden or kept safe before. If the Dragon Lords can't keep it secure, who can?"

Gallenius nodded. "I would agree."

Ignatius accepted the silver ouroboros from Salidar. "Thank you. I can assure you all that it will be kept secure."

He turned back to Ellen. "You were going to rescue some people?"

"Oh, yes, now in fact," she answered, letting Smokey slip from her arms, who promptly began grooming himself. "The rest of y'all should stay out of sight."

"If you would permit me to offer some advice?" Ignatius opened his palms.

"Of course, please do."

"Allow me to accompany you. A number of gargoyles currently stand watch above the circle. All life forms within are held in a stasis field of my doing, and shall remain so until I have determined the appropriate disposition of each. I know you have mastered the ability to transit within a single realm—that is obviously how you made your own escape and rescued these two gentlemen. However, that will not work with the stasis spell now in play; only I can release those whom you would rescue. I will do so at your request, but it would be best if we were simply to walk to them. I assure you it is safe."

"I understand; please, m'lord, accompany me," Ellen requested. "Oh! Did you stop the rain, too?"

Ignatius smiled and shook his head. "No, not I. Nature does as she pleases, of course."

"Right," Ellen conceded, not entirely convinced. "After this, I think we should talk, in detail, yes?"

"Yes," Ignatius nodded, "we probably should."

ELLEN WAS NOT PREPARED for the carnage. Transiting only a short distance within the realm during the melee had spared her most of this horror; but now, she had to walk through a battlefield held in suspension. Everything was wet—not only from the rain. Carefully stepping around combatants, pools of rain-diluted blood, and bits of viscera, she did her best to keep her gorge down.

Although they were now held in stasis, it was clear the warring predators had taken quite a toll on one another. Bloodied bodies, and pieces thereof, were littered everywhere. All of the bats were down, some torn to shreds. The velociraptors had fared somewhat better, but only two remained upright, both severely wounded. The saber-toothed cats bore wounds as well, but none seemed so severe. The other predator bodies around the huge felines told a sufficiently blatant tale.

When Ellen passed near one of the fauns, she stopped. He appeared dead, yet she had seen Silenos resurrect him with necromancy. She pointed, "Is he—"

"Dead? Oh, yes," Ignatius assured her. "I erased any trace of necromancy with either of the fauns. They had actually been dead for some time—decades, perhaps. Their master repeatedly resurrected them as needed. When I remove my stasis spell, their corpses will decompose commensurate with the time elapsed since their first death. It will happen rather quickly, I suspect."

"Oh, I'm not sure I'd want to see that."

Ignatius nodded. "I understand. Shall we proceed?"

"Yes, let's," she answered gratefully. "The others are at the altar, or at least they were."

The three were still there, in their statue-like poses, their eyes alert.

Ignatius pointed to Mab. "Her, I know; and I recall warning her not to perform any magic here. Now, there must be a reckoning. These others, I do not know. This one has a pet lizard—interesting. Him, I know not—however, I sense the taint of necromancy upon him."

"Well, I don't really know either of them. They just showed up with her." Ellen pointed to the Dark Elf. "You could ask the others about them, couldn't you?"

"Good idea," Ignatius acknowledged. "I think I will release my stasis spells on these three, but I shall keep them silent until we are among the trees. Then I will hear what they have to say. They were briefly with you, so would you explain the circumstances to them? I shall see to it that they comply, of course."

"No problem."

Ignatius made a simple hand gesture. All three *statues* seemed to come alive; but, none could speak.

"Look at me!" Ellen demanded. "Listen! I'm going to lead you out of here. Follow me, touch nothing, and don't speak—you won't be able to anyway, at least not yet. Let's go!"

Ellen wove a convoluted path through the frozen tableau of embattled predators. Three wide-eyed people followed, occasionally stumbling while gaping at shocking scenes. Ignatius brought up the rear.

In moments, they were beyond the tree line, and apparently alone.

"You are safe here. I don't know all of you. I am Ellen, the Steward. The ordeal with Silenos is over. He is gone." She gestured to her companion. "This is Lord Ignatius, Avatar of the Dragon Lords. We have some questions."

Ignatius nodded to Ellen, and made a simple gesture to remove the spell of silence.

He faced Mab, who scowled at him. "We meet again. Tell me why you are here."

Mab glared daggers at Daegon, and faced Ignatius. "Very well, I will share my tragic tale of betrayal. I am a victim of foul treachery . . ."

Ignatius listened until her tale wound down. "I see. Thank you. Now please remain silent."

Somewhat surprised, Mab complied, but sneered at Daegon.

Ignatius turned to Circe. "We have not met. Who are you and why are you here?"

The sea witch gently stroked the lizard upon her shoulder to calm it. "I am called Circe, from Mer. I am a businesswoman . . ."

Ignatius listened to her as well. "I see, thank you. Now please remain silent."

Finally he turned to Daegon. "We have not met, either. Who are you and why are you here?"

Daegon straightened his robe. "I am called Daegon, late of the Realm of Dark Elves, I am an alchemist . . ."

Ellen thought Ignatius listened most intently to Daegon.

When Daegon finished, Ignatius said, "Thank you, please remain silent. Now, all of you stay right here. We shall return shortly. My associates will keep you company."

Half a dozen armored gargoyles silently stepped forth from the trees.

ONCE ALONE, ELLEN TUGGED at Ignatius' sleeve, bringing him to a stop. "I have a question of my own, m'lord, if we might take a moment?"

"Of course, what can I do for you?"

"Silenos bragged about his 'unsurpassed skill' with stasis spells. We know he used some versions when he kidnapped the Council members—you know about that, right?"

"Yes, you may assume I was well informed."

"Am I right in assuming any such stasis spells of his would have no further effect, or dissipate, or whatever, with his death? I ask because we recovered the missing Council members, but they were still bespelled. I don't know if those who have been working to counter those spells have had any success."

Ignatius stroked his chin. "I see. I think it entirely likely those spells ceased to function, as did his stasis spells here, with his demise. I had to invoke my own stasis spell here to bring that overall melee to a halt. Of course, those you just rescued were subject to my spell as well."

Ellen sighed in relief. "In that case, could I ask that you wait here for a few minutes? I should go check on the recovered Council members. I'll be right back."

Ignatius grinned. "I am sure you will. By all means, go! I shall wait right here. One thing, do not mention my involvement; that is to be kept secret."

"I understand—be right back!"

Pop!

SHE WAS BACK IN UNDER two minutes, all smiles. "You were right! Everyone is fine; they'll be returning to the Council Realm for a briefing from me later tonight. Don't worry, I'll keep your name out of it."

"That would be best," he confirmed. "Now could you ask your friends to meet with me here? I would speak with them out of earshot of those three now in the gargoyles' custody."

Ellen nodded and returned in a moment with her friends.

"Lord Ignatius, I told them the Council members are okay!" Ellen declared. "And how your involvement here is to be considered *classified, need to know* and all that."

"Excellent," acknowledged the Avatar of the Dragon Lords, and turned to the group. "This information may go no further without my explicit permission; do each of you understand?"

Trey and Hawk acknowledged with nods and assurances.

Salidar murmured, "Yes, m'lord."

Gallenius raised a hand. "The Guildmaster?"

Ignatius shrugged. "Authorized, but no further. Agreed?"

"Aye, m'lord, agreed," Gallenius confirmed.

"Now, as to Mab, Circe, and Daegon—you all were close enough to hear what they had to say, correct?" Ignatius asked. "Do any of you know any of them? Or know of facts different from what they have told us?"

"I suspect each of us knows something," Gallenius conceded, "but Salidar may know all three the best. I would hear him out, m'lord."

"Very well, Salidar, please enlighten me." Ignatius folded his arms.

"As you wish, m'lord," he began, but added, "This may take a while. I would ask anyone else to fill in any gaps as I go, if you please."

"Fair enough," Ignatius acknowledged. "Proceed."

And so he did, for almost an hour.

AFTER EVERYONE HAD added what they could, Ignatius thanked them.

Walking a few paces, he stretched his stiffened back, and signaled for a gargoyle to attend him. Moments later, the gargoyle hurried off to follow his new instructions.

Ellen took that opportunity to ask, "So, what now?"

Ignatius shrugged. "First, I have to finish cleaning up this mess." He waved a hand toward the stone circle. "Then, I must deal with Mab, Circe, and Daegon. I have not yet reached any decisions in that regard. Oh, you should know that the sorcery Silenos had commenced in Mer, to effect a realm-scale sacrifice, has been negated. It took the form of a noxious fog that has since been eliminated."

She nodded. "That's good; but you know his plan would not have worked anyway, because we did not give him the real iron ouroboros. He could not form the real infinity key."

"Yes, I am aware; remember that I was well informed." He smiled, a twinkle in his eye, but his tone turned serious. "The Realm of Mer would have paid a dear price had that pernicious spell progressed further; its continued expansion could not be tolerated. Of course, everything in Mer is fine now.

"More disturbing is the fact that Silenos did manage to bring Crom to the gate—that was too close—and it cost Silenos his life. Had he managed to let Crom slip through, we would all be in dire straits."

Surprised and a bit confused, she countered, "But surely, the Dragon Lords would have interceded, wouldn't they?"

Ignatius looked around and locked eyes with her. "Ellen, we will speak of this at another time. Not here, not now."

"What? Why? What do you mean?"

But Ignatius merely shook his head as a gargoyle stepped to his side and bent to his ear.

Ignatius listened, then nodded. The gargoyle departed.

"We *are* going to talk, later—right?" Ellen asked.

"We will; I promise. Now join me; it is time to deal with Mab, Circe, and Daegon."

"You've decided?"

"For the most part, yes, albeit tentative decisions. But first, I want to show you something."

He led her past the tree line to where she could see the area of the stone circle. It was empty; no predators, no blood, no gore.

"What the—?" she blurted. "It looks like nothing ever happened here! What did you do?"

"Me? Nothing," he admitted. "However, the gargoyles have been busy. The dead creatures have been buried. Those that survived have been returned to their native realms. Curiously, the big lizards and the saber-toothed cats are from the same realm; and there, they have been returned."

Ellen shook her head in confusion. "But wait—how did they . . . Oh, yeah, Mab admitted she left a portal open. And I . . . oh, man, I think I'm partially responsible, too. So the cats and the velociraptors were from the same realm all along?"

Ignatius nodded, "Quite so. At any rate, all trace of what happened here, in Olmus, is gone. As you said, *like nothing ever happened here.*"

"Now what?" she asked.

"Actually, that comment *like nothing ever happened* gives me an idea. I can alter a person's memories to a degree, like locking certain memories away; they are always there, but impossible to recall. Do you follow me?"

Ellen's face turned grim. "Oh yes, I know exactly what you mean. That very thing happened to Hawk; but, he overcame it and recovered his memories."

"Yes, that can happen with a very strong-willed individual. However, I refer to something far more permanent, a level of mind-wiping. Some consider it somewhat drastic, but I feel it may be warranted in this case, especially since the alternative is quite severe."

"So, you mean to do that to Circe, Daegon and Mab?" she asked.

"Essentially, yes, to varying degrees. I must eliminate any personal memories of Olmus from all three; they should have never come here in the first place. As for Daegon, I will also purge his memory of any knowledge of necromancy; I now know for certain he is a secret practitioner."

"And Mab, er, Diere?" she prompted.

Ignatius frowned. "Yes, she presents a far more troubling case. In the past, her transgressions would have merited a justified penalty of *true-death,* the obliteration of her *true name,* and all record of her existence purged. But times have changed; less draconian measures are now preferred. She may live, but I feel her memory may require the most severe *adjustment.*"

Ellen shuddered. "I can't stand her, and would never trust her. But, what you suggest, 'the most severe adjustment' sounds really harsh. Uh, I assume her skill with magic would be affected?"

"Assuredly, such learned skills and abilities reside within one's memory. Please understand that short of true-death, there may be no other choice.

"Consider the facts. She has effectively been deposed; she is not yet fully aware of that fact. She is thought to be dead by many. Were she to suddenly show up in her home realm, especially with drastically altered memories and limited abilities, she would not likely survive a fortnight."

"That is probably true," Ellen admitted. "She has a host of enemies, even in her home realm."

"Understand, Ellen, that I share these possible dispositions with you in confidence. So, I will expect your discretion. I shall see to it that none of the three have any personal memory of you as well."

"That might be for the best." Ellen acknowledged the inherent wisdom therein. "Of course, I shall be discreet, m'lord."

"Thank you, my dear Lady Steward. To be candid, discussing this with you is helpful for me. I find myself considering alternatives that I might have overlooked. I now know what must be done."

"May I speak of this with those whom I might deem have a need to know?"

"What? Just whom do you mean?"

She looked him squarely in the eye. "Those upon whom I rely, my close-knit family and friends."

"Ah, I see, and I know of whom you speak. I have no problem with them; they have proven to be quite trustworthy." He paused. "I would ask that you convey such information in the broadest of terms, generalities rather than details. I think you will find that may work out for the best."

"Really?" Ellen asked truly intrigued.

"Oh yes, indeed. Now, let us be about this business."

"Okay, but remember, we've still gotta talk, right, uh, m'lord?"

Ignatius chuckled. "We do, and we will—I promise."

CH 40

THE SMELLS IN THE SLIGHTLY warm Delafaire Farm kitchen were enticing. Millie bustled about, making sure everything would be good and hot when served.

The dogs and Smokey had taken up strategic positions around the room, out of the way, yet well placed to savor all the aromas, knowing full well they would share in this bountiful repast.

This would be an early supper, but an important one for everyone. Ellen had promised to tell the complete story, now that she had seen it through to the end, and those involved were home and safe.

Yes, everyone was home, safe and sound; that suited Millie just fine.

Miska and Brona had been keeping Millie company while everyone else was gone. They were so sweet to one another. Millie chuckled to herself; it was like watching a pair of high school kids going steady.

Ellen, Hawk, and Trey had come back last night; but, they had gone out again, something about an emergency Council meeting. They came back before too long; so, that was good. Of course, Hawk and Trey couldn't stay. It was late; they had to get on home.

Mark and Stacy had returned late last night, too, safe and sound.

Now, everyone would be coming to supper, even Madeline and Armand, and Ellen's doctor, Marie and her husband, Zack. Barnabas and Padraic were expected as well. This was going to be a fine evening. In fact, this was the first time they would be using the dining room, because everybody could be easily accommodated at the long dining table.

In truth, putting on a supper for such a large group, a real dinner party, tickled Millie no end. She loved this sort of thing, despite the inherent work. She enjoyed the creativity of it all, and knew she had a real flair for it.

Relishing in the challenge, she had diligently prepared a multicourse menu.

An assortment of oysters, fried, on the half shell, and sautéed in clarified butter would serve as appetizers, followed by a shrimp bisque for the soup. A romaine salad, with sourdough croûtons, would be offered with an assortment of dressings, and chilled plates of cheeses. A light lemon sorbet to follow would cleanse the palate. The entree would be two dishes; Cornish hens with oyster dressing, and crabmeat-stuffed pork loin. Vegetables would include rosemary potatoes, butter beans, field peas with snaps, mustard greens, and rice. Wedges of warm jalapeño cornbread would be on the table. Desserts would be strawberry pie and vanilla ice cream, or rum-laced bread pudding with crème Chantilly.

These were awesome desserts, among her specialties. Millie realized some guests might opt for both—well, why not?

She had selected several wines; two Chablis, two reds, and a California white zinfandel. Of course, there would be sweet tea and lemonade for those who might so choose. Brandies and Irish Coffees would cap the meal.

Wiping her hands on her apron, Millie surveyed the kitchen with a practiced eye. Hands on her hips, she smiled at the pets and murmured to herself, “Hmm, everything is going to be fine—just as it should be.”

AND SO IT WAS.

The meal went superbly; the food was wonderful. The pets, having been given samples of the Cornish hen and pork loin mixed with their regular food, now lay about pleasantly satiated.

The guests were amazed and delighted with the skill of the chef. Millie, basking a little uncomfortably in the effusive praise, was more than a bit grateful when Ellen rose and tapped the side of her wineglass to garner everyone's attention.

"If I could have your attention please? Thank you. First, let me thank my mother for this sumptuous supper—"

Applause broke out around the table amid cries of "Hear hear! Compliments to the chef! Kudos!"

Millie blushed and waved down the good-natured commotion.

"Seriously, thanks, Mom," Ellen repeated, taking control. "Now, as promised, I'll give you all a synopsis of what happened. I'm sure you'll have questions, which I'll gladly answer, but please wait until I'm done, okay?"

Affirmative nods and mumbles of assent went around the room.

"As you know, Trey, Hawk, and I attended the Council meeting last night. All the missing members were in attendance, and they had a lot of questions." She rolled her eyes. "I mean a *lot* of questions. We told them what we could, but there are some things they are better off not knowing—some of which you will hear this evening. So, what you learn here, tonight, must stay among us. Is that clear?"

A few eyebrows rose, but everyone agreed.

"Good! I can't overemphasize how important that is." Ellen paused; the room grew dead quiet.

"Before the kidnapping, the Council had authorized us, the Realm of Man, to investigate suspected acts of necromancy. We took the position that following up on the kidnapping was a logical progression of that mandate, since a suspected necromancer, Silenos, was clearly involved. As far as the Council knows, only we were involved in the events that followed; they are unaware of any other assets who may have played a role.

It has been made very clear that it is best that the Council knows no further details in that regard."

Armand raised his hand. "You mean Storm Haven, I presume?"

Madeline lightly swatted her husband's arm. "Couldn't hold your questions until she was through, like she asked, could you?"

Amused chuckles circulated around the table.

Ellen smiled. "Yes, Storm Haven, and others. Understand that they insisted most strongly on this. Consequently, the Realm of Man has been given credit for solving the mystery of the incidents of necromancy and foiling the kidnapping scheme. The Council is aware that Silenos planned to sacrifice Mer—"

"And you!" Hawk interjected.

Ellen gave him a *look*. "Yes, and me, in an effort to break the seal on the banishment of the Old Ones. In that, Silenos failed, and it cost him his life. The old proscription against any attempted residence or even travel to Olmus has been emphatically reinforced; that realm is taboo.

"The Council is aware that there are sentient beings indigenous to Olmus, various goblin tribes, who apparently had nothing to do with Silenos, and went into hiding. The Council has decreed that they are to be left alone. Of course, the entire realm being declared off-limits, that concern is effectively moot.

"Now, unknown to any outside this room, three others were there: Lady Diere, also known as Queen Mab; Circe, a sea witch from Mer; and Daegon, an alchemist who served the former Queen Mab. Daegon is an avowed enemy of Diere, whom he believes killed his Queen Mab to supplant her in a coup d'etat. All three would have served as sacrifices, too, had Silenos succeeded. When it was over, Lord Ignatius, Avatar of the Dragon Lords, dealt with these three."

"Dealt with?" asked Zack. "Meaning what?"

Marie turned her head toward her husband. "You too? Really?"

Zack winced. "Oh, sorry . . ."

Ellen smiled. "As far as I know, all three are fine. They just have some sizable gaps in their memories. Circe was sent back to Mer, but she'll have no memory of Olmus, anything that happened there, or any of us.

"As for Daegon and Diere, their respective memories were far more severely redacted to the point that they have little of their past lives available for recall. You all know about Diere, er, Mab, and the havoc she wreaked. Daegon, it turned out, was also a secret necromancer, although nowhere near the level of Silenos.

"We've been told that while Diere and Daegon are still alive, they're not the same people they were before—not even close. They were not returned to their home realms. We do not know where they ended up—somewhere in the *wild*."

The room grew quiet.

"Can we ask questions, now?" Armand asked, while flinching and leaning away from his wife.

Ellen smiled. "Sure, go ahead."

Armand sat straighter. "What became of Papa George and his minions? Weren't they suspected of being in Olmus as well?"

"I can answer that," Trey offered. "You're right, Papa George, his driver and muscle, Vito Smith, and his meth cook, 'Teddy Pots' Rasmussen were operating a drug lab on Olmus. They intended to distribute the drugs, primarily methamphetamine, in various realms, to include Mer and here. They got into some sort of disagreement with some organized-crime figures here. That led to a confrontation a few days ago during a meeting in New Orleans. Violence ensued, and the deaths of some well-connected members of organized-crime families resulted. Papa George,

Vito, and Teddy Pots were arrested at the scene of the homicides and are still in custody."

Hawk spoke up. "The state and federal prosecutors are currently working out how they will proceed, since there are concurrent jurisdictional issues, but there's no way any of them will make bail. Papa George and Vito aren't talking, of course. However, Teddy is; consequently, he's pending a forensic psychiatric examination because he insists on telling the truth—uh, as he believes it, that is—to anyone who will listen. You can imagine how his story is being received."

"Yeah," Trey nodded sympathetically and added, "it looks like Teddy will get some long-term care for his mental-health issues.

"But Papa George has a bigger problem; the old-school crime families will hold him responsible for the deaths of their members. He may be going to jail for a long time, but he won't be out of their reach—and he knows it."

"He'll probably try to cut a deal," Hawk reasoned, "but Teddy has already played the delusional 'truth card'—that wouldn't work with the *wiseguys* anyway. So, if Papa George can't offer something of major significance, there's no deal in his future. In all probability, he's totally screwed."

"At least we think that's the case," Trey cautioned. "Of course, the drug lab on Olmus is gone, destroyed—we checked. The indigenous goblin tribes scavenged the site. Even if someone were to look for it, they'd find no trace of it. Of course, the entire realm is now forbidden."

"There was some meth stored on Mer, in Circe's shop in Derinseum," Hawk added. "That has been quietly confiscated and destroyed as well."

"So, any more questions?" Ellen asked.

Of course there were more questions and subsequent discussion.

TAKING NOTE OF THE time, Padraic stood.

"If you will all forgive me, I should be going. I still have to meet with Lord Nightshade this evening."

"I meant to ask," Ellen probed, "do you plan to stay in the Realm of the Dark Elves for now?"

"I do, at Nightshade's invitation. With Diere, er, Mab gone, still considered *missing,* although presumed dead by many, I am certain Nightshade intends to orchestrate putting Malvana, who is currently serving as regent, permanently on the throne. This, I expect him to confide in me tonight."

"Really?" Mark remarked. "That will certainly stir the pot. Would he have her as monarch of the Unseelie Court as well?"

Padraic nodded, "I think it likely, although that will be a tall order. He must get her seated on the throne of Dark Elves first. The prominent houses of the realm are already posturing and taking subtle positions to their presumed advantage should the House of Hawthorne lose its grip on the throne."

"Is that likely?" Ellen asked.

"Oh yes, virtually inevitable," Padraic insisted. "Between Diere and her predecessor, Celeste, all other eligible candidates within the House of Hawthorne were either subdued or compromised to the degree that none are now truly viable candidates. The throne will assuredly go to another ascendant house. I suspect if Nightshade has his way, it will be the House of Tanist."

"And you would help him?" Mark asked.

"Well, yes." Padraic shrugged. "I might; we'll see. I like Malvana. She is young—for an elf—and impressionable; but, I think she is innately shrewd and fair-minded, if a bit naive."

Ellen rose and held her glass out in a toast. "To you, Padraic, and your predilection for getting involved in the most interesting, and often ironic, developments—and still be a rogue at heart. I do wish you well. Try to be safe, please."

Everyone rose and joined in the tongue-in-cheek toast.

Barnabas announced, "I, too, should be on my way back to Mer. Thank you for a wonderful evening; and of course, thank you for recovering my daughter, Brona."

Brona blushed and dropped her eyes, but still clung to Miska's arm.

"So, Barnabas, you'll go back to the Keys of Osiris?" Ellen asked.

He shrugged, "It is my home. Since that foul fog, and that other, uh, *contagion* is gone—"

"Thanks to Lord Ignatius and his gargoyles," Ellen interjected.

"Indeed, for which I am deeply grateful. Now there's no reason for me not to return. Although," Barnabas teased, "I understand my daughter would wish to stay here, with Miska."

Brona turned beet-red, turning her face into Miska's shoulder; but, her smile couldn't be any wider.

"M-miss Ellen!" Miska sputtered, "W-we were going to talk to you, uh, about that—I mean—"

Everyone erupted in laughter.

Ellen rescued the embarrassed Were. "Miska! It's all right! Of course, Brona can stay as long as she wants—she's family! And as far as I'm concerned, you are, too!"

"Yeah, y'all can set up housekeeping at the cabin," teased Mark. That earned him a slap on the arm from Stacy, and a big mischievous grin.

Ellen tilted her head. "Actually, Mark has a good point. If you like, consider the cabin yours to use, and Delafaire Farm your home, for as long as you'd like."

In wide-eyed surprise, Brona broke her self-conscious silence. "In truth, cousin?"

Hand over her heart Ellen intoned, "Indeed, verily and vouchsafed, cousin."

"Thank you!" Brona blurted, and hugged Miska mightily, who winced at her strength but smiled broadly nonetheless.

Millie went to Ellen and hugged her. "That was sweet of you."

Ellen hugged her back. "Family, Mom, it's all about family."

Trey glanced to Hawk and nodded. "I'm afraid we've gotta get going, too."

"Yeah, we've got court in the morning," Hawk remarked. "Thanks for supper, Miss Millie."

Madeline nudged her husband. "Armand, I'm tired. We should think about going."

Marie echoed the thought. "We should, too. I have an early morning meeting with Dr. Hollis."

Ellen raised a hand. "One moment, everyone—I have a final toast before we say good night. Please charge your glasses."

Everyone complied, rose, and looked to Ellen.

She raised her glass and smiled.

"To you, the members of our Middle Earth Society, without whom we could have never accomplished all that we did—your knowledge, analysis, ongoing support and guidance are appreciated beyond words. Thank you."

"Hear-hear!" echoed around the table amidst a host of congratulatory comments and well-wishes.

Over the next few minutes, the guests who had to leave prepared for departure and thanked their hosts.

"We'll walk y'all out," Ellen offered, linking arms with her mother.

"Us, too," Stacy chimed in, tugging Mark up from the table. "Come on, Brona—you and Miska, too."

Grinning broadly, the couple followed.

THEY SAID THEIR GOOD-byes on the front porch, beneath the soft glow of the porch lights.

After those who were departing had gone, and those who would stay had gone back to the kitchen, Ellen lingered on the front porch with the the Chows, Max and Sophie, and the cat, Smokey.

Sitting in the rocking chair, she smiled as a cooling night breeze set a few errant hairs to fluttering at her cheek. The events of the past few days somehow seemed distant. She relished the peacefulness of the moment. Looking out from the softly lit porch, the grounds seemed swallowed in the velvet dark. Crickets and tree frogs began a subtle serenade—and suddenly stopped.

Ellen sensed the arrival of a transit globe before it appeared. She stood. The pets stood with her, fully alert, peering into the night.

The globe formed at the very edge of illumination; a sole figure stepped forth.

Ellen smiled and murmured to the pets, "It's okay."

Waving her hand, she declared, "Welcome, Lord Ignatius! To what do I owe the honor?"

The short man bowed. "Ah, Lady Ellen, I am merely keeping a promise."

She smiled. "That we talk?"

He approached the steps, stopped, and gestured to the porch. "Indeed, may I?"

She gestured toward another rocking chair. "Of course. Please, join me. Can I offer you any refreshment?"

"No, thank you." He settled into the indicated rocker as she resumed her seat. "This is quite lovely."

"Thank you."

He leaned slightly toward her. "Can we speak here in confidence—just us two?"

"Of course. What's on your mind?"

Folding his hands in his lap, he rocked gently. "My purpose is twofold; to share certain information, and to convey an invitation."

"An invitation?"

"Yes," he raised a finger, "but let me give you the information first, especially since it is for your ears alone."

Her eyebrows rose. "Really? Very well, please, go on."

"You'll remember how insistent I was about not mentioning my involvement in recent events, yes? You may be aware of an old belief, some mistakenly consider it a prophecy, that in times of crisis the Dragon Lords would return to assess and rectify the situation. Some even think the mere appearance of their avatar would herald a judgment in which the Dragon Lords would purge all life from the realms and start over. This is gross exaggeration, warped beyond belief, and simply wrong in so many ways.

"The original intent was that the Council Realms should self-govern and see to it that necromancy was not tolerated within their spheres of influence. Should a crisis beyond their collective, and presumed cooperative, ability to handle arise, the Dragon Lords might intervene—that is all.

"Over time, this became muddled in the retelling and reinterpreted as some sort of prophetic dogma engendering unnecessary fear and potential panic among those living within the Council Realms. For too long this has been perceived as sacrosanct truth, rather than the perverted rumor it actually is. Worse, there is little that can be done to correct the situation."

"Little?" she echoed. "Really? I should think correcting the misconception would be relatively easy; just have a Dragon Lord appear at a Council meeting and do so."

He was silent for a long moment. "Sadly, I do not believe that is an option."

"Why not? It seems pretty straightforward to me."

He stopped rocking. His voice dropped so low, she could barely hear him.

"I have not seen a dragon since I was appointed to serve as avatar; that was a very long time ago."

Stunned, she had no words.

"Ellen, I share this with you in confidence; you must not divulge this to anyone. Understand I am not suggesting there are no more dragons—I just have not seen one for some time. I do not know why."

She found her voice. "But then, how do you, uh, know what to do? Or what needs to be done?"

He opened his palms. "I receive instructions from gargoyle messengers. I know someone is there; someone is monitoring what happens in the realms."

"So, you receive instructions, and act accordingly?" she reasoned.

"That is an accurate assessment," he confirmed.

"So, why not attend the Council meetings?" she pressed. "I mean, you *are* the avatar, right? If the avatar supposedly represents a member realm's interest, why aren't you attending the meetings?"

He leaned back and set the chair rocking once more. "I was advised not to attend the meetings; I don't know why. However, I have speculated that it might have to do with the perverse belief in the so-called *prophecy* that even the mere appearance of an avatar of the Dragon Lords will presage some disaster and precipitate some degree of panic."

"Oh, yeah, that is a problem, one without a ready solution," she concluded.

He shrugged in chagrin. "I know; such is my life."

She spent a moment in quiet reflection; this was a lot to digest.

"Ignatius, I gotta ask; why tell me all this?"

He smiled at her. "Simple, I was instructed to do so."

She gaped at him, stunned and wordless once more.

"Actually, I have more to tell you, if I may?"

She managed to close her mouth and nod.

"You were concerned regarding the final dispositions of the alchemist, Daegon, and Lady Diere. You are aware there are many other realms beyond those few of the Council, actually, vast numbers of habitable worlds. None, that I am aware of, are as technologically advanced as your home realm, but some are well provisioned with some technology. It is one of these realms to which Daegon and Diere were sent. As you know, their memories have been severely redacted, and they have no knowledge of each other. They are safe, and are discreetly monitored."

Her curiosity piqued, she asked, "*Some technology?* Like what, exactly?"

He rolled his eyes and shrugged. "Oh, I suppose something like your home realm, but well over a century ago. Think in terms of the 1890s and early 1900s; gas lights, fledgling understanding of electricity, and widespread use of steam power. However, there are considerable differences."

Her face beamed in smiling surprise. "OMG! That is so cool! Has it got a name?"

"Yes, they call it Victoria Crossing."

"Ha-ha!" Ellen laughed in delight. "Victoria Crossing! That is so *steampunk!* That's great!"

He smiled, yet his confusion was evident. "I'm pleased you are so amused. *Steampunk?* Have I missed something?"

"No-no, it's nothing to worry about," she assured him. "It's just a popular subculture thing, kind of a well-intentioned fantasy hobby in my home realm that celebrates that time period. It's fun! Wait—can I visit this realm?"

"As a matter of fact, your question segues nicely into the final aspect of my task, the invitation."

"Oh, really?" She grinned, already liking where this appeared to be going.

Ignatius opened his hand to display an opal the size of a robin's egg. Reflections of the porch lights flowed across its surface as he tilted his hand.

"This gem is part of your invitation to visit someone in the Realm of Victoria Crossing. I am sure you know how to use such a stone to craft the appropriate transit globe, yes?"

"I do." She gestured toward the opal. "A gem once in a dragon's hoard and thus capable of holding the required spell, I presume. But just whom am I to visit—not Daegon or Diere, surely?"

"No." He shook his head. "Neither would recognize you, now having no memory of you. No, the invitation to visit comes from your grandfather."

"My *grandfather?"* She snatched her hand back. "Are you serious?"

"Quite serious," Ignatius intoned. "I am well aware of your lineage. I assure you this gem and the invitation comes from your grandfather, Oberon."

She squared her shoulders. "How does he even know about me—or my father? I was under the impression he was never told about the birth of my father! Until this moment, Oberon—*my grandfather?*—has never acknowledged me. So, why now?"

"It would not be my place to explain, even if I could," Ignatius conceded. "Perhaps, you should ask him when you visit?"

"If I visit," she corrected. "I'll have to think about this. Do you know him?"

"I do." Ignatius considered the opal in his hand. "I can tell you that he has watched you for some time, albeit from a distance. I think he is impressed with you. He would not invite you lightly; he surely has a reason."

"And probably a purpose, no doubt," she groused. "I don't like feeling like I'm being used; and, somehow I do in this circumstance."

"Forgive me, that was not my intent. I merely conveyed his invitation. I apologize if you perceived it as otherwise." He extended his hand. "Please, take the opal. Whether or not you choose to use it is entirely at your discretion."

Her shoulders slumped. “Forgive me, Ignatius. I did not mean to snap at you. Thank you for the information, and for conveying the invitation. I have not made a decision; but, I will accept the gem.” She took it from his palm. “Did he indicate when he might expect me to visit?”

“No, Ellen, he did not. It may well be that this is an open-ended invitation, to be used at a time of your choosing. I know that Oberon does not care much about the passage of time, or so it appears.”

Ellen nodded. “I understand. In fact, I think that may be for the best. I am not inclined to go anywhere just now. I think I’d rather just relax here at home for a while. Were you supposed to wait for an answer?”

Ignatius shook his head. “He did not ask that of me. Would you like to send him an answer?”

She smiled impishly. “Yeah, tell him I’ll think about it—and that might take some time.”

“As you wish, m’lady.” Ignatius chuckled. “There is one other matter I should mention.”

“What might that be?”

“As you know, I have taken steps to secure the silver ouroboros in the Dragon Lords’ home realm. I must encourage you to do the same with the iron ouroboros. The two should never again come together, as you well know.”

Ellen sighed. “That’s a problem—I don’t have it. I have no idea where it is; I never did.”

“But—” Ignatius balked, clearly confused. “You are the Steward. The iron ouroboros was given to the last Steward for safekeeping. You are her heir—you must have it, surely!”

She shook her head. “Sorry to disappoint you, but I knew nothing about it until a short time ago. If Maude Delafaire had it, she never told me. I suppose it was given to her in the expectation she would hide it in some inaccessible realm in the *wild*, but I really have no clue where."

Ignatius was crestfallen. "That is somehow both disconcerting and yet reassuring. So, essentially the iron ouroboros is to be considered lost?"

Ellen shrugged. "May as well be, I suppose."

He sighed heavily. "Alas, perhaps that's for the best."

She tilted her head and stared into the night. "Yeah, who knows?"

He stood. "Well, I have enjoyed our visit, m'lady. My mission is complete; I should take my leave."

She stood. "Thank you, m'lord. It was good to see you; feel free to visit me anytime. Safe journey."

ALONE ONCE MORE WITH the pets on the porch, she studied the opal. Even in the soft light of the porch lamps it was beautiful, and felt slightly warm to the touch. She slipped it into a pocket, sat, and resumed rocking. The crickets and tree frogs started up again, softly.

She smiled, feeling completely at peace.

Smokey leapt into her lap and began purring gently as she absently scratched his head. Max and Sophie sat before her and stared into her eyes.

"Don't worry, guys; I'm home to stay for a while, perhaps a long while. Maybe I shouldn't care all that much about the passage of time either—apparently, that runs in the family.

"Okay, I'll admit Victoria Crossing, a steampunk realm, sounds intriguing. But the truth is I'm tired; and, I'm way behind in updating the journal. Now that I'm home, I think I'm gonna stay."

She could swear the animals were smiling.

She stood up, still cradling Smokey. "Okay, guys, let's go in."

She pulled at the screen door and held it open with her elbow. Before she could open the heavy wooden door, Max and Sophie nudged up against her knees, stopping her. Surprised, she paused, knowing the dogs wouldn't do this without a reason.

"What?" she whispered.

Smokey reached out a paw and swatted at the knocker—the large *iron ring* knocker.

Ellen's breath caught in her throat. She leaned forward, peering at the heavy knocker in the barely adequate porch light.

Could it be? No way! Or is it? All this time—right in front of our noses?

She focused on the iron ring, her senses probing, but found nothing, just old iron.

Of course, Maude would have seen to that; old iron is what one would expect to find. No, Maude is far too shrewd; she would not disappoint. My gut says there is something here. I must look deeper yet.

She set Smokey down, and refocused her concentration on the knocker.

It took several moments. Ever so slowly, she peeled back metaphysical layers of glamour-like illusion until she discerned a faint glimmering of intent. She sensed a rather distinct familiarity in the crafting.

Aha! Maude, that's your hand in this, you clever rascal! This is indeed it! You hid it in plain sight!

Ellen stepped back, and shook her head.

The iron ouroboros—hidden in plain sight!

The very idea was brilliant; and no one was ever the wiser.

Smiling, she looked at the pets gathered at her feet.

"You guys knew, all this time, you knew, didn't you? She hid it so well. It stays right here. We'll just keep this our secret, okay?"

Accepting tail wags and an audible purr as tokens of acceptance and compliance, Ellen opened the heavy door and ushered the pets into the house.

As she gently closed and locked the door, she had a vision of a delightfully pleased Maude, smiling and winking.

Well done, Steward, well done indeed . . .

THE END . . ?

(perhaps not . . .)

About the Author

M.D. Ironz is the pseudonym of a former government official, based in an undisclosed location in North America, and now serving as a confidential consultant on matters of intelligence, security, and investigations.

www.ingramcontent.com/pod-product-compliance
Lightning Source LLC
Chambersburg PA
CBHW010142030826
48979CB00028B/2158/J

* 9 7 8 1 7 3 3 7 5 9 4 8 9 *